ROXANA

THE FORTUNATE MISTRESS

OR A HISTORY OF THE LIFE OF MADEMOISELLE DE BELEAU

KNOWN BY THE NAME OF THE LADY ROXANA

By

Daniel Defoe

Authored by Daniel Defoe (1660-1731).
First published in 1724.
This unabridged edition is based on the "The New Roxana" edition from 1775.
The original language and grammar has been preserved.
Published by CreateSpace Independent Publishing 2015.
Part of the "Immortal Classics"-series.
ISBN-13: 978-1518699832.
ISBN-10: 1518699839.

AUTHOR'S PREFACE

The history of this beautiful lady is to speak for itself; if it is not as beautiful as the lady herself is reported to be; if it is not as diverting as the reader can desire, and much more than he can reasonably expect; and if all the most diverting parts of it are not adapted to the instruction and improvement of the reader, the relator says it must be from the defect of his performance; dressing up the story in worse clothes than the lady whose words he speaks, prepared for the world.

He takes the liberty to say that this story differs from most of the modern performances of this kind, though some of them have met with a very good reception in the world. I say, it differs from them in this great and essential article, namely, that the foundation of this is laid in truth of fact; and so the work is not a story, but a history.

The scene is laid so near the place where the main part of it was transacted that it was necessary to conceal names and persons, lest what cannot be yet entirely forgot in that part of the town should be remembered, and the facts traced back too plainly by the many people yet living, who would know the persons by the particulars.

It is not always necessary that the names of persons should be discovered, though the history may be many ways useful; and if we should be always obliged to name the persons, or not to relate the story, the consequence might be only this—that many a pleasant and delightful history would be buried in the dark, and the world deprived both of the pleasure and the profit of it.

The writer says he was particularly acquainted with this lady's first husband, the brewer, and with his father, and also with his bad circumstances, and knows that first part of the story to be truth.

This may, he hopes, be a pledge for the credit of the rest, though the latter part of her history lay abroad, and could not be so well vouched as the first; yet, as she has told it herself, we have the less reason to question the truth of that part also.

In the manner she has told the story, it is evident she does not insist upon her justification in any one part of it; much less does she recommend her conduct, or, indeed, any part of it, except her repentance, to our imitation. On the contrary, she makes frequent excursions, in a just censuring and condemning her own practice. How often does she reproach herself in the most passionate manner, and guide us to just reflections in the like cases!

It is true she met with unexpected success in all her wicked courses; but even in the highest elevations of her prosperity she makes frequent acknowledgments that the pleasure of her wickedness was not worth the repentance; and that all the satisfaction she had, all the joy in the view of her prosperity—no, nor all the wealth she rolled in, the gaiety of her appearance, the equipages and the honours she was attended with, could quiet her mind, abate the reproaches of her conscience, or procure her an hour's sleep when just reflection kept her waking.

The noble inferences that are drawn from this one part are worth all the rest of the story, and abundantly justify, as they are the professed design of, the publication.

If there are any parts in her story which, being obliged to relate a wicked action, seem to describe it too plainly, the writer says all imaginable care has been taken to keep clear of indecencies and immodest expressions; and it is hoped you will find nothing to prompt a vicious mind, but everywhere much to discourage and expose it.

Scenes of crime can scarce be represented in such a manner but some may make a criminal use of them; but when vice is painted in its low-prized colours, it is not to make people in love with it, but to expose it; and if the reader makes a wrong use of the figures, the wickedness is his own.

In the meantime, the advantages of the present work are so great, and the virtuous reader has room for so much improvement, that we make no question the story, however meanly told, will find a passage to his best hours, and be read both with profit and delight.

A HISTORY OF THE LIFE OF ROXANA

I was born, as my friends told me, at the city of Poitiers, in the province or county of Poitou, in France, from whence I was brought to England by my parents, who fled for their religion about the year 1683, when the Protestants were banished from France by the cruelty of their persecutors.

I, who knew little or nothing of what I was brought over hither for, was well enough pleased with being here. London, a large and gay city, took with me mighty well, who, from my being a child, loved a crowd, and to see a great many fine folks.

I retained nothing of France but the language, my father and mother being people of better fashion than ordinarily the people called refugees at that time were; and having fled early, while it was easy to secure their effects, had, before their coming over, remitted considerable sums of money, or, as I remember, a considerable value in French brandy, paper, and other goods; and these selling very much to advantage here, my father was in very good circumstances at his coming over, so that he was far from applying to the rest of our nation that were here for countenance and relief. On the contrary, he had his door continually thronged with miserable objects of the poor starving creatures who at that time fled hither for shelter on account of conscience, or something else.

I have indeed heard my father say that he was pestered with a great many of those who, for any religion they had, might e'en have stayed where they were, but who flocked over hither in droves, for what they call in English a livelihood; hearing with what open arms the refugees were received in England, and how they fell readily into business, being, by the charitable assistance of the people in London, encouraged to work in their manufactories in Spitalfields, Canterbury, and other places, and that they had a much better price for their work than in France, and the like.

My father, I say, told me that he was more pestered with the clamours of these people than of those who were truly refugees, and fled in distress merely for conscience.

I was about ten years old when I was brought over hither, where, as I have said, my father lived in very good circumstances, and died in about eleven years more; in which time, as I had accomplished myself for the sociable part of the world, so I had acquainted myself with some of our English neighbours, as is the custom in London; and as, while I was young, I had picked up three or four playfellows and companions suitable to my years, so, as we grew bigger, we learned to call one another intimates and friends; and this forwarded very much the finishing me for conversation and the world.

I went to English schools, and being young, I learned the English tongue perfectly well, with all the customs of the English young women; so that I retained nothing of the French but the speech; nor did I so much as keep any remains of the French language tagged to my way of speaking, as most foreigners do, but spoke what we call natural English, as if I had been born here.

Being to give my own character, I must be excused to give it as impartially as possible, and as if I was speaking of another body; and the sequel will lead you to judge whether I flatter myself or no.

I was (speaking of myself at about fourteen years of age) tall, and very well made; sharp as a hawk in matters of common knowledge; quick and smart in discourse; apt to be satirical; full of repartee; and a little too forward in conversation, or, as we call it in English, bold, though perfectly modest in my behaviour. Being French born, I danced, as some say, naturally, loved it extremely, and sang well also, and so well that, as you will hear, it was afterwards some advantage to me. With all these things, I wanted neither wit, beauty, or money. In this manner I set out into the world, having all the advantages that any young woman could desire, to recommend me to others, and form a prospect of happy living to myself.

At about fifteen years of age, my father gave me, as he called it in French, 25,000 livres, that is to say, two thousand pounds portion, and married me to an eminent brewer in the city. Pardon me if I conceal his name; for though he was the foundation of my ruin, I cannot take so severe a revenge upon him.

With this thing called a husband I lived eight years in good fashion, and for some part of the time kept a coach, that is to say, a kind of mock coach; for all the week the horses were kept at work in the dray-carts; but on Sunday I had the privilege to go abroad in my chariot, either to church or otherways, as my husband and I could agree about it, which, by the way, was not very often; but of that hereafter.

Before I proceed in the history of the married part of my life, you must allow me to give as impartial an account of my husband as I have done of myself. He was a jolly, handsome fellow, as any woman need wish for a companion; tall and well made; rather a little too large, but not so as to be ungenteel; he danced well, which I think was the first thing that brought us together. He had an old father who managed the business carefully, so that he had little of that part lay on him, but now and then to appear and show himself; and he took the advantage of it, for he troubled himself very little about it, but went abroad, kept company, hunted much, and loved it exceedingly.

After I have told you that he was a handsome man and a good sportsman, I have indeed said all; and unhappy was I, like other young people of our sex, I chose him for being a handsome, jolly fellow, as I have said; for he was otherwise a weak, empty-headed, untaught creature, as any woman could ever desire to be coupled with. And here I must take the liberty, whatever I have to reproach myself with in my after conduct, to turn to my fellow-creatures, the young ladies of this country, and speak to them by way of precaution. If you have any regard to your future happiness, any view of living comfortably with a husband, any hope of preserving your fortunes, or restoring them after any disaster, never, ladies, marry a fool; any husband rather than a fool. With some other husbands you may be unhappy, but with a fool you will be miserable; with another husband you may, I say, be unhappy, but with a fool you must; nay, if he would, he cannot make you easy; everything he does is so awkward, everything he says is so empty, a woman of any sense cannot but be

6

surfeited and sick of him twenty times a day. What is more shocking than for a woman to bring a handsome, comely fellow of a husband into company, and then be obliged to blush for him every time she hears him speak? to hear other gentlemen talk sense, and he able to say nothing? and so look like a fool, or, which is worse, hear him talk nonsense, and be laughed at for a fool.

In the next place, there are so many sorts of fools, such an infinite variety of fools, and so hard it is to know the worst of the kind, that I am obliged to say, "No fool, ladies, at all, no kind of fool, whether a mad fool or a sober fool, a wise fool or a silly fool; take anything but a fool; nay, be anything, be even an old maid, the worst of nature's curses, rather than take up with a fool."

But to leave this awhile, for I shall have occasion to speak of it again; my case was particularly hard, for I had a variety of foolish things complicated in this unhappy match.

First, and which I must confess is very unsufferable, he was a conceited fool, tout opiniatre; everything he said was right, was best, and was to the purpose, whoever was in company, and whatever was advanced by others, though with the greatest modesty imaginable. And yet, when he came to defend what he had said by argument and reason, he would do it so weakly, so emptily, and so nothing to the purpose, that it was enough to make anybody that heard him sick and ashamed of him.

Secondly, he was positive and obstinate, and the most positive in the most simple and inconsistent things, such as were intolerable to bear.

These two articles, if there had been no more, qualified him to be a most unbearable creature for a husband; and so it may be supposed at first sight what a kind of life I led with him. However, I did as well as I could, and held my tongue, which was the only victory I gained over him; for when he would talk after his own empty rattling way with me, and I would not answer, or enter into discourse with him on the point he was upon, he would rise up in the greatest passion imaginable, and go away, which was the cheapest way I had to be delivered.

I could enlarge here much upon the method I took to make my life passable and easy with the most incorrigible temper in the world; but it is too long, and the articles too trifling. I shall mention some of them as the circumstances I am to relate shall necessarily bring them in.

After I had been married about four years, my own father died, my mother having been dead before. He liked my match so ill, and saw so little room to be satisfied with the conduct of my husband, that though he left me five thousand livres, and more, at his death, yet he left it in the hands of my elder brother, who, running on too rashly in his adventures as a merchant, failed, and lost not only what he had, but what he had for me too, as you shall hear presently.

Thus I lost the last gift of my father's bounty by having a husband not fit to be trusted with it: there's one of the benefits of marrying a fool.

Within two years after my own father's death my husband's father also died, and, as I thought, left him a considerable addition to his estate, the whole trade of the brewhouse, which was a very good one, being now his own.

But this addition to his stock was his ruin, for he had no genius to business, he had no knowledge of his accounts; he bustled a little about it, indeed, at first, and put on a face of business, but he soon grew slack; it was below him to inspect his books, he committed all that to his clerks and book-keepers; and while he found money in cash to pay the maltman and the excise, and put some in his pocket, he was perfectly easy and indolent, let the main chance go how it would.

I foresaw the consequence of this, and attempted several times to persuade him to apply himself to his business; I put him in mind how his customers complained of the neglect of his servants on one hand, and how abundance broke in his debt, on the other hand, for want of the clerk's care to secure him, and the like; but he thrust me by, either with hard words, or fraudulently, with representing the cases otherwise than they were.

However, to cut short a dull story, which ought not to be long, he began to find his trade sunk, his stock declined, and that, in short, he could not carry on his business, and once or twice his brewing utensils were extended for the excise; and, the last time, he was put to great extremities to clear them.

This alarmed him, and he resolved to lay down his trade; which, indeed, I was not sorry for; foreseeing that if he did not lay it down in time, he would be forced to do it another way, namely, as a bankrupt. Also I was willing he should draw out while he had something left, lest I should come to be stripped at home, and be turned out of doors with my children; for I had now five children by him, the only work (perhaps) that fools are good for.

I thought myself happy when he got another man to take his brewhouse clear off his hands; for, paying down a large sum of money, my husband found himself a clear man, all his debts paid, and with between two and three thousand pounds in his pocket; and being now obliged to remove from the brewhouse, we took a house at ——, a village about two miles out of town; and happy I thought myself, all things considered, that I was got off clear, upon so good terms; and had my handsome fellow had but one capful of wit, I had been still well enough.

I proposed to him either to buy some place with the money, or with part of it, and offered to join my part to it, which was then in being, and might have been secured; so we might have lived tolerably at least during his life. But as it is the part of a fool to be void of counsel, so he neglected it, lived on as he did before, kept his horses and men, rid every day out to the forest a-hunting, and nothing was done all this while; but the money decreased apace, and I thought I saw my ruin hastening on without any possible way to prevent it.

I was not wanting with all that persuasions and entreaties could perform, but it was all fruitless; representing to him how fast our money wasted, and what would be our condition when it was gone, made no impression on him; but like one stupid, he went on, not valuing all that tears and lamentations could be supposed to do; nor did he abate his figure or equipage, his horses or servants, even to the last, till he had not a hundred pounds left in the whole world.

It was not above three years that all the ready money was thus spending off; yet he spent it, as I may say, foolishly too, for he kept no valuable company neither, but generally with huntsmen and horse-coursers, and men meaner than himself, which is another consequence of a man's being a fool; such can never take delight in men more wise and capable than themselves, and that makes them converse with scoundrels, drink, belch with porters, and keep company always below themselves.

This was my wretched condition, when one morning my husband told me he was sensible he was come to a miserable condition, and he would go and seek his fortune somewhere or other. He had said something to that purpose several times before that, upon my pressing him to consider his circumstances, and the circumstances of his family, before it should be too late; but as I found he had no meaning in anything of that kind, as, indeed, he had not much in anything he ever said, so I thought they were but words of course now. When he had said he would be gone, I used to wish secretly, and even say in my thoughts, I wish you would, for if you go on thus you will starve us all.

He stayed, however, at home all that day, and lay at home that night; early the next morning he gets out of bed, goes to a window which looked out towards the stable, and sounds his French horn, as he called it, which was his usual signal to call his men to go out a-hunting.

It was about the latter end of August, and so was light yet at five o'clock, and it was about that time that I heard him and his two men go out and shut the yard gates after them. He said nothing to me more than as usual when he used to go out upon hissport; neither did I rise, or say anything to him that was material, but went to sleep again after he was gone, for two hours or thereabouts.

It must be a little surprising to the reader to tell him at once, that after this I never saw my husband more; but, to go farther, I not only never saw him more, but I never heard from him, or of him, neither of any or either of his two servants, or of the horses, either what became of them, where or which way they went, or what they did or intended to do, no more than if the ground had opened and swallowed them all up, and nobody had known it, except as hereafter.

I was not, for the first night or two, at all surprised, no, nor very much the first week or two, believing that if anything evil had befallen them, I should soon enough have heard of that; and also knowing, that as he had two servants and three horses with him, it would be the strangest thing in the world that anything could befall them all but that I must some time or other hear of them.

But you will easily allow, that as time ran on, a week, two weeks, a month, two months, and so on, I was dreadfully frighted at last, and the more when I looked into my own circumstances, and considered the condition in which I was left with five children, and not one farthing subsistence for them, other than about seventy pounds in money, and what few things of value I had about me, which, though considerable in themselves, were yet nothing to feed a family, and for a length of time too.

THE BREWER AND HIS MEN

I heard him and his two men go out and shut the yard gates after them

What to do I knew not, nor to whom to have recourse: to keep in the house where I was, I could not, the rent being too great; and to leave it without his orders, if my husband should return, I could not think of that neither; so that I continued extremely perplexed, melancholy, and discouraged to the last degree.

I remained in this dejected condition near a twelvemonth. My husband had two sisters, who were married, and lived very well, and some other near relations that I knew of, and I hoped would do something for me; and I frequently sent to these, to know if they could give me any account of my vagrant creature. But they all declared to me in answer, that they knew nothing about him; and, after frequent sending, began to think me troublesome, and to let me know they thought so too, by their treating my maid with very slight and unhandsome returns to her inquiries.

This grated hard, and added to my affliction; but I had no recourse but to my tears, for I had not a friend of my own left me in the world. I should have observed, that it was about half a year before this elopement of my husband that the disaster I mentioned above befell my brother, who broke, and that in such bad circumstances, that I had the mortification to hear, not only that he was in prison, but that there would be little or nothing to be had by way of composition.

Misfortunes seldom come alone: this was the forerunner of my husband's flight; and as my expectations were cut off on that side, my husband gone, and my family of children on my hands, and nothing to subsist them, my condition was the most deplorable that words can express.

I had some plate and some jewels, as might be supposed, my fortune and former circumstances considered; and my husband, who had never stayed to be distressed, had not been put to the necessity of rifling me, as husbands usually do in such cases. But as I had seen an end of all the ready money during the long time I had lived in a state of expectation for my husband, so I began to make away one thing after another, till those few things of value which I had began to lessen apace, and I saw nothing but misery and the utmost distress before me, even to have my children starve before my face. I leave any one that is a mother of children, and has lived in plenty and in good fashion, to consider and reflect what must be my condition. As to my husband, I had now no hope or expectation of seeing him any more; and indeed, if I had, he was a man of all the men in the world the least able to help me, or to have turned his hand to the gaining one shilling towards lessening our distress; he neither had the capacity or the inclination; he could have been no clerk, for he scarce wrote a legible hand; he was so far from being able to write sense, that he could not make sense of what others wrote; he was so far from understanding good English, that he could not spell good English; to be out of all business was his delight, and he would stand leaning against a post for half-an-hour together, with a pipe in his mouth, with all the tranquillity in the world, smoking, like Dryden's countryman, that whistled as he went for want of thought, and this even when his family was, as it were, starving, that little he had wasting, and that we were all bleeding to death; he not knowing, and as little considering, where to get another shilling when the last was spent.

This being his temper, and the extent of his capacity, I confess I did not see so much loss in his parting with me as at first I thought I did; though it was hard and cruel to the last degree in him, not giving me the least notice of his design; and indeed, that which I was most astonished at was, that seeing he must certainly have intended this excursion some few moments at least before he put it in practice, yet he did not come and take what little stock of money we had left, or at least a share of it, to bear his expense for a little while; but he did not; and I am morally certain he had not five guineas with him in the world when he went away. All that I could come to the knowledge of about him was, that he left his hunting-horn, which he called the French horn, in the stable, and his hunting-saddle, went away in a handsome furniture, as they call it, which he used sometimes to travel with, having an embroidered housing, a case of pistols, and other things belonging to them; and one of his servants had another saddle with pistols, though plain, and the other a long gun; so that they did not go out as sportsmen, but rather as travellers; what part of the world they went to I never heard for many years.

As I have said, I sent to his relations, but they sent me short and surly answers; nor did any one of them offer to come to see me, or to see the children, or so much as to inquire after them, well perceiving that I was in a condition that was likely to be soon troublesome to them. But it was no time now to dally with them or with the world; I left off sending to them, and went myself among them, laid my circumstances open to them, told them my whole case, and the condition I was reduced to, begged they would advise me what course to take, laid myself as low as they could desire, and entreated them to consider that I was not in a condition to help myself, and that without some assistance we must all inevitably perish. I told them that if I had had but one child, or two children, I would have done my endeavour to have worked for them with my needle, and should only have come to them to beg them to help me to some work, that I might get our bread by my labour; but to think of one single woman, not bred to work, and at a loss where to get employment, to get the bread of five children, that was not possible—some of my children being young too, and none of them big enough to help one another.

It was all one; I received not one farthing of assistance from anybody, was hardly asked to sit down at the two sisters' houses, nor offered to eat or drink at two more near relations'. The fifth, an ancient gentlewoman, aunt-in-law to my husband, a widow, and the least able also of any of the rest, did, indeed, ask me to sit down, gave me a dinner, and refreshed me with a kinder treatment than any of the rest, but added the melancholy part, viz., that she would have helped me, but that, indeed, she was not able, which, however, I was satisfied was very true.

Here I relieved myself with the constant assistant of the afflicted, I mean tears; for, relating to her how I was received by the other of my husband's relations, it made me burst into tears, and I cried vehemently for a great while together, till I made the good old gentlewoman cry too several times.

However, I came home from them all without any relief, and went on at home till I was reduced to such inexpressible distress that is not to be described. I had been several times after this at the old aunt's, for I prevailed with her to promise me to go and talk with the other relations, at least, that, if possible, she could bring some of them to take off the children, or to contribute something towards their maintenance. And, to do her justice, she did use her endeavour with them; but all was to no purpose, they would do nothing, at least that way. I think, with much entreaty, she obtained, by a kind of collection among them all, about eleven or twelve shillings in money, which, though it was a present comfort, was yet not to be named as capable to deliver me from any part of the load that lay upon me.

There was a poor woman that had been a kind of a dependent upon our family, and whom I had often, among the rest of the relations, been very kind to; my maid put it into my head one morning to send to this poor woman, and to see whether she might not be able to help in this dreadful case.

I must remember it here, to the praise of this poor girl, my maid, that though I was not able to give her any wages, and had told her so—nay, I was not able to pay her the wages that I was in arrears to her—yet she would not leave me; nay, and as long as she had any money, when I had none, she would help me out of her own, for which, though I acknowledged her kindness and fidelity, yet it was but a bad coin that she was paid in at last, as will appear in its place.

Amy (for that was her name) put it into my thoughts to send for this poor woman to come to me; for I was now in great distress, and I resolved to do so. But just the very morning that I intended it, the old aunt, with the poor woman in her company, came to see me; the good old gentlewoman was, it seems, heartily concerned for me, and had been talking again among those people, to see what she could do for me, but to very little purpose.

You shall judge a little of my present distress by the posture she found me in. I had five little children, the eldest was under ten years old, and I had not one shilling in the house to buy them victuals, but had sent Amy out with a silver spoon to sell it, and bring home something from the butcher's; and I was in a parlour, sitting on the ground, with a great heap of old rags, linen, and other things about me, looking them over, to see if I had anything among them that would sell or pawn for a little money, and had been crying ready to burst myself, to think what I should do next.

At this juncture they knocked at the door. I thought it had been Amy, so I did not rise up; but one of the children opened the door, and they came directly into the room where I was, and where they found me in that posture, and crying vehemently, as above. I was surprised at their coming, you may be sure, especially seeing the person I had but just before resolved to send for; but when they saw me, how I looked, for my eyes were swelled with crying, and what a condition I was in as to the house, and the heaps of things that were about me, and especially when I told them what I was doing, and on what occasion, they sat down, like Job's three comforters, and said not one word to me for a great while, but both of them cried as fast and as heartily as I did.

The truth was, there was no need of much discourse in the case, the thing spoke itself; they saw me in rags and dirt, who was but a little before riding in my coach; thin, and looking almost like one starved, who was before fat and beautiful. The house, that was before handsomely furnished with pictures and ornaments, cabinets, pier-glasses, and everything suitable, was now stripped and naked, most of the goods having been seized by the landlord for rent, or sold to buy necessaries; in a word, all was misery and distress, the face of ruin was everywhere to be seen; we had eaten up almost everything, and little remained, unless, like one of the pitiful women of Jerusalem, I should eat up my very children themselves.

After these two good creatures had sat, as I say, in silence some time, and had then looked about them, my maid Amy came in, and brought with her a small breast of mutton and two great bunches of turnips, which she intended to stew for our dinner. As for me, my heart was so overwhelmed at seeing these two friends—for such they were, though poor—and at their seeing me in such a condition, that I fell into another violent fit of crying, so that, in short, I could not speak to them again for a great while longer.

During my being in such an agony, they went to my maid Amy at another part of the same room and talked with her. Amy told them all my circumstances, and set them forth in such moving terms, and so to the life, that I could not upon any terms have done it like her myself, and, in a word, affected them both with it in such a manner, that the old aunt came to me, and though hardly able to speak for tears, "Look ye, cousin," said she, in a few words, "things must not stand thus; some course must be taken, and that forthwith; pray, where were these children born?" I told her the parish where we lived before, that four of them were born there, and one in the house where I now was, where the landlord, after having seized my goods for the rent past, not then knowing my circumstances, had now given me leave to live for a whole year more without any rent, being moved with compassion; but that this year was now almost expired.

Upon hearing this account, they came to this resolution, that the children should be all carried by them to the door of one of the relations mentioned above, and be set down there by the maid Amy, and that I, the mother, should remove for some days, shut up the doors, and be gone; that the people should be told, that if they did not think fit to take some care of the children, they might send for the churchwardens if they thought that better, for that they were born in that parish, and there they must be provided for; as for the other child, which was born in the parish of ——, that was already taken care of by the parish officers there, for indeed they were so sensible of the distress of the family that they had at first word done what was their part to do.

This was what these good women proposed, and bade me leave the rest to them. I was at first sadly afflicted at the thoughts of parting with my children, and especially at that terrible thing, their being taken into the parish keeping; and then a hundred terrible things came into my thoughts, viz., of parish children being starved at nurse; of their being ruined, let grow crooked, lamed, and the like, for want of being taken care of; and this sunk my very heart within me.

But the misery of my own circumstances hardened my heart against my own flesh and blood; and when I considered they must inevitably be starved, and I too if I continued to keep them about me, I began to be reconciled to parting with them all, anyhow and anywhere, that I might be freed from the dreadful necessity of seeing them all perish, and perishing with them myself. So I agreed to go away out of the house, and leave the management of the whole matter to my maid Amy and to them; and accordingly I did so, and the same afternoon they carried them all away to one of their aunts.

Amy, a resolute girl, knocked at the door, with the children all with her, and bade the eldest, as soon as the door was open, run in, and the rest after her. She set them all down at the door before she knocked, and when she knocked she stayed till a maid-servant came to the door; "Sweetheart," said she, "pray go in and tell your mistress here are her little cousins come to see her from —," naming the town where we lived, at which the maid offered to go back. "Here, child," says Amy, "take one of 'em in your hand, and I'll bring the rest;" so she gives her the least, and the wench goes in mighty innocently, with the little one in her hand, upon which Amy turns the rest in after her, shuts the door softly, and marches off as fast as she could.

Just in the interval of this, and even while the maid and her mistress were quarrelling (for the mistress raved and scolded her like a mad woman, and had ordered her to go and stop the maid Amy, and turn all the children out of the doors again; but she had been at the door, and Amy was gone, and the wench was out of her wits, and the mistress too), I say, just at this juncture came the poor old woman, not the aunt, but the other of the two that had been with me, and knocks at the door: the aunt did not go, because she had pretended to advocate for me, and they would have suspected her of some contrivance; but as for the other woman, they did not so much as know that she had kept up any correspondence with me.

Amy and she had concerted this between them, and it was well enough contrived that they did so. When she came into the house, the mistress was fuming, and raging like one distracted, and called the maid all the foolish jades and sluts that she could think of, and that she would take the children and turn them all out into the streets. The good poor woman, seeing her in such a passion, turned about as if she would be gone again, and said, "Madam, I'll come again another time, I see you are engaged." "No, no, Mrs. —," says the mistress, "I am not much engaged, sit down; this senseless creature here has brought in my fool of a brother's whole house of children upon me, and tells me that a wench brought them to the door and thrust them in, and bade her carry them to me; but it shall be no disturbance to me, for I have ordered them to be set in the street without the door, and so let the churchwardens take care of them, or else make this dull jade carry 'em back to —

again, and let her that brought them into the world look after them if she will; what does she send her brats to me for?"

"The last indeed had been the best of the two," says the poor woman, "if it had been to be done; and that brings me to tell you my errand, and the occasion of my coming, for I came on purpose about this very business, and to have prevented this being put upon you if I could, but I see I am come too late."

"How do you mean too late?" says the mistress. "What! have you been concerned in this affair, then? What! have you helped bring this family slur upon us?" "I hope you do not think such a thing of me, madam," says the poor woman; "but I went this morning to ——, to see my old mistress and benefactor, for she had been very kind to me, and when I came to the door I found all fast locked and bolted, and the house looking as if nobody was at home.

"I knocked at the door, but nobody came, till at last some of the neighbours' servants called to me and said, 'There's nobody lives there, mistress; what do you knock for?' I seemed surprised at that. 'What, nobody lives there!' said I; 'what d'ye mean? Does not Mrs. —— live there?' The answer was, 'No, she is gone;' at which I parleyed with one of them, and asked her what was the matter. 'Matter!' says she, 'why, it is matter enough: the poor gentlewoman has lived there all alone, and without anything to subsist her a long time, and this morning the landlord turned her out of doors.'

"'Out of doors!' says I; 'what! with all her children? Poor lambs, what is become of them?' 'Why, truly, nothing worse,' said they, 'can come to them than staying here, for they were almost starved with hunger; so the neighbours, seeing the poor lady in such distress, for she stood crying and wringing her hands over her children like one distracted, sent for the churchwardens to take care of the children; and they, when they came, took the youngest, which was born in this parish, and have got it a very good nurse, and taken care of it; but as for the other four, they had sent them away to some of their father's relations, and who were very substantial people, and who, besides that, lived in the parish where they were born.'

"I was not so surprised at this as not presently to foresee that this trouble would be brought upon you or upon Mr. ——; so I came immediately to bring word of it, that you might be prepared for it, and might not be surprised; but I see they have been too nimble for me, so that I know not what to advise. The poor woman, it seems, is turned out of doors into the street; and another of the neighbours there told me, that when they took her children from her she swooned away, and when they recovered her out of that, she ran distracted, and is put into a madhouse by the parish, for there is nobody else to take any care of her."

This was all acted to the life by this good, kind, poor creature; for though her design was perfectly good and charitable, yet there was not one word of it true in fact; for I was not turned out of doors by the landlord, nor gone distracted. It was true, indeed, that at parting with my poor children I fainted, and was like one mad when I came to myself and found they were gone; but I remained in the house a good while after that, as you shall hear.

While the poor woman was telling this dismal story, in came the gentlewoman's husband, and though her heart was hardened against all pity, who was really and nearly related to the children, for they were the children of her own brother, yet the good man was quite softened with the dismal relation of the circumstances of the family; and when the poor woman had done, he said to his wife, "This is a dismal case, my dear, indeed, and something must be done." His wife fell a-raving at him: "What," says she, "do you want to have four children to keep? Have we not children of our own? Would you have these brats come and eat up my children's bread? No, no, let 'em go to the parish, and let them take care of them; I'll take care of my own."

"Come, come, my dear," says the husband, "charity is a duty to the poor, and he that gives to the poor lends to the Lord; let us lend our heavenly Father a little of our children's bread, as you call it; it will be a store well laid up for them, and will be the best security that our children shall never come to want charity, or be turned out of doors, as these poor innocent creatures are." "Don't tell me of security," says the wife, "'tis a good security for our children to keep what we have together, and provide for them, and then 'tis time enough to help keep other folks' children. Charity begins at home."

"Well, my dear," says he again, "I only talk of putting out a little money to interest: our Maker is a good borrower; never fear making a bad debt there, child, I'll be bound for it."

"Don't banter me with your charity and your allegories," says the wife angrily; "I tell you they are my relations, not yours, and they shall not roost here; they shall go to the parish."

"All your relations are my relations now," says the good gentleman very calmly, "and I won't see your relations in distress, and not pity them, any more than I would my own; indeed, my dear, they shan't go to the parish. I assure you, none of my wife's relations shall come to the parish, if I can help it."

"What! will you take four children to keep?" says the wife.

"No, no, my dear," says he, "there's your sister ——, I'll go and talk with her; and your uncle — —, I'll send for him, and the rest. I'll warrant you, when we are all together, we will find ways and means to keep four poor little creatures from beggary and starving, or else it would be very hard; we are none of us in so bad circumstances but we are able to spare a mite for the fatherless. Don't shut up your bowels of compassion against your own flesh and blood. Could you hear these poor innocent children cry at your door for hunger, and give them no bread?"

"Prithee, what need they cry at our door?" says she. "'Tis the business of the parish to provide for them; they shan't cry at our door. If they do, I'll give them nothing." "Won't you?" says he; "but I will. Remember that dreadful Scripture is directly against us, Prov. xxi. , 'Whoso stoppeth his ears at the cry of the poor, he also shall cry himself, but shall not be heard.'"

"Well, well," says she, "you must do what you will, because you pretend to be master; but if I had my will I would send them where they ought to be sent: I would send them from whence they came."

Then the poor woman put in, and said, "But, madam, that is sending them to starve indeed, for the parish has no obligation to take care of 'em, and so they will lie and perish in the street."

"Or be sent back again," says the husband, "to our parish in a cripple-cart, by the justice's warrant, and so expose us and all the relations to the last degree among our neighbours, and among those who know the good old gentleman their grandfather, who lived and flourished in this parish so many years, and was so well beloved among all people, and deserved it so well."

"I don't value that one farthing, not I," says the wife; "I'll keep none of them."

"Well, my dear," says her husband, "but I value it, for I won't have such a blot lie upon the family, and upon your children; he was a worthy, ancient, and good man, and his name is respected among all his neighbours; it will be a reproach to you, that are his daughter, and to our children, that are his grandchildren, that we should let your brother's children perish, or come to be a charge to the public, in the very place where your family once flourished. Come, say no more; I will see what can be done."

Upon this he sends and gathers all the relations together at a tavern hard by, and sent for the four little children, that they might see them; and they all, at first word, agreed to have them taken care of, and, because his wife was so furious that she would not suffer one of them to be kept at home, they agreed to keep them all together for a while; so they committed them to the poor woman that had managed the affair for them, and entered into obligations to one another to supply the needful sums for their maintenance; and, not to have one separated from the rest, they sent for the youngest from the parish where it was taken in, and had them all brought up together.

It would take up too long a part of this story to give a particular account with what a charitable tenderness this good person, who was but an uncle-in-law to them, managed that affair; how careful he was of them; went constantly to see them, and to see that they were well provided for, clothed, put to school, and, at last, put out in the world for their advantage; but it is enough to say he acted more like a father to them than an uncle-in-law, though all along much against his wife's consent, who was of a disposition not so tender and compassionate as her husband.

You may believe I heard this with the same pleasure which I now feel at the relating it again; for I was terribly affrighted at the apprehensions of my children being brought to misery and distress, as those must be who have no friends, but are left to parish benevolence.

I was now, however, entering on a new scene of life. I had a great house upon my hands, and some furniture left in it; but I was no more able to maintain myself and my maid Amy in it than I was my five children; nor had I anything to subsist with but what I might get by working, and that was not a town where much work was to be had.

My landlord had been very kind indeed after he came to know my circumstances; though, before he was acquainted with that part, he had gone so far as to seize my goods, and to carry some of them off too.

But I had lived three-quarters of a year in his house after that, and had paid him no rent, and, which was worse, I was in no condition to pay him any. However, I observed he came oftener to see me, looked kinder upon me, and spoke more friendly to me, than he used to do, particularly the last two or three times he had been there. He observed, he said, how poorly I lived, how low I was reduced, and the like; told me it grieved him for my sake; and the last time of all he was kinder still, told me he came to dine with me, and that I should give him leave to treat me; so he called my maid Amy, and sent her out to buy a joint of meat; he told her what she should buy; but naming two or three things, either of which she might take, the maid, a cunning wench, and faithful to me as the skin to my back, did not buy anything outright, but brought the butcher along with her, with both the things that she had chosen, for him to please himself. The one was a large, very good leg of veal; the other a piece of the fore-ribs of roasting beef. He looked at them, but made me chaffer with the butcher for him, and I did so, and came back to him and told him what the butcher had demanded for either of them, and what each of them came to. So he pulls out eleven shillings and threepence, which they came to together, and bade me take them both; the rest, he said, would serve another time.

I was surprised, you may be sure, at the bounty of a man that had but a little while ago been my terror, and had torn the goods out of my house like a fury; but I considered that my distresses had mollified his temper, and that he had afterwards been so compassionate as to give me leave to live rent free in the house a whole year.

But now he put on the face, not of a man of compassion only, but of a man of friendship and kindness, and this was so unexpected that it was surprising. We chatted together, and were, as I may call it, cheerful, which was more than I could say I had been for three years before. He sent for wine and beer too, for I had none; poor Amy and I had drank nothing but water for many weeks, and indeed I have often wondered at the faithful temper of the poor girl, for which I but ill requited her at last.

When Amy was come with the wine, he made her fill a glass to him, and with the glass in his hand he came to me and kissed me, which I was, I confess, a little surprised at, but more at what followed; for he told me, that as the sad condition which I was reduced to had made him pity me, so my conduct in it, and the courage I bore it with, had given him a more than ordinary respect for me, and made him very thoughtful for my good; that he was resolved for the present to do something to relieve me, and to employ his thoughts in the meantime, to see if he could for the future put me into a way to support myself.

While he found me change colour, and look surprised at his discourse, for so I did, to be sure, he turns to my maid Amy, and looking at her, he says to me, "I say all this, madam, before your maid, because both she and you shall know that I have no ill design, and that I have, in mere kindness, resolved to do something for you if I can; and as I have been a witness of the uncommon honesty and fidelity of Mrs. Amy here to you in all your distresses, I know she may be trusted with so honest a design as mine is; for I assure you, I bear a proportioned regard to your maid too, for her affection to you."

Amy made him a curtsey, and the poor girl looked so confounded with joy that she could not speak, but her colour came and went, and every now and then she blushed as red as scarlet, and the next minute looked as pale as death. Well, having said this, he sat down, made me sit down, and then drank to me, and made me drink two glasses of wine together; "For," says he, "you have need of it;" and so indeed I had. When he had done so, "Come, Amy," says he, "with your mistress's leave, you shall have a glass too." So he made her drink two glasses also; and then rising up, "And now, Amy," says he, "go and get dinner; and you, madam," says he to me, "go up and dress you, and come down and smile and be merry;" adding, "I'll make you easy if I can;" and in the meantime, he said, he would walk in the garden.

When he was gone, Amy changed her countenance indeed, and looked as merry as ever she did in her life. "Dear madam," says she, "what does this gentleman mean?" "Nay, Amy," said I, "he means to do us good, you see, don't he? I know no other meaning he can have, for he can get nothing by me." "I warrant you, madam," says she, "he'll ask you a favour by-and-by." "No, no, you are mistaken, Amy, I dare say," said I; "you have heard what he said, didn't you?" "Ay," says Amy, "it's no matter for that, you shall see what he will do after dinner." "Well, well, Amy," says I, "you have hard thoughts of him. I cannot be of your opinion: I don't see anything in him yet that looks like it." "As to that, madam," says Amy, "I don't see anything of it yet neither; but what should move a gentleman to take pity of us as he does?" "Nay," says I, "that's a hard thing too, that we should judge a man to be wicked because he's charitable, and vicious because he's kind." "Oh, madam," says Amy, "there's abundance of charity begins in that vice; and he is not so unacquainted with things as not to know that poverty is the strongest incentive—a temptation against which no virtue is powerful enough to stand out. He knows your condition as well as you do." "Well, and what then?" "Why, then, he knows too that you are young and handsome, and he has the surest bait in the world to take you with."

"Well, Amy," said I, "but he may find himself mistaken too in such a thing as that." "Why, madam," says Amy, "I hope you won't deny him if he should offer it."

"What d'ye mean by that, hussy?" said I. "No, I'd starve first."

"I hope not, madam, I hope you would be wiser; I'm sure if he will set you up, as he talks of, you ought to deny him nothing; and you will starve if you do not consent, that's certain."

"What! consent to lie with him for bread? Amy," said I, "how can you talk so!"

"Nay, madam," says Amy, "I don't think you would for anything else; it would not be lawful for anything else, but for bread, madam; why, nobody can starve, there's no bearing that, I'm sure."

"Ay," says I, "but if he would give me an estate to live on, he should not lie with me, I assure you."

"Why, look you, madam; if he would but give you enough to live easy upon, he should lie with me for it with all my heart."

"That's a token, Amy, of inimitable kindness to me," said I, "and I know how to value it; but there's more friendship than honesty in it, Amy."

"Oh, madam," says Amy, "I'd do anything to get you out of this sad condition; as to honesty, I think honesty is out of the question when starving is the case. Are not we almost starved to death?"

"I am indeed," said I, "and thou art for my sake; but to be a whore, Amy!" and there I stopped.

"Dear madam," says Amy, "if I will starve for your sake, I will be a whore or anything for your sake; why, I would die for you if I were put to it."

"Why, that's an excess of affection, Amy," said I, "I never met with before; I wish I may be ever in condition to make you some returns suitable. But, however, Amy, you shall not be a whore to him, to oblige him to be kind to me; no, Amy, nor I won't be a whore to him, if he would give me much more than he is able to give me or do for me."

"Why, madam," says Amy, "I don't say I will go and ask him; but I say, if he should promise to do so and so for you, and the condition was such that he would not serve you unless I would let him lie with me, he should lie with me as often as he would, rather than you should not have his assistance. But this is but talk, madam; I don't see any need of such discourse, and you are of opinion that there will be no need of it."

"Indeed so I am, Amy; but," said I, "if there was, I tell you again, I'd die before I would consent, or before you should consent for my sake."

Hitherto I had not only preserved the virtue itself, but the virtuous inclination and resolution; and had I kept myself there I had been happy, though I had perished of mere hunger; for, without question, a woman ought rather to die than to prostitute her virtue and honour, let the temptation be what it will.

But to return to my story; he walked about the garden, which was, indeed, all in disorder, and overrun with weeds, because I had not been able to hire a gardener to do anything to it, no, not so much as to dig up ground enough to sow a few turnips and carrots for family use. After he had viewed it, he came in, and sent Amy to fetch a poor man, a gardener, that used to help our man-servant, and carried him into the garden, and ordered him to do several things in it, to put it into a little order; and this took him up near an hour.

By this time I had dressed me as well as I could; for though I had good linen left still, yet I had but a poor head-dress, and no knots, but old fragments; no necklace, no earrings; all those things were gone long ago for mere bread.

However, I was tight and clean, and in better plight than he had seen me in a great while, and he looked extremely pleased to see me so; for, he said, I looked so disconsolate and so afflicted before, that it grieved him to see me; and he bade me pluck up a good heart, for he hoped to put me in a condition to live in the world, and be beholden to nobody.

I told him that was impossible, for I must be beholden to him for it, for all the friends I had in the world would not or could not do so much for me as that he spoke of "Well, widow," says he (so he called me, and so indeed I was in the worst sense that desolate word could be used in), "if you are beholden to me, you shall be beholden to nobody else."

By this time dinner was ready, and Amy came in to lay the cloth, and indeed it was happy there was none to dine but he and I, for I had but six plates left in the house, and but two dishes; however, he knew how things were, and bade me make no scruple about bringing out what I had. He hoped to see me in a better plight. He did not come, he said, to be entertained, but to entertain me, and comfort and encourage me. Thus he went on, speaking so cheerfully to me, and such cheerful things, that it was a cordial to my very soul to hear him speak.

Well, we went to dinner. I'm sure I had not ate a good meal hardly in a twelvemonth, at least not of such a joint of meat as the loin of veal was. I ate, indeed, very heartily, and so did he, and he made me drink three or four glasses of wine; so that, in short, my spirits were lifted up to a degree I had not been used to, and I was not only cheerful, but merry; and so he pressed me to be.

I told him I had a great deal of reason to be merry, seeing he had been so kind to me, and had given me hopes of recovering me from the worst circumstances that ever woman of any sort of fortune was sunk into; that he could not but believe that what he had said to me was like life from the dead; that it was like recovering one sick from the brink of the grave; how I should ever make him a return any way suitable was what I had not yet had time to think of; I could only say that I should never forget it while I had life, and should be always ready to acknowledge it.

He said that was all he desired of me; that his reward would be the satisfaction of having rescued me from misery; that he found he was obliging one that knew what gratitude meant; that he would make it his business to make me completely easy, first or last, if it lay in his power; and in the meantime he bade me consider of anything that I thought he might do for me, for my advantage, and in order to make me perfectly easy.

After we had talked thus, he bade me be cheerful. "Come," says he, "lay aside these melancholy things, and let us be merry." Amy waited at the table, and she smiled and laughed, and was so merry she could hardly contain it, for the girl loved me to an excess hardly to be described; and it was such an unexpected thing to hear any one talk to her mistress, that the wench was beside herself almost, and, as soon as dinner was over, Amy went upstairs, and put on her best clothes too, and came down dressed like a gentlewoman.

We sat together talking of a thousand things—of what had been, and what was to be—all the rest of the day, and in the evening he took his leave of me, with a thousand expressions of kindness and tenderness and true affection to me, but offered not the least of what my maid Amy had suggested.

At his going away he took me in his arms, protested an honest kindness to me; said a thousand kind things to me, which I cannot now recollect; and, after kissing me twenty times or thereabouts, put a guinea into my hand, which, he said, was for my present supply, and told me that he would see me again before it was out; also he gave Amy half-a-crown.

When he was gone, "Well, Amy," said I, "are you convinced now that he is an honest as well as a true friend, and that there has been nothing, not the least appearance of anything, of what you imagined in his behaviour?" "Yes," says Amy, "I am, but I admire at it. He is such a friend as the world, sure, has not abundance of to show."

"I am sure," says I, "he is such a friend as I have long wanted, and as I have as much need of as any creature in the world has or ever had." And, in short, I was so overcome with the comfort of it that I sat down and cried for joy a good while, as I had formerly cried for sorrow. Amy and I went to bed that night (for Amy lay with me) pretty early, but lay chatting almost all night about it, and the girl was so transported that she got up two or three times in the night and danced about the room in her shift; in short, the girl was half distracted with the joy of it; a testimony still of her violent affection for her mistress, in which no servant ever went beyond her.

We heard no more of him for two days, but the third day he came again; then he told me, with the same kindness, that he had ordered me a supply of household goods for the furnishing the house; that, in particular, he had sent me back all the goods that he had seized for rent, which consisted, indeed, of the best of my former furniture. "And now," says he, "I'll tell you what I have had in my head for you for your present supply, and that is," says he, "that the house being well furnished, you shall let it out to lodgings for the summer gentry," says he, "by which you will easily get a good comfortable subsistence, especially seeing you shall pay me no rent for two years, nor after neither, unless you can afford it."

This was the first view I had of living comfortably indeed, and it was a very probable way, I must confess, seeing we had very good conveniences, six rooms on a floor, and three stories high. While he was laying down the scheme of my management, came a cart to the door with a load of goods, and an upholsterer's man to put them up. They were chiefly the furniture of two rooms which he had carried away for his two years' rent, with two fine cabinets, and some pier-glasses out of the parlour, and several other valuable things.

These were all restored to their places, and he told me he gave them me freely, as a satisfaction for the cruelty he had used me with before; and the furniture of one room being finished and set up, he told me he would furnish one chamber for himself, and would come and be one of my lodgers, if I would give him leave.

I told him he ought not to ask me leave, who had so much right to make himself welcome. So the house began to look in some tolerable figure, and clean; the garden also, in about a fortnight's work, began to look something less like a wilderness than it used to do; and he ordered me to put up a bill for letting rooms, reserving one for himself, to come to as he saw occasion.

When all was done to his mind, as to placing the goods, he seemed very well pleased, and we dined together again of his own providing; and the upholsterer's man gone, after dinner he took me by the hand. "Come now, madam," says he, "you must show me your house" (for he had a mind to see everything over again). "No, sir," said I; "but I'll go show you your house, if you please;" so we went up through all the rooms, and in the room which was appointed for himself Amy was doing something. "Well, Amy," says he, "I intend to lie with you to-morrow night." "To-night if you please, sir," says Amy very innocently; "your room is quite ready." "Well, Amy," says he, "I am glad you are so willing." "No," says Amy, "I mean your chamber is ready to-night," and away she run out of the room, ashamed enough; for the girl meant no harm, whatever she had said to me in private.

However, he said no more then; but when Amy was gone he walked about the room, and looked at everything, and taking me by the hand he kissed me, and spoke a great many kind, affectionate things to me indeed; as of his measures for my advantage, and what he would do to raise me again in the world; told me that my afflictions and the conduct I had shown in bearing them to such an extremity, had so engaged him to me that he valued me infinitely above all the women in the world; that though he was under such engagements that he could not marry me (his wife and he had been parted for some reasons, which make too long a story to intermix with mine), yet that he would be everything else that a woman could ask in a husband; and with that he kissed me again, and took me in his arms, but offered not the least uncivil action to me, and told me he hoped I would not deny him all the favours he should ask, because he resolved to ask nothing of me but what it was fit for a woman of virtue and modesty, for such he knew me to be, to yield.

I confess the terrible pressure of my former misery, the memory of which lay heavy upon my mind, and the surprising kindness with which he had delivered me, and, withal, the expectations of what he might still do for me, were powerful things, and made me have scarce the power to deny him anything he would ask. However, I told him thus, with an air of tenderness too, that he had done so much for me that I thought I ought to deny him nothing; only I hoped and depended upon him that he would not take the advantage of the infinite obligations I was under to him, to desire anything of me the yielding to which would lay me lower in his esteem than I desired to be; that as I took him to be a man of honour, so I knew he could not like me better for doing anything that was below a woman of honesty and good manners to do.

23

He told me that he had done all this for me, without so much as telling me what kindness or real affection he had for me, that I might not be under any necessity of yielding to him in anything for want of bread; and he would no more oppress my gratitude now than he would my necessity before, nor ask anything, supposing he would stop his favours or withdraw his kindness, if he was denied; it was true, he said, he might tell me more freely his mind now than before, seeing I had let him see that I accepted his assistance, and saw that he was sincere in his design of serving me; that he had gone thus far to show me that he was kind to me, but that now he would tell me that he loved me, and yet would demonstrate that his love was both honourable, and that what he should desire was what he might honestly ask and I might honestly grant.

I answered that, within those two limitations, I was sure I ought to deny him nothing, and I should think myself not ungrateful only, but very unjust, if I should; so he said no more, but I observed he kissed me more, and took me in his arms in a kind of familiar way, more than usual, and which once or twice put me in mind of my maid Amy's words; and yet, I must acknowledge, I was so overcome with his goodness to me in those many kind things he had done that I not only was easy at what he did and made no resistance, but was inclined to do the like, whatever he had offered to do. But he went no farther than what I have said, nor did he offer so much as to sit down on the bedside with me, but took his leave, said he loved me tenderly, and would convince me of it by such demonstrations as should be to my satisfaction. I told him I had a great deal of reason to believe him, that he was full master of the whole house and of me, as far as was within the bounds we had spoken of, which I believe he would not break, and asked him if he would not lodge there that night.

He said he could not well stay that night, business requiring him in London, but added, smiling, that he would come the next day and take a night's lodging with me. I pressed him to stay that night, and told him I should be glad a friend so valuable should be under the same roof with me; and indeed I began at that time not only to be much obliged to him, but to love him too, and that in a manner that I had not been acquainted with myself.

Oh! let no woman slight the temptation that being generously delivered from trouble is to any spirit furnished with gratitude and just principles. This gentleman had freely and voluntarily delivered me from misery, from poverty, and rags; he had made me what I was, and put me into a way to be even more than I ever was, namely, to live happy and pleased, and on his bounty I depended. What could I say to this gentleman when he pressed me to yield to him, and argued the lawfulness of it? But of that in its place.

I pressed him again to stay that night, and told him it was the first completely happy night that I had ever had in the house in my life, and I should be very sorry to have it be without his company, who was the cause and foundation of it all; that we would be innocently merry, but that it could never be without him; and, in short, I courted him so, that he said he could not deny me, but he would take his horse and go to London, do the business he had to do, which, it seems, was to pay a foreign bill that was due that night, and would else be protested, and that he would come back in three hours at farthest, and sup with me; but bade me get nothing there, for since I was resolved to be merry, which was what he desired above all things, he would send me something from London. "And we will make it a wedding supper, my dear," says he; and with that word took me in his arms, and kissed me so vehemently that I made no question but he intended to do everything else that Amy had talked of.

I started a little at the word wedding. "What do ye mean, to call it by such a name?" says I; adding, "We will have a supper, but t' other is impossible, as well on your side as mine." He laughed. "Well," says he, "you shall call it what you will, but it may be the same thing, for I shall satisfy you it is not so impossible as you make it."

"I don't understand you," said I. "Have not I a husband and you a wife?"

"Well, well," says he, "we will talk of that after supper;" so he rose up, gave me another kiss, and took his horse for London.

This kind of discourse had fired my blood, I confess, and I knew not what to think of it. It was plain now that he intended to lie with me, but how he would reconcile it to a legal thing, like a marriage, that I could not imagine. We had both of us used Amy with so much intimacy, and trusted her with everything, having such unexampled instances of her fidelity, that he made no scruple to kiss me and say all these things to me before her; nor had he cared one farthing, if I would have let him lie with me, to have had Amy there too all night. When he was gone, "Well, Amy," says I, "what will all this come to now? I am all in a sweat at him." "Come to, madam?" says Amy. "I see what it will come to; I must put you to bed to-night together." "Why, you would not be so impudent, you jade you," says I, "would you?" "Yes, I would," says she, "with all my heart, and think you both as honest as ever you were in your lives."

"What ails the slut to talk so?" said I. "Honest! How can it be honest?" "Why, I'll tell you, madam," says Amy; "I sounded it as soon as I heard him speak, and it is very true too; he calls you widow, and such indeed you are; for, as my master has left you so many years, he is dead, to be sure; at least he is dead to you; he is no husband. You are, and ought to be, free to marry who you will; and his wife being gone from him, and refusing to lie with him, then he is a single man again as much as ever; and though you cannot bring the laws of the land to join you together, yet, one refusing to do the office of a wife, and the other of a husband, you may certainly take one another fairly."

"Nay, Amy," says I, "if I could take him fairly, you may be sure I'd take him above all the men in the world; it turned the very heart within me when I heard him say he loved me. How could it be otherwise, when you know what a condition I was in before, despised and trampled on by all the world? I could have took him in my arms and kissed him as freely as he did me, if it had not been for shame."
"Ay, and all the rest too," says Amy, "at the first word. I don't see how you can think of denying him anything. Has he not brought you out of the devil's clutches, brought you out of the blackest misery that ever poor lady was reduced to? Can a woman deny such a man anything?"

"Nay, I don't know what to do, Amy," says I. "I hope he won't desire anything of that kind of me; I hope he won't attempt it. If he does, I know not what to say to him."

"Not ask you!" says Amy. "Depend upon it, he will ask you, and you will grant it too. I am sure my mistress is no fool. Come, pray, madam, let me go air you a clean shift; don't let him find you in foul linen the wedding-night."

"But that I know you to be a very honest girl, Amy," says I, "you would make me abhor you. Why, you argue for the devil, as if you were one of his privy councillors."

"It's no matter for that, madam, I say nothing but what I think. You own you love this gentleman, and he has given you sufficient testimony of his affection to you; your conditions are alike unhappy, and he is of opinion that he may take another woman, his first wife having broke her honour, and living from him; and that though the laws of the land will not allow him to marry formally, yet that he may take another woman into his arms, provided he keeps true to the other woman as a wife; nay, he says it is usual to do so, and allowed by the custom of the place, in several countries abroad. And, I must own, I am of the same mind; else it is in the power of a whore, after she has jilted and abandoned her husband, to confine him from the pleasure as well as convenience of a woman all the days of his life, which would be very unreasonable, and, as times go, not tolerable to all people; and the like on your side, madam."

Had I now had my senses about me, and had my reason not been overcome by the powerful attraction of so kind, so beneficent a friend; had I consulted conscience and virtue, I should have repelled this Amy, however faithful and honest to me in other things, as a viper and engine of the devil. I ought to have remembered that neither he or I, either by the laws of God or man, could come together upon any other terms than that of notorious adultery. The ignorant jade's argument, that he had brought me out of the hands of the devil, by which she meant the devil of poverty and distress, should have been a powerful motive to me not to plunge myself into the jaws of hell, and into the power of the real devil, in recompense for that deliverance. I should have looked upon all the good this man had done for me to have been the particular work of the goodness of Heaven, and that goodness should have moved me to a return of duty and humble obedience. I should have received the mercy thankfully, and applied it soberly, to the praise and honour of my Maker; whereas, by this wicked course, all the bounty and kindness of this gentleman became a snare to me, was a mere bait to the devil's hook; I received his kindness at the dear expense of body and soul, mortgaging faith, religion, conscience, and modesty for (as I may call it) a morsel of bread; or, if you will, ruined my soul from a principle of gratitude, and gave myself up to the devil, to show myself grateful to my benefactor. I must do the gentleman that justice as to say I verily believe that he did nothing but what he thought was lawful; and I must do that justice upon myself as to say I did what my own conscience convinced me, at the very time I did it, was horribly unlawful, scandalous, and abominable.

But poverty was my snare; dreadful poverty! The misery I had been in was great, such as would make the heart tremble at the apprehensions of its return; and I might appeal to any that has had any experience of the world, whether one so entirely destitute as I was of all manner of all helps or friends, either to support me or to assist me to support myself, could withstand the proposal; not that I plead this as a justification of my conduct, but that it may move the pity even of those that abhor the crime.

Besides this, I was young, handsome, and, with all the mortifications I had met with, was vain, and that not a little; and, as it was a new thing, so it was a pleasant thing to be courted, caressed, embraced, and high professions of affection made to me, by a man so agreeable and so able to do me good.

Add to this, that if I had ventured to disoblige this gentleman, I had no friend in the world to have recourse to; I had no prospect—no, not of a bit of bread; I had nothing before me but to fall back into the same misery that I had been in before.

Amy had but too much rhetoric in this cause; she represented all those things in their proper colours; she argued them all with her utmost skill; and at last the merry jade, when she came to dress me, "Look ye, madam," said she, "if you won't consent, tell him you will do as Rachel did to Jacob, when she could have no children—put her maid to bed to him; tell him you cannot comply with him, but there's Amy, he may ask her the question; she has promised me she won't deny you."

"And would you have me say so, Amy?" said I.

"No, madam; but I would really have you do so. Besides, you are undone if you do not; and if my doing it would save you from being undone, as I said before, he shall, if he will; if he asks me, I won't deny him, not I; hang me if I do," says Amy.

"Well, I know not what to do," says I to Amy.

"Do!" says Amy. "Your choice is fair and plain. Here you may have a handsome, charming gentleman, be rich, live pleasantly and in plenty, or refuse him, and want a dinner, go in rags, live in tears; in short, beg and starve. You know this is the case, madam," says Amy. "I wonder how you can say you know not what to do."

"Well, Amy," says I, "the case is as you say, and I think verily I must yield to him; but then," said I, moved by conscience, "don't talk any more of your cant of its being lawful that I ought to marry again, and that he ought to marry again, and such stuff as that; 'tis all nonsense," says I, "Amy, there's nothing in it; let me hear no more of that, for if I yield, 'tis in vain to mince the matter, I am a whore, Amy; neither better nor worse, I assure you."

"I don't think so, madam, by no means," says Amy. "I wonder how you can talk so;" and then she run on with her argument of the unreasonableness that a woman should be obliged to live single, or a man to live single, in such cases as before. "Well, Amy," said I, "come, let us dispute no more, for the longer I enter into that part, the greater my scruples will be; but if I let it alone, the necessity of my present circumstances is such that I believe I shall yield to him, if he should importune me much about it; but I should be glad he would not do it at all, but leave me as I am."

"As to that, madam, you may depend," says Amy, "he expects to have you for his bedfellow to-night. I saw it plainly in his management all day; and at last he told you so too, as plain, I think, as he could." "Well, well, Amy," said I, "I don't know what to say; if he will he must, I think; I don't know how to resist such a man, that has done so much for me." "I don't know how you should," says Amy.

Thus Amy and I canvassed the business between us; the jade prompted the crime which I had but too much inclination to commit, that is to say, not as a crime, for I had nothing of the vice in my constitution; my spirits were far from being high, my blood had no fire in it to kindle the flame of desire; but the kindness and good humour of the man and the dread of my own circumstances concurred to bring me to the point, and I even resolved, before he asked, to give up my virtue to him whenever he should put it to the question.

In this I was a double offender, whatever he was, for I was resolved to commit the crime, knowing and owning it to be a crime; he, if it was true as he said, was fully persuaded it was lawful, and in that persuasion he took the measures and used all the circumlocutions which I am going to speak of.

About two hours after he was gone, came a Leadenhall basket-woman, with a whole load of good things for the mouth (the particulars are not to the purpose), and brought orders to get supper by eight o'clock. However, I did not intend to begin to dress anything till I saw him; and he gave me time enough, for he came before seven, so that Amy, who had gotten one to help her, got everything ready in time.

We sat down to supper about eight, and were indeed very merry. Amy made us some sport, for she was a girl of spirit and wit, and with her talk she made us laugh very often, and yet the jade managed her wit with all the good manners imaginable.

But to shorten the story. After supper he took me up into his chamber, where Amy had made a good fire, and there he pulled out a great many papers, and spread them upon a little table, and then took me by the hand, and after kissing me very much, he entered into a discourse of his circumstances and of mine, how they agreed in several things exactly; for example, that I was abandoned of a husband in the prime of my youth and vigour, and he of a wife in his middle age; how the end of marriage was destroyed by the treatment we had either of us received, and it would be very hard that we should be tied by the formality of the contract where the essence of it was destroyed. I interrupted him, and told him there was a vast difference between our circumstances, and that in the most essential part, namely, that he was rich, and I was poor; that he was above the world, and I infinitely below it; that his circumstances were very easy, mine miserable, and this was an inequality the most essential that could be imagined. "As to that, my dear," says he, "I have taken such measures as shall make an equality still;" and with that he showed me a contract in writing, wherein he engaged himself to me to cohabit constantly with me, to provide for me in all respects as a wife, and repeating in the preamble a long account of the nature and reason of our living together, and an obligation in the penalty of £7000 never to abandon me; and at last showed me a bond for £500, to be paid to me, or to my assigns, within three months after his death.

He read over all these things to me, and then, in a most moving, affectionate manner, and in words not to be answered, he said, "Now, my dear, is this not sufficient? Can you object anything against it? If not, as I believe you will not, then let us debate this matter no longer." With that he pulled out a silk purse, which had threescore guineas in it, and threw them into my lap, and concluded all the rest of his discourse with kisses and protestations of his love, of which indeed I had abundant proof.

Pity human frailty, you that read of a woman reduced in her youth and prime to the utmost misery and distress, and raised again, as above, by the unexpected and surprising bounty of a stranger; I say, pity her if she was not able, after all these things, to make any more resistance.

However, I stood out a little longer still. I asked him how he could expect that I could come into a proposal of such consequence the very first time it was moved to me; and that I ought, if I consented to it, to capitulate with him that he should never upbraid me with easiness and consenting too soon. He said no; but, on the contrary, he would take it as a mark of the greatest kindness I could show him. Then he went on to give reasons why there was no occasion to use the ordinary ceremony of delay, or to wait a reasonable time of courtship, which was only to avoid scandal; but, as this was private, it had nothing of that nature in it; that he had been courting me some time by the best of courtship, viz., doing acts of kindness to me; and that he had given testimonies of his sincere affection to me by deeds, not by flattering trifles and the usual courtship of words, which were often found to have very little meaning; that he took me, not as a mistress, but as his wife, and protested it was clear to him he might lawfully do it, and that I was perfectly at liberty, and assured me, by all that it was possible for an honest man to say, that he would treat me as his wife as long as he lived. In a word, he conquered all the little resistance I intended to make; he protested he loved me above all the world, and begged I would for once believe him; that he had never deceived me, and never would, but would make it his study to make my life comfortable and happy, and to make me forget the misery I had gone through. I stood still a while, and said nothing; but seeing him eager for my answer, I smiled, and looking up at him, "And must I, then," says I, "say yes at first asking? Must I depend upon your promise? Why, then," said I, "upon the faith of that promise, and in the sense of that inexpressible kindness you have shown me, you shall be obliged, and I will be wholly yours to the end of my life;" and with that I took his hand, which held me by the hand, and gave it a kiss.

And thus, in gratitude for the favours I received from a man, was all sense of religion and duty to God, all regard to virtue and honour, given up at once, and we were to call one another man and wife, who, in the sense of the laws both of God and our country, were no more than two adulterers; in short, a whore and a rogue. Nor, as I have said above, was my conscience silent in it, though it seems his was; for I sinned with open eyes, and thereby had a double guilt upon me. As I always said, his notions were of another kind, and he either was before of the opinion, or argued himself into it now, that we were both free and might lawfully marry.

But I was quite of another side—nay, and my judgment was right, but my circumstances were my temptation; the terrors behind me looked blacker than the terrors before me; and the dreadful argument of wanting bread, and being run into the horrible distresses I was in before, mastered all my resolution, and I gave myself up as above.

The rest of the evening we spent very agreeably to me; he was perfectly good-humoured, and was at that time very merry. Then he made Amy dance with him, and I told him I would put Amy to bed to him. Amy said, with all her heart; she never had been a bride in her life. In short, he made the girl so merry that, had he not been to lie with me the same night, I believe he would have played the fool with Amy for half-an-hour, and the girl would no more have refused him than I intended to do. Yet before, I had always found her a very modest wench as any I ever saw in all my life; but, in short, the mirth of that night, and a few more such afterwards, ruined the girl's modesty for ever, as shall appear by-and-by, in its place.

So far does fooling and toying sometimes go that I know nothing a young woman has to be more cautious of; so far had this innocent girl gone in jesting between her and I, and in talking that she would let him lie with her, if he would but be kinder to me, that at last she let him lie with her in earnest; and so empty was I now of all principle, that I encouraged the doing it almost before my face.

I say but too justly that I was empty of principle, because, as above, I had yielded to him, not as deluded to believe it lawful, but as overcome by his kindness, and terrified at the fear of my own misery if he should leave me. So with my eyes open, and with my conscience, as I may say, awake, I sinned, knowing it to be a sin, but having no power to resist. When this had thus made a hole in my heart, and I was come to such a height as to transgress against the light of my own conscience, I was then fit for any wickedness, and conscience left off speaking where it found it could not be heard.

But to return to our story. Having consented, as above, to his proposal, we had not much more to do. He gave me my writings, and the bond for my maintenance during his life, and for five hundred pounds after his death. And so far was he from abating his affection to me afterwards, that two years after we were thus, as he called it, married, he made his will, and gave me a thousand pounds more, and all my household stuff, plate, &c., which was considerable too.

Amy put us to bed, and my new friend—I cannot call him husband—was so well pleased with Amy for her fidelity and kindness to me that he paid her all the arrear of her wages that I owed her, and gave her five guineas over; and had it gone no farther, Amy had richly deserved what she had, for never was a maid so true to her mistress in such dreadful circumstances as I was in. Nor was what followed more her own fault than mine, who led her almost into it at first, and quite into it at last; and this may be a farther testimony what a hardness of crime I was now arrived to, which was owing to the conviction, that was from the beginning upon me, that I was a whore, not a wife; nor could I ever frame my mouth to call him husband or to say "my husband" when I was speaking of him.

We lived, surely, the most agreeable life, the grand exception only excepted, that ever two lived together. He was the most obliging, gentlemanly man, and the most tender of me, that ever woman gave herself up to. Nor was there ever the least interruption to our mutual kindness, no, not to the last day of his life. But I must bring Amy's disaster in at once, that I may have done with her.

Amy was dressing me one morning, for now I had two maids, and Amy was my chambermaid. "Dear madam," says Amy, "what! a'nt you with child yet?" "No, Amy," says I; "nor any sign of it."

"Law, madam!" says Amy, "what have you been doing? Why, you have been married a year and a half. I warrant you master would have got me with child twice in that time." "It may be so, Amy," says I. "Let him try, can't you?" "No," says Amy; "you'll forbid it now. Before, I told you he should, with all my heart; but I won't now, now he's all your own." "Oh," says I, "Amy, I'll freely give you my consent. It will be nothing at all to me. Nay, I'll put you to bed to him myself one night or other, if you are willing." "No, madam, no," says Amy, "not now he's yours."

"Why, you fool you," says I, "don't I tell you I'll put you to bed to him myself?" "Nay, nay," says Amy, "if you put me to bed to him, that's another case; I believe I shall not rise again very soon." "I'll venture that, Amy," says I.

After supper that night, and before we were risen from table, I said to him, Amy being by, "Hark ye, Mr. ——, do you know that you are to lie with Amy to-night?" "No, not I," says he; but turns to Amy, "Is it so, Amy?" says he. "No, sir," says she. "Nay, don't say no, you fool; did not I promise to put you to bed to him?" But the girl said "No," still, and it passed off.

At night, when we came to go to bed, Amy came into the chamber to undress me, and her master slipped into bed first; then I began, and told him all that Amy had said about my not being with child, and of her being with child twice in that time. "Ay, Mrs. Amy," says he, "I believe so too. Come hither, and, we'll try." But Amy did not go. "Go, you fool," says I, "can't you? I freely give you both leave." But Amy would not go. "Nay, you whore," says I, "you said, if I would put you to bed, you would with all your heart." And with that I sat her down, pulled off her stockings and shoes, and all her clothes piece by piece, and led her to the bed to him. "Here," says I, "try what you can do with your maid Amy." She pulled back a little, would not let me pull off her clothes at first, but it was hot weather, and she had not many clothes on, and particularly no stays on; and at last, when she saw I was in earnest, she let me do what I would. So I fairly stripped her, and then I threw open the bed and thrust her in.

I need say no more. This is enough to convince anybody that I did not think him my husband, and that I had cast off all principle and all modesty, and had effectually stifled conscience.

Amy, I dare say, began now to repent, and would fain have got out of bed again; but he said to her, "Nay, Amy, you see your mistress has put you to bed; 'tis all her doing; you must blame her." So he held her fast, and the wench being naked in the bed with him, it was too late to look back, so she lay still and let him do what he would with her.

Had I looked upon myself as a wife, you cannot suppose I would have been willing to have let my husband lie with my maid, much less before my face, for I stood by all the while; but as I thought myself a whore, I cannot say but that it was something designed in my thoughts that my maid should be a whore too, and should not reproach me with it.

Amy, however, less vicious than I, was grievously out of sorts the next morning, and cried and took on most vehemently, that she was ruined and undone, and there was no pacifying her; she was a whore, a slut, and she was undone! undone! and cried almost all day. I did all I could to pacify her. "A whore!" says I. "Well, and am not I a whore as well as you?" "No, no," says Amy; "no, you are not, for you are married." "Not I, Amy," says I; "I do not pretend to it. He may marry you to-morrow, if he will, for anything I could do to hinder it. I am not married. I do not look upon it as anything." Well, all did not pacify Amy, but she cried two or three days about it; but it wore off by degrees.

But the case differed between Amy and her master exceedingly; for Amy retained the same kind temper she always had; but, on the contrary, he was quite altered, for he hated her heartily, and could, I believe, have killed her after it, and he told me so, for he thought this a vile action; whereas what he and I had done he was perfectly easy in, thought it just, and esteemed me as much his wife as if we had been married from our youth, and had neither of us known any other; nay, he loved me, I believe, as entirely as if I had been the wife of his youth. Nay, he told me it was true, in one sense, that he had two wives, but that I was the wife of his affection, the other the wife of his aversion.

I was extremely concerned at the aversion he had taken to my maid Amy, and used my utmost skill to get it altered; for though he had, indeed, debauched the wench, I knew that I was the principal occasion of it; and as he was the best-humoured man in the world, I never gave him over till I prevailed with him to be easy with her, and as I was now become the devil's agent, to make others as wicked as myself, I brought him to lie with her again several times after that, till at last, as the poor girl said, so it happened, and she was really with child.

She was terribly concerned at it, and so was he too. "Come, my dear," says I, "when Rachel put her handmaid to bed to Jacob, she took the children as her own. Don't be uneasy; I'll take the child as my own. Had not I a hand in the frolic of putting her to bed to you? It was my fault as much as yours." So I called Amy, and encouraged her too, and told her that I would take care of the child and her too, and added the same argument to her. "For," says I, "Amy, it was all my fault. Did not I drag your clothes off your back, and put you to bed to him?" Thus I, that had, indeed, been the cause of all the wickedness between them, encouraged them both, when they had any remorse about it, and rather prompted them to go on with it than to repent it.

When Amy grew big she went to a place I had provided for her, and the neighbours knew nothing but that Amy and I was parted. She had a fine child indeed, a daughter, and we had it nursed; and Amy came again in about half a year to live with her old mistress; but neither my gentleman, or Amy either, cared for playing that game over again; for, as he said, the jade might bring him a houseful of children to keep.

We lived as merrily and as happily after this as could be expected, considering our circumstances; I mean as to the pretended marriage, &c.; and as to that, my gentleman had not the least concern about him for it. But as much as I was hardened, and that was as much as I believe ever any wicked creature was, yet I could not help it, there was and would be hours of intervals and of dark reflections which came involuntarily in, and thrust in sighs into the middle of all my songs; and there would be sometimes a heaviness of heart which intermingled itself with all my joy, and which would often fetch a tear from my eye. And let others pretend what they will, I believe it impossible to be otherwise with anybody. There can be no substantial satisfaction in a life of known wickedness; conscience will, and does often, break in upon them at particular times, let them do what they can to prevent it.

But I am not to preach, but to relate; and whatever loose reflections were, and how often soever those dark intervals came on, I did my utmost to conceal them from him; ay, and to suppress and smother them too in myself; and, to outward appearance, we lived as cheerfully and agreeably as it was possible for any couple in the world to live.

After I had thus lived with him something above two years, truly I found myself with child too. My gentleman was mightily pleased at it, and nothing could be kinder than he was in the preparations he made for me, and for my lying-in, which was, however, very private, because I cared for as little company as possible; nor had I kept up my neighbourly acquaintance, so that I had nobody to invite upon such an occasion.

I was brought to bed very well (of a daughter too, as well as Amy), but the child died at about six weeks old, so all that work was to do over again—that is to say, the charge, the expense, the travail, &c.

The next year I made him amends, and brought him a son, to his great satisfaction. It was a charming child, and did very well. After this my husband, as he called himself, came to me one evening, and told me he had a very difficult thing happened to him, which he knew not what to do in, or how to resolve about, unless I would make him easy; this was, that his occasions required him to go over to France for about two months.

"Well, my dear," says I, "and how shall I make you easy?"

"Why, by consenting to let me go," says he; "upon which condition, I'll tell you the occasion of my going, that you may judge of the necessity there is for it on my side." Then, to make me easy in his going, he told me he would make his will before he went, which should be to my full satisfaction.

I told him the last part was so kind that I could not decline the first part, unless he would give me leave to add that, if it was not for putting him to an extraordinary expense, I would go over along with him.

He was so pleased with this offer that he told me he would give me full satisfaction for it, and accept of it too; so he took me to London with him the next day, and there he made his will, and showed it to me, and sealed it before proper witnesses, and then gave it to me to keep. In this will he gave a thousand pounds to a person that we both knew very well, in trust, to pay it, with the interest from the time of his decease, to me or my assigns; then he willed the payment of my jointure, as he called it, viz., his bond of five hundred pounds after his death; also, he gave me all my household stuff, plate, &c.

This was a most engaging thing for a man to do to one under my circumstances; and it would have been hard, as I told him, to deny him anything, or to refuse to go with him anywhere. So we settled everything as well as we could, left Amy in charge with the house, and for his other business, which was in jewels, he had two men he intrusted, who he had good security for, and who managed for him, and corresponded with him.

Things being thus concerted, we went away to France, arrived safe at Calais, and by easy journeys came in eight days more to Paris, where we lodged in the house of an English merchant of his acquaintance, and was very courteously entertained.

My gentleman's business was with some persons of the first rank, and to whom he had sold some jewels of very good value, and received a great sum of money in specie; and, as he told me privately, he gained three thousand pistoles by his bargain, but would not suffer the most intimate friend he had there to know what he had received; for it is not so safe a thing in Paris to have a great sum of money in keeping as it might be in London.

We made this journey much longer than we intended, and my gentleman sent for one of his managers in London to come over to us in Paris with some diamonds, and sent him back to London again to fetch more. Then other business fell into his hands so unexpectedly that I began to think we should take up our constant residence there, which I was not very averse to, it being my native country, and I spoke the language perfectly well. So we took a good house in Paris, and lived very well there; and I sent for Amy to come over to me, for I lived gallantly, and my gentleman was two or three times going to keep me a coach, but I declined it, especially at Paris, but as they have those conveniences by the day there, at a certain rate, I had an equipage provided for me whenever I pleased, and I lived here in a very good figure, and might have lived higher if I pleased.

But in the middle of all this felicity a dreadful disaster befell me, which entirely unhinged all my affairs, and threw me back into the same state of life that I was in before; with this one happy exception, however, that whereas before I was poor, even to misery, now I was not only provided for, but very rich.

My gentleman had the name in Paris for a rich man, and indeed he was so, though not so immensely rich as people imagined; but that which was fatal to him was, that he generally

34

carried a shagreen case in his pocket, especially when he went to court, or to the houses of any of the princes of the blood, in which he had jewels of very great value.

It happened one day that, being to go to Versailles to wait upon the Prince of ——, he came up into my chamber in the morning, and laid out his jewel-case, because he was not going to show any jewels, but to get a foreign bill accepted, which he had received from Amsterdam; so, when he gave me the case, he said, "My dear, I think I need not carry this with me, because it may be I may not come back till night, and it is too much to venture." I returned, "Then, my dear, you shan't go." "Why?" says he. "Because, as they are too much for you, so you are too much for me to venture, and you shall not go, unless you will promise me not to stay so as to come back in the night."

"I hope there's no danger," said he, "seeing that I have nothing about me of any value; and therefore, lest I should, take that too," says he, and gives me his gold watch and a rich diamond which he had in a ring, and always wore on his finger.

"Well, but, my dear," says I, "you make me more uneasy now than before; for if you apprehend no danger, why do you use this caution? and if you apprehend there is danger, why do you go at all?"

"There is no danger," says he, "if I do not stay late, and I do not design to do so."

"Well, but promise me, then, that you won't," says I, "or else I cannot let you go."

"I won't indeed, my dear," says he, "unless I am obliged to it. I assure you I do not intend it; but if I should, I am not worth robbing now, for I have nothing about me but about six pistoles in my little purse and that little ring," showing me a small diamond ring, worth about ten or twelve pistoles, which he put upon his finger, in the room of the rich one he usually wore.

THE JEWELLER IS ABOUT TO LEAVE FOR VERSAILLES

And gives me his gold watch and a rich diamond which he had in a ring, and always wore on his finger

I still pressed him not to stay late, and he said he would not. "But if I am kept late," says he, "beyond my expectation, I'll stay all night, and come next morning." This seemed a very good caution; but still my mind was very uneasy about him, and I told him so, and entreated him not to go. I told him I did not know what might be the reason, but that I had a strange terror upon my mind about his going, and that if he did go, I was persuaded some harm would attend him. He smiled, and returned, "Well, my dear, if it should be so, you are now richly provided for; all that I have here I give to you." And with that he takes up the casket or case, "Here," says he, "hold your hand; there is a good estate for you in this case; if anything happens to me 'tis all your own. I give it you for yourself;" and with that he put the casket, the fine ring, and his gold watch all into my hands, and the key of his scrutoire besides, adding, "And in my scrutoire there is some money; it is all your own."

I stared at him as if I was frighted, for I thought all his face looked like a death's-head; and then immediately I thought I perceived his head all bloody, and then his clothes looked bloody too, and immediately it all went off, and he looked as he really did. Immediately I fell a-crying, and hung about him. "My dear," said I, "I am frighted to death; you shall not go. Depend upon it some mischief will befall you." I did not tell him how my vapourish fancy had represented him to me; that, I thought, was not proper. Besides, he would only have laughed at me, and would have gone away with a jest about it; but I pressed him seriously not to go that day, or, if he did, to promise me to come home to Paris again by daylight. He looked a little graver then than he did before, told me he was not apprehensive of the least danger, but if there was, he would either take care to come in the day, or, as he had said before, would stay all night.

But all these promises came to nothing, for he was set upon in the open day and robbed by three men on horseback, masked, as he went; and one of them, who, it seems, rifled him while the rest stood to stop the coach, stabbed him into the body with a sword, so that he died immediately. He had a footman behind the coach, who they knocked down with the stock or butt-end of a carbine. They were supposed to kill him because of the disappointment they met with in not getting his case or casket of diamonds, which they knew he carried about him; and this was supposed because, after they had killed him, they made the coachman drive out of the road a long way over the heath, till they came to a convenient place, where they pulled him out of the coach and searched his clothes more narrowly than they could do while he was alive. But they found nothing but his little ring, six pistoles, and the value of about seven livres in small moneys.

This was a dreadful blow to me, though I cannot say I was so surprised as I should otherwise have been, for all the while he was gone my mind was oppressed with the weight of my own thoughts, and I was as sure that I should never see him any more that I think nothing could be like it. The impression was so strong that I think nothing could make so deep a wound that was imaginary; and I was so dejected and disconsolate that, when I received the news of his disaster, there was no room for any extraordinary alteration in me.

I had cried all that day, ate nothing, and only waited, as I might say, to receive the dismal news, which I had brought to me about five o'clock in the afternoon.

I was in a strange country, and, though I had a pretty many acquaintances, had but very few friends that I could consult on this occasion. All possible inquiry was made after the rogues that had been thus barbarous, but nothing could be heard of them; nor was it possible that the footman could make any discovery of them by his description, for they knocked him down immediately, so that he knew nothing of what was done afterwards. The coachman was the only man that could say anything, and all his account amounted to no more than this, that one of them had soldier's clothes, but he could not remember the particulars of his mounting, so as to know what regiment he belonged to; and as to their faces, that he could know nothing of, because they had all of them masks on.

I had him buried as decently as the place would permit a Protestant stranger to be buried, and made some of the scruples and difficulties on that account easy by the help of money to a certain person, who went impudently to the curate of the parish of St. Sulpitius, in Paris, and told him that the gentleman that was killed was a Catholic; that the thieves had taken from him a cross of gold, set with diamonds, worth six thousand livres; that his widow was a Catholic, and had sent by him sixty crowns to the church of ——, for masses to be said for the repose of his soul. Upon all which, though not one word was true, he was buried with all the ceremonies of the Roman Church.

I think I almost cried myself to death for him, for I abandoned myself to all the excesses of grief; and indeed I loved him to a degree inexpressible; and considering what kindness he had shown me at first, and how tenderly he had used me to the last, what could I do less?

Then the manner of his death was terrible and frightful to me, and, above all, the strange notices I had of it. I had never pretended to the second-sight, or anything of that kind, but certainly, if any one ever had such a thing, I had it at this time, for I saw him as plainly in all those terrible shapes as above; first, as a skeleton, not dead only, but rotten and wasted; secondly, as killed, and his face bloody; and, thirdly, his clothes bloody, and all within the space of one minute, or indeed of a very few moments.

These things amazed me, and I was a good while as one stupid. However, after some time I began to recover, and look into my affairs. I had the satisfaction not to be left in distress, or in danger of poverty. On the contrary, besides what he had put into my hands fairly in his lifetime, which amounted to a very considerable value, I found above seven hundred pistoles in gold in his scrutoire, of which he had given me the key; and I found foreign bills accepted for about twelve thousand livres; so that, in a word, I found myself possessed of almost ten thousand pounds sterling in a very few days after the disaster.

The first thing I did upon this occasion was to send a letter to my maid, as I still called her, Amy, wherein I gave her an account of my disaster, how my husband, as she called him (for I never called him so), was murdered; and as I did not know how his relations, or his wife's friends might act upon that occasion, I ordered her to convey away all the plate, linen, and other things of value, and to secure them in a person's hands that I directed her to, and then to sell or dispose of the furniture of the house, if she could, and so, without acquainting anybody with the reason of her going, withdraw; sending notice to his head manager at London that the house was quitted by the tenant, and they might come and take possession of it for the executors. Amy was so dexterous, and did her work so nimbly, that she gutted the house, and sent the key to the said manager, almost as soon as he had notice of the misfortune that befell their master.

Upon their receiving the surprising news of his death, the head manager came over to Paris, and came to the house. I made no scruple of calling myself Madame ——, the widow of Monsieur ——, the English jeweller. And as I spoke French naturally, I did not let him know but that I was his wife, married in France, and that I had not heard that he had any wife in England, but pretended to be surprised, and exclaim against him for so base an action; and that I had good friends in Poictou, where I was born, who would take care to have justice done me in England out of his estate.

I should have observed that, as soon as the news was public of a man being murdered, and that he was a jeweller, fame did me the favour as to publish presently that he was robbed of his casket of jewels, which he always carried about him. I confirmed this, among my daily lamentations for his disaster, and added that he had with him a fine diamond ring, which he was known to wear frequently about him, valued at one hundred pistoles, a gold watch, and a great quantity of diamonds of inestimable value in his casket, which jewels he was carrying to the Prince of ——, to show some of them to him; and the prince owned that he had spoken to him to bring some such jewels, to let him see them. But I sorely repented this part afterward, as you shall hear.

This rumour put an end to all inquiry after his jewels, his ring, or his watch; and as for the seven hundred pistoles, that I secured. For the bills which were in hand, I owned I had them, but that, as I said I brought my husband thirty thousand livres portion, I claimed the said bills, which came to not above twelve thousand livres, for my amende; and this, with the plate and the household stuff, was the principal of all his estate which they could come at. As to the foreign bill which he was going to Versailles to get accepted, it was really lost with him; but his manager, who had remitted the bill to him, by way of Amsterdam, bringing over the second bill, the money was saved, as they call it, which would otherwise have been also gone; the thieves who robbed and murdered him were, to be sure, afraid to send anybody to get the bill accepted, for that would undoubtedly have discovered them.

By this time my maid Amy was arrived, and she gave me an account of her management, and how she had secured everything, and that she had quitted the house, and sent the key to the head manager of his business, and let me know how much she had made of everything very punctually and honestly.

I should have observed, in the account of his dwelling with me so long at ——, that he never passed for anything there but a lodger in the house; and though he was landlord, that did not alter the case. So that at his death, Amy coming to quit the house and give them the key, there was no affinity between that and the case of their master who was newly killed.

I got good advice at Paris from an eminent lawyer, a counsellor of the Parliament there, and laying my case before him, he directed me to make a process in dower upon the estate, for making good my new fortune upon matrimony, which accordingly I did; and, upon the whole, the manager went back to England well satisfied that he had gotten the unaccepted bill of exchange, which was for two thousand five hundred pounds, with some other things, which together amounted to seventeen thousand livres; and thus I got rid of him.

I was visited with great civility on this sad occasion of the loss of my husband, as they thought him, by a great many ladies of quality. And the Prince of ——, to whom it was reported he was carrying the jewels, sent his gentleman with a very handsome compliment of condolence to me; and his gentleman, whether with or without order, hinted as if his Highness did intend to have visited me himself, but that some accident, which he made a long story of, had prevented him.

By the concourse of ladies and others that thus came to visit me, I began to be much known; and as I did not forget to set myself out with all possible advantage, considering the dress of a widow, which in those days was a most frightful thing; I say, as I did thus from my own vanity, for I was not ignorant that I was very handsome; I say, on this account I was soon made very public, and was known by the name of La belle veufeu de Poictou, or the pretty widow of Poictou. As I was very well pleased to see myself thus handsomely used in my affliction, it soon dried up all my tears; and though I appeared as a widow, yet, as we say in England, it was of a widow comforted. I took care to let the ladies see that I knew how to receive them; that I was not at a loss how to behave to any of them; and, in short, I began to be very popular there. But I had an occasion afterwards which made me decline that kind of management, as you shall hear presently.

About four days after I had received the compliments of condolence from the Prince ——, the same gentleman he had sent before came to tell me that his Highness was coming to give me a visit. I was indeed surprised at that, and perfectly at a loss how to behave. However, as there was no remedy, I prepared to receive him as well as I could. It was not many minutes after but he was at the door, and came in, introduced by his own gentleman, as above, and after by my woman Amy.

He treated me with abundance of civility, and condoled handsomely on the loss of my husband, and likewise the manner of it. He told me he understood he was coming to Versailles to himself, to show him some jewels; that it was true that he had discoursed with him about jewels, but could not imagine how any villains should hear of his coming at that time with them; that he had not ordered him to attend with them at Versailles, but told him that he would come to Paris by such a day, so that he was no way accessory to the disaster. I told him gravely I knew very well that all his Highness had said of that part was true; that these villains knew his profession, and knew, no doubt, that he always carried a casket of jewels about him, and that he always wore a diamond ring on his finger worth a hundred pistoles, which report had magnified to five hundred; and that, if he had been going to any other place, it would have been the same thing. After this his Highness rose up to go, and told me he had resolved, however, to make me some reparation; and with these words put a silk purse into my hand with a hundred pistoles, and told me he would make me a farther compliment of a small pension, which his gentleman would inform me of.

You may be sure I behaved with a due sense of so much goodness, and offered to kneel to kiss his hand; but he took me up and saluted me, and sat down again (though before he made as if he was going away), making me sit down by him.

He then began to talk with me more familiarly; told me he hoped I was not left in bad circumstances; that Mr. —— was reputed to be very rich, and that he had gained lately great sums by some jewels, and he hoped, he said, that I had still a fortune agreeable to the condition I had lived in before.

I replied, with some tears, which, I confess, were a little forced, that I believed, if Mr. —— had lived, we should have been out of danger of want, but that it was impossible to estimate the loss which I had sustained, besides that of the life of my husband; that, by the opinion of those that knew something of his affairs, and of what value the jewels were which he intended to have shown to his Highness, he could not have less about him than the value of a hundred thousand livres; that it was a fatal blow to me, and to his whole family, especially that they should be lost in such a manner.

His Highness returned, with an air of concern, that he was very sorry for it; but he hoped, if I settled in Paris, I might find ways to restore my fortune; at the same time he complimented me upon my being very handsome, as he was pleased to call it, and that I could not fail of admirers. I stood up and humbly thanked his Highness, but told him I had no expectations of that kind; that I thought I should be obliged to go over to England, to look after my husband's effects there, which, I was told, were considerable, but that I did not know what justice a poor stranger would get among them; and as for Paris, my fortune being so impaired, I saw nothing before me but to go back to Poictou to my friends, where some of my relations, I hoped, might do something for me, and added that one of my brothers was an abbot at ——, near Poictiers.

He stood up, and taking me by the hand, led me to a large looking-glass, which made up the pier in the front of the parlour. "Look there, madam," said he; "is it fit that that face" (pointing to my figure in the glass) "should go back to Poictou? No, madam," says he; "stay and make some gentleman of quality happy, that may, in return, make you forget all your sorrows;" and with that he took me in his arms, and kissing me twice, told me he would see me again, but with less ceremony.

Some little time after this, but the same day, his gentleman came to me again, and with great ceremony and respect, delivered me a black box tied with a scarlet riband and sealed with a noble coat-of-arms, which, I suppose, was the prince's.

There was in it a grant from his Highness, or an assignment—I know not which to call it— with a warrant to his banker to pay me two thousand livres a year during my stay in Paris, as the widow of Monsieur ——, the jeweller, mentioning the horrid murder of my late husband as the occasion of it, as above.

I received it with great submission, and expressions of being infinitely obliged to his master, and of my showing myself on all occasions his Highness's most obedient servant; and after giving my most humble duty to his Highness, with the utmost acknowledgments of the obligation, &c., I went to a little cabinet, and taking out some money, which made a little sound in taking it out, offered to give him five pistoles.

He drew back, but with the greatest respect, and told me he humbly thanked me, but that he durst not take a farthing; that his Highness would take it so ill of him, he was sure he would never see his face more; but that he would not fail to acquaint his Highness what respect I had offered; and added, "I assure you, madam, you are more in the good graces of my master, the Prince of ——, than you are aware of; and I believe you will hear more of him."

Now I began to understand him, and resolved, if his Highness did come again, he should see me under no disadvantages, if I could help it. I told him, if his Highness did me the honour to see me again, I hoped he would not let me be so surprised as I was before; that I would be glad to have some little notice of it, and would be obliged to him if he would procure it me. He told me he was very sure that when his Highness intended to visit me he should be sent before to give me notice of it, and that he would give me as much warning of it as possible.

He came several times after this on the same errand, that is, about the settlement, the grant requiring several things yet to be done for making it payable without going every time to the prince again for a fresh warrant. The particulars of this part I did not understand; but as soon as it was finished, which was above two months, the gentleman came one afternoon, and said his Highness designed to visit me in the evening, but desired to be admitted without ceremony.

I prepared not my rooms only, but myself; and when he came in there was nobody appeared in the house but his gentleman and my maid Amy; and of her I bid the gentleman acquaint his Highness that she was an Englishwoman, that she did not understand a word of French, and that she was one also that might be trusted.

When he came into my room, I fell down at his feet before he could come to salute me, and with words that I had prepared, full of duty and respect, thanked him for his bounty and goodness to a poor, desolate woman, oppressed under the weight of so terrible a disaster; and refused to rise till he would allow me the honour to kiss his hand.

"Levez vous donc," says the prince, taking me in his arms; "I design more favours for you than this trifle;" and going on, he added, "You shall for the future find a friend where you did not look for it, and I resolve to let you see how kind I can be to one who is to me the most agreeable creature on earth."

I was dressed in a kind of half mourning, had turned off my weeds, and my head, though I had yet no ribands or lace, was so dressed as failed not to set me out with advantage enough, for I began to understand his meaning; and the prince professed I was the most beautiful creature on earth. "And where have I lived," says he, "and how ill have I been served, that I should never till now be showed the finest woman in France!"

This was the way in all the world the most likely to break in upon my virtue, if I had been mistress of any; for I was now become the vainest creature upon earth, and particularly of my beauty, which as other people admired, so I became every day more foolishly in love with myself than before.

He said some very kind things to me after this, and sat down with me for an hour or more, when, getting up and calling his gentleman by his name, he threw open the door: "Au boire," says he; upon which his gentleman immediately brought up a little table covered with a fine damask cloth, the table no bigger than he could bring in his two hands, but upon it was set two decanters, one of champagne and the other of water, six silver plates, and a service of fine sweetmeats in fine china dishes, on a set of rings standing up about twenty inches high, one above another. Below was three roasted partridges and a quail. As soon as his gentleman had set it all down, he ordered him to withdraw. "Now," says the prince, "I intend to sup with you."

When he sent away his gentleman, I stood up and offered to wait on his Highness while he ate; but he positively refused, and told me, "No; to-morrow you shall be the widow of Monsieur —, the jeweller, but to-night you shall be my mistress; therefore sit here," says he, "and eat with me, or I will get up and serve."

I would then have called up my woman Amy, but I thought that would not be proper neither; so I made my excuse, that since his Highness would not let his own servant wait, I would not presume to let my woman come up; but if he would please to let me wait, it would be my honour to fill his Highness's wine. But, as before, he would by no means allow me; so we sat and ate together.

THE VISIT OF THE PRINCE
And refused to rise till he would allow me the honour to kiss his hand
"Now, madam," says the prince, "give me leave to lay aside my character; let us talk together with the freedom of equals. My quality sets me at a distance from you, and makes you ceremonious. Your beauty exalts you to more than an equality. I must, then, treat you as lovers do their mistresses, but I cannot speak the language; it is enough to tell you how agreeable you are to me, how I am surprised at your beauty, and resolve to make you happy, and to be happy with you."

I knew not what to say to him a good while, but blushed, and looking up towards him, said I was already made happy in the favour of a person of such rank, and had nothing to ask of his Highness but that he would believe me infinitely obliged.

After he had eaten, he poured the sweetmeats into my lap; and the wine being out, he called his gentleman again to take away the table, who, at first, only took the cloth and the remains of what was to eat away; and, laying another cloth, set the table on one side of the room with a noble service of plate upon it, worth at least two hundred pistoles. Then, having set the two decanters again upon the table, filled as before, he withdrew; for I found the fellow understood his business very well, and his lord's business too.

About half-an-hour after, the prince told me that I offered to wait a little before, that if I would now take the trouble he would give me leave to give him some wine; so I went to the table, filled a glass of wine, and brought it to him on a fine salver, which the glasses stood on, and brought the bottle or decanter for water in my other hand, to mix as he thought fit.

He smiled, and bid me look on that salver, which I did, and admired it much, for it was a very fine one indeed. "You may see," says he, "I resolve to have more of your company, for my servant shall leave you that plate for my use." I told him I believed his Highness would not take it ill that I was not furnished fit to entertain a person of his rank, and that I would take great care of it, and value myself infinitely upon the honour of his Highness's visit.

It now began to grow late, and he began to take notice of it. "But," says he, "I cannot leave you; have you not a spare lodging for one night?" I told him I had but a homely lodging to entertain such a guest. He said something exceeding kind on that head, but not fit to repeat, adding that my company would make him amends.

About midnight he sent his gentleman of an errand, after telling him aloud that he intended to stay here all night. In a little time his gentleman brought him a nightgown, slippers, two caps, a neckcloth, and shirt, which he gave me to carry into his chamber, and sent his man home; and then, turning to me, said I should do him the honour to be his chamberlain of the household, and his dresser also. I smiled, and told him I would do myself the honour to wait on him upon all occasions.

About one in the morning, while his gentleman was yet with him, I begged leave to withdraw, supposing he would go to bed; but he took the hint, and said, "I'm not going to bed yet; pray let me see you again."

I took this time to undress me, and to come in a new dress, which was, in a manner, une dishabille, but so fine, and all about me so clean and so agreeable, that he seemed surprised. "I thought," says he, "you could not have dressed to more advantage than you had done before; but now," says he, "you charm me a thousand times more, if that be possible."

"It is only a loose habit, my lord," said I, "that I may the better wait on your Highness." He pulls me to him. "You are perfectly obliging," says he; and, sitting on the bedside, says he, "Now you shall be a princess, and know what it is to oblige the gratefullest man alive;" and with that he took me in his arms.... I can go no farther in the particulars of what passed at that time, but it ended in this, that, in short, I lay with him all night.

I have given you the whole detail of this story to lay it down as a black scheme of the way how unhappy women are ruined by great men; for, though poverty and want is an irresistible temptation to the poor, vanity and great things are as irresistible to others. To be courted by a prince, and by a prince who was first a benefactor, then an admirer; to be called handsome, the finest woman in France, and to be treated as a woman fit for the bed of a prince—these are things a woman must have no vanity in her, nay, no corruption in her, that is not overcome by it; and my case was such that, as before, I had enough of both.

I had now no poverty attending me; on the contrary, I was mistress of ten thousand pounds before the prince did anything for me. Had I been mistress of my resolution, had I been less obliging, and rejected the first attack, all had been safe; but my virtue was lost before, and the devil, who had found the way to break in upon me by one temptation, easily mastered me now by another; and I gave myself up to a person who, though a man of high dignity, was yet the most tempting and obliging that ever I met with in my life.

I had the same particular to insist upon here with the prince that I had with my gentleman before. I hesitated much at consenting at first asking, but the prince told me princes did not court like other men; that they brought more powerful arguments; and he very prettily added that they were sooner repulsed than other men, and ought to be sooner complied with; intimating, though very genteely, that after a woman had positively refused him once, he could not, like other men, wait with importunities and stratagems, and laying long sieges; but as such men as he stormed warmly, so, if repulsed, they made no second attacks; and, indeed, it was but reasonable; for as it was below their rank to be long battering a woman's constancy, so they ran greater hazards in being exposed in their amours than other men did.

I took this for a satisfactory answer, and told his Highness that I had the same thoughts in respect to the manner of his attacks; for that his person and his arguments were irresistible; that a person of his rank and a munificence so unbounded could not be withstood; that no virtue was proof against him, except such as was able, too, to suffer martyrdom; that I thought it impossible I could be overcome, but that now I found it was impossible I should not be overcome; that so much goodness, joined with so much greatness, would have conquered a saint; and that I confessed he had the victory over me, by a merit infinitely superior to the conquest he had made.

He made me a most obliging answer; told me abundance of fine things, which still flattered my vanity, till at last I began to have pride enough to believe him, and fancied myself a fit mistress for a prince.

As I had thus given the prince the last favour, and he had all the freedom with me that it was possible for me to grant, so he gave me leave to use as much freedom with him another way, and that was to have everything of him I thought fit to command; and yet I did not ask of him with an air of avarice, as if I was greedily making a penny of him, but I managed him with such art that he generally anticipated my demands. He only requested of me that I would not think of taking another house, as I had intimated to his Highness that I intended, not thinking it good enough to receive his visits in; but he said my house was the most convenient that could possibly be found in all Paris for an amour, especially for him, having a way out into three streets, and not overlooked by any neighbours, so that he could pass and repass without observation; for one of the back-ways opened into a narrow dark alley, which alley was a thoroughfare or passage out of one street into another; and any person that went in or out by the door had no more to do but to see that there was nobody following him in the alley before he went in at the door. This request, I knew, was reasonable, and therefore I assured him I would not change my dwelling, seeing his Highness did not think it too mean for me to receive him in.

He also desired me that I would not take any more servants or set up any equipage, at least for the present; for that it would then be immediately concluded I had been left very rich, and then I should be thronged with the impertinence of admirers, who would be attracted by the money, as well as by the beauty of a young widow, and he should be frequently interrupted in his visits; or that the world would conclude I was maintained by somebody, and would be indefatigable to find out the person; so that he should have spies peeping at him every time he went out or in, which it would be impossible to disappoint; and that he should presently have it talked over all the toilets in Paris that the Prince de —— had got the jeweller's widow for a mistress.

This was too just to oppose, and I made no scruple to tell his Highness that, since he had stooped so low as to make me his own, he ought to have all the satisfaction in the world that I was all his own; that I would take all the measures he should please to direct me to avoid the impertinent attacks of others; and that, if he thought fit, I would be wholly within doors, and have it given out that I was obliged to go to England to solicit my affairs there, after my husband's misfortune, and that I was not expected there again for at least a year or two. This he liked very well; only he said that he would by no means have me confined; that it would injure my health, and that I should then take a country-house in some village, a good way off of the city, where it should not be known who I was, and that he should be there sometimes to divert me.

I made no scruple of the confinement, and told his Highness no place could be a confinement where I had such a visitor, and so I put off the country-house, which would have been to remove myself farther from him and have less of his company; so I made the house be, as it were, shut up. Amy, indeed, appeared, and when any of the neighbours and servants inquired, she answered, in broken French, that I was gone to England to look after my affairs, which presently went current through the streets about us. For you are to note that the people of Paris, especially the women, are the most busy and impertinent inquirers into the conduct of their neighbours, especially that of a single woman, that are in the world, though there are no greater intriguers in the universe than themselves; and perhaps that may be the reason of it, for it is an old but a sure rule, that

"When deep intrigues are close and shy,
The guilty are the first that spy."

Thus his Highness had the most easy, and yet the most undiscoverable, access to me imaginable, and he seldom failed to come two or three nights in a week, and sometimes stayed two or three nights together. Once he told me he was resolved I should be weary of his company, and that he would learn to know what it was to be a prisoner; so he gave out among his servants that he was gone to ——, where he often went a-hunting, and that he should not return under a fortnight; and that fortnight he stayed wholly with me, and never went out of my doors.

Never woman in such a station lived a fortnight in so complete a fulness of human delight; for to have the entire possession of one of the most accomplished princes in the world, and of the politest, best-bred man; to converse with him all day, and, as he professed, charm him all night, what could be more inexpressibly pleasing, and especially to a woman of a vast deal of pride, as I was?

To finish the felicity of this part, I must not forget that the devil had played a new game with me, and prevailed with me to satisfy myself with this amour, as a lawful thing; that a prince of such grandeur and majesty, so infinitely superior to me, and one who had made such an introduction by an unparalleled bounty, I could not resist; and, therefore, that it was very lawful for me to do it, being at that time perfectly single, and unengaged to any other man, as I was, most certainly, by the unaccountable absence of my first husband, and the murder of my gentleman who went for my second.

It cannot be doubted but that I was the easier to persuade myself of the truth of such a doctrine as this when it was so much for my ease and for the repose of my mind to have it be so:—

"In things we wish, 'tis easy to deceive;
What we would have, we willingly believe."
Besides, I had no casuists to resolve this doubt; the same devil that put this into my head bade me go to any of the Romish clergy, and, under the pretence of confession, state the case exactly, and I should see they would either resolve it to be no sin at all or absolve me upon the easiest penance. This I had a strong inclination to try, but I know not what scruple put me off of it, for I could never bring myself to like having to do with those priests. And though it was strange that I, who had thus prostituted my chastity and given up all sense of virtue in two such particular cases, living a life of open adultery, should scruple anything, yet so it was. I argued with myself that I could not be a cheat in anything that was esteemed sacred; that I could not be of one opinion, and then pretend myself to be of another; nor could I go to confession, who knew nothing of the manner of it, and should betray myself to the priest to be a Huguenot, and then might come into trouble; but, in short, though I was a whore, yet I was a Protestant whore, and could not act as if I was popish, upon any account whatsoever.

But, I say, I satisfied myself with the surprising occasion, that as it was all irresistible, so it was all lawful; for that Heaven would not suffer us to be punished for that which it was not possible for us to avoid; and with these absurdities I kept conscience from giving me any considerable disturbance in all this matter; and I was as perfectly easy as to the lawfulness of it as if I had been married to the prince and had had no other husband; so possible is it for us to roll ourselves up in wickedness, till we grow invulnerable by conscience; and that sentinel, once dozed, sleeps fast, not to be awakened while the tide of pleasure continues to flow, or till something dark and dreadful brings us to ourselves again.

I have, I confess, wondered at the stupidity that my intellectual part was under all that while; what lethargic fumes dozed the soul; and how was it possible that I, who in the case before, where the temptation was many ways more forcible and the arguments stronger and more irresistible, was yet under a continued inquietude on account of the wicked life I led, could now live in the most profound tranquillity and with an uninterrupted peace, nay, even rising up to satisfaction and joy, and yet in a more palpable state of adultery than before; for before, my gentleman, who called me wife, had the pretence of his wife being parted from him, refusing to do the duty of her office as a wife to him. As for me, my circumstances were the same; but as for the prince, as he had a fine and extraordinary lady, or princess, of his own, so he had had two or three mistresses more besides me, and made no scruple of it at all.

However, I say, as to my own part, I enjoyed myself in perfect tranquillity; and as the prince was the only deity I worshipped, so I was really his idol; and however it was with his princess, I assure you his other mistresses found a sensible difference, and though they could never find me out, yet I had good intelligence that they guessed very well that their lord had got some new favourite that robbed them of his company, and, perhaps, of some of his usual bounty too. And now I must mention the sacrifices he made to his idol, and they were not a few, I assure you.

As he loved like a prince, so he rewarded like a prince; for though he declined my making a figure, as above, he let me see that he was above doing it for the saving the expense of it, and so he told me, and that he would make it up in other things. First of all, he sent me a toilet, with all the appurtenances of silver, even so much as the frame of the table; and then for the house, he gave me the table, or sideboard of plate, I mentioned above, with all things belonging to it of massy silver; so that, in short, I could not for my life study to ask him for anything of plate which I had not.

He could, then, accommodate me in nothing more but jewels and clothes, or money for clothes. He sent his gentleman to the mercer's, and bought me a suit, or whole piece, of the finest brocaded silk, figured with gold, and another with silver, and another of crimson; so that I had three suits of clothes, such as the Queen of France would not have disdained to have worn at that time. Yet I went out nowhere; but as those were for me to put on when I went out of mourning, I dressed myself in them, one after another, always when his Highness came to see me.

I had no less than five several morning dresses besides these, so that I need never be seen twice in the same dress; to these he added several parcels of fine linen and of lace, so much that I had no room to ask for more, or, indeed, for so much.

I took the liberty once, in our freedoms, to tell him he was too bountiful, and that I was too chargeable to him for a mistress, and that I would be his faithful servant at less expense to him; and that he not only left me no room to ask him for anything, but that he supplied me with such a profusion of good things that I could scarce wear them, or use them, unless I kept a great equipage, which, he knew, was no way convenient for him or for me. He smiled, and took me in his arms, and told me he was resolved, while I was his, I should never be able to ask him for anything, but that he would be daily asking new favours of me.

After we were up (for this conference was in bed), he desired I would dress me in the best suit of clothes I had. It was a day or two after the three suits were made and brought home. I told him, if he pleased, I would rather dress me in that suit which I knew he liked best. He asked me how I could know which he would like best before he had seen them. I told him I would presume for once to guess at his fancy by my own; so I went away and dressed me in the second suit, brocaded with silver, and returned in full dress, with a suit of lace upon my head, which would have been worth in England two hundred pounds sterling; and I was every way set out as well as Amy could dress me, who was a very genteel dresser too. In this figure I came to him, out of my dressing-room, which opened with folding-doors into his bedchamber.

He sat as one astonished a good while, looking at me, without speaking a word, till I came quite up to him, kneeled on one knee to him, and almost, whether he would or no, kissed his hand. He took me up, and stood up himself, but was surprised when, taking me in his arms, he perceived tears to run down my cheeks. "My dear," says he aloud, "what mean these tears?" "My lord," said I, after some little check, for I could not speak presently, "I beseech you to believe me, they are not tears of sorrow, but tears of joy. It is impossible for me to see myself snatched from the misery I was fallen into, and at once to be in the arms of a prince of such goodness, such immense bounty, and be treated in such a manner; it is not possible, my lord," said I, "to contain the satisfaction of it; and it will break out in an excess in some measure proportioned to your immense bounty, and to the affection which your Highness treats me with, who am so infinitely below you."

It would look a little too much like a romance here to repeat all the kind things he said to me on that occasion, but I can't omit one passage. As he saw the tears drop down my cheek, he pulls out a fine cambric handkerchief, and was going to wipe the tears off, but checked his hand, as if he was afraid to deface something; I say, he checked his hand, and tossed the handkerchief to me to do it myself. I took the hint immediately, and with a kind of pleasant disdain, "How, my lord," said I, "have you kissed me so often, and don't you know whether I am painted or not? Pray let your Highness satisfy yourself that you have no cheats put upon you; for once let me be vain enough to say I have not deceived you with false colours." With this I put a handkerchief into his hand, and taking his hand into mine, I made him wipe my face so hard that he was unwilling to do it, for fear of hurting me.

He appeared surprised more than ever, and swore, which was the first time that I had heard him swear from my first knowing him, that he could not have believed there was any such skin without paint in the world. "Well, my lord," said I, "your Highness shall have a further demonstration than this, as to that which you are pleased to accept for beauty, that it is the mere work of nature;" and with that I stepped to the door and rung a little bell for my woman Amy, and bade her bring me a cup full of hot water, which she did; and when it was come, I desired his Highness to feel if it was warm, which he did, and I immediately washed my face all over with it before him. This was, indeed, more than satisfaction, that is to say, than believing, for it was an undeniable demonstration, and he kissed my cheeks and breasts a thousand times, with expressions of the greatest surprise imaginable.

Nor was I a very indifferent figure as to shape; though I had had two children by my gentleman, and six by my true husband, I say I was no despisable shape; and my prince (I must be allowed the vanity to call him so) was taking his view of me as I walked from one end of the room to the other. At last he leads me to the darkest part of the room, and standing behind me, bade me hold up my head, when, putting both his hands round my neck, as if he was spanning my neck to see how small it was, for it was long and small, he held my neck so long and so hard in his hand that I complained he hurt me a little. What he did it for I knew not, nor had I the least suspicion but that he was spanning my neck; but when I said he hurt me, he seemed to let go, and in half a minute more led me to a pier-glass, and behold I saw my neck clasped with a fine necklace of diamonds; whereas I felt no more what he was doing than if he had really done nothing at all, nor did I suspect it in the least. If I had an ounce of blood in me that did not fly up into my face, neck, and breasts, it must be from some interruption in the vessels. I was all on fire with the sight, and began to wonder what it was that was coming to me.

However, to let him see that I was not unqualified to receive benefits, I turned about: "My lord," says I, "your Highness is resolved to conquer, by your bounty, the very gratitude of your servants; you will leave no room for anything but thanks, and make those thanks useless too, by their bearing no proportion to the occasion."

"I love, child," says he, "to see everything suitable. A fine gown and petticoat, a fine laced head, a fine face and neck, and no necklace, would not have made the object perfect. But why that blush, my dear?" says the prince. "My lord," said I, "all your gifts call for blushes, but, above all, I blush to receive what I am so ill able to merit, and may become so ill also."

Thus far I am a standing mark of the weakness of great men in their vice, that value not squandering away immense wealth upon the most worthless creatures; or, to sum it up in a word, they raise the value of the object which they pretend to pitch upon by their fancy; I say, raise the value of it at their own expense; give vast presents for a ruinous favour, which is so far from being equal to the price that nothing will at last prove more absurd than the cost men are at to purchase their own destruction.

I could not, in the height of all this fine doings—I say, I could not be without some just reflection, though conscience was, as I said, dumb, as to any disturbance it gave me in my wickedness. My vanity was fed up to such a height that I had no room to give way to such reflections. But I could not but sometimes look back with astonishment at the folly of men of quality, who, immense in their bounty as in their wealth, give to a profusion and without bounds to the most scandalous of our sex, for granting them the liberty of abusing themselves and ruining both.

I, that knew what this carcase of mine had been but a few years before; how overwhelmed with grief, drowned in tears, frightened with the prospect of beggary, and surrounded with rags and fatherless children; that was pawning and selling the rags that covered me for a dinner, and sat on the ground despairing of help and expecting to be starved, till my children were snatched from me to be kept by the parish; I, that was after this a whore for bread, and, abandoning conscience and virtue, lived with another woman's husband; I, that was despised by all my relations, and my husband's too; I, that was left so entirely desolate, friendless, and helpless that I knew not how to get the least help to keep me from starving,—that I should be caressed by a prince, for the honour of having the scandalous use of my prostituted body, common before to his inferiors, and perhaps would not have denied one of his footmen but a little while before, if I could have got my bread by it.

I say, I could not but reflect upon the brutality and blindness of mankind; that because nature had given me a good skin and some agreeable features, should suffer that beauty to be such a bait to appetite as to do such sordid, unaccountable things to obtain the possession of it.

It is for this reason that I have so largely set down the particulars of the caresses I was treated with by the jeweller, and also by this prince; not to make the story an incentive to the vice, which I am now such a sorrowful penitent for being guilty of (God forbid any should make so vile a use of so good a design), but to draw the just picture of a man enslaved to the rage of his vicious appetite; how he defaces the image of God in his soul, dethrones his reason, causes conscience to abdicate the possession, and exalts sense into the vacant throne; how he deposes the man and exalts the brute.

Oh! could we hear the reproaches this great man afterwards loaded himself with when he grew weary of this admired creature, and became sick of his vice, how profitable would the report of them be to the reader of this story! But had he himself also known the dirty history of my actings upon the stage of life that little time I had been in the world, how much more severe would those reproaches have been upon himself! But I shall come to this again.

I lived in this gay sort of retirement almost three years, in which time no amour of such a kind, sure, was ever carried up so high. The prince knew no bounds to his munificence; he could give me nothing, either for my wearing, or using, or eating, or drinking, more than he had done from the beginning.

His presents were after that in gold, and very frequent and large, often a hundred pistoles, never less than fifty at a time; and I must do myself the justice that I seemed rather backward to receive than craving and encroaching. Not that I had not an avaricious temper, nor was it that I did not foresee that this was my harvest, in which I was to gather up, and that it would not last long; but it was that really his bounty always anticipated my expectations, and even my wishes; and he gave me money so fast that he rather poured it in upon me than left me room to ask it; so that, before I could spend fifty pistoles, I had always a hundred to make it up.

After I had been near a year and a half in his arms as above, or thereabouts, I proved with child. I did not take any notice of it to him till I was satisfied that I was not deceived; when one morning early, when we were in bed together, I said to him, "My lord, I doubt your Highness never gives yourself leave to think what the case should be if I should have the honour to be with child by you." "Why, my dear," says he, "we are able to keep it if such a thing should happen; I hope you are not concerned about that." "No, my lord," said I; "I should think myself very happy if I could bring your Highness a son; I should hope to see him a lieutenant-general of the king's armies by the interest of his father, and by his own merit." "Assure yourself, child," says he, "if it should be so, I will not refuse owning him for my son, though it be, as they call it, a natural son; and shall never slight or neglect him, for the sake of his mother." Then he began to importune me to know if it was so, but I positively denied it so long, till at last I was able to give him the satisfaction of knowing it himself by the motion of the child within me.

He professed himself overjoyed at the discovery, but told me that now it was absolutely necessary for me to quit the confinement which, he said, I had suffered for his sake, and to take a house somewhere in the country, in order for health as well as for privacy, against my lying-in. This was quite out of my way; but the prince, who was a man of pleasure, had, it seems, several retreats of this kind, which he had made use of, I suppose, upon like occasions. And so, leaving it, as it were, to his gentleman, he provided a very convenient house, about four miles south of Paris, at the village of ——, where I had very agreeable lodgings, good gardens, and all things very easy to my content. But one thing did not please me at all, viz., that an old woman was provided, and put into the house to furnish everything necessary to my lying-in, and to assist at my travail.

I did not like this old woman at all; she looked so like a spy upon me, or (as sometimes I was frighted to imagine) like one set privately to despatch me out of the world, as might best suit with the circumstance of my lying-in. And when his Highness came the next time to see me, which was not many days, I expostulated a little on the subject of the old woman; and by the management of my tongue, as well as by the strength of reasoning, I convinced him that it would not be at all convenient; that it would be the greater risk on his side; and at first or last it would certainly expose him and me also. I assured him that my servant, being an Englishwoman, never knew to that hour who his Highness was; that I always called him the Count de Clerac, and that she knew nothing else of him, nor ever should; that if he would give me leave to choose proper persons for my use, it should be so ordered that not one of them should know who he was, or perhaps ever see his face; and that, for the reality of the child that should be born, his Highness, who had alone been at the first of it, should, if he pleased, be present in the room all the time, so that he would need no witnesses on that account.

This discourse fully satisfied him, so that he ordered his gentleman to dismiss the old woman the same day; and without any difficulty I sent my maid Amy to Calais, and thence to Dover, where she got an English midwife and an English nurse to come over on purpose to attend an English lady of quality, as they styled me, for four months certain.

The midwife, Amy had agreed to pay a hundred guineas to, and bear her charges to Paris, and back again to Dover. The poor woman that was to be my nurse had twenty pounds, and the same terms for charges as the other.

I was very easy when Amy returned, and the more because she brought with the midwife a good motherly sort of woman, who was to be her assistant, and would be very helpful on occasion; and bespoke a man midwife at Paris too, if there should be any necessity for his help. Having thus made provision for everything, the Count, for so we all called him in public, came as often to see me as I could expect, and continued exceeding kind, as he had always been. One day, conversing together upon the subject of my being with child, I told him how all things were in order, but that I had a strange apprehension that I should die with that child. He smiled. "So all the ladies say, my dear," says he, "when they are with child." "Well, however, my lord," said I, "it is but just that care should be taken that what you have bestowed in your excess of bounty upon me should not be lost;" and upon this I pulled a paper out of my bosom, folded up, but not sealed, and I read it to him, wherein I had left order that all the plate and jewels and fine furniture which his Highness had given me should be restored to him by my women, and the keys be immediately delivered to his gentleman in case of disaster.

Then I recommended my woman, Amy, to his favour for a hundred pistoles, on condition she gave the keys up as above to his gentleman, and his gentleman's receipt for them. When he saw this, "My dear child," said he, and took me in his arms, "what! have you been making your will and disposing of your effects? Pray, who do you make your universal heir?" "So far as to do justice to your Highness, in case of mortality, I have, my lord," said I, "and who should I dispose the valuable things to, which I have had from your hand as pledges of your favour and testimonies of your bounty, but to the giver of them? If the child should live, your Highness will, I don't question, act like yourself in that part, and I shall have the utmost satisfaction that it will be well used by your direction."

I could see he took this very well. "I have forsaken all the ladies in Paris," says he, "for you, and I have lived every day since I knew you to see that you know how to merit all that a man of honour can do for you. Be easy, child; I hope you shall not die, and all you have is your own, to do what with it you please."

I was then within about two months of my time, and that soon wore off. When I found my time was come, it fell out very happily that he was in the house, and I entreated he would continue a few hours in the house, which he agreed to. They called his Highness to come into the room, if he pleased, as I had offered and as I desired him; and I sent word I would make as few cries as possible to prevent disturbing him. He came into the room once, and called to me to be of good courage, it would soon be over, and then he withdrew again; and in about half-an-hour more Amy carried him the news that I was delivered, and had brought him a charming boy. He gave her ten pistoles for her news, stayed till they had adjusted things about me, and then came into the room again, cheered me and spoke kindly to me, and looked on the child, then withdrew, and came again the next day to visit me.

Since this, and when I have looked back upon these things with eyes unpossessed with crime, when the wicked part has appeared in its clearer light and I have seen it in its own natural colours, when no more blinded with the glittering appearances which at that time deluded me, and as in like cases, if I may guess at others by myself, too much possessed the mind; I say, since this I have often wondered with what pleasure or satisfaction the prince could look upon the poor innocent infant, which, though his own, and that he might that way have some attachment in his affections to it, yet must always afterwards be a remembrancer to him of his most early crime, and, which was worse, must bear upon itself, unmerited, an eternal mark of infamy, which should be spoken of, upon all occasions, to its reproach, from the folly of its father and wickedness of its mother.

Great men are indeed delivered from the burthen of their natural children, or bastards, as to their maintenance. This is the main affliction in other cases, where there is not substance sufficient without breaking into the fortunes of the family. In those cases either a man's legitimate children suffer, which is very unnatural, or the unfortunate mother of that illegitimate birth has a dreadful affliction, either of being turned off with her child, and be left to starve, &c., or of seeing the poor infant packed off with a piece of money to those she-butchers who take children off their hands, as 'tis called, that is to say, starve them, and, in a word, murder them.

Great men, I say, are delivered from this burthen, because they are always furnished to supply the expense of their out-of-the-way offspring, by making little assignments upon the Bank of Lyons or the townhouse of Paris, and settling those sums, to be received for the maintenance of such expense as they see cause.

Thus, in the case of this child of mine, while he and I conversed, there was no need to make any appointment as an appanage or maintenance for the child or its nurse, for he supplied me more than sufficiently for all those things; but afterwards, when time, and a particular circumstance, put an end to our conversing together (as such things always meet with a period, and generally break off abruptly), I say, after that, I found he appointed the children a settled allowance, by an assignment of annual rent upon the Bank of Lyons, which was sufficient for bringing them handsomely, though privately, up in the world, and that not in a manner unworthy of their father's blood, though I came to be sunk and forgotten in the case; nor did the children ever know anything of their mother to this day, other than as you may have an account hereafter.

But to look back to the particular observation I was making, which I hope may be of use to those who read my story, I say it was something wonderful to me to see this person so exceedingly delighted at the birth of this child, and so pleased with it; for he would sit and look at it, and with an air of seriousness sometimes a great while together, and particularly, I observed, he loved to look at it when it was asleep.

It was indeed a lovely, charming child, and had a certain vivacity in its countenance that is far from being common to all children so young; and he would often say to me that he believed there was something extraordinary in the child, and he did not doubt but he would come to be a great man.

I could never hear him say so, but though secretly it pleased me, yet it so closely touched me another way that I could not refrain sighing, and sometimes tears; and one time in particular it so affected me that I could not conceal it from him; but when he saw tears run down my face, there was no concealing the occasion from him; he was too importunate to be denied in a thing of that moment; so I frankly answered, "It sensibly affects me, my lord," said I, "that, whatever the merit of this little creature may be, he must always have a bend on his arms. The disaster of his birth will be always, not a blot only to his honour, but a bar to his fortunes in the world. Our affection will be ever his affliction, and his mother's crime be the son's reproach. The blot can never be wiped out by the most glorious action; nay, if it lives to raise a family," said I, "the infamy must descend even to its innocent posterity."

He took the thought, and sometimes told me afterwards that it made a deeper impression on him than he discovered to me at that time; but for the present he put it off with telling me these things could not be helped; that they served for a spur to the spirits of brave men, inspired them with the principles of gallantry, and prompted them to brave actions; that though it might be true that the mention of illegitimacy might attend the name, yet that personal virtue placed a man of honour above the reproach of his birth; that, as he had no share in the offence, he would have no concern at the blot; when, having by his own merit placed himself out of the reach of scandal, his fame should drown the memory of his beginning; that as it was usual for men of quality to make such little escapes, so the number of their natural children were so great, and they generally took such good care of their education, that some of the greatest men in the world had a bend in their coats-of-arms, and that it was of no consequence to them, especially when their fame began to rise upon the basis of their acquired merit; and upon this he began to reckon up to me some of the greatest families in France and in England also.

This carried off our discourse for a time; but I went farther with him once, removing the discourse from the part attending our children to the reproach which those children would be apt to throw upon us, their originals; and when speaking a little too feelingly on the subject, he began to receive the impression a little deeper than I wished he had done. At last he told me I had almost acted the confessor to him; that I might, perhaps, preach a more dangerous doctrine to him than we should either of us like, or than I was aware of. "For, my dear," says he, "if once we come to talk of repentance we must talk of parting."

If tears were in my eyes before, they flowed too fast now to be restrained, and I gave him but too much satisfaction by my looks that I had yet no reflections upon my mind strong enough to go that length, and that I could no more think of parting than he could.

He said a great many kind things, which were great, like himself, and, extenuating our crime, intimated to me that he could no more part with me than I could with him; so we both, as I may say, even against our light and against our conviction, concluded to sin on; indeed, his affection to the child was one great tie to him, for he was extremely fond of it.

The child lived to be a considerable man. He was first an officer of the Garde du Corps of France, and afterwards colonel of a regiment of dragoons in Italy, and on many extraordinary occasions showed that he was not unworthy such a father, but many ways deserving a legitimate birth and a better mother; of which hereafter.

I think I may say now that I lived indeed like a queen; or, if you will have me confess that my condition had still the reproach of a whore, I may say I was, sure, the queen of whores; for no woman was ever more valued or more caressed by a person of such quality only in the station of a mistress. I had, indeed, one deficiency which women in such circumstances seldom are chargeable with, namely, I craved nothing of him, I never asked him for anything in my life, nor suffered myself to be made use of, as is too much the custom of mistresses, to ask favours for others. His bounty always prevented me in the first, and my strict concealing myself in the last, which was no less to my convenience than his.

The only favour I ever asked of him was for his gentleman, who he had all along entrusted with the secret of our affair, and who had once so much offended him by some omissions in his duty that he found it very hard to make his peace. He came and laid his case before my woman Amy, and begged her to speak to me to intercede for him, which I did, and on my account he was received again and pardoned, for which the grateful dog requited me by getting to bed to his benefactress, Amy, at which I was very angry. But Amy generously acknowledged that it was her fault as much as his; that she loved the fellow so much that she believed if he had not asked her she should have asked him. I say, this pacified me, and I only obtained of her that she should not let him know that I knew it.

I might have interspersed this part of my story with a great many pleasant parts and discourses which happened between my maid Amy and I, but I omit them on account of my own story, which has been so extraordinary. However, I must mention something as to Amy and her gentleman.

I inquired of Amy upon what terms they came to be so intimate, but Amy seemed backward to explain herself. I did not care to press her upon a question of that nature, knowing that she might have answered my question with a question, and have said, "Why, how did I and the prince come to be so intimate?" So I left off farther inquiring into it, till, after some time, she told it me all freely of her own accord, which, to cut it short, amounted to no more than this, that, like mistress like maid, as they had many leisure hours together below, while they waited respectively when his lord and I were together above; I say, they could hardly avoid the usual question one to another, namely, why might not they do the same thing below that we did above?

On that account, indeed, as I said above, I could not find in my heart to be angry with Amy. I was, indeed, afraid the girl would have been with child too, but that did not happen, and so there was no hurt done; for Amy had been hanselled before, as well as her mistress, and by the same party too, as you have heard.

After I was up again, and my child provided with a good nurse, and, withal, winter coming on, it was proper to think of coming to Paris again, which I did; but as I had now a coach and horses, and some servants to attend me, by my lord's allowance, I took the liberty to have them come to Paris sometimes, and so to take a tour into the garden of the Tuileries and the other pleasant places of the city. It happened one day that my prince (if I may call him so) had a mind to give me some diversion, and to take the air with me; but, that he might do it and not be publicly known, he comes to me in a coach of the Count de ——, a great officer of the court, attended by his liveries also; so that, in a word, it was impossible to guess by the equipage who I was or who I belonged to; also, that I might be the more effectually concealed, he ordered me to be taken up at a mantua-maker's house, where he sometimes came, whether upon other amours or not was no business of mine to inquire. I knew nothing whither he intended to carry me; but when he was in the coach with me, he told me he had ordered his servants to go to court with me, and he would show me some of the beau monde. I told him I cared not where I went while I had the honour to have him with me. So he carried me to the fine palace of Meudon, where the Dauphin then was, and where he had some particular intimacy with one of the Dauphin's domestics, who procured a retreat for me in his lodgings while we stayed there, which was three or four days.

While I was there the king happened to come thither from Versailles, and making but a short stay, visited Madame the Dauphiness, who was then living. The prince was here incognito, only because of his being with me, and therefore, when he heard that the king was in the gardens, he kept close within the lodgings; but the gentleman in whose lodgings we were, with his lady and several others, went out to see the king, and I had the honour to be asked to go with them.

After we had seen the king, who did not stay long in the gardens, we walked up the broad terrace, and crossing the hall towards the great staircase, I had a sight which confounded me at once, as I doubt not it would have done to any woman in the world. The horse guards, or what they call there the gens d'armes, had, upon some occasion, been either upon duty or been reviewed, or something (I did not understand that part) was the matter that occasioned their being there, I know not what; but, walking in the guard-chamber, and with his jack-boots on, and the whole habit of the troop, as it is worn when our horse guards are upon duty, as they call it, at St. James's Park; I say, there, to my inexpressible confusion, I saw Mr. ——, my first husband, the brewer.

I could not be deceived; I passed so near him that I almost brushed him with my clothes, and looked him full in the face, but having my fan before my face, so that he could not know me. However, I knew him perfectly well, and I heard him speak, which was a second way of knowing him. Besides being, you may be sure, astonished and surprised at such a sight, I turned about after I had passed him some steps, and pretending to ask the lady that was with me some questions, I stood as if I had viewed the great hall, the outer guard-chamber, and some things; but I did it to take a full view of his dress, that I might farther inform myself.

While I stood thus amusing the lady that was with me with questions, he walked, talking with another man of the same cloth, back again, just by me; and to my particular satisfaction, or dissatisfaction—take it which way you will—I heard him speak English, the other being, it seems, an Englishman.

I then asked the lady some other questions. "Pray, madam," says I, "what are these troopers here? Are they the king's guards?" "No," says she; "they are the gens d'armes; a small detachment of them, I suppose, attended the king to-day, but they are not his Majesty's ordinary guard." Another lady that was with her said, "No, madam, it seems that is not the case, for I heard them saying the gens d'armes were here to-day by special order, some of them being to march towards the Rhine, and these attend for orders; but they go back to-morrow to Orleans, where they are expected."

This satisfied me in part, but I found means after this to inquire whose particular troop it was that the gentlemen that were here belonged to; and with that I heard they would all be at Paris the week after.

Two days after this we returned for Paris, when I took occasion to speak to my lord, that I heard the gens d'armes were to be in the city the next week, and that I should be charmed with seeing them march if they came in a body. He was so obliging in such things that I need but just name a thing of that kind and it was done; so he ordered his gentleman (I should now call him Amy's gentleman) to get me a place in a certain house, where I might see them march.

As he did not appear with me on this occasion, so I had the liberty of taking my woman Amy with me, and stood where we were very well accommodated for the observation which I was to make. I told Amy what I had seen, and she was as forward to make the discovery as I was to have her, and almost as much surprised at the thing itself. In a word, the gens d'armes entered the city, as was expected, and made a most glorious show indeed, being new clothed and armed, and being to have their standards blessed by the Archbishop of Paris. On this occasion they indeed looked very gay; and as they marched very leisurely, I had time to take as critical a view and make as nice a search among them as I pleased. Here, in a particular rank, eminent for one monstrous-sized man on the right; here, I say, I saw my gentleman again, and a very handsome, jolly fellow he was, as any in the troop, though not so monstrous large as that great one I speak of, who, it seems, was, however, a gentleman of a good family in Gascony, and was called the giant of Gascony.

It was a kind of a good fortune to us, among the other circumstances of it, that something caused the troops to halt in their march a little before that particular rank came right against that window which I stood in, so that then we had occasion to take our full view of him at a small distance, and so as not to doubt of his being the same person.

Amy, who thought she might, on many accounts, venture with more safety to be particular than I could, asked her gentleman how a particular man, who she saw there among the gens d'armes, might be inquired after and found out; she having seen an Englishman riding there which was supposed to be dead in England for several years before she came out of London and that his wife had married again. It was a question the gentleman did not well understand how to answer; but another person that stood by told her, if she would tell him the gentleman's name, he would endeavour to find him out for her, and asked jestingly if he was her lover. Amy put that off with a laugh, but still continued her inquiry, and in such a manner as the gentleman easily perceived she was in earnest; so he left bantering, and asked her in what part of the troop he rode. She foolishly told him his name, which she should not have done; and pointing to the cornet that troop carried, which was not then quite out of sight, she let him easily know whereabouts he rode, only she could not name the captain. However, he gave her such directions afterwards that, in short, Amy, who was an indefatigable girl, found him out. It seems he had not changed his name, not supposing any inquiry would be made after him here; but, I say, Amy found him out, and went boldly to his quarters, asked for him, and he came out to her immediately.

I believe I was not more confounded at my first seeing him at Meudon than he was at seeing Amy. He started and turned pale as death. Amy believed if he had seen her at first, in any convenient place for so villainous a purpose, he would have murdered her.

But he started, as I say above, and asked in English, with an admiration, "What are you?" "Sir," says she, "don't you know me?" "Yes," says he, "I knew you when you were alive; but what are you now?—whether ghost or substance I know not." "Be not afraid, sir, of that," says Amy; "I am the same Amy that I was in your service, and do not speak to you now for any hurt, but that I saw you accidentally yesterday ride among the soldiers; I thought you might be glad to hear from your friends at London." "Well, Amy," says he then (having a little recovered himself), "how does everybody do? What! is your mistress here?" Thus they begun:—

Amy. My mistress, sir, alas! not the mistress you mean; poor gentlewoman, you left her in a sad condition.

Gent. Why, that's true, Amy; but it could not be helped; I was in a sad condition myself.

Amy. I believe so, indeed, sir, or else you had not gone away as you did; for it was a very terrible condition you left them all in, that I must say.

Gent. What did they do after I was gone?

Amy. Do, sir! Very miserably, you may be sure. How could it be otherwise?

Gent. Well, that's true indeed; but you may tell me, Amy, what became of them, if you please; for though I went so away, it was not because I did not love them all very well, but because I could not bear to see the poverty that was coming upon them, and which it was not in my power to help. What could I do?

Amy. Nay, I believe so indeed; and I have heard my mistress say many times she did not doubt but your affliction was as great as hers, almost, wherever you were.

Gent. Why, did she believe I was alive, then?

Amy. Yes, sir; she always said she believed you were alive, because she thought she should have heard something of you if you had been dead.

Gent. Ay, ay; my perplexity was very great indeed, or else I had never gone away.

Amy. It was very cruel, though, to the poor lady, sir, my mistress; she almost broke her heart for you at first, for fear of what might befall you, and at last because she could not hear from you.

Gent. Alas, Amy! what could I do? Things were driven to the last extremity before I went. I could have done nothing but help starve them all if I had stayed; and, besides, I could not bear to see it.

Amy. You know, sir, I can say little to what passed before, but I am a melancholy witness to the sad distresses of my poor mistress as long as I stayed with her, and which would grieve your heart to hear them.

[Here she tells my whole story to the time that the parish took off one of my children, and which she perceived very much affected him; and he shook his head, and said some things very bitter when he heard of the cruelty of his own relations to me.]

Gent. Well, Amy, I have heard enough so far. What did she do afterwards?

Amy. I can't give you any farther account, sir; my mistress would not let me stay with her any longer. She said she could neither pay me or subsist me. I told her I would serve her without any wages, but I could not live without victuals, you know; so I was forced to leave her, poor lady, sore against my will; and I heard afterwards that the landlord seized her goods, so she was, I suppose, turned out of doors; for as I went by the door, about a month after, I saw the house shut up; and, about a fortnight after that, I found there were workmen at work, fitting it up, as I suppose, for a new tenant. But none of the neighbours could tell me what was become of my poor mistress, only that they said she was so poor that it was next to begging; that some of the neighbouring gentlefolks had relieved her, or that else she must have starved.

Then she went on, and told him that after that they never heard any more of (me) her mistress, but that she had been seen once or twice in the city very shabby and poor in clothes, and it was thought she worked with her needle for her bread.

All this the jade said with so much cunning, and managed and humoured it so well, and wiped her eyes and cried so artificially, that he took it all as it was intended he should, and once or twice she saw tears in his eyes too. He told her it was a moving, melancholy story, and it had almost broke his heart at first, but that he was driven to the last extremity, and could do nothing but stay and see them all starve, which he could not bear the thoughts of, but should have pistolled himself if any such thing had happened while he was there; that he left (me) his wife all the money he had in the world but £25, which was as little as he could take with him to seek his fortune in the world. He could not doubt but that his relations, seeing they were all rich, would have taken the poor children off, and not let them come to the parish; and that his wife was young and handsome, and, he thought, might marry again, perhaps, to her advantage, and for that very reason he never wrote to her or let her know he was alive, that she might in a reasonable term of years marry, and perhaps mend her fortunes; that he resolved never to claim her, because he should rejoice to hear that she had settled to her mind; and that he wished there had been a law made to empower a woman to marry if her husband was not heard of in so long a time, which time, he thought, should not be above four years, which was long enough to send word in to a wife or family from any part of the world.

Amy said she could say nothing to that but this, that she was satisfied her mistress would marry nobody unless she had certain intelligence that he had been dead from somebody that saw him buried. "But, alas!" says Amy, "my mistress was reduced to such dismal circumstances that nobody would be so foolish to think of her, unless it had been somebody to go a-begging with her."

Amy then, seeing him so perfectly deluded, made a long and lamentable outcry how she had been deluded away to marry a poor footman. "For he is no worse or better," says she, "though he calls himself a lord's gentleman. And here," says Amy, "he has dragged me over into a strange country to make a beggar of me;" and then she falls a-howling again, and snivelling, which, by the way, was all hypocrisy, but acted so to the life as perfectly deceived him, and he gave entire credit to every word of it.

"Why, Amy," says he, "you are very well dressed; you don't look as if you were in danger of being a beggar." "Ay, hang 'em!" says Amy, "they love to have fine clothes here, if they have never a smock under them. But I love to have money in cash, rather than a chestful of fine clothes. Besides, sir," says she, "most of the clothes I have were given me in the last place I had, when I went away from my mistress."

Upon the whole of the discourse, Amy got out of him what condition he was in and how he lived, upon her promise to him that if ever she came to England, and should see her old mistress, she should not let her know that he was alive. "Alas, sir!" says Amy, "I may never come to see England again as long as I live; and if I should, it would be ten thousand to one whether I shall see my old mistress, for how should I know which way to look for her, or what part of England she may be in?—not I," says she. "I don't so much as know how to inquire for her; and if I should," says Amy, "ever be so happy as to see her, I would not do her so much mischief as to tell her where you were, sir, unless she was in a condition to help herself and you too." This farther deluded him, and made him entirely open in his conversing with her. As to his own circumstances, he told her she saw him in the highest preferment he had arrived to, or was ever like to arrive to; for, having no friends or acquaintance in France, and, which was worse, no money, he never expected to rise; that he could have been made a lieutenant to a troop of light horse but the week before, by the favour of an officer in the gens d'armes who was his friend, but that he must have found eight thousand livres to have paid for it to the gentleman who possessed it, and had leave given him to sell. "But where could I get eight thousand livres," says he, "that have never been master of five hundred livres ready money at a time since I came into France?"

"Oh dear, sir!" says Amy, "I am very sorry to hear you say so. I fancy if you once got up to some preferment, you would think of my old mistress again, and do something for her. Poor lady," says Amy, "she wants it, to be sure;" and then she falls a-crying again. "It is a sad thing indeed," says she, "that you should be so hard put to it for money, when you had got a friend to recommend you, and should lose it for want of money." "Ay, so it was, Amy, indeed," says he; "but what can a stranger do that has neither money or friends?" Here Amy puts in again on my account. "Well," says she, "my poor mistress has had the loss, though she knows nothing of it. Oh dear! how happy it would have been! To be sure, sir, you would have helped her all you could." "Ay," says he, "Amy, so I would with all my heart; and even as I am, I would send her some relief, if I thought she wanted it, only that then letting her know I was alive might do her some prejudice, in case of her settling, or marrying anybody."

"Alas," says Amy, "marry! Who will marry her in the poor condition she is in?" And so their discourse ended for that time.

All this was mere talk on both sides, and words of course; for on farther inquiry, Amy found that he had no such offer of a lieutenant's commission, or anything like it; and that he rambled in his discourse from one thing to another; but of that in its place.

You may be sure that this discourse, as Amy at first related it, was moving to the last degree upon me, and I was once going to have sent him the eight thousand livres to purchase the commission he had spoken of; but as I knew his character better than anybody, I was willing to search a little farther into it, and so I set Amy to inquire of some other of the troop, to see what character he had, and whether there was anything in the story of a lieutenant's commission or no.

But Amy soon came to a better understanding of him, for she presently learnt that he had a most scoundrel character; that there was nothing of weight in anything he said; but that he was, in short, a mere sharper, one that would stick at nothing to get money, and that there was no depending on anything he said; and that more especially about the lieutenant's commission, she understood that there was nothing at all in it, but they told her how he had often made use of that sham to borrow money, and move gentlemen to pity him and lend him money, in hopes to get him preferment; that he had reported that he had a wife and five children in England, who he maintained out of his pay, and by these shifts had run into debt in several places; and upon several complaints for such things, he had been threatened to be turned out of the gens d'armes; and that, in short, he was not to be believed in anything he said, or trusted on any account.

Upon this information, Amy began to cool in her farther meddling with him, and told me it was not safe for me to attempt doing him any good, unless I resolved to put him upon suspicions and inquiries which might be to my ruin, in the condition I was now in.

I was soon confirmed in this part of his character, for the next time that Amy came to talk with him, he discovered himself more effectually; for, while she had put him in hopes of procuring one to advance the money for the lieutenant's commission for him upon easy conditions, he by degrees dropped the discourse, then pretended it was too late, and that he could not get it, and then descended to ask poor Amy to lend him five hundred pistoles.

Amy pretended poverty, that her circumstances were but mean, and that she could not raise such a sum; and this she did to try him to the utmost. He descended to three hundred, then to one hundred, then to fifty, and then to a pistole, which she lent him, and he, never intending to pay it, played out of her sight as much as he could. And thus being satisfied that he was the same worthless thing he had ever been, I threw off all thoughts of him;

whereas, had he been a man of any sense and of any principle of honour, I had it in my thoughts to retire to England again, send for him over, and have lived honestly with him. But as a fool is the worst of husbands to do a woman good, so a fool is the worst husband a woman can do good to. I would willingly have done him good, but he was not qualified to receive it or make the best use of it. Had I sent him ten thousand crowns instead of eight thousand livres, and sent it with express condition that he should immediately have bought himself the commission he talked of with part of the money, and have sent some of it to relieve the necessities of his poor miserable wife at London, and to prevent his children to be kept by the parish, it was evident he would have been still but a private trooper, and his wife and children should still have starved at London, or been kept of mere charity, as, for aught he knew, they then were.

Seeing, therefore, no remedy, I was obliged to withdraw my hand from him, that had been my first destroyer, and reserve the assistance that I intended to have given him for another more desirable opportunity. All that I had now to do was to keep myself out of his sight, which was not very difficult for me to do, considering in what station he lived.

Amy and I had several consultations then upon the main question, namely, how to be sure never to chop upon him again by chance, and to be surprised into a discovery, which would have been a fatal discovery indeed. Amy proposed that we should always take care to know where the gens d'armes were quartered, and thereby effectually avoid them; and this was one way.

But this was not so as to be fully to my satisfaction; no ordinary way of inquiring where the gens d'armes were quartered was sufficient to me; but I found out a fellow who was completely qualified for the work of a spy (for France has plenty of such people). This man I employed to be a constant and particular attendant upon his person and motions; and he was especially employed and ordered to haunt him as a ghost, that he should scarce let him be ever out of his sight. He performed this to a nicety, and failed not to give me a perfect journal of all his motions from day to day, and, whether for his pleasure or his business, was always at his heels.

This was somewhat expensive, and such a fellow merited to be well paid, but he did his business so exquisitely punctual that this poor man scarce went out of the house without my knowing the way he went, the company he kept, when he went abroad, and when he stayed at home.

By this extraordinary conduct I made myself safe, and so went out in public or stayed at home as I found he was or was not in a possibility of being at Paris, at Versailles, or any place I had occasion to be at. This, though it was very chargeable, yet as I found it absolutely necessary, so I took no thought about the expense of it, for I knew I could not purchase my safety too dear.

By this management I found an opportunity to see what a most insignificant, unthinking life the poor, indolent wretch, who, by his unactive temper, had at first been my ruin, now lived; how he only rose in the morning to go to bed at night; that, saving the necessary motion of the troops, which he was obliged to attend, he was a mere motionless animal, of no consequence in the world; that he seemed to be one who, though he was indeed alive, had no manner of business in life but to stay to be called out of it. He neither kept any company, minded any sport, played at any game, or indeed did anything of moment; but, in short, sauntered about like one that it was not two livres value whether he was dead or alive; that when he was gone, would leave no remembrance behind him that ever he was here; that if ever he did anything in the world to be talked of, it was only to get five beggars and starve his wife. The journal of his life, which I had constantly sent me every week, was the least significant of anything of its kind that was ever seen, as it had really nothing of earnest in it, so it would make no jest to relate it. It was not important enough so much as to make the reader merry withal, and for that reason I omit it.

Yet this nothing-doing wretch was I obliged to watch and guard against, as against the only thing that was capable of doing me hurt in the world. I was to shun him as we would shun a spectre, or even the devil, if he was actually in our way; and it cost me after the rate of a hundred and fifty livres a month, and very cheap too, to have this creature constantly kept in view. That is to say, my spy undertook never to let him be out of his sight an hour, but so as that he could give an account of him, which was much the easier for to be done considering his way of living; for he was sure that, for whole weeks together, he would be ten hours of the day half asleep on a bench at the tavern-door where he quartered, or drunk within the house. Though this wicked life he led sometimes moved me to pity him, and to wonder how so well-bred, gentlemanly a man as he once was could degenerate into such a useless thing as he now appeared, yet at the same time it gave me most contemptible thoughts of him, and made me often say I was a warning for all the ladies of Europe against marrying of fools. A man of sense falls in the world and gets up again, and a woman has some chance for herself; but with a fool, once fall, and ever undone; once in the ditch, and die in the ditch; once poor, and sure to starve.

But it is time to have done with him. Once I had nothing to hope for but to see him again; now my only felicity was, if possible, never to see him, and, above all, to keep him from seeing me, which, as above, I took effectual care of.

I was now returned to Paris. My little son of honour, as I called him, was left at ——, where my last country-seat then was, and I came to Paris at the prince's request. Thither he came to me as soon as I arrived, and told me he came to give me joy of my return, and to make his acknowledgments for that I had given him a son. I thought, indeed, he had been going to give me a present, and so he did the next day, but in what he said then he only jested with me. He gave me his company all the evening, supped with me about midnight, and did me the honour, as I then called it, to lodge me in his arms all the night, telling me, in jest, that the best thanks for a son born was giving the pledge for another.

But as I hinted, so it was; the next morning he laid me down on my toilet a purse with three hundred pistoles. I saw him lay it down, and understood what he meant, but I took no notice of it till I came to it, as it were, casually; then I gave a great cry out, and fell a-scolding in my way, for he gave me all possible freedom of speech on such occasions. I told him he was unkind, that he would never give me an opportunity to ask for anything, and that he forced me to blush by being too much obliged, and the like; all which I knew was very agreeable to him, for as he was bountiful beyond measure, so he was infinitely obliged by my being so backward to ask any favours; and I was even with him, for I never asked him for a farthing in my life.

Upon this rallying him, he told me I had either perfectly studied the art of humour, or else what was the greatest difficulty to others was natural to me, adding that nothing could be more obliging to a man of honour than not to be soliciting and craving.

I told him nothing could be craving upon him, that he left no room for it; that I hoped he did not give merely to avoid the trouble of being importuned. I told him he might depend upon it that I should be reduced very low indeed before I offered to disturb him that way.

He said a man of honour ought always to know what he ought to do; and as he did nothing but what he knew was reasonable, he gave me leave to be free with him if I wanted anything; that he had too much value for me to deny me anything if I asked, but that it was infinitely agreeable to him to hear me say that what he did was to my satisfaction.

We strained compliments thus a great while, and as he had me in his arms most part of the time, so upon all my expressions of his bounty to me he put a stop to me with his kisses, and would admit me to go on no farther.

I should in this place mention that this prince was not a subject of France, though at that time he resided at Paris and was much at court, where, I suppose, he had or expected some considerable employment. But I mention it on this account, that a few days after this he came to me and told me he was come to bring me not the most welcome news that ever I heard from him in his life. I looked at him a little surprised; but he returned, "Do not be uneasy; it is as unpleasant to me as to you, but I come to consult with you about it and see if it cannot be made a little easy to us both."

I seemed still more concerned and surprised. At last he said it was that he believed he should be obliged to go into Italy, which, though otherwise it was very agreeable to him, yet his parting with me made it a very dull thing but to think of.

I sat mute, as one thunderstruck, for a good while; and it presently occurred to me that I was going to lose him, which, indeed, I could but ill bear the thoughts of; and as he told me I turned pale. "What's the matter?" said he hastily. "I have surprised you indeed," and stepping to the sideboard fills a dram of cordial water, which was of his own bringing, and comes to me. "Be not surprised," said he; "I'll go nowhere without you;" adding several other things so kind as nothing could exceed it.

I might indeed turn pale, for I was very much surprised at first, believing that this was, as it often happens in such cases, only a project to drop me, and break off an amour which he had now carried on so long; and a thousand thoughts whirled about my head in the few moments while I was kept in suspense, for they were but a few. I say, I was indeed surprised, and might, perhaps, look pale, but I was not in any danger of fainting that I knew of.

However, it not a little pleased me to see him so concerned and anxious about me, but I stopped a little when he put the cordial to my mouth, and taking the glass in my hand, I said, "My lord, your words are infinitely more of a cordial to me than this citron; for as nothing can be a greater affliction than to lose you, so nothing can be a greater satisfaction than the assurance that I shall not have that misfortune."

He made me sit down, and sat down by me, and after saying a thousand kind things to me, he turns upon me with a smile: "Why, will you venture yourself to Italy with me?" says he. I stopped a while, and then answered that I wondered he would ask me that question, for I would go anywhere in the world, or all over the world, wherever he should desire me, and give me the felicity of his company.

Then he entered into a long account of the occasion of his journey, and how the king had engaged him to go, and some other circumstances which are not proper to enter into here; it being by no means proper to say anything that might lead the reader into the least guess at the person.

But to cut short this part of the story, and the history of our journey and stay abroad, which would almost fill up a volume of itself, I say we spent all that evening in cheerful consultations about the manner of our travelling, the equipage and figure he should go in, and in what manner I should go. Several ways were proposed, but none seemed feasible, till at last I told him I thought it would be so troublesome, so expensive, and so public that it would be many ways inconvenient to him; and though it was a kind of death to me to lose him, yet that, rather than so very much perplex his affairs, I would submit to anything.

At the next visit I filled his head with the same difficulties, and then at last came over him with a proposal that I would stay in Paris, or where else he should direct; and when I heard of his safe arrival, would come away by myself, and place myself as near him as I could.

This gave him no satisfaction at all, nor would he hear any more of it; but if I durst venture myself, as he called it, such a journey, he would not lose the satisfaction of my company; and as for the expense, that was not to be named; neither, indeed, was there room to name it, for I found that he travelled at the king's expense, as well for himself as for all his equipage, being upon a piece of secret service of the last importance.

But after several debates between ourselves, he came to this resolution, viz., that he would travel incognito, and so he should avoid all public notice either of himself or of who went with him; and that then he should not only carry me with him, but have a perfect leisure of enjoying my agreeable company (as he was pleased to call it) all the way.

This was so obliging that nothing could be more so. Upon this foot he immediately set to work to prepare things for his journey, and, by his directions, so did I too. But now I had a terrible difficulty upon me, and which way to get over it I knew not; and that was, in what manner to take care of what I had to leave behind me. I was rich, as I have said, very rich, and what to do with it I knew not; nor who to leave in trust I knew not. I had nobody but Amy in the world, and to travel without Amy was very uncomfortable, or to leave all I had in the world with her, and, if she miscarried, be ruined at once, was still a frightful thought; for Amy might die, and whose hands things might fall into I knew not. This gave me great uneasiness, and I knew not what to do; for I could not mention it to the prince, lest he should see that I was richer than he thought I was.

But the prince made all this easy to me; for in concerting measures for our journey he started the thing himself, and asked me merrily one evening who I would trust with all my wealth in my absence.

"My wealth, my lord," said I, "except what I owe to your goodness is but small, but yet that little I have, I confess, causes some thoughtfulness, because I have no acquaintance in Paris that I dare trust with it, nor anybody but my woman to leave in the house; and how to do without her upon the road I do not well know."

"As to the road, be not concerned," says the prince; "I'll provide you servants to your mind; and as for your woman, if you can trust her, leave her here, and I'll put you in a way how to secure things as well as if you were at home." I bowed, and told him I could not be put into better hands than his own, and that, therefore, I would govern all my measures by his directions; so we talked no more of it that night.

The next day he sent me in a great iron chest, so large that it was as much as six lusty fellows could get up the steps into the house; and in this I put, indeed, all my wealth; and for my safety he ordered a good, honest, ancient man and his wife to be in the house with her, to keep her company, and a maid-servant and boy; so that there was a good family, and Amy was madam, the mistress of the house.

Things being thus secured, we set out incog., as he called it; but we had two coaches and six horses, two chaises, and about eight men-servants on horseback, all very well armed.

Never was woman better used in this world that went upon no other account than I did. I had three women-servants to wait on me, one whereof was an old Madame ——, who thoroughly understood her business, and managed everything as if she had been major-domo; so I had no trouble. They had one coach to themselves, and the prince and I in the other; only that sometimes, where he knew it necessary, I went into their coach, and one particular gentleman of the retinue rode with him.

I shall say no more of the journey than that when we came to those frightful mountains, the Alps, there was no travelling in our coaches, so he ordered a horse-litter, but carried by mules, to be provided for me, and himself went on horseback. The coaches went some other way back to Lyons. Then we had coaches hired at Turin, which met us at Suza; so that we were accommodated again, and went by easy journeys afterwards to Rome, where his business, whatever it was, called him to stay some time, and from thence to Venice.

He was as good as his word, indeed; for I had the pleasure of his company, and, in a word, engrossed his conversation almost all the way. He took delight in showing me everything that was to be seen, and particularly in telling me something of the history of everything he showed me.

What valuable pains were here thrown away upon one who he was sure, at last, to abandon with regret! How below himself did a man of quality and of a thousand accomplishments behave in all this! It is one of my reasons for entering into this part, which otherwise would not be worth relating. Had I been a daughter or a wife, of whom it might be said that he had a just concern in their instruction or improvement, it had been an admirable step; but all this to a whore; to one who he carried with him upon no account that could be rationally agreeable, and none but to gratify the meanest of human frailties—this was the wonder of it. But such is the power of a vicious inclination. Whoring was, in a word, his darling crime, the worst excursion he made, for he was otherwise one of the most excellent persons in the world. No passions, no furious excursions, no ostentatious pride; the most humble, courteous, affable person in the world. Not an oath, not an indecent word, or the least blemish in behaviour was to be seen in all his conversation, except as before excepted; and it has given me occasion for many dark reflections since, to look back and think that I should be the snare of such a person's life; that I should influence him to so much wickedness, and that I should be the instrument in the hand of the devil to do him so much prejudice.

We were near two years upon this grand tour, as it may be called, during most of which I resided at Rome or at Venice, having only been twice at Florence and once at Naples. I made some very diverting and useful observations in all these places, and particularly of the conduct of the ladies; for I had opportunity to converse very much among them, by the help of the old witch that travelled with us. She had been at Naples and at Venice, and had lived in the former several years, where, as I found, she had lived but a loose life, as indeed the women of Naples generally do; and, in short, I found she was fully acquainted with all the intriguing arts of that part of the world.

Here my lord bought me a little female Turkish slave, who, being taken at sea by a Maltese man-of-war, was brought in there, and of her I learnt the Turkish language, their way of dressing and dancing, and some Turkish, or rather Moorish, songs, of which I made use to my advantage on an extraordinary occasion some years after, as you shall hear in its place. I need not say I learnt Italian too, for I got pretty well mistress of that before I had been there a year; and as I had leisure enough and loved the language, I read all the Italian books I could come at.
I began to be so in love with Italy, especially with Naples and Venice, that I could have been very well satisfied to have sent for Amy and have taken up my residence there for life.

As to Rome, I did not like it at all. The swarms of ecclesiastics of all kinds on one side, and the scoundrel rabbles of the common people on the other, make Rome the unpleasantest place in the world to live in. The innumerable number of valets, lackeys, and other servants is such that they used to say that there are very few of the common people in Rome but what have been footmen, or porters, or grooms to cardinals or foreign ambassadors. In a word, they have an air of sharping and cozening, quarrelling and scolding, upon their general behaviour; and when I was there the footmen made such a broil between two great families in Rome, about which of their coaches (the ladies being in the coaches on either side) should give way to the other, that there was about thirty people wounded on both sides, five or six killed outside, and both the ladies frighted almost to death.

But I have no mind to write the history of my travels on this side of the world, at least not now; it would be too full of variety.

I must not, however, omit that the prince continued in all this journey the most kind, obliging person to me in the world, and so constant that, though we were in a country where it is well known all manner of liberties are taken, I am yet well assured he neither took the liberty he knew he might have, or so much as desired it.

I have often thought of this noble person on that account. Had he been but half so true, so faithful and constant, to the best lady in the world—I mean his princess—how glorious a virtue had it been in him! And how free had he been from those just reflections which touched him in her behalf when it was too late!

We had some very agreeable conversations upon this subject, and once he told me, with a kind of more than ordinary concern upon his thoughts, that he was greatly beholden to me for taking this hazardous and difficult journey, for that I had kept him honest. I looked up in his face, and coloured as red as fire. "Well, well," says he, "do not let that surprise you, I do say you have kept me honest." "My lord," said I, "'tis not for me to explain your words, but I wish I could turn them my own way. I hope," says I, "and believe we are both as honest as we can be in our circumstances." "Ay, ay," says he; "and honester than I doubt I should have been if you had not been with me. I cannot say but if you had not been here I should have wandered among the gay world here, in Naples, and in Venice too, for 'tis not such a crime here as 'tis in other places. But I protest," says he, "I have not touched a woman in Italy but yourself; and more than that, I have not so much as had any desire to it. So that, I say, you have kept me honest."

I was silent, and was glad that he interrupted me, or kept me from speaking, with kissing me, for really I knew not what to say. I was once going to say that if his lady, the princess, had been with him, she would doubtless have had the same influence upon his virtue, with infinitely more advantage to him; but I considered this might give him offence; and, besides, such things might have been dangerous to the circumstance I stood in, so it passed off. But I must confess I saw that he was quite another man as to women than I understood he had always been before, and it was a particular satisfaction to me that I was thereby convinced that what he said was true, and that he was, as I may say, all my own.

I was with child again in this journey, and lay in at Venice, but was not so happy as before. I brought him another son, and a very fine boy it was, but it lived not above two months; nor, after the first touches of affection (which are usual, I believe, to all mothers) were over, was I sorry the child did not live, the necessary difficulties attending it in our travelling being considered.

After these several perambulations, my lord told me his business began to close, and we would think of returning to France, which I was very glad of, but principally on account of my treasure I had there, which, as you have heard, was very considerable. It is true I had letters very frequently from my maid Amy, with accounts that everything was very safe, and that was very much to my satisfaction. However, as the prince's negotiations were at an end, and he was obliged to return, I was very glad to go; so we returned from Venice to Turin, and in the way I saw the famous city of Milan. From Turin we went over the mountains again, as before, and our coaches met us at Pont à Voisin, between Chambery and Lyons; and so, by easy journeys, we arrived safely at Paris, having been absent two years, wanting about eleven days, as above.

I found the little family we left just as we left them, and Amy cried for joy when she saw me, and I almost did the same.

The prince took his leave of me the night before, for, as he told me, he knew he should be met upon the road by several persons of quality, and perhaps by the princess herself; so we lay at two different inns that night, lest some should come quite to the place, as indeed it happened.

After this I saw him not for above twenty days, being taken up in his family, and also with business; but he sent me his gentleman to tell me the reason of it, and bid me not be uneasy, and that satisfied me effectually.

In all this affluence of my good fortune I did not forget that I had been rich and poor once already alternately, and that I ought to know that the circumstances I was now in were not to be expected to last always; that I had one child, and expected another; and if I had bred often, it would something impair me in the great article that supported my interest—I mean, what he called beauty; that as that declined, I might expect the fire would abate, and the warmth with which I was now so caressed would cool, and in time, like the other mistresses of great men, I might be dropped again; and that therefore it was my business to take care that I should fall as softly as I could.

I say, I did not forget, therefore, to make as good provision for myself as if I had had nothing to have subsisted on but what I now gained; whereas I had not less than ten thousand pounds, as I said above, which I had amassed, or secured rather, out of the ruins of my faithful friend the jeweller, and which he, little thinking of what was so near him when he went out, told me, though in a kind of a jest, was all my own, if he was knocked on the head, and which, upon that title, I took care to preserve.

My greatest difficulty now was how to secure my wealth and to keep what I had got; for I had greatly added to this wealth by the generous bounty of the Prince ——, and the more by the private, retired mode of living, which he rather desired for privacy than parsimony; for he supplied me for a more magnificent way of life than I desired, if it had been proper.

I shall cut short the history of this prosperous wickedness with telling you I brought him a third son, within little more than eleven months after our return from Italy; that now I lived a little more openly, and went by a particular name which he gave me abroad, but which I must omit, viz., the Countess de ——; and had coaches and servants, suitable to the quality he had given me the appearance of; and, which is more than usually happens in such cases, this held eight years from the beginning, during which time, as I had been very faithful to him, so I must say, as above, that I believe he was so separated to me, that whereas he usually had two or three women, which he kept privately, he had not in all that time meddled with any of them, but that I had so perfectly engrossed him that he dropped them all. Not, perhaps, that he saved much by it, for I was a very chargeable mistress to him, that I must acknowledge, but it was all owing to his particular affection to me, not to my extravagance, for, as I said, he never gave me leave to ask him for anything, but poured in his favours and presents faster than I expected, and so fast as I could not have the assurance to make the least mention of desiring more. Nor do I speak this of my own guess, I mean about his constancy to me and his quitting all other women; but the old harridan, as I may call her, whom he made the guide of our travelling, and who was a strange old creature, told me a thousand stories of his gallantry, as she called it, and how, as he had no less than three mistresses at one time, and, as I found, all of her procuring, he had of a sudden dropped them all, and that he was entirely lost to both her and them; that they did believe he had fallen into some new hands, but she could never hear who, or where, till he sent for her to go this journey; and then the old hag complimented me upon his choice; that she did not wonder I had so engrossed him; so much beauty, &c.; and there she stopped.

Upon the whole, I found by her what was, you may be sure, to my particular satisfaction, viz., that, as above, I had him all my own. But the highest tide has its ebb; and in all things of this kind there is a reflux which sometimes, also, is more impetuously violent than the first aggression. My prince was a man of a vast fortune, though no sovereign, and therefore there was no probability that the expense of keeping a mistress could be injurious to him, as to his estate. He had also several employments, both out of France as well as in it; for, as above, I say he was not a subject of France, though he lived in that court. He had a princess, a wife with whom he had lived several years, and a woman (so the voice of fame reported) the most valuable of her sex, of birth equal to him, if not superior, and of fortune proportionable; but in beauty, wit, and a thousand good qualities superior, not to most women, but even to all her sex; and as to her virtue, the character which was justly her due was that of, not only the best of princesses, but even the best of women.

They lived in the utmost harmony, as with such a princess it was impossible to be otherwise. But yet the princess was not insensible that her lord had his foibles, that he did make some excursions, and particularly that he had one favourite mistress, which sometimes engrossed him more than she (the princess) could wish, or be easily satisfied with. However, she was so good, so generous, so truly kind a wife, that she never gave him any uneasiness on this account; except so much as must arise from his sense of her bearing the affront of it with such patience, and such a profound respect for him as was in itself enough to have reformed him, and did sometimes shock his generous mind, so as to keep him at home, as I may call it, a great while together. And it was not long before I not only perceived it by his absence, but really got a knowledge of the reason of it, and once or twice he even acknowledged it to me.

It was a point that lay not in me to manage. I made a kind of motion once or twice to him to leave me, and keep himself to her, as he ought by the laws and rites of matrimony to do, and argued the generosity of the princess to him, to persuade him; but I was a hypocrite, for had I prevailed with him really to be honest, I had lost him, which I could not bear the thoughts of; and he might easily see I was not in earnest. One time in particular, when I took upon me to talk at this rate, I found, when I argued so much for the virtue and honour, the birth, and, above all, the generous usage he found in the person of the princess with respect to his private amours, and how it should prevail upon him, &c., I found it began to affect him, and he returned, "And do you indeed," says he, "persuade me to leave you? Would you have me think you sincere?" I looked up in his face, smiling. "Not for any other favourite, my lord," says I; "that would break my heart; but for madam the princess!" said I; and then I could say no more. Tears followed, and I sat silent a while. "Well," said he, "if ever I do leave you, it shall be on the virtuous account; it shall be for the princess; I assure you it shall be for no other woman." "That's enough, my lord," said I; "there I ought to submit; and while I am assured it shall be for no other mistress, I promise your Highness I will not repine; or that, if I do, it shall be a silent grief; it shall not interrupt your felicity."

All this while I said I knew not what, and said what I was no more able to do than he was able to leave me; which, at that time, he owned he could not do—no, not for the princess herself.

But another turn of affairs determined this matter, for the princess was taken very ill, and, in the opinion of all her physicians, very dangerously so. In her sickness she desired to speak with her lord, and to take her leave of him. At this grievous parting she said so many passionate, kind things to him, lamented that she had left him no children (she had had three, but they were dead); hinted to him that it was one of the chief things which gave her satisfaction in death, as to this world, that she should leave him room to have heirs to his family, by some princess that should supply her place; with all humility, but with a Christian earnestness, recommended to him to do justice to such princess, whoever it should be, from whom, to be sure, he would expect justice; that is to say, to keep to her singly, according to the solemnest part of the marriage covenant; humbly asked his Highness's pardon if she had any way offended him; and appealing to Heaven, before whose tribunal she was to appear, that she had never violated her honour or her duty to him, and praying to Jesus and the blessed Virgin for his Highness; and thus, with the most moving and most passionate expressions of her affection to him, took her last leave of him, and died the next day.

This discourse, from a princess so valuable in herself and so dear to him, and the loss of her following so immediately after, made such deep impressions on him that he looked back with detestation upon the former part of his life, grew melancholy and reserved, changed his society and much of the general conduct of his life, resolved on a life regulated most strictly by the rules of virtue and piety, and, in a word, was quite another man.

The first part of his reformation was a storm upon me; for, about ten days after the princess's funeral, he sent a message to me by his gentleman, intimating, though in very civil terms, and with a short preamble or introduction, that he desired I would not take it ill that he was obliged to let me know that he could see me no more. His gentleman told me a long story of the new regulation of life his lord had taken up; and that he had been so afflicted for the loss of his princess that he thought it would either shorten his life or he would retire into some religious house, to end his days in solitude.

I need not direct anybody to suppose how I received this news. I was indeed exceedingly surprised at it, and had much ado to support myself when the first part of it was delivered, though the gentleman delivered his errand with great respect, and with all the regard to me that he was able, and with a great deal of ceremony, also telling me how much he was concerned to bring me such a message.

But when I heard the particulars of the story at large, and especially that of the lady's discourse to the prince a little before her death, I was fully satisfied. I knew very well he had done nothing but what any man must do that had a true sense upon him of the justice of the princess's discourse to him, and of the necessity there was of his altering his course of life, if he intended to be either a Christian or an honest man. I say, when I heard this I was perfectly easy. I confess it was a circumstance that it might be reasonably expected should have wrought something also upon me; I that had so much to reflect upon more than the prince; that had now no more temptation of poverty, or of the powerful motive which Amy used with me—namely, comply and live, deny and starve; I say, I that had no poverty to introduce vice, but was grown not only well supplied, but rich; and not only rich, but was very rich; in a word, richer than I knew how to think of, for the truth of it was, that thinking of it sometimes almost distracted me, for want of knowing how to dispose of it, and for fear of losing it all again by some cheat or trick, not knowing anybody that I could commit the trust of it to.

Besides, I should add, at the close of this affair, that the prince did not, as I may say, turn me off rudely and with disgust, but with all the decency and goodness peculiar to himself, and that could consist with a man reformed and struck with the sense of his having abused so good a lady as his late princess had been. Nor did he send me away empty, but did everything like himself; and, in particular, ordered his gentleman to pay the rent of the house and all the expense of his two sons, and to tell me how they were taken care of, and where, and also that I might at all times inspect the usage they had, and if I disliked anything it should be rectified; and having thus finished everything, he retired into Lorraine, or somewhere that way, where he had an estate, and I never heard of him more—I mean, not as a mistress.

Now I was at liberty to go to any part of the world, and take care of my money myself. The first thing that I resolved to do was to go directly to England, for there, I thought, being among my country-folks—for I esteemed myself an Englishwoman, though I was born in France—there, I say, I thought I could better manage things than in France; at least, that I would be in less danger of being circumvented and deceived; but how to get away with such a treasure as I had with me was a difficult point, and what I was greatly at a loss about.

There was a Dutch merchant in Paris, that was a person of great reputation for a man of substance and of honesty, but I had no manner of acquaintance with him, nor did I know how to get acquainted with him, so as to discover my circumstances to him; but at last I employed my maid Amy (such I must be allowed to call her, notwithstanding what has been said of her, because she was in the place of a maid-servant); I say, I employed my maid Amy to go to him, and she got a recommendation to him from somebody else, I knew not who, so that she got access to him well enough.

But now was my case as bad as before, for when I came to him what could I do? I had money and jewels to a vast value, and I might leave all those with him; that I might indeed do; and so I might with several other merchants in Paris, who would give me bills for it, payable at London; but then I ran a hazard of my money, and I had nobody at London to send the bills to, and so to stay till I had an account that they were accepted; for I had not one friend in London that I could have recourse to, so that indeed I knew not what to do.

In this case I had no remedy but that I must trust somebody, so I sent Amy to this Dutch merchant, as I said above. He was a little surprised when Amy came to him and talked to him of remitting a sum of about twelve thousand pistoles to England, and began to think she came to put some cheat upon him; but when he found that Amy was but a servant, and that I came to him myself, the case was altered presently.

When I came to him myself, I presently saw such a plainness in his dealing and such honesty in his countenance that I made no scruple to tell him my whole story, viz., that I was a widow, that I had some jewels to dispose of, and also some money which I had a mind to send to England, and to follow there myself; but being but a woman, and having no correspondence in London, or anywhere else, I knew not what to do, or how to secure my effects.

He dealt very candidly with me, but advised me, when he knew my case so particularly, to take bills upon Amsterdam, and to go that way to England; for that I might lodge my treasure in the bank there, in the most secure manner in the world, and that there he could recommend me to a man who perfectly understood jewels, and would deal faithfully with me in the disposing them.

I thanked him, but scrupled very much the travelling so far in a strange country, and especially with such a treasure about me; that, whether known or concealed, I did not know how to venture with it. Then he told me he would try to dispose of them there, that is, at Paris, and convert them into money, and so get me bills for the whole; and in a few days he brought a Jew to me, who pretended to buy the jewels. As soon as the Jew saw the jewels I saw my folly, and it was ten thousand to one but I had been ruined, and perhaps put to death in as cruel a manner as possible; and I was put in such a fright by it that I was once upon the point of flying for my life, and leaving the jewels and money too in the hands of the Dutchman, without any bills or anything else. The case was thus:—

As soon as the Jew saw the jewels he falls a-jabbering, in Dutch or Portuguese, to the merchant; and I could presently perceive that they were in some great surprise, both of them. The Jew held up his hands, looked at me with some horror, then talked Dutch again, and put himself into a thousand shapes, twisting his body and wringing up his face this way and that way in his discourse, stamping with his feet, and throwing abroad his hands, as if he was not in a rage only, but in a mere fury. Then he would turn and give a look at me like the devil. I thought I never saw anything so frightful in my life.

At length I put in a word. "Sir," says I to the Dutch merchant, "what is all this discourse to my business? What is this gentleman in all these passions about? I wish, if he is to treat with me, he would speak that I may understand him; or if you have business of your own between you that is to be done first, let me withdraw, and I'll come again when you are at leisure."

"No, no, madam," says the Dutchman very kindly, "you must not go; all our discourse is about you and your jewels, and you shall hear it presently; it concerns you very much, I assure you." "Concern me!" says I. "What can it concern me so much as to put this gentleman into such agonies, and what makes him give me such devil's looks as he does? Why, he looks as if he would devour me."

The Jew understood me presently, continuing in a kind of rage, and spoke in French: "Yes, madam, it does concern you much, very much, very much," repeating the words, shaking his head; and then turning to the Dutchman, "Sir," says he, "pray tell her what is the case." "No," says the merchant, "not yet; let us talk a little farther of it by ourselves;" upon which they withdrew into another room, where still they talked very high, but in a language I did not understand. I began to be a little surprised at what the Jew had said, you may be sure, and eager to know what he meant, and was very impatient till the Dutch merchant came back, and that so impatient that I called one of his servants to let him know I desired to speak with him. When he came in I asked his pardon for being so impatient, but told him I could not be easy till he had told me what the meaning of all this was. "Why, madam," says the Dutch merchant, "in short, the meaning is what I am surprised at too. This man is a Jew, and understands jewels perfectly well, and that was the reason I sent for him, to dispose of them to him for you; but as soon as he saw them, he knew the jewels very distinctly, and flying out in a passion, as you see he did, told me, in short, that they were the very parcel of jewels which the English jeweller had about him who was robbed going to Versailles, about eight years ago, to show them the Prince de ——, and that it was for these very jewels that the poor gentleman was murdered; and he is in all this agony to make me ask you how you came by them; and he says you ought to be charged with the robbery and murder, and put to the question to discover who were the persons that did it, that they might be brought to justice." While he said this the Jew came impudently back into the room without calling, which a little surprised me again.

The Dutch merchant spoke pretty good English, and he knew that the Jew did not understand English at all, so he told me the latter part, when he came into the room, in English, at which I smiled, which put the Jew into his mad fit again, and shaking his head and making his devil's faces again, he seemed to threaten me for laughing, saying, in French, this was an affair I should have little reason to laugh at, and the like. At this I laughed again, and flouted him, letting him see that I scorned him, and turning to the Dutch merchant, "Sir," says I, "that those jewels were belonging to Mr. ——, the English jeweller" (naming his name readily), "in that," says I, "this person is right; but that I should be questioned how I came to have them is a token of his ignorance, which, however, he might have managed with a little more good manners, till I told him who I am, and both he and you too will be more easy in that part when I should tell you that I am the unhappy widow of that Mr. —— who was so barbarously murdered going to Versailles, and that he was not robbed of those jewels, but of others, Mr. —— having left those behind him with me, lest he should be robbed. Had I, sir, come otherwise by them, I should not have been weak enough to have exposed them to sale here, where the thing was done, but have carried them farther off."

This was an agreeable surprise to the Dutch merchant, who, being an honest man himself, believed everything I said, which, indeed, being all really and literally true, except the deficiency of my marriage, I spoke with such an unconcerned easiness that it might plainly be seen that I had no guilt upon me, as the Jew suggested.

The Jew was confounded when he heard that I was the jeweller's wife. But as I had raised his passion with saying he looked at me with the devil's face, he studied mischief in his heart, and answered, that should not serve my turn; so called the Dutchman out again, when he told him that he resolved to prosecute this matter farther.

There was one kind chance in this affair, which, indeed, was my deliverance, and that was, that the fool could not restrain his passion, but must let it fly to the Dutch merchant, to whom, when they withdrew a second time, as above, he told that he would bring a process against me for the murder, and that it should cost me dear for using him at that rate; and away he went, desiring the Dutch merchant to tell him when I would be there again. Had he suspected that the Dutchman would have communicated the particulars to me, he would never have been so foolish as to have mentioned that part to him.

But the malice of his thoughts anticipated him, and the Dutch merchant was so good as to give me an account of his design, which, indeed, was wicked enough in its nature; but to me it would have been worse than otherwise it would to another, for, upon examination, I could not have proved myself to be the wife of the jeweller, so the suspicion might have been carried on with the better face; and then I should also have brought all his relations in England upon me, who, finding by the proceedings that I was not his wife, but a mistress, or, in English, a whore, would immediately have laid claim to the jewels, as I had owned them to be his.

This thought immediately rushed into my head as soon as the Dutch merchant had told me what wicked things were in the head of that cursed Jew; and the villain (for so I must call him) convinced the Dutch merchant that he was in earnest by an expression which showed the rest of his design, and that was, a plot to get the rest of the jewels into his hand.

When first he hinted to the Dutchman that the jewels were such a man's (meaning my husband's), he made wonderful exclamations on account of their having been concealed so long. Where must they have lain? And what was the woman that brought them? And that she (meaning me) ought to be immediately apprehended and put into the hands of justice. And this was the time that, as I said, he made such horrid gestures and looked at me so like a devil.

The merchant, hearing him talk at that rate, and seeing him in earnest, said to him, "Hold your tongue a little; this is a thing of consequence. If it be so, let you and I go into the next room and consider of it there;" and so they withdrew, and left me.

Here, as before, I was uneasy, and called him out, and, having heard how it was, gave him that answer, that I was his wife, or widow, which the malicious Jew said should not serve my turn. And then it was that the Dutchman called him out again; and in this time of his withdrawing, the merchant, finding, as above, that he was really in earnest, counterfeited a little to be of his mind, and entered into proposals with him for the thing itself.

In this they agreed to go to an advocate, or counsel, for directions how to proceed, and to meet again the next day, against which time the merchant was to appoint me to come again with the jewels, in order to sell them. "No," says the merchant, "I will go farther with her than so; I will desire her to leave the jewels with me, to show to another person, in order to get the better price for them." "That's right," says the Jew; "and I'll engage she shall never be mistress of them again; they shall either be seized by us," says he, "in the king's name, or she shall be glad to give them up to us to prevent her being put to the torture."

The merchant said "Yes" to everything he offered, and they agreed to meet the next morning about it, and I was to be persuaded to leave the jewels with him, and come to them the next day at four o'clock in order to make a good bargain for them; and on these conditions they parted. But the honest Dutchman, filled with indignation at the barbarous design, came directly to me and told me the whole story. "And now, madam," says he, "you are to consider immediately what you have to do."

I told him, if I was sure to have justice, I would not fear all that such a rogue could do to me; but how such things were carried on in France I knew not. I told him the greatest difficulty would be to prove our marriage, for that it was done in England, and in a remote part of England too; and, which was worse, it would be hard to produce authentic vouchers of it, because we were married in private. "But as to the death of your husband,[madam, what can be said to that?" said he. "Nay," said I, "what can they say to it? In England," added I, "if they would offer such an injury to any one, they must prove the fact or give just reason for their suspicions. That my husband was murdered, that every one knows; but that he was robbed, or of what, or how much, that none knows—no, not myself; and why was I not questioned for it then? I have lived in Paris ever since, lived publicly, and no man had yet the impudence to suggest such a thing of me."

"I am fully satisfied of that," says the merchant; "but as this is a rogue who will stick at nothing, what can we say? And who knows what he may swear? Suppose he should swear that he knows your husband had those particular jewels with him the morning when he went out, and that he showed them to him to consider their value, and what price he should ask the Prince de — for them?"

"Nay, by the same rule," said I, "he may swear that I murdered my husband, if he finds it for his turn." "That's true," said he; "and if he should, I do not see what could save you;" but added, "I have found out his more immediate design. His design is to have you carried to the Châtelet, that the suspicion may appear just, and then to get the jewels out of your hands if possible; then, at last, to drop the prosecution on your consenting to quit the jewels to him; and how you will do to avoid this is the question which I would have you consider of."

"My misfortune, sir," said I, "is that I have no time to consider, and I have no person to consider with or advise about it. I find that innocence may be oppressed by such an impudent fellow as this; he that does not value perjury has any man's life at his mercy. But, sir," said I, "is the justice such here that, while I may be in the hands of the public and under prosecution, he may get hold of my effects and get my jewels into his hands?"

"I don't know," says he, "what may be done in that case; but if not he, if the court of justice should get hold of them I do not know but you may find it as difficult to get them out of their hands again, and, at least, it may cost you half as much as they are worth; so I think it would be a much better way to prevent their coming at them at all."

"But what course can I take to do that," says I, "now they have got notice that I have them? If they get me into their hands they will oblige me to produce them, or perhaps sentence me to prison till I do."

"Nay," says he, "as this brute says, too, put you to the question—that is, to the torture, on pretence of making you confess who were the murderers of your husband."

"Confess!" said I. "How can I confess what I know nothing of?"

"If they come to have you to the rack," said he, "they will make you confess you did it yourself, whether you did it or no, and then you are cast."

The very word rack frighted me to death almost, and I had no spirit left in me. "Did it myself!" said I. "That's impossible!"

"No, madam," says he, "'tis far from impossible. The most innocent people in the world have been forced to confess themselves guilty of what they never heard of, much less had any hand in."

"What, then, must I do?" said I. "What would you advise me to?"

"Why," says he, "I would advise you to be gone. You intended to go away in four or five days, and you may as well go in two days; and if you can do so, I shall manage it so that he shall not suspect your being gone for several days after." Then he told me how the rogue would have me ordered to bring the jewels the next day for sale, and that then he would have me apprehended; how he had made the Jew believe he would join with him in his design, and that he (the merchant) would get the jewels into his hands. "Now," says the merchant, "I shall give you bills for the money you desired, immediately, and such as shall not fail of being paid. Take your jewels with you, and go this very evening to St. Germain-en-Laye; I'll send a man thither with you, and from thence he shall guide you to-morrow to Rouen, where there lies a ship of mine, just ready to sail for Rotterdam; you shall have your passage in that ship on my account, and I will send orders for him to sail as soon as you are on board, and a letter to my friend at Rotterdam to entertain and take care of you."

This was too kind an offer for me, as things stood, not to be accepted, and be thankful for; and as to going away, I had prepared everything for parting, so that I had little to do but to go back, take two or three boxes and bundles, and such things, and my maid Amy, and be gone.

Then the merchant told me the measures he had resolved to take to delude the Jew while I made my escape, which was very well contrived indeed. "First," said he, "when he comes to-morrow I shall tell him that I proposed to you to leave the jewels with me, as we agreed, but that you said you would come and bring them in the afternoon, so that we must stay for you till four o'clock; but then, at that time, I will show a letter from you, as if just come in, wherein you shall excuse your not coming, for that some company came to visit you, and prevented you; but that you desire me to take care that the gentleman be ready to buy your jewels, and that you will come to-morrow at the same hour, without fail.

"When to-morrow is come, we shall wait at the time, but you not appearing, I shall seem most dissatisfied, and wonder what can be the reason; and so we shall agree to go the next day to get out a process against you. But the next day, in the morning, I'll send to give him notice that you have been at my house, but he not being there, have made another appointment, and that I desire to speak with him. When he comes, I'll tell him you appear perfectly blind as to your danger, and that you appeared much disappointed that he did not come, though you could not meet the night before; and obliged me to have him here to-morrow at three o'clock. When to-morrow comes," says he, "you shall send word that you are taken so ill that you cannot come out for that day, but that you will not fail the next day; and the next day you shall neither come or send, nor let us ever hear any more of you; for by that time you shall be in Holland, if you please."

I could not but approve all his measures, seeing they were so well contrived, and in so friendly a manner, for my benefit; and as he seemed to be so very sincere, I resolved to put my life in his hands. Immediately I went to my lodgings, and sent away Amy with such bundles as I had prepared for my travelling. I also sent several parcels of my fine furniture to the merchant's house to be laid up for me, and bringing the key of the lodgings with me, I came back to his house. Here we finished our matters of money, and I delivered into his hands seven thousand eight hundred pistoles in bills and money, a copy of an assignment on the townhouse of Paris for four thousand pistoles, at three per cent. interest, attested, and a procuration for receiving the interest half-yearly; but the original I kept myself.

I could have trusted all I had with him, for he was perfectly honest, and had not the least view of doing me any wrong. Indeed, after it was so apparent that he had, as it were, saved my life, or at least saved me from being exposed and ruined—I say, after this, how could I doubt him in anything?

When I came to him, he had everything ready as I wanted, and as he had proposed. As to my money, he gave me first of all an accepted bill, payable at Rotterdam, for four thousand pistoles, and drawn from Genoa upon a merchant at Rotterdam, payable to a merchant at Paris, and endorsed by him to my merchant; this, he assured me, would be punctually paid; and so it was, to a day. The rest I had in other bills of exchange, drawn by himself upon other merchants in Holland. Having secured my jewels too, as well as I could, he sent me away the same evening in a friend's coach, which he had procured for me, to St. Germain, and the next morning to Rouen. He also sent a servant of his own on horseback with me, who provided everything for me, and who carried his orders to the captain of the ship, which lay about three miles below Rouen, in the river, and by his directions I went immediately on board. The third day after I was on board the ship went away, and we were out at sea the next day after that; and thus I took my leave of France, and got clear of an ugly business, which, had it gone on, might have ruined me, and sent me back as naked to England as I was a little before I left it.

And now Amy and I were at leisure to look upon the mischiefs that we had escaped; and had I had any religion or any sense of a Supreme Power, managing, directing, and governing in both causes and events in this world, such a case as this would have given anybody room to have been very thankful to the Power who had not only put such a treasure into my hand, but given me such an escape from the ruin that threatened me; but I had none of those things about me. I had, indeed, a grateful sense upon my mind of the generous friendship of my deliverer, the Dutch merchant, by whom I was so faithfully served, and by whom, as far as relates to second causes, I was preserved from destruction.

I say, I had a grateful sense upon my mind of his kindness and faithfulness to me, and I resolved to show him some testimony of it as soon as I came to the end of my rambles, for I was yet but in a state of uncertainty, and sometimes that gave me a little uneasiness too. I had paper indeed for my money, and he had showed himself very good to me in conveying me away, as above; but I had not seen the end of things yet, for unless the bills were paid, I might still be a great loser by my Dutchman, and he might, perhaps, have contrived all that affair of the Jew to put me into a fright and get me to run away, and that as if it were to save my life; that if the bills should be refused, I was cheated with a witness, and the like. But these were but surmises, and, indeed, were perfectly without cause, for the honest man acted as honest men always do, with an upright and disinterested principle, and with a sincerity not often to be found in the world. What gain he made by the exchange was just, and was nothing but what was his due, and was in the way of his business; but otherwise he made no advantage of me at all.

When I passed in the ship between Dover and Calais and saw beloved England once more under my view—England, which I counted my native country, being the place I was bred up in, though not born there—a strange kind of joy possessed my mind, and I had such a longing desire to be there that I would have given the master of the ship twenty pistoles to have stood over and set me on shore in the Downs; and when he told me he could not do it—that is, that he durst not do it if I would have given him a hundred pistoles—I secretly wished that a storm would rise that might drive the ship over to the coast of England, whether they would or not, that I might be set on shore anywhere upon English ground.

This wicked wish had not been out of my thoughts above two or three hours, but the master steering away to the north, as was his course to do, we lost sight of land on that side, and only had the Flemish shore in view on our right hand, or, as the seamen call it, the starboard side; and then, with the loss of the sight, the wish for landing in England abated, and I considered how foolish it was to wish myself out of the way of my business; that if I had been on shore in England, I must go back to Holland on account of my bills, which were so considerable, and I having no correspondence there, that I could not have managed it without going myself. But we had not been out of sight of England many hours before the weather began to change; the winds whistled and made a noise, and the seamen said to one another that it would blow hard at night. It was then about two hours before sunset, and we were passed by Dunkirk, and I think they said we were in sight of Ostend; but then the wind grew high and the sea swelled, and all things looked terrible, especially to us that understood nothing but just what we saw before us; in short, night came on, and very dark it was; the wind freshened and blew harder and harder, and about two hours within night it blew a terrible storm.

I was not quite a stranger to the sea, having come from Rochelle to England when I was a child, and gone from London, by the River Thames, to France afterward, as I have said. But I began to be alarmed a little with the terrible clamour of the men over my head, for I had never been in a storm, and so had never seen the like, or heard it; and once offering to look out at the door of the steerage, as they called it, it struck me with such horror (the darkness, the fierceness of the wind, the dreadful height of the waves, and the hurry the Dutch sailors were in, whose language I did not understand one word of, neither when they cursed or when they prayed); I say, all these things together filled me with terror, and, in short, I began to be very much frighted.

When I was come back into the great cabin, there sat Amy, who was very sea-sick, and I had a little before given her a sup of cordial waters to help her stomach. When Amy saw me come back and sit down without speaking, for so I did, she looked two or three times up at me; at last she came running to me. "Dear madam," says she, "what is the matter? What makes you look so pale? Why, you an't well; what is the matter?" I said nothing still, but held up my hands two or three times. Amy doubled her importunities; upon that I said no more but, "Step to the steerage-door, and look out, as I did;" so she went away immediately, and looked too, as I had bidden her; but the poor girl came back again in the greatest amazement and horror that ever I saw any poor creature in, wringing her hands and crying out she was undone! she was undone! she should be drowned! they were all lost! Thus she ran about the cabin like a mad thing, and as perfectly out of her senses as any one in such a case could be supposed to be. I was frighted myself, but when I saw the girl in such a terrible agony, it brought me a little to myself, and I began to talk to her and put her in a little hope. I told her there was many a ship in a storm that was not cast away, and I hoped we should not be drowned; that it was true the storm was very dreadful, but I did not see that the seamen were so much concerned as we were. And so I talked to her as well as I could, though my heart was full enough of it, as well as Amy's; and death began to stare in my face; ay, and something else too—that is to say, conscience, and my mind was very much disturbed; but I had nobody to comfort me.

But Amy being in so much worse a condition—that is to say, so much more terrified at the storm than I was—I had something to do to comfort her. She was, as I have said, like one distracted, and went raving about the cabin, crying out she was undone! undone! she should be drowned! and the like. And at last, the ship giving a jerk, by the force, I suppose, of some violent wave, it threw poor Amy quite down, for she was weak enough before with being sea-sick, and as it threw her forward, the poor girl struck her head against the bulk-head, as the seamen call it, of the cabin, and laid her as dead as a stone upon the floor or deck; that is to say, she was so to all appearance.

I cried out for help, but it had been all one to have cried out on the top of a mountain where nobody had been within five miles of me, for the seamen were so engaged and made so much noise that nobody heard me or came near me. I opened the great cabin door, and looked into the steerage to cry for help, but there, to increase my fright, was two seamen on their knees at prayers, and only one man who steered, and he made a groaning noise too, which I took to be saying his prayers, but it seems it was answering to those above, when they called to him to tell him which way to steer.

Here was no help for me, or for poor Amy, and there she lay still so, and in such a condition, that I did not know whether she was dead or alive. In this fright I went to her, and lifted her a little way up, setting her on the deck, with her back to the boards of the bulk-head; and I got a little bottle out of my pocket, and I held it to her nose, and rubbed her temples and what else I could do, but still Amy showed no signs of life, till I felt for her pulse, but could hardly distinguish her to be alive. However, after a great while, she began to revive, and in about half-an-hour she came to herself, but remembered nothing at first of what had happened to her for a good while more.

When she recovered more fully, she asked me where she was. I told her she was in the ship yet, but God knows how long it might be. "Why, madam," says she, "is not the storm over?" "No, no," says I, "Amy." "Why, madam," says she, "it was calm just now" (meaning when she was in the swooning fit occasioned by her fall). "Calm, Amy!" says I. "'Tis far from calm. It may be it will be calm by-and-by, when we are all drowned and gone to heaven."

"Heaven, madam!" says she. "What makes you talk so? Heaven! I go to heaven! No, no; if I am drowned I am damned! Don't you know what a wicked creature I have been? I have been a whore to two men, and have lived a wretched, abominable life of vice and wickedness for fourteen years. Oh, madam! you know it, and God knows it, and now I am to die—to be drowned! Oh! what will become of me? I am undone for ever!—ay, madam, for ever! to all eternity! Oh! I am lost! I am lost! If I am drowned, I am lost for ever!"

All these, you will easily suppose, must be so many stabs into the very soul of one in my own case. It immediately occurred to me, "Poor Amy! what art thou that I am not? What hast thou been that I have not been? Nay, I am guilty of my own sin and thine too." Then it came to my remembrance that I had not only been the same with Amy, but that I had been the devil's instrument to make her wicked; that I had stripped her, and prostituted her to the very man that I had been naught with myself; that she had but followed me, I had been her wicked example; and I had led her into all; and that, as we had sinned together, now we were likely to sink together.

All this repeated itself to my thoughts at that very moment, and every one of Amy's cries sounded thus in my ears: "I am the wicked cause of it all! I have been thy ruin, Amy! I have brought thee to this, and now thou art to suffer for the sin I have enticed thee to! And if thou art lost for ever, what must I be? what must be my portion?"

It is true this difference was between us, that I said all these things within myself, and sighed and mourned inwardly; but Amy, as her temper was more violent, spoke aloud, and cried, and called out aloud, like one in agony.

I had but small encouragement to give her, and indeed could say but very little, but I got her to compose herself a little, and not let any of the people of the ship understand what she meant or what she said; but even in her greatest composure she continued to express herself with the utmost dread and terror on account of the wicked life she had lived, crying out she should be damned, and the like, which was very terrible to me, who knew what condition I was in myself.

Upon these serious considerations, I was very penitent too for my former sins, and cried out, though softly, two or three times, "Lord, have mercy upon me!" To this I added abundance of resolutions of what a life I would live if it should please God but to spare my life but this one time; how I would live a single and a virtuous life, and spend a great deal of what I had thus wickedly got in acts of charity and doing good.

Under these dreadful apprehensions I looked back on the life I had led with the utmost contempt and abhorrence. I blushed, and wondered at myself how I could act thus, how I could divest myself of modesty and honour, and prostitute myself for gain; and I thought, if ever it should please God to spare me this one time from death, it would not be possible that I should be the same creature again.

Amy went farther; she prayed, she resolved, she vowed to lead a new life, if God would spare her but this time. It now began to be daylight, for the storm held all night long, and it was some comfort to see the light of another day, which none of us expected; but the sea went mountains high, and the noise of the water was as frightful to us as the sight of the waves; nor was any land to be seen, nor did the seamen know whereabout they were. At last, to our great joy, they made land, which was in England, and on the coast of Suffolk; and the ship being in the utmost distress, they ran for the shore at all hazards, and with great difficulty got into Harwich, where they were safe, as to the danger of death; but the ship was so full of water and so much damaged that if they had not laid her on shore the same day she would have sunk before night, according to the opinion of the seamen, and of the workmen on shore too who were hired to assist them in stopping their leaks.

Amy was revived as soon as she heard they had espied land, and went out upon the deck; but she soon came in again to me. "Oh, madam!" says she, "there's the land indeed to be seen. It looks like a ridge of clouds, and may be all a cloud for aught I know; but if it be land, 'tis a great way off, and the sea is in such a combustion, we shall all perish before we can reach it. 'Tis the dreadfullest sight to look at the waves that ever was seen. Why, they are as high as mountains; we shall certainly be all swallowed up, for all the land is so near."

I had conceived some hope that, if they saw land, we should be delivered; and I told her she did not understand things of that nature; that she might be sure if they saw land they would go directly towards it, and would make into some harbour; but it was, as Amy said, a frightful distance to it. The land looked like clouds, and the sea went as high as mountains, so that no hope appeared in the seeing the land, but we were in fear of foundering before we could reach it. This made Amy so desponding still; but as the wind, which blew from the east, or that way, drove us furiously towards the land, so when, about half-an-hour after, I stepped to the steerage-door and looked out, I saw the land much nearer than Amy represented it; so I went in and encouraged Amy again, and indeed was encouraged myself.

In about an hour, or something more, we saw, to our infinite satisfaction, the open harbour of Harwich, and the vessel standing directly towards it, and in a few minutes more the ship was in smooth water, to our inexpressible comfort; and thus I had, though against my will and contrary to my true interest, what I wished for, to be driven away to England, though it was by a storm.

Nor did this incident do either Amy or me much service, for, the danger being over, the fears of death vanished with it; ay, and our fear of what was beyond death also. Our sense of the life we had lived went off, and with our return to life our wicked taste of life returned, and we were both the same as before, if not worse. So certain is it that the repentance which is brought about by the mere apprehensions of death wears off as those apprehensions wear off, and deathbed repentance, or storm repentance, which is much the same, is seldom true.

However, I do not tell you that this was all at once neither; the fright we had at sea lasted a little while afterwards; at least the impression was not quite blown off as soon as the storm; especially poor Amy. As soon as she set her foot on shore she fell flat upon the ground and kissed it, and gave God thanks for her deliverance from the sea; and turning to me when she got up, "I hope, madam," says she, "you will never go upon the sea again."

I know not what ailed me, not I; but Amy was much more penitent at sea, and much more sensible of her deliverance when she landed and was safe, than I was. I was in a kind of stupidity, I know not well what to call it; I had a mind full of horror in the time of the storm, and saw death before me as plainly as Amy, but my thoughts got no vent, as Amy's did. I had a silent, sullen kind of grief, which could not break out either in words or tears, and which was therefore much the worse to bear.

I had a terror upon me for my wicked life past, and firmly believed I was going to the bottom, launching into death, where I was to give an account of all my past actions; and in this state, and on that account, I looked back upon my wickedness with abhorrence, as I have said above, but I had no sense of repentance from the true motive of repentance; I saw nothing of the corruption of nature, the sin of my life, as an offence against God, as a thing odious to the holiness of His being, as abusing His mercy and despising His goodness. In short, I had no thorough effectual repentance, no sight of my sins in their proper shape, no view of a Redeemer, or hope in Him. I had only such a repentance as a criminal has at the place of execution, who is sorry, not that he has committed the crime, as it is a crime, but sorry that he is to be hanged for it.

It is true Amy's repentance wore off too, as well as mine, but not so soon. However, we were both very grave for a time.

As soon as we could get a boat from the town we went on shore, and immediately went to a public-house in the town of Harwich, where we were to consider seriously what was to be done, and whether we should go up to London or stay till the ship was refitted, which, they said, would be a fortnight, and then go for Holland, as we intended, and as business required.

Reason directed that I should go to Holland, for there I had all my money to receive, and there I had persons of good reputation and character to apply to, having letters to them from the honest Dutch merchant at Paris, and they might perhaps give me a recommendation again to merchants in London, and so I should get acquaintance with some people of figure, which was what I loved; whereas now I knew not one creature in the whole city of London, or anywhere else, that I could go and make myself known to. Upon these considerations, I resolved to go to Holland, whatever came of it.

But Amy cried and trembled, and was ready to fall into fits, when I did but mention going upon the sea again, and begged of me not to go, or if I would go, that I would leave her behind, though I was to send her a-begging. The people in the inn laughed at her, and jested with her, asked her if she had any sins to confess that she was ashamed should be heard of, and that she was troubled with an evil conscience; told her, if she came to sea, and to be in a storm, if she had lain with her master, she would certainly tell her mistress of it, and that it was a common thing for poor maids to confess all the young men they had lain with; that there was one poor girl that went over with her mistress, whose husband was a ......r, in ......, in the city of London, who confessed, in the terror of a storm, that she had lain with her master, and all the apprentices, so often, and in such-and-such places, and made the poor mistress, when she returned to London, fly at her husband, and make such a stir as was indeed the ruin of the whole family. Amy could bear all that well enough, for though she had indeed lain with her master, it was with her mistress's knowledge and consent, and, which was worse, was her mistress's own doing. I record it to the reproach of my own vice, and to expose the excesses of such wickedness as they deserve to be exposed.

I thought Amy's fear would have been over by that time the ship would be gotten ready, but I found the girl was rather worse and worse; and when I came to the point that we must go on board or lose the passage, Amy was so terrified that she fell into fits; so the ship went away without us.

But my going being absolutely necessary, as above, I was obliged to go in the packet-boat some time after, and leave Amy behind at Harwich, but with directions to go to London and stay there to receive letters and orders from me what to do. Now I was become, from a lady of pleasure, a woman of business, and of great business too, I assure you.

I got me a servant at Harwich to go over with me, who had been at Rotterdam, knew the place, and spoke the language, which was a great help to me, and away I went. I had a very quick passage and pleasant weather, and, coming to Rotterdam, soon found out the merchant to whom I was recommended, who received me with extraordinary respect. And first he acknowledged the accepted bill for four thousand pistoles, which he afterwards paid punctually; other bills that I had also payable at Amsterdam he procured to be received for me; and whereas one of the bills for one thousand two hundred crowns was protested at Amsterdam, he paid it me himself, for the honour of the indorser, as he called it, which was my friend the merchant at Paris.

There I entered into a negotiation by his means for my jewels, and he brought me several jewellers to look on them, and particularly one to value them, and to tell me what every particular was worth. This was a man who had great skill in jewels, but did not trade at that time, and he was desired by the gentleman that I was with to see that I might not be imposed upon.

All this work took me up near half a year, and by managing my business thus myself, and having large sums to do with, I became as expert in it as any she-merchant of them all. I had credit in the bank for a large sum of money, and bills and notes for much more.

After I had been here about three months, my maid Amy writes me word that she had received a letter from her friend, as she called him. That, by the way, was the prince's gentleman, that had been Amy's extraordinary friend indeed, for Amy owned to me he had lain with her a hundred times, that is to say, as often as he pleased, and perhaps in the eight years which that affair lasted it might be a great deal oftener. This was what she called her friend, who she corresponded with upon this particular subject, and, among other things, sent her this particular news, that my extraordinary friend, my real husband, who rode in the gens d'armes, was dead, that he was killed in a rencounter, as they call it, or accidental scuffle among the troopers; and so the jade congratulated me upon my being now a real free woman. "And now, madam," says she at the end of her letter, "you have nothing to do but to come hither and set up a coach and a good equipage, and if beauty and a good fortune won't make you a duchess, nothing will." But I had not fixed my measures yet. I had no inclination to be a wife again. I had had such bad luck with my first husband, I hated the thoughts of it. I found that a wife is treated with indifference, a mistress with a strong passion; a wife is looked upon as but an upper servant, a mistress is a sovereign; a wife must give up all she has, have every reserve she makes for herself be thought hard of, and be upbraided with her very pin-money, whereas a mistress makes the saying true, that what the man has is hers, and what she has is her own; the wife bears a thousand insults, and is forced to sit still and bear it, or part, and be undone; a mistress insulted helps herself immediately, and takes another.

These were my wicked arguments for whoring, for I never set against them the difference another way—I may say, every other way; how that, first, a wife appears boldly and honourably with her husband, lives at home, and possesses his house, his servants, his equipages, and has a right to them all, and to call them her own; entertains his friends, owns his children, and has the return of duty and affection from them, as they are here her own, and claims upon his estate, by the custom of England, if he dies and leaves her a widow.

The whore skulks about in lodgings, is visited in the dark, disowned upon all occasions before God and man; is maintained, indeed, for a time, but is certainly condemned to be abandoned at last, and left to the miseries of fate and her own just disaster. If she has any children, her endeavour is to get rid of them, and not maintain them; and if she lives, she is certain to see them all hate her, and be ashamed of her. While the vice rages, and the man is in the devil's hand, she has him; and while she has him, she makes a prey of him; but if he happens to fall sick, if any disaster befalls him, the cause of all lies upon her. He is sure to lay all his misfortunes at her door; and if once he comes to repentance, or makes but one step towards a reformation, he begins with her—leaves her, uses her as she deserves, hates her, abhors her, and sees her no more; and that with this never-failing addition, namely, that the more sincere and unfeigned his repentance is, the more earnestly he looks up, and the more effectually he looks in, the more his aversion to her increases, and he curses her from the bottom of his soul; nay, it must be a kind of excess of charity if he so much as wishes God may forgive her.

The opposite circumstances of a wife and whore are such and so many, and I have since seen the difference with such eyes, as I could dwell upon the subject a great while; but my business is history. I had a long scene of folly yet to run over. Perhaps the moral of all my story may bring me back again to this part, and if it does I shall speak of it fully.

While I continued in Holland I received several letters from my friend (so I had good reason to call him) the merchant in Paris, in which he gave me a farther account of the conduct of that rogue the Jew, and how he acted after I was gone; how impatient he was while the said merchant kept him in suspense, expecting me to come again; and how he raged when he found I came no more.

It seems, after he found I did not come, he found out by his unwearied inquiry where I had lived, and that I had been kept as a mistress by some great person; but he could never learn by who, except that he learnt the colour of his livery. In pursuit of this inquiry he guessed at the right person, but could not make it out, or offer any positive proof of it; but he found out the prince's gentleman, and talked so saucily to him of it that the gentleman treated him, as the French call it, à coup de baton—that is to say, caned him very severely, as he deserved; and that not satisfying him, or curing his insolence, he was met one night late upon the Pont Neuf, in Paris, by two men, who, muffling him up in a great cloak, carried him into a more private place and cut off both his ears, telling him it was for talking impudently of his superiors; adding that he should take care to govern his tongue better and behave with more manners, or the next time they would cut his tongue out of his head.

This put a check to his sauciness that way; but he comes back to the merchant and threatened to begin a process against him for corresponding with me, and being accessory to the murder of the jeweller, &c.

The merchant found by his discourse that he supposed I was protected by the said Prince de —; nay, the rogue said he was sure I was in his lodgings at Versailles, for he never had so much as the least intimation of the way I was really gone; but that I was there he was certain, and certain that the merchant was privy to it. The merchant bade him defiance. However, he gave him a great deal of trouble and put him to a great charge, and had like to have brought him in for a party to my escape; in which case he would have been obliged to have produced me, and that in the penalty of some capital sum of money.

But the merchant was too many for him another way, for he brought an information against him for a cheat; wherein laying down the whole fact, how he intended falsely to accuse the widow of the jeweller for the supposed murder of her husband; that he did it purely to get the jewels from her; and that he offered to bring him (the merchant) in, to be confederate with him, and to share the jewels between them; proving also his design to get the jewels into his hands, and then to have dropped the prosecution upon condition of my quitting the jewels to him. Upon this charge he got him laid by the heels; so he was sent to the Conciergerie—that is to say, to Bridewell—and the merchant cleared. He got out of jail in a little while, though not without the help of money, and continued teasing the merchant a long while, and at last threatening to assassinate and murder him. So the merchant, who, having buried his wife about two months before, was now a single man, and not knowing what such a villain might do, thought fit to quit Paris, and came away to Holland also.

It is most certain that, speaking of originals, I was the source and spring of all that trouble and vexation to this honest gentleman; and as it was afterwards in my power to have made him full satisfaction, and did not, I cannot say but I added ingratitude to all the rest of my follies; but of that I shall give a fuller account presently.

I was surprised one morning, when, being at the merchant's house who he had recommended me to in Rotterdam, and being busy in his counting-house, managing my bills, and preparing to write a letter to him to Paris, I heard a noise of horses at the door, which is not very common in a city where everybody passes by water; but he had, it seems, ferried over the Maas from Willemstadt, and so came to the very door, and I, looking towards the door upon hearing the horses, saw a gentleman alight and come in at the gate. I knew nothing, and expected nothing, to be sure, of the person; but, as I say, was surprised, and indeed more than ordinarily surprised, when, coming nearer to me, I saw it was my merchant of Paris, my benefactor, and indeed my deliverer.

I confess it was an agreeable surprise to me, and I was exceeding glad to see him, who was so honourable and so kind to me, and who indeed had saved my life. As soon as he saw me he ran to me, took me in his arms, and kissed me with a freedom that he never offered to take with me before. "Dear Madam ——," says he, "I am glad to see you safe in this country; if you had stayed two days longer in Paris you had been undone." I was so glad to see him that I could not speak a good while, and I burst out into tears without speaking a word for a minute; but I recovered that disorder, and said, "The more, sir, is my obligation to you that saved my life;" and added, "I am glad to see you here, that I may consider how to balance an account in which I am so much your debtor." "You and I will adjust that matter easily," says he, "now we are so near together. Pray where do you lodge?" says he.

"In a very honest, good house," said I, "where that gentleman, your friend, recommended me," pointing to the merchant in whose house we then were.

"And where you may lodge too, sir," says the gentleman, "if it suits with your business and your other conveniency."

"With all my heart," says he. "Then, madam," adds he, turning to me, "I shall be near you, and have time to tell you a story which will be very long, and yet many ways very pleasant to you; how troublesome that devilish fellow, the Jew, has been to me on your account, and what a hellish snare he had laid for you, if he could have found you."

"I shall have leisure too, sir," said I, "to tell you all my adventures since that, which have not been a few, I assure you."

In short, he took up his lodgings in the same house where I lodged, and the room he lay in opened, as he was wishing it would, just opposite to my lodging-room, so we could almost call out of bed to one another; and I was not at all shy of him on that score, for I believed him perfectly honest, and so indeed he was; and if he had not, that article was at present no part of my concern.

It was not till two or three days, and after his first hurries of business were over, that we began to enter into the history of our affairs on every side, but when we began, it took up all our conversation for almost a fortnight. First, I gave him a particular account of everything that happened material upon my voyage, and how we were driven into Harwich by a very terrible storm; how I had left my woman behind me, so frighted with the danger she had been in that she durst not venture to set her foot into a ship again any more, and that I had not come myself if the bills I had of him had not been payable in Holland; but that money, he might see, would make a woman go anywhere.

He seemed to laugh at all our womanish fears upon the occasion of the storm, telling me it was nothing but what was very ordinary in those seas, but that they had harbours on every coast so near that they were seldom in danger of being lost indeed. "For," says he, "if they cannot fetch one coast, they can always stand away for another, and run afore it," as he called it, "for one side or other." But when I came to tell him what a crazy ship it was, and how, even when they got into Harwich, and into smooth water, they were fain to run the ship on shore, or she would have sunk in the very harbour; and when I told him that when I looked out at the cabin-door I saw the Dutchmen, one upon his knees here, and another there, at their prayers, then indeed he acknowledged I had reason to be alarmed; but, smiling, he added, "But you, madam," says he, "are so good a lady, and so pious, you would but have gone to heaven a little the sooner; the difference had not been much to you."

I confess when he said this it made all the blood turn in my veins, and I thought I should have fainted. "Poor gentleman," thought I, "you know little of me. What would I give to be really what you really think me to be!" He perceived the disorder, but said nothing till I spoke; when, shaking my head, "Oh, sir!" said I, "death in any shape has some terror in it, but in the frightful figure of a storm at sea and a sinking ship, it comes with a double, a treble, and indeed an inexpressible horror; and if I were that saint you think me to be (which God knows I am not), it is still very dismal. I desire to die in a calm, if I can." He said a great many good things, and very prettily ordered his discourse between serious reflection and compliment, but I had too much guilt to relish it as it was meant, so I turned it off to something else, and talked of the necessity I had on me to come to Holland, but I wished myself safe on shore in England again.

He told me he was glad I had such an obligation upon me to come over into Holland, however, but hinted that he was so interested in my welfare, and, besides, had such further designs upon me, that if I had not so happily been found in Holland he was resolved to have gone to England to see me, and that it was one of the principal reasons of his leaving Paris.

I told him I was extremely obliged to him for so far interesting himself in my affairs, but that I had been so far his debtor before that I knew not how anything could increase the debt; for I owed my life to him already, and I could not be in debt for anything more valuable than that. He answered in the most obliging manner possible, that he would put it in my power to pay that debt, and all the obligations besides that ever he had, or should be able to lay upon me.

I began to understand him now, and to see plainly that he resolved to make love to me, but I would by no means seem to take the hint; and, besides, I knew that he had a wife with him in Paris; and I had, just then at least, no gust to any more intriguing. However, he surprised me into a sudden notice of the thing a little while after by saying something in his discourse that he did, as he said, in his wife's days. I started at that word, "What mean you by that, sir?" said I. "Have you not a wife at Paris?" "No, madam, indeed," said he; "my wife died the beginning of September last," which, it seems, was but a little after I came away.

We lived in the same house all this while, and as we lodged not far off of one another, opportunities were not wanting of as near an acquaintance as we might desire; nor have such opportunities the least agency in vicious minds to bring to pass even what they might not intend at first.

However, though he courted so much at a distance, yet his pretensions were very honourable; and as I had before found him a most disinterested friend, and perfectly honest in his dealings, even when I trusted him with all I had, so now I found him strictly virtuous, till I made him otherwise myself, even almost whether he would or no, as you shall hear.

It was not long after our former discourse, when he repeated what he had insinuated before, namely, that he had yet a design to lay before me, which, if I would agree to his proposals, would more than balance all accounts between us. I told him I could not reasonably deny him anything; and except one thing, which I hoped and believed he would not think of, I should think myself very ungrateful if I did not do everything for him that lay in my power.

He told me what he should desire of me would be fully in my power to grant, or else he should be very unfriendly to offer it; and still all this while he declined making the proposal, as he called it, and so for that time we ended our discourse, turning it off to other things. So that, in short, I began to think he might have met with some disaster in his business, and might have come away from Paris in some discredit, or had had some blow on his affairs in general; and as really I had kindness enough to have parted with a good sum to have helped him, and was in gratitude bound to have done so, he having so effectually saved to me all I had, so I resolved to make him the offer the first time I had an opportunity, which two or three days after offered itself, very much to my satisfaction.

He had told me at large, though on several occasions, the treatment he had met with from the Jew, and what expense he had put him to; how at length he had cast him, as above, and had recovered good damage of him, but that the rogue was unable to make him any considerable reparation. He had told me also how the Prince de ——'s gentleman had resented his treatment of his master, and how he had caused him to be used upon the Pont Neuf, &c., as I have mentioned above, which I laughed at most heartily.

"It is a pity," said I, "that I should sit here and make that gentleman no amends; if you would direct me, sir," said I, "how to do it, I would make him a handsome present, and acknowledge the justice he had done to me, as well as to the prince, his master." He said he would do what I directed in it; so I told him I would send him five hundred crowns. "That's too much," said he, "for you are but half interested in the usage of the Jew; it was on his master's account he corrected him, not on yours." Well, however, we were obliged to do nothing in it, for neither of us knew how to direct a letter to him, or to direct anybody to him; so I told him I would leave it till I came to England, for that my woman, Amy, corresponded with him, and that he had made love to her.

"Well, but, sir," said I, "as, in requital for his generous concern for me, I am careful to think of him, it is but just that what expense you have been obliged to be at, which was all on my account, should be repaid you; and therefore," said I, "let me see—." And there I paused, and began to reckon up what I had observed, from his own discourse, it had cost him in the several disputes and hearings which he had with that dog of a Jew, and I cast them up at something above 2130 crowns; so I pulled out some bills which I had upon a merchant in Amsterdam, and a particular account in bank, and was looking on them in order to give them to him; when he, seeing evidently what I was going about, interrupted me with some warmth, and told me he would have nothing of me on that account, and desired I would not pull out my bills and papers on that score; that he had not told me the story on that account, or with any such view; that it had been his misfortune first to bring that ugly rogue to me, which, though it was with a good design, yet he would punish himself with the expense he had been at for his being so unlucky to me; that I could not think so hard of him as to suppose he would take money of me, a widow, for serving me, and doing acts of kindness to me in a strange country, and in distress too; but he said he would repeat what he had said before, that he kept me for a deeper reckoning, and that, as he had told me, he would put me into a posture to even all that favour, as I called it, at once, so we should talk it over another time, and balance all together.

Now I expected it would come out, but still he put it off, as before, from whence I concluded it could not be matter of love, for that those things are not usually delayed in such a manner, and therefore it must be matter of money. Upon which thought I broke the silence, and told him, that as he knew I had, by obligation, more kindness for him than to deny any favour to him that I could grant, and that he seemed backward to mention his case, I begged leave of him to give me leave to ask him whether anything lay upon his mind with respect to his business and effects in the world; that if it did, he knew what I had in the world as well as I did, and that, if he wanted money, I would let him have any sum for his occasion, as far as five or six thousand pistoles, and he should pay me as his own affairs would permit; and that, if he never paid me, I would assure him that I would never give him any trouble for it.

He rose up with ceremony, and gave me thanks in terms that sufficiently told me he had been bred among people more polite and more courteous than is esteemed the ordinary usage of the Dutch; and after his compliment was over he came nearer to me, and told me he was obliged to assure me, though with repeated acknowledgments of my kind offer, that he was not in any want of money; that he had met with no uneasiness in any of his affairs— no, not of any kind whatever, except that of the loss of his wife and one of his children, which indeed had troubled him much; but that this was no part of what he had to offer me, and by granting which I should balance all obligations; but that, in short, it was that, seeing Providence had (as it were for that purpose) taken his wife from him, I would make up the loss to him; and with that he held me fast in his arms, and, kissing me, would not give me leave to say no, and hardly to breathe.

At length, having got room to speak, I told him that, as I had said before, I could deny him but one thing in the world; I was very sorry he should propose that thing only that I could not grant.

I could not but smile, however, to myself that he should make so many circles and roundabout motions to come at a discourse which had no such rarity at the bottom of it, if he had known all. But there was another reason why I resolved not to have him, when, at the same time, if he had courted me in a manner less honest or virtuous, I believe I should not have denied him; but I shall come to that part presently.

He was, as I have said, long a-bringing it out, but when he had brought it out he pursued it with such importunities as would admit of no denial; at least he intended they should not;

but I resisted them obstinately, and yet with expressions of the utmost kindness and respect for him that could be imagined, often telling him there was nothing else in the world that I could deny him, and showing him all the respect, and upon all occasions treating him with intimacy and freedom, as if he had been my brother.

He tried all the ways imaginable to bring his design to pass, but I was inflexible. At last he thought of a way which, he flattered himself, would not fail; nor would he have been mistaken, perhaps, in any other woman in the world but me. This was, to try if he could take me at an advantage and get to bed to me, and then, as was most rational to think, I should willingly enough marry him afterwards.

We were so intimate together that nothing but man and wife could, or at least ought, to be more; but still our freedoms kept within the bounds of modesty and decency. But one evening, above all the rest, we were very merry, and I fancied he pushed the mirth to watch for his advantage, and I resolved that I would at least feign to be as merry as he; and that, in short, if he offered anything he should have his will easily enough.

About one o'clock in the morning—for so long we sat up together—I said, "Come, 'tis one o'clock; I must go to bed." "Well," says he, "I'll go with you." "No, no;" says I; "go to your own chamber." He said he would go to bed with me. "Nay," says I, "if you will, I don't know what to say; if I can't help it, you must." However, I got from him, left him, and went into my chamber, but did not shut the door, and as he could easily see that I was undressing myself, he steps to his own room, which was but on the same floor, and in a few minutes undresses himself also, and returns to my door in his gown and slippers.

I thought he had been gone indeed, and so that he had been in jest; and, by the way, thought either he had no mind to the thing, or that he never intended it; so I shut my door—that is, latched it, for I seldom locked or bolted it—and went to bed. I had not been in bed a minute but he comes in his gown to the door and opens it a little way, but not enough to come in or look in, and says softly, "What! are you really gone to bed?" "Yes, yes," says I; "get you gone." "No, indeed," says he, "I shall not be gone; you gave me leave before to come to bed, and you shan't say 'Get you gone' now." So he comes into my room, and then turns about and fastens the door, and immediately comes to the bedside to me. I pretended to scold and struggle, and bid him begone with more warmth than before; but it was all one; he had not a rag of clothes on but his gown and slippers and shirt, so he throws off his gown, and throws open the bed, and came in at once.

I made a seeming resistance, but it was no more indeed; for, as above, I resolved from the beginning he should lie with me if he would, and, for the rest, I left it to come after.

Well, he lay with me that night, and the two next, and very merry we were all the three days between; but the third night he began to be a little more grave. "Now, my dear," says he, "though I have pushed this matter farther than ever I intended, or than I believe you expected from me, who never made any pretences to you but what were very honest, yet to heal it all up, and let you see how sincerely I meant at first, and how honest I will ever be to you, I am ready to marry you still, and desire you to let it be done to-morrow morning; and I will give you the same fair conditions of marriage as I would have done before."

This, it must be owned, was a testimony that he was very honest, and that he loved me sincerely; but I construed it quite another way, namely, that he aimed at the money. But how surprised did he look, and how was he confounded, when he found me receive his proposal with coldness and indifference, and still tell him that it was the only thing I could not grant!

He was astonished. "What! not take me now," says he, "when I have been abed with you!" I answered coldly, though respectfully still, "It is true, to my shame be it spoken," says I, "that you have taken me by surprise, and have had your will of me; but I hope you will not take it ill that I cannot consent to marry for all that. If I am with child," said I, "care must be taken to manage that as you shall direct; I hope you won't expose me for my having exposed myself to you, but I cannot go any farther." And at that point I stood, and would hear of no matrimony by any means.

Now, because this may seem a little odd, I shall state the matter clearly, as I understood it myself. I knew that, while I was a mistress, it is customary for the person kept to receive from them that keep; but if I should be a wife, all I had then was given up to the husband, and I was henceforth to be under his authority only; and as I had money enough, and needed not fear being what they call a cast-off mistress, so I had no need to give him twenty thousand pounds to marry me, which had been buying my lodging too dear a great deal.

Thus his project of coming to bed to me was a bite upon himself, while he intended it for a bite upon me; and he was no nearer his aim of marrying me than he was before. All his arguments he could urge upon the subject of matrimony were at an end, for I positively declined marrying him; and as he had refused the thousand pistoles which I had offered him in compensation for his expenses and loss at Paris with the Jew, and had done it upon the hopes he had of marrying me, so when he found his way difficult still, he was amazed, and, I had some reason to believe, repented that he had refused the money.

But thus it is when men run into wicked measures to bring their designs about. I, that was infinitely obliged to him before, began to talk to him as if I had balanced accounts with him now, and that the favour of lying with a whore was equal, not to the thousand pistoles only, but to all the debt I owed him for saving my life and all my effects.

But he drew himself into it, and though it was a dear bargain, yet it was a bargain of his own making; he could not say I had tricked him into it. But as he projected and drew me in to lie with him, depending that was a sure game in order to a marriage, so I granted him the favour, as he called it, to balance the account of favours received from him, and keep the thousand pistoles with a good grace.

He was extremely disappointed in this article, and knew not how to manage for a great while; and as I dare say, if he had not expected to have made it an earnest for marrying me, he would not have attempted me the other way, so, I believed, if it had not been for the money which he knew I had, he would never have desired to marry me after he had lain with me. For where is the man that cares to marry a whore, though of his own making? And as I knew him to be no fool, so I did him no wrong when I supposed that, but for the money, he would not have had any thoughts of me that way, especially after my yielding as I had done; in which it is to be remembered that I made no capitulation for marrying him when I yielded to him, but let him do just what he pleased, without any previous bargain.

Well, hitherto we went upon guesses at one another's designs; but as he continued to importune me to marry, though he had lain with me, and still did lie with me as often as he pleased, and I continued to refuse to marry him, though I let him lie with me whenever he desired it; I say, as these two circumstances made up our conversation, it could not continue long thus, but we must come to an explanation.

One morning, in the middle of our unlawful freedoms—that is to say, when we were in bed together—he sighed, and told me he desired my leave to ask me one question, and that I would give him an answer to it with the same ingenious freedom and honesty that I had used to treat him with. I told him I would. Why, then, his question was, why I would not marry him, seeing I allowed him all the freedom of a husband. "Or," says he, "my dear, since you have been so kind as to take me to your bed, why will you not make me your own, and take me for good and all, that we may enjoy ourselves without any reproach to one another?"

I told him, that as I confessed it was the only thing I could not comply with him in, so it was the only thing in all my actions that I could not give him a reason for; that it was true I had let him come to bed to me, which was supposed to be the greatest favour a woman could grant; but it was evident, and he might see it, that, as I was sensible of the obligation I was under to him for saving me from the worst circumstance it was possible for me to be brought to, I could deny him nothing; and if I had had any greater favour to yield him, I should have done it, that of matrimony only excepted, and he could not but see that I loved him to an extraordinary degree, in every part of my behaviour to him; but that as to marrying, which was giving up my liberty, it was what once he knew I had done, and he had seen how it had hurried me up and down in the world, and what it had exposed me to; that I had an aversion to it, and desired he would not insist upon it. He might easily see I had no aversion to him; and that, if I was with child by him, he should see a testimony of my kindness to the father, for that I would settle all I had in the world upon the child.

He was mute a good while. At last says he, "Come, my dear, you are the first woman in the world that ever lay with a man and then refused to marry him, and therefore there must be some other reason for your refusal; and I have therefore one other request, and that is, if I guess at the true reason, and remove the objection, will you then yield to me?" I told him if he removed the objection I must needs comply, for I should certainly do everything that I had no objection against.

"Why then, my dear, it must be that either you are already engaged or married to some other man, or you are not willing to dispose of your money to me, and expect to advance yourself higher with your fortune. Now, if it be the first of these, my mouth will be stopped, and I have no more to say; but if it be the last, I am prepared effectually to remove the objection, and answer all you can say on that subject."

I took him up short at the first of these, telling him he must have base thoughts of me indeed, to think that I could yield to him in such a manner as I had done, and continue it with so much freedom as he found I did, if I had a husband or were engaged to any other man; and that he might depend upon it that was not my case, nor any part of my case.

"Why then," said he, "as to the other, I have an offer to make to you that shall take off all the objection, viz., that I will not touch one pistole of your estate more than shall be with your own voluntary consent, neither now or at any other time, but you shall settle it as you please for your life, and upon who you please after your death;" that I should see he was able to maintain me without it, and that it was not for that that he followed me from Paris.

I was indeed surprised at that part of his offer, and he might easily perceive it; it was not only what I did not expect, but it was what I knew not what answer to make to. He had, indeed, removed my principal objection—nay, all my objections, and it was not possible for me to give any answer; for, if upon so generous an offer I should agree with him, I then did as good as confess that it was upon the account of my money that I refused him; and that though I could give up my virtue and expose myself, yet I would not give up my money, which, though it was true, yet was really too gross for me to acknowledge, and I could not pretend to marry him upon that principle neither. Then as to having him, and make over all my estate out of his hands, so as not to give him the management of what I had, I thought it would be not only a little Gothic and inhuman, but would be always a foundation of unkindness between us, and render us suspected one to another; so that, upon the whole, I was obliged to give a new turn to it, and talk upon a kind of an elevated strain, which really was not in my thoughts, at first, at all; for I own, as above, the divesting myself of my estate and putting my money out of my hand was the sum of the matter that made me refuse to marry; but, I say, I gave it a new turn upon this occasion, as follows:—

I told him I had, perhaps, different notions of matrimony from what the received custom had given us of it; that I thought a woman was a free agent as well as a man, and was born free, and, could she manage herself suitably, might enjoy that liberty to as much purpose as the men do; that the laws of matrimony were indeed otherwise, and mankind at this time acted quite upon other principles, and those such that a woman gave herself entirely away from herself, in marriage, and capitulated, only to be, at best, but an upper servant, and from the time she took the man she was no better or worse than the servant among the Israelites, who had his ears bored—that is, nailed to the door-post—who by that act gave himself up to be a servant during life; that the very nature of the marriage contract was, in short, nothing but giving up liberty, estate, authority, and everything to the man, and the woman was indeed a mere woman ever after—that is to say, a slave.

He replied, that though in some respects it was as I had said, yet I ought to consider that, as an equivalent to this, the man had all the care of things devolved upon him; that the weight of business lay upon his shoulders, and as he had the trust, so he had the toil of life upon him; his was the labour, his the anxiety of living; that the woman had nothing to do but to eat the fat and drink the sweet; to sit still and look around her, be waited on and made much of, be served and loved and made easy, especially if the husband acted as became him; and that, in general, the labour of the man was appointed to make the woman live quiet and unconcerned in the world; that they had the name of subjection without the thing; and if in inferior families they had the drudgery of the house and care of the provisions upon them, yet they had indeed much the easier part; for, in general, the women had only the care of managing—that is, spending what their husbands get; and that a woman had the name of subjection, indeed, but that they generally commanded, not the men only, but all they had; managed all for themselves; and where the man did his duty, the woman's life was all ease and tranquillity, and that she had nothing to do but to be easy, and to make all that were about her both easy and merry.

I returned, that while a woman was single, she was a masculine in her politic capacity; that she had then the full command of what she had, and the full direction of what she did; that she was a man in her separate capacity, to all intents and purposes that a man could be so to himself; that she was controlled by none, because accountable to none, and was in subjection to none. So I sung these two lines of Mr. —'s:—

"Oh! 'tis pleasant to be free,
The sweetest Miss is Liberty."
I added, that whoever the woman was that had an estate, and would give it up to be the slave of a great man, that woman was a fool, and must be fit for nothing but a beggar; that it was my opinion a woman was as fit to govern and enjoy her own estate without a man as a man was without a woman; and that, if she had a mind to gratify herself as to sexes, she might entertain a man as a man does a mistress; that while she was thus single she was her own, and if she gave away that power she merited to be as miserable as it was possible that any creature could be.

All he could say could not answer the force of this as to argument; only this, that the other way was the ordinary method that the world was guided by; that he had reason to expect I should be content with that which all the world was contented with; that he was of the opinion that a sincere affection between a man and his wife answered all the objections that I had made about the being a slave, a servant, and the like; and where there was a mutual love there could be no bondage, but that there was but one interest, one aim, one design, and all conspired to make both very happy.

"Ay," said I, "that is the thing I complain of. The pretence of affection takes from a woman everything that can be called herself; she is to have no interest, no aim, no view; but all is the interest, aim, and view of the husband; she is to be the passive creature you spoke of," said I. "She is to lead a life of perfect indolence, and living by faith, not in God, but in her husband, she sinks or swims, as he is either fool or wise man, unhappy or prosperous; and in the middle of what she thinks is her happiness and prosperity, she is engulfed in misery and beggary, which she had not the least notice, knowledge, or suspicion of. How often have I seen a woman living in all the splendour that a plentiful fortune ought to allow her, with her coaches and equipages, her family and rich furniture, her attendants and friends, her visitors and good company, all about her to-day; to-morrow surprised with a disaster, turned out of all by a commission of bankrupt, stripped to the clothes on her back; her jointure, suppose she had it, is sacrificed to the creditors so long as her husband lived, and she turned into the street, and left to live on the charity of her friends, if she has any, or follow the monarch, her husband, into the Mint, and live there on the wreck of his fortunes, till he is forced to run away from her even there; and then she sees her children starve, herself miserable, breaks her heart, and cries herself to death! This," says I, "is the state of many a lady that has had £10,000 to her portion."

He did not know how feelingly I spoke this, and what extremities I had gone through of this kind; how near I was to the very last article above, viz., crying myself to death; and how I really starved for almost two years together.

But he shook his head, and said, where had I lived? and what dreadful families had I lived among, that had frighted me into such terrible apprehensions of things? that these things indeed might happen where men run into hazardous things in trade, and, without prudence or due consideration, launched their fortunes in a degree beyond their strength, grasping at adventures beyond their stocks, and the like; but that, as he was stated in the world, if I would embark with him, he had a fortune equal with mine; that together we should have no occasion of engaging in business any more, but that in any part of the world where I had a mind to live, whether England, France, Holland, or where I would, we might settle, and live as happily as the world could make any one live; that if I desired the management of our estate, when put together, if I would not trust him with mine, he would trust me with his; that we would be upon one bottom, and I should steer. "Ay," says I, "you'll allow me to steer—that is, hold the helm—but you'll con the ship, as they call it; that is, as at sea, a boy serves to stand at the helm, but he that gives him the orders is pilot."

He laughed at my simile. "No," says he; "you shall be pilot then; you shall con the ship." "Ay," says I, "as long as you please; but you can take the helm out of my hand when you please, and bid me go spin. It is not you," says I, "that I suspect, but the laws of matrimony puts the power into your hands, bids you do it, commands you to command, and binds me, forsooth, to obey. You, that are now upon even terms with me, and I with you," says I, "are the next hour set up upon the throne, and the humble wife placed at your footstool; all the rest, all that you call oneness of interest, mutual affection, and the like, is courtesy and kindness then, and a woman is indeed infinitely obliged where she meets with it, but can't help herself where it fails."

Well, he did not give it over yet, but came to the serious part, and there he thought he should be too many for me. He first hinted that marriage was decreed by Heaven; that it was the fixed state of life, which God had appointed for man's felicity, and for establishing a legal posterity; that there could be no legal claim of estates by inheritance but by children born in wedlock; that all the rest was sunk under scandal and illegitimacy; and very well he talked upon that subject indeed.

But it would not do; I took him short there. "Look you, sir," said I, "you have an advantage of me there indeed, in my particular case, but it would not be generous to make use of it. I readily grant that it were better for me to have married you than to admit you to the liberty I have given you, but as I could not reconcile my judgment to marriage, for the reasons above, and had kindness enough for you, and obligation too much on me to resist you, I suffered your rudeness and gave up my virtue. But I have two things before me to heal up that breach of honour without that desperate one of marriage, and those are, repentance for what is past, and putting an end to it for time to come."

He seemed to be concerned to think that I should take him in that manner. He assured me that I misunderstood him; that he had more manners as well as more kindness for me, and more justice than to reproach me with what he had been the aggressor in, and had surprised me into; that what he spoke referred to my words above, that the woman, if she thought fit, might entertain a man, as a man did a mistress; and that I seemed to mention that way of living as justifiable, and setting it as a lawful thing, and in the place of matrimony.

Well, we strained some compliments upon those points, not worth repeating; and I added, I supposed when he got to bed to me he thought himself sure of me; and, indeed, in the ordinary course of things, after he had lain with me he ought to think so, but that, upon the same foot of argument which I had discoursed with him upon, it was just the contrary; and when a woman had been weak enough to yield up the last point before wedlock, it would be adding one weakness to another to take the man afterwards, to pin down the shame of it upon herself all the days of her life, and bind herself to live all her time with the only man that could upbraid her with it; that in yielding at first, she must be a fool, but to take the man is to be sure to be called fool; that to resist a man is to act with courage and vigour, and to cast off the reproach, which, in the course of things, drops out of knowledge and dies. The man goes one way and the woman another, as fate and the circumstances of living direct; and if they keep one another's counsel, the folly is heard no more of. "But to take the man," says I, "is the most preposterous thing in nature, and (saving your presence) is to befoul one's self, and live always in the smell of it. No, no," added I; "after a man has lain with me as a mistress, he ought never to lie with me as a wife. That's not only preserving the crime in memory, but it is recording it in the family. If the woman marries the man afterwards, she bears the reproach of it to the last hour. If her husband is not a man of a hundred thousand, he some time or other upbraids her with it. If he has children, they fail not one way or other to hear of it. If the children are virtuous, they do their mother the justice to hate her for it; if they are wicked, they give her the mortification of doing the like, and giving her for the example. On the other hand, if the man and the woman part, there is an end of the crime and an end of the clamour; time wears out the memory of it, or a woman may remove but a few streets, and she soon outlives it, and hears no more of it."

He was confounded at this discourse, and told me he could not say but I was right in the main. That as to that part relating to managing estates, it was arguing à la cavalier; it was in some sense right, if the women were able to carry it on so, but that in general the sex were not capable of it; their heads were not turned for it, and they had better choose a person capable and honest, that knew how to do them justice as women, as well as to love them; and that then the trouble was all taken off of their hands.

I told him it was a dear way of purchasing their ease, for very often when the trouble was taken off of their hands, so was their money too; and that I thought it was far safer for the sex not to be afraid of the trouble, but to be really afraid of their money; that if nobody was trusted, nobody would be deceived, and the staff in their own hands was the best security in the world.

He replied, that I had started a new thing in the world; that however I might support it by subtle reasoning, yet it was a way of arguing that was contrary to the general practice, and that he confessed he was much disappointed in it; that, had he known I would have made such a use of it, he would never have attempted what he did, which he had no wicked design in, resolving to make me reparation, and that he was very sorry he had been so unhappy; that he was very sure he should never upbraid me with it hereafter, and had so good an opinion of me as to believe I did not suspect him; but seeing I was positive in refusing him, notwithstanding what had passed, he had nothing to do but secure me from reproach by going back again to Paris, that so, according to my own way of arguing, it might die out of memory, and I might never meet with it again to my disadvantage.

I was not pleased with this part at all, for I had no mind to let him go neither, and yet I had no mind to give him such hold of me as he would have had; and thus I was in a kind of suspense, irresolute, and doubtful what course to take.

I was in the house with him, as I have observed, and I saw evidently that he was preparing to go back to Paris; and particularly I found he was remitting money to Paris, which was, as I understood afterwards, to pay for some wines which he had given order to have bought for him at Troyes, in Champagne, and I knew not what course to take; and, besides that, I was very loth to part with him. I found also that I was with child by him, which was what I had not yet told him of, and sometimes I thought not to tell him of it at all; but I was in a strange place, and had no acquaintance, though I had a great deal of substance, which indeed, having no friends there, was the more dangerous to me.

This obliged me to take him one morning when I saw him, as I thought, a little anxious about his going, and irresolute. Says I to him, "I fancy you can hardly find in your heart to leave me now." "The more unkind is it in you," said he, "severely unkind, to refuse a man that knows not how to part with you."

"I am so far from being unkind to you," said I, "that I will go over all the world with you if you desire me to, except to Paris, where you know I can't go."

"It is a pity so much love," said he, "on both sides should ever separate."

"Why, then," said I, "do you go away from me?"

"Because," said he, "you won't take me."

"But if I won't take you," said I, "you may take me anywhere but to Paris."

He was very loth to go anywhere, he said, without me, but he must go to Paris or the East Indies.

I told him I did not use to court, but I durst venture myself to the East Indies with him, if there was a necessity of his going.

He told me, God be thanked he was in no necessity of going anywhere, but that he had a tempting invitation to go to the Indies.

I answered, I would say nothing to that, but that I desired he would go anywhere but to Paris, because there he knew I must not go.

He said he had no remedy but to go where I could not go, for he could not bear to see me if he must not have me.

I told him that was the unkindest thing he could say of me, and that I ought to take it very ill, seeing I knew how very well to oblige him to stay, without yielding to what he knew I could not yield to.

This amazed him, and he told me I was pleased to be mysterious, but that he was sure it was in nobody's power to hinder him going, if he resolved upon it, except me, who had influence enough upon him to make him do anything.

Yes, I told him, I could hinder him, because I knew he could no more do an unkind thing by me than he could do an unjust one; and to put him out of his pain, I told him I was with child.

He came to me, and taking me in his arms and kissing me a thousand times almost, said, why would I be so unkind not to tell him that before?

I told him 'twas hard, that to have him stay, I should be forced to do as criminals do to avoid the gallows, plead my belly; and that I thought I had given him testimonies enough of an affection equal to that of a wife, if I had not only lain with him, been with child by him, shown myself unwilling to part with him, but offered to go to the East Indies with him; and except one thing that I could not grant, what could he ask more?

He stood mute a good while, but afterwards told me he had a great deal more to say if I could assure him that I would not take ill whatever freedom he might use with me in his discourse.

I told him he might use any freedom in words with me; for a woman who had given leave to such other freedoms as I had done had left herself no room to take anything ill, let it be what it would.

"Why, then," he said, "I hope you believe, madam, I was born a Christian, and that I have some sense of sacred things upon my mind. When I first broke in upon my own virtue and assaulted yours; when I surprised and, as it were, forced you to that which neither you intended or I designed but a few hours before, it was upon a presumption that you would certainly marry me, if once I could go that length with you, and it was with an honest resolution to make you my wife.

"But I have been surprised with such a denial that no woman in such circumstances ever gave to a man; for certainly it was never known that any woman refused to marry a man that had first lain with her, much less a man that had gotten her with child. But you go upon different notions from all the world, and though you reason upon it so strongly that a man knows hardly what to answer, yet I must own there is something in it shocking to nature, and something very unkind to yourself. But, above all, it is unkind to the child that is yet unborn, who, if we marry, will come into the world with advantage enough, but if not, is ruined before it is born; must bear the eternal reproach of what it is not guilty of; must be branded from its cradle with a mark of infamy, be loaded with the crimes and follies of its parents, and suffer for sins that it never committed. This I take to be very hard, and, indeed, cruel to the poor infant not yet born, who you cannot think of with any patience, if you have the common affection of a mother, and not do that for it which should at once place it on a level with the rest of the world, and not leave it to curse its parents for what also we ought to be ashamed of. I cannot, therefore," says he, "but beg and entreat you, as you are a Christian and a mother, not to let the innocent lamb you go with be ruined before it is born, and leave it to curse and reproach us hereafter for what may be so easily avoided.

"Then, dear madam," said he, with a world of tenderness (and I thought I saw tears in his eyes), "allow me to repeat it, that I am a Christian, and consequently I do not allow what I have rashly, and without due consideration, done; I say, I do not approve of it as lawful, and therefore, though I did, with the view I have mentioned, one unjustifiable action, I cannot say that I could satisfy myself to live in a continual practice of what in judgment we must both condemn; and though I love you above all the women in the world, and have done enough to convince you of it by resolving to marry you after what has passed between us, and by offering to quit all pretensions to any part of your estate, so that I should, as it were, take a wife after I had lain with her, and without a farthing portion, which, as my circumstances are, I need not do; I say, notwithstanding my affection to you, which is inexpressible, yet I cannot give up soul as well as body, the interest of this world and the hopes of another; and you cannot call this my disrespect to you."

If ever any man in the world was truly valuable for the strictest honesty of intention, this was the man; and if ever woman in her senses rejected a man of merit on so trivial and frivolous a pretence, I was the woman; but surely it was the most preposterous thing that ever woman did.

He would have taken me as a wife, but would not entertain me as a whore. Was ever woman angry with any gentleman on that head? And was ever woman so stupid to choose to be a whore, where she might have been an honest wife? But infatuations are next to being possessed of the devil. I was inflexible, and pretended to argue upon the point of a woman's liberty as before, but he took me short, and with more warmth than he had yet used with me, though with the utmost respect, replied, "Dear madam, you argue for liberty, at the same time that you restrain yourself from that liberty which God and nature has directed you to take, and, to supply the deficiency, propose a vicious liberty, which is neither honourable or religious. Will you propose liberty at the expense of modesty?"

I returned, that he mistook me; I did not propose it; I only said that those that could not be content without concerning the sexes in that affair might do so indeed; might entertain a man as men do a mistress, if they thought fit, but he did not hear me say I would do so; and though, by what had passed, he might well censure me in that part, yet he should find, for the future, that I should freely converse with him without any inclination that way.

He told me he could not promise that for himself, and thought he ought not to trust himself with the opportunity, for that, as he had failed already, he was loth to lead himself into the temptation of offending again, and that this was the true reason of his resolving to go back to Paris; not that he could willingly leave me, and would be very far from wanting my invitation; but if he could not stay upon terms that became him, either as an honest man or a Christian, what could he do? And he hoped, he said, I could not blame him that he was unwilling anything that was to call him father should upbraid him with leaving him in the world to be called bastard; adding that he was astonished to think how I could satisfy myself to be so cruel to an innocent infant not yet born; professed he could neither bear the thoughts of it, much less bear to see it, and hoped I would not take it ill that he could not stay to see me delivered, for that very reason.

I saw he spoke this with a disturbed mind, and that it was with some difficulty that he restrained his passion, so I declined any farther discourse upon it; only said I hoped he would consider of it. "Oh, madam!" says he, "do not bid me consider; 'tis for you to consider;" and with that he went out of the room, in a strange kind of confusion, as was easy to be seen in his countenance.

If I had not been one of the foolishest as well as wickedest creatures upon earth, I could never have acted thus. I had one of the honestest, completest gentlemen upon earth at my hand. He had in one sense saved my life, but he had saved that life from ruin in a most remarkable manner. He loved me even to distraction, and had come from Paris to Rotterdam on purpose to seek me. He had offered me marriage even after I was with child by him, and had offered to quit all his pretensions to my estate, and give it up to my own management, having a plentiful estate of his own. Here I might have settled myself out of the reach even of disaster itself; his estate and mine would have purchased even then above two thousand pounds a year, and I might have lived like a queen—nay, far more happy than a queen; and, which was above all, I had now an opportunity to have quitted a life of crime and debauchery, which I had been given up to for several years, and to have sat down quiet in plenty and honour, and to have set myself apart to the great work which I have since seen so much necessity of and occasion for—I mean that of repentance.

But my measure of wickedness was not yet full. I continued obstinate against matrimony, and yet I could not bear the thoughts of his going away neither. As to the child, I was not very anxious about it. I told him I would promise him it should never come to him to upbraid him with its being illegitimate; that if it was a boy, I would breed it up like the son of a gentleman, and use it well for his sake; and after a little more such talk as this, and seeing him resolved to go, I retired, but could not help letting him see the tears run down my cheeks. He came to me and kissed me, entreated me, conjured me by the kindness he had shown me in my distress, by the justice he had done me in my bills and money affairs, by the respect which made him refuse a thousand pistoles from me for his expenses with that traitor the Jew, by the pledge of our misfortunes—so he called it—which I carried with me, and by all that the sincerest affection could propose to do, that I would not drive him away.

But it would not do. I was stupid and senseless, deaf to all his importunities, and continued so to the last. So we parted, only desiring me to promise that I would write him word when I was delivered, and how he might give me an answer; and this I engaged my word I would do. And upon his desiring to be informed which way I intended to dispose of myself, I told him I resolved to go directly to England, and to London, where I proposed to lie in; but since he resolved to leave me, I told him I supposed it would be of no consequence to him what became of me.

He lay in his lodgings that night, but went away early in the morning, leaving me a letter in which he repeated all he had said, recommended the care of the child, and desired of me that as he had remitted to me the offer of a thousand pistoles which I would have given him for the recompense of his charges and trouble with the Jew, and had given it me back, so he desired I would allow him to oblige me to set apart that thousand pistoles, with its improvement, for the child, and for its education; earnestly pressing me to secure that little portion for the abandoned orphan when I should think fit, as he was sure I would, to throw away the rest upon something as worthless as my sincere friend at Paris. He concluded with moving me to reflect, with the same regret as he did, on our follies we had committed together; asked me forgiveness for being the aggressor in the fact, and forgave me everything, he said, but the cruelty of refusing him, which he owned he could not forgive me so heartily as he should do, because he was satisfied it was an injury to myself, would be an introduction to my ruin, and that I would seriously repent of it. He foretold some fatal things which, he said, he was well assured I should fall into, and that at last I would be ruined by a bad husband; bid me be the more wary, that I might render him a false prophet; but to remember that, if ever I came into distress, I had a fast friend at Paris, who would not upbraid me with the unkind things past, but would be always ready to return me good for evil.

This letter stunned me. I could not think it possible for any one that had not dealt with the devil to write such a letter, for he spoke of some particular things which afterwards were to befall me with such an assurance that it frighted me beforehand; and when those things did come to pass, I was persuaded he had some more than human knowledge. In a word, his advices to me to repent were very affectionate, his warnings of evil to happen to me were very kind, and his promises of assistance, if I wanted him, were so generous that I have seldom seen the like; and though I did not at first set much by that part because I looked upon them as what might not happen, and as what was improbable to happen at that time, yet all the rest of his letter was so moving that it left me very melancholy, and I cried four-and-twenty hours after, almost without ceasing, about it; and yet even all this while, whatever it was that bewitched me, I had not one serious wish that I had taken him. I wished heartily, indeed, that I could have kept him with me, but I had a mortal aversion to marrying him, or indeed anybody else, but formed a thousand wild notions in my head that I was yet gay enough, and young and handsome enough, to please a man of quality, and that I would try my fortune at London, come of it what would.

Thus blinded by my own vanity, I threw away the only opportunity I then had to have effectually settled my fortunes, and secured them for this world; and I am a memorial to all that shall read my story, a standing monument of the madness and distraction which pride and infatuations from hell run us into, how ill our passions guide us, and how dangerously we act when we follow the dictates of an ambitious mind.

I was rich, beautiful, and agreeable, and not yet old. I had known something of the influence I had had upon the fancies of men even of the highest rank. I never forgot that the Prince de — had said, with an ecstasy, that I was the finest woman in France. I knew I could make a figure at London, and how well I could grace that figure. I was not at a loss how to behave, and having already been adored by princes, I thought of nothing less than of being mistress to the king himself. But I go back to my immediate circumstances at that time.

I got over the absence of my honest merchant but slowly at first. It was with infinite regret that I let him go at all; and when I read the letter he left I was quite confounded. As soon as he was out of call and irrecoverable I would have given half I had in the world for him back again; my notion of things changed in an instant, and I called myself a thousand fools for casting myself upon a life of scandal and hazard, when, after the shipwreck of virtue, honour, and principle, and sailing at the utmost risk in the stormy seas of crime and abominable levity, I had a safe harbour presented, and no heart to cast anchor in it.

His predictions terrified me; his promises of kindness if I came to distress melted me into tears, but frighted me with the apprehensions of ever coming into such distress, and filled my head with a thousand anxieties and thoughts how it should be possible for me, who had now such a fortune, to sink again into misery.

Then the dreadful scene of my life, when I was left with my five children, &c., as I have related, represented itself again to me, and I sat considering what measures I might take to bring myself to such a state of desolation again, and how I should act to avoid it.

But these things wore off gradually. As to my friend the merchant, he was gone, and gone irrecoverably, for I durst not follow him to Paris, for the reasons mentioned above. Again, I was afraid to write to him to return, lest he should have refused, as I verily believed he would; so I sat and cried intolerably for some days—nay, I may say for some weeks; but, I say, it wore off gradually, and as I had a pretty deal of business for managing my effects, the hurry of that particular part served to divert my thoughts, and in part to wear out the impressions which had been made upon my mind.

I had sold my jewels, all but the diamond ring which my gentleman the jeweller used to wear, and this, at proper times, I wore myself; as also the diamond necklace which the prince had given me, and a pair of extraordinary earrings worth about 600 pistoles; the other, which was a fine casket, he left with me at his going to Versailles, and a small case with some rubies and emeralds, &c. I say I sold them at the Hague for 7600 pistoles. I had received all the bills which the merchant had helped me to at Paris, and with the money I brought with me, they made up 13,900 pistoles more; so that I had in ready money, and in account in the bank at Amsterdam, above one-and-twenty thousand pistoles, besides jewels; and how to get this treasure to England was my next care.

The business I had had now with a great many people for receiving such large sums and selling jewels of such considerable value gave me opportunity to know and converse with several of the best merchants of the place, so that I wanted no direction now how to get my money remitted to England. Applying, therefore, to several merchants, that I might neither risk it all on the credit of one merchant, nor suffer any single man to know the quantity of money I had; I say, applying myself to several merchants, I got bills of exchange payable in London for all my money. The first bills I took with me; the second bills I left in trust (in case of any disaster at sea) in the hands of the first merchant, him to whom I was recommended by my friend from Paris.

Having thus spent nine months in Holland, refused the best offer ever woman in my circumstances had, parted unkindly, and indeed barbarously, with the best friend and honestest man in the world, got all my money in my pocket, and a bastard in my belly, I took shipping at the Brill in the packet-boat, and arrived safe at Harwich, where my woman Amy was come by my direction to meet me.

I would willingly have given ten thousand pounds of my money to have been rid of the burthen I had in my belly, as above; but it could not be, so I was obliged to bear with that part, and get rid of it by the ordinary method of patience and a hard travail.

I was above the contemptible usage that women in my circumstances oftentimes meet with. I had considered all that beforehand; and having sent Amy beforehand, and remitted her money to do it, she had taken me a very handsome house in —— Street, near Charing Cross; had hired me two maids and a footman, who she had put in a good livery; and having hired a glass coach and four horses, she came with them and the man-servant to Harwich to meet me, and had been there near a week before I came, so I had nothing to do but to go away to London to my own house, where I arrived in very good health, and where I passed for a French lady, by the title of ——.

My first business was to get all my bills accepted, which, to cut the story short, was all both accepted and currently paid; and I then resolved to take me a country lodging somewhere near the town, to be incognito, till I was brought to bed; which, appearing in such a figure and having such an equipage, I easily managed without anybody's offering the usual insults of parish inquiries. I did not appear in my new house for some time, and afterwards I thought fit, for particular reasons, to quit that house, and not to come to it at all, but take handsome large apartments in the Pall Mall, in a house out of which was a private door into the king's garden, by the permission of the chief gardener, who had lived in the house.

I had now all my effects secured; but my money being my great concern at that time, I found it a difficulty how to dispose of it so as to bring me in an annual interest. However, in some time I got a substantial safe mortgage for £14,000 by the assistance of the famous Sir Robert Clayton, for which I had an estate of £1800 a year bound to me, and had £700 per annum interest for it.

This, with some other securities, made me a very handsome estate of above a thousand pounds a year; enough, one would think, to keep any woman in England from being a whore.

I lay in at ——, about four miles from London, and brought a fine boy into the world, and, according to my promise, sent an account of it to my friend at Paris, the father of it; and in the letter told him how sorry I was for his going away, and did as good as intimate that, if he would come once more to see me, I should use him better than I had done. He gave me a very kind and obliging answer, but took not the least notice of what I had said of his coming over, so I found my interest lost there for ever. He gave me joy of the child, and hinted that he hoped I would make good what he had begged for the poor infant as I had promised, and I sent him word again that I would fulfil his order to a tittle; and such a fool and so weak I was in this last letter, notwithstanding what I have said of his not taking notice of my invitation, as to ask his pardon almost for the usage I gave him at Rotterdam, and stooped so low as to expostulate with him for not taking notice of my inviting him to come to me again, as I had done; and, which was still more, went so far as to make a second sort of an offer to him, telling him, almost in plain words, that if he would come over now I would have him; but he never gave me the least reply to it at all, which was as absolute a denial to me as he was ever able to give; so I sat down, I cannot say contented, but vexed heartily that I had made the offer at all, for he had, as I may say, his full revenge of me in scorning to answer, and to let me twice ask that of him which he with so much importunity begged of me before.

I was now up again, and soon came to my City lodging in the Pall Mall, and here I began to make a figure suitable to my estate, which was very great; and I shall give you an account of my equipage in a few words, and of myself too.

I paid £60 a year for my new apartments, for I took them by the year; but then they were handsome lodgings indeed, and very richly furnished. I kept my own servants to clean and look after them, found my own kitchen ware and firing. My equipage was handsome, but not very great; I had a coach, a coachman, a footman, my woman Amy, who I now dressed like a gentlewoman and made her my companion, and three maids; and thus I lived for a time. I dressed to the height of every mode, went extremely rich in clothes, and as for jewels, I wanted none. I gave a very good livery, laced with silver, and as rich as anybody below the nobility could be seen with; and thus I appeared, leaving the world to guess who or what I was, without offering to put myself forward.

I walked sometimes in the Mall with my woman Amy, but I kept no company and made no acquaintances, only made as gay a show as I was able to do, and that upon all occasions. I found, however, the world was not altogether so unconcerned about me as I seemed to be about them; and first I understood that the neighbours began to be mighty inquisitive about me, as who I was, and what my circumstances were.

Amy was the only person that could answer their curiosity or give any account of me; and she, a tattling woman and a true gossip, took care to do that with all the art that she was mistress of. She let them know that I was the widow of a person of quality in France, that I was very rich, that I came over hither to look after an estate that fell to me by some of my relations who died here, that I was worth £40,000 all in my own hands, and the like.

This was all wrong in Amy, and in me too, though we did not see it at first, for this recommended me indeed to those sort of gentlemen they call fortune-hunters, and who always besieged ladies, as they called it—on purpose to take them prisoners, as I called it— that is to say, to marry the women and have the spending of their money. But if I was wrong in refusing the honourable proposals of the Dutch merchant, who offered me the disposal of my whole estate, and had as much of his own to maintain me with, I was right now in refusing those offers which came generally from gentlemen of good families and good estates, but who, living to the extent of them, were always needy and necessitous, and wanted a sum of money to make themselves easy, as they call it—that is to say, to pay off encumbrances, sisters' portions, and the like; and then the woman is prisoner for life, and may live as they give her leave. This life I had seen into clearly enough, and therefore I was not to be catched that way. However, as I said, the reputation of my money brought several of those sort of gentry about me, and they found means, by one stratagem or other, to get access to my ladyship; but, in short, I answered them well enough, that I lived single and was happy; that as I had no occasion to change my condition for an estate, so I did not see that by the best offer that any of them could make me I could mend my fortune; that I might be honoured with titles indeed, and in time rank on public occasions with the peeresses (I mention that because one that offered at me was the eldest son of a peer), but that I was as well without the title as long as I had the estate, and while I had £2000 a year of my own I was happier than I could be in being prisoner of state to a nobleman, for I took the ladies of that rank to be little better.

As I have mentioned Sir Robert Clayton, with whom I had the good fortune to become acquainted, on account of the mortgage which he helped me to, it is necessary to take notice that I had much advantage in my ordinary affairs by his advice, and therefore I called it my good fortune; for as he paid me so considerable an annual income as £700 a year, so I am to acknowledge myself much a debtor, not only to the justice of his dealings with me, but to the prudence and conduct which he guided me to, by his advice, for the management of my estate. And as he found I was not inclined to marry, he frequently took occasion to hint how soon I might raise my fortune to a prodigious height if I would but order my family economy so far within my revenue as to lay up every year something to add to the capital.

I was convinced of the truth of what he said, and agreed to the advantages of it. You are to take it as you go that Sir Robert supposed by my own discourse, and especially by my woman Amy, that I had £2000 a year income. He judged, as he said, by my way of living that I could not spend above one thousand, and so, he added, I might prudently lay by

£1000 every year to add to the capital; and by adding every year the additional interest or income of the money to the capital, he proved to me that in ten years I should double the £1000 per annum that I laid by. And he drew me out a table, as he called it, of the increase, for me to judge by; and by which, he said, if the gentlemen of England would but act so, every family of them would increase their fortunes to a great degree, just as merchants do by trade; whereas now, says Sir Robert, by the humour of living up to the extent of their fortunes, and rather beyond, the gentlemen, says he, ay, and the nobility too, are almost all of them borrowers, and all in necessitous circumstances.

As Sir Robert frequently visited me, and was (if I may say so from his own mouth) very well pleased with my way of conversing with him, for he knew nothing, not so much as guessed at what I had been; I say, as he came often to see me, so he always entertained me with this scheme of frugality; and one time he brought another paper, wherein he showed me, much to the same purpose as the former, to what degree I should increase my estate if I would come into his method of contracting my expenses; and by this scheme of his, it appeared that, laying up a thousand pounds a year, and every year adding the interest to it, I should in twelve years' time have in bank one-and-twenty thousand and fifty-eight pounds, after which I might lay up two thousand pounds a year.

I objected that I was a young woman, that I had been used to live plentifully, and with a good appearance, and that I knew not how to be a miser.

He told me that if I thought I had enough it was well, but that if I desired to have more, this was the way; that in another twelve years I should be too rich, so that I should not know what to do with it.

"Ay, sir," says I, "you are contriving how to make me a rich old woman, but that won't answer my end; I had rather have £20,000 now than £60,000 when I am fifty years old."
"Then, madam," says he, "I suppose your honour has no children?"

"None, Sir Robert," said I, "but what are provided for." So I left him in the dark as much as I found him. However, I considered his scheme very well, though I said no more to him at that time, and I resolved, though I would make a very good figure, I say I resolved to abate a little of my expense, and draw in, live closer, and save something, if not so much as he proposed to me. It was near the end of the year that Sir Robert made this proposal to me, and when the year was up I went to his house in the City, and there I told him I came to thank him for his scheme of frugality; that I had been studying much upon it, and though I had not been able to mortify myself so much as to lay up a thousand pounds a year, yet, as I had not come to him for my interest half-yearly, as was usual, I was now come to let him know that I had resolved to lay up that seven hundred pounds a year, and never use a penny of it, desiring him to help me to put it out to advantage.

Sir Robert, a man thoroughly versed in arts of improving money, but thoroughly honest, said to me, "Madam, I am glad you approve of the method that I proposed to you; but you have begun wrong; you should have come for your interest at the half-year, and then you had had the money to put out. Now you have lost half a year's interest of £350, which is £9; for I had but per cent, on the mortgage."

"Well, well, sir," says I, "can you put this out for me now?"

"Let it lie, madam," says he, "till the next year, and then I'll put out your £1400 together, and in the meantime I'll pay you interest for the £700." So he gave me his bill for the money, which he told me should be no less than £6 per cent. Sir Robert Clayton's bill was what nobody would refuse, so I thanked him and let it lie; and next year I did the same, and the third year Sir Robert got me a good mortgage for £2200 at £6 per cent interest. So I had £132 a year added to my income, which was a very satisfying article.

But I return to my history. As I have said, I found that my measures were all wrong; the posture I set up in exposed me to innumerable visitors of the kind I have mentioned above. I was cried up for a vast fortune, and one that Sir Robert Clayton managed for; and Sir Robert Clayton was courted for me as much as I was for myself. But I had given Sir Robert his cue. I had told him my opinion of matrimony, in just the same terms as I had done my merchant, and he came into it presently. He owned that my observation was just, and that if I valued my liberty, as I knew my fortune, and that it was in my own hands, I was to blame if I gave it away to any one.

But Sir Robert knew nothing of my design, that I aimed at being a kept mistress, and to have a handsome maintenance; and that I was still for getting money, and laying it up too, as much as he could desire me, only by a worse way.

However, Sir Robert came seriously to me one day, and told me he had an offer of matrimony to make to me that was beyond all that he had heard had offered themselves, and this was a merchant. Sir Robert and I agreed exactly in our notions of a merchant. Sir Robert said, and I found it to be true, that a true-bred merchant is the best gentleman in the nation; that in knowledge, in manners, in judgment of things, the merchant outdid many of the nobility; that having once mastered the world, and being above the demand of business, though no real estate, they were then superior to most gentlemen, even in estate; that a merchant in flush business and a capital stock is able to spend more money than a gentleman of £5000 a year estate; that while a merchant spent, he only spent what he got, and not that, and that he laid up great sums every year; that an estate is a pond, but that a trade was a spring; that if the first is once mortgaged, it seldom gets clear, but embarrassed the person for ever; but the merchant had his estate continually flowing; and upon this he named me merchants who lived in more real splendour and spent more money than most of the noblemen in England could singly expend, and that they still grew immensely rich.

He went on to tell me that even the tradesmen in London, speaking of the better sort of trades, could spend more money in their families, and yet give better fortunes to their children, than, generally speaking, the gentry of England from £1000 a year downward could do, and yet grow rich too.

The upshot of all this was to recommend to me rather the bestowing my fortune upon some eminent merchant, who lived already in the first figure of a merchant, and who, not being in want or scarcity of money, but having a flourishing business and a flowing cash, would at the first word settle all my fortune on myself and children, and maintain me like a queen.

This was certainly right, and had I taken his advice, I had been really happy; but my heart was bent upon an independency of fortune, and I told him I knew no state of matrimony but what was at best a state of inferiority, if not of bondage; that I had no notion of it; that I lived a life of absolute liberty now, was free as I was born, and having a plentiful fortune, I did not understand what coherence the words "honour and obey" had with the liberty of a free woman; that I knew no reason the men had to engross the whole liberty of the race, and make the woman, notwithstanding any disparity of fortune, be subject to the laws of marriage, of their own making; that it was my misfortune to be a woman, but I was resolved it should not be made worse by the sex; and, seeing liberty seemed to be the men's property, I would be a man-woman, for, as I was born free, I would die so.

Sir Robert smiled, and told me I talked a kind of Amazonian language; that he found few women of my mind, or that, if they were, they wanted resolution to go on with it; that, notwithstanding all my notions, which he could not but say had once some weight in them, yet he understood I had broke in upon them, and had been married. I answered, I had so; but he did not hear me say that I had any encouragement from what was past to make a second venture; that I was got well out of the toil, and if I came in again I should have nobody to blame but myself.

Sir Robert laughed heartily at me, but gave over offering any more arguments, only told me he had pointed me out for some of the best merchants in London, but since I forbade him he would give me no disturbance of that kind. He applauded my way of managing my money, and told me I should soon be monstrous rich; but he neither knew or mistrusted that, with all this wealth, I was yet a whore, and was not averse to adding to my estate at the farther expense of my virtue.

But to go on with my story as to my way of living. I found, as above, that my living as I did would not answer; that it only brought the fortune-hunters and bites about me, as I have said before, to make a prey of me and my money; and, in short, I was harassed with lovers, beaux, and fops of quality, in abundance, but it would not do. I aimed at other things, and was possessed with so vain an opinion of my own beauty, that nothing less than the king himself was in my eye. And this vanity was raised by some words let fall by a person I conversed with, who was, perhaps, likely enough to have brought such a thing to pass, had it been sooner; but that game began to be pretty well over at court. However, the having mentioned such a thing, it seems a little too publicly, it brought abundance of people about me, upon a wicked account too.

And now I began to act in a new sphere. The court was exceedingly gay and fine, though fuller of men than of women, the queen not affecting to be very much in public. On the other hand, it is no slander upon the courtiers to say, they were as wicked as anybody in reason could desire them. The king had several mistresses, who were prodigious fine, and there was a glorious show on that side indeed. If the sovereign gave himself a loose, it could not be expected the rest of the court should be all saints; so far was it from that, though I would not make it worse than it was, that a woman that had anything agreeable in her appearance could never want followers.

I soon found myself thronged with admirers, and I received visits from some persons of very great figure, who always introduced themselves by the help of an old lady or two who were now become my intimates; and one of them, I understood afterwards, was set to work on purpose to get into my favour, in order to introduce what followed.

The conversation we had was generally courtly, but civil. At length some gentlemen proposed to play, and made what they called a party. This, it seems, was a contrivance of one of my female hangers-on, for, as I said, I had two of them, who thought this was the way to introduce people as often as she pleased; and so indeed it was. They played high and stayed late, but begged my pardon, only asked leave to make an appointment for the next night. I was as gay and as well pleased as any of them, and one night told one of the gentlemen, my Lord —, that seeing they were doing me the honour of diverting themselves at my apartment, and desired to be there sometimes, I did not keep a gaming-table, but I would give them a little ball the next day if they pleased, which they accepted very willingly.

Accordingly, in the evening the gentlemen began to come, where I let them see that I understood very well what such things meant. I had a large dining-room in my apartments, with five other rooms on the same floor, all which I made drawing-rooms for the occasion, having all the beds taken down for the day. In three of these I had tables placed, covered with wine and sweetmeats, the fourth had a green table for play, and the fifth was my own room, where I sat, and where I received all the company that came to pay their compliments to me. I was dressed, you may be sure, to all the advantage possible, and had all the jewels on that I was mistress of. My Lord —, to whom I had made the invitation, sent me a set of fine music from the playhouse, and the ladies danced, and we began to be very merry, when about eleven o'clock I had notice given me that there were some gentlemen coming in masquerade. I seemed a little surprised, and began to apprehend some disturbance, when my Lord — perceiving it, spoke to me to be easy, for that there was a party of the guards at the door which should be ready to prevent any rudeness; and another gentleman gave me a hint as if the king was among the masks. I coloured as red as blood itself could make a face look, and expressed a great surprise; however, there was no going back, so I kept my station in my drawing-room, but with the folding-doors wide open.

A while after the masks came in, and began with a dance à la comique, performing wonderfully indeed. While they were dancing I withdrew, and left a lady to answer for me that I would return immediately. In less than half-an-hour I returned, dressed in the habit of a Turkish princess; the habit I got at Leghorn, when my foreign prince bought me a Turkish slave, as I have said. The Maltese man-of-war had, it seems, taken a Turkish vessel going from Constantinople to Alexandria, in which were some ladies bound for Grand Cairo in Egypt; and as the ladies were made slaves, so their fine clothes were thus exposed; and with this Turkish slave I bought the rich clothes too. The dress was extraordinary fine indeed; I had bought it as a curiosity, having never seen the like. The robe was a fine Persian or India damask, the ground white, and the flowers blue and gold, and the train held five yards. The dress under it was a vest of the same, embroidered with gold, and set with some pearl in the work and some turquoise stones. To the vest was a girdle five or six inches wide, after the Turkish mode; and on both ends where it joined, or hooked, was set with diamonds for eight inches either way, only they were not true diamonds, but nobody knew that but myself.

The turban, or head-dress, had a pinnacle on the top, but not above five inches, with a piece of loose sarcenet hanging from it; and on the front, just over the forehead, was a good jewel which I had added to it.

This habit, as above, cost me about sixty pistoles in Italy, but cost much more in the country from whence it came; and little did I think when I bought it that I should put it to such a use as this, though I had dressed myself in it many times by the help of my little Turk, and afterwards between Amy and I, only to see how I looked in it. I had sent her up before to get it ready, and when I came up I had nothing to do but slip it on, and was down in my drawing-room in a little more than a quarter of an hour. When I came there the room was full of company; but I ordered the folding-doors to be shut for a minute or two till I had received the compliments of the ladies that were in the room, and had given them a full view of my dress.

But my Lord ——, who happened to be in the room, slipped out at another door, and brought back with him one of the masks, a tall, well-shaped person, but who had no name, being all masked; nor would it have been allowed to ask any person's name on such an occasion. The person spoke in French to me, that it was the finest dress he had ever seen, and asked me if he should have the honour to dance with me. I bowed, as giving my consent, but said, as I had been a Mahometan, I could not dance after the manner of this country; I supposed their music would not play à la Moresque. He answered merrily. I had a Christian's face, and he'd venture it that I could dance like a Christian; adding that so much beauty could not be Mahometan. Immediately the folding-doors were flung open, and he led me into the room. The company were under the greatest surprise imaginable; the very music stopped awhile to gaze, for the dress was indeed exceedingly surprising, perfectly new, very agreeable, and wonderful rich.

The gentleman, whoever he was, for I never knew, led me only à courant, and then asked me if I had a mind to dance an antic—that is to say, whether I would dance the antic as they had danced in masquerade, or anything by myself. I told him anything else rather, if he pleased; so we danced only two French dances, and he led me to the drawing-room door, when he retired to the rest of the masks. When he left me at the drawing-room door I did not go in, as he thought I would have done, but turned about and showed myself to the whole room, and calling my woman to me, gave her some directions to the music, by which the company presently understood that I would give them a dance by myself. Immediately all the house rose up and paid me a kind of a compliment by removing back every way to make me room, for the place was exceedingly full. The music did not at first hit the tune that I directed, which was a French tune, so I was forced to send my woman to them again, standing all this while at my drawing-room door; but as soon as my woman spoke to them again, they played it right, and I, to let them see it was so, stepped forward to the middle of the room. Then they began it again, and I danced by myself a figure which I learnt in France, when the Prince de —— desired I would dance for his diversion. It was, indeed, a very fine figure, invented by a famous master at Paris, for a lady or a gentleman to dance single; but being perfectly new, it pleased the company exceedingly, and they all thought it had been Turkish; nay, one gentleman had the folly to expose himself so much as to say, and I think swore too, that he had seen it danced at Constantinople, which was ridiculous enough.

At the finishing the dance the company clapped, and almost shouted; and one of the gentlemen cried out "Roxana! Roxana! by ——," with an oath; upon which foolish accident I had the name of Roxana presently fixed upon me all over the court end of town as effectually as if I had been christened Roxana. I had, it seems, the felicity of pleasing everybody that night to an extreme; and my ball, but especially my dress, was the chat of the town for that week; and so the name of Roxana was the toast at and about the court; no other health was to be named with it.

Now things began to work as I would have them, and I began to be very popular, as much as I could desire. The ball held till (as well as I was pleased with the show) I was sick of the night; the gentlemen masked went off about three o'clock in the morning, the other gentlemen sat down to play; the music held it out, and some of the ladies were dancing at six in the morning.

But I was mighty eager to know who it was danced with me. Some of the lords went so far as to tell me I was very much honoured in my company; one of them spoke so broad as almost to say it was the king, but I was convinced afterwards it was not; and another replied if he had been his Majesty he should have thought it no dishonour to lead up a Roxana; but to this hour I never knew positively who it was; and by his behaviour I thought he was too young, his Majesty being at that time in an age that might be discovered from a young person, even in his dancing.

Be that as it would, I had five hundred guineas sent me the next morning, and the messenger was ordered to tell me that the persons who sent it desired a ball again at my lodgings on the next Tuesday, but that they would have my leave to give the entertainment themselves. I was mighty well pleased with this, to be sure, but very inquisitive to know who the money came from; but the messenger was silent as death as to that point, and bowing always at my inquiries, begged me to ask no questions which he could not give an obliging answer to.

I forgot to mention, that the gentlemen that played gave a hundred guineas to the box, as they called it, and at the end of their play they asked for my gentlewoman of the bedchamber, as they called her (Mrs. Amy, forsooth), and gave it her, and gave twenty guineas more among the servants.

These magnificent doings equally both pleased and surprised me, and I hardly knew where I was; but especially that notion of the king being the person that danced with me, puffed me up to that degree, that I not only did not know anybody else, but indeed was very far from knowing myself.

I had now, the next Tuesday, to provide for the like company. But, alas! it was all taken out of my hand. Three gentlemen, who yet were, it seems, but servants, came on the Saturday, and bringing sufficient testimonies that they were right, for one was the same who brought the five hundred guineas; I say, three of them came, and brought bottles of all sorts of wines, and hampers of sweetmeats to such a quantity, it appeared they designed to hold the trade on more than once, and that they would furnish everything to a profusion.

However, as I found a deficiency in two things, I made provision of about twelve dozen of fine damask napkins, with tablecloths of the same, sufficient to cover all the tables, with three tablecloths upon every table, and sideboards in proportion. Also I bought a handsome quantity of plate, necessary to have served all the sideboards; but the gentlemen would not suffer any of it to be used, telling me they had bought fine china dishes and plates for the whole service, and that in such public places they could not be answerable for the plate. So it was set all up in a large glass cupboard in the room I sat in, where it made a very good show indeed.

On Tuesday there came such an appearance of gentlemen and ladies, that my apartments were by no means able to receive them, and those who in particular appeared as principals gave order below to let no more company come up. The street was full of coaches with coronets, and fine glass chairs, and, in short, it was impossible to receive the company. I kept my little room as before, and the dancers filled the great room; all the drawing-rooms also were filled, and three rooms below stairs, which were not mine.

It was very well that there was a strong party of the guards brought to keep the door, for without that there had been such a promiscuous crowd, and some of them scandalous too, that we should have been all disorder and confusion; but the three head servants managed all that, and had a word to admit all the company by.

It was uncertain to me, and is to this day, who it was that danced with me the Wednesday before, when the ball was my own; but that the king was at this assembly was out of question with me, by circumstances that, I suppose, I could not be deceived in, and particularly that there were five persons who were not masked; three of them had blue garters, and they appeared not to me till I came out to dance.

This meeting was managed just as the first, though with much more magnificence, because of the company. I placed myself (exceedingly rich in clothes and jewels) in the middle of my little room, as before, and made my compliment to all the company as they passed me, as I did before. But my Lord ——, who had spoken openly to me the first night, came to me, and, unmasking, told me the company had ordered him to tell me they hoped they should see me in the dress I had appeared in the first day, which had been so acceptable that it had been the occasion of this new meeting. "And, madam," says he, "there are some in this assembly who it is worth your while to oblige."

I bowed to my Lord —, and immediately withdrew. While I was above, a-dressing in my new habit, two ladies, perfectly unknown to me, were conveyed into my apartment below, by the order of a noble person, who, with his family, had been in Persia; and here, indeed, I thought I should have been outdone, or perhaps balked.

One of these ladies was dressed most exquisitely fine indeed, in the habit of a virgin lady of quality of Georgia, and the other in the same habit of Armenia, with each of them a woman slave to attend them.

The ladies had their petticoats short to their ankles, but plaited all round, and before them short aprons, but of the finest point that could be seen. Their gowns were made with long antique sleeves hanging down behind, and a train let down. They had no jewels, but their heads and breasts were dressed up with flowers, and they both came in veiled.

Their slaves were bareheaded, but their long, black hair was braided in locks hanging down behind to their waists, and tied up with ribands. They were dressed exceeding rich, and were as beautiful as their mistresses; for none of them had any masks on. They waited in my room till I came down, and all paid their respects to me after the Persian manner, and sat down on a safra—that is to say, almost crosslegged, on a couch made up of cushions laid on the ground.

This was admirably fine, and I was indeed startled at it. They made their compliment to me in French, and I replied in the same language. When the doors were opened, they walked into the dancing-room, and danced such a dance as indeed nobody there had ever seen, and to an instrument like a guitar, with a small low-sounding trumpet, which indeed was very fine, and which my Lord — had provided.
They danced three times all alone, for nobody indeed could dance with them. The novelty pleased, truly, but yet there was something wild and bizarre in it, because they really acted to the life the barbarous country whence they came; but as mine had the French behaviour under the Mahometan dress, it was every way as new, and pleased much better indeed.

As soon as they had shown their Georgian and Armenian shapes, and danced, as I have said, three times, they withdrew, paid their compliment to me (for I was queen of the day), and went off to undress.

Some gentlemen then danced with ladies all in masks; and when they stopped, nobody rose up to dance, but all called out "Roxana, Roxana." In the interval, my Lord — had brought another masked person into my room, who I knew not, only that I could discern it was not the same person that led me out before. This noble person (for I afterwards understood it was the Duke of —), after a short compliment, led me out into the middle of the room.

I was dressed in the same vest and girdle as before, but the robe had a mantle over it, which is usual in the Turkish habit, and it was of crimson and green, the green brocaded with gold; and my tyhiaai, or head-dress, varied a little from that I had before, as it stood higher, and had some jewels about the rising part, which made it look like a turban crowned.

I had no mask, neither did I paint, and yet I had the day of all the ladies that appeared at the ball, I mean of those that appeared with faces on. As for those masked, nothing could be said of them, no doubt there might be many finer than I was; it must be confessed that the habit was infinitely advantageous to me, and everybody looked at me with a kind of pleasure, which gave me great advantage too.

After I had danced with that noble person, I did not offer to dance by myself, as I had before; but they all called out "Roxana" again; and two of the gentlemen came into the drawing-room to entreat me to give them the Turkish dance, which I yielded to readily, so I came out and danced just as at first.

While I was dancing, I perceived five persons standing all together, and among them only one with his hat on. It was an immediate hint to me who it was, and had at first almost put me into some disorder; but I went on, received the applause of the house, as before, and retired into my own room. When I was there, the five gentlemen came across the room to my side, and, coming in, followed by a throng of great persons, the person with his hat on said, "Madam Roxana, you perform to admiration." I was prepared, and offered to kneel to kiss his hand, but he declined it, and saluted me, and so, passing back again through the great room, went away.

I do not say here who this was, but I say I came afterwards to know something more plainly. I would have withdrawn, and disrobed, being somewhat too thin in that dress, unlaced and open-breasted, as if I had been in my shift; but it could not be, and I was obliged to dance afterwards with six or eight gentlemen most, if not all of them, of the first rank; and I was told afterwards that one of them was the Duke of M[onmou]th.
About two or three o'clock in the morning the company began to decrease; the number of women especially dropped away home, some and some at a time; and the gentlemen retired downstairs, where they unmasked and went to play.

Amy waited at the room where they played, sat up all night to attend them, and in the morning when they broke up they swept the box into her lap, when she counted out to me sixty-two guineas and a half; and the other servants got very well too. Amy came to me when they were all gone; "Law, madam," says Amy, with a long gaping cry, "what shall I do with all this money?" And indeed the poor creature was half mad with joy.

I was now in my element. I was as much talked of as anybody could desire, and I did not doubt but something or other would come of it; but the report of my being so rich rather was a balk to my view than anything else; for the gentlemen that would perhaps have been troublesome enough otherwise, seemed to be kept off, for Roxana was too high for them.

There is a scene which came in here which I must cover from human eyes or ears. For three years and about a month Roxana lived retired, having been obliged to make an excursion in a manner, and with a person which duty and private vows obliges her not to reveal, at least not yet.

At the end of this time I appeared again; but, I must add, that as I had in this time of retreat made hay, &c., so I did not come abroad again with the same lustre, or shine with so much advantage as before. For as some people had got at least a suspicion of where I had been, and who had had me all the while, it began to be public that Roxana was, in short, a mere Roxana, neither better nor worse, and not that woman of honour and virtue that was at first supposed.

You are now to suppose me about seven years come to town, and that I had not only suffered the old revenue, which I hinted was managed by Sir Robert Clayton, to grow, as was mentioned before, but I had laid up an incredible wealth, the time considered; and had I yet had the least thought of reforming, I had all the opportunity to do it with advantage that ever woman had. For the common vice of all whores, I mean money, was out of the question, nay, even avarice itself seemed to be glutted; for, including what I had saved in reserving the interest of £14,000, which, as above, I had left to grow, and including some very good presents I had made to me in mere compliment upon these shining masquerading meetings, which I held up for about two years, and what I made of three years of the most glorious retreat, as I call it, that ever woman had, I had fully doubled my first substance, and had near £5000 in money which I kept at home, besides abundance of plate and jewels, which I had either given me or had bought to set myself out for public days.

In a word, I had now five-and-thirty thousand pounds estate; and as I found ways to live without wasting either principal or interest, I laid up £2000 every year at least out of the mere interest, adding it to the principal, and thus I went on.

After the end of what I call my retreat, and out of which I brought a great deal of money, I appeared again, but I seemed like an old piece of plate that had been hoarded up some years, and comes out tarnished and discoloured; so I came out blown, and looked like a cast-off mistress; nor, indeed, was I any better, though I was not at all impaired in beauty except that I was a little fatter than I was formerly, and always granting that I was four years older.

However, I preserved the youth of my temper, was always bright, pleasant in company, and agreeable to everybody, or else everybody flattered me; and in this condition I came abroad to the world again. And though I was not so popular as before, and indeed did not seek it, because I knew it could not be, yet I was far from being without company, and that of the greatest quality (of subjects I mean), who frequently visited me, and sometimes we had meetings for mirth and play at my apartments, where I failed not to divert them in the most agreeable manner possible.

Nor could any of them make the least particular application to me, from the notion they had of my excessive wealth, which, as they thought, placed me above the meanness of a maintenance, and so left no room to come easily about me.

But at last I was very handsomely attacked by a person of honour, and (which recommended him particularly to me) a person of a very great estate. He made a long introduction to me upon the subject of my wealth. "Ignorant creature!" said I to myself, considering him as a lord, "was there ever woman in the world that could stoop to the baseness of being a whore, and was above taking the reward of her vice! No, no, depend upon it, if your lordship obtains anything of me, you must pay for it; and the notion of my being so rich serves only to make it cost you the dearer, seeing you cannot offer a small matter to a woman of £2000 a year estate."

After he had harangued upon that subject a good while, and had assured me he had no design upon me, that he did not come to make a prize of me, or to pick my pocket, which, by the way, I was in no fear of, for I took too much care of my money to part with any of it that way, he then turned his discourse to the subject of love, a point so ridiculous to me without the main thing, I mean the money, that I had no patience to hear him make so long a story of it.

I received him civilly, and let him see I could bear to hear a wicked proposal without being affronted, and yet I was not to be brought into it too easily. He visited me a long while, and, in short, courted me as closely and assiduously as if he had been wooing me to matrimony. He made me several valuable presents, which I suffered myself to be prevailed with to accept, but not without great difficulty.

Gradually I suffered also his other importunities; and when he made a proposal of a compliment or appointment to me for a settlement, he said that though I was rich, yet there was not the less due from him to acknowledge the favours he received; and that if I was to be his I should not live at my own expense, cost what it would. I told him I was far from being extravagant, and yet I did not live at the expense of less than £500 a year out of my own pocket; that, however, I was not covetous of settled allowances, for I looked upon that as a kind of golden chain, something like matrimony; that though I knew how to be true to a man of honour, as I knew his lordship to be, yet I had a kind of aversion to the bonds; and though I was not so rich as the world talked me up to be, yet I was not so poor as to bind myself to hardships for a pension.

He told me he expected to make my life perfectly easy, and intended it so; that he knew of no bondage there could be in a private engagement between us; that the bonds of honour he knew I would be tied by, and think them no burthen; and for other obligations, he scorned to expect anything from me but what he knew as a woman of honour I could grant. Then as to maintenance, he told me he would soon show me that he valued me infinitely above £500 a year, and upon this foot we began.

I seemed kinder to him after this discourse, and as time and private conversation made us very intimate, we began to come nearer to the main article, namely, the £500 a year. He offered that at first word, and to acknowledge it as an infinite favour to have it be accepted of; and I, that thought it was too much by all the money, suffered myself to be mastered, or prevailed with to yield, even on but a bare engagement upon parole.

When he had obtained his end that way, I told him my mind. "Now you see, my lord," said I, "how weakly I have acted, namely, to yield to you without any capitulation, or anything secured to me but that which you may cease to allow when you please. If I am the less valued for such a confidence, I shall be injured in a manner that I will endeavour not to deserve."

He told me that he would make it evident to me that he did not seek me by way of bargain, as such things were often done; that as I had treated him with a generous confidence, so I should find I was in the hands of a man of honour, and one that knew how to value the obligation; and upon this he pulled out a goldsmith's bill for £300, which (putting it into my hand), he said, he gave me as a pledge that I should not be a loser by my not having made a bargain with him.

This was engaging indeed, and gave me a good idea of our future correspondence; and, in short, as I could not refrain treating him with more kindness than I had done before, so one thing begetting another, I gave him several testimonies that I was entirely his own by inclination as well as by the common obligation of a mistress, and this pleased him exceedingly.

Soon after this private engagement I began to consider whether it were not more suitable to the manner of life I now led to be a little less public; and, as I told my lord, it would rid me of the importunities of others, and of continual visits from a sort of people who he knew of, and who, by the way, having now got the notion of me which I really deserved, began to talk of the old game, love and gallantry, and to offer at what was rude enough—things as nauseous to me now as if I had been married and as virtuous as other people. The visits of these people began indeed to be uneasy to me, and particularly as they were always very tedious and impertinent; nor could my Lord —— be pleased with them at all if they had gone on. It would be diverting to set down here in what manner I repulsed these sort of people; how in some I resented it as an affront, and told them that I was sorry they should oblige me to vindicate myself from the scandal of such suggestions by telling them that I could see them no more, and by desiring them not to give themselves the trouble of visiting me, who, though I was not willing to be uncivil, yet thought myself obliged never to receive any visit from any gentleman after he had made such proposals as those to me. But these things would be too tedious to bring in here. It was on this account I proposed to his lordship my taking new lodgings for privacy; besides, I considered that as I might live very handsomely, and yet not so publicly, so I needed not spend so much money by a great deal; and if I made £500 a year of this generous person, it was more than I had any occasion to spend by a great deal.

My lord came readily into this proposal, and went further than I expected, for he found out a lodging for me in a very handsome house, where yet he was not known—I suppose he had employed somebody to find it out for him—and where he had a convenient way to come into the garden by a door that opened into the park, a thing very rarely allowed in those times.

By this key he could come in at what time of night or day he pleased; and as we had also a little door in the lower part of the house which was always left upon a lock, and his was the master-key, so if it was twelve, one, or two o'clock at night, he could come directly into my bedchamber. N.B.—I was not afraid I should be found abed with anybody else, for, in a word, I conversed with nobody at all.

It happened pleasantly enough one night, his lordship had stayed late, and I, not expecting him that night, had taken Amy to bed with me, and when my lord came into the chamber we were both fast asleep. I think it was near three o'clock when he came in, and a little merry, but not at all fuddled or what they call in drink; and he came at once into the room.

Amy was frighted out of her wits, and cried out. I said calmly, "Indeed, my lord, I did not expect you to-night, and we have been a little frighted to-night with fire." "Oh!" says he, "I see you have got a bedfellow with you." I began to make an apology. "No, no," says my lord, "you need no excuse, 'tis not a man bedfellow, I see;" but then, talking merrily enough, he catched his words back: "But, hark ye," says he, "now I think on 't, how shall I be satisfied it is not a man bedfellow?" "Oh," says I, "I dare say your lordship is satisfied 'tis poor Amy." "Yes," says he, "'tis Mrs. Amy; but how do I know what Amy is? it may be Mr. Amy for aught I know; I hope you'll give me leave to be satisfied." I told him, yes, by all means, I would have his lordship satisfied; but I supposed he knew who she was.

Well, he fell foul of poor Amy, and indeed I thought once he would have carried the jest on before my face, as was once done in a like case; but his lordship was not so hot neither, but he would know whether Amy was Mr. Amy or Mrs. Amy, and so, I suppose, he did; and then being satisfied in that doubtful case, he walked to the farther end of the room, and went into a little closet and sat down.

In the meantime Amy and I got up, and I bid her run and make the bed in another chamber for my lord, and I gave her sheets to put into it; which she did immediately, and I put my lord to bed there, and when I had done, at his desire went to bed to him. I was backward at first to come to bed to him, and made my excuse because I had been in bed with Amy, and had not shifted me; but he was past those niceties at that time; and as long as he was sure it was Mrs. Amy, and not Mr. Amy, he was very well satisfied, and so the jest passed over. But Amy appeared no more all that night, or the next day, and when she did, my lord was so merry with her upon his eclaircissement, as he called it, that Amy did not know what to do with herself.

Not that Amy was such a nice lady in the main, if she had been fairly dealt with, as has appeared in the former part of this work; but now she was surprised, and a little hurried, that she scarce knew where she was; and besides, she was, as to his lordship, as nice a lady as any in the world, and for anything he knew of her she appeared as such. The rest was to us only that knew of it.

I held this wicked scene of life out eight years, reckoning from my first coming to England; and though my lord found no fault, yet I found, without much examining, that any one who looked in my face might see I was above twenty years old; and yet, without flattering myself, I carried my age, which was above fifty, very well too.

I may venture to say that no woman ever lived a life like me, of six-and-twenty years of wickedness, without the least signals of remorse, without any signs of repentance, or without so much as a wish to put an end to it; I had so long habituated myself to a life of vice, that really it appeared to be no vice to me. I went on smooth and pleasant, I wallowed in wealth, and it flowed in upon me at such a rate, having taken the frugal measures that the good knight directed, so that I had at the end of the eight years two thousand eight hundred pounds coming yearly in, of which I did not spend one penny, being maintained by my allowance from my Lord ——, and more than maintained by above £200 per annum; for though he did not contract for £500 a year, as I made dumb signs to have it be, yet he gave me money so often, and that in such large parcels, that I had seldom so little as seven to eight hundred pounds a year of him, one year with another.

THE DUTCH MERCHANT CALLS ON ROXANA

I must go back here, after telling openly the wicked things I did, to mention something which, however, had the face of doing good. I remembered that when I went from England, which was fifteen years before, I had left five little children, turned out as it were to the wide world, and to the charity of their father's relations; the eldest was not six years old, for we had not been married full seven years when their father went away.

After my coming to England I was greatly desirous to hear how things stood with them, and whether they were all alive or not, and in what manner they had been maintained; and yet I resolved not to discover myself to them in the least, or to let any of the people that had the breeding of them up know that there was such a body left in the world as their mother.

Amy was the only body I could trust with such a commission, and I sent her into Spitalfields, to the old aunt and to the poor woman that were so instrumental in disposing the relations to take some care of the children, but they were both gone, dead and buried some years. The next inquiry she made was at the house where she carried the poor children, and turned them in at the door. When she came there she found the house inhabited by other people, so that she could make little or nothing of her inquiries, and came back with an answer that indeed was no answer to me, for it gave me no satisfaction at all. I sent her back to inquire in the neighbourhood what was become of the family that lived in that house; and if they were removed, where they lived, and what circumstances they were in; and, withal, if she could, what became of the poor children, and how they lived, and where; how they had been treated; and the like.

She brought me back word upon this second going, that she heard, as to the family, that the husband, who, though but uncle-in-law to the children, had yet been kindest to them, was dead; and that the widow was left but in mean circumstances—that is to say, she did not want, but that she was not so well in the world as she was thought to be when her husband was alive; that, as to the poor children, two of them, it seems, had been kept by her, that is to say, by her husband, while he lived, for that it was against her will, that we all knew; but the honest neighbours pitied the poor children, they said, heartily; for that their aunt used them barbarously, and made them little better than servants in the house to wait upon her and her children, and scarce allowed them clothes fit to wear.

These were, it seems, my eldest and third, which were daughters; the second was a son, the fourth a daughter, and the youngest a son.
To finish the melancholy part of this history of my two unhappy girls, she brought me word that as soon as they were able to go out and get any work they went from her, and some said she had turned them out of doors; but it seems she had not done so, but she used them so cruelly that they left her, and one of them went to service to a neighbour's, a little way off, who knew her, an honest, substantial weaver's wife, to whom she was chambermaid, and in a little time she took her sister out of the Bridewell of her aunt's house, and got her a place too.

This was all melancholy and dull. I sent her then to the weaver's house, where the eldest had lived, but found that, her mistress being dead, she was gone, and nobody knew there whither she went, only that they heard she had lived with a great lady at the other end of the town; but they did not know who that lady was.

These inquiries took us up three or four weeks, and I was not one jot the better for it, for I could hear nothing to my satisfaction. I sent her next to find out the honest man who, as in the beginning of my story I observed, made them be entertained, and caused the youngest to be fetched from the town where we lived, and where the parish officers had taken care of him. This gentleman was still alive; and there she heard that my youngest daughter and eldest son was dead also; but that my youngest son was alive, and was at that time about seventeen years old, and that he was put out apprentice by the kindness and charity of his uncle, but to a mean trade, and at which he was obliged to work very hard.

Amy was so curious in this part that she went immediately to see him, and found him all dirty and hard at work. She had no remembrance at all of the youth, for she had not seen him since he was about two years old; and it was evident he could have no knowledge of her.

However, she talked with him, and found him a good, sensible, mannerly youth; that he knew little of the story of his father or mother, and had no view of anything but to work hard for his living; and she did not think fit to put any great things into his head, lest it should take him off of his business, and perhaps make him turn giddy-headed and be good for nothing; but she went and found out that kind man, his benefactor, who had put him out, and finding him a plain, well-meaning, honest, and kind-hearted man, she opened her tale to him the easier. She made a long story, how she had a prodigious kindness for the child, because she had the same for his father and mother; told him that she was the servant-maid that brought all of them to their aunt's door, and run away and left them; that their poor mother wanted bread, and what came of her after she would have been glad to know. She added that her circumstances had happened to mend in the world, and that, as she was in condition, so she was disposed to show some kindness to the children if she could find them out.

He received her with all the civility that so kind a proposal demanded, gave her an account of what he had done for the child, how he had maintained him, fed and clothed him, put him to school, and at last put him out to a trade. She said he had indeed been a father to the child. "But, sir," says she, "'tis a very laborious, hard-working trade, and he is but a thin, weak boy." "That's true," says he; "but the boy chose the trade, and I assure you I gave £20 with him, and am to find him clothes all his apprenticeship; and as to its being a hard trade," says he, "that's the fate of his circumstances, poor boy. I could not well do better for him."

"Well, sir, as you did all for him in charity," says she, "it was exceeding well; but, as my resolution is to do something for him, I desire you will, if possible, take him away again from that place, where he works so hard, for I cannot bear to see the child work so very hard for his bread, and I will do something for him that shall make him live without such hard labour."

He smiled at that. "I can, indeed," says he, "take him away, but then I must lose my £20 that I gave with him."

"Well, sir," said Amy, "I'll enable you to lose that £20 immediately;" and so she put her hand in her pocket and pulls out her purse.

He begun to be a little amazed at her, and looked her hard in the face, and that so very much that she took notice of it, and said, "Sir, I fancy by your looking at me you think you know me, but I am assured you do not, for I never saw your face before. I think you have done enough for the child, and that you ought to be acknowledged as a father to him; but you ought not to lose by your kindness to him, more than the kindness of bringing him up obliges you to; and therefore there's the £20," added she, "and pray let him be fetched away."

"Well, madam," says he, "I will thank you for the boy, as well as for myself; but will you please to tell me what I must do with him?"

"Sir," says Amy, "as you have been so kind to keep him so many years, I beg you will take him home again one year more, and I'll bring you a hundred pounds more, which I will desire you to lay out in schooling and clothes for him, and to pay you for his board. Perhaps I may put him in a condition to return your kindness."

He looked pleased, but surprised very much, and inquired of Amy, but with very great respect, what he should go to school to learn, and what trade she would please to put him out to.

Amy said he should put him to learn a little Latin, and then merchants' accounts, and to write a good hand, for she would have him be put to a Turkey merchant.

"Madam," says he, "I am glad for his sake to hear you talk so; but do you know that a Turkey merchant will not take him under £400 or £500?"

"Yes, sir," says Amy, "I know it very well."

"And," says he, "that it will require as many thousands to set him up?"

"Yes, sir," says Amy, "I know that very well too;" and, resolving to talk very big, she added, "I have no children of my own, and I resolve to make him my heir, and if £10,000 be required to set him up, he shall not want it. I was but his mother's servant when he was born, and I mourned heartily for the disaster of the family, and I always said, if ever I was worth anything in the world, I would take the child for my own, and I'll be as good as my word now, though I did not then foresee that it would be with me as it has been since." And so Amy told him a long story how she was troubled for me, and what she would give to hear whether I was dead or alive, and what circumstances I was in; that if she could but find me, if I was ever so poor, she would take care of me, and make a gentlewoman of me again.

He told her that, as to the child's mother, she had been reduced to the last extremity, and was obliged (as he supposed she knew) to send the children all among her husband's friends; and if it had not been for him, they had all been sent to the parish; but that he obliged the other relations to share the charge among them; that he had taken two, whereof he had lost the eldest, who died of the smallpox, but that he had been as careful of this as of his own, and had made very little difference in their breeding up, only that when he came to put him out he thought it was best for the boy to put him to a trade which he might set up in without a stock, for otherwise his time would be lost; and that as to his mother, he had never been able to hear one word of her, no, not though he had made the utmost inquiry after her; that there went a report that she had drowned herself, but that he could never meet with anybody that could give him a certain account of it.

Amy counterfeited a cry for her poor mistress; told him she would give anything in the world to see her, if she was alive; and a great deal more such-like talk they had about that; then they returned to speak of the boy.

He inquired of her why she did not seek after the child before, that he might have been brought up from a younger age, suitable to what she designed to do for him.

She told him she had been out of England, and was but newly returned from the East Indies. That she had been out of England, and was but newly returned, was true, but the latter was false, and was put in to blind him, and provide against farther inquiries; for it was not a strange thing for young women to go away poor to the East Indies, and come home vastly rich. So she went on with directions about him, and both agreed in this, that the boy should by no means be told what was intended for him, but only that he should be taken home again to his uncle's, that his uncle thought the trade too hard for him, and the like.

About three days after this Amy goes again, and carried him the hundred pounds she promised him, but then Amy made quite another figure than she did before; for she went in my coach, with two footmen after her, and dressed very fine also, with jewels and a gold watch; and there was indeed no great difficulty to make Amy look like a lady, for she was a very handsome, well-shaped woman, and genteel enough. The coachman and servants were particularly ordered to show her the same respect as they would to me, and to call her Madam Collins, if they were asked any questions about her.

When the gentleman saw what a figure she made it added to the former surprise, and he entertained her in the most respectful manner possible, congratulated her advancement in fortune, and particularly rejoiced that it should fall to the poor child's lot to be so provided for, contrary to all expectation.

Well, Amy talked big, but very free and familiar, told them she had no pride in her good fortune (and that was true enough, for, to give Amy her due, she was far from it, and was as good-humoured a creature as ever lived); that she was the same as ever; and that she always loved this boy, and was resolved to do something extraordinary for him.

Then she pulled out her money, and paid him down a hundred and twenty pounds, which, she said, she paid him that he might be sure he should be no loser by taking him home again, and that she would come and see him again, and talk farther about things with him, so that all might be settled for him, in such a manner as accidents, such as mortality, or anything else, should make no alteration to the child's prejudice.

At this meeting the uncle brought his wife out, a good, motherly, comely, grave woman, who spoke very tenderly of the youth, and, as it appeared, had been very good to him, though she had several children of her own. After a long discourse, she put in a word of her own. "Madam," says she, "I am heartily glad of the good intentions you have for this poor orphan, and I rejoice sincerely in it for his sake; but, madam, you know, I suppose, that there are two sisters alive too; may we not speak a word for them? Poor girls," says she, "they have not been so kindly used as he has, and are turned out to the wide world."

"Where are they, madam?" says Amy.

"Poor creatures," says the gentlewoman, "they are out at service, nobody knows where but themselves; their case is very hard."

"Well, madam," says Amy, "though if I could find them I would assist them, yet my concern is for my boy, as I call him, and I will put him into a condition to take care of his sisters."

"But, madam," says the good, compassionate creature, "he may not be so charitable perhaps by his own inclination, for brothers are not fathers, and they have been cruelly used already, poor girls; we have often relieved them, both with victuals and clothes too, even while they were pretended to be kept by their barbarous aunt."

"Well, madam," says Amy, "what can I do for them? They are gone, it seems, and cannot be heard of. When I see them 'tis time enough."

She pressed Amy then to oblige their brother, out of the plentiful fortune he was like to have, to do something for his sisters when he should be able.

Amy spoke coldly of that still, but said she would consider of it; and so they parted for that time. They had several meetings after this, for Amy went to see her adopted son, and ordered his schooling, clothes, and other things, but enjoined them not to tell the young man anything, but that they thought the trade he was at too hard for him, and they would keep him at home a little longer, and give him some schooling to fit him for other business; and Amy appeared to him as she did before, only as one that had known his mother and had some kindness for him.

Thus this matter passed on for near a twelvemonth, when it happened that one of my maid-servants having asked Amy leave (for Amy was mistress of the servants, and took and put out such as she pleased)—I say, having asked leave to go into the city to see her friends, came home crying bitterly, and in a most grievous agony she was, and continued so several days till Amy, perceiving the excess, and that the maid would certainly cry herself sick, she took an opportunity with her and examined her about it.

The maid told her a long story, that she had been to see her brother, the only brother she had in the world, and that she knew he was put out apprentice to a —; but there had come a lady in a coach to his uncle —, who had brought him up, and made him take him home again; and so the wench run on with the whole story just as 'tis told above, till she came to that part that belonged to herself. "And there," says she, "I had not let them know where I lived, and the lady would have taken me, and, they say, would have provided for me too, as she has done for my brother; but nobody could tell where to find me, and so I have lost it all, and all the hopes of being anything but a poor servant all my days;" and then the girl fell a-crying again.

Amy said, "What's all this story? Who could this lady be? It must be some trick, sure." "No," she said, "it was not a trick, for she had made them take her brother home from apprentice, and bought him new clothes, and put him to have more learning; and the gentlewoman said she would make him her heir."

"Her heir!" says Amy. "What does that amount to? It may be she had nothing to leave him; she might make anybody her heir."

"No, no," says the girl; "she came in a fine coach and horses, and I don't know how many footmen to attend her, and brought a great bag of gold and gave it to my uncle —, he that brought up my brother, to buy him clothes and to pay for his schooling and board."

"He that brought up your brother?" says Amy. "Why, did not he bring you up too as well as your brother? Pray who brought you up, then?"

Here the poor girl told a melancholy story, how an aunt had brought up her and her sister, and how barbarously she had used them, as we have heard.

By this time Amy had her head full enough, and her heart too, and did not know how to hold it, or what to do, for she was satisfied that this was no other than my own daughter, for she told her all the history of her father and mother, and how she was carried by their maid to her aunt's door, just as is related in the beginning of my story.

Amy did not tell me this story for a great while, nor did she well know what course to take in it; but as she had authority to manage everything in the family, she took occasion some time after, without letting me know anything of it, to find some fault with the maid and turn her away.

Her reasons were good, though at first I was not pleased when I heard of it, but I was convinced afterwards that she was in the right, for if she had told me of it I should have been in great perplexity between the difficulty of concealing myself from my own child and the inconvenience of having my way of living be known among my first husband's relations, and even to my husband himself; for as to his being dead at Paris, Amy, seeing me resolved against marrying any more, had told me that she had formed that story only to make me easy when I was in Holland if anything should offer to my liking.

However, I was too tender a mother still, notwithstanding what I had done, to let this poor girl go about the world drudging, as it were, for bread, and slaving at the fire and in the kitchen as a cook-maid; besides, it came into my head that she might perhaps marry some poor devil of a footman, or a coachman, or some such thing, and be undone that way, or, which was worse, be drawn in to lie with some of that coarse, cursed kind, and be with child, and be utterly ruined that way; and in the midst of all my prosperity this gave me great uneasiness.

As to sending Amy to her, there was no doing that now, for, as she had been servant in the house, she knew Amy as well as Amy knew me; and no doubt, though I was much out of her sight, yet she might have had the curiosity to have peeped at me, and seen me enough to know me again if I had discovered myself to her; so that, in short, there was nothing to be done that way.

However, Amy, a diligent indefatigable creature, found out another woman, and gave her her errand, and sent her to the honest man's house in Spitalfields, whither she supposed the girl would go after she was out of her place; and bade her talk with her, and tell her at a distance that as something had been done for her brother, so something would be done for her too; and, that she should not be discouraged, she carried her £20 to buy her clothes, and bid her not go to service any more, but think of other things; that she should take a lodging in some good family, and that she should soon hear farther.

The girl was overjoyed with this news, you may be sure, and at first a little too much elevated with it, and dressed herself very handsomely indeed, and as soon as she had done so came and paid a visit to Madam Amy, to let her see how fine she was. Amy congratulated her, and wished it might be all as she expected, but admonished her not to be elevated with it too much; told her humility was the best ornament of a gentlewoman, and a great deal of good advice she gave her, but discovered nothing.

All this was acted in the first years of my setting up my new figure here in town, and while the masks and balls were in agitation; and Amy carried on the affair of setting out my son into the world, which we were assisted in by the sage advice of my faithful counsellor, Sir Robert Clayton, who procured us a master for him, by whom he was afterwards sent abroad to Italy, as you shall hear in its place; and Amy managed my daughter too very well, though by a third hand.

My amour with my Lord —— began now to draw to an end, and indeed, notwithstanding his money, it had lasted so long that I was much more sick of his lordship than he could be of me. He grew old and fretful, and captious, and I must add, which made the vice itself begin to grow surfeiting and nauseous to me, he grew worse and wickeder the older he grew, and that to such degree as is not fit to write of, and made me so weary of him that upon one of his capricious humours, which he often took occasion to trouble me with, I took occasion to be much less complaisant to him than I used to be; and as I knew him to be hasty, I first took care to put him into a little passion, and then to resent it, and this brought us to words, in which I told him I thought he grew sick of me; and he answered in a heat that truly so he was. I answered that I found his lordship was endeavouring to make me sick too; that I had met with several such rubs from him of late, and that he did not use me as he used to do, and I begged his lordship he would make himself easy. This I spoke with an air of coldness and indifference such as I knew he could not bear; but I did not downright quarrel with him and tell him I was sick of him too, and desire him to quit me, for I knew that would come of itself; besides, I had received a great deal of handsome usage from him, and I was loth to have the breach be on my side, that he might not be able to say I was ungrateful.

THE AMOUR DRAWS TO AN END

I told him I thought he grew sick of me; and he
answered in a heat that truly so he was

THE AMOUR DRAWS TO AN END
I told him I thought he grew sick of me; and he answered in a heat that truly so he was
But he put the occasion into my hands, for he came no more to me for two months; indeed I expected a fit of absence, for such I had had several times before, but not for above a fortnight or three weeks at most; but after I had stayed a month, which was longer than ever he kept away yet, I took a new method with him, for I was resolved now it should be in my power to continue or not, as I thought fit. At the end of a month, therefore, I removed, and took lodgings at Kensington Gravel Pits, at that part next to the road to Acton, and left nobody in my lodgings but Amy and a footman, with proper instructions how to behave when his lordship, being come to himself, should think fit to come again, which I knew he would.

About the end of two months, he came in the dusk of the evening as usual. The footman answered him, and told him his lady was not at home, but there was Mrs. Amy above; so he did not order her to be called down, but went upstairs into the dining-room, and Mrs. Amy came to him. He asked where I was. "My lord," said she, "my mistress has been removed a good while from hence, and lives at Kensington." "Ah, Mrs. Amy! how came you to be here, then?" "My lord," said she, "we are here till the quarter-day, because the goods are not removed, and to give answers if any comes to ask for my lady." "Well, and what answer are you to give to me?" "Indeed, my lord," says Amy, "I have no particular answer to your lordship, but to tell you and everybody else where my lady lives, that they may not think she's run away." "No, Mrs. Amy," says he, "I don't think she's run away; but, indeed, I can't go after her so far as that." Amy said nothing to that, but made a courtesy, and said she believed I would be there again for a week or two in a little time. "How little time, Mrs Amy?" says my lord. "She comes next Tuesday," says Amy. "Very well," says my lord; "I'll call and see her then;" and so he went away.

Accordingly I came on the Tuesday, and stayed a fortnight, but he came not; so I went back to Kensington, and after that I had very few of his lordship's visits, which I was very glad of, and in a little time after was more glad of it than I was at first, and upon a far better account too.

For now I began not to be sick of his lordship only, but really I began to be sick of the vice; and as I had good leisure now to divert and enjoy myself in the world as much as it was possible for any woman to do that ever lived in it, so I found that my judgment began to prevail upon me to fix my delight upon nobler objects than I had formerly done, and the very beginning of this brought some just reflections upon me relating to things past, and to the former manner of my living; and though there was not the least hint in all this from what may be called religion or conscience, and far from anything of repentance, or anything that was akin to it, especially at first, yet the sense of things, and the knowledge I had of the world, and the vast variety of scenes that I had acted my part in, began to work upon my senses, and it came so very strong upon my mind one morning when I had been lying awake some time in my bed, as if somebody had asked me the question, What was I a whore for now? It occurred naturally upon this inquiry, that at first I yielded to the importunity of my circumstances, the misery of which the devil dismally aggravated, to draw me to comply; for I confess I had strong natural aversions to the crime at first, partly owing to a virtuous education, and partly to a sense of religion; but the devil, and that greater devil of poverty, prevailed; and the person who laid siege to me did it in such an obliging, and I may almost say irresistible, manner, all still managed by the evil spirit; for I must be allowed to believe that he has a share in all such things, if not the whole management of them. But, I say, it was carried on by that person in such an irresistible manner that, as I said when I related the fact, there was no withstanding it; these circumstances, I say, the devil managed not only to bring me to comply, but he continued them as arguments to fortify my mind against all reflection, and to keep me in that horrid course I had engaged in, as if it were honest and lawful.

But not to dwell upon that now; this was a pretence, and here was something to be said, though I acknowledge it ought not to have been sufficient to me at all; but, I say, to leave that, all this was out of doors; the devil himself could not form one argument, or put one reason into my head now, that could serve for an answer—no, not so much as a pretended answer to this question, why I should be a whore now.

It had for a while been a little kind of excuse to me that I was engaged with this wicked old lord, and that I could not in honour forsake him; but how foolish and absurd did it look to repeat the word "honour" on so vile an occasion! as if a woman should prostitute her honour in point of honour—horrid inconsistency! Honour called upon me to detest the crime and the man too, and to have resisted all the attacks which, from the beginning, had been made upon my virtue; and honour, had it been consulted, would have preserved me honest from the beginning:

"For 'honesty' and 'honour' are the same."

This, however, shows us with what faint excuses and with what trifles we pretend to satisfy ourselves, and suppress the attempts of conscience, in the pursuit of agreeable crime, and in the possessing those pleasures which we are loth to part with.

130

But this objection would now serve no longer, for my lord had in some sort broke his engagements (I won't call it honour again) with me, and had so far slighted me as fairly to justify my entire quitting of him now; and so, as the objection was fully answered, the question remained still unanswered, Why am I a whore now? Nor indeed had I anything to say for myself, even to myself; I could not without blushing, as wicked as I was, answer that I loved it for the sake of the vice, and that I delighted in being a whore, as such; I say, I could not say this, even to myself, and all alone, nor indeed would it have been true. I was never able, in justice and with truth, to say I was so wicked as that; but as necessity first debauched me, and poverty made me a whore at the beginning, so excess of avarice for getting money and excess of vanity continued me in the crime, not being able to resist the flatteries of great persons; being called the finest woman in France; being caressed by a prince; and afterwards, I had pride enough to expect and folly enough to believe, though indeed without ground, by a great monarch. These were my baits, these the chains by which the devil held me bound, and by which I was indeed too fast held for any reasoning that I was then mistress of to deliver me from.

But this was all over now; avarice could have no pretence. I was out of the reach of all that fate could be supposed to do to reduce me; now I was so far from poor, or the danger of it, that I had £50,000 in my pocket at least; nay, I had the income of £50,000, for I had £2500 a year coming in upon very good land security, besides three or four thousand pounds in money, which I kept by me for ordinary occasions, and, besides, jewels, and plate, and goods which were worth near £5600 more; these put together, when I ruminated on it all in my thoughts, as you may be sure I did often, added weight still to the question, as above, and it sounded continually in my head, "What next? What am I a whore for now?"

It is true this was, as I say, seldom out of my thoughts, but yet it made no impressions upon me of that kind which might be expected from a reflection of so important a nature, and which had so much of substance and seriousness in it.

But, however, it was not without some little consequences, even at that time, and which gave a little turn to my way of living at first, as you shall hear in its place.

But one particular thing intervened besides this which gave me some uneasiness at this time, and made way for other things that followed. I have mentioned in several little digressions the concern I had upon me for my children, and in what manner I had directed that affair; I must go on a little with that part, in order to bring the subsequent parts of my story together.

My boy, the only son I had left that I had a legal right to call "son," was, as I have said, rescued from the unhappy circumstances of being apprentice to a mechanic, and was brought up upon a new foot; but though this was infinitely to his advantage, yet it put him back near three years in his coming into this world; for he had been near a year at the drudgery he was first put to, and it took up two years more to form him for what he had hopes given him he should hereafter be, so that he was full nineteen years old, or rather twenty years, before he came to be put out as I intended; at the end of which time I put him to a very flourishing Italian merchant, and he again sent him to Messina, in the island of Sicily; and a little before the juncture I am now speaking of I had letters from him—that is to say, Mrs. Amy had letters from him, intimating that he was out of his time, and that he had an opportunity to be taken into an English house there, on very good terms, if his support from hence might answer what he was bid to hope for; and so begged that what would be done for him might be so ordered that he might have it for his present advancement, referring for the particulars to his master, the merchant in London, who he had been put apprentice to here; who, to cut the story short, gave such a satisfactory account of it, and of my young man, to my steady and faithful counsellor, Sir Robert Clayton, that I made no scruple to pay £4000, which was £1000 more than he demanded, or rather proposed, that he might have encouragement to enter into the world better than he expected.

His master remitted the money very faithfully to him; and finding, by Sir Robert Clayton, that the young gentleman—for so he called him—was well supported, wrote such letters on his account as gave him a credit at Messina equal in value to the money itself.

I could not digest it very well that I should all this while conceal myself thus from my own child, and make all this favour due, in his opinion, to a stranger; and yet I could not find in my heart to let my son know what a mother he had, and what a life she lived; when, at the same time that he must think himself infinitely obliged to me, he must be obliged, if he was a man of virtue, to hate his mother, and abhor the way of living by which all the bounty he enjoyed was raised.

This is the reason of mentioning this part of my son's story, which is otherwise no ways concerned in my history, but as it put me upon thinking how to put an end to that wicked course I was in, that my own child, when he should afterwards come to England in a good figure, and with the appearance of a merchant, should not be ashamed to own me.

But there was another difficulty, which lay heavier upon me a great deal, and that was my daughter, who, as before, I had relieved by the hands of another instrument, which Amy had procured. The girl, as I have mentioned, was directed to put herself into a good garb, take lodgings, and entertain a maid to wait upon her, and to give herself some breeding—that is to say, to learn to dance, and fit herself to appear as a gentlewoman; being made to hope that she should, some time or other, find that she should be put into a condition to support her character, and to make herself amends for all her former troubles. She was only charged not to be drawn into matrimony till she was secured of a fortune that might assist to dispose of herself suitable not to what she then was, but what she was to be.

The girl was too sensible of her circumstances not to give all possible satisfaction of that kind, and indeed she was mistress of too much understanding not to see how much she should be obliged to that part for her own interest.

It was not long after this, but being well equipped, and in everything well set out, as she was directed, she came, as I have related above, and paid a visit to Mrs. Amy, and to tell her of her good fortune. Amy pretended to be much surprised at the alteration, and overjoyed for her sake, and began to treat her very well, entertained her handsomely, and when she would have gone away, pretended to ask my leave, and sent my coach home with her; and, in short, learning from her where she lodged, which was in the city, Amy promised to return her visit, and did so; and, in a word, Amy and Susan (for she was my own name) began an intimate acquaintance together.

There was an inexpressible difficulty in the poor girl's way, or else I should not have been able to have forborne discovering myself to her, and this was, her having been a servant in my particular family; and I could by no means think of ever letting the children know what a kind of creature they owed their being to, or giving them an occasion to upbraid their mother with her scandalous life, much less to justify the like practice from my example.

Thus it was with me; and thus, no doubt, considering parents always find it that their own children are a restraint to them in their worst courses, when the sense of a superior power has not the same influence. But of that hereafter.

There happened, however, one good circumstance in the case of this poor girl, which brought about a discovery sooner than otherwise it would have been, and it was thus. After she and Amy had been intimate for some time, and had exchanged several visits, the girl, now grown a woman, talking to Amy of the gay things that used to fall out when she was servant in my family, spoke of it with a kind of concern that she could not see (me) her lady; and at last she adds, "'Twas very strange, madam," says she to Amy, "but though I lived near two years in the house, I never saw my mistress in my life, except it was that public night when she danced in the fine Turkish habit, and then she was so disguised that I knew nothing of her afterwards."

Amy was glad to hear this, but as she was a cunning girl from the beginning, she was not to be bit, and so she laid no stress upon that at first, but gave me an account of it; and I must confess it gave me a secret joy to think that I was not known to her, and that, by virtue of that only accident, I might, when other circumstances made room for it, discover myself to her, and let her know she had a mother in a condition fit to be owned.

It was a dreadful restraint to me before, and this gave me some very sad reflections, and made way for the great question I have mentioned above; and by how much the circumstance was bitter to me, by so much the more agreeable it was to understand that the girl had never seen me, and consequently did not know me again if she was to be told who I was.

However, the next time she came to visit Amy, I was resolved to put it to a trial, and to come into the room and let her see me, and to see by that whether she knew me or not; but Amy put me by, lest indeed, as there was reason enough to question, I should not be able to contain or forbear discovering myself to her; so it went off for that time.

But both these circumstances, and that is the reason of mentioning them, brought me to consider of the life I lived, and to resolve to put myself into some figure of life in which I might not be scandalous to my own family, and be afraid to make myself known to my own children, who were my own flesh and blood.

There was another daughter I had, which, with all our inquiries, we could not hear of, high nor low, for several years after the first. But I return to my own story.

Being now in part removed from my old station, I seemed to be in a fair way of retiring from my old acquaintances, and consequently from the vile, abominable trade I had driven so long; so that the door seemed to be, as it were, particularly open to my reformation, if I had any mind to it in earnest; but, for all that, some of my old friends, as I had used to call them, inquired me out, and came to visit me at Kensington, and that more frequently than I wished they would do; but it being once known where I was, there was no avoiding it, unless I would have downright refused and affronted them; and I was not yet in earnest enough with my resolutions to go that length.

The best of it was, my old lewd favourite, who I now heartily hated, entirely dropped me. He came once to visit me, but I caused Amy to deny me, and say I was gone out. She did it so oddly, too, that when his lordship went away, he said coldly to her, "Well, well, Mrs. Amy, I find your mistress does not desire to be seen; tell her I won't trouble her any more," repeating the words "any more" two or three times over, just at his going away.

I reflected a little on it at first as unkind to him, having had so many considerable presents from him, but, as I have said, I was sick of him, and that on some accounts which, if I could suffer myself to publish them, would fully justify my conduct. But that part of the story will not bear telling, so I must leave it, and proceed.

I had begun a little, as I have said above, to reflect upon my manner of living, and to think of putting a new face upon it, and nothing moved me to it more than the consideration of my having three children, who were now grown up; and yet that while I was in that station of life I could not converse with them or make myself known to them; and this gave me a great deal of uneasiness. At last I entered into talk on this part of it with my woman Amy.

We lived at Kensington, as I have said, and though I had done with my old wicked l——, as above, yet I was frequently visited, as I said, by some others; so that, in a word, I began to be known in the town, not by name only, but by my character too, which was worse.

It was one morning when Amy was in bed with me, and I had some of my dullest thoughts about me, that Amy, hearing me sigh pretty often, asked me if I was not well. "Yes, Amy, I am well enough," says I, "but my mind is oppressed with heavy thoughts, and has been so a good while;" and then I told her how it grieved me that I could not make myself known to my own children, or form any acquaintances in the world. "Why so?" says Amy. "Why, prithee, Amy," says I, "what will my children say to themselves, and to one another, when they find their mother, however rich she may be, is at best but a whore, a common whore? And as for acquaintance, prithee, Amy, what sober lady or what family of any character will visit or be acquainted with a whore?"

"Why, all that's true, madam," says Amy; "but how can it be remedied now?" "'Tis true, Amy," said I, "the thing cannot be remedied now, but the scandal of it, I fancy, may be thrown off."

"Truly," says Amy, "I do not see how, unless you will go abroad again, and live in some other nation where nobody has known us or seen us, so that they cannot say they ever saw us before."

That very thought of Amy put what follows into my head, and I returned, "Why, Amy," says I, "is it not possible for me to shift my being from this part of the town and go and live in another part of the city, or another part of the country, and be as entirely concealed as if I had never been known?"

"Yes," says Amy, "I believe it might; but then you must put off all your equipages and servants, coaches and horses, change your liveries—nay, your own clothes, and, if it was possible, your very face."

"Well," says I, "and that's the way, Amy, and that I'll do, and that forthwith; for I am not able to live in this manner any longer." Amy came into this with a kind of pleasure particular to herself—that is to say, with an eagerness not to be resisted; for Amy was apt to be precipitant in her motions, and was for doing it immediately. "Well," says I, "Amy, as soon as you will; but what course must we take to do it? We cannot put off servants, and coach and horses, and everything, leave off housekeeping, and transform ourselves into a new shape all in a moment; servants must have warning, and the goods must be sold off, and a thousand things;" and this began to perplex us, and in particular took us up two or three days' consideration.

At last Amy, who was a clever manager in such cases, came to me with a scheme, as she called it. "I have found it out, madam," says she, "I have found a scheme how you shall, if you have a mind to it, begin and finish a perfect entire change of your figure and circumstances in one day, and shall be as much unknown, madam, in twenty-four hours, as you would be in so many years."

"Come, Amy," says I, "let us hear of it, for you please me mightily with the thoughts of it." "Why, then," says Amy, "let me go into the city this afternoon, and I'll inquire out some honest, plain sober family, where I will take lodgings for you, as for a country gentlewoman that desires to be in London for about half a year, and to board yourself and a kinswoman— that is, half a servant, half a companion, meaning myself; and so agree with them by the month. To this lodging (if I hit upon one to your mind) you may go to-morrow morning in a hackney-coach, with nobody but me, and leave such clothes and linen as you think fit, but, to be sure, the plainest you have; and then you are removed at once; you never need set your foot in this house again" (meaning where we then were), "or see anybody belonging to it. In the meantime I'll let the servants know that you are going over to Holland upon extraordinary business, and will leave off your equipages, and so I'll give them warning, or, if they will accept of it, give them a month's wages. Then I'll sell off your furniture as well as I can. As to your coach, it is but having it new painted and the lining changed, and getting new harness and hammercloths, and you may keep it still or dispose of it as you think fit. And only take care to let this lodging be in some remote part of the town, and you may be as perfectly unknown as if you had never been in England in your life."

This was Amy's scheme, and it pleased me so well that I resolved not only to let her go, but was resolved to go with her myself; but Amy put me off of that, because, she said, she should have occasion to hurry up and down so long that if I was with her it would rather hinder than further her, so I waived it.

In a word, Amy went, and was gone five long hours; but when she came back I could see by her countenance that her success had been suitable to her pains, for she came laughing and gaping. "O madam!" says she, "I have pleased you to the life;" and with that she tells me how she had fixed upon a house in a court in the Minories; that she was directed to it merely by accident; that it was a female family, the master of the house being gone to New England, and that the woman had four children, kept two maids, and lived very handsomely, but wanted company to divert her; and that on that very account she had agreed to take boarders.

Amy agreed for a good, handsome price, because she was resolved I should be used well; so she bargained to give her £35 for the half-year, and £50 if we took a maid, leaving that to my choice; and that we might be satisfied we should meet with nothing very gay, the people were Quakers, and I liked them the better.

I was so pleased that I resolved to go with Amy the next day to see the lodgings, and to see the woman of the house, and see how I liked them; but if I was pleased with the general, I was much more pleased with the particulars, for the gentlewoman—I must call her so, though she was a Quaker—was a most courteous, obliging, mannerly person, perfectly well-bred and perfectly well-humoured, and, in short, the most agreeable conversation that ever I met with; and, which was worth all, so grave, and yet so pleasant and so merry, that 'tis scarcely possible for me to express how I was pleased and delighted with her company; and particularly, I was so pleased that I would go away no more; so I e'en took up my lodging there the very first night.

In the meantime, though it took up Amy almost a month so entirely to put off all the appearances of housekeeping, as above, it need take me up no time to relate it; 'tis enough to say that Amy quitted all that part of the world and came pack and package to me, and here we took up our abode.

I was now in a perfect retreat indeed, remote from the eyes of all that ever had seen me, and as much out of the way of being ever seen or heard of by any of the gang that used to follow me as if I had been among the mountains in Lancashire; for when did a blue garter or a coach-and-six come into a little narrow passage in the Minories or Goodman's Fields? And as there was no fear of them, so really I had no desire to see them, or so much as to hear from them any more as long as I lived.

I seemed in a little hurry while Amy came and went so every day at first, but when that was over I lived here perfectly retired, and with a most pleasant and agreeable lady; I must call her so, for, though a Quaker, she had a full share of good breeding, sufficient to her if she had been a duchess; in a word, she was the most agreeable creature in her conversation, as I said before, that ever I met with.

I pretended, after I had been there some time, to be extremely in love with the dress of the Quakers, and this pleased her so much that she would needs dress me up one day in a suit of her own clothes; but my real design was to see whether it would pass upon me for a disguise.

Amy was struck with the novelty, though I had not mentioned my design to her, and when the Quaker was gone out of the room says Amy, "I guess your meaning; it is a perfect disguise to you. Why, you look quite another body; I should not have known you myself. Nay," says Amy, "more than that, it makes you look ten years younger than you did."

Nothing could please me better than that, and when Amy repeated it, I was so fond of it that I asked my Quaker (I won't call her landlady; 'tis indeed too coarse a word for her, and she deserved a much better)—I say, I asked her if she would sell it. I told her I was so fond of it that I would give her enough to buy her a better suit. She declined it at first, but I soon perceived that it was chiefly in good manners, because I should not dishonour myself, as she called it, to put on her old clothes; but if I pleased to accept of them, she would give me them for my dressing-clothes, and go with me, and buy a suit for me that might be better worth my wearing.

But as I conversed in a very frank, open manner with her, I bid her do the like with me; that I made no scruples of such things, but that if she would let me have them I would satisfy her. So she let me know what they cost, and to make her amends I gave her three guineas more than they cost her.

This good (though unhappy) Quaker had the misfortune to have had a bad husband, and he was gone beyond sea. She had a good house, and well furnished, and had some jointure of her own estate which supported her and her children, so that she did not want; but she was not at all above such a help as my being there was to her; so she was as glad of me as I was of her.

However, as I knew there was no way to fix this new acquaintance like making myself a friend to her, I began with making her some handsome presents and the like to her children. And first, opening my bundles one day in my chamber, I heard her in another room, and called her in with a kind of familiar way. There I showed her some of my fine clothes, and having among the rest of my things a piece of very fine new holland, which I had bought a little before, worth about s. an ell, I pulled it out: "Here, my friend," says I, "I will make you a present, if you will accept of it;" and with that I laid the piece of Holland in her lap.

I could see she was surprised, and that she could hardly speak. "What dost thou mean?" says she. "Indeed I cannot have the face to accept so fine a present as this;" adding, "'Tis fit for thy own use, but 'tis above my wear, indeed." I thought she had meant she must not wear it so fine because she was a Quaker. So I returned, "Why, do not you Quakers wear fine linen neither?" "Yes," says she, "we wear fine linen when we can afford it, but this is too good for me." However, I made her take it, and she was very thankful too. But my end was answered another way, for by this I engaged her so, that as I found her a woman of understanding, and of honesty too, I might, upon any occasion, have a confidence in her, which was, indeed, what I very much wanted.

By accustoming myself to converse with her, I had not only learned to dress like a Quaker, but so used myself to "thee" and "thou" that I talked like a Quaker too, as readily and naturally as if I had been born among them; and, in a word, I passed for a Quaker among all people that did not know me. I went but little abroad, but I had been so used to a coach that I knew not how well to go without one; besides, I thought it would be a farther disguise to me, so I told my Quaker friend one day that I thought I lived too close, that I wanted air. She proposed taking a hackney-coach sometimes, or a boat; but I told her I had always had a coach of my own till now, and I could find in my heart to have one again.

She seemed to think it strange at first, considering how close I lived, but had nothing to say when she found I did not value the expense; so, in short, I resolved I would have a coach. When we came to talk of equipages, she extolled the having all things plain. I said so too; so I left it to her direction, and a coachmaker was sent for, and he provided me a plain coach, no gilding or painting, lined with a light grey cloth, and my coachman had a coat of the same, and no lace on his hat.

When all was ready I dressed myself in the dress I bought of her, and said, "Come, I'll be a Quaker to-day, and you and I'll go abroad;" which we did, and there was not a Quaker in the town looked less like a counterfeit than I did. But all this was my particular plot, to be the more completely concealed, and that I might depend upon being not known, and yet need not be confined like a prisoner and be always in fear; so that all the rest was grimace.

We lived here very easy and quiet, and yet I cannot say I was so in my mind; I was like a fish out of water. I was as gay and as young in my disposition as I was at five-and-twenty; and as I had always been courted, flattered, and used to love it, so I missed it in my conversation; and this put me many times upon looking back upon things past.

I had very few moments in my life which, in their reflection, afforded me anything but regret: but of all the foolish actions I had to look back upon in my life, none looked so preposterous and so like distraction, nor left so much melancholy on my mind, as my parting with my friend, the merchant of Paris, and the refusing him upon such honourable and just conditions as he had offered; and though on his just (which I called unkind) rejecting my invitation to come to him again, I had looked on him with some disgust, yet now my mind run upon him continually, and the ridiculous conduct of my refusing him, and I could never be satisfied about him. I flattered myself that if I could but see him I could yet master him, and that he would presently forget all that had passed that might be thought unkind; but as there was no room to imagine anything like that to be possible, I threw those thoughts off again as much as I could.

However, they continually returned, and I had no rest night or day for thinking of him, who I had forgot above eleven years. I told Amy of it, and we talked it over sometimes in bed, almost whole nights together. At last Amy started a thing of her own head, which put it in a way of management, though a wild one too. "You are so uneasy, madam," says she, "about this Mr. ——, the merchant at Paris; come," says she, "if you'll give me leave, I'll go over and see what's become of him."

"Not for ten thousand pounds," said I; "no, nor if you met him in the street, not to offer to speak to him on my account." "No," says Amy, "I would not speak to him at all; or if I did, I warrant you it shall not look to be upon your account. I'll only inquire after him, and if he is in being, you shall hear of him; if not, you shall hear of him still, and that may be enough."

"Why," says I, "if you will promise me not to enter into anything relating to me with him, nor to begin any discourse at all unless he begins it with you, I could almost be persuaded to let you go and try."

Amy promised me all that I desired; and, in a word, to cut the story short, I let her go, but tied her up to so many particulars that it was almost impossible her going could signify anything; and had she intended to observe them, she might as well have stayed at home as have gone, for I charged her, if she came to see him, she should not so much as take notice that she knew him again; and if he spoke to her, she should tell him she was come away from me a great many years ago, and knew nothing what was become of me; that she had been come over to France six years ago, and was married there, and lived at Calais; or to that purpose.

Amy promised me nothing, indeed; for, as she said, it was impossible for her to resolve what would be fit to do, or not to do, till she was there upon the spot, and had found out the gentleman, or heard of him; but that then, if I would trust her, as I had always done, she would answer for it that she would do nothing but what should be for my interest, and what she would hope I should be very well pleased with.

With this general commission, Amy, notwithstanding she had been so frighted at the sea, ventured her carcass once more by water, and away she goes to France. She had four articles of confidence in charge to inquire after for me, and, as I found by her, she had one for herself—I say, four for me, because, though her first and principal errand was to inform myself of my Dutch merchant, yet I gave her in charge to inquire, second, after my husband, who I left a trooper in the gens d'armes; third, after that rogue of a Jew, whose very name I hated, and of whose face I had such a frightful idea that Satan himself could not counterfeit a worse; and, lastly, after my foreign prince. And she discharged herself very well of them all, though not so successful as I wished.

Amy had a very good passage over the sea, and I had a letter from her, from Calais, in three days after she went from London. When she came to Paris she wrote me an account, that as to her first and most important inquiry, which was after the Dutch merchant, her account was, that he had returned to Paris, lived three years there, and quitting that city, went to live at Rouen; so away goes Amy for Rouen.

But as she was going to bespeak a place in the coach to Rouen, she meets very accidentally in the street with her gentleman, as I called him—that is to say, the Prince de —— 's gentleman, who had been her favourite, as above.

You may be sure there were several other kind things happened between Amy and him, as you shall hear afterwards; but the two main things were, first, that Amy inquired about his lord, and had a full account of him, of which presently; and, in the next place, telling him whither she was going and for what, he bade her not go yet, for that he would have a particular account of it the next day from a merchant that knew him; and, accordingly, he brought her word the next day that he had been for six years before that gone for Holland, and that he lived there still.

This, I say, was the first news from Amy for some time—I mean about my merchant. In the meantime Amy, as I have said, inquired about the other persons she had in her instructions. As for the prince, the gentleman told her he was gone into Germany, where his estate lay, and that he lived there; that he had made great inquiry after me; that he (his gentleman) had made all the search he had been able for me, but that he could not hear of me; that he believed, if his lord had known I had been in England, he would have gone over to me; but that, after long inquiry, he was obliged to give it over; but that he verily believed, if he could have found me, he would have married me; and that he was extremely concerned that he could hear nothing of me.

I was not at all satisfied with Amy's account, but ordered her to go to Rouen herself, which she did, and there with much difficulty (the person she was directed to being dead)—I say, with much difficulty she came to be informed that my merchant had lived there two years, or something more, but that, having met with a very great misfortune, he had gone back to Holland, as the French merchant said, where he had stayed two years; but with this addition, viz., that he came back again to Rouen, and lived in good reputation there another year; and afterwards he was gone to England, and that he lived in London. But Amy could by no means learn how to write to him there, till, by great accident, an old Dutch skipper, who had formerly served him, coming to Rouen, Amy was told of it; and he told her that he lodged in St. Laurence Pountney's Lane, in London, but was to be seen every day upon the Exchange, in the French walk.

This, Amy thought, it was time enough to tell me of when she came over; and, besides, she did not find this Dutch skipper till she had spent four or five months and been again in Paris, and then come back to Rouen for farther information. But in the meantime she wrote to me from Paris that he was not to be found by any means; that he had been gone from Paris seven or eight years; that she was told he had lived at Rouen, and she was agoing thither to inquire, but that she had heard afterwards that he was gone also from thence to Holland, so she did not go.

This, I say, was Amy's first account; and I, not satisfied with it, had sent her an order to go to Rouen to inquire there also, as above.

While this was negotiating, and I received these accounts from Amy at several times, a strange adventure happened to me which I must mention just here. I had been abroad to take the air as usual with my Quaker, as far as Epping Forest, and we were driving back towards London, when, on the road between Bow and Mile End, two gentlemen on horseback came riding by, having overtaken the coach and passed it, and went forwards towards London.

They did not ride apace though they passed the coach, for we went very softly; nor did they look into the coach at all, but rode side by side, earnestly talking to one another and inclining their faces sideways a little towards one another, he that went nearest the coach with his face from it, and he that was farthest from the coach with his face towards it, and passing in the very next tract to the coach, I could hear them talk Dutch very distinctly. But it is impossible to describe the confusion I was in when I plainly saw that the farthest of the two, him whose face looked towards the coach, was my friend the Dutch merchant of Paris.

If it had been possible to conceal my disorder from my friend the Quaker I would have done it, but I found she was too well acquainted with such things not to take the hint. "Dost thou understand Dutch?" said she. "Why?" said I. "Why," says she, "it is easy to suppose that thou art a little concerned at somewhat those men say; I suppose they are talking of thee." "Indeed, my good friend," said I, "thou art mistaken this time, for I know very well what they are talking of, but 'tis all about ships and trading affairs." "Well," says she, "then one of them is a man friend of thine, or somewhat is the case; for though thy tongue will not confess it, thy face does."

I was going to have told a bold lie, and said I knew nothing of them; but I found it was impossible to conceal it, so I said, "Indeed, I think I know the farthest of them; but I have neither spoken to him or so much as seen him for about eleven years." "Well, then," says she, "thou hast seen him with more than common eyes when thou didst see him, or else seeing him now would not be such a surprise to thee." "Indeed," said I, "it is true I am a little surprised at seeing him just now, for I thought he had been in quite another part of the world; and I can assure you I never saw him in England in my life." "Well, then, it is the more likely he is come over now on purpose to seek thee." "No, no," said I, "knight-errantry is over; women are not so hard to come at that men should not be able to please themselves without running from one kingdom to another." "Well, well," says she, "I would have him see thee for all that, as plainly as thou hast seen him." "No, but he shan't," says I, "for I am sure he don't know me in this dress, and I'll take care he shan't see my face, if I can help it;" so I held up my fan before my face, and she saw me resolute in that, so she pressed me no farther.

We had several discourses upon the subject, but still I let her know I was resolved he should not know me; but at last I confessed so much, that though I would not let him know who I was or where I lived, I did not care if I knew where he lived and how I might inquire about him. She took the hint immediately, and her servant being behind the coach, she called him to the coach-side and bade him keep his eye upon that gentleman, and as soon as the coach came to the end of Whitechapel he should get down and follow him closely, so as to see where he put up his horse, and then to go into the inn and inquire, if he could, who he was and where he lived.

The fellow followed diligently to the gate of an inn in Bishopsgate Street, and seeing him go in, made no doubt but he had him fast; but was confounded when, upon inquiry, he found the inn was a thoroughfare into another street, and that the two gentlemen had only rode through the inn, as the way to the street where they were going; and so, in short, came back no wiser than he went.

My kind Quaker was more vexed at the disappointment, at least apparently so, than I was; and asking the fellow if he was sure he knew the gentleman again if he saw him, the fellow said he had followed him so close and took so much notice of him, in order to do his errand as it ought to be done, that he was very sure he should know him again; and that, besides, he was sure he should know his horse.

This part was, indeed, likely enough; and the kind Quaker, without telling me anything of the matter, caused her man to place himself just at the corner of Whitechapel Church wall every Saturday in the afternoon, that being the day when the citizens chiefly ride abroad to take the air, and there to watch all the afternoon and look for him.

It was not till the fifth Saturday that her man came, with a great deal of joy, and gave her an account that he had found out the gentleman; that he was a Dutchman, but a French merchant; that he came from Rouen, and his name was ——, and that he lodged at Mr. ——'s, on Laurence Pountney's Hill. I was surprised, you may be sure, when she came and told me one evening all the particulars, except that of having set her man to watch. "I have found out thy Dutch friend," says she, "and can tell thee how to find him too." I coloured again as red as fire. "Then thou hast dealt with the evil one, friend," said I very gravely. "No, no," says she, "I have no familiar; but I tell thee I have found him for thee, and his name is So-and-so, and he lives as above recited."

I was surprised again at this, not being able to imagine how she should come to know all this. However, to put me out of pain, she told me what she had done. "Well," said I, "thou art very kind, but this is not worth thy pains; for now I know it, 'tis only to satisfy my curiosity; for I shall not send to him upon any account." "Be that as thou wilt," says she. "Besides," added she, "thou art in the right to say so to me, for why should I be trusted with it? Though, if I were, I assure thee I should not betray thee." "That's very kind," said I, "and I believe thee; and assure thyself, if I do send to him, thou shalt know it, and be trusted with it too."

During this interval of five weeks I suffered a hundred thousand perplexities of mind. I was thoroughly convinced I was right as to the person, that it was the man. I knew him so well, and saw him so plain, I could not be deceived. I drove out again in the coach (on pretence of air) almost every day in hopes of seeing him again, but was never so lucky as to see him;

and now I had made the discovery I was as far to seek what measures to take as I was before.

To send to him, or speak to him first if I should see him, so as to be known to him, that I resolved not to do, if I died for it. To watch him about his lodging, that was as much below my spirit as the other. So that, in a word, I was at a perfect loss how to act or what to do.

At length came Amy's letter, with the last account which she had at Rouen from the Dutch skipper, which, confirming the other, left me out of doubt that this was my man; but still no human invention could bring me to the speech of him in such a manner as would suit with my resolutions. For, after all, how did I know what his circumstances were? whether married or single? And if he had a wife, I knew he was so honest a man he would not so much as converse with me, or so much as know me if he met me in the street.

In the next place, as he entirely neglected me, which, in short, is the worst way of slighting a woman, and had given no answer to my letters, I did not know but he might be the same man still; so I resolved that I could do nothing in it unless some fairer opportunity presented, which might make my way clearer to me; for I was determined he should have no room to put any more slights upon me.

In these thoughts I passed away near three months; till at last, being impatient, I resolved to send for Amy to come over, and tell her how things stood, and that I would do nothing till she came. Amy, in answer, sent me word she would come away with all speed, but begged of me that I would enter into no engagement with him, or anybody, till she arrived; but still keeping me in the dark as to the thing itself which she had to say; at which I was heartily vexed, for many reasons.

But while all these things were transacting, and letters and answers passed between Amy and I a little slower than usual, at which I was not so well pleased as I used to be with Amy's despatch—I say, in this time the following scene opened.

It was one afternoon, about four o'clock, my friendly Quaker and I sitting in her chamber upstairs, and very cheerful, chatting together (for she was the best company in the world), when somebody ringing hastily at the door, and no servant just then in the way, she ran down herself to the door, when a gentleman appears, with a footman attending, and making some apologies, which she did not thoroughly understand, he speaking but broken English, he asked to speak with me, by the very same name that I went by in her house, which, by the way, was not the name that he had known me by.

She, with very civil language, in her way, brought him into a very handsome parlour below stairs, and said she would go and see whether the person who lodged in her house owned that name, and he should hear farther.

I was a little surprised, even before I knew anything of who it was, my mind foreboding the thing as it happened (whence that arises let the naturalists explain to us); but I was frighted and ready to die when my Quaker came up all gay and crowing. "There," says she, "is the

Dutch French merchant come to see thee." I could not speak one word to her nor stir off of my chair, but sat as motionless as a statue. She talked a thousand pleasant things to me, but they made no impression on me. At last she pulled me and teased me. "Come, come," says she, "be thyself, and rouse up. I must go down again to him; what shall I say to him?" "Say," said I, "that you have no such body in the house." "That I cannot do," says she, "because it is not the truth. Besides, I have owned thou art above. Come, come, go down with me." "Not for a thousand guineas," said I. "Well," says she, "I'll go and tell him thou wilt come quickly." So, without giving me time to answer her, away she goes.

A million of thoughts circulated in my head while she was gone, and what to do I could not tell; I saw no remedy but I must speak with him, but would have given £500 to have shunned it; yet had I shunned it, perhaps then I would have given £500 again that I had seen him. Thus fluctuating and unconcluding were my thoughts, what I so earnestly desired I declined when it offered itself; and what now I pretended to decline was nothing but what I had been at the expense of £40 or £50 to send Amy to France for, and even without any view, or, indeed, any rational expectation of bringing it to pass; and what for half a year before I was so uneasy about that I could not be quiet night or day till Amy proposed to go over to inquire after him. In short, my thoughts were all confused and in the utmost disorder. I had once refused and rejected him, and I repented it heartily; then I had taken ill his silence, and in my mind rejected him again, but had repented that too. Now I had stooped so low as to send after him into France, which if he had known, perhaps, he had never come after me; and should I reject him a third time! On the other hand, he had repented too, in his turn, perhaps, and not knowing how I had acted, either in stooping to send in search after him or in the wickeder part of my life, was come over hither to seek me again; and I might take him, perhaps, with the same advantages as I might have done before, and would I now be backward to see him! Well, while I was in this hurry my friend the Quaker comes up again, and perceiving the confusion I was in, she runs to her closet and fetched me a little pleasant cordial; but I would not taste it. "Oh," says she, "I understand thee. Be not uneasy; I'll give thee something shall take off all the smell of it; if he kisses thee a thousand times he shall be no wiser." I thought to myself, "Thou art perfectly acquainted with affairs of this nature; I think you must govern me now;" so I began to incline to go down with her. Upon that I took the cordial, and she gave me a kind of spicy preserve after it, whose flavour was so strong, and yet so deliciously pleasant, that it would cheat the nicest smelling, and it left not the least taint of the cordial on the breath.

Well, after this, though with some hesitation still, I went down a pair of back-stairs with her, and into a dining-room, next to the parlour in which he was; but there I halted, and desired she would let me consider of it a little. "Well, do so," says she, and left me with more readiness than she did before. "Do consider, and I'll come to thee again."

Though I hung back with an awkwardness that was really unfeigned, yet when she so readily left me I thought it was not so kind, and I began to think she should have pressed me still on to it; so foolishly backward are we to the thing which, of all the world, we most desire; mocking ourselves with a feigned reluctance, when the negative would be death to us. But she was too cunning for me; for while I, as it were, blamed her in my mind for not carrying me to him, though, at the same time, I appeared backward to see him, on a sudden she unlocks the folding-doors, which looked into the next parlour, and throwing them open. "There," says she (ushering him in), "is the person who, I suppose, thou inquirest for;" and the same moment, with a kind decency, she retired, and that so swift that she would not give us leave hardly to know which way she went.

I stood up, but was confounded with a sudden inquiry in my thoughts how I should receive him, and with a resolution as swift as lightning, in answer to it, said to myself, "It shall be coldly." So on a sudden I put on an air of stiffness and ceremony, and held it for about two minutes; but it was with great difficulty.

He restrained himself too, on the other hand, came towards me gravely, and saluted me in form; but it was, it seems, upon his supposing the Quaker was behind him, whereas she, as I said, understood things too well, and had retired as if she had vanished, that we might have full freedom; for, as she said afterwards, she supposed we had seen one another before, though it might have been a great while ago.

Whatever stiffness I had put on my behaviour to him, I was surprised in my mind, and angry at his, and began to wonder what kind of a ceremonious meeting it was to be. However, after he perceived the woman was gone he made a kind of a hesitation, looking a little round him. "Indeed," said he, "I thought the gentlewoman was not withdrawn;" and with that he took me in his arms and kissed me three or four times; but I, that was prejudiced to the last degree with the coldness of his first salutes, when I did not know the cause of it, could not be thoroughly cleared of the prejudice though I did know the cause, and thought that even his return, and taking me in his arms, did not seem to have the same ardour with which he used to receive me, and this made me behave to him awkwardly, and I know not how for a good while; but this by the way.

He began with a kind of an ecstasy upon the subject of his finding me out; how it was possible that he should have been four years in England, and had used all the ways imaginable, and could never so much as have the least intimation of me, or of any one like me; and that it was now above two years that he had despaired of it, and had given over all inquiry; and that now he should chop upon me, as it were, unlooked and unsought for.

I could easily have accounted for his not finding me if I had but set down the detail of my real retirement; but I gave it a new, and indeed a truly hypocritical turn. I told him that any one that knew the manner of life I led might account for his not finding me; that the retreat I had taken up would have rendered it a hundred thousand to one odds that he ever found me at all; that, as I had abandoned all conversation, taken up another name, lived remote from London, and had not preserved one acquaintance in it, it was no wonder he had not met with me; that even my dress would let him see that I did not desire to be known by anybody.

Then he asked if I had not received some letters from him. I told him no, he had not thought fit to give me the civility of an answer to the last I wrote to him, and he could not suppose I should expect a return after a silence in a case where I had laid myself so low and exposed myself in a manner I had never been used to; that indeed I had never sent for any letters after that to the place where I had ordered his to be directed; and that, being so justly, as I thought, punished for my weakness, I had nothing to do but to repent of being a fool, after I had strictly adhered to a just principle before; that, however, as what I did was rather from motions of gratitude than from real weakness, however it might be construed by him, I had the satisfaction in myself of having fully discharged the debt. I added, that I had not wanted occasions of all the seeming advancements which the pretended felicity of a marriage life was usually set off with, and might have been what I desired not to name; but that, however low I had stooped to him, I had maintained the dignity of female liberty against all the attacks either of pride or avarice; and that I had been infinitely obliged to him for giving me an opportunity to discharge the only obligation that endangered me, without subjecting me to the consequence; and that I hoped he was satisfied I had paid the debt by offering myself to be chained, but was infinitely debtor to him another way for letting me remain free.

He was so confounded at this discourse that he knew not what to say, and for a good while he stood mute indeed; but recovering himself a little, he said I run out into a discourse he hoped was over and forgotten, and he did not intend to revive it; that he knew I had not had his letters, for that, when he first came to England, he had been at the place to which they were directed, and found them all lying there but one, and that the people had not known how to deliver them; that he thought to have had a direction there how to find me, but had the mortification to be told that they did not so much as know who I was; that he was under a great disappointment; and that I ought to know, in answer to all my resentments, that he had done a long and, he hoped, a sufficient penance for the slight that I had supposed he had put upon me; that it was true (and I could not suppose any other) that upon the repulse I had given them in a case so circumstanced as his was, and after such earnest entreaties and such offers as he had made me, he went away with a mind heartily grieved and full of resentment; that he had looked back on the crime he had committed with some regret, but on the cruelty of my treatment of the poor infant I went with at that time with the utmost detestation, and that this made him unable to send an agreeable answer to me; for which reason he had sent none at all for some time; but that in about six or seven months, those resentments wearing off by the return of his affection to me and his concern in the poor child ——. There he stopped, and indeed tears stood in his eyes; while in a parenthesis he only added, and to this minute he did not know whether it was dead or alive. He then went on: Those resentments wearing off, he sent me several letters—I think he said seven or eight—but received no answer; that then his business obliging him to go to Holland, he came to England, as in his way, but found, as above, that his letters had not been called for, but that he left them at the house after paying the postage of them; and going then back to France, he was yet uneasy, and could not refrain the knight-errantry of coming to England again to seek me, though he knew neither where or of who to inquire for me, being disappointed in all his inquiries before; that he had yet taken up his residence here, firmly believing that one time or other he should meet me, or hear of me, and that some kind chance would at last throw him in my way; that he had lived thus above four years, and though his hopes were vanished, yet he had not any thoughts of removing any more in the world, unless it should be at last, as it is with other old men, he might have some inclination to go home to die in his own country, but that he had not thought of it yet; that if I would consider all these steps, I would find some reasons to forget his first resentments, and to think that penance, as he called it, which he had undergone in search of me an amende honorable, in reparation of the affront given to the kindness of my letter of invitation; and that we might at last make ourselves some satisfaction on both sides for the mortifications past.

I confess I could not hear all this without being moved very much, and yet I continued a little stiff and formal too a good while. I told him that before I could give him any reply to the rest of his discourse I ought to give him the satisfaction of telling him that his son was alive, and that indeed, since I saw him so concerned about it, and mention it with such affection, I was sorry that I had not found out some way or other to let him know it sooner; but that I thought, after his slighting the mother, as above, he had summed up his affection to the child in the letter he had wrote to me about providing for it; and that he had, as other fathers often do, looked upon it as a birth which, being out of the way, was to be forgotten, as its beginning was to be repented of; that in providing sufficiently for it he had done more than all such fathers used to do, and might be well satisfied with it.

He answered me that he should have been very glad if I had been so good but to have given him the satisfaction of knowing the poor unfortunate creature was yet alive, and he would have taken some care of it upon himself, and particularly by owning it for a legitimate child, which, where nobody had known to the contrary, would have taken off the infamy which would otherwise cleave to it, and so the child should not itself have known anything of its own disaster; but that he feared it was now too late.

He added that I might see by all his conduct since that what unhappy mistake drew him into the thing at first, and that he would have been very far from doing the injury to me, or being instrumental to add une miserable (that was his word) to the world, if he had not been drawn into it by the hopes he had of making me his own; but that, if it was possible to rescue the child from the consequences of its unhappy birth, he hoped I would give him leave to do it, and he would let me see that he had both means and affection still to do it; and that, notwithstanding all the misfortunes that had befallen him, nothing that belonged to him, especially by a mother he had such a concern for as he had for me, should ever want what he was in a condition to do for it.

I could not hear this without being sensibly touched with it. I was ashamed that he should show that he had more real affection for the child, though he had never seen it in his life, than I that bore it, for indeed I did not love the child, nor love to see it; and though I had provided for it, yet I did it by Amy's hand, and had not seen it above twice in four years, being privately resolved that when it grew up it should not be able to call me mother.

However, I told him the child was taken care of, and that he need not be anxious about it, unless he suspected that I had less affection for it than he that had never seen it in his life; that he knew what I had promised him to do for it, namely, to give it the thousand pistoles which I had offered him, and which he had declined; that I assured him I had made my will, and that I had left it £5000, and the interest of it till he should come of age, if I died before that time; that I would still be as good as that to it; but if he had a mind to take it from me into his government, I would not be against it; and to satisfy him that I would perform what I said, I would cause the child to be delivered to him, and the £5000 also for its support, depending upon it that he would show himself a father to it by what I saw of his affection to it now.

I had observed that he had hinted two or three times in his discourse, his having had misfortunes in the world, and I was a little surprised at the expression, especially at the repeating it so often; but I took no notice of that part yet.

He thanked me for my kindness to the child with a tenderness which showed the sincerity of all he had said before, and which increased the regret with which, as I said, I looked back on the little affection I had showed to the poor child. He told me he did not desire to take him from me, but so as to introduce him into the world as his own, which he could still do, having lived absent from his other children (for he had two sons and a daughter which were brought up at Nimeguen, in Holland, with a sister of his) so long that he might very well send another son of ten years old to be bred up with them, and suppose his mother to be dead or alive, as he found occasion; and that, as I had resolved to do so handsomely for the child, he would add to it something considerable, though, having had some great disappointments (repeating the words), he could not do for it as he would otherwise have done.

I then thought myself obliged to take notice of his having so often mentioned his having met with disappointments. I told him I was very sorry to hear he had met with anything afflicting to him in the world; that I would not have anything belonging to me add to his loss, or weaken him in what he might do for his other children; and that I would not agree to his having the child away, though the proposal was infinitely to the child's advantage, unless he would promise me that the whole expense should be mine, and that, if he did not think £5000 enough for the child, I would give it more.

We had so much discourse upon this and the old affairs that it took up all our time at his first visit. I was a little importunate with him to tell me how he came to find me out, but he put it off for that time, and only obtaining my leave to visit me again, he went away; and indeed my heart was so full with what he had said already that I was glad when he went away. Sometimes I was full of tenderness and affection for him, and especially when he expressed himself so earnestly and passionately about the child; other times I was crowded with doubts about his circumstances. Sometimes I was terrified with apprehensions lest, if I should come into a close correspondence with him, he should any way come to hear what kind of life I had led at Pall Mall and in other places, and it might make me miserable afterwards; from which last thought I concluded that I had better repulse him again than receive him. All these thoughts, and many more, crowded in so fast, I say, upon me that I wanted to give vent to them and get rid of him, and was very glad when he was gone away.

We had several meetings after this, in which still we had so many preliminaries to go through that we scarce ever bordered upon the main subject. Once, indeed, he said something of it, and I put it off with a kind of a jest. "Alas!" says I, "those things are out of the question now; 'tis almost two ages since those things were talked between us," says I. "You see I am grown an old woman since that." Another time he gave a little push at it again, and I laughed again. "Why, what dost thou talk of?" said I in a formal way. "Dost thou not see I am turned Quaker? I cannot speak of those things now." "Why," says he, "the Quakers marry as well as other people, and love one another as well. Besides," says he, "the Quakers' dress does not ill become you," and so jested with me again, and so it went off for a third time. However, I began to be kind to him in process of time, as they call it, and we grew very intimate; and if the following accident had not unluckily intervened, I had certainly married him, or consented to marry him, the very next time he had asked me.

I had long waited for a letter from Amy, who, it seems, was just at that time gone to Rouen the second time, to make her inquiries about him; and I received a letter from her at this unhappy juncture, which gave me the following account of my business:—

I. That for my gentleman, who I had now, as I may say, in my arms, she said he had been gone from Paris, as I have hinted, having met with some great losses and misfortunes; that he had been in Holland on that very account, whither he had also carried his children; that he was after that settled for some time at Rouen; that she had been at Rouen, and found there (by a mere accident), from a Dutch skipper, that he was at London, had been there above three years; that he was to be found upon the Exchange, on the French walk; and that he lodged at St. Laurence Pountney's Lane, and the like; so Amy said she supposed I might soon find him out, but that she doubted he was poor, and not worth looking after. This she did because of the next clause, which the jade had most mind to on many accounts.

II. That as to the Prince ——; that, as above, he was gone into Germany, where his estate lay; that he had quitted the French service, and lived retired; that she had seen his gentleman, who remained at Paris to solicit his arrears, &c.; that he had given her an account how his lord had employed him to inquire for me and find me out, as above, and told her what pains he had taken to find me; that he had understood that I was gone to England; that he once had orders to go to England to find me; that his lord had resolved, if he could have found me, to have called me a countess, and so have married me, and have carried me into Germany with him; and that his commission was still to assure me that the prince would marry me if I would come to him, and that he would send him an account that he had found me, and did not doubt but he would have orders to come over to England to attend me in a figure suitable to my quality.

Amy, an ambitious jade, who knew my weakest part—namely, that I loved great things, and that I loved to be flattered and courted—said abundance of kind things upon this occasion, which she knew were suitable to me and would prompt my vanity; and talked big of the prince's gentleman having orders to come over to me with a procuration to marry me by proxy (as princes usually do in like cases), and to furnish me with an equipage, and I know not how many fine things; but told me, withal, that she had not yet let him know that she belonged to me still, or that she knew where to find me, or to write to me; because she was willing to see the bottom of it, and whether it was a reality or a gasconade. She had indeed told him that, if he had any such commission, she would endeavour to find me out, but no more.

III. For the Jew, she assured me that she had not been able to come at a certainty what was become of him, or in what part of the world he was; but that thus much she had learned from good hands, that he had committed a crime, in being concerned in a design to rob a rich banker at Paris; and that he was fled, and had not been heard of there for above six years.

IV. For that of my husband, the brewer, she learned, that being commanded into the field upon an occasion of some action in Flanders, he was wounded at the battle of Mons, and died of his wounds in the Hospital of the Invalids; so there was an end of my four inquiries, which I sent her over to make.

This account of the prince, and the return of his affection to me, with all the flattering great things which seemed to come along with it; and especially as they came gilded and set out by my maid Amy—I say this account of the prince came to me in a very unlucky hour, and in the very crisis of my affair.

The merchant and I had entered into close conferences upon the grand affair. I had left off talking my platonics, and of my independency, and being a free woman, as before; and he having cleared up my doubts too, as to his circumstances and the misfortunes he had spoken of, I had gone so far that we had begun to consider where we should live, and in what figure, what equipage, what house, and the like.

I had made some harangues upon the delightful retirement of a country life, and how we might enjoy ourselves so effectually without the encumbrances of business and the world; but all this was grimace, and purely because I was afraid to make any public appearance in the world, for fear some impertinent person of quality should chop upon me again and cry out, "Roxana, Roxana, by ——!" with an oath, as had been done before.

My merchant, bred to business and used to converse among men of business, could hardly tell how to live without it; at least it appeared he should be like a fish out of water, uneasy and dying. But, however, he joined with me; only argued that we might live as near London as we could, that he might sometimes come to 'Change and hear how the world should go abroad, and how it fared with his friends and his children.

I answered that if he chose still to embarrass himself with business, I supposed it would be more to his satisfaction to be in his own country, and where his family was so well known, and where his children also were.

He smiled at the thoughts of that, and let me know that he should be very willing to embrace such an offer; but that he could not expect it of me, to whom England was, to be sure, so naturalised now as that it would be carrying me out of my native country, which he would not desire by any means, however agreeable it might be to him.

I told him he was mistaken in me; that as I had told him so much of a married state being a captivity, and the family being a house of bondage, that when I married I expected to be but an upper servant; so, if I did notwithstanding submit to it, I hoped he should see I knew how to act the servant's part, and do everything to oblige my master; that if I did not resolve to go with him wherever he desired to go, he might depend I would never have him. "And did I not," said I, "offer myself to go with you to the East Indies?"

All this while this was indeed but a copy of my countenance; for, as my circumstances would not admit of my stay in London, at least not so as to appear publicly, I resolved, if I took him, to live remote in the country, or go out of England with him.

But in an evil hour, just now came Amy's letter, in the very middle of all these discourses; and the fine things she had said about the prince began to make strange work with me. The notion of being a princess, and going over to live where all that had happened here would have been quite sunk out of knowledge as well as out of memory (conscience excepted), was mighty taking. The thoughts of being surrounded with domestics, honoured with titles, be called her Highness, and live in all the splendour of a court, and, which was still more, in the arms of a man of such rank, and who, I knew, loved and valued me—all this, in a word, dazzled my eyes, turned my head, and I was as truly crazed and distracted for about a fortnight as most of the people in Bedlam, though perhaps not quite so far gone.

When my gentleman came to me the next time I had no notion of him; I wished I had never received him at all. In short, I resolved to have no more to say to him, so I feigned myself indisposed; and though I did come down to him and speak to him a little, yet I let him see that I was so ill that I was (as we say) no company, and that it would be kind in him to give me leave to quit him for that time.

The next morning he sent a footman to inquire how I did; and I let him know I had a violent cold, and was very ill with it. Two days after he came again, and I let him see me again, but feigned myself so hoarse that I could not speak to be heard, and that it was painful to me but to whisper; and, in a word, I held him in this suspense near three weeks.

During this time I had a strange elevation upon my mind; and the prince, or the spirit of him, had such a possession of me that I spent most of this time in the realising all the great things of a life with the prince, to my mind pleasing my fancy with the grandeur I was supposing myself to enjoy, and with wickedly studying in what manner to put off this gentleman and be rid of him for ever.

I cannot but say that sometimes the baseness of the action stuck hard with me; the honour and sincerity with which he had always treated me, and, above all, the fidelity he had showed me at Paris, and that I owed my life to him—I say, all these stared in my face, and I frequently argued with myself upon the obligation I was under to him, and how base would it be now too, after so many obligations and engagements, to cast him off.

But the title of highness, and of a princess, and all those fine things, as they came in, weighed down all this; and the sense of gratitude vanished as if it had been a shadow.

At other times I considered the wealth I was mistress of; that I was able to live like a princess, though not a princess; and that my merchant (for he had told me all the affair of his misfortunes) was far from being poor, or even mean; that together we were able to make up an estate of between three and four thousand pounds a year, which was in itself equal to some princes abroad. But though this was true, yet the name of princess, and the flutter of it—in a word, the pride—weighed them down; and all these arguings generally ended to the disadvantage of my merchant; so that, in short, I resolved to drop him, and give him a final answer at his next coming; namely, that something had happened in my affairs which had caused me to alter my measures unexpectedly, and, in a word, to desire him to trouble himself no farther.

I think, verily, this rude treatment of him was for some time the effect of a violent fermentation in my blood; for the very motion which the steady contemplation of my fancied greatness had put my spirits into had thrown me into a kind of fever, and I scarce knew what I did.

I have wondered since that it did not make me mad; nor do I now think it strange to hear of those who have been quite lunatic with their pride, that fancied themselves queens and empresses, and have made their attendants serve them upon the knee, given visitors their hand to kiss, and the like; for certainly, if pride will not turn the brain, nothing can.

However, the next time my gentleman came, I had not courage enough, or not ill nature enough, to treat him in the rude manner I had resolved to do, and it was very well I did not; for soon after, I had another letter from Amy, in which was the mortifying news, and indeed surprising to me, that my prince (as I, with a secret pleasure, had called him) was very much hurt by a bruise he had received in hunting and engaging with a wild boar, a cruel and desperate sport which the noblemen of Germany, it seems, much delight in.

This alarmed me indeed, and the more because Amy wrote me word that his gentleman was gone away express to him, not without apprehensions that he should find his master was dead before his coming home; but that he (the gentleman) had promised her that as soon as he arrived he would send back the same courier to her with an account of his master's health, and of the main affair; and that he had obliged Amy to stay at Paris fourteen days for his return; she having promised him before to make it her business to go to England and to find me out for his lord if he sent her such orders; and he was to send her a bill for fifty pistoles for her journey. So Amy told me she waited for the answer.

This was a blow to me several ways; for, first, I was in a state of uncertainty as to his person, whether he was alive or dead; and I was not unconcerned in that part, I assure you; for I had an inexpressible affection remaining for his person, besides the degree to which it was revived by the view of a firmer interest in him. But this was not all, for in losing him I forever lost the prospect of all the gaiety and glory that had made such an impression upon my imagination.

In this state of uncertainty, I say, by Amy's letter, I was like still to remain another fortnight; and had I now continued the resolution of using my merchant in the rude manner I once intended, I had made perhaps a sorry piece of work of it indeed, and it was very well my heart failed me as it did.

However, I treated him with a great many shuffles, and feigned stories to keep him off from any closer conferences than we had already had, that I might act afterwards as occasion might offer, one way or other. But that which mortified me most was, that Amy did not write, though the fourteen days were expired. At last, to my great surprise, when I was, with the utmost impatience, looking out at the window, expecting the postman that usually brought the foreign letters—I say I was agreeably surprised to see a coach come to the yard-gate where we lived, and my woman Amy alight out of it and come towards the door, having the coachman bringing several bundles after her.

I flew like lightning downstairs to speak to her, but was soon damped with her news. "Is the prince alive or dead, Amy?" says I. She spoke coldly and slightly. "He is alive, madam," said she. "But it is not much matter; I had as lieu he had been dead." So we went upstairs again to my chamber, and there we began a serious discourse of the whole matter.

First, she told me a long story of his being hurt by a wild boar, and of the condition he was reduced to, so that every one expected he should die, the anguish of the wound having thrown him into a fever, with abundance of circumstances too long to relate here; how he recovered of that extreme danger, but continued very weak; how the gentleman had been homme de parole, and had sent back the courier as punctually as if it had been to the king; that he had given a long account of his lord, and of his illness and recovery; but the sum of the matter, as to me, was, that as to the lady, his lord was turned penitent, was under some vows for his recovery, and could not think any more on that affair; and especially, the lady being gone, and that it had not been offered to her, so there was no breach of honour; but that his lord was sensible of the good offices of Mrs. Amy, and had sent her the fifty pistoles for her trouble, as if she had really gone the journey.

I was, I confess, hardly able to bear the first surprise of this disappointment. Amy saw it, and gapes out (as was her way), "Lawd, madam! never be concerned at it; you see he is gotten among the priests, and I suppose they have saucily imposed some penance upon him, and, it may be, sent him of an errand barefoot to some Madonna or Nôtredame, or other; and he is off of his amours for the present. I'll warrant you he'll be as wicked again as ever he was when he is got thorough well, and gets but out of their hands again. I hate this out-o'-season repentance. What occasion had he, in his repentance, to be off of taking a good wife? I should have been glad to see you have been a princess, and all that; but if it can't be, never afflict yourself; you are rich enough to be a princess to yourself; you don't want him, that's the best of it."

Well, I cried for all that, and was heartily vexed, and that a great while; but as Amy was always at my elbow, and always jogging it out of my head with her mirth and her wit, it wore off again.

Then I told Amy all the story of my merchant, and how he had found me out when I was in such a concern to find him; how it was true that he lodged in St. Laurence Pountney's Lane; and how I had had all the story of his misfortune, which she had heard of, in which he had lost above £8000 sterling; and that he had told me frankly of it before she had sent me any account of it, or at least before I had taken any notice that I had heard of it.

Amy was very joyful at that part. "Well, madam, then," says Amy, "what need you value the story of the prince, and going I know not whither into Germany to lay your bones in another world, and learn the devil's language, called High Dutch? You are better here by half," says Amy. "Lawd, madam!" says she; "why, are you not as rich as Crœsus?"

Well, it was a great while still before I could bring myself off of this fancied sovereignty; and I, that was so willing once to be mistress to a king, was now ten thousand times more fond of being wife to a prince.

So fast a hold has pride and ambition upon our minds, that when once it gets admission, nothing is so chimerical but, under this possession, we can form ideas of in our fancy and realise to our imagination. Nothing can be so ridiculous as the simple steps we take in such cases; a man or a woman becomes a mere malade imaginaire, and, I believe, may as easily die with grief or run mad with joy (as the affair in his fancy appears right or wrong) as if all was real, and actually under the management of the person.

I had indeed two assistants to deliver me from this snare, and these were, first, Amy, who knew my disease, but was able to do nothing as to the remedy; the second, the merchant, who really brought the remedy, but knew nothing of the distemper.

I remember, when all these disorders were upon my thoughts, in one of the visits my friend the merchant made me, he took notice that he perceived I was under some unusual disorder; he believed, he said, that my distemper, whatever it was, lay much in my head, and it being summer weather and very hot, proposed to me to go a little way into the air.

I started at his expression. "What!" says I; "do you think, then, that I am crazed? You should, then, propose a madhouse for my cure." "No, no," says he, "I do not mean anything like that; I hope the head may be distempered and not the brain." Well, I was too sensible that he was right, for I knew I had acted a strange, wild kind of part with him; but he insisted upon it, and pressed me to go into the country. I took him short again. "What need you," says I, "send me out of your way? It is in your power to be less troubled with me, and with less inconvenience to us both."

He took that ill, and told me I used to have a better opinion of his sincerity, and desired to know what he had done to forfeit my charity. I mention this only to let you see how far I had gone in my measures of quitting him—that is to say, how near I was of showing him how base, ungrateful, and how vilely I could act; but I found I had carried the jest far enough, and that a little matter might have made him sick of me again, as he was before; so I began by little and little to change my way of talking to him, and to come to discourse to the purpose again as we had done before.

A while after this, when we were very merry and talking familiarly together, he called me, with an air of particular satisfaction, his princess. I coloured at the word, for it indeed touched me to the quick; but he knew nothing of the reason of my being touched with it. "What d'ye mean by that?" said I. "Nay," says he, "I mean nothing but that you are a princess to me." "Well," says I, "as to that I am content, and yet I could tell you I might have been a princess if I would have quitted you, and believe I could be so still." "It is not in my power to make you a princess," says he, "but I can easily make you a lady here in England, and a countess too if you will go out of it."

I heard both with a great deal of satisfaction, for my pride remained though it had been balked, and I thought with myself that this proposal would make me some amends for the loss of the title that had so tickled my imagination another way, and I was impatient to understand what he meant, but I would not ask him by any means; so it passed off for that time.

When he was gone I told Amy what he had said, and Amy was as impatient to know the manner how it could be as I was; but the next time (perfectly unexpected to me) he told me that he had accidentally mentioned a thing to me last time he was with me, having not the least thought of the thing itself; but not knowing but such a thing might be of some weight to me, and that it might bring me respect among people where I might appear, he had thought since of it, and was resolved to ask me about it.

I made light of it, and told him that, as he knew I had chosen a retired life, it was of no value to me to be called lady or countess either; but that if he intended to drag me, as I might call it, into the world again, perhaps it might be agreeable to him; but, besides that, I could not judge of the thing, because I did not understand how either of them was to be done.

He told me that money purchased titles of honour in almost all parts of the world, though money could not give principles of honour, they must come by birth and blood; that, however, titles sometimes assist to elevate the soul and to infuse generous principles into the mind, and especially where there was a good foundation laid in the persons; that he hoped we should neither of us misbehave if we came to it; and that as we knew how to wear a title without undue elevations, so it might sit as well upon us as on another; that as to England, he had nothing to do but to get an act of naturalisation in his favour, and he knew where to purchase a patent for baronet—that is say, to have the honour and title transferred to him; but if I intended to go abroad with him, he had a nephew, the son of his eldest brother, who had the title of count, with the estate annexed, which was but small, and that he had frequently offered to make it over to him for a thousand pistoles, which was not a great deal of money, and considering it was in the family already, he would, upon my being willing, purchase it immediately.

I told him I liked the last best, but then I would not let him buy it unless he would let me pay the thousand pistoles. "No, no," says he, "I refused a thousand pistoles that I had more right to have accepted than that, and you shall not be at so much expense now." "Yes," says I, "you did refuse it, and perhaps repented it afterwards." "I never complained," said he. "But I did," says I, "and often repented it for you." "I do not understand you," says he. "Why," said I, "I repented that I suffered you to refuse it." "Well, well," said he, "we may talk of that hereafter, when you shall resolve which part of the world you will make your settled residence in." Here he talked very handsomely to me, and for a good while together; how it had been his lot to live all his days out of his native country, and to be often shifting and changing the situation of his affairs; and that I myself had not always had a fixed abode, but that now, as neither of us was very young, he fancied I would be for taking up our abode where, if possible, we might remove no more; that as to his part, he was of that opinion entirely, only with this exception, that the choice of the place should be mine, for that all places in the world were alike to him, only with this single addition, namely, that I was with him.

I heard him with a great deal of pleasure, as well for his being willing to give me the choice as for that I resolved to live abroad, for the reason I have mentioned already, namely, lest I should at any time be known in England, and all that story of Roxana and the balls should come out; as also I was not a little tickled with the satisfaction of being still a countess, though I could not be a princess.

I told Amy all this story, for she was still my privy councillor; but when I asked her opinion, she made me laugh heartily. "Now, which of the two shall I take, Amy?" said I. "Shall I be a lady—that is, a baronet's lady in England, or a countess in Holland?" The ready-witted jade, that knew the pride of my temper too, almost as well as I did myself, answered (without the least hesitation), "Both, madam. Which of them?" says she (repeating the words). "Why not both of them? and then you will be really a princess; for, sure, to be a lady in English and a countess in Dutch may make a princess in High Dutch." Upon the whole, though Amy was in jest, she put the thought into my head, and I resolved that, in short, I would be both of them, which I managed as you shall hear.

First, I seemed to resolve that I would live and settle in England, only with this condition, namely, that I would not live in London. I pretended that it would choke me up; that I wanted breath when I was in London, but that anywhere else I would be satisfied; and then I asked him whether any seaport town in England would not suit him; because I knew, though he seemed to leave off, he would always love to be among business, and conversing with men of business; and I named several places, either nearest for business with France or with Holland; as Dover or Southampton, for the first; and Ipswich, or Yarmouth, or Hull for the last; but I took care that we would resolve upon nothing; only by this it seemed to be certain that we should live in England.

It was time now to bring things to a conclusion, and so in about six weeks' time more we settled all our preliminaries; and, among the rest, he let me know that he should have the bill for his naturalisation passed time enough, so that he would be (as he called it) an Englishman before we married. That was soon perfected, the Parliament being then sitting, and several other foreigners joining in the said bill to save the expense.

It was not above three or four days after, but that, without giving me the least notice that he had so much as been about the patent for baronet, he brought it me in a fine embroidered bag, and saluting me by the name of my Lady —— (joining his own surname to it), presented it to me with his picture set with diamonds, and at the same time gave me a breast-jewel worth a thousand pistoles, and the next morning we were married. Thus I put an end to all the intriguing part of my life—a life full of prosperous wickedness; the reflections upon which were so much the more afflicting as the time had been spent in the grossest crimes, which, the more I looked back upon, the more black and horrid they appeared, effectually drinking up all the comfort and satisfaction which I might otherwise have taken in that part of life which was still before me.

The first satisfaction, however, that I took in the new condition I was in was in reflecting that at length the life of crime was over, and that I was like a passenger coming back from the Indies, who, having, after many years' fatigues and hurry in business, gotten a good estate, with innumerable difficulties and hazards, is arrived safe at London with all his effects, and has the pleasure of saying he shall never venture upon the seas any more.

When we were married we came back immediately to my lodgings (for the church was but just by), and we were so privately married that none but Amy and my friend the Quaker was acquainted with it. As soon as we came into the house he took me in his arms, and kissing me, "Now you are my own," says he. "Oh that you had been so good to have done this eleven years ago!" "Then," said I, "you, perhaps, would have been tired of me long ago; it is much better now, for now all our happy days are to come. Besides," said I, "I should not have been half so rich;" but that I said to myself, for there was no letting him into the reason of it. "Oh!" says he, "I should not have been tired of you; but, besides having the satisfaction of your company, it had saved me that unlucky blow at Paris, which was a dead loss to me of above eight thousand pistoles, and all the fatigues of so many years' hurry and business;" and then he added, "But I'll make you pay for it all, now I have you." I started a little at the words. "Ay," said I, "do you threaten already? Pray what d'ye mean by that?" and began to look a little grave.

"I'll tell you," says he, "very plainly what I mean;" and still he held me fast in his arms. "I intend from this time never to trouble myself with any more business, so I shall never get one shilling for you more than I have already; all that you will lose one way. Next, I intend not to trouble myself with any of the care or trouble of managing what either you have for me or what I have to add to it; but you shall e'en take it all upon yourself, as the wives do in Holland; so you will pay for it that way too, for all the drudgery shall be yours. Thirdly, I intend to condemn you to the constant bondage of my impertinent company, for I shall tie you like a pedlar's pack at my back. I shall scarce ever be from you; for I am sure I can take delight in nothing else in this world." "Very well," says I; "but I am pretty heavy. I hope you'll set me down sometimes when you are aweary." "As for that," says he, "tire me if you can."

This was all jest and allegory; but it was all true, in the moral of the fable, as you shall hear in its place. We were very merry the rest of the day, but without any noise or clutter; for he brought not one of his acquaintance or friends, either English or foreigner. The honest Quaker provided us a very noble dinner indeed, considering how few we were to eat it; and every day that week she did the like, and would at last have it be all at her own charge, which I was utterly averse to; first, because I knew her circumstances not to be very great, though not very low; and next, because she had been so true a friend, and so cheerful a comforter to me, ay, and counsellor too, in all this affair, that I had resolved to make her a present that should be some help to her when all was over.

But to return to the circumstances of our wedding. After being very merry, as I have told you, Amy and the Quaker put us to bed, the honest Quaker little thinking we had been abed together eleven years before. Nay, that was a secret which, as it happened, Amy herself did not know. Amy grinned and made faces, as if she had been pleased; but it came out in so many words, when he was not by, the sum of her mumbling and muttering was, that this should have been done ten or a dozen years before; that it would signify little now; that was to say, in short, that her mistress was pretty near fifty, and too old to have any children. I chid her; the Quaker laughed, complimented me upon my not being so old as Amy pretended, that I could not be above forty, and might have a house full of children yet. But Amy and I too knew better than she how it was, for, in short, I was old enough to have done breeding, however I looked; but I made her hold her tongue.

In the morning my Quaker landlady came and visited us before we were up, and made us eat cakes and drink chocolate in bed; and then left us again, and bid us take a nap upon it, which I believe we did. In short, she treated us so handsomely, and with such an agreeable cheerfulness, as well as plenty, as made it appear to me that Quakers may, and that this Quaker did, understand good manners as well as any other people.

I resisted her offer, however, of treating us for the whole week; and I opposed it so long that I saw evidently that she took it ill, and would have thought herself slighted if we had not accepted it. So I said no more, but let her go on, only told her I would be even with her; and so I was. However, for that week she treated us as she said she would, and did it so very fine, and with such a profusion of all sorts of good things, that the greatest burthen to her was how to dispose of things that were left; for she never let anything, how dainty or however large, be so much as seen twice among us.

I had some servants indeed, which helped her off a little; that is to say, two maids, for Amy was now a woman of business, not a servant, and ate always with us. I had also a coachman and a boy. My Quaker had a man-servant too, but had but one maid; but she borrowed two more of some of her friends for the occasion, and had a man-cook for dressing the victuals.

She was only at a loss for plate, which she gave me a whisper of; and I made Amy fetch a large strong-box, which I had lodged in a safe hand, in which was all the fine plate which I had provided on a worse occasion, as is mentioned before; and I put it into the Quaker's hand, obliging her not to use it as mine, but as her own, for a reason I shall mention presently.

I was now my Lady —, and I must own I was exceedingly pleased with it; 'twas so big and so great to hear myself called "her ladyship," and "your ladyship," and the like, that I was like the Indian king at Virginia, who, having a house built for him by the English, and a lock put upon the door, would sit whole days together with the key in his hand, locking and unlocking, and double-locking, the door, with an unaccountable pleasure at the novelty; so I could have sat a whole day together to hear Amy talk to me, and call me "your ladyship" at every word; but after a while the novelty wore off and the pride of it abated, till at last truly I wanted the other title as much as I did that of ladyship before.

We lived this week in all the innocent mirth imaginable, and our good-humoured Quaker was so pleasant in her way that it was particularly entertaining to us. We had no music at all, or dancing; only I now and then sung a French song to divert my spouse, who desired it, and the privacy of our mirth greatly added to the pleasure of it. I did not make many clothes for my wedding, having always a great many rich clothes by me, which, with a little altering for the fashion, were perfectly new. The next day he pressed me to dress, though we had no company. At last, jesting with him, I told him I believed I was able to dress me so, in one kind of dress that I had by me, that he would not know his wife when he saw her, especially if anybody else was by. No, he said, that was impossible, and he longed to see that dress. I told him I would dress me in it, if he would promise me never to desire me to appear in it before company. He promised he would not, but wanted to know why too; as husbands, you know, are inquisitive creatures, and love to inquire after anything they think is kept from them; but I had an answer ready for him. "Because," said I, "it is not a decent dress in this country, and would not look modest." Neither, indeed, would it, for it was but one degree off from appearing in one's shift, but was the usual wear in the country where they were used. He was satisfied with my answer, and gave me his promise never to ask me to be seen in it before company. I then withdrew, taking only Amy and the Quaker with me; and Amy dressed me in my old Turkish habit which I danced in formerly, &c., as before. The Quaker was charmed with the dress, and merrily said, that if such a dress should come to be worn here, she should not know what to do; she should be tempted not to dress in the Quaker's way any more.

When all the dress was put on, I loaded it with jewels, and in particular I placed the large breast-jewel which he had given me of a thousand pistoles upon the front of the tyhaia, or head-dress, where it made a most glorious show indeed. I had my own diamond necklace on, and my hair was tout brilliant, all glittering with jewels.

His picture set with diamonds I had placed stitched to my vest, just, as might be supposed, upon my heart (which is the compliment in such cases among the Eastern people); and all being open at the breast, there was no room for anything of a jewel there.
In this figure, Amy holding the train of my robe, I came down to him. He was surprised, and perfectly astonished. He knew me, to be sure, because I had prepared him, and because there was nobody else there but the Quaker and Amy; but he by no means knew Amy, for she had dressed herself in the habit of a Turkish slave, being the garb of my little Turk which I had at Naples, as I have said; she had her neck and arms bare, was bareheaded, and her hair braided in a long tassel hanging down her back; but the jade could neither hold her countenance or her chattering tongue, so as to be concealed long.

Well, he was so charmed with this dress that he would have me sit and dine in it; but it was so thin, and so open before, and the weather being also sharp, that I was afraid of taking cold; however, the fire being enlarged and the doors kept shut, I sat to oblige him, and he professed he never saw so fine a dress in his life. I afterwards told him that my husband (so he called the jeweller that was killed) bought it for me at Leghorn, with a young Turkish slave which I parted with at Paris; and that it was by the help of that slave that I learned how to dress in it, and how everything was to be worn, and many of the Turkish customs also, with some of their language. This story agreeing with the fact, only changing the person, was very natural, and so it went off with him; but there was good reason why I should not receive any company in this dress—that is to say, not in England. I need not repeat it; you will hear more of it.

But when I came abroad I frequently put it on, and upon two or three occasions danced in it, but always at his request.

We continued at the Quaker's lodgings for above a year; for now, making as though it was difficult to determine where to settle in England to his satisfaction, unless in London, which was not to mine, I pretended to make him an offer, that, to oblige him, I began to incline to go and live abroad with him; that I knew nothing could be more agreeable to him, and that as to me, every place was alike; that, as I had lived abroad without a husband so many years, it could be no burthen to me to live abroad again, especially with him. Then we fell to straining our courtesies upon one another. He told me he was perfectly easy at living in England, and had squared all his affairs accordingly; for that, as he had told me he intended to give over all business in the world, as well the care of managing it as the concern about it, seeing we were both in condition neither to want it or to have it be worth our while, so I might see it was his intention, by his getting himself naturalised, and getting the patent of baronet, &c. Well, for all that, I told him I accepted his compliment, but I could not but know that his native country, where his children were breeding up, must be most agreeable to him, and that, if I was of such value to him, I would be there then, to enhance the rate of his satisfaction; that wherever he was would be a home to me, and any place in the world would be England to me if he was with me; and thus, in short, I brought him to give me leave to oblige him with going to live abroad, when, in truth, I could not have been perfectly easy at living in England, unless I had kept constantly within doors, lest some time or other the dissolute life I had lived here should have come to be known, and all those wicked things have been known too, which I now began to be very much ashamed of.

When we closed up our wedding week, in which our Quaker had been so very handsome to us, I told him how much I thought we were obliged to her for her generous carriage to us; how she had acted the kindest part through the whole, and how faithful a friend she had been to me upon all occasions; and then letting him know a little of her family unhappiness, I proposed that I thought I not only ought to be grateful to her, but really to do something extraordinary for her, towards making her easy in her affairs. And I added, that I had no hangers-on that should trouble him; that there was nobody belonged to me but what was thoroughly provided for, and that, if I did something for this honest woman that was considerable, it should be the last gift I would give to anybody in the world but Amy; and as for her, we were not agoing to turn her adrift, but whenever anything offered for her, we would do as we saw cause; that, in the meantime, Amy was not poor, that she had saved together between seven and eight hundred pounds. By the way, I did not tell him how, and by what wicked ways she got it, but that she had it; and that was enough to let him know she would never be in want of us.

My spouse was exceedingly pleased with my discourse about the Quaker, made a kind of a speech to me upon the subject of gratitude, told me it was one of the brightest parts of a gentlewoman, that it was so twisted with honesty, nay, and even with religion too, that he questioned whether either of them could be found where gratitude was not to be found; that in this act there was not only gratitude, but charity; and that to make the charity still more Christian-like, the object too had real merit to attract it; he therefore agreed to the thing with all his heart, only would have had me let him pay it out of his effects.

I told him, as for that, I did not design, whatever I had said formerly, that we should have two pockets; and that though I had talked to him of being a free woman, and an independent, and the like, and he had offered and promised that I should keep all my own estate in my own hands; yet, that since I had taken him, I would e'en do as other honest wives did—where I thought fit to give myself, I should give what I had too; that if I reserved anything, it should be only in case of mortality, and that I might give it to his children afterwards, as my own gift; and that, in short, if he thought fit to join stocks, we would see to-morrow morning what strength we could both make up in the world, and bringing it all together, consider, before we resolved upon the place of removing, how we should dispose of what we had, as well as of ourselves. This discourse was too obliging, and he too much of a man of sense not to receive it as it was meant. He only answered, we would do in that as we should both agree; but the thing under our present care was to show not gratitude only, but charity and affection too, to our kind friend the Quaker; and the first word he spoke of was to settle a thousand pounds upon her for her life—that is to say, sixty pounds a year—but in such a manner as not to be in the power of any person to reach but herself. This was a great thing, and indeed showed the generous principles of my husband, and for that reason I mention it; but I thought that a little too much too, and particularly because I had another thing in view for her about the plate; so I told him I thought, if he gave her a purse with a hundred guineas as a present first, and then made her a compliment of £40 per annum for her life, secured any such way as she should desire, it would be very handsome.

He agreed to that; and the same day, in the evening, when we were just going to bed, he took my Quaker by the hand, and, with a kiss, told her that we had been very kindly treated by her from the beginning of this affair, and his wife before, as she (meaning me) had informed him; and that he thought himself bound to let her see that she had obliged friends who knew how to be grateful; that for his part of the obligation he desired she would accept of that, for an acknowledgment in part only (putting the gold into her hand), and that his wife would talk with her about what farther he had to say to her; and upon that, not giving her time hardly to say "Thank ye," away he went upstairs into our bedchamber, leaving her confused and not knowing what to say.

When he was gone she began to make very handsome and obliging representations of her goodwill to us both, but that it was without expectation of reward; that I had given her several valuable presents before—and so, indeed, I had; for, besides the piece of linen which I had given her at first, I had given her a suit of damask table-linen, of the linen I bought for my balls, viz., three table-cloths and three dozen of napkins; and at another time I gave her a little necklace of gold beads, and the like; but that is by the way. But she mentioned them, I say, and how she was obliged by me on many other occasions; that she was not in condition to show her gratitude any other way, not being able to make a suitable return; and that now we took from her all opportunity, to balance my former friendship, and left her more in debt than she was before. She spoke this in a very good kind of manner, in her own way, but which was very agreeable indeed, and had as much apparent sincerity, and I verily believe as real as was possible to be expressed; but I put a stop to it, and bade her say no more, but accept of what my spouse had given her, which was but in part, as she had heard him say. "And put it up," says I, "and come and sit down here, and give me leave to say something else to you on the same head, which my spouse and I have settled between ourselves in your behalf." "What dost thee mean?" says she, and blushed, and looked surprised, but did not stir. She was going to speak again, but I interrupted her, and told her she should make no more apologies of any kind whatever, for I had better things than all this to talk to her of; so I went on, and told her, that as she had been so friendly and kind to us on every occasion, and that her house was the lucky place where we came together, and that she knew I was from her own mouth acquainted in part with her circumstances, we were resolved she should be the better for us as long as she lived. Then I told what we had resolved to do for her, and that she had nothing more to do but to consult with me how it should be effectually secured for her, distinct from any of the effects which were her husband's; and that if her husband did so supply her that she could live comfortably, and not want it for bread or other necessaries, she should not make use of it, but lay up the income of it, and add it every year to the principal, so to increase the annual payment, which in time, and perhaps before she might come to want it, might double itself; that we were very willing whatever she should so lay up should be to herself, and whoever she thought fit after her; but that the forty pounds a year must return to our family after her life, which we both wished might be long and happy.

Let no reader wonder at my extraordinary concern for this poor woman, or at my giving my bounty to her a place in this account. It is not, I assure you, to make a pageantry of my charity, or to value myself upon the greatness of my soul, that should give in so profuse a manner as this, which was above my figure, if my wealth had been twice as much as it was; but there was another spring from whence all flowed, and 'tis on that account I speak of it. Was it possible I could think of a poor desolate woman with four children, and her husband gone from her, and perhaps good for little if he had stayed—I say, was I, that had tasted so deep of the sorrows of such a kind of widowhood, able to look on her, and think of her circumstances, and not be touched in an uncommon manner? No, no; I never looked on her and her family, though she was not left so helpless and friendless as I had been, without remembering my own condition, when Amy was sent out to pawn or sell my pair of stays to buy a breast of mutton and a bunch of turnips; nor could I look on her poor children, though not poor and perishing, like mine, without tears; reflecting on the dreadful condition that mine were reduced to, when poor Amy sent them all into their aunt's in Spitalfields, and run away from them. These were the original springs, or fountain-head, from whence my affectionate thoughts were moved to assist this poor woman.

When a poor debtor, having lain long in the Compter, or Ludgate, or the King's Bench for debt, afterwards gets out, rises again in the world, and grows rich, such a one is a certain benefactor to the prisoners there, and perhaps to every prison he passes by as long as he lives, for he remembers the dark days of his own sorrow; and even those who never had the experience of such sorrows to stir up their minds to acts of charity would have the same charitable, good disposition did they as sensibly remember what it is that distinguishes them from others by a more favourable and merciful Providence.

This, I say, was, however, the spring of my concern for this honest, friendly, and grateful Quaker; and as I had so plentiful a fortune in the world, I resolved she should taste the fruit of her kind usage to me in a manner that she could not expect.

All the while I talked to her I saw the disorder of her mind; the sudden joy was too much for her, and she coloured, trembled, changed, and at last grew pale, and was indeed near fainting, when she hastily rung a little bell for her maid, who coming in immediately, she beckoned to her—for speak she could not—to fill her a glass of wine; but she had no breath to take it in, and was almost choked with that which she took in her mouth. I saw she was ill, and assisted her what I could, and with spirits and things to smell to just kept her from fainting, when she beckoned to her maid to withdraw, and immediately burst out in crying, and that relieved her. When she recovered herself a little she flew to me, and throwing her arms about my neck, "Oh!" says she, "thou hast almost killed me;" and there she hung, laying her head in my neck for half a quarter of an hour, not able to speak, but sobbing like a child that had been whipped.

I was very sorry that I did not stop a little in the middle of my discourse and make her drink a glass of wine before it had put her spirits into such a violent motion; but it was too late, and it was ten to one odds but that it had killed her.

But she came to herself at last, and began to say some very good things in return for my kindness. I would not let her go on, but told her I had more to say to her still than all this, but that I would let it alone till another time. My meaning was about the box of plate, good part of which I gave her, and some I gave to Amy; for I had so much plate, and some so large, that I thought if I let my husband see it he might be apt to wonder what occasion I could ever have for so much, and for plate of such a kind too; as particularly a great cistern for bottles, which cost a hundred and twenty pounds, and some large candlesticks too big for any ordinary use. These I caused Amy to sell; in short, Amy sold above three hundred pounds' worth of plate; what I gave the Quaker was worth above sixty pounds, and I gave Amy above thirty pounds' worth, and yet I had a great deal left for my husband.

Nor did our kindness to the Quaker end with the forty pounds a year, for we were always, while we stayed with her, which was above ten months, giving her one good thing or another; and, in a word, instead of lodging with her, she boarded with us, for I kept the house, and she and all her family ate and drank with us, and yet we paid her the rent of the house too; in short, I remembered my widowhood, and I made this widow's heart glad many a day the more upon that account.

And now my spouse and I began to think of going over to Holland, where I had proposed to him to live, and in order to settle all the preliminaries of our future manner of living, I began to draw in my effects, so as to have them all at command upon whatever occasion we thought fit; after which, one morning I called my spouse up to me: "Hark ye, sir," said I to him, "I have two very weighty questions to ask of you. I don't know what answer you will give to the first, but I doubt you will be able to give but a sorry answer to the other, and yet, I assure you, it is of the last importance to yourself, and towards the future part of your life, wherever it is to be."

He did not seem to be much alarmed, because he could see I was speaking in a kind of merry way. "Let's hear your questions, my dear," says he, "and I'll give the best answer I can to them." "Why, first," says I:

"I. You have married a wife here, made her a lady, and put her in expectation of being something else still when she comes abroad. Pray have you examined whether you are able to supply all her extravagant demands when she comes abroad, and maintain an expensive Englishwoman in all her pride and vanity? In short, have you inquired whether you are able to keep her?

"II. You have married a wife here, and given her a great many fine things, and you maintain her like a princess, and sometimes call her so. Pray what portion have you had with her? what fortune has she been to you? and where does her estate lie, that you keep her so fine? I am afraid that you keep her in a figure a great deal above her estate, at least above all that you have seen of it yet. Are you sure you han't got a bite, and that you have not made a beggar a lady?"

"Well," says he, "have you any more questions to ask? Let's have them all together; perhaps they may be all answered in a few words, as well as these two." "No," says I, "these are the two grand questions—at least for the present." "Why, then," says he, "I'll answer you in a few words; that I am fully master of my own circumstances, and, without farther inquiry, can let my wife you speak of know, that as I have made her a lady I can maintain her as a lady, wherever she goes with me; and this whether I have one pistole of her portion, or whether she has any portion or no; and as I have not inquired whether she has any portion or not, so she shall not have the less respect showed her from me, or be obliged to live meaner, or be anyways straitened on that account; on the contrary, if she goes abroad to live with me in my own country, I will make her more than a lady, and support the expense of it too, without meddling with anything she has; and this, I suppose," says he, "contains an answer to both your questions together."

He spoke this with a great deal more earnestness in his countenance than I had when I proposed my questions, and said a great many kind things upon it, as the consequence of former discourses, so that I was obliged to be in earnest too. "My dear," says I, "I was but in jest in my questions; but they were proposed to introduce what I am going to say to you in earnest; namely, that if I am to go abroad, 'tis time I should let you know how things stand, and what I have to bring you with your wife; how it is to be disposed and secured, and the like; and therefore come," says I, "sit down, and let me show you your bargain here; I hope you will find that you have not got a wife without a fortune."

He told me then, that since he found I was in earnest, he desired that I would adjourn it till to-morrow, and then we would do as the poor people do after they marry, feel in their pockets, and see how much money they can bring together in the world. "Well," says I, "with all my heart;" and so we ended our talk for that time.

As this was in the morning, my spouse went out after dinner to his goldsmith's, as he said, and about three hours after returns with a porter and two large boxes with him; and his servant brought another box, which I observed was almost as heavy as the two that the porter brought, and made the poor fellow sweat heartily; he dismissed the porter, and in a little while after went out again with his man, and returning at night, brought another porter with more boxes and bundles, and all was carried up, and put into a chamber, next to our bedchamber; and in the morning he called for a pretty large round table, and began to unpack.

When the boxes were opened, I found they were chiefly full of books, and papers, and parchments, I mean books of accounts, and writings, and such things as were in themselves of no moment to me, because I understood them not; but I perceived he took them all out, and spread them about him upon the table and chairs, and began to be very busy with them; so I withdrew and left him; and he was indeed so busy among them, that he never missed me till I had been gone a good while; but when he had gone through all his papers, and come to open a little box, he called for me again. "Now," says he, and called me his countess, "I am ready to answer your first question; if you will sit down till I have opened this box, we will see how it stands."

So we opened the box; there was in it indeed what I did not expect, for I thought he had sunk his estate rather than raised it; but he produced me in goldsmiths' bills, and stock in the English East India Company, about sixteen thousand pounds sterling; then he gave into my hands nine assignments upon the Bank of Lyons in France, and two upon the rents of the town-house in Paris, amounting in the whole to 5800 crowns per annum, or annual rent, as it is called there; and lastly, the sum of 30,000 rixdollars in the Bank of Amsterdam; besides some jewels and gold in the box to the value of about £1500 or £1600, among which was a very good necklace of pearl of about £200 value; and that he pulled out and tied about my neck, telling me that should not be reckoned into the account.

I was equally pleased and surprised, and it was with an inexpressible joy that I saw him so rich.

"You might well tell me," said I, "that you were able to make me countess, and maintain me as such." In short, he was immensely rich; for besides all this, he showed me, which was the reason of his being so busy among the books, I say, he showed me several adventures he had abroad in the business of his merchandise; as particularly an eighth share in an East India ship then abroad; an account-courant with a merchant at Cadiz in Spain; about £3000 lent upon bottomry, upon ships gone to the Indies; and a large cargo of goods in a merchant's hands, for sale at Lisbon in Portugal; so that in his books there was about £12,000 more; all which put together, made about £27,000 sterling, and £1320 a year.

I stood amazed at this account, as well I might, and said nothing to him for a good while, and the rather because I saw him still busy looking over his books. After a while, as I was going to express my wonder, "Hold, my dear," says he, "this is not all neither;" then he pulled me out some old seals, and small parchment rolls, which I did not understand; but he told me they were a right of reversion which he had to a paternal estate in his family, and a mortgage of 14,000 rixdollars, which he had upon it, in the hands of the present possessor; so that was about £3000 more.

"But now hold again," says he, "for I must pay my debts out of all this, and they are very great, I assure you;" and the first he said was a black article of 8000 pistoles, which he had a lawsuit about at Paris, but had it awarded against him, which was the loss he had told me of, and which made him leave Paris in disgust; that in other accounts he owed about £5300 sterling; but after all this, upon the whole, he had still £17,000 clear stock in money, and £1320 a year in rent.

After some pause, it came to my turn to speak. "Well," says I, "'tis very hard a gentleman with such a fortune as this should come over to England, and marry a wife with nothing; it shall never," says I, "be said, but what I have, I'll bring into the public stock;" so I began to produce.

First, I pulled out the mortgage which good Sir Robert had procured for me, the annual rent £700 per annum; the principal money £14,000.

Secondly, I pulled out another mortgage upon land, procured by the same faithful friend, which at three times had advanced £12,000.

Thirdly, I pulled him out a parcel of little securities, procured by several hands, by fee-farm rents, and such petty mortgages as those times afforded, amounting to £10,800 principal money, and paying six hundred and thirty-six pounds a-year. So that in the whole there was two thousand and fifty-six pounds a year ready money constantly coming in.

When I had shown him all these, I laid them upon the table, and bade him take them, that he might be able to give me an answer to the second question. What fortune he had with his wife? And laughed a little at it.

He looked at them awhile, and then handed them all back again to me: "I will not touch them," says he, "nor one of them, till they are all settled in trustees' hands for your own use, and the management wholly your own."

I cannot omit what happened to me while all this was acting; though it was cheerful work in the main, yet I trembled every joint of me, worse for aught I know than ever Belshazzar did at the handwriting on the wall, and the occasion was every way as just. "Unhappy wretch," said I to myself, "shall my ill-got wealth, the product of prosperous lust, and of a vile and vicious life of whoredom and adultery, be intermingled with the honest well-gotten estate of this innocent gentleman, to be a moth and a caterpillar among it, and bring the judgments of heaven upon him, and upon what he has, for my sake? Shall my wickedness blast his comforts? Shall I be fire in his flax? and be a means to provoke heaven to curse his blessings? God forbid! I'll keep them asunder if it be possible."

This is the true reason why I have been so particular in the account of my vast acquired stock; and how his estate, which was perhaps the product of many years' fortunate industry, and which was equal if not superior to mine at best, was, at my request, kept apart from mine, as is mentioned above.

I have told you how he gave back all my writings into my own hands again. "Well," says I, "seeing you will have it be kept apart, it shall be so, upon one condition, which I have to propose, and no other." "And what is the condition?" says he. "Why," says I, "all the pretence I can have for the making over my own estate to me is, that in case of your mortality, I may have it reserved for me, if I outlive you." "Well," says he, "that is true" "But then," said I, "the annual income is always received by the husband, during his life, as 'tis supposed, for the mutual subsistence of the family; now," says I, "here is £2000 a year, which I believe is as much as we shall spend, and I desire none of it may be saved; and all the income of your own estate, the interest of the £17,000 and the £1320 a year, may be constantly laid by for the increase of your estate; and so," added I, "by joining the interest every year to the capital you will perhaps grow as rich as you would do if you were to trade with it all, if you were obliged to keep house out of it too."

He liked the proposal very well, and said it should be so; and this way I, in some measure, satisfied myself that I should not bring my husband under the blast of a just Providence, for mingling my cursed ill-gotten wealth with his honest estate. This was occasioned by the reflections which, at some certain intervals of time, came into my thoughts of the justice of heaven, which I had reason to expect would some time or other still fall upon me or my effects, for the dreadful life I had lived.

And let nobody conclude from the strange success I met with in all my wicked doings, and the vast estate which I had raised by it, that therefore I either was happy or easy. No, no, there was a dart struck into the liver; there was a secret hell within, even all the while, when our joy was at the highest; but more especially now, after it was all over, and when, according to all appearance, I was one of the happiest women upon earth; all this while, I say, I had such constant terror upon my mind, as gave me every now and then very terrible shocks, and which made me expect something very frightful upon every accident of life.

In a word, it never lightened or thundered, but I expected the next flash would penetrate my vitals, and melt the sword (soul) in this scabbard of flesh; it never blew a storm of wind, but I expected the fall of some stack of chimneys, or some part of the house, would bury me in its ruins; and so of other things.

But I shall perhaps have occasion to speak of all these things again by-and-by; the case before us was in a manner settled; we had full four thousand pounds per annum for our future subsistence, besides a vast sum in jewels and plate; and besides this, I had about eight thousand pounds reserved in money which I kept back from him, to provide for my two daughters, of whom I have much yet to say.

With this estate, settled as you have heard, and with the best husband in the world, I left England again; I had not only, in human prudence, and by the nature of the thing, being now married and settled in so glorious a manner,—I say, I had not only abandoned all the gay and wicked course which I had gone through before, but I began to look back upon it with that horror and that detestation which is the certain companion, if not the forerunner, of repentance.

Sometimes the wonders of my present circumstances would work upon me, and I should have some raptures upon my soul, upon the subject of my coming so smoothly out of the arms of hell, that I was not ingulfed in ruin, as most who lead such lives are, first or last; but this was a flight too high for me; I was not come to that repentance that is raised from a sense of Heaven's goodness; I repented of the crime, but it was of another and lower kind of repentance, and rather moved by my fears of vengeance, than from a sense of being spared from being punished, and landed safe after a storm.

The first thing which happened after our coming to the Hague (where we lodged for a while) was, that my spouse saluted me one morning with the title of countess, as he said he intended to do, by having the inheritance to which the honour was annexed made over to him. It is true, it was a reversion, but it soon fell, and in the meantime, as all the brothers of a count are called counts, so I had the title by courtesy, about three years before I had it in reality.

I was agreeably surprised at this coming so soon, and would have had my spouse have taken the money which it cost him out of my stock, but he laughed at me, and went on.

I was now in the height of my glory and prosperity, and I was called the Countess de ——; for I had obtained that unlooked for, which I secretly aimed at, and was really the main reason of my coming abroad. I took now more servants, lived in a kind of magnificence that I had not been acquainted with, was called "your honour" at every word, and had a coronet behind my coach; though at the same time I knew little or nothing of my new pedigree.
The first thing that my spouse took upon him to manage, was to declare ourselves married eleven years before our arriving in Holland; and consequently to acknowledge our little son, who was yet in England, to be legitimate; order him to be brought over, and added to his family, and acknowledge him to be our own.

This was done by giving notice to his people at Nimeguen, where his children (which were two sons and a daughter) were brought up, that he was come over from England, and that he was arrived at the Hague with his wife, and should reside there some time, and that he would have his two sons brought down to see him; which accordingly was done, and where I entertained them with all the kindness and tenderness that they could expect from their mother-in-law; and who pretended to be so ever since they were two or three years old.

This supposing us to have been so long married was not difficult at all, in a country where we had been seen together about that time, viz., eleven years and a half before, and where we had never been seen afterwards till we now returned together: this being seen together was also openly owned and acknowledged, of course, by our friend the merchant at

Rotterdam, and also by the people in the house where we both lodged in the same city, and where our first intimacies began, and who, as it happened, were all alive; and therefore, to make it the more public, we made a tour to Rotterdam again, lodged in the same house, and was visited there by our friend the merchant, and afterwards invited frequently to his house, where he treated us very handsomely.

This conduct of my spouse, and which he managed very cleverly, was indeed a testimony of a wonderful degree of honesty and affection to our little son; for it was done purely for the sake of the child.

I call it an honest affection, because it was from a principle of honesty that he so earnestly concerned himself to prevent the scandal which would otherwise have fallen upon the child, who was itself innocent; and as it was from this principle of justice that he so earnestly solicited me, and conjured me by the natural affections of a mother, to marry him when it was yet young within me and unborn, that the child might not suffer for the sin of its father and mother; so, though at the same time he really loved me very well, yet I had reason to believe that it was from this principle of justice to the child that he came to England again to seek me with design to marry me, and, as he called it, save the innocent lamb from infamy worse than death.

It was with a just reproach to myself that I must repeat it again, that I had not the same concern for it, though it was the child of my own body; nor had I ever the hearty affectionate love to the child that he had. What the reason of it was I cannot tell; and, indeed, I had shown a general neglect of the child through all the gay years of my London revels, except that I sent Amy to look upon it now and then, and to pay for its nursing; as for me, I scarce saw it four times in the first four years of its life, and often wished it would go quietly out of the world; whereas a son which I had by the jeweller, I took a different care of, and showed a different concern for, though I did not let him know me; for I provided very well for him, had him put out very well to school, and when he came to years fit for it, let him go over with a person of honesty and good business, to the Indies; and after he had lived there some time, and began to act for himself, sent him over the value of £2000, at several times, with which he traded and grew rich; and, as 'tis to be hoped, may at last come over again with forty or fifty thousand pounds in his pocket, as many do who have not such encouragement at their beginning.

I also sent him over a wife, a beautiful young lady, well-bred, an exceeding good-natured pleasant creature; but the nice young fellow did not like her, and had the impudence to write to me, that is, to the person I employed to correspond with him, to send him another, and promised that he would marry her I had sent him, to a friend of his, who liked her better than he did; but I took it so ill, that I would not send him another, and withal, stopped another article of £1000 which I had appointed to send him. He considered of it afterwards, and offered to take her; but then truly she took so ill the first affront he put upon her, that she would not have him, and I sent him word I thought she was very much in the right. However, after courting her two years, and some friends interposing, she took him, and made him an excellent wife, as I knew she would, but I never sent him the thousand pounds cargo, so that he lost that money for misusing me, and took the lady at last without it.

My new spouse and I lived a very regular, contemplative life; and, in itself, certainly a life filled with all human felicity. But if I looked upon my present situation with satisfaction, as I certainly did, so, in proportion, I on all occasions looked back on former things with detestation, and with the utmost affliction; and now, indeed, and not till now, those reflections began to prey upon my comforts, and lessen the sweets of my other enjoyments. They might be said to have gnawed a hole in my heart before; but now they made a hole quite through it: now they ate into all my pleasant things, made bitter every sweet, and mixed my sighs with every smile.

Not all the affluence of a plentiful fortune; not a hundred thousand pounds estate (for, between us, we had little less); not honour and titles, attendants and equipages; in a word, not all the things we call pleasure, could give me any relish, or sweeten the taste of things to me; at least, not so much but I grew sad, heavy, pensive, and melancholy; slept little, and ate little; dreamed continually of the most frightful and terrible things imaginable: nothing but apparitions of devils and monsters, falling into gulfs, and off from steep and high precipices, and the like; so that in the morning, when I should rise, and be refreshed with the blessing of rest, I was hag-ridden with frights and terrible things formed merely in the imagination, and was either tired and wanted sleep, or overrun with vapours, and not fit for conversing with my family, or any one else.

My husband, the tenderest creature in the world, and particularly so to me, was in great concern for me, and did everything that lay in his power to comfort and restore me; strove to reason me out of it; then tried all the ways possible to divert me: but it was all to no purpose, or to but very little.

My only relief was sometimes to unbosom myself to poor Amy, when she and I was alone; and she did all she could to comfort me. But all was to little effect there; for, though Amy was the better penitent before, when we had been in the storm, Amy was just where she used to be now, a wild, gay, loose wretch, and not much the graver for her age; for Amy was between forty and fifty by this time too.

But to go on with my own story. As I had no comforter, so I had no counsellor; it was well, as I often thought, that I was not a Roman Catholic; for what a piece of work should I have made, to have gone to a priest with such a history as I had to tell him; and what penance would any father confessor have obliged me to perform, especially if he had been honest, and true to his office!

However, as I had none of the recourse, so I had none of the absolution, by which the criminal confessing goes away comforted; but I went about with a heart loaded with crime, and altogether in the dark as to what I was to do; and in this condition I languished near two years. I may well call it languishing, for if Providence had not relieved me, I should have died in little time. But of that hereafter.

I must now go back to another scene, and join it to this end of my story, which will complete all my concern with England, at least all that I shall bring into this account.

I have hinted at large what I had done for my two sons, one at Messina, and the other in the Indies; but I have not gone through the story of my two daughters. I was so in danger of being known by one of them, that I durst not see her, so as to let her know who I was; and for the other, I could not well know how to see her, and own her, and let her see me, because she must then know that I would not let her sister know me, which would look strange; so that, upon the whole, I resolved to see neither of them at all. But Amy managed all that for me; and when she had made gentlewomen of them both, by giving them a good, though late education, she had like to have blown up the whole case, and herself and me too, by an unhappy discovery of herself to the last of them, that is, to her who was our cook-maid, and who, as I said before, Amy had been obliged to turn away, for fear of the very discovery which now happened. I have observed already in what manner Amy managed her by a third person; and how the girl, when she was set up for a lady, as above, came and visited Amy at my lodgings; after which, Amy going, as was her custom, to see the girl's brother (my son) at the honest man's house in Spitalfields, both the girls were there, merely by accident, at the same time; and the other girl unawares discovered the secret, namely, that this was the lady that had done all this for them.

Amy was greatly surprised at it; but as she saw there was no remedy, she made a jest of it, and so after that conversed openly, being still satisfied that neither of them could make much of it, as long as they knew nothing of me. So she took them together one time, and told them the history, as she called it, of their mother, beginning at the miserable carrying them to their aunt's; she owned she was not their mother herself, but described her to them. However, when she said she was not their mother, one of them expressed herself very much surprised, for the girl had taken up a strong fancy that Amy was really her mother, and that she had, for some particular reasons, concealed it from her; and therefore, when she told her frankly that she was not her mother, the girl fell a-crying, and Amy had much ado to keep life in her. This was the girl who was at first my cook-maid in the Pall Mall. When Amy had brought her to again a little, and she had recovered her first disorder, Amy asked what ailed her? The poor girl hung about her, and kissed her, and was in such a passion still, though she was a great wench of nineteen or twenty years old, that she could not be brought to speak a great while. At last, having recovered her speech, she said still, "But oh! Do not say you a'n't my mother! I'm sure you are my mother;" and then the girl cried again like to kill herself. Amy could not tell what to do with her a good while; she was loth to say again she was not her mother, because she would not throw her into a fit of crying again; but she went round about a little with her. "Why, child," says she, "why would you have me be your mother? If it be because I am so kind to you, be easy, my dear," says Amy; "I'll be as kind to you still, as if I was your mother."

"Ay, but," says the girl, "I am sure you are my mother too; and what have I done that you won't own me, and that you will not be called my mother? Though I am poor, you have made me a gentlewoman," says she, "and I won't do anything to disgrace you; besides," added she, "I can keep a secret, too, especially for my own mother, sure;" then she calls Amy her dear mother, and hung about her neck again, crying still vehemently.

This last part of the girl's words alarmed Amy, and, as she told me, frighted her terribly; nay, she was so confounded with it, that she was not able to govern herself, or to conceal her disorder from the girl herself, as you shall hear. Amy was at a full stop, and confused to the last degree; and the girl, a sharp jade, turned it upon her. "My dear mother," says she, "do not be uneasy about it; I know it all; but do not be uneasy, I won't let my sister know a word of it, or my brother either, without you giving me leave; but don't disown me now you have found me; don't hide yourself from me any longer; I can't bear that," says she, "it will break my heart."

"I think the girl's mad," says Amy; "why, child, I tell thee, if I was thy mother I would not disown thee; don't you see I am as kind to you as if I was your mother?" Amy might as well have sung a song to a kettledrum, as talk to her. "Yes," says the girl, "you are very good to me indeed;" and that was enough to make anybody believe she was her mother too; but, however, that was not the case, she had other reasons to believe, and to know, that she was her mother; and it was a sad thing she would not let her call her mother, who was her own child.

Amy was so heart-full with the disturbance of it, that she did not enter farther with her into the inquiry, as she would otherwise have done; I mean, as to what made the girl so positive; but comes away, and tells me the whole story.

I was thunderstruck with the story at first, and much more afterwards, as you shall hear; but, I say, I was thunderstruck at first, and amazed, and said to Amy, "There must be something or other in it more than we know of." But, having examined farther into it, I found the girl had no notion of anybody but of Amy; and glad I was that I was not concerned in the pretence, and that the girl had no notion of me in it. But even this easiness did not continue long; for the next time Amy went to see her, she was the same thing, and rather more violent with Amy than she was before. Amy endeavoured to pacify her by all the ways imaginable: first, she told her she took it ill that she would not believe her; and told her, if she would not give over such a foolish whimsey, she would leave her to the wide world as she found her.

This put the girl into fits, and she cried ready to kill herself, and hung about Amy again like a child. "Why," says Amy, "why can you not be easy with me, then, and compose yourself, and let me go on to do you good, and show you kindness, as I would do, and as I intend to do? Can you think that if I was your mother, I would not tell you so? What whimsey is this that possesses your mind?" says Amy. Well, the girl told her in a few words (but those few such as frighted Amy out of her wits, and me too) that she knew well enough how it was. "I know," says she, "when you left ——," naming the village, "where I lived when my father went away from us all, that you went over to France; I know that too, and who you went with," says the girl; "did not my Lady Roxana come back again with you? I know it all well enough; though I was but a child, I have heard it all." And thus she run on with such discourse as put Amy out of all temper again; and she raved at her like a bedlam, and told her she would never come near her any more; she might go a-begging again if she would; she'd have nothing to do with her. The girl, a passionate wench, told her she knew the worst of it, she could go to service again, and if she would not own her own child, she must do as she pleased; then she fell into a passion of crying again, as if she would kill herself.

In short, this girl's conduct terrified Amy to the last degree, and me too; and was it not that we knew the girl was quite wrong in some things, she was yet so right in some other, that it gave me a great deal of perplexity; but that which put Amy the most to it, was that the girl (my daughter) told her that she (meaning me, her mother) had gone away with the jeweller, and into France too; she did not call him the jeweller, but with the landlord of the house; who, after her mother fell into distress, and that Amy had taken all the children from her, made much of her, and afterwards married her.

In short, it was plain the girl had but a broken account of things, but yet that she had received some accounts that had a reality in the bottom of them, so that, it seems, our first measures, and the amour with the jeweller, were not so concealed as I thought they had been; and, it seems, came in a broken manner to my sister-in-law, who Amy carried the children to, and she made some bustle, it seems, about it. But, as good luck was, it was too late, and I was removed and gone, none knew whither, or else she would have sent all the children home to me again, to be sure.

This we picked out of the girl's discourse, that is to say, Amy did, at several times; but it all consisted of broken fragments of stories, such as the girl herself had heard so long ago, that she herself could make very little of it; only that in the main, that her mother had played the whore; had gone away with the gentleman that was landlord of the house; that he married her; that she went into France. And, as she had learned in my family, where she was a servant, that Mrs. Amy and her Lady Roxana had been in France together, so she put all these things together, and joining them with the great kindness that Amy now showed her, possessed the creature that Amy was really her mother, nor was it possible for Amy to conquer it for a long time.

But this, after I had searched into it, as far as by Amy's relation I could get an account of it, did not disquiet me half so much as that the young slut had got the name of Roxana by the end, and that she knew who her Lady Roxana was, and the like; though this, neither, did not hang together, for then she would not have fixed upon Amy for her mother. But some time after, when Amy had almost persuaded her out of it, and that the girl began to be so confounded in her discourses of it, that she made neither head nor tail, at last the passionate creature flew out in a kind of rage, and said to Amy, that if she was not her mother, Madam Roxana was her mother then, for one of them, she was sure, was her mother; and then all this that Amy had done for her was by Madam Roxana's order. "And I am sure," says she, "it was my Lady Roxana's coach that brought the gentlewoman, whoever it was, to my uncle's in Spitalfields, for the coachman told me so." Amy fell a-laughing at her aloud, as was her usual way; but, as Amy told me, it was but on one side of her mouth, for she was so confounded at her discourse, that she was ready to sink into the ground; and so was I too when she told it me.

However, Amy brazened her out of it all; told her, "Well, since you think you are so high-born as to be my Lady Roxana's daughter, you may go to her and claim your kindred, can't you? I suppose," says Amy, "you know where to find her?" She said she did not question to find her, for she knew where she was gone to live privately; but, though, she might be removed again. "For I know how it is," says she, with a kind of a smile or a grin; "I know how it all is, well enough."

Amy was so provoked, that she told me, in short, she began to think it would be absolutely necessary to murder her. That expression filled me with horror, all my blood ran chill in my veins, and a fit of trembling seized me, that I could not speak a good while; at last. "What, is the devil in you, Amy?" said I. "Nay, nay," says she, "let it be the devil or not the devil, if I thought she knew one tittle of your history, I would despatch her if she were my own daughter a thousand times." "And I," says I in a rage, "as well as I love you, would be the first that should put the halter about your neck, and see you hanged with more satisfaction than ever I saw you in my life; nay," says I, "you would not live to be hanged, I believe I should cut your throat with my own hand; I am almost ready to do it," said I, "as 'tis, for your but naming the thing." With that, I called her cursed devil, and bade her get out of the room.

I think it was the first time that ever I was angry with Amy in all my life; and when all was done, though she was a devilish jade in having such a thought, yet it was all of it the effect of her excess of affection and fidelity to me.

But this thing gave me a terrible shock, for it happened just after I was married, and served to hasten my going over to Holland; for I would not have been seen, so as to be known by the name of Roxana, no, not for ten thousand pounds; it would have been enough to have ruined me to all intents and purposes with my husband, and everybody else too; I might as well have been the "German princess."

Well, I set Amy to work; and give Amy her due, she set all her wits to work to find out which way this girl had her knowledge, but, more particularly, how much knowledge she had—that is to say, what she really knew, and what she did not know, for this was the main thing with me; how she could say she knew who Madam Roxana was, and what notions she had of that affair, was very mysterious to me, for it was certain she could not have a right notion of me, because she would have it be that Amy was her mother.

I scolded heartily at Amy for letting the girl ever know her, that is to say, know her in this affair; for that she knew her could not be hid, because she, as I might say, served Amy, or rather under Amy, in my family, as is said before; but she (Amy) talked with her at first by another person, and not by herself; and that secret came out by an accident, as I have said above.

Amy was concerned at it as well as I, but could not help it; and though it gave us great uneasiness, yet, as there was no remedy, we were bound to make as little noise of it as we could, that it might go no farther. I bade Amy punish the girl for it, and she did so, for she parted with her in a huff, and told her she should see she was not her mother, for that she could leave her just where she found her; and seeing she could not be content to be served by the kindness of a friend, but that she would needs make a mother of her, she would, for the future, be neither mother or friend, and so bid her go to service again, and be a drudge as she was before.

The poor girl cried most lamentably, but would not be beaten out of it still; but that which dumbfoundered Amy more than all the rest was that when she had berated the poor girl a long time, and could not beat her out of it, and had, as I have observed, threatened to leave her, the girl kept to what she said before, and put this turn to it again, that she was sure, if Amy wa'n't, my Lady Roxana was her mother, and that she would go find her out; adding, that she made no doubt but she could do it, for she knew where to inquire the name of her new husband.

Amy came home with this piece of news in her mouth to me. I could easily perceive when she came in that she was mad in her mind, and in a rage at something or other, and was in great pain to get it out; for when she came first in, my husband was in the room. However, Amy going up to undress her, I soon made an excuse to follow her, and coming into the room, "What the d—l is the matter, Amy?" says I; "I am sure you have some bad news." "News," says Amy aloud; "ay, so I have; I think the d—l is in that young wench. She'll ruin us all and herself too; there's no quieting her." So she went on and told me all the particulars; but sure nothing was so astonished as I was when she told me that the girl knew I was married, that she knew my husband's name, and would endeavour to find me out. I thought I should have sunk down at the very words. In the middle of all my amazement, Amy starts up and runs about the room like a distracted body. "I must put an end to it, that I will; I can't bear it—I must murder her, I'll kill the b——;" and swears by her Maker, in the most serious tone in the world, and then repeated it over three or four times, walking to and again in the room. "I will, in short, I will kill her, if there was not another wench in the world."

"Prithee hold thy tongue, Amy," says I; "why, thou art mad." "Ay, so I am," says she, "stark mad; but I'll be the death of her for all that, and then I shall be sober again." "But you sha'n't," says I, "you sha'n't hurt a hair of her head; why, you ought to be hanged for what you have done already, for having resolved on it is doing it; as to the guilt of the fact you are a murderer already, as much as if you had done it already."

"I know that," says Amy, "and it can be no worse; I'll put you out of your pain, and her too; she shall never challenge you for her mother in this world, whatever she may in the next." "Well, well," says I, "be quiet, and do not talk thus, I can't bear it." So she grew a little soberer after a while.

I must acknowledge, the notion of being discovered carried with it so many frightful ideas, and hurried my thoughts so much, that I was scarce myself any more than Amy, so dreadful a thing is a load of guilt upon the mind.

And yet when Amy began the second time to talk thus abominably of killing the poor child, of murdering her, and swore by her Maker that she would, so that I began to see that she was in earnest, I was farther terrified a great deal, and it helped to bring me to myself again in other cases.

We laid our heads together then to see if it was possible to discover by what means she had learned to talk so, and how she (I mean my girl) came to know that her mother had married a husband; but it would not do, the girl would acknowledge nothing, and gave but a very imperfect account of things still, being disgusted to the last degree with Amy's leaving her so abruptly as she did.

Well, Amy went to the house where the boy was; but it was all one, there they had only heard a confused story of the lady somebody, they knew not who, which the same wench had told them, but they gave no heed to it at all. Amy told them how foolishly the girl had acted, and how she had carried on the whimsey so far, in spite of all they could say to her; that she had taken it so ill, she would see her no more, and so she might e'en go to service again if she would, for she (Amy) would have nothing to do with her unless she humbled herself and changed her note, and that quickly too.

The good old gentleman, who had been the benefactor to them all, was greatly concerned at it, and the good woman his wife was grieved beyond all expressing, and begged her ladyship (meaning Amy), not to resent it; they promised, too, they would talk with her about it, and the old gentlewoman added, with some astonishment, "Sure she cannot be such a fool but she will be prevailed with to hold her tongue, when she has it from your own mouth that you are not her mother, and sees that it disobliges your ladyship to have her insist upon it." And so Amy came away with some expectation that it would be stopped here.

But the girl was such a fool for all that, and persisted in it obstinately, notwithstanding all they could say to her; nay, her sister begged and entreated her not to play the fool, for that it would ruin her too, and that the lady (meaning Amy) would abandon them both.

Well, notwithstanding this, she insisted, I say, upon it, and which was worse, the longer it lasted the more she began to drop Amy's ladyship, and would have it that the Lady Roxana was her mother, and that she had made some inquiries about it, and did not doubt but she should find her out.

When it was come to this, and we found there was nothing to be done with the girl, but that she was so obstinately bent upon the search after me, that she ventured to forfeit all she had in view; I say, when I found it was come to this, I began to be more serious in my preparations of my going beyond sea, and particularly, it gave me some reason to fear that there was something in it. But the following accident put me beside all my measures, and struck me into the greatest confusion that ever I was in my life.

I was so near going abroad that my spouse and I had taken measures for our going off; and because I would be sure not to go too public, but so as to take away all possibility of being seen, I had made some exception to my spouse against going in the ordinary public passage boats. My pretence to him was the promiscuous crowds in those vessels, want of convenience, and the like. So he took the hint, and found me out an English merchant-ship, which was bound for Rotterdam, and getting soon acquainted with the master, he hired his whole ship, that is to say, his great cabin, for I do not mean his ship for freight, that so we had all the conveniences possible for our passage; and all things being near ready, he brought home the captain one day to dinner with him, that I might see him, and be acquainted a little with him. So we came after dinner to talk of the ship and the conveniences on board, and the captain pressed me earnestly to come on board and see the ship, intimating that he would treat us as well as he could; and in discourse I happened to say I hoped he had no other passengers. He said no, he had not; but, he said, his wife had courted him a good while to let her go over to Holland with him, for he always used that trade, but he never could think of venturing all he had in one bottom; but if I went with him he thought to take her and her kinswoman along with him this voyage, that they might both wait upon me; and so added, that if we would do him the honour to dine on board the next day, he would bring his wife on board, the better to make us welcome.

Who now could have believed the devil had any snare at the bottom of all this? or that I was in any danger on such an occasion, so remote and out of the way as this was? But the event was the oddest that could be thought of. As it happened, Amy was not at home when we accepted this invitation, and so she was left out of the company; but instead of Amy, we took our honest, good-humoured, never-to-be-omitted friend the Quaker, one of the best creatures that ever lived, sure; and who, besides a thousand good qualities unmixed with one bad one, was particularly excellent for being the best company in the world; though I think I had carried Amy too, if she had not been engaged in this unhappy girl's affair. For on a sudden the girl was lost, and no news was to be heard of her; and Amy had haunted her to every place she could think of, that it was likely to find her in; but all the news she could hear of her was, that she was gone to an old comrade's house of hers, which she called sister, and who was married to a master of a ship, who lived at Redriff; and even this the jade never told me. It seems, when this girl was directed by Amy to get her some breeding, go to the boarding-school, and the like, she was recommended to a boarding-school at Camberwell, and there she contracted an acquaintance with a young lady (so they are all called), her bedfellow, that they called sisters, and promised never to break off their acquaintance.

But judge you what an unaccountable surprise I must be in when I came on board the ship and was brought into the captain's cabin, or what they call it, the great cabin of the ship, to see his lady or wife, and another young person with her, who, when I came to see her near hand, was my old cook-maid in the Pall Mall, and, as appeared by the sequel of the story, was neither more or less than my own daughter. That I knew her was out of doubt; for though she had not had opportunity to see me very often, yet I had often seen her, as I must needs, being in my own family so long.

If ever I had need of courage, and a full presence of mind, it was now; it was the only valuable secret in the world to me, all depended upon this occasion; if the girl knew me, I was undone; and to discover any surprise or disorder had been to make her know me, or guess it, and discover herself.

I was once going to feign a swooning and fainting away, and so falling on the ground, or floor, put them all into a hurry and fright, and by that means to get an opportunity to be continually holding something to my nose to smell to, and so hold my hand or my handkerchief, or both, before my mouth; then pretend I could not bear the smell of the ship, or the closeness of the cabin. But that would have been only to remove into a clearer air upon the quarter-deck, where we should, with it, have had a clearer light too; and if I had pretended the smell of the ship, it would have served only to have carried us all on shore to the captain's house, which was hard by; for the ship lay so close to the shore, that we only walked over a plank to go on board, and over another ship which lay within her; so this not appearing feasible, and the thought not being two minutes old, there was no time, for the two ladies rose up, and we saluted, so that I was bound to come so near my girl as to kiss her, which I would not have done had it been possible to have avoided it, but there was no room to escape.

I cannot but take notice here, that notwithstanding there was a secret horror upon my mind, and I was ready to sink when I came close to her to salute her, yet it was a secret inconceivable pleasure to me when I kissed her, to know that I kissed my own child, my own flesh and blood, born of my body, and who I had never kissed since I took the fatal farewell of them all, with a million of tears, and a heart almost dead with grief, when Amy and the good woman took them all away, and went with them to Spitalfields. No pen can describe, no words can express, I say, the strange impression which this thing made upon my spirits. I felt something shoot through my blood, my heart fluttered, my head flashed, and was dizzy, and all within me, as I thought, turned about, and much ado I had not to abandon myself to an excess of passion at the first sight of her, much more when my lips touched her face. I thought I must have taken her in my arms and kissed her again a thousand times, whether I would or no.

But I roused up my judgment, and shook it off, and with infinite uneasiness in my mind, I sat down. You will not wonder if upon this surprise I was not conversable for some minutes, and that the disorder had almost discovered itself. I had a complication of severe things upon me, I could not conceal my disorder without the utmost difficulty, and yet upon my concealing it depended the whole of my prosperity; so I used all manner of violence with myself to prevent the mischief which was at the door.

Well, I saluted her, but as I went first forward to the captain's lady, who was at the farther end of the cabin, towards the light, I had the occasion offered to stand with my back to the light, when I turned about to her, who stood more on my left hand, so that she had not a fair sight of me, though I was so near her. I trembled, and knew neither what I did or said, I was in the utmost extremity, between so many particular circumstances as lay upon me, for I was to conceal my disorder from everybody at the utmost peril, and at the same time expected everybody would discern it. I was to expect she would discover that she knew me, and yet was, by all means possible, to prevent it. I was to conceal myself, if possible, and yet had not the least room to do anything towards it. In short, there was no retreat, no shifting anything off, no avoiding or preventing her having a full sight of me, nor was there any counterfeiting my voice, for then my husband would have perceived it. In short, there was not the least circumstance that offered me any assistance, or any favourable thing to help me in this exigence.

After I had been upon the rack for near half-an-hour, during which I appeared stiff and reserved, and a little too formal, my spouse and the captain fell into discourses about the ship and the sea, and business remote from us women; and by-and-by the captain carried him out upon the quarter-deck, and left us all by ourselves in the great cabin. Then we began to be a little freer one with another, and I began to be a little revived by a sudden fancy of my own—namely, I thought I perceived that the girl did not know me, and the chief reason of my having such a notion was because I did not perceive the least disorder in her countenance, or the least change in her carriage, no confusion, no hesitation in her discourse; nor, which I had my eye particularly upon, did I observe that she fixed her eyes much upon me, that is to say, not singling me out to look steadily at me, as I thought would have been the case, but that she rather singled out my friend the Quaker, and chatted with her on several things; but I observed, too, that it was all about indifferent matters.

This greatly encouraged me, and I began to be a little cheerful; but I was knocked down again as with a thunderclap, when turning to the captain's wife, and discoursing of me, she said to her, "Sister, I cannot but think my lady to be very much like such a person." Then she named the person, and the captain's wife said she thought so too. The girl replied again, she was sure she had seen me before, but she could not recollect where; I answered (though her speech was not directed to me) that I fancied she had not seen me before in England, but asked if she had lived in Holland. She said, No, no, she had never been out of England, and I added, that she could not then have known me in England, unless it was very lately, for I had lived at Rotterdam a great while. This carried me out of that part of the broil pretty well, and to make it go off better, when a little Dutch boy came into the cabin, who belonged to the captain, and who I easily perceived to be Dutch, I jested and talked Dutch to him, and was merry about the boy, that is to say, as merry as the consternation I was still in would let me be.

However, I began to be thoroughly convinced by this time that the girl did not know me, which was an infinite satisfaction to me, or, at least, that though she had some notion of me, yet that she did not think anything about my being who I was, and which, perhaps, she would have been as glad to have known as I would have been surprised if she had; indeed, it was evident that, had she suspected anything of the truth, she would not have been able to have concealed it.

Thus this meeting went off, and, you may be sure, I was resolved, if once I got off of it, she should never see me again to revive her fancy; but I was mistaken there too, as you shall hear. After we had been on board, the captain's lady carried us home to her house, which was but just on shore, and treated us there again very handsomely, and made us promise that we would come again and see her before we went to concert our affairs for the voyage and the like, for she assured us that both she and her sister went the voyage at that time for our company, and I thought to myself, "Then you'll never go the voyage at all;" for I saw from that moment that it would be no way convenient for my ladyship to go with them, for that frequent conversation might bring me to her mind, and she would certainly claim her kindred to me in a few days, as indeed would have been the case.

It is hardly possible for me to conceive what would have been our part in this affair had my woman Amy gone with me on board this ship; it had certainly blown up the whole affair, and I must for ever after have been this girl's vassal, that is to say, have let her into the secret, and trusted to her keeping it too, or have been exposed and undone. The very thought filled me with horror.

But I was not so unhappy neither, as it fell out, for Amy was not with us, and that was my deliverance indeed; yet we had another chance to get over still. As I resolved to put off the voyage, so I resolved to put off the visit, you may be sure, going upon this principle, namely, that I was fixed in it that the girl had seen her last of me, and should never see me more.

However, to bring myself well off, and, withal, to see, if I could, a little farther into the matter, I sent my friend the Quaker to the captain's lady to make the visit promised, and to make my excuse that I could not possibly wait on her, for that I was very much out of order; and in the end of the discourse I bade her insinuate to them that she was afraid I should not be able to get ready to go the voyage as soon as the captain would be obliged to go, and that perhaps we might put it off to his next voyage. I did not let the Quaker into any other reason for it than that I was indisposed; and not knowing what other face to put upon that part, I made her believe that I thought I was a-breeding.

It was easy to put that into her head, and she of course hinted to the captain's lady that she found me so very ill that she was afraid I would miscarry, and then, to be sure, I could not think of going.

She went, and she managed that part very dexterously, as I knew she would, though she knew not a word of the grand reason of my indisposition; but I was all sunk and dead-hearted again when she told me she could not understand the meaning of one thing in her visit, namely, that the young woman, as she called her, that was with the captain's lady, and who she called sister, was most impertinently inquisitive into things; as who I was? how long I had been in England? where I had lived? and the like; and that, above all the rest, she inquired if I did not live once at the other end of the town.

"I thought her inquiries so out of the way," says the honest Quaker, "that I gave her not the least satisfaction; but as I saw by thy answers on board the ship, when she talked of thee, that thou didst not incline to let her be acquainted with thee, so I was resolved that she should not be much the wiser for me; and when she asked me if thou ever lived'st here or there, I always said, No, but that thou wast a Dutch lady, and was going home again to thy family, and lived abroad."

I thanked her very heartily for that part, and indeed she served me in it more than I let her know she did: in a word, she thwarted the girl so cleverly, that if she had known the whole affair she could not have done it better.

But, I must acknowledge, all this put me upon the rack again, and I was quite discouraged, not at all doubting but that the jade had a right scent of things, and that she knew and remembered my face, but had artfully concealed her knowledge of me till she might perhaps do it more to my disadvantage. I told all this to Amy, for she was all the relief I had. The poor soul (Amy) was ready to hang herself, that, as she said, she had been the occasion of it all; and that if I was ruined (which was the word I always used to her), she had ruined me; and she tormented herself about it so much, that I was sometimes fain to comfort her and myself too.

What Amy vexed herself at was, chiefly, that she should be surprised so by the girl, as she called her; I mean surprised into a discovery of herself to the girl; which indeed was a false step of Amy's, and so I had often told her. But it was to no purpose to talk of that now, the business was, how to get clear of the girl's suspicions, and of the girl too, for it looked more threatening every day than other; and if I was uneasy at what Amy had told me of her rambling and rattling to her (Amy), I had a thousand times as much reason to be uneasy now, when she had chopped upon me so unhappily as this; and not only had seen my face, but knew too where I lived, what name I went by, and the like.

And I am not come to the worst of it yet neither, for a few days after my friend the Quaker had made her visit, and excused me on the account of indisposition, as if they had done it in over and above kindness, because they had been told I was not well, they come both directly to my lodgings to visit me: the captain's wife and my daughter (who she called sister), and the captain, to show them the place; the captain only brought them to the door, put them in, and went away upon some business.

Had not the kind Quaker, in a lucky moment, come running in before them, they had not only clapped in upon me, in the parlour, as it had been a surprise, but which would have been a thousand times worse, had seen Amy with me; I think if that had happened, I had had no remedy but to take the girl by herself, and have made myself known to her, which would have been all distraction.

But the Quaker, a lucky creature to me, happened to see them come to the door, before they rung the bell, and instead of going to let them in, came running in with some confusion in her countenance, and told me who was a-coming; at which Amy run first and I after her, and bid the Quaker come up as soon as she had let them in.

I was going to bid her deny me, but it came into my thoughts, that having been represented so much out of order, it would have looked very odd; besides, I knew the honest Quaker, though she would do anything else for me, would not lie for me, and it would have been hard to have desired it of her.

After she had let them in, and brought them into the parlour, she came up to Amy and I, who were hardly out of the fright, and yet were congratulating one another that Amy was not surprised again.

They paid their visit in form, and I received them as formally, but took occasion two or three times to hint that I was so ill that I was afraid I should not be able to go to Holland, at least not so soon as the captain must go off; and made my compliment how sorry I was to be disappointed of the advantage of their company and assistance in the voyage; and sometimes I talked as if I thought I might stay till the captain returned, and would be ready to go again; then the Quaker put in, that then I might be too far gone, meaning with child, that I should not venture at all; and then (as if she should be pleased with it) added, she hoped I would stay and lie in at her house; so as this carried its own face with it, 'twas well enough.

But it was now high time to talk of this to my husband, which, however, was not the greatest difficulty before me; for after this and other chat had taken up some time, the young fool began her tattle again; and two or three times she brought it in, that I was so like a lady that she had the honour to know at the other end of the town, that she could not put that lady out of her mind when I was by, and once or twice I fancied the girl was ready to cry; by and by she was at it again, and at last I plainly saw tears in her eyes; upon which I asked her if the lady was dead, because she seemed to be in some concern for her. She made me much easier by her answer than ever she did before; she said she did not really know, but she believed she was dead.

This, I say, a little relieved my thoughts, but I was soon down again; for, after some time, the jade began to grow talkative; and as it was plain that she had told all that her head could retain of Roxana, and the days of joy which I had spent at that part of the town, another accident had like to have blown us all up again.

I was in a kind of dishabille when they came, having on a loose robe, like a morning-gown, but much after the Italian way; and I had not altered it when I went up, only dressed my head a little; and as I had been represented as having been lately very ill, so the dress was becoming enough for a chamber.

This morning vest, or robe, call it as you please, was more shaped to the body than we wear them since, showing the body in its true shape, and perhaps a little too plainly if it had been to be worn where any men were to come; but among ourselves it was well enough, especially for hot weather; the colour was green, figured, and the stuff a French damask, very rich.

This gown or vest put the girl's tongue a running again, and her sister, as she called her, prompted it; for as they both admired my vest, and were taken up much about the beauty of the dress, the charming damask, the noble trimming, and the like, my girl puts in a word to the sister (captain's wife), "This is just such a thing as I told you," says she, "the lady danced in." "What," says the captain's wife, "the Lady Roxana that you told me of? Oh! that's a charming story," says she, "tell it my lady." I could not avoid saying so too, though from my soul I wished her in heaven for but naming it; nay, I won't say but if she had been carried t'other way it had been much as one to me, if I could but have been rid of her, and her story too, for when she came to describe the Turkish dress, it was impossible but the Quaker, who was a sharp, penetrating creature, should receive the impression in a more dangerous manner than the girl, only that indeed she was not so dangerous a person; for if she had known it all, I could more freely have trusted her than I could the girl, by a great deal, nay, I should have been perfectly easy in her.

However, as I have said, her talk made me dreadfully uneasy, and the more when the captain's wife mentioned but the name of Roxana. What my face might do towards betraying me I knew not, because I could not see myself, but my heart beat as if it would have jumped out at my mouth, and my passion was so great, that, for want of vent, I thought I should have burst. In a word, I was in a kind of a silent rage, for the force I was under of restraining my passion was such as I never felt the like of. I had no vent, nobody to open myself to, or to make a complaint to, for my relief; I durst not leave the room by any means, for then she would have told all the story in my absence, and I should have been perpetually uneasy to know what she had said, or had not said; so that, in a word, I was obliged to sit and hear her tell all the story of Roxana, that is to say, of myself, and not know at the same time whether she was in earnest or in jest, whether she knew me or no; or, in short, whether I was to be exposed, or not exposed.

She began only in general with telling where she lived, what a place she had of it, how gallant a company her lady had always had in the house; how they used to sit up all night in the house gaming and dancing; what a fine lady her mistress was, and what a vast deal of money the upper servants got; as for her, she said, her whole business was in the next house, so that she got but little, except one night that there was twenty guineas given to be divided among the servants, when, she said, she got two guineas and a half for her share.

She went on, and told them how many servants there was, and how they were ordered; but, she said, there was one Mrs. Amy who was over them all; and that she, being the lady's favourite, got a great deal. She did not know, she said, whether Amy was her Christian name or her surname, but she supposed it was her surname; that they were told she got threescore pieces of gold at one time, being the same night that the rest of the servants had the twenty guineas divided among them.

I put in at that word, and said it was a vast deal to give away. "Why," says I, "it was a portion for a servant." "O madam!" says she, "it was nothing to what she got afterwards; we that were servants hated her heartily for it; that is to say, we wished it had been our lot in her stead." Then I said again, "Why, it was enough to get her a good husband, and settle her for the world, if she had sense to manage it." "So it might, to be sure, madam," says she, "for we were told she laid up above £500; but, I suppose, Mrs. Amy was too sensible that her character would require a good portion to put her off."

"Oh," said I, "if that was the case it was another thing."

"Nay," says she, "I don't know, but they talked very much of a young lord that was very great with her."

"And pray what came of her at last?" said I, for I was willing to hear a little (seeing she would talk of it) what she had to say, as well of Amy as of myself.

"I don't know, madam," said she, "I never heard of her for several years, till t'other day I happened to see her."

"Did you indeed?" says I (and made mighty strange of it); "what! and in rags, it may be," said I; "that's often the end of such creatures."

"Just the contrary, madam," says she. "She came to visit an acquaintance of mine, little thinking, I suppose, to see me, and, I assure you, she came in her coach."

"In her coach!" said I; "upon my word, she had made her market then; I suppose she made hay while the sun shone. Was she married, pray?"

"I believe she had been married, madam," says she, "but it seems she had been at the East Indies; and if she was married, it was there, to be sure. I think she said she had good luck in the Indies."

"That is, I suppose," said I, "had buried her husband there."

"I understood it so, madam," says she, "and that she had got his estate."

"Was that her good luck?" said I; "it might be good to her, as to the money indeed, but it was but the part of a jade to call it good luck."

Thus far our discourse of Mrs. Amy went, and no farther, for she knew no more of her; but then the Quaker unhappily, though undesignedly, put in a question, which the honest good-humoured creature would have been far from doing if she had known that I had carried on the discourse of Amy on purpose to drop Roxana out of the conversation.

But I was not to be made easy too soon. The Quaker put in, "But I think thou saidst something was behind of thy mistress; what didst thou call her? Roxana, was it not? Pray, what became of her?"

"Ay, ay, Roxana," says the captain's wife; "pray, sister, let's hear the story of Roxana; it will divert my lady, I'm sure."

"That's a damned lie," said I to myself; "if you knew how little 't would divert me, you would have too much advantage over me." Well, I saw no remedy, but the story must come on, so I prepared to hear the worst of it.

"Roxana!" says she, "I know not what to say of her; she was so much above us, and so seldom seen, that we could know little of her but by report; but we did sometimes see her too; she was a charming woman indeed, and the footmen used to say that she was to be sent for to court."

"To court!" said I; "why, she was at court, wasn't she? the Pall Mall is not far from Whitehall."

"Yes, madam," says she, "but I mean another way."

"I understand thee," says the Quaker; "thou meanest, I suppose, to be mistress to the king."

"Yes, madam," said she.

I cannot help confessing what a reserve of pride still was left in me; and though I dreaded the sequel of the story, yet when she talked how handsome and how fine a lady this Roxana was, I could not help being pleased and tickled with it, and put in questions two or three times of how handsome she was; and was she really so fine a woman as they talked of; and the like, on purpose to hear her repeat what the people's opinion of me was, and how I had behaved.

"Indeed," says she, at last, "she was a most beautiful creature as ever I saw in my life." "But then," said I, "you never had the opportunity to see her but when she was set out to the best advantage."

"Yes, yes, madam," says she, "I have seen her several times in her déshabille. And I can assure you, she was a very fine woman; and that which was more still, everybody said she did not paint."

This was still agreeable to me one way; but there was a devilish sting in the tail of it all, and this last article was one; wherein she said she had seen me several times in my déshabille. This put me in mind that then she must certainly know me, and it would come out at last; which was death to me but to think of.

"Well, but, sister," says the captain's wife, "tell my lady about the ball; that's the best of all the story; and of Roxana's dancing in a fine outlandish dress."

"That's one of the brightest parts of her story indeed," says the girl. "The case was this: we had balls and meetings in her ladyship's apartments every week almost; but one time my lady invited all the nobles to come such a time, and she would give them a ball; and there was a vast crowd indeed," says she.

"I think you said the king was there, sister, didn't you?"

"No, madam," says she, "that was the second time, when they said the king had heard how finely the Turkish lady danced, and that he was there to see her; but the king, if his Majesty was there, came disguised."

"That is, what they call incog.," says my friend the Quaker; "thou canst not think the king would disguise himself." "Yes," says the girl, "it was so; he did not come in public with his guards, but we all knew which was the king well enough, that is to say, which they said was the king."

"Well," says the captain's wife, "about the Turkish dress; pray let us hear that." "Why," says she, "my lady sat in a fine little drawing-room, which opened into the great room, and where she received the compliments of the company; and when the dancing began, a great lord," says she, "I forget who they called him (but he was a very great lord or duke, I don't know which), took her out, and danced with her; but after a while, my lady on a sudden shut the drawing-room, and ran upstairs with her woman, Mrs. Amy; and though she did not stay long (for I suppose she had contrived it all beforehand), she came down dressed in the strangest figure that ever I saw in my life; but it was exceeding fine."

Here she went on to describe the dress, as I have done already; but did it so exactly, that I was surprised at the manner of her telling it; there was not a circumstance of it left out.

I was now under a new perplexity, for this young slut gave so complete an account of everything in the dress, that my friend the Quaker coloured at it, and looked two or three times at me, to see if I did not do so too; for (as she told me afterwards) she immediately perceived it was the same dress that she had seen me have on, as I have said before. However, as she saw I took no notice of it, she kept her thought private to herself; and I did so too, as well as I could.

I put in two or three times, that she had a good memory, that could be so particular in every part of such a thing.

"Oh, madam!" says she, "we that were servants, stood by ourselves in a corner, but so as we could see more than some strangers; besides," says she, "it was all our conversation for several days in the family, and what one did not observe another did." "Why," says I to her, "this was no Persian dress; only, I suppose your lady was some French comedian, that is to say, a stage Amazon, that put on a counterfeit dress to please the company, such as they used in the play of Tamerlane at Paris, or some such."

"No, indeed, madam," says she, "I assure you my lady was no actress; she was a fine modest lady, fit to be a princess; everybody said if she was a mistress, she was fit to be a mistress to none but the king; and they talked her up for the king as if it had really been so. Besides, madam," says she, "my lady danced a Turkish dance; all the lords and gentry said it was so; and one of them swore he had seen it danced in Turkey himself, so that it could not come from the theatre at Paris; and then the name Roxana," says she, "was a Turkish name."

"Well," said I, "but that was not your lady's name, I suppose?"

"No, no, madam," said she, "I know that. I know my lady's name and family very well; Roxana was not her name, that's true, indeed."

Here she run me aground again, for I durst not ask her what was Roxana's real name, lest she had really dealt with the devil, and had boldly given my own name in for answer; so that I was still more and more afraid that the girl had really gotten the secret somewhere or other; though I could not imagine neither how that could be.

In a word, I was sick of the discourse, and endeavoured many ways to put an end to it, but it was impossible; for the captain's wife, who called her sister, prompted her, and pressed her to tell it, most ignorantly thinking that it would be a pleasant tale to all of us.

Two or three times the Quaker put in, that this Lady Roxana had a good stock of assurance; and that it was likely, if she had been in Turkey, she had lived with, or been kept by, some great bashaw there. But still she would break in upon all such discourse, and fly out into the most extravagant praises of her mistress, the famed Roxana. I run her down as some scandalous woman; that it was not possible to be otherwise; but she would not hear of it; her lady was a person of such and such qualifications that nothing but an angel was like her, to be sure; and yet, after all she could say, her own account brought her down to this, that, in short, her lady kept little less than a gaming ordinary; or, as it would be called in the times since that, an assembly for gallantry and play.

All this while I was very uneasy, as I said before, and yet the whole story went off again without any discovery, only that I seemed a little concerned that she should liken me to this gay lady, whose character I pretended to run down very much, even upon the foot of her own relation.

But I was not at the end of my mortifications yet, neither, for now my innocent Quaker threw out an unhappy expression, which put me upon the tenters again. Says she to me, "This lady's habit, I fancy, is just such a one as thine, by the description of it;" and then turning to the captain's wife, says she, "I fancy my friend has a finer Turkish or Persian dress, a great deal." "Oh," says the girl, "'tis impossible to be finer; my lady's," says she, "was all covered with gold and diamonds; her hair and head-dress, I forget the name they gave it," said she, "shone like the stars, there were so many jewels in it."

I never wished my good friend the Quaker out of my company before now; but, indeed, I would have given some guineas to have been rid of her just now; for beginning to be curious in the comparing the two dresses, she innocently began a description of mine; and nothing terrified me so much as the apprehension lest she should importune me to show it, which I was resolved I would never agree to. But before it came to this, she pressed my girl to describe the tyhaia, or head-dress, which she did so cleverly that the Quaker could not help saying mine was just such a one; and after several other similitudes, all very vexatious to me, out comes the kind motion to me to let the ladies see my dress; and they joined their eager desires of it, even to importunity.

I desired to be excused, though I had little to say at first why I declined it; but at last it came into my head to say it was packed up with my other clothes that I had least occasion for, in order to be sent on board the captain's ship; but that if we lived to come to Holland together (which, by the way, I resolved should never happen), then, I told them, at unpacking my clothes, they should see me dressed in it; but they must not expect I should dance in it, like the Lady Roxana in all her fine things.

This carried it off pretty well; and getting over this, got over most of the rest, and I began to be easy again; and, in a word, that I may dismiss the story too, as soon as may be, I got rid at last of my visitors, who I had wished gone two hours sooner than they intended it.

As soon as they were gone, I ran up to Amy, and gave vent to my passions by telling her the whole story, and letting her see what mischiefs one false step of hers had like, unluckily, to have involved us all in; more, perhaps, than we could ever have lived to get through. Amy was sensible of it enough, and was just giving her wrath a vent another way, viz., by calling the poor girl all the damned jades and fools (and sometimes worse names) that she could think of, in the middle of which up comes my honest, good Quaker, and put an end to our discourse. The Quaker came in smiling (for she was always soberly cheerful). "Well," says she, "thou art delivered at last; I come to joy thee of it; I perceived thou wert tired grievously of thy visitors."

"Indeed," says I, "so I was; that foolish young girl held us all in a Canterbury story; I thought she would never have done with it." "Why, truly, I thought she was very careful to let thee know she was but a cook-maid." "Ay," says I, "and at a gaming-house, or gaming-ordinary, and at t'other end of the town too; all which (by the way) she might know would add very little to her good name among us citizens."

"I can't think," says the Quaker, "but she had some other drift in that long discourse; there's something else in her head," says she, "I am satisfied of that." Thought I, "Are you satisfied of it? I am sure I am the less satisfied for that; at least 'tis but small satisfaction to me to hear you say so. What can this be?" says I; "and when will my uneasiness have an end?" But this was silent, and to myself, you may be sure. But in answer to my friend the Quaker, I returned by asking her a question or two about it; as what she thought was in it, and why she thought there was anything in it. "For," says I, "she can have nothing in it relating to me."

"Nay," says the kind Quaker, "if she had any view towards thee, that's no business of mine; and I should be far from desiring thee to inform me."

This alarmed me again; not that I feared trusting the good-humoured creature with it, if there had been anything of just suspicion in her; but this affair was a secret I cared not to communicate to anybody. However, I say, this alarmed me a little; for as I had concealed everything from her, I was willing to do so still; but as she could not but gather up abundance of things from the girl's discourse, which looked towards me, so she was too penetrating to be put off with such answers as might stop another's mouth. Only there was this double felicity in it, first, that she was not inquisitive to know or find anything out, and not dangerous if she had known the whole story. But, as I say, she could not but gather up several circumstances from the girl's discourse, as particularly the name of Amy, and the several descriptions of the Turkish dress which my friend the Quaker had seen, and taken so much notice of, as I have said above.

As for that, I might have turned it off by jesting with Amy, and asking her who she lived with before she came to live with me. But that would not do, for we had unhappily anticipated that way of talking, by having often talked how long Amy had lived with me; and, which was still worse, by having owned formerly that I had had lodgings in the Pall Mall; so that all those things corresponded too well. There was only one thing that helped me out with the Quaker, and that was the girl's having reported how rich Mrs. Amy was grown, and that she kept her coach. Now, as there might be many more Mrs. Amys besides mine, so it was not likely to be my Amy, because she was far from such a figure as keeping her coach; and this carried it off from the suspicions which the good friendly Quaker might have in her head.

But as to what she imagined the girl had in her head, there lay more real difficulty in that part a great deal, and I was alarmed at it very much, for my friend the Quaker told me that she observed the girl was in a great passion when she talked of the habit, and more when I had been importuned to show her mine, but declined it. She said she several times perceived her to be in disorder, and to restrain herself with great difficulty; and once or twice she muttered to herself that she had found it out, or that she would find it out, she could not tell whether; and that she often saw tears in her eyes; that when I said my suit of Turkish clothes was put up, but that she should see it when we arrived in Holland, she heard her say softly she would go over on purpose then.

After she had ended her observations, I added: "I observed, too, that the girl talked and looked oddly, and that she was mighty inquisitive, but I could not imagine what it was she aimed at." "Aimed at," says the Quaker, "'tis plain to me what she aims at. She believes thou art the same Lady Roxana that danced in the Turkish vest, but she is not certain." "Does she believe so?" says I; "if I had thought that, I would have put her out of her pain." "Believe so!" says the Quaker; "yes, and I began to think so too, and should have believed so still, if thou had'st not satisfied me to the contrary by thy taking no notice of it, and by what thou hast said since." "Should you have believed so?" said I warmly; "I am very sorry for that. Why, would you have taken me for an actress, or a French stage-player?" "No," says the good kind creature, "thou carriest it too far; as soon as thou madest thy reflections upon her, I knew it could not be; but who could think any other when she described the Turkish dress which thou hast here, with the head-tire and jewels, and when she named thy maid Amy too, and several other circumstances concurring? I should certainly have believed it," said she, "if thou hadst not contradicted it; but as soon as I heard thee speak, I concluded it was otherwise." "That was very kind," said I, "and I am obliged to you for doing me so much justice; it is more, it seems, than that young talking creature does." "Nay," says the Quaker, "indeed she does not do thee justice; for she as certainly believes it still as ever she did." "Does she?" said I. "Ay," says the Quaker; "and I warrant thee she'll make thee another visit about it." "Will she?" said I; "then I believe I shall downright affront her." "No, thou shalt not affront her," says she (full of her good-humour and temper), "I'll take that part off thy hands, for I'll affront her for thee, and not let her see thee." I thought that was a very kind offer, but was at a loss how she would be able to do it; and the thought of seeing her there again half distracted me, not knowing what temper she would come in, much less what manner to receive her in; but my fast friend and constant comforter, the Quaker, said she perceived the girl was impertinent, and that I had no inclination to converse with her, and she was resolved I should not be troubled with her. But I shall have occasion to say more of this presently, for this girl went farther yet than I thought she had.

It was now time, as I said before, to take measures with my husband, in order to put off my voyage; so I fell into talk with him one morning as he was dressing, and while I was in bed. I pretended I was very ill; and as I had but too easy a way to impose upon him, because he so absolutely believed everything I said, so I managed my discourse as that he should understand by it I was a-breeding, though I did not tell him so.

189

However, I brought it about so handsomely that, before he went out of the room, he came and sat down by my bedside, and began to talk very seriously to me upon the subject of my being so every day ill, and that, as he hoped I was with child, he would have me consider well of it, whether I had not best alter my thoughts of the voyage to Holland; for that being sea-sick, and which was worse, if a storm should happen, might be very dangerous to me. And after saying abundance of the kindest things that the kindest of husbands in the world could say, he concluded that it was his request to me, that I would not think any more of going till after all should be over; but that I would, on the contrary, prepare to lie-in where I was, and where I knew, as well as he, I could be very well provided, and very well assisted.

This was just what I wanted, for I had, as you have heard, a thousand good reasons why I should put off the voyage, especially with that creature in company; but I had a mind the putting it off should be at his motion, not my own; and he came into it of himself, just as I would have had it. This gave me an opportunity to hang back a little, and to seem as if I was unwilling. I told him I could not abide to put him to difficulties and perplexities in his business; that now he had hired the great cabin in the ship, and, perhaps, paid some of the money, and, it may be, taken freight for goods; and to make him break it all off again would be a needless charge to him, or, perhaps, a damage to the captain.

As to that, he said, it was not to be named, and he would not allow it to be any consideration at all; that he could easily pacify the captain of the ship by telling him the reason of it, and that if he did make him some satisfaction for the disappointment, it should not be much.

"But, my dear," says I, "you ha'n't heard me say I am with child, neither can I say so; and if it should not be so at last, then I shall have made a fine piece of work of it indeed; besides," says I, "the two ladies, the captain's wife and her sister, they depend upon our going over, and have made great preparations, and all in compliment to me; what must I say to them?"

"Well, my dear," says he, "if you should not be with child, though I hope you are, yet there is no harm done; the staying three or four months longer in England will be no damage to me, and we can go when we please, when we are sure you are not with child, or, when it appearing that you are with child, you shall be down and up again; and as for the captain's wife and sister, leave that part to me; I'll answer for it there shall be no quarrel raised upon that subject. I'll make your excuse to them by the captain himself, so all will be well enough there, I'll warrant you."

This was as much as I could desire, and thus it rested for awhile. I had indeed some anxious thoughts about this impertinent girl, but believed that putting off the voyage would have put an end to it all, so I began to be pretty easy; but I found myself mistaken, for I was brought to the point of destruction by her again, and that in the most unaccountable manner imaginable.

My husband, as he and I had agreed, meeting the captain of the ship, took the freedom to tell him that he was afraid he must disappoint him, for that something had fallen out which had obliged him to alter his measures, and that his family could not be ready to go time enough for him.

"I know the occasion, sir," says the captain; "I hear your lady has got a daughter more than she expected; I give you joy of it." "What do you mean by that?" says my spouse. "Nay, nothing," says the captain, "but what I hear the women tattle over the tea-table. I know nothing, but that you don't go the voyage upon it, which I am sorry for; but you know your own affairs," added the captain, "that's no business of mine."

"Well, but," says my husband, "I must make you some satisfaction for the disappointment," and so pulls out his money. "No, no," says the captain; and so they fell to straining their compliments one upon another; but, in short, my spouse gave him three or four guineas, and made him take it. And so the first discourse went off again, and they had no more of it.

But it did not go off so easily with me, for now, in a word, the clouds began to thicken about me, and I had alarms on every side. My husband told me what the captain had said, but very happily took it that the captain had brought a tale by halves, and having heard it one way, had told it another; and that neither could he understand the captain, neither did the captain understand himself, so he contented himself to tell me, he said, word for word, as the captain delivered it.

How I kept my husband from discovering my disorder you shall hear presently; but let it suffice to say just now, that if my husband did not understand the captain, nor the captain understand himself, yet I understood them both very well; and, to tell the truth, it was a worse shock than ever I had yet. Invention supplied me, indeed, with a sudden motion to avoid showing my surprise; for as my spouse and I was sitting by a little table near the fire, I reached out my hand, as if I had intended to take a spoon which lay on the other side, and threw one of the candles off of the table; and then snatching it up, started up upon my feet, and stooped to the lap of my gown and took it in my hand. "Oh!" says I, "my gown's spoiled; the candle has greased it prodigiously." This furnished me with an excuse to my spouse to break off the discourse for the present, and call Amy down; and Amy not coming presently, I said to him, "My dear, I must run upstairs and put it off, and let Amy clean it a little." So my husband rose up too, and went into a closet where he kept his papers and books, and fetched a book out, and sat down by himself to read.

Glad I was that I had got away, and up I run to Amy, who, as it happened, was alone. "Oh, Amy!" says I, "we are all utterly undone." And with that I burst out a-crying, and could not speak a word for a great while.

I cannot help saying that some very good reflections offered themselves upon this head. It presently occurred, what a glorious testimony it is to the justice of Providence, and to the concern Providence has in guiding all the affairs of men (even the least as well as the greatest), that the most secret crimes are, by the most unforeseen accidents, brought to light and discovered.

Another reflection was, how just it is that sin and shame follow one another so constantly at the heels; that they are not like attendants only, but, like cause and consequence, necessarily connected one with another; that the crime going before, the scandal is certain to follow; and that 'tis not in the power of human nature to conceal the first, or avoid the last.

"What shall I do, Amy?" said I, as soon as I could speak, "and what will become of me?" And then I cried again so vehemently that I could say no more a great while. Amy was frighted almost out of her wits, but knew nothing what the matter was; but she begged to know, and persuaded me to compose myself, and not cry so. "Why, madam, if my master should come up now," says she, "he will see what a disorder you are in; he will know you have been crying, and then he will want to know the cause of it." With that I broke out again. "Oh, he knows it already, Amy," says I, "he knows all! 'Tis all discovered, and we are undone!" Amy was thunderstruck now indeed. "Nay," says Amy, "if that be true, we are undone indeed; but that can never be; that's impossible, I'm sure."

"No, no," says I, "'tis far from impossible, for I tell you 'tis so." And by this time, being a little recovered, I told her what discourse my husband and the captain had had together, and what the captain had said. This put Amy into such a hurry that she cried, she raved, she swore and cursed like a mad thing; then she upbraided me that I would not let her kill the girl when she would have done it, and that it was all my own doing, and the like. Well, however, I was not for killing the girl yet. I could not bear the thoughts of that neither.

We spent half-an-hour in these extravagances, and brought nothing out of them neither; for indeed we could do nothing or say nothing that was to the purpose; for if anything was to come out-of-the-way, there was no hindering it, or help for it; so after thus giving a vent to myself by crying, I began to reflect how I had left my spouse below, and what I had pretended to come up for; so I changed my gown that I pretended the candle fell upon, and put on another, and went down.

When I had been down a good while, and found my spouse did not fall into the story again, as I expected, I took heart, and called for it. "My dear," said I, "the fall of the candle put you out of your history, won't you go on with it?" "What history?" says he. "Why," says I, "about the captain." "Oh," says he, "I had done with it. I know no more than that the captain told a broken piece of news that he had heard by halves, and told more by halves than he heard it,—namely, of your being with child, and that you could not go the voyage."

I perceived my husband entered not into the thing at all, but took it for a story, which, being told two or three times over, was puzzled, and come to nothing, and that all that was meant by it was what he knew, or thought he knew already—viz., that I was with child, which he wished might be true.

His ignorance was a cordial to my soul, and I cursed them in my thoughts that should ever undeceive him; and as I saw him willing to have the story end there, as not worth being farther mentioned, I closed it too, and said I supposed the captain had it from his wife; she might have found somebody else to make her remarks upon; and so it passed off with my husband well enough, and I was still safe there, where I thought myself in most danger. But

I had two uneasinesses still; the first was lest the captain and my spouse should meet again, and enter into farther discourse about it; and the second was lest the busy impertinent girl should come again, and when she came, how to prevent her seeing Amy, which was an article as material as any of the rest; for seeing Amy would have been as fatal to me as her knowing all the rest.

As to the first of these, I knew the captain could not stay in town above a week, but that his ship being already full of goods, and fallen down the river, he must soon follow, so I contrived to carry my husband somewhere out of town for a few days, that they might be sure not to meet.

My greatest concern was where we should go. At last I fixed upon North Hall; not, I said, that I would drink the waters, but that I thought the air was good, and might be for my advantage. He, who did everything upon the foundation of obliging me, readily came into it, and the coach was appointed to be ready the next morning; but as we were settling matters, he put in an ugly word that thwarted all my design, and that was, that he had rather I would stay till afternoon, for that he should speak to the captain the next morning if he could, to give him some letters, which he could do, and be back again about twelve o'clock.

I said, "Ay, by all means." But it was but a cheat on him, and my voice and my heart differed; for I resolved, if possible, he should not come near the captain, nor see him, whatever came of it.

In the evening, therefore, a little before we went to bed, I pretended to have altered my mind, and that I would not go to North Hall, but I had a mind to go another way, but I told him I was afraid his business would not permit him. He wanted to know where it was. I told him, smiling, I would not tell him, lest it should oblige him to hinder his business. He answered with the same temper, but with infinitely more sincerity, that he had no business of so much consequence as to hinder him going with me anywhere that I had a mind to go. "Yes," says I, "you want to speak with the captain before he goes away." "Why, that's true," says he, "so I do," and paused awhile; and then added, "but I'll write a note to a man that does business for me to go to him; 'tis only to get some bills of loading signed, and he can do it." When I saw I had gained my point, I seemed to hang back a little. "My dear," says I, "don't hinder an hour's business for me; I can put it off for a week or two rather than you shall do yourself any prejudice." "No, no," says he, "you shall not put it off an hour for me, for I can do my business by proxy with anybody but my wife." And then he took me in his arms and kissed me. How did my blood flush up into my face when I reflected how sincerely, how affectionately, this good-humoured gentleman embraced the most cursed piece of hypocrisy that ever came into the arms of an honest man! His was all tenderness, all kindness, and the utmost sincerity; mine all grimace and deceit;—a piece of mere manage and framed conduct to conceal a past life of wickedness, and prevent his discovering that he had in his arms a she-devil, whose whole conversation for twenty-five years had been black as hell, a complication of crime, and for which, had he been let into it, he must have abhorred me and the very mention of my name. But there was no help for me in it; all I had to satisfy myself was that it was my business to be what I was, and conceal what I had been; that all the satisfaction I could make him was to live virtuously for the time to come, not being able to retrieve what had been in time past; and this I resolved upon, though, had the great temptation offered, as it did afterwards, I had reason to question my stability. But of that hereafter.

After my husband had kindly thus given up his measures to mine, we resolved to set out in the morning early. I told him that my project, if he liked it, was to go to Tunbridge, and he, being entirely passive in the thing, agreed to it with the greatest willingness; but said if I had not named Tunbridge, he would have named Newmarket, there being a great court there, and abundance of fine things to be seen. I offered him another piece of hypocrisy here, for I pretended to be willing to go thither, as the place of his choice, but indeed I would not have gone for a thousand pounds; for the court being there at that time, I durst not run the hazard of being known at a place where there were so many eyes that had seen me before. So that, after some time, I told my husband that I thought Newmarket was so full of people at that time, that we should get no accommodation; that seeing the court and the crowd was no entertainment at all to me, unless as it might be so to him, that if he thought fit, we would rather put it off to another time; and that if, when we went to Holland, we should go by Harwich, we might take a round by Newmarket and Bury, and so come down to Ipswich, and go from thence to the seaside. He was easily put off from this, as he was from anything else that I did not approve; and so, with all imaginable facility, he appointed to be ready early in the morning to go with me for Tunbridge.

I had a double design in this, viz., first, to get away my spouse from seeing the captain any more; and secondly, to be out of the way myself, in case this impertinent girl, who was now my plague, should offer to come again, as my friend the Quaker believed she would, and as indeed happened within two or three days afterwards.

Having thus secured my going away the next day, I had nothing to do but to furnish my faithful agent the Quaker with some instructions what to say to this tormentor (for such she proved afterwards), and how to manage her, if she made any more visits than ordinary.

I had a great mind to leave Amy behind too, as an assistant, because she understood so perfectly well what to advise upon any emergence; and Amy importuned me to do so. But I know not what secret impulse prevailed over my thoughts against it; I could not do it for fear the wicked jade should make her away, which my very soul abhorred the thoughts of; which, however, Amy found means to bring to pass afterwards, as I may in time relate more particularly.

It is true I wanted as much to be delivered from her as ever a sick man did from a third-day ague; and had she dropped into the grave by any fair way, as I may call it, I mean, had she died by any ordinary distemper, I should have shed but very few tears for her. But I was not arrived to such a pitch of obstinate wickedness as to commit murder, especially such as to murder my own child, or so much as to harbour a thought so barbarous in my mind. But, as I said, Amy effected all afterwards without my knowledge, for which I gave her my hearty curse, though I could do little more; for to have fallen upon Amy had been to have murdered myself. But this tragedy requires a longer story than I have room for here. I return to my journey.

My dear friend the Quaker was kind, and yet honest, and would do anything that was just and upright to serve me, but nothing wicked or dishonourable. That she might be able to say boldly to the creature, if she came, she did not know where I was gone, she desired I would not let her know; and to make her ignorance the more absolutely safe to herself, and likewise to me, I allowed her to say that she heard us talk of going to Newmarket, &c. She liked that part, and I left all the rest to her, to act as she thought fit; only charged her, that if the girl entered into the story of the Pall Mall, she should not entertain much talk about it, but let her understand that we all thought she spoke of it a little too particularly; and that the lady (meaning me) took it a little ill to be so likened to a public mistress, or a stage-player, and the like; and so to bring her, if possible, to say no more of it. However, though I did not tell my friend the Quaker how to write to me, or where I was, yet I left a sealed paper with her maid to give her, in which I gave her a direction how to write to Amy, and so, in effect, to myself.

It was but a few days after I was gone, but the impatient girl came to my lodgings on pretence to see how I did, and to hear if I intended to go the voyage, and the like. My trusty agent was at home, and received her coldly at the door; but told her that the lady, which she supposed she meant, was gone from her house.

This was a full stop to all she could say for a good while; but as she stood musing some time at the door, considering what to begin a talk upon, she perceived my friend the Quaker looked a little uneasy, as if she wanted to go in and shut the door, which stung her to the quick; and the wary Quaker had not so much as asked her to come in; for seeing her alone she expected she would be very impertinent, and concluded that I did not care how coldly she received her.

But she was not to be put off so. She said if the Lady —— was not to be spoken with, she desired to speak two or three words with her, meaning my friend the Quaker. Upon that the Quaker civilly but coldly asked her to walk in, which was what she wanted. Note.—She did not carry her into her best parlour, as formerly, but into a little outer room, where the servants usually waited.

By the first of her discourse she did not stick to insinuate as if she believed I was in the house, but was unwilling to be seen; and pressed earnestly that she might speak but two words with me; to which she added earnest entreaties, and at last tears.

"I am sorry," says my good creature the Quaker, "thou hast so ill an opinion of me as to think I would tell thee an untruth, and say that the Lady —— was gone from my house if she was not! I assure thee I do not use any such method; nor does the Lady —— desire any such kind of service from me, as I know of. If she had been in the house, I should have told thee so."

She said little to that, but said it was business of the utmost importance that she desired to speak with me about, and then cried again very much.

195

"Thou seem'st to be sorely afflicted," says the Quaker, "I wish I could give thee any relief; but if nothing will comfort thee but seeing the Lady ——, it is not in my power."

"I hope it is," says she again; "to be sure it is of great consequence to me, so much that I am undone without it."

"Thou troublest me very much to hear thee say so," says the Quaker; "but why, then, didst thou not speak to her apart when thou wast here before?"

"I had no opportunity," says she, "to speak to her alone, and I could not do it in company; if I could have spoken but two words to her alone, I would have thrown myself at her foot, and asked her blessing."

"I am surprised at thee; I do not understand thee," says the Quaker.

"Oh!" says she, "stand my friend if you have any charity, or if you have any compassion for the miserable; for I am utterly undone!"
"Thou terrifiest me," says the Quaker, "with such passionate expressions, for verily I cannot comprehend thee!"

"Oh!" says she, "she is my mother! she is my mother! and she does not own me!"

"Thy mother!" says the Quaker, and began to be greatly moved indeed. "I am astonished at thee: what dost thou mean?"

"I mean nothing but what I say," says she. "I say again, she is my mother, and will not own me;" and with that she stopped with a flood of tears.

"Not own thee!" says the Quaker; and the tender good creature wept too. "Why," says she, "she does not know thee, and never saw thee before."

"No," says the girl, "I believe she does not know me, but I know her; and I know that she is my mother."

"It's impossible, thou talk'st mystery!" says the Quaker; "wilt thou explain thyself a little to me?"

"Yes, yes," says she, "I can explain it well enough. I am sure she is my mother, and I have broke my heart to search for her; and now to lose her again, when I was so sure I had found her, will break my heart more effectually."

"Well, but if she be thy mother," says the Quaker, "how can it be that she should not know thee?"

"Alas!" says she, "I have been lost to her ever since I was a child; she has never seen me."

"And hast thou never seen her?" says the Quaker.

"Yes," says she, "I have seen her; often enough I saw her; for when she was the Lady Roxana I was her housemaid, being a servant, but I did not know her then, nor she me; but it has all come out since. Has she not a maid named Amy?" Note.—The honest Quaker was nonplussed, and greatly surprised at that question.

"Truly," says she, "the Lady —— has several women servants, but I do not know all their names."

"But her woman, her favourite," adds the girl; "is not her name Amy?"

"Why, truly," says the Quaker, with a very happy turn of wit, "I do not like to be examined; but lest thou shouldest take up any mistakes by reason of my backwardness to speak, I will answer thee for once, that what her woman's name is I know not, but they call her Cherry."

N.B.—My husband gave her that name in jest on our wedding-day, and we had called her by it ever after; so that she spoke literally true at that time.

The girl replied very modestly that she was sorry if she gave her any offence in asking; that she did not design to be rude to her, or pretend to examine her; but that she was in such an agony at this disaster that she knew not what she did or said; and that she should be very sorry to disoblige her, but begged of her again, as she was a Christian and a woman, and had been a mother of children, that she would take pity on her, and, if possible, assist her, so that she might but come to me and speak a few words to me.

The tender-hearted Quaker told me the girl spoke this with such moving eloquence that it forced tears from her; but she was obliged to say that she neither knew where I was gone or how to write to me; but that if she did ever see me again she would not fail to give me an account of all she had said to her, or that she should yet think fit to say, and to take my answer to it, if I thought fit to give any.

Then the Quaker took the freedom to ask a few particulars about this wonderful story, as she called it; at which the girl, beginning at the first distresses of my life, and indeed of her own, went through all the history of her miserable education, her service under the Lady Roxana, as she called me, and her relief by Mrs. Amy, with the reasons she had to believe that as Amy owned herself to be the same that lived with her mother, and especially that Amy was the Lady Roxana's maid too, and came out of France with her, she was by those circumstances, and several others in her conversation, as fully convinced that the Lady Roxana was her mother, as she was that the Lady —— at her house (the Quaker's) was the very same Roxana that she had been servant to.

My good friend the Quaker, though terribly shocked at the story, and not well knowing what to say, yet was too much my friend to seem convinced in a thing which she did not know to be true, and which, if it was true, she could see plainly I had a mind should not be known; so she turned her discourse to argue the girl out of it. She insisted upon the slender

197

evidence she had of the fact itself, and the rudeness of claiming so near a relation of one so much above her, and of whose concern in it she had no knowledge, at least no sufficient proof; that as the lady at her house was a person above any disguises, so she could not believe that she would deny her being her daughter, if she was really her mother; that she was able sufficiently to have provided for her if she had not a mind to have her known; and, therefore, seeing she had heard all she had said of the Lady Roxana, and was so far from owning herself to be the person, so she had censured that sham lady as a cheat and a common woman; and that 'twas certain she could never be brought to own a name and character she had so justly exposed.

Besides, she told her that her lodger, meaning me, was not a sham lady, but the real wife of a knight-baronet; and that she knew her to be honestly such, and far above such a person as she had described. She then added that she had another reason why it was not very possible to be true. "And that is," says she, "thy age is in the way; for thou acknowledgest that thou art four-and twenty years old, and that thou wast the youngest of three of thy mother's children; so that, by thy account, thy mother must be extremely young, or this lady cannot be thy mother; for thou seest," says she, "and any one may see, she is but a young woman now, and cannot be supposed to be above forty years old, if she is so much; and is now big with child at her going into the country; so that I cannot give any credit to thy notion of her being thy mother; and if I might counsel thee, it should be to give over that thought, as an improbable story that does but serve to disorder thee, and disturb thy head; for," added she, "I perceive thou art much disturbed indeed."

But this was all nothing; she could be satisfied with nothing but seeing me; but the Quaker defended herself very well, and insisted on it that she could not give her any account of me; and finding her still importunate, she affected at last being a little disgusted that she should not believe her, and added, that indeed, if she had known where I was gone, she would not have given any one an account of it, unless I had given her orders to do so. "But seeing she has not acquainted me," says she, "where she has gone, 'tis an intimation to me she was not desirous it should be publicly known;" and with this she rose up, which was as plain a desiring her to rise up too and begone as could be expressed, except the downright showing her the door.

Well, the girl rejected all this, and told her she could not indeed expect that she (the Quaker) should be affected with the story she had told her, however moving, or that she should take any pity on her. That it was her misfortune, that when she was at the house before, and in the room with me, she did not beg to speak a word with me in private, or throw herself upon the floor at my feet, and claim what the affection of a mother would have done for her; but since she had slipped her opportunity, she would wait for another; that she found by her (the Quaker's) talk, that she had not quite left her lodgings, but was gone into the country, she supposed for the air; and she was resolved she would take so much knight-errantry upon her, that she would visit all the airing-places in the nation, and even all the kingdom over, ay, and Holland too, but she would find me; for she was satisfied she could so convince me that she was my own child, that I would not deny it; and she was sure I was so tender and compassionate, I would not let her perish after I was convinced that she was my own flesh and blood; and in saying she would visit all the airing-places in

England, she reckoned them all up by name, and began with Tunbridge, the very place I was gone to; then reckoning up Epsom, North Hall, Barnet, Newmarket, Bury, and at last, the Bath; and with this she took her leave.

My faithful agent the Quaker failed not to write to me immediately; but as she was a cunning as well as an honest woman, it presently occurred to her that this was a story which, whether true or false, was not very fit to come to my husband's knowledge; that as she did not know what I might have been, or might have been called in former times, and how far there might have been something or nothing in it, so she thought if it was a secret I ought to have the telling it myself; and if it was not, it might as well be public afterwards as now; and that, at least, she ought to leave it where she found it, and not hand it forwards to anybody without my consent. These prudent measures were inexpressibly kind, as well as seasonable; for it had been likely enough that her letter might have come publicly to me, and though my husband would not have opened it, yet it would have looked a little odd that I should conceal its contents from him, when I had pretended so much to communicate all my affairs.

In consequence of this wise caution, my good friend only wrote me in few words, that the impertinent young woman had been with her, as she expected she would; and that she thought it would be very convenient that, if I could spare Cherry, I would send her up (meaning Amy), because she found there might be some occasion for her.

As it happened, this letter was enclosed to Amy herself, and not sent by the way I had at first ordered; but it came safe to my hands; and though I was alarmed a little at it, yet I was not acquainted with the danger I was in of an immediate visit from this teasing creature till afterwards; and I ran a greater risk, indeed, than ordinary, in that I did not send Amy up under thirteen or fourteen days, believing myself as much concealed at Tunbridge as if I had been at Vienna.

But the concern of my faithful spy (for such my Quaker was now, upon the mere foot of her own sagacity), I say, her concern for me, was my safety in this exigence, when I was, as it were, keeping no guard for myself; for, finding Amy not come up, and that she did not know how soon this wild thing might put her designed ramble in practice, she sent a messenger to the captain's wife's house, where she lodged, to tell her that she wanted to speak with her. She was at the heels of the messenger, and came eager for some news; and hoped, she said, the lady (meaning me) had been come to town.

The Quaker, with as much caution as she was mistress of, not to tell a downright lie, made her believe she expected to hear of me very quickly; and frequently, by the by, speaking of being abroad to take the air, talked of the country about Bury, how pleasant it was, how wholesome, and how fine an air; how the downs about Newmarket were exceeding fine, and what a vast deal of company there was, now the court was there; till at last, the girl began to conclude that my ladyship was gone thither; for, she said, she knew I loved to see a great deal of company.

"Nay," says my friend, "thou takest me wrong; I did not suggest," says she, "that the person thou inquirest after is gone thither, neither do I believe she is, I assure thee." Well, the girl smiled, and let her know that she believed it for all that; so, to clench it fast, "Verily," says she, with great seriousness, "thou dost not do well, for thou suspectest everything and believest nothing. I speak solemnly to thee that I do not believe they are gone that way; so if thou givest thyself the trouble to go that way, and art disappointed, do not say that I have deceived thee." She knew well enough that if this did abate her suspicion it would not remove it, and that it would do little more than amuse her; but by this she kept her in suspense till Amy came up, and that was enough.

When Amy came up, she was quite confounded to hear the relation which the Quaker gave her, and found means to acquaint me of it; only letting me know, to my great satisfaction, that she would not come to Tunbridge first, but that she would certainly go to Newmarket or Bury first.

However, it gave me very great uneasiness; for as she resolved to ramble in search after me over the whole country, I was safe nowhere, no, not in Holland itself. So indeed I did not know what to do with her; and thus I had a bitter in all my sweet, for I was continually perplexed with this hussy, and thought she haunted me like an evil spirit.

In the meantime Amy was next door to stark-mad about her; she durst not see her at my lodgings for her life; and she went days without number to Spitalfields, where she used to come, and to her former lodging, and could never meet with her. At length she took up a mad resolution that she would go directly to the captain's house in Redriff and speak with her. It was a mad step, that's true; but as Amy said she was mad, so nothing she could do could be otherwise. For if Amy had found her at Redriff, she (the girl) would have concluded presently that the Quaker had given her notice, and so that we were all of a knot; and that, in short, all she had said was right. But as it happened, things came to hit better than we expected; for that Amy going out of a coach to take water at Tower Wharf, meets the girl just come on shore, having crossed the water from Redriff. Amy made as if she would have passed by her, though they met so full that she did not pretend she did not see her, for she looked fairly upon her first, but then turning her head away with a slight, offered to go from her; but the girl stopped, and spoke first, and made some manners to her.

Amy spoke coldly to her, and a little angry; and after some words, standing in the street or passage, the girl saying she seemed to be angry, and would not have spoken to her, "Why," says Amy, "how can you expect I should have any more to say to you after I had done so much for you, and you have behaved so to me?" The girl seemed to take no notice of that now, but answered, "I was going to wait on you now." "Wait on me!" says Amy; "what do you mean by that?" "Why," says she again, with a kind of familiarity, "I was going to your lodgings."

Amy was provoked to the last degree at her, and yet she thought it was not her time to resent, because she had a more fatal and wicked design in her head against her; which, indeed, I never knew till after it was executed, nor durst Amy ever communicate it to me; for as I had always expressed myself vehemently against hurting a hair of her head, so she was resolved to take her own measures without consulting me any more.

In order to this, Amy gave her good words, and concealed her resentment as much as she could; and when she talked of going to her lodging, Amy smiled and said nothing, but called for a pair of oars to go to Greenwich; and asked her, seeing she said she was going to her lodging, to go along with her, for she was going home, and was all alone.

Amy did this with such a stock of assurance that the girl was confounded, and knew not what to say; but the more she hesitated, the more Amy pressed her to go; and talking very kindly to her, told her if she did not go to see her lodgings she might go to keep her company, and she would pay a boat to bring her back again; so, in a word, Amy prevailed on her to go into the boat with her, and carried her down to Greenwich.

'Tis certain that Amy had no more business at Greenwich than I had, nor was she going thither; but we were all hampered to the last degree with the impertinence of this creature; and, in particular, I was horribly perplexed with it.
As they were in the boat, Amy began to reproach her with ingratitude in treating her so rudely who had done so much for her, and been so kind to her; and to ask her what she had got by it, or what she expected to get. Then came in my share, the Lady Roxana. Amy jested with that, and bantered her a little, and asked her if she had found her yet.

But Amy was both surprised and enraged when the girl told her roundly that she thanked her for what she had done for her, but that she would not have her think she was so ignorant as not to know that what she (Amy) had done was by her mother's order, and who she was beholden to for it. That she could never make instruments pass for principals, and pay the debt to the agent when the obligation was all to the original. That she knew well enough who she was, and who she was employed by. That she knew the Lady — very well (naming the name that I now went by), which was my husband's true name, and by which she might know whether she had found out her mother or no.

Amy wished her at the bottom of the Thames; and had there been no watermen in the boat, and nobody in sight, she swore to me she would have thrown her into the river. I was horribly disturbed when she told me this story, and began to think this would, at last, all end in my ruin; but when Amy spoke of throwing her into the river and drowning her, I was so provoked at her that all my rage turned against Amy, and I fell thoroughly out with her. I had now kept Amy almost thirty years, and found her on all occasions the faithfullest creature to me that ever woman had—I say, faithful to me; for, however wicked she was, still she was true to me; and even this rage of hers was all upon my account, and for fear any mischief should befall me.

But be that how it would, I could not bear the mention of her murdering the poor girl, and it put me so beside myself, that I rose up in a rage, and bade her get out of my sight, and out of my house; told her I had kept her too long, and that I would never see her face more. I had before told her that she was a murderer, and a bloody-minded creature; that she could not but know that I could not bear the thought of it, much less the mention of it; and that it was the impudentest thing that ever was known to make such a proposal to me, when she knew that I was really the mother of this girl, and that she was my own child; that it was wicked enough in her, but that she must conclude I was ten times wickeder than herself if I could come into it; that the girl was in the right, and I had nothing to blame her for; but that it was owing to the wickedness of my life that made it necessary for me to keep her from a discovery; but that I would not murder my child, though I was otherwise to be ruined by it. Amy replied, somewhat rough and short, Would I not? but she would, she said, if she had an opportunity; and upon these words it was that I bade her get out of my sight and out of my house; and it went so far that Amy packed up her alls, and marched off; and was gone for almost good and all. But of that in its order; I must go back to her relation of the voyage which they made to Greenwich together.

They held on the wrangle all the way by water; the girl insisted upon her knowing that I was her mother, and told her all the history of my life in the Pall Mall, as well after her being turned away as before, and of my marriage since; and which was worse, not only who my present husband was, but where he had lived, viz., at Rouen in France. She knew nothing of Paris or of where we was going to live, namely, at Nimeguen; but told her in so many words that if she could not find me here, she would go to Holland after me.

They landed at Greenwich, and Amy carried her into the park with her, and they walked above two hours there in the farthest and remotest walks; which Amy did because, as they talked with great heat, it was apparent they were quarrelling, and the people took notice of it.

They walked till they came almost to the wilderness at the south side of the park; but the girl, perceiving Amy offered to go in there among the woods and trees, stopped short there, and would go no further; but said she would not go in there.

Amy smiled, and asked her what was the matter? She replied short, she did not know where she was, nor where she was going to carry her, and she would go no farther; and without any more ceremony, turns back, and walks apace away from her. Amy owned she was surprised, and came back too, and called to her, upon which the girl stopped, and Amy coming up to her, asked her what she meant?

The girl boldly replied she did not know but she might murder her; and that, in short, she would not trust herself with her, and never would come into her company again alone.

It was very provoking, but, however, Amy kept her temper with much difficulty, and bore it, knowing that much might depend upon it; so she mocked her foolish jealousy, and told her she need not be uneasy for her, she would do her no harm, and would have done her good if she would have let her; but since she was of such a refractory humour, she should not trouble herself, for she should never come into her company again; and that neither she or her brother or sister should ever hear from her or see her any more; and so she should have the satisfaction of being the ruin of her brother and sisters as well as of herself.

The girl seemed a little mollified at that, and said that for herself, she knew the worst of it, she could seek her fortune; but it was hard her brother and sister should suffer on her score; and said something that was tender and well enough on that account. But Amy told her it was for her to take that into consideration; for she would let her see that it was all her own; that she would have done them all good, but that having been used thus, she would do no more for any of them; and that she should not need to be afraid to come into her company again, for she would never give her occasion for it any more. This, by the way, was false in the girl too; for she did venture into Amy's company again after that, once too much, as I shall relate by itself.

They grew cooler, however, afterwards, and Amy carried her into a house at Greenwich, where she was acquainted, and took an occasion to leave the girl in a room awhile, to speak to the people in the house, and so prepare them to own her as a lodger in the house; and then going in to her again told her there she lodged, if she had a mind to find her out, or if anybody else had anything to say to her. And so Amy dismissed her, and got rid of her again; and finding an empty hackney-coach in the town, came away by land to London, and the girl, going down to the water-side, came by boat.

This conversation did not answer Amy's end at all, because it did not secure the girl from pursuing her design of hunting me out; and though my indefatigable friend the Quaker amused her three or four days, yet I had such notice of it at last that I thought fit to come away from Tunbridge upon it. And where to go I knew not; but, in short, I went to a little village upon Epping Forest, called Woodford, and took lodgings in a private house, where I lived retired about six weeks, till I thought she might be tired of her search, and have given me over.

Here I received an account from my trusty Quaker that the wench had really been at Tunbridge, had found out my lodgings, and had told her tale there in a most dismal tone; that she had followed us, as she thought, to London; but the Quaker had answered her that she knew nothing of it, which was indeed true; and had admonished her to be easy, and not hunt after people of such fashion as we were, as if we were thieves; that she might be assured, that since I was not willing to see her, I would not be forced to it; and treating me thus would effectually disoblige me. And with such discourses as these she quieted her; and she (the Quaker) added that she hoped I should not be troubled much more with her.

It was in this time that Amy gave me the history of her Greenwich voyage, when she spoke of drowning and killing the girl in so serious a manner, and with such an apparent resolution of doing it, that, as I said, put me in a rage with her, so that I effectually turned her away from me, as I have said above, and she was gone; nor did she so much as tell me whither or which way she was gone. On the other hand, when I came to reflect on it that now I had neither assistant or confidant to speak to, or receive the least information from, my friend the Quaker excepted, it made me very uneasy.

I waited and expected and wondered from day to day, still thinking Amy would one time or other think a little and come again, or at least let me hear of her; but for ten days together I heard nothing of her. I was so impatient that I got neither rest by day or sleep by night, and what to do I knew not. I durst not go to town to the Quaker's for fear of meeting that vexatious creature, my girl, and I could get no intelligence where I was; so I got my spouse, upon pretence of wanting her company, to take the coach one day and fetch my good Quaker to me.

When I had her, I durst ask her no questions, nor hardly knew which end of the business to begin to talk of; but of her own accord she told me that the girl had been three or four times haunting her for news from me; and that she had been so troublesome that she had been obliged to show herself a little angry with her; and at last told her plainly that she need give herself no trouble in searching after me by her means, for she (the Quaker) would not tell her if she knew; upon which she refrained awhile. But, on the other hand, she told me it was not safe for me to send my own coach for her to come in, for she had some reason to believe that she (my daughter) watched her door night and day; nay, and watched her too every time she went in and out; for she was so bent upon a discovery that she spared no pains, and she believed she had taken a lodging very near their house for that purpose.

I could hardly give her a hearing of all this for my eagerness to ask for Amy; but I was confounded when she told me she had heard nothing of her. It is impossible to express the anxious thoughts that rolled about in my mind, and continually perplexed me about her; particularly I reproached myself with my rashness in turning away so faithful a creature that for so many years had not only been a servant but an agent; and not only an agent, but a friend, and a faithful friend too.

Then I considered too that Amy knew all the secret history of my life; had been in all the intrigues of it, and been a party in both evil and good; and at best there was no policy in it; that as it was very ungenerous and unkind to run things to such an extremity with her, and for an occasion, too, in which all the fault she was guilty of was owing to her excessive care for my safety, so it must be only her steady kindness to me, and an excess of generous friendship for me, that should keep her from ill-using me in return for it; which ill-using me was enough in her power, and might be my utter undoing.

These thoughts perplexed me exceedingly, and what course to take I really did not know. I began, indeed, to give Amy quite over, for she had now been gone above a fortnight, and as she had taken away all her clothes, and her money too, which was not a little, and so had no occasion of that kind to come any more, so she had not left any word where she was gone, or to which part of the world I might send to hear of her.

And I was troubled on another account too, viz., that my spouse and I too had resolved to do very handsomely for Amy, without considering what she might have got another way at all; but we had said nothing of it to her, and so I thought, as she had not known what was likely to fall in her way, she had not the influence of that expectation to make her come back.

Upon the whole, the perplexity of this girl, who hunted me as if, like a hound, she had had a hot scent, but was now at a fault, I say, that perplexity, and this other part of Amy being gone, issued in this—I resolved to be gone, and go over to Holland; there, I believed, I should be at rest. So I took occasion one day to tell my spouse that I was afraid he might take it ill that I had amused him thus long, and that at last I doubted I was not with child; and that since it was so, our things being packed up, and all in order for going to Holland, I would go away now when he pleased.

My spouse, who was perfectly easy whether in going or staying, left it all entirely to me; so I considered of it, and began to prepare again for my voyage. But, alas! I was irresolute to the last degree. I was, for want of Amy, destitute; I had lost my right hand; she was my steward, gathered in my rents (I mean my interest money) and kept my accounts, and, in a word, did all my business; and without her, indeed, I knew not how to go away nor how to stay. But an accident thrust itself in here, and that even in Amy's conduct too, which frighted me away, and without her too, in the utmost horror and confusion.

I have related how my faithful friend the Quaker was come to me, and what account she gave me of her being continually haunted by my daughter; and that, as she said, she watched her very door night and day. The truth was, she had set a spy to watch so effectually that she (the Quaker) neither went in or out but she had notice of it.

This was too evident when, the next morning after she came to me (for I kept her all night), to my unspeakable surprise I saw a hackney-coach stop at the door where I lodged, and saw her (my daughter) in the coach all alone. It was a very good chance, in the middle of a bad one, that my husband had taken out the coach that very morning, and was gone to London. As for me, I had neither life or soul left in me; I was so confounded I knew not what to do or to say.

My happy visitor had more presence of mind than I, and asked me if I had made no acquaintance among the neighbours. I told her, yes, there was a lady lodged two doors off that I was very intimate with. "But hast thou no way out backward to go to her?" says she. Now it happened there was a back-door in the garden, by which we usually went and came to and from the house, so I told her of it. "Well, well," says she, "go out and make a visit then, and leave the rest to me." Away I run, told the lady (for I was very free there) that I was a widow to-day, my spouse being gone to London, so I came not to visit her, but to dwell with her that day, because also our landlady had got strangers come from London. So having framed this orderly lie, I pulled some work out of my pocket, and added I did not come to be idle.

As I went out one way, my friend the Quaker went the other to receive this unwelcome guest. The girl made but little ceremony, but having bid the coachman ring at the gate, gets down out of the coach and comes to the door, a country girl going to the door (belonging to the house), for the Quaker forbid any of my maids going. Madam asked for my Quaker by name, and the girl asked her to walk in.

Upon this, my Quaker, seeing there was no hanging back, goes to her immediately, but put all the gravity upon her countenance that she was mistress of, and that was not a little indeed.

When she (the Quaker) came into the room (for they had showed my daughter into a little parlour), she kept her grave countenance, but said not a word, nor did my daughter speak a good while; but after some time my girl began and said, "I suppose you know me, madam?"

"Yes," says the Quaker, "I know thee." And so the dialogue went on.

Girl. Then you know my business too?

Quaker. No, verily, I do not know any business thou canst have here with me.

Girl. Indeed, my business is not chiefly with you.

Qu. Why, then, dost thou come after me thus far?

Girl. You know whom I seek. [And with that she cried.]

Qu. But why shouldst thou follow me for her, since thou know'st that I assured thee more than once that I knew not where she was?

Girl. But I hoped you could.

Qu. Then thou must hope that I did not speak the truth, which would be very wicked.

Girl. I doubt not but she is in this house.

Qu. If those be thy thoughts, thou may'st inquire in the house; so thou hast no more business with me. Farewell! [Offers to go.]

Girl. I would not be uncivil; I beg you to let me see her.

Qu. I am here to visit some of my friends, and I think thou art not very civil in following me hither.

Girl. I came in hopes of a discovery in my great affair which you know of.

Qu. Thou cam'st wildly, indeed; I counsel thee to go back again, and be easy; I shall keep my word with thee, that I would not meddle in it, or give thee any account, if I knew it, unless I had her orders.

ROXANA'S DAUGHTER AND THE QUAKER

Here the girl importuned her again with the utmost
earnestness, and cried bitterly

Girl. If you knew my distress you could not be so cruel.

Qu Thou hast told me all thy story, and I think it might be more cruelty to tell thee than not to tell thee; for I understand she is resolved not to see thee, and declares she is not thy mother. Will'st thou be owned where thou hast no relation?

Girl. Oh, if I could but speak to her, I would prove my relation to her so that she could not deny it any longer.

Qu. Well, but thou canst not come to speak with her, it seems.

Girl. I hope you will tell me if she is here. I had a good account that you were come out to see her, and that she sent for you.
Qu. I much wonder how thou couldst have such an account. If I had come out to see her, thou hast happened to miss the house, for I assure thee she is not to be found in this house.

Here the girl importuned her again with the utmost earnestness, and cried bitterly, insomuch that my poor Quaker was softened with it, and began to persuade me to consider of it, and, if it might consist with my affairs, to see her, and hear what she had to say; but this was afterwards. I return to the discourse.

The Quaker was perplexed with her a long time; she talked of sending back the coach, and lying in the town all night. This, my friend knew, would be very uneasy to me, but she durst not speak a word against it; but on a sudden thought, she offered a bold stroke, which, though dangerous if it had happened wrong, had its desired effect.

She told her that, as for dismissing her coach, that was as she pleased, she believed she would not easily get a lodging in the town; but that as she was in a strange place, she would so much befriend her, that she would speak to the people of the house, that if they had room, she might have a lodging there for one night, rather than be forced back to London before she was free to go.

This was a cunning, though a dangerous step, and it succeeded accordingly, for it amused the creature entirely, and she presently concluded that really I could not be there then, otherwise she would never have asked her to lie in the house; so she grew cold again presently as to her lodging there, and said, No, since it was so, she would go back that afternoon, but she would come again in two or three days, and search that and all the towns round in an effectual manner, if she stayed a week or two to do it; for, in short, if I was in England or Holland she would find me.

"In truth," says the Quaker, "thou wilt make me very hurtful to thee, then." "Why so?" says she, "Because wherever I go, thou wilt put thyself to great expense, and the country to a great deal of unnecessary trouble." "Not unnecessary," says she. "Yes, truly," says the Quaker; "it must be unnecessary, because it will be to no purpose. I think I must abide in my own house to save thee that charge and trouble."

She said little to that, except that, she said, she would give her as little trouble as possible; but she was afraid she should sometimes be uneasy to her, which she hoped she would excuse. My Quaker told her she would much rather excuse her if she would forbear; for that if she would believe her, she would assure her she should never get any intelligence of me by her.

That set her into tears again; but after a while, recovering herself, she told her perhaps she might be mistaken; and she (the Quaker) should watch herself very narrowly, or she might one time or other get some intelligence from her, whether she would or no; and she was satisfied she had gained some of her by this journey, for that if I was not in the house, I was not far off; and if I did not remove very quickly, she would find me out. "Very well," says my Quaker; "then if the lady is not willing to see thee, thou givest me notice to tell her, that she may get out of thy way."

She flew out in a rage at that, and told my friend that if she did, a curse would follow her, and her children after her, and denounced such horrid things upon her as frighted the poor tender-hearted Quaker strangely, and put her more out of temper than ever I saw her before; so that she resolved to go home the next morning, and I, that was ten times more uneasy than she, resolved to follow her, and go to London too; which, however, upon second thoughts, I did not, but took effectual measures not to be seen or owned if she came any more; but I heard no more of her for some time.

I stayed there about a fortnight, and in all that time I heard no more of her, or of my Quaker about her; but after about two days more, I had a letter from my Quaker, intimating that she had something of moment to say, that she could not communicate by letter, but wished I would give myself the trouble to come up, directing me to come with the coach into Goodman's Fields, and then walk to her back-door on foot, which being left open on purpose, the watchful lady, if she had any spies, could not well see me.

My thoughts had for so long time been kept, as it were, waking, that almost everything gave me the alarm, and this especially, so that I was very uneasy; but I could not bring matters to bear to make my coming to London so clear to my husband as I would have done; for he liked the place, and had a mind, he said, to stay a little longer, if it was not against my inclination; so I wrote my friend the Quaker word that I could not come to town yet; and that, besides, I could not think of being there under spies, and afraid to look out of doors; and so, in short, I put off going for near a fortnight more.

At the end of that time she wrote again, in which she told me that she had not lately seen the impertinent visitor which had been so troublesome; but that she had seen my trusty agent Amy, who told her she had cried for six weeks without intermission; that Amy had given her an account how troublesome the creature had been, and to what straits and perplexities I was driven by her hunting after and following me from place to place; upon which Amy had said, that, notwithstanding I was angry with her, and had used her so hardly for saying something about her of the same kind, yet there was an absolute necessity of securing her, and removing her out of the way; and that, in short, without asking my leave, or anybody's leave, she should take care she should trouble her mistress (meaning me) no more; and that after Amy had said so, she had indeed never heard any more of the girl; so that she supposed Amy had managed it so well as to put an end to it.

The innocent, well-meaning creature, my Quaker, who was all kindness and goodness in herself, and particularly to me, saw nothing in this; but she thought Amy had found some way to persuade her to be quiet and easy, and to give over teasing and following me, and rejoiced in it for my sake; as she thought nothing of any evil herself, so she suspected none in anybody else, and was exceeding glad of having such good news to write to me; but my thoughts of it run otherwise.

I was struck, as with a blast from heaven, at the reading her letter; I fell into a fit of trembling from head to foot, and I ran raving about the room like a mad woman. I had nobody to speak a word to, to give vent to my passion; nor did I speak a word for a good while, till after it had almost overcome me. I threw myself on the bed, and cried out, "Lord, be merciful to me, she has murdered my child!" and with that a flood of tears burst out, and I cried vehemently for above an hour.

My husband was very happily gone out a-hunting, so that I had the opportunity of being alone, and to give my passions some vent, by which I a little recovered myself. But after my crying was over, then I fell in a new rage at Amy; I called her a thousand devils and monsters and hard-hearted tigers; I reproached her with her knowing that I abhorred it, and had let her know it sufficiently, in that I had, at it were, kicked her out of doors, after so many years' friendship and service, only for naming it to me.

Well, after some time, my spouse came in from his sport, and I put on the best looks I could to deceive him; but he did not take so little notice of me as not to see I had been crying, and that something troubled me, and he pressed me to tell him. I seemed to bring it out with reluctance, but told him my backwardness was more because I was ashamed that such a trifle should have any effect upon me, than for any weight that was in it; so I told him I had been vexing myself about my woman Amy's not coming again; that she might have known me better than not to believe I should have been friends with her again, and the like; and that, in short, I had lost the best servant by my rashness that ever woman had.

"Well, well," says he, "if that be all your grief, I hope you will soon shake it off; I'll warrant you in a little while we shall hear of Mrs. Amy again." And so it went off for that time. But it did not go off with me; for I was uneasy and terrified to the last degree, and wanted to get some farther account of the thing. So I went away to my sure and certain comforter, the Quaker, and there I had the whole story of it; and the good innocent Quaker gave me joy of my being rid of such an unsufferable tormentor.

"Rid of her! Ay," says I, "if I was rid of her fairly and honourably; but I don't know what Amy may have done. Sure, she ha'n't made her away?" "Oh fie!" says my Quaker; "how canst thou entertain such a notion! No, no. Made her away? Amy didn't talk like that; I dare say thou may'st be easy in that; Amy has nothing of that in her head, I dare say," says she; and so threw it, as it were, out of my thoughts.

But it would not do; it run in my head continually; night and day I could think of nothing else; and it fixed such a horror of the fact upon my spirits, and such a detestation of Amy, who I looked upon as the murderer, that, as for her, I believe if I could have seen her I should certainly have sent her to Newgate, or to a worse place, upon suspicion; indeed, I think I could have killed her with my own hands.

As for the poor girl herself, she was ever before my eyes; I saw her by night and by day; she haunted my imagination, if she did not haunt the house; my fancy showed me her in a hundred shapes and postures; sleeping or waking, she was with me. Sometimes I thought I saw her with her throat cut; sometimes with her head cut, and her brains knocked out; other times hanged up upon a beam; another time drowned in the great pond at Camberwell. And all these appearances were terrifying to the last degree; and that which was still worse, I could really hear nothing of her; I sent to the captain's wife in Redriff, and she answered me, she was gone to her relations in Spitalfields. I sent thither, and they said she was there about three weeks ago, but that she went out in a coach with the gentlewoman that used to be so kind to her, but whither she was gone they knew not, for she had not been there since. I sent back the messenger for a description of the woman she went out with; and they described her so perfectly, that I knew it to be Amy, and none but Amy.

I sent word again that Mrs. Amy, who she went out with, left her in two or three hours, and that they should search for her, for I had a reason to fear she was murdered. This frighted them all intolerably. They believed Amy had carried her to pay her a sum of money, and that somebody had watched her after her having received it, and had robbed and murdered her.

I believed nothing of that part; but I believed, as it was, that whatever was done, Amy had done it; and that, in short, Amy had made her away; and I believed it the more, because Amy came no more near me, but confirmed her guilt by her absence.

Upon the whole, I mourned thus for her for above a month; but finding Amy still come not near me, and that I must put my affairs in a posture that I might go to Holland, I opened all my affairs to my dear trusty friend the Quaker, and placed her, in matters of trust, in the room of Amy; and with a heavy, bleeding heart for my poor girl, I embarked with my spouse, and all our equipage and goods, on board another Holland's trader, not a packet-boat, and went over to Holland, where I arrived, as I have said.

I must put in a caution, however, here, that you must not understand me as if I let my friend the Quaker into any part of the secret history of my former life; nor did I commit the grand reserved article of all to her, viz., that I was really the girl's mother, and the Lady Roxana; there was no need of that part being exposed; and it was always a maxim with me, that secrets should never be opened without evident utility. It could be of no manner of use to me or her to communicate that part to her; besides, she was too honest herself to make it safe to me; for though she loved me very sincerely, and it was plain by many circumstances that she did so, yet she would not lie for me upon occasion, as Amy would, and therefore it was not advisable on any terms to communicate that part; for if the girl, or any one else, should have come to her afterwards, and put it home to her, whether she knew that I was the girl's mother or not, or was the same as the Lady Roxana or not, she either would not have denied it, or would have done it with so ill a grace, such blushing, such hesitations and falterings in her answers, as would have put the matter out of doubt, and betrayed herself and the secret too.

For this reason, I say, I did not discover anything of that kind to her; but I placed her, as I have said, in Amy's stead in the other affairs of receiving money, interests, rents, and the like, and she was as faithful as Amy could be, and as diligent.

But there fell out a great difficulty here, which I knew not how to get over; and this was how to convey the usual supply of provision and money to the uncle and the other sister, who depended, especially the sister, upon the said supply for her support; and indeed, though Amy had said rashly that she would not take any more notice of the sister, and would leave her to perish, as above, yet it was neither in my nature, or Amy's either, much less was it in my design; and therefore I resolved to leave the management of what I had reserved for that work with my faithful Quaker, but how to direct her to manage them was the great difficulty.

Amy had told them in so many words that she was not their mother, but that she was the maid Amy, that carried them to their aunt's; that she and their mother went over to the East Indies to seek their fortune, and that there good things had befallen them, and that their mother was very rich and happy; that she (Amy) had married in the Indies, but being now a widow, and resolving to come over to England, their mother had obliged her to inquire them out, and do for them as she had done; and that now she was resolved to go back to the Indies again; but that she had orders from their mother to do very handsomely by them; and, in a word, told them she had £2000 apiece for them, upon condition that they proved sober, and married suitably to themselves, and did not throw themselves away upon scoundrels.

The good family in whose care they had been, I had resolved to take more than ordinary notice of; and Amy, by my order, had acquainted them with it, and obliged my daughters to promise to submit to their government, as formerly, and to be ruled by the honest man as by a father and counsellor; and engaged him to treat them as his children. And to oblige him effectually to take care of them, and to make his old age comfortable both to him and his wife, who had been so good to the orphans, I had ordered her to settle the other £2000, that is to say, the interest of it, which was £120 a year, upon them, to be theirs for both their lives, but to come to my two daughters after them. This was so just, and was so prudently managed by Amy, that nothing she ever did for me pleased me better. And in this posture, leaving my two daughters with their ancient friend, and so coming away to me (as they thought to the East Indies), she had prepared everything in order to her going over with me to Holland; and in this posture that matter stood when that unhappy girl, who I have said so much of, broke in upon all our measures, as you have heard, and, by an obstinacy never to be conquered or pacified, either with threats or persuasions, pursued her search after me (her mother) as I have said, till she brought me even to the brink of destruction; and would, in all probability, have traced me out at last, if Amy had not, by the violence of her passion, and by a way which I had no knowledge of, and indeed abhorred, put a stop to her, of which I cannot enter into the particulars here.

However, notwithstanding this, I could not think of going away and leaving this work so unfinished as Amy had threatened to do, and for the folly of one child to leave the other to starve, or to stop my determined bounty to the good family I have mentioned. So, in a word, I committed the finishing it all to my faithful friend the Quaker, to whom I communicated as much of the whole story as was needful to empower her to perform what Amy had promised, and to make her talk so much to the purpose, as one employed more remotely than Amy had been, needed to be.

To this purpose she had, first of all, a full possession of the money; and went first to the honest man and his wife, and settled all the matter with them; when she talked of Mrs. Amy, she talked of her as one that had been empowered by the mother of the girls in the Indies, but was obliged to go back to the Indies, and had settled all sooner if she had not been hindered by the obstinate humour of the other daughter; that she had left instructions with her for the rest; but that the other had affronted her so much that she was gone away without doing anything for her; and that now, if anything was done, it must be by fresh orders from the East Indies.

I need not say how punctually my new agent acted; but, which was more, she brought the old man and his wife, and my other daughter, several times to her house, by which I had an opportunity, being there only as a lodger, and a stranger, to see my other girl, which I had never done before, since she was a little child.

The day I contrived to see them I was dressed up in a Quaker's habit, and looked so like a Quaker, that it was impossible for them, who had never seen me before, to suppose I had ever been anything else; also my way of talking was suitable enough to it, for I had learned that long before.

I have not time here to take notice what a surprise it was to me to see my child; how it worked upon my affections; with what infinite struggle I mastered a strong inclination that I had to discover myself to her; how the girl was the very counterpart of myself, only much handsomer; and how sweetly and modestly she behaved; how, on that occasion, I resolved to do more for her than I had appointed by Amy, and the like.

It is enough to mention here, that as the settling this affair made way for my going on board, notwithstanding the absence of my old agent Amy, so, however, I left some hints for Amy too, for I did not yet despair of my hearing from her; and that if my good Quaker should ever see her again, she should let her see them; wherein, particularly, ordering her to leave the affair of Spitalfields just as I had done, in the hands of my friend, she should come away to me; upon this condition, nevertheless, that she gave full satisfaction to my friend the Quaker that she had not murdered my child; for if she had, I told her I would never see her face more. However, notwithstanding this, she came over afterwards, without giving my friend any of that satisfaction, or any account that she intended to come over.

I can say no more now, but that, as above, being arrived in Holland, with my spouse and his son, formerly mentioned, I appeared there with all the splendour and equipage suitable to our new prospect, as I have already observed.

Here, after some few years of flourishing and outwardly happy circumstances, I fell into a dreadful course of calamities, and Amy also; the very reverse of our former good days. The blast of Heaven seemed to follow the injury done the poor girl by us both, and I was brought so low again, that my repentance seemed to be only the consequence of my misery, as my misery was of my crime.

CONTINUATION

In resolving to go to Holland with my husband, and take possession of the title of countess as soon as possible, I had a view of deceiving my daughter, were she yet alive, and seeking me out; for it seldom happens that a nobleman, or his lady, are called by their surnames, and as she was a stranger to our noble title, might have inquired at our next door neighbours for Mr. ——, the Dutch merchant, and not have been one jot the wiser for her inquiry. So one evening, soon after this resolution, as I and my husband were sitting together when supper was over, and talking of several various scenes in life, I told him that, as there was no likelihood of my being with child, as I had some reason to suspect I was some time before, I was ready to go with him to any part of the world, whenever he pleased. I said, that great part of my things were packed up, and what was not would not be long about, and that I had little occasion to buy any more clothes, linen, or jewels, whilst I was in England, having a large quantity of the richest and best of everything by me already. On saying these words, he took me in his arms, and told me that he looked on what I had now spoken with so great an emphasis, to be my settled resolution, and the fault should not lie on his side if it miscarried being put in practice.

The next morning he went out to see some merchants, who had received advice of the arrival of some shipping which had been in great danger at sea, and whose insurance had run very high; and it was this interval that gave me an opportunity of my coming to a final resolution. I now told the Quaker, as she was sitting at work in her parlour, that we should very speedily leave her, and although she daily expected it, yet she was really sorry to hear that we had come to a full determination; she said abundance of fine things to me on the happiness of the life I did then, and was going to live; believing, I suppose, that a countess could not have a foul conscience; but at that very instant, I would have, had it been in my power, resigned husband, estate, title, and all the blessings she fancied I had in the world, only for her real virtue, and the sweet peace of mind, joined to a loving company of children, which she really possessed.

When my husband returned, he asked me at dinner if I persevered in my resolution of leaving England; to which I answered in the affirmative. "Well," says he, "as all my affairs will not take up a week's time to settle, I will be ready to go from London with you in ten days' time." We fixed upon no particular place or abode, but in general concluded to go to Dover, cross the Channel to Calais, and proceed from thence by easy journeys to Paris, where after staying about a week, we intended to go through part of France, the Austrian Netherlands, and so on to Amsterdam, Rotterdam, or the Hague, as we were to settle before we went from Paris. As my husband did not care to venture all our fortune in one bottom, so our goods, money, and plate were consigned to several merchants, who had been his intimates many years, and he took notes of a prodigious value in his pocket, besides what he gave me to take care of during our journey. The last thing to be considered was, how we should go ourselves, and what equipage we should take with us; my thoughts were wholly taken up about it some time; I knew I was going to be a countess, and did not care to appear anything mean before I came to that honour; but, on the other hand, if I left London in any public way, I might possibly hear of inquiries after me in the road, that I had been acquainted with before. At last I said we would discharge all our servants, except two footmen, who should travel with us to Dover, and one maid to wait on me, that had lived with me only since the retreat of Amy, and she was to go through, if she was willing; and as to the carriage of us, a coach should be hired for my husband, myself, and maid, and two horses were to be hired for the footmen, who were to return with them to London.

When the Quaker had heard when and how we intended to go, she begged, as there would be a spare seat in the coach, to accompany us as far as Dover, which we both readily consented to; no woman could be a better companion, neither was there any acquaintance that we loved better, or could show more respect to us.

The morning before we set out, my husband sent for a master coachman to know the price of a handsome coach, with six able horses, to go to Dover. He inquired how many days we intended to be on the journey? My husband said he would go but very easy, and chose to be three days on the road; that they should stay there two days, and be three more returning to London, with a gentlewoman (meaning the Quaker) in it. The coachman said it would be an eight days' journey, and he would have ten guineas for it. My husband consented to pay him his demand, and he received orders to be ready at the door by seven of the clock the next morning: I was quite prepared to go, having no person to take leave of but the Quaker, and she had desired to see us take the packet-boat at Dover, before we parted with her; and the last night of my stay in London was spent very agreeably with the Quaker and her family. My husband, who stayed out later than usual, in taking his farewell of several merchants of his acquaintance, came home about eleven o'clock, and drank a glass or two of wine with us before we went to bed.

The next morning, the whole family got up about five o'clock, and I, with my husband's consent, made each of the Quaker's daughters a present of a diamond ring, valued at £20, and a guinea apiece to all the servants, without exception. We all breakfasted together, and at the hour appointed, the coach and attendants came to the door; this drew several people about it, who were all very inquisitive to know who was going into the country, and what is never forgot on such occasions, all the beggars in the neighbourhood were prepared to give us their benedictions in hopes of an alms. When the coachmen had packed up what boxes were designed for our use, we, namely, my husband, the Quaker, myself, and the waiting-maid, all got into the coach, the footmen were mounted on horses behind, and in this manner the coach, after I had given a guinea to one of the Quaker's daughters equally to divide among the beggars at the door, drove away from the house, and I took leave of my lodging in the Minories, as well as of London.

At St. George's Church, Southwark, we were met by three gentlemen on horseback, who were merchants of my husband's acquaintance, and had come out on purpose, to go half a day's journey with us; and as they kept talking to us at the coach side, we went a good pace, and were very merry together; we stopped at the best house of entertainment on Shooter's Hill.

Here we stopped for about an hour, and drank some wine, and my husband, whose chief study was how to please and divert me, caused me to alight out of the coach; which the gentlemen who accompanied us observing, alighted also. The waiter showed us upstairs into a large room, whose window opened to our view a fine prospect of the river Thames, which here, they say, forms one of the most beautiful meanders. It was within an hour of high water, and such a number of ships coming in under sail quite astonished as well as delighted me, insomuch that I could not help breaking out into such-like expressions, "My dear, what a fine sight this is; I never saw the like before! Pray will they get to London this tide?" At which the good-natured gentleman smiled, and said, "Yes, my dear; why, there is London, and as the wind is quite fair for them, some of them will come to an anchor in about half-an-hour, and all within an hour."

I was so taken up with looking down the river that, till my husband spoke, I had not once looked up the river; but when I did, and saw London, the Monument, the cathedral church of St. Paul, and the steeples belonging to the several parish churches, I was transported into an ecstasy, and could not refrain from saying, "Sure that cannot be the place we are now just come from, it must be further off, for that looks to be scarce three miles off, and we have been three hours, by my watch, coming from our lodgings in the Minories! No, no, it is not London, it is some other place!"

Upon which one of the gentlemen present offered to convince me that the place I saw was London if I would go up to the top of the house, and view it from the turret. I accepted the offer, and I, my husband, and the three gentlemen were conducted by the master of the house upstairs into the turret. If I was delighted before with my prospect, I was now ravished, for I was elevated above the room I was in before upwards of thirty feet. I seemed a little dizzy, for the turret being a lantern, and giving light all ways, for some time I thought myself suspended in the air; but sitting down, and having eat a mouthful of biscuit and drank a glass of sack, I soon recovered, and then the gentleman who had undertaken to convince me that the place I was shown was really London, thus began, after having drawn aside one of the windows.

"You see, my lady," says the gentleman, "the greatest, the finest, the richest, and the most populous city in the world, at least in Europe, as I can assure your ladyship, upon my own knowledge, it deserves the character I have given it." "But this, sir, will never convince me that the place you now show me is London, though I have before heard that London deserves the character you have with so much cordiality bestowed upon it. And this I can testify, that London, in every particular you have mentioned, greatly surpasses Paris, which is allowed by all historians and travellers to be the second city in Europe."

Here the gentleman, pulling out his pocket-glass, desired me to look through it, which I did; and then he directed me to look full at St. Paul's, and to make that the centre of my future observation, and thereupon he promised me conviction.

Whilst I took my observation, I sat in a high chair, made for that purpose, with a convenience before you to hold the glass. I soon found the cathedral, and then I could not help saying I have been several times up to the stone gallery, but not quite so often up to the iron gallery. Then I brought my eye to the Monument, and was obliged to confess I knew it to be such. The gentleman then moved the glass and desired me to look, which doing, I said, "I think I see Whitehall and St. James's Park, and I see also two great buildings like barns, but I do not know what they are." "Oh," says the gentleman, "they are the Parliament House and Westminster Abbey." "They may be so," said I; and continuing looking, I perceived the very house at Kensington which I had lived in some time; but of that I took no notice, yet I found my colour come, to think what a life of gaiety and wickedness I had lived. The gentleman, perceiving my disorder, said, "I am afraid I have tired your ladyship; I will make but one remove, more easterly, and then I believe you will allow the place we see to be London."

He might have saved himself the trouble, for I was thoroughly convinced of my error; but to give myself time to recover, and to hide my confusion, I seemed not yet to be quite convinced. I looked, and the first object that presented itself was Aldgate Church, which, though I confess to my shame, I seldom saw the inside of it, yet I was well acquainted with the outside, for many times my friend the Quaker and I had passed and repassed by it when we used to go in the coach to take an airing. I saw the church, or the steeple of the church, so plain, and knew it so well, that I could not help saying, with some earnestness, "My dear, I see our church; the church, I mean, belonging to our neighbourhood; I am sure it is Aldgate Church." Then I saw the Tower, and all the shipping; and, taking my eye from the glass, I thanked the gentleman for the trouble I had given him, and said to him that I was fully convinced that the place I saw was London, and that it was the very place we came from that morning.

When we came to Sittingbourne, our servant soon brought us word that although we were at the best inn in the town, yet there was nothing in the larder fit for our dinner. The landlord came in after him and began to make excuses for his empty cupboard. He told us, withal, that if we would please to stay, he would kill a calf, a sheep, a hog, or anything we had a fancy to. We ordered him to kill a pig and some pigeons, which, with a dish of fish, a cherry pie, and some pastry, made up a tolerable dinner. We made up two pounds ten shillings, for we caused the landlord, his wife, and two daughters, to dine with us, and help us off with our wine. Our landlady and her two daughters, with a glass or two given to the cook, managed two bottles of white wine. This operated so strong upon one of the young wenches that, my spouse being gone out into the yard, her tongue began to run; and, looking at me, she says to her mother, "La! mother, how much like the lady her ladyship is" (speaking of me), "the young woman who lodged here the other night, and stayed here part of the next day, and then set forward for Canterbury, described. The lady is the same person, I'm sure."

This greatly alarmed me, and made me very uneasy, for I concluded this young woman could be no other than my daughter, who was resolved to find me out, whether I would or no. I desired the girl to describe the young woman she mentioned, which she did, and I was convinced it was my own daughter. I asked in what manner she travelled, and whether she had any company. I was answered that she was on foot, and that she had no company; but that she always travelled from place to place in company; that her method was, when she came into any town, to go to the best inns and inquire for the lady she sought; and then, when she had satisfied herself that the lady, whom she called her mother, was not to be found in that town or neighbourhood, she then begged the favour of the landlady of the inn where she was, to put her into such a company that she knew that she might go safe to the next town; that this was the manner of her proceeding at her house, and she believed she had practised it ever since she set out from London; and she hoped to meet with her mother, as she called her, upon the road.

I asked my landlady whether she described our coach and equipage, but she said the young woman did not inquire concerning equipage, but only described a lady "so like your ladyship, that I have often, since I saw your ladyship, took you to be the very person she was looking for."

Amidst the distractions of my mind, this afforded me some comfort, that my daughter was not in the least acquainted with the manner in which we travelled. My husband and the landlord returned, and that put an end to the discourse.

I left this town with a heavy heart, feeling my daughter would infallibly find me out at Canterbury; but, as good luck would have it, she had left that city before we came thither, some time. I was very short in one thing, that I had not asked my landlady at Sittingbourne how long it was since my daughter was there. But when I came to Canterbury I was a very anxious and indefatigable in inquiring after my daughter, and I found that she had been at the inn where we then were, and had inquired for me, as I found by the description the people gave of myself.

Here I learnt my daughter had left Canterbury a week. This pleased me; and I was determined to stay in Canterbury one day, to view the cathedral, and see the antiquities of this metropolis.

As we had sixteen miles to our journey's end that night, for it was near four o'clock before we got into our coach again, the coachman drove with great speed, and at dusk in the evening we entered the west gate of the city, and put up at an inn in High Street (near St. Mary Bredman's church), which generally was filled with the best of company. The anxiety of my mind, on finding myself pursued by this girl, and the fatigue of my journey, had made me much out of order, my head ached, and I had no stomach.

This made my husband (but he knew not the real occasion of my illness) and the Quaker very uneasy, and they did all in their power to persuade me to eat anything I could fancy.

At length the landlady of the inn, who perceived I was more disturbed in my mind than sick, advised me to eat one poached egg, drink a glass of sack, eat a toast, and go to bed, and she warranted, she said, I should be well by the morning. This was immediately done; and I must acknowledge, that the sack and toast cheered me wonderfully, and I began to take heart again; and my husband would have the coachman in after supper, on purpose to divert me and the honest Quaker, who, poor creature, seemed much more concerned at my misfortune than I was myself.

I went soon to bed, but for fear I should be worse in the night, two maids of the inn were ordered to sit up in an adjoining chamber; the Quaker and my waiting-maid lay in a bed in the same room, and my husband by himself in another apartment.

While my maid was gone down on some necessary business, and likewise to get me some burnt wine, which I was to drink going to bed, or rather when I was just got into bed, the Quaker and I had the following dialogue:

Quaker. The news thou heardest at Sittingbourne has disordered thee. I am glad the young woman has been out of this place a week; she went indeed for Dover; and when she comes there and canst not find thee, she may go to Deal, and so miss of thee.

Roxana. What I most depend upon is, that as we do not travel by any particular name, but the general one of the baronet and his lady, and the girl hath no notion what sort of equipage we travelled with, it was not easy to make a discovery of me, unless she accidentally, in her travels, light upon you (meaning the Quaker), or upon me; either of which must unavoidably blow the secret I had so long laboured to conceal.

Quaker. As thou intendest to stay here to-morrow, to see the things which thou callest antiquities, and which are more properly named the relics of the Whore of Babylon; suppose thou wert to send Thomas, who at thy command followeth after us, to the place called Dover, to inquire whether such a young woman has been inquiring for thee. He may go out betimes in the morning, and may return by night, for it is but twelve or fourteen miles at farthest thither.

Roxana. I like thy scheme very well; and I beg the favour of you in the morning, as soon as you are up, to send Tom to Dover, with such instructions as you shall think proper.

After a good night's repose I was well recovered, to the great satisfaction of all that were with me.

The good-natured Quaker, always studious to serve and oblige me, got up about five o'clock in the morning, and going down into the inn-yard, met with Tom, gave him his instructions, and he set out for Dover before six o'clock.

As we were at the best inn in the city, so we could readily have whatever we pleased, and whatever the season afforded; but my husband, the most indulgent man that ever breathed, having observed how heartily I ate my dinner at Rochester two days before, ordered the very same bill of fare, and of which I made a heartier meal than I did before. We were very merry, and after we had dined, we went to see the town-house, but as it was near five o'clock I left the Quaker behind me, to receive what intelligence she could get concerning my daughter, from the footman, who was expected to return from Dover at six.

We came to the inn just as it was dark, and then excusing myself to my husband, I immediately ran up into my chamber, where I had appointed the Quaker to be against my return. I ran to her with eagerness, and inquired what news from Dover, by Tom, the footman.

219

She said, Tom had been returned two hours; that he got to Dover that morning between seven and eight, and found, at the inn he put up at, there had been an inquisitive young woman to find out a gentleman that was a Dutch merchant, and a lady who was her mother; that the young woman perfectly well described his lady; that he found that she had visited every public inn in the town; that she said she would go to Deal, and that if she did not find the lady, her mother, there, she would go by the first ship to the Hague, and go from thence, to Amsterdam and Rotterdam, searching all the towns through which she passed in the United Provinces.

This account pleased me very well, especially when I understood that she had been gone from Dover five days. The Quaker comforted me, and said it was lucky this busy creature had passed the road before us, otherwise she might easily have found means to have overtaken us, for, as she observed, the wench had such an artful way of telling her story, that she moved everybody to compassion; and she did not doubt but that if we had been before, as we were behind, she would have got those who would have assisted her with a coach, &c., to have pursued us, and they might have come up with us.

I was of the honest Quaker's sentiments. I grew pretty easy, called Tom, and gave him half a guinea for his diligence; then I and the Quaker went into the parlour to my husband, and soon after supper came in, and I ate moderately, and we spent the remainder of the evening, for the clock had then tolled nine, very cheerfully; for my Quaker was so rejoiced at my good fortune, as she called it, that she was very alert, and exceeding good company; and her wit, and she had no small share of it, I thought was better played off than ever I had heard it before.

My husband asked me how I should choose to go on board; I desired him to settle it as he pleased, telling him it was a matter of very great indifference to me, as he was to go with me. "That may be true, my dear," says he, "but I ask you for a reason or two, which I will lay before you, viz., if we hire a vessel for ourselves, we may set sail when we please, have the liberty of every part of the ship to ourselves, and land at what port, either in Holland or France, we might make choice of. Besides," added he, "another reason I mention it to you is, that I know you do not love much company, which, in going into the packet-boat, it is almost impossible to avoid." "I own, my dear," said I, "your reasons are very good; I have but one thing to say against them, which is, that the packet-boat, by its frequent voyages, must of course be furnished with experienced seamen, who know the seas too well even to run any hazard." (At this juncture the terrible voyage I and Amy made from France to Harwich came so strong in my mind, that I trembled so as to be taken notice of by my husband.) "Besides," added I, "the landlord may send the master of one of them to you, and I think it may be best to hire the state cabin, as they call it, to ourselves, by which method we shall avoid company, without we have an inclination to associate ourselves with such passengers we may happen to like; and the expense will be much cheaper than hiring a vessel to go the voyage with us alone, and every whit as safe."

The Quaker, who had seriously listened to our discourse, gave it as her opinion that the method I had proposed was by far the safest, quickest, and cheapest. "Not," said she, "as I think thou wouldest be against any necessary expense, though I am certain thou wouldest not fling thy money away."

Soon after, my husband ordered the landlord to send for one of the masters of the packet-boats, of whom he hired the great cabin, and agreed to sail from thence the next day, if the wind and the tide answered.

The settling our method of going over sea had taken up the time till the dinner was ready, which we being informed of, came out of a chamber we had been in all the morning, to a handsome parlour, where everything was placed suitable to our rank; there was a large, old-fashioned service of plate, and a sideboard genteelly set off. The dinner was excellent, and well dressed.

After dinner, we entered into another discourse, which was the hiring of servants to go with us from Dover to Paris; a thing frequently done by travellers; and such are to be met with at every stage inn. Our footmen set out this morning on their return to London, and the Quaker and coach was to go the next day. My new chambermaid, whose name was Isabel, was to go through the journey, on condition of doing no other business than waiting on me. In a while we partly concluded to let the hiring of men-servants alone till we came to Calais, for they could be of no use to us on board a ship, the sailor's or cabin boy's place being to attend the cabin passengers as well as his master.

To divert ourselves, we took a walk after we had dined, round about the town, and coming to the garrison, and being somewhat thirsty, all went into the sutler's for a glass of wine. A pint was called for and brought; but the man of the house came in with it raving like a madman, saying, "Don't you think you are a villain, to ask for a pot of ale when I know you have spent all your money, and are ignorant of the means of getting more, without you hear of a place, which I look upon to be very unlikely?" "Don't be in such a passion, landlord," said my husband. "Pray, what is the matter?" "Oh, nothing, sir," says he; "but a young fellow in the sutling room, whom I find to have been a gentleman's servant, wants a place; and having spent all his money, would willingly run up a score with me, knowing I must get him a master if ever I intend to have my money." "Pray, sir," said my husband, "send the young fellow to me; if I like him, and can agree with him, it is possible I may take him into my service." The landlord took care we should not speak to him twice, he went and fetched him in himself, and my husband examined him before he spoke, as to his size, mien, and garb. The young man was clean dressed, of a middling stature, a dark complexion, and about twenty-seven years old.

"I hear, young man," says he to him, "that you want a place; it may perhaps be in my power to serve you. Let me know at once what education you have had, if you have any family belonging to you, or if you are fit for a gentleman's service, can bring any person of reputation to your character, and are willing to go and live in Holland with me: we will not differ about your wages."

The young fellow made a respectful bow to each of us, and addressed himself to my husband as follows: "Sir," said he, "in me you behold the eldest child of misfortune. I am but young, as you may see; I have no comers after me, and having lived with several gentlemen, some of whom are on their travels, others settled in divers parts of the world, besides what are dead, makes me unable to produce a character without a week's notice to write to London, and I should not doubt but by the return of the post to let you see some letters as would satisfy you in any doubts about me. My education," continued he, "is but very middling, being taken from school before I had well learnt to read, write, and cast accounts; and as to my parentage, I cannot well give you any account of them: all that I know is, that my father was a brewer, and by his extravagance ran out a handsome fortune, and afterwards left my poor mother almost penniless, with five small children, of which I was the second, though not above five years old. My mother knew not what to do with us, so she sent a poor girl, our maid, whose name I have forgot this many years, with us all to a relation's, and there left us, and I never saw or heard of or from them any more. Indeed, I inquired among the neighbours, and all that I could learn was that my mother's goods were seized, that she was obliged to apply to the parish for relief, and died of grief soon after. For my part," says he, "I was put into the hands of my father's sister, where, by her cruel usage, I was forced to run away at nine years of age; and the numerous scenes of life I have since gone through are more than would fill a small volume. Pray, sir," added he, "let it satisfy you that I am thoroughly honest, and should be glad to serve you at any rate; and although I cannot possibly get a good character from anybody at present, yet I defy the whole world to give me an ill one, either in public or private life."

If I had had the eyes of Argus I should have seen with them all on this occasion. I knew that this was my son, and one that, among all my inquiry, I could never get any account of. The Quaker seeing my colour come and go, and also tremble, said, "I verily believe thou art not well; I hope this Kentish air, which was always reckoned aguish, does not hurt thee?" "I am taken very sick of a sudden," said I; "so pray let me go to our inn that I may go to my chamber." Isabel being called in, she and the Quaker attended me there, leaving the young fellow with my spouse. When I was got into my chamber I was seized with such a grief as I had never known before; and flinging myself down upon the bed, burst into a flood of tears, and soon after fainted away. Soon after, I came a little to myself, and the Quaker begged of me to tell her what was the cause of my sudden indisposition. "Nothing at all," says I, "as I know of; but a sudden chilliness seized my blood, and that, joined to a fainting of the spirits, made me ready to sink."

Presently after my husband came to see how I did, and finding me somewhat better, he told me that he had a mind to hire the young man I had left him with, for he believed he was honest and fit for our service. "My dear," says I, "I did not mind him. I would desire you to be cautious who we pick up on the road; but as I have the satisfaction of hiring my maids, I shall never trouble myself with the men-servants, that is wholly your province. However," added I (for I was very certain he was my son, and was resolved to have him in my service, though it was my interest to keep my husband off, in order to bring him on), "if you like the fellow, I am not averse to your hiring one servant in England. We are not obliged to trust him with much before we see his conduct, and if he does not prove as you may expect, you may turn him off whenever you please." "I believe," said my husband, "he has been ingenuous in his relation to me; and as a man who has seen great variety of life, and may have been the shuttlecock of fortune, the butt of envy, and the mark of malice, I will hire him when he comes to me here anon, as I have ordered him."

As I knew he was to be hired, I resolved to be out of the way when he came to my husband; so about five o'clock I proposed to the Quaker to take a walk on the pier and see the shipping, while the tea-kettle was boiling. We went, and took Isabel with us, and as we were going along I saw my son Thomas (as I shall for the future call him) going to our inn; so we stayed out about an hour, and when we returned my husband told me he had hired the man, and that he was to come to him as a servant on the morrow morning. "Pray, my dear," said I, "did you ask where he ever lived, or what his name is?" "Yes," replied my husband, "he says his name is Thomas ——; and as to places, he has mentioned several families of note, and among others, he lived at my Lord ——'s, next door to the great French lady's in Pall Mall, whose name he tells me was Roxana." I was now in a sad dilemma, and was fearful I should be known by my own son; and the Quaker took notice of it, and afterwards told me she believed fortune had conspired that all the people I became acquainted with, should have known the Lady Roxana. "I warrant," said she, "this young fellow is somewhat acquainted with the impertinent wench that calls herself thy daughter."

I was very uneasy in mind, but had one thing in my favour, which was always to keep myself at a very great distance from my servants; and as the Quaker was to part with us the next day or night, he would have nobody to mention the name Roxana to, and so of course it would drop.

We supped pretty late at night, and were very merry, for my husband said all the pleasant things he could think of, to divert me from the supposed illness he thought I had been troubled with in the day. The Quaker kept up the discourse with great spirit, and I was glad to receive the impression, for I wanted the real illness to be drove out of my head.

The next morning, after breakfast, Thomas came to his new place. He appeared very clean, and brought with him a small bundle, which I supposed to be linen tied up in a handkerchief. My husband sent him to order some porters belonging to the quay to fetch our boxes to the Custom-house, where they were searched, for which we paid one shilling; and he had orders to give a crown for head money, as they called it; their demand by custom is but sixpence a head, but we appeared to our circumstances in everything. As soon as our baggage was searched, it was carried from the Custom-house on board the packet-boat, and there lodged in the great cabin as we had ordered it.

This took up the time till dinner, and when we were sitting together after we had both dined, the captain came to tell us that the wind was very fair, and that he was to sail at high water, which would be about ten o'clock at night. My husband asked him to stay and drink part of a bottle of wine with him, which he did; and their discourse being all in the maritime strain, the Quaker and I retired and left them together, for I had something to remind her of in our discourse before we left London. When we got into the garden, which was rather neat than fine, I repeated all my former requests to her about my children, Spitalfields, Amy, &c., and we sat talking together till Thomas was sent to tell us the captain was going, on which we returned; but, by the way, I kissed her and put a large gold medal into her hand, as a token of my sincere love, and desired that she would never neglect the things she had promised to perform, and her repeated promise gave me great satisfaction.

The captain, who was going out of the parlour as we returned in, was telling my husband he would send six of his hands to conduct us to the boat, about a quarter of an hour before he sailed, and as the moon was at the full, he did not doubt of a pleasant passage.

Our next business was to pay off the coachman, to whom my husband gave half a guinea extraordinary, to set the Quaker down at the house he took us all up at, which he promised to perform.

As it was low water, we went on board to see the cabin that we were to go our voyage in, and the captain would detain us to drink a glass of the best punch, I think, I ever tasted.

When we returned to the inn, we ordered supper to be ready by eight o'clock, that we might drink a parting glass to settle it, before we went on board; for my husband, who knew the sea very well, said a full stomach was the forerunner of sea-sickness, which I was willing to avoid.

We invited the landlord, his wife, and daughter, to supper with us, and having sat about an hour afterwards, the captain himself, with several sailors, came to fetch us to the vessel. As all was paid, we had nothing to hinder us but taking a final leave of the Quaker, who would go to see us safe in the vessel, where tears flowed from both our eyes; and I turned short in the boat, while my husband took his farewell, and he then followed me, and I never saw the Quaker or England any more.

We were no sooner on board than we hoisted sail; the anchors being up, and the wind fair, we cut the waves at a great rate, till about four o'clock in the morning, when a French boat came to fetch the mail to carry it to the post-house, and the boat cast her anchors, for we were a good distance from the shore, neither could we sail to the town till next tide, the present one being too far advanced in the ebb.

We might have gone on shore in the boat that carried the mail, but my husband was sleeping in the cabin when it came to the packet-boat, and I did not care to disturb him; however, we had an opportunity soon after, for my husband awaking, and two other boats coming up with oars to see for passengers, Thomas came to let us know we might go on shore, if we pleased. My husband paid the master of the packet-boat for our passage, and Thomas, with the sailors' assistance, got our boxes into the wherry, so we sailed for Calais; but before our boat came to touch ground, several men, whose bread I suppose it is, rushed into the water, without shoes or stockings, to carry us on shore; so having paid ten shillings for the wherry, we each of us was carried from the boat to the land by two men, and our goods brought after us; here was a crown to be paid, to save ourselves from being wet, by all which a man that is going a travelling may see that it is not the bare expense of the packet-boat that will carry him to Calais.

It would be needless to inform the reader of all the ceremonies that we passed through at this place before we were suffered to proceed on our journey; however, our boxes having been searched at the Custom-house, my husband had them plumbed, as they called it, to hinder any further inquiry about them; and we got them all to the Silver Lion, a noted inn, and the post-house of this place, where we took a stage-coach for ourselves, and the next morning, having well refreshed ourselves, we all, viz., my husband, self, and chambermaid within the coach, and Thomas behind (beside which my husband hired two horsemen well armed, who were pretty expensive, to travel with us), set forward on our journey.

We were five days on our journey from Calais to Paris, which we went through with much satisfaction, for, having fine weather and good attendance, we had nothing to hope for.

When we arrived at Paris (I began to be sorry I had ever proposed going to it for fear of being known, but as we were to stay there but a few days, I was resolved to keep very retired), we went to a merchant's house of my husband's acquaintance in the Rue de la Bourle, near the Carmelites, in the Faubourg de St. Jacques.

This being a remote part of the city, on the south side, and near several pleasant gardens, I thought it would be proper to be a little indisposed, that my husband might not press me to go with him to see the curiosities; for he could do the most needful business, such as going to the bankers to exchange bills, despatching of letters, settling affairs with merchants, &c., without my assistance; and I had a tolerable plea for my conduct, such as the great fatigue of our journey, being among strangers, &c.; so we stayed at Paris eight days without my going to any particular places, except going one day to the gardens of Luxembourg, another to the church of Notre Dame on the Isle of Paris, a third to the Hôtel Royale des Invalides, a fourth to the gardens of the Tuileries, a fifth to the suburbs of St. Lawrence, to see the fair which was then holding there; a sixth to the gardens of the Louvre, a seventh to the playhouse, and the eighth stayed all day at home to write a letter to the Quaker, letting her know where I then was, and how soon we should go forwards in our journey, but did not mention where we intended to settle, as, indeed, we had not yet settled that ourselves.

One of the days, viz., that in which I went to the gardens of the Tuileries, I asked Thomas several questions about his father, mother, and other relations, being resolved, notwithstanding he was my own son, as he did not know it, to turn him off by some stratagem or another, if he had any manner of memory of me, either as his mother, or the Lady Roxana. I asked him if he had any particular memory of his mother or father; he answered, "No, I scarce remember anything of either of them," said he, "but I have heard from several people that I had one brother and three sisters, though I never saw them all, to know them, notwithstanding I lived with an aunt four years; I often asked after my mother, and some people said she went away with a man, but it was allowed by most people, that best knew her, that she, being brought to the greatest distress, was carried to the workhouse belonging to the parish, where she died soon after with grief."

Nothing could give me more satisfaction than what Thomas had related; so now, I thought I would ask about the Lady Roxana (for he had been my next-door neighbour when I had that title conferred on me). "Pray, Thomas," said I, "did not you speak of a great person of quality, whose name I have forgot, that lived next door to my Lord ——'s when you was his valet? pray who was she? I suppose a foreigner, by the name you called her." "Really, my lady," replied he, "I do not know who she was; all I can say of her is, that she kept the greatest company, and was a beautiful woman, by report, but I never saw her; she was called the Lady Roxana, was a very good mistress, but her character was not so good as to private life as it ought to be. Though I once had an opportunity," continued he, "of seeing a fine outlandish dress she danced in before the king, which I took as a great favour, for the cook took me up when the lady was out, and she desired my lady's woman to show it to me."

All this answered right, and I had nothing to do but to keep my Turkish dress out of the way, to be myself unknown to my child, for as he had never seen Roxana, so he knew nothing of me.

In the interval, my husband had hired a stage-coach to carry us to the city of Menin, where he intended to go by water down the river Lys to Ghent, and there take coach to Isabella fort, opposite the city of Anvers, and cross the river to that place, and go from thence by land to Breda; and as he had agreed and settled this patrol, I was satisfied, and we set out next day. We went through several handsome towns and villages before we took water, but by water we went round part of the city of Courtrai, and several fortified towns. At Anvers we hired a coach to Breda, where we stayed two days to refresh ourselves, for we had been very much fatigued; as Willemstadt was situated so as to be convenient for our taking water for Rotterdam, we went there, and being shipped, had a safe and speedy voyage to that city.

As we had resolved in our journey to settle at the Hague, we did not intend to stay any longer at Rotterdam, than while my husband had all our wealth delivered to him from the several merchants he had consigned it to. This business took up a month, during which time we lived in ready-furnished lodgings on the Great Quay, where all the respect was shown us as was due to our quality.

Here my husband hired two more men-servants, and I took two maids, and turned Isabel, who was a well-bred, agreeable girl, into my companion; but that I might not be too much fatigued, my husband went to the Hague first, and left me, with three maids and Thomas, at Rotterdam, while he took a house, furnished it, and had everything ready for my reception, which was done with great expedition. One of his footmen came with a letter to me one morning, to let me know his master would come by the scow next day to take me home, in which he desired that I would prepare for my departure. I soon got everything ready, and the next morning, on the arrival of the scow, I saw my husband; and we both, with all the servants, left the city of Rotterdam, and safely got to the Hague the afternoon following.

It was now the servants had notice given them to call me by the name of "my lady," as the honour of baronetage had entitled me, and with which title I was pretty well satisfied, but should have been more so had not I yet the higher title of countess in view.
I now lived in a place where I knew nobody, neither was I known, on which I was pretty careful whom I became acquainted with; our circumstances were very good, my husband loving, to the greatest degree, my servants respectful; and, in short, I lived the happiest life woman could enjoy, had my former crimes never crept into my guilty conscience.

I was in this happy state of life when I wrote a letter to the Quaker, in which I gave her a direction where she might send to me. And about a fortnight after, as I was one afternoon stepping into my coach in order to take an airing, the postman came to our door with letters, one of which was directed to me, and as soon as I saw it was the Quaker's hand, I bid the coachman put up again, and went into my closet to read the contents, which were as follows:

"Dear Friend,—I have had occasion to write to thee several times since we saw each other, but as this is my first letter, so it shall contain all the business thou wouldst know. I got safe to London, by thy careful ordering of the coach, and the attendants were not at all wanting in their duty. When I had been at home a few days, thy woman, Mrs. Amy, came to see me, so I took her to task as thou ordered me, about murdering thy pretended daughter; she declared her innocence, but said she had procured a false evidence to swear a large debt against her, and by that means had put her into a prison, and fee'd the keepers to hinder her from sending any letter or message out of the prison to any person whatever. This, I suppose, was the reason thou thought she was murdered, because thou wert relieved from her by this base usage. However, when I heard of it, I checked Amy very much, but was well satisfied to hear she was alive. After this I did not hear from Amy for above a month, and in the interim (as I knew thou wast safe), I sent a friend of mine to pay the debt, and release the prisoner, which he did, but was so indiscreet as to let her know who was the benefactress. My next care was to manage thy Spitalfields business, which I did with much exactness. And the day that I received thy last letter, Amy came to me again, and I read as much of it to her as she was concerned in: nay, I entreated her to drink tea with me, and after it one glass of citron, in which she drank towards thy good health, and she told me she would come to see thee as soon as possible. Just as she was gone, I was reading thy letter again in the little parlour, and that turbulent creature (thy pretended daughter) came to me, as she said, to return thanks for the favour I had done her, so I accidentally laid thy letter down in the window, while I went to fetch her a glass of cordial, for she looked sadly; and before I returned I heard the street door shut, on which I went back without the liquor, not knowing who might have come in, but missing her, I thought she might be gone to stand at the door, and the wind had blown it to; but I was never the nearer, she was sought for in vain. So when I believed her to be quite gone, I looked to see if I missed anything, which I did not; but at last, to my great surprise, I missed your letter, which she certainly took and made off with. I was so terrified at this unhappy chance that I fainted away, and had not one of my maidens come in at that juncture, it might have been attended with fatal consequences. I would advise thee to prepare thyself to see her, for I verily believe she will come to thee. I dread your knowing of this, but hope the best. Before I went to fetch the unhappy cordial, she told me, as she had often done before, that she was the eldest daughter, that the captain's wife was your second daughter, and her sister, and that the youngest sister was dead. She also said there were two brothers, the eldest of whom had never been seen by any of them since he run away from an uncle's at nine years of age, and that the youngest had been taken care of by an old lady that kept her coach, whom he took to be his godmother. She gave me a long history in what manner she was arrested and flung into Whitechapel jail, how hardly she fared there; and at length the keeper's wife, to whom she told her pitiful story, took compassion of her, and recommended her to the bounty of a certain lady who lived in that neighbourhood, that redeemed prisoners for small sums, and who lay for their fees, every return of the day of her nativity; that she was one of the six the lady had discharged; that the lady prompted her to seek after her mother; that she thereupon did seek thee in all the towns and villages between London and Dover; that not finding thee at Dover she went to Deal; and that at length, she being tired of seeking thee, she returned by shipping to London, where she was no sooner arrived but she was immediately arrested and flung into the Marshalsea prison, where she lived in a miserable condition, without the use of pen, ink, and paper, and without the liberty of having any one of her friends come near her. 'In this condition I was,' continued she, 'when you sent and paid my debt for me, and discharged me.' When she had related all this she fell into such a fit of crying, sighing, and sobbing, from which, when she was a little recovered, she broke out into loud exclamations against the wickedness of the people in England, that they could be so unchristian as to arrest her twice, when she said it was as true as the Gospel that she never did owe to any one person the sum of one shilling in all her life; that she could not think who it was that should owe her so much ill-will, for that she was not conscious to herself that she had any ways offended any person in the whole universal world, except Mrs. Amy, in the case of her mother, which, she affirmed, she was acquitted of by all men, and hoped she should be so by her Maker; and that if she (Mrs. Amy) had any hand in her sufferings, God would forgive her, as she heartily did. 'But then,' she added, 'I will not stay in England, I will go all over the world, I will go to France, to Paris; I know my mother did once live there, and if I do not find her there, I will go through Holland, to Amsterdam, to Rotterdam; in short, I will go till I find my mother out, if I should die in the pursuit.' I should be glad to hear of thine and thy spouse's welfare, and remain with much sincerity, your sincere friend,

"M.P.
"The ninth of the month called October.

"P.S.—If thou hast any business to transact in this city, pray let me know; I shall use my best endeavours to oblige thee; my daughters all join with me in willing thee a hearty farewell."

I concealed my surprise for a few minutes, only till I could get into the summer-house, at the bottom of our large garden; but when I was shut in, no living soul can describe the agony I was in, I raved, tore, fainted away, swore, prayed, wished, cried, and promised, but all availed nothing, I was now stuck in to see the worst of it, let what would happen.

At last I came to the following resolution, which was to write a letter to the Quaker, and in it enclose a fifty pound bank-bill, and tell the Quaker to give that to the young woman if she called again, and also to let her know a fifty pound bill should be sent her every year, so long as she made no inquiry after me, and kept herself retired in England. Although this opened myself too full to the Quaker, yet I thought I had better venture my character abroad, than destroy my peace at home.
Soon after, my husband came home, and he perceived I had been crying, and asked what was the reason. I told him that I had shed tears both for joy and sorrow: "For," said I, "I have received one of the tenderest letters from Amy, as it was possible for any person, and she tells me in it," added I, "that she will soon come to see me; which so overjoyed me, that I

cried, and after it, I went to read the letter a second time, as I was looking out of the summer-house window over the canal; and in unfolding it, I accidentally let it fall in, by which mischance it is lost, for which I am very sorry, as I intended you should see it." "Pray, my dear," said he, "do not let that give you any uneasiness; if Amy comes, and you approve of it, you have my consent to take her into the house, in what capacity you please. I am very glad," continued he, "that you have nothing of more consequence to be uneasy at, I fancy you would make but an indifferent helpmate if you had." Oh! thought I to myself, if you but knew half the things that lie on my conscience, I believe you would think that I bear them out past all example.

About ten days afterwards, as we were sitting at dinner with two gentlemen, one of the footmen came to the door, and said, "My lady, here is a gentlewoman at the door who desires to speak with you: she says her name is Mrs. Amy."

I no sooner heard her name, but I was ready to swoon away, but I ordered the footman to call Isabel, and ask the gentlewoman to walk up with her into my dressing-room; which he immediately did, and there I went to have my first interview with her. She kissed me for joy when she saw me, and I sent Isabel downstairs, for I was in pain till I had some private conversation with my old confidante.

There was not much ceremony between us, before I told her all the material circumstances that had happened in her absence, especially about the girl's imprisonments which she had contrived, and how she had got my letter at the Quaker's, the very day she had been there. "Well," says Amy, when I had told her all, "I find nothing is to ensue, if she lives, but your ruin; you would not agree to her death, so I will not make myself uneasy about her life; it might have been rectified, but you were angry with me for giving you the best of counsel, viz., when I proposed to murder her."

"Hussy," said I, in the greatest passion imaginable, "how dare you mention the word murder? You wretch you, I could find in my heart, if my husband and the company were gone, to kick you out of my house. Have you not done enough to kill her, in throwing her into one of the worst jails in England, where, you see, that Providence in a peculiar manner appeared to her assistance. Away! thou art a wicked wretch; thou art a murderer in the sight of God."

"I will say no more," says Amy, "but if I could have found her, after thy friend the Quaker had discharged her out of the Marshalsea prison, I had laid a scheme to have her taken up for a theft, and by that means got her transported for fourteen years. She will be with you soon, I am sure; I believe she is now in Holland."

While we were in this discourse, I found the gentlemen who dined with us were going, so we came downstairs, and I went into the parlour to take leave of them before their departure. When they were gone, my husband told me he had been talking with them about taking upon him the title of Count or Earl of ——, as he had told me of, and as an opportunity now offered, he was going to put it in execution.

I told him I was so well settled, as not to want anything this world could afford me, except the continuance of his life and love (though the very thing he had mentioned, joined with the death of my daughter, in the natural way, would have been much more to my satisfaction). "Well, my dear," says he, "the expense will be but small, and as I promised you the title, it shall not be long before the honour shall be brought home to your toilette." He was as good as his word, for that day week he brought the patent home to me, in a small box covered with crimson velvet and two gold hinges. "There, my lady countess," says he, "long may you live to bear the title, for I am certain you are a credit to it." In a few days after, I had the pleasure to see our equipage, as coach, chariot, &c., all new painted, and a coronet fixed at the proper place, and, in short, everything was proportioned to our quality, so that our house vied with most of the other nobility.

It was at this juncture that I was at the pinnacle of all my worldly felicity, notwithstanding my soul was black with the foulest crimes. And, at the same time, I may begin to reckon the beginning of my misfortunes, which were in embryo, but were very soon brought forth, and hurried me on to the greatest distress.

As I was sitting one day talking to Amy in our parlour, and the street door being left open by one of the servants, I saw my daughter pass by the window, and without any ceremony she came to the parlour door, and opening of it, came boldly in. I was terribly amazed, and asked her who she wanted, as if I had not known her, but Amy's courage was quite lost, and she swooned away. "Your servant, my lady," says she; "I thought I should never have had the happiness to see you tête-à-tête, till your agent, the Quaker, in Haydon Yard, in the Minories, carelessly left a direction for me in her own window; however, she is a good woman, for she released me out of a jail in which, I believe, that base wretch" (pointing to Amy, who was coming to herself) "caused me to be confined." As soon as Amy recovered, she flew at her like a devil, and between them there was so much noise as alarmed the servants, who all came to see what was the matter. Amy had pulled down one of my husband's swords, drawn it, and was just going to run her through the body, as the servants came in, who not knowing anything of the matter, some of them secured Amy, others held the girl, and the rest were busy about me, to prevent my fainting away, which was more than they could do, for I fell into strong fits, and in the interim they turned the girl out of the house, who was fully bent on revenge.

My lord, as I now called him, was gone out a-hunting. I was satisfied he knew nothing of it, as yet, and when Amy and I were thoroughly come to ourselves, we thought it most advisable to find the girl out, and give her a handsome sum of money to keep her quiet. So Amy went out, but in all her searching could hear nothing of her; this made me very uneasy. I guessed she would contrive to see my lord before he came home, and so it proved, as you shall presently hear.

When night came on, that I expected his return, I wondered I did not see him. Amy sat up in my chamber with me, and was as much concerned as was possible. Well, he did not come in all that night, but the next morning, about ten o'clock, he rapped at the door, with the girl along with him. When it was opened, he went into the great parlour, and bid Thomas go call down his lady. This was the crisis. I now summoned up all my resolution, and took Amy down with me, to see if we could not baffle the girl, who, to an inch, was her mother's own child.

It will be necessary here to give a short account of our debate, because on it all my future misery depended, and it made me lose my husband's love, and own my daughter; who would not rest there, but told my lord how many brothers and sisters she had.

When we entered the room, my lord was walking very gravely about it, but with his brows knit, and a wild confusion in his face, as if all the malice and revenge of a Dutchman had joined to put me out of countenance before I spoke a word.

"Pray, madam," says he, "do you know this young woman? I expect a speedy and positive answer, without the least equivocation."

"Really, my lord," replied I, "to give you an answer as quick as you desire, I declare I do not."

"Do not!" said he, "what do you mean by that? She tells me that you are her mother, and that her father ran away from you, and left two sons, and two daughters besides herself, who were all sent to their relations for provision, after which you ran away with a jeweller to Paris. Do you know anything of this? answer me quickly."

"My lord," said the girl, "there is Mrs. Amy, who was my mother's servant at the time (as she told me herself about three months ago), knows very well I am the person I pretend to be, and caused me to be thrown into jail for debts I knew nothing of, because I should not find out my mother to make myself known to her before she left England."

After this she told my lord everything she knew of me, even in the character of Roxana, and described my dress so well, that he knew it to be mine.

ROXANA IS CONFRONTED WITH HER DAUGHTER

"Pray, madam," says he, "do you know this young woman?"

When she had quite gone through her long relation, "Well, madam," says he, "now let me see if I cannot tell how far she has told the truth in relation to you. When I first became acquainted with you, it was on the sale of those jewels, in which I stood so much your friend, at a time that you were in the greatest distress, your substance being in the hands of the Jew; you then passed for a jeweller's widow; this agrees with her saying you ran away with a jeweller. In the next place, you would not consent to marry me about twelve years ago; I suppose then your real husband was living, for nothing else could tally with your condescension to me in everything except marriage. Since that time, your refusing to come to Holland in the vessel I had provided for you, under a distant prospect of your being with child, though in reality it was your having a child too much, as the captain told me of, when I, being ignorant of the case, did not understand him. Now," continued he, "she says that you are the identical Lady Roxana which made so much noise in the world, and has even described the robe and head-dress you wore on that occasion, and in that I know she is right; for, to my own knowledge, you have that very dress by you now; I having seen you dressed in it at our lodging at the Quaker's. From all these circumstances," says he, "I may be assured that you have imposed grossly upon me, and instead of being a woman of honour as I took you for, I find that you have been an abandoned wretch, and had nothing to recommend you but a sum of money and a fair countenance, joined to a false unrelenting heart."

These words of my lord's struck such a damp upon my spirits, as made me unable to speak in my turn. But at last, I spoke as follows: "My lord, I have most patiently stood to hear all it was possible for you to allege against me, which has no other proof than imagination. That I was the wife of a brewer, I have no reason now to deny, neither had I any occasion before to acknowledge it. I brought him a handsome fortune, which, joined to his, made us appear in a light far superior to our neighbours. I had also five children by him, two sons and three daughters, and had my husband been as wise as rich, we might have lived happily together now. But it was not so, for he minded nothing but sporting, in almost every branch; and closely following of it soon run out all his substance, and then left me in an unhappy, helpless condition. I did not send my children to my relations till the greatest necessity drove me, and after that, hearing my husband was dead, I married the jeweller, who was afterwards murdered. If I had owned how many children I had, the jeweller would not have married me, and the way of life I was in would not keep my family, so I was forced to deny them in order to get them bread. Neither can I say that I have either heard or known anything of my children since, excepting that I heard they were all taken care of; and this was the very reason I would not marry you, when you offered it some years since, for these children lay seriously at my heart, and as I did not want money, my inclination was to come to England, and not entail five children upon you the day of marriage."

"Pray, madam," said my lord, interrupting me, "I do not find that you kept up to your resolutions when you got there; you were so far from doing your duty as a parent, that you even neglected the civility of acquaintances, for they would have asked after them, but your whole scheme has been to conceal yourself as much as possible, and even when you were found out, denied yourself, as witness the case of your daughter here. As to the character of Lady Roxana, which you so nicely managed," said he, "did that become a woman that had five children, whose necessity had obliged you to leave them, to live in a continual scene of pageantry and riot, I could almost say debauchery? Look into your conduct, and see if you deserve to have the title or the estate you now so happily enjoy."

After this speech, he walked about the room in a confused manner for some minutes, and then addressed himself to Amy. "Pray, Mrs. Amy," says he, "give me your judgment in this case, for although I know you are as much as possible in your lady's interest, yet I cannot think you have so little charity as to think she acted like a woman of worth and discretion. Do you really think, as you knew all of them from infants, that this young woman is your lady's daughter?"

Amy, who always had spirits enough about her, said at once she believed the girl was my daughter. "And truly," says she, "I think your man Thomas is her eldest son, for the tale he tells of his birth and education suits exactly with our then circumstances."

"Why, indeed," said my lord, "I believe so too, for I now recollect that when we first took him into our service at Dover, he told me he was the son of a brewer in London; that his father had run away from his mother, and left her in a distressed condition with five children, of which he was second child, or eldest son."

Thomas was then called into the parlour, and asked what he knew of his family; he repeated all as above, concerning his father's running away and leaving me; but said that he had often asked and inquired after them, but without any success, and concluded, that he believed his brothers and sisters were distributed in several places, and that his mother died in the greatest distress, and was buried by the parish.

"Indeed," said my lord, "it is my opinion that Thomas is one of your sons; do not you think the same?" addressing himself to me.

"From the circumstances that have been related, my lord," said I, "I now believe that these are both my children; but you would have thought me a mad woman to have countenanced and taken this young woman in as my child, without a thorough assurance of it; for that would have been running myself to a certain expense and trouble, without the least glimpse of real satisfaction."

"Pray," said my lord to my daughter, "let me know what is become of your brothers and sisters; give me the best account of them that you can."

"My lord," replied she, "agreeably to your commands, I will inform you to the best of my knowledge; and to begin with myself, who am the eldest of the five. I was put to a sister of my father's with my youngest brother, who, by mere dint of industry, gave us maintenance and education, suitable to her circumstances; and she, with my uncle's consent, let me go to service when I was advanced in years; and among the variety of places I lived at, Lady Roxana's was one."

"Yes," said Thomas, "I knew her there, when I was a valet at my Lord D——'s, the next door; it was there I became acquainted with her; and she, by the consent of the gentlewoman," pointing to Amy, "let me see the Lady Roxana's fine vestment, which she danced in at the grand ball."

"Well," continued my daughter, "after I left this place, I was at several others before I became acquainted with Mrs. Amy a second time (I knew her before as Roxana's woman), who told me one day some things relating to my mother, and from thence I concluded if she was not my mother herself (as I at first thought she was), she must be employed by her; for no stranger could profess so much friendship, where there was no likelihood of any return, after being so many years asunder.

"After this, I made it my business to find your lady out if possible, and was twice in her company, once on board the ship you were to have come to Holland in, and once at the Quaker's house in the Minories, London; but as I gave her broad hints of whom I took her for, and my lady did not think proper to own me, I began to think I was mistaken, till your voyage to Holland was put off. Soon after, I was flung into Whitechapel jail for a false debt, but, through the recommendation of the jailer's wife to the annual charity of the good Lady Roberts, of Mile End, I was discharged. Whereupon I posted away, seeking my mother all down the Kent Road as far as Dover and Deal, at which last place not finding her, I came in a coaster to London, and landing in Southwark, was immediately arrested, and confined in the Marshalsea prison, where I remained some time, deprived of every means to let any person without the prison know my deplorable state and condition, till my chum, a young woman, my bedfellow, who was also confined for debt, was, by a gentleman, discharged. This young woman of her own free will, went, my lord, to your lodgings in the Minories, and acquainted your landlady, the Quaker, where I was, and for what sum I was confined, who immediately sent and paid the pretended debt, and so I was a second time discharged. Upon which, going to the Quaker's to return her my thanks soon after a letter from your lady to her, with a direction in it where to find you, falling into my hands, I set out the next morning for the Hague; and I humbly hope your pardon, my lord, for the liberty I have taken; and you may be assured, that whatever circumstances of life I happen to be in, I will be no disgrace to your lordship or family."

"Well," said my husband, "what can you say of your mother's second child, who, I hear, was a son?"

"My lord," said I, "it is in my power to tell you, that Thomas there is the son you mention; their circumstances are the same, with this difference, that she was brought up under the care of a good aunt, and the boy forced to run away from a bad one, and shift for his bread ever since; so if she is my daughter, he is my son, and to oblige you, my lord, I own her, and to please myself I will own him, and they two are brother and sister." I had no sooner done speaking, than Thomas fell down before me, and asked my blessing, after which, he addressed himself to my lord as follows:

"My lord," said he, "out of your abundant goodness you took me into your service at Dover. I told you then the circumstances I was in, which will save your lordship much time by preventing a repetition; but, if your lordship pleases, it shall be carefully penned down, for such a variety of incidents has happened to me in England, Wales, Scotland, Ireland, Holland, France, and the Isle of Man, in which I have travelled for about eighteen years past, as may prove an agreeable amusement to you, when you are cloyed with better company; for as I have never been anything above a common servant, so my stories shall only consist of facts, and such as are seldom to be met with, as they are all in low life."

"Well, Thomas," said my lord, "take your own time to do it, and I will reward you for your trouble."

"Now, madam," said my lord to my daughter, "if you please to proceed." "My lord," continued she, "my mother's third child, which was a daughter, lived with the relation I did, and got a place to wait upon a young lady whose father and mother were going to settle at Boulogne, in France; she went with them, and having stayed at this gentleman's (who was a French merchant) two years, was married to a man with the consent of the family she lived in; and her master, by way of fortune, got him to be master of a French and Holland coaster, and this was the very person whose ship you hired to come to Holland in; the captain's wife was my own sister, consequently my lady's second daughter; as to my youngest sister, she lived with the uncle and aunt Thomas ran away from, and died of the smallpox soon after. My youngest brother was put out apprentice to a carpenter, where he improved in his business, till a gentlewoman came to his master and mistress (which I take by the description they gave me, to be Mrs. Amy), who had him put out to an education fit for a merchant, and then sent him to the Indies, where he is now settled, and in a fair way to get a large estate. This, my lord, is the whole account I can at present give of them, and although it may seem very strange, I assure you, it is all the just truth."

When she had finished her discourse, my lord turned to me, and said, that since I that was her mother had neglected doing my duty, though sought so much after, he would take it upon himself to see both the girl and Thomas provided for, without any advising or letting me know anything about them; and added, with a malicious sneer, "I must take care of the child I have had by you too, or it will have but an indifferent parent to trust to in case of my decease."

This finished the discourse, and my lord withdrew into his study, in a humour that I am unable to describe, and left me, Amy, Thomas, and my daughter Susanna, as I must now call her, in the parlour together. We sat staring at each other some time, till at last Amy said, "I suppose, my lady, you have no farther business with your new daughter; she has told her story, and may now dispose of herself to the best advantage she can." "No," said I, "I have nothing to say to her, only that she shall never be admitted into my presence again." The poor girl burst out into tears, and said, "Pray, my lady, excuse me, for I am certain that were you in my circumstances, you would have done the very action I have, and would expect a pardon for committing the offence."

After this, I said to Thomas, "Keep what has been said to yourself, and I shall speak to you by-and-by;" and then I withdrew, and went upstairs to my closet, leaving Amy with Susanna, who soon dismissed her, and followed me.

When Amy came to me, "Now, my lady," says she, "what do you think of this morning's work? I believe my lord is not so angry as we were fearful of." "You are mistaken in your lord, Amy," said I, "and are not so well acquainted with the deep and premeditated revenge of Dutchmen as I am, and although it may not be my husband's temper, yet I dread it as much, but shall see more at dinner time."

Soon after this, my husband called Thomas, and bid him order the cloth for his dinner to be laid in his study, and bid him tell his mother that he would dine by himself. When I heard this, I was more shocked than I had been yet. "Now his anger begins to work, Amy," said I, "how must I act?" "I do not know," answered she, "but I will go into the study, and try what can be done, and, as a faithful mediator, will try to bring you together." She was not long before she returned, and bursting into tears, "I know not what to do," says she, "for your husband is in a deep study, and when I told him you desired him to dine with you in the parlour as usual, he only said, 'Mrs. Amy, go to your lady, tell her to dine when and where she pleases, and pray obey her as your lady; but let her know from me that she has lost the tenderness I had for her as a wife, by the little thought she had of her children.'"

Nothing could have shocked me more than the delivery of this message by Amy. I, almost bathed in tears, went to him myself; found him in a melancholy posture reading in Milton's "Paradise Regained." He looked at me very sternly when I entered his study, told me he had nothing to say to me at that time, and if I had a mind not to disturb him, I must leave him for the present. "My lord," said I, "supposing all that has been said by this girl was truth, what reason have you to be in this unforgiving humour? What have I done to you to deserve this usage? Have you found any fault with me since I had the happiness of being married to you? Did you ever find me in any company that you did not approve of? Have you any reason to think that I have wasted any of your substance? If you have none of these things to allege against me, for heaven's sake do not let us now make our lives unhappy, for my having had legitimate children by a lawful husband, at a time that you think it no crime to have had a natural son by me, which I had the most reason to repent of."

I spoke the latter part of these words with a small air of authority, that he might think me the less guilty; but, I believe, he only looked on what I had said as a piece of heroism; for he soon after delivered himself in the following speech: "Madam, do you not think that you have used me in a very deceitful manner? If you think that I have not had that usage, I will, in a few words, prove the contrary. When first I knew you, soon after the jeweller's death at Paris, you never mentioned, in all that intricate affair I was engaged in for you, so much as your having any children; that, as your circumstances then were, could have done you no harm, but, on the contrary, it would have moved the compassion of your bitter enemy the Jew, if he had any. Afterwards, when I first saw you in London, and began to treat with you about marriage, your children, which, to all prudent women, are the first things provided for, were so far neglected as not to be spoken of, though mine were mentioned to you; and as our fortunes were very considerable, yours might very well have been put into the opposite scale with them. Another great piece of your injustice was when I offered to settle your own fortune upon yourself, you would not consent to it; I do not look on that piece of condescension out of love to me, but a thorough hatred you had to your own flesh and blood; and lastly, your not owning your daughter, though she strongly hinted who she was to you when she was twice in your company, and even followed you from place to place while you were in England. Now, if you can reconcile this piece of inhumanity with yourself, pray try what you can say to me about your never telling me the life you led in Pall Mall, in the character of Roxana? You scrupled to be happily married to me, and soon after came to England, and was a reputed whore to any nobleman that would come up to your price, and lived with one a considerable time, and was taken by several people to be his lawful wife. If any gentleman should ask me what I have taken to my bed, what must I answer? I must say an inhuman false-hearted whore, one that had not tenderness enough to own her own children, and has too little virtue, in my mind, to make a good wife.

"I own I would," says he, "have settled your own estate upon you with great satisfaction, but I will not do it now; you may retire to your chamber, and when I have any occasion to speak with you, I will send a messenger to you; so, my undeserving lady countess, you may walk out of the room."

I was going to reply to all this, but instead of hearing me, he began to speak against the Quaker, who, he supposed, knew all the intrigues of my life; but I cleared her innocence, by solemnly declaring it was a thorough reformation of my past life that carried me to live at the Quaker's house, who knew nothing of me before I went to live with her, and that she was, I believed, a virtuous woman.

I went away prodigiously chagrined. I knew not what course to take; I found expostulation signified nothing, and all my hopes depended on what I might say to him after we were gone to bed at night. I sent in for Amy, and having told her our discourse, she said she knew not what to think of him, but hoped it would, by great submission, wear off by degrees. I could eat but little dinner, and Amy was more sorrowful than hungry, and after we had dined, we walked by ourselves in the garden, to know what we had best pursue. As we were walking about, Thomas came to us, and told us that the young woman who had caused all the words, had been at the door, and delivered a letter to my lord's footman, who had carried it upstairs, and that she was ordered to go to his lordship in his study, which struck me with a fresh and sensible grief. I told Thomas, as he was to be her brother, to learn what my lord had said to her, if he could, as she came down; on which he went into the house to obey his order.

He was not gone in above a quarter of an hour before he came to me again, and told me she was gone, and that my lord had given her a purse of twenty guineas, with orders to live retired, let nobody know who or what she was, and come to him again in about a month's time. I was very much satisfied to hear this, and was in hopes of its proving a happy omen; and I was better pleased about two hours after, when Thomas came to me to let me know that my lord had given him thirty guineas, and bid him take off his livery, and new clothe himself, for he intended to make him his first clerk, and put him in the way of making his fortune. I now thought it was impossible for me to be poor, and was inwardly rejoiced that my children (meaning Thomas and Susanna) were in the high road to grow rich.

As Amy and I had dined by ourselves, my lord kept his study all the day, and at night, after supper, Isabel came and told me that my lord's man had received orders to make his bed in the crimson room, which name it received from the colour of the bed and furniture, and was reserved against the coming of strangers, or sickness. When she had delivered her message she withdrew, and I told Amy it would be to no purpose to go to him again, but I would have her lie in a small bed, which I ordered immediately to be carried into my chamber. Before we went to bed, I went to his lordship to know why he would make us both look so little among our own servants, as to part, bed and board, so suddenly. He only said, "My Lady Roxana knows the airs of quality too well to be informed that a scandal among nobility does not consist in parting of beds; if you cannot lie by yourself, you may send a letter to my Lord ——, whom you lived with as a mistress in London; perhaps he may want a bedfellow as well as you, and come to you at once; you are too well acquainted with him to stand upon ceremony."

I left him, with my heart full of malice, grief, shame, and revenge. I did not want a good will to do any mischief; but I wanted an unlimited power to put all my wicked thoughts in execution.

Amy and I lay in our chamber, and the next morning at breakfast we were talking of what the servants (for there were thirteen of them in all, viz., two coachmen, four footmen, a groom, and postillion, two women cooks, two housemaids, and a laundry-maid, besides Isabel, who was my waiting-maid, and Amy, who acted as housekeeper) could say of the disturbance that was in the family. "Pho!" said Amy, "never trouble your head about that, for family quarrels are so common in noblemen's houses, both here and in England, that there are more families parted, both in bed and board, than live lovingly together. It can be no surprise to the servants, and if your neighbours should hear it, they will only think you are imitating the air of nobility, and have more of that blood in you than you appeared to have when you and your lord lived happily together."

The time, I own, went very sluggishly on. I had no company but Amy and Isabel, and it was given out among the servants of noblemen and gentry that I was very much indisposed, for I thought it a very improper time either to receive or pay visits.

In this manner I lived till the month was up that my daughter was to come again to my lord, for although I went morning, noon, and night, into his apartment to see him, I seldom had a quarter of an hour's discourse with him, and oftentimes one of his valets would be sent to tell me his lord was busy, a little before the time I usually went, which I found was to prevent my going in to him, but this was only when he was in an ill humour, as his man called it.
Whether my lord used to make himself uneasy for want of mine or other company, I cannot tell, but the servants complained every day, as I heard by Amy, that his lordship ate little or nothing, and would sometimes shed tears when he sat down by himself to breakfast,

dinner, or supper; and, indeed, I began to think that he looked very thin, his countenance grew pale, and that he had every other sign of a grieved or broken heart.

My daughter came to him one Monday morning, and stayed with him in his study near two hours. I wondered at the reason of it, but could guess at nothing certain; and at last she went away, but I fixed myself so as to see her as she passed by me, and she appeared to have a countenance full of satisfaction.

In the evening, when I went in as usual, he spoke to me in a freer style than he had done since our breach. "Well, madam" (for he had not used the words "my lady" at any time after my daughter's coming to our house), said he, "I think I have provided for your daughter." "As how, my lord, pray will you let me know?" said I. "Yes," replied he, "as I have reason to think you will be sorry to hear of her welfare in any shape, I will tell you. A gentleman who is going factor for the Dutch East India Company, on the coast of Malabar, I have recommended her to; and he, on my character and promise of a good fortune, will marry her very soon, for the Company's ships sail in about twelve days; so, in a fortnight, like a great many mothers as there are nowadays, you may rejoice at having got rid of one of your children, though you neither know where, how, or to whom."

Although I was very glad my lord spoke to me at all, and more especially so at my daughter's going to be married, and settling in the Indies, yet his words left so sharp a sting behind them as was exceeding troublesome to me to wear off. I did not dare venture to make any further inquiries, but was very glad of what I heard, and soon bidding my lord goodnight, went and found Amy, who was reading a play in the chamber.

I waited with the greatest impatience for this marriage; and when I found the day was fixed, I made bold to ask my lord if I should not be present in his chamber when the ceremony was performed. This favor was also denied me. I then asked my lord's chaplain to speak to him on that head, but he was deaf to his importunities, and bade him tell me that I very well knew his mind. The wedding was performed on a Wednesday evening, in my lord's presence, and he permitted nobody to be there but a sister of the bridegroom's, and Thomas (now my lord's secretary or chief clerk), who was brother to the bride, and who gave her away. They all supped together after the ceremony was over in the great dining-room, where the fortune was paid, which was £2000 (as I heard from Thomas afterwards), and the bonds for the performance of the marriage were redelivered.

Next morning my lord asked me if I was willing to see my daughter before she sailed to the Indies. "My lord," said I, "as the seeing of her was the occasion of this great breach that has happened between us, so if your lordship will let me have a sight of her and a reconciliation with you at the same time, there is nothing can be more desirable to me, or would more contribute to my happiness during the rest of my life."

"No, madam," says he, "I would have you see your daughter, to be reconciled to her, and give her your blessing (if a blessing can proceed from you) at parting; but our reconciliation will never be completed till one of us comes near the verge of life, if then; for I am a man that am never reconciled without ample amends, which is a thing that is not in your power to give, without you can alter the course of nature and recall time."

On hearing him declare himself so open, I told him that my curse instead of my blessing would pursue my daughter for being the author of all the mischiefs that had happened between us. "No, madam," said he, "if you had looked upon her as a daughter heretofore, I should have had no occasion to have had any breach with you. The whole fault lies at your own door; for whatever your griefs may inwardly be, I would have you recollect they were of your own choosing."

I found I was going to give way to a very violent passion, which would perhaps be the worse for me, so I left the room and went up to my own chamber, not without venting bitter reproaches both against my daughter and her unknown husband.

However, the day she was to go on shipboard, she breakfasted with my lord, and as soon as it was over, and my lord was gone into his study to fetch something out, I followed him there, and asked him if he would give me leave to present a gold repeating watch to my daughter before she went away. I thought he seemed somewhat pleased with this piece of condescension in me, though it was done more to gain his goodwill than to express any value I had for her. He told me that he did not know who I could better make such a present to, and I might give it to her if I pleased. Accordingly I went and got it out of my cabinet in a moment, and bringing it to my lord, desired he would give it her from me. He asked me if I would not give it her myself. I told him no; I wished her very well, but had nothing to say to her till I was restored to his lordship's bed and board.

About two hours after all this, the coach was ordered to the door, and my daughter and her new husband, the husband's sister, and my son Thomas, all went into it, in order to go to the house of a rich uncle of the bridegroom's, where they were to dine before they went on board, and my lord went there in a sedan about an hour after. And having eaten their dinner, which on this occasion was the most elegant, they all went on board the Indiaman, where my lord and my son Thomas stayed till the ship's crew was hauling in their anchors to sail, and then came home together in the coach, and it being late in the evening, he told Thomas he should sup with him that night, after which they went to bed in their several apartments.

Next morning when I went to see my lord as usual, he told me that as he had handsomely provided for my daughter, and sent her to the Indies with a man of merit and fortune, he sincerely wished her great prosperity. "And," he added, "to let you see, madam, that I should never have parted from my first engagements of love to you, had you not laid yourself so open to censure for your misconduct, my next care shall be to provide for your son Thomas in a handsome manner, before I concern myself with my son by you."

This was the subject of our discourse, with which I was very well pleased. I only wished my daughter had been married and sent to the Indies before I had married myself; but I began to hope that the worst would be over when Thomas was provided for too, and the son my lord had by me, who was now at the university, was at home; which I would have brought to pass could my will be obeyed, but I was not to enjoy that happiness.

My lord and I lived with a secret discontent of each other for near a twelvemonth before I saw any provision made for my son Thomas, and then I found my lord bought him a very large plantation in Virginia, and was furnishing him to go there in a handsome manner; he also gave him four quarter parts in four large trading West India vessels, in which he boarded a great quantity of merchandise to traffic with when he came to the end of his journey, so that he was a very rich man before he (what we call) came into the world.

The last article that was to be managed, was to engage my son to a wife before he left Holland; and it happened that the gentleman who was the seller of the plantation my husband bought, had been a Virginia planter in that colony a great many years; but his life growing on the decline, and his health very dubious, he had come to Holland with an intent to sell his plantation, and then had resolved to send for his wife, son, and daughter, to come to him with the return of the next ships. This gentleman had brought over with him the pictures of all his family, which he was showing to my lord at the same time he was paying for the effects; and on seeing the daughter's picture, which appeared to him very beautiful, my lord inquired if she was married. "No, my lord," says the planter, "but I believe I shall dispose of her soon after she comes to me." "How old is your daughter?" said my lord. "Why, my lord," replied the planter, "she is twenty-two years of age." Then my lord asked my son if he should like that young lady for a wife. "Nothing, my lord," said Thomas, "could lay a greater obligation upon me than your lordship's providing me with a wife."

"Now, sir," said my lord to the planter, "what do you say to a match between this young gentleman and your daughter? Their ages are agreeable, and if you can, or will, give her more fortune than he has, his shall be augmented. You partly know his substance, by the money I have now paid you."

This generous proposal of my lord's pleased the planter to a great degree, and he declared to my lord that he thought nothing could be a greater favour done him, for two reasons; one of which was, that he was certain the young gentleman was as good as he appeared, because he had taken for his plantation so large a sum of money as none but a gentleman could pay. The next reason was, that this marriage, to be performed as soon as my son arrived there, would be a great satisfaction to his wife, whose favourite the daughter was. "For," added he, "my wife will not only have the pleasure of seeing her daughter settled on what was our own hereditary estate, but also see her married to a man of substance, without the danger of crossing the seas to be matched to a person equal to herself."

"Pray, sir," said my lord, "let me hear what fortune you are willing to give with your daughter; you have but two children, and I know you must be rich." "Why, my lord," replied the planter, "there is no denying that; but you must remember I have a son as well as a daughter to provide for, and he I intend to turn into the mercantile way as soon as he arrives safe from Virginia. I have, my lord," continued he, "a very large stock-in-trade there, as warehouses of tobacco, &c., lodged in the custom-houses of the ports, to the value of £7000, to which I will add £3000 in money, and I hope you will look upon that as a very competent estate; and when the young gentleman's fortune is joined to that, I believe he will be the richest man in the whole American colonies of his age."

It was then considered between my lord and Thomas, that no woman with a quarter of that fortune would venture herself over to the West Indies with a man that had ten times as much; so it being hinted to the planter that my lord had agreed to the proposals, they promised to meet the next morning to settle the affair.

In the evening, my lord, with Thomas in his company, hinted the above discourse to me. I was frightened almost out of my wits to think what a large sum of money had been laid out for my son, but kept what I thought to myself. It was agreed that my son was to marry the old planter's daughter, and a lawyer was sent for, with instructions to draw up all the writings for the marriage-settlement, &c., and the next morning a messenger came from the planter with a note to my lord, letting him know, if it was not inconvenient, he would wait on his lordship to breakfast. He came soon after with a Dutch merchant of great estate, who was our neighbour at The Hague, where they settled every point in question, and the articles were all drawn up and signed by the several parties the next day before dinner.

There was nothing now remaining but my son's departure to his new plantation in Virginia. Great despatch was made that he might be ready to sail in one of his own ships, and take the advantage of an English convoy, which was almost ready to sail. My lord sent several valuable presents to my son's lady, as did her father; and as I was at liberty in this case to do as I would, and knowing my lord had a very great value for my son, I thought that the richer my presents were, the more he would esteem me (but there was nothing in it, the enmity he took against me had taken root in his heart); so I sent her a curious set of china, the very best I could buy, with a silver tea-kettle and lamp, tea-pot, sugar-dish, cream-pot, teaspoons, &c., and as my lord had sent a golden repeater, I added to it a golden equipage, with my lord's picture hanging to it, finely painted; (This was another thing I did purposely to please him, but it would not do.) A few days after, he came to take his leave of me, by my lord's order, and at my parting with him I shed abundance of tears, to think I was then in an almost strange place, no child that could then come near me, and under so severe a displeasure of my lord, that I had very little hopes of ever being friends with him again.

My life did not mend after my son was gone; all I could do would not persuade my lord to have any free conversation with me. And at this juncture it was that the foolish jade Amy, who was now advanced in years, was catched in a conversation with one of my lord's men, which was not to her credit; for, it coming to his ears, she was turned out of the house by my lord's orders, and was never suffered to come into it again during his lifetime, and I did not dare to speak a word in her favour for fear he should retort upon me, "Like mistress, like maid."

I could hear nothing of Amy for the first three months after she had left me, till one day, as I was looking out of a dining-room window, I saw her pass by, but I did not dare ask her to come in, for fear my lord should hear of her being there, which would have been adding fuel to the fire; however, she, looking up at the house, saw me. I made a motion to her to stay a little about the door, and in the meantime I wrote a note, and dropped it out of the window, in which I told her how I had lived in her absence, and desired her to write me a letter, and carry it the next day to my sempstress's house, who would take care to deliver it to me herself.

I told Isabel that she should let me know when the milliner came again, for I had some complaints to her about getting up my best suit of Brussels lace nightclothes. On the Saturday following, just after I had dined, Isabel came into my apartment. "My lady," says she, "the milliner is in the parlour; will you be pleased to have her sent upstairs, or will your ladyship be pleased to go down to her?" "Why, send her up, Isabel," said I, "she is as able to come to me as I am to go to her; I will see her here."

When the milliner came into my chamber, I sent Isabel to my dressing-room to fetch a small parcel of fine linen which lay there, and in the interim she gave me Amy's letter, which I put into my pocket, and, having pretended to be angry about my linen, I gave her the small bundle Isabel brought, and bid her be sure to do them better for the future.

She promised me she would, and went about her business; and when she was gone, I opened Amy's letter, and having read it, found it was to the following purpose, viz., that she had opened a coffee-house, and furnished the upper part of it to let out in lodgings; that she kept two maids and a man, but that the trade of it did not answer as she had reason to expect; she was willing to leave it off, and retire into the country to settle for the rest of her life, but was continually harassed by such disturbance in her conscience as made her unfit to resolve upon anything, and wished there was a possibility for her to see me, that she might open her mind with the same freedom as formerly, and have my advice upon some particular affairs; and such-like discourse.

It was a pretty while before I heard from Amy again, and when I did, the letter was in much the same strain as the former, excepting that things were coming more to a crisis; for she told me in it that her money was so out, that is, lent as ready money to traders, and trusted for liquors in her house, that if she did not go away this quarter, she should be obliged to run away the next. I very much lamented her unfortunate case, but that could be no assistance to her, as I had it not now in my power to see her when I would, or give her what I pleased, as it had always used to be; so all I could do was to wish her well, and leave her to take care of herself.

About this time it was that I perceived my lord began to look very pale and meagre, and I had a notion he was going into a consumption, but did not dare tell him so, for fear he should say I was daily looking for his death, and was now overjoyed that I saw a shadow of it; nevertheless, he soon after began to find himself in a very bad state of health, for he said to me one morning, that my care would not last long, for he believed he was seized by a distemper it was impossible for him to get over. "My lord," said I, "you do not do me justice in imagining anything concerning me that does not tend to your own happiness, for if your body is out of order, my mind suffers for it." Indeed, had he died then, without making a will, it might have been well for me; but he was not so near death as that; and, what was worse, the distemper, which proved a consumption (which was occasioned chiefly by much study, watchings, melancholy thoughts, wilful and obstinate neglect of taking care of his body, and such like things), held him nine weeks and three days after this, before it carried him off.

He now took country lodgings, most delightfully situated both for air and prospect, and had a maid and man to attend him. I begged on my knees to go with him, but could not get that favour granted; for, if I could, it might have been the means of restoring me to his favour, but our breach was too wide to be thoroughly reconciled, though I used all the endearing ways I had ever had occasion for to creep into his favour.

Before he went out of town he locked and sealed up every room in the house, excepting my bedchamber, dressing-room, one parlour, and all the offices and rooms belonging to the servants; and, as he had now all my substance in his power, I was in a very poor state for a countess, and began to wish, with great sincerity, that I had never seen him, after I had lived so happy a life as I did at the Quaker's. For notwithstanding our estates joined together, when we were first married, amounted to £3376 per annum, and near £18,000 ready money, besides jewels, plate, goods, &c., of a considerable value, yet we had lived in a very high manner since our taking the title of earl and countess upon us; setting up a great house, and had a number of servants; our equipage, such as coach, chariot, horses, and their attendants; a handsome fortune my lord had given to my daughter, and a very noble one to my son, whom he loved very well, not for his being my son, but for the courteous behaviour of him in never aspiring to anything above a valet after he knew who he was, till my lord made him his secretary or clerk. Besides all these expenses, my lord, having flung himself into the trade to the Indies, both East and West, had sustained many great and uncommon losses, occasioned by his merchandise being mostly shipped in English bottoms; and that nation having declared war against the crown of Spain, he was one of the first and greatest sufferers by that power; so that, on the whole, our estate, which was as above, dwindled to about £1000 per annum, and our home stock, viz., about £17,000, was entirely gone. This, I believe, was another great mortification to his lordship, and one of the main things that did help to hasten his end; for he was observed, both by me and all his servants, to be more cast down at hearing of his losses, that were almost daily sent to him, than he was at what had happened between him and me.

Nothing could give more uneasiness than the damage our estate sustained by this traffic. He looked upon it as a mere misfortune that no person could avoid; but I, besides that, thought it was a judgment upon me, to punish me in the loss of all my ill-got gain. But when I found that his own fortune began to dwindle as well as mine, I was almost ready to think it was possible his lordship might have been as wicked a liver as I had, and the same vengeance as had been poured upon me for my repeated crimes might also be a punishment for him.

As his lordship was in a bad state of health, and had removed to a country lodging, his study and counting-house, as well as his other rooms, were locked and sealed up; all business was laid aside, excepting such letters as came to him were carried to his lordship to be opened, read, and answered. I also went to see him morning and evening, but he would not suffer me to stay with him a single night. I might have had another room in the same house, but was not willing the people who kept it should know that there was a misunderstanding between us; so I contented myself to be a constant visitor, but could not persuade him to

244

forgive me the denying of my daughter, and acting the part of Roxana, because I had kept those two things an inviolable secret from him and everybody else but Amy, and it was carelessness in her conduct at last that was the foundation of all my future misery.

As my lord's weakness increased, so his ill temper, rather than diminish, increased also. I could do nothing to please him, and began to think that he was only pettish because he found it was his turn to go out of the world first. A gentleman that lived near him, as well as his chaplain, persuaded him to have a physician, to know in what state his health was; and by all I could learn, the doctor told him to settle his worldly affairs as soon as he conveniently could. "For," says he, "although your death is not certain, still your life is very precarious."

The first thing he did after this was to send for the son he had by me from the university. He came the week afterwards, and the tutor with him, to take care of his pupil. The next day after my lord came home, and sending for six eminent men that lived at The Hague he made his will, and signed it in the presence of them all; and they, with the chaplain, were appointed the executors of it, and guardians of my son.

As I was in a great concern at his making his will unknown to me, and before we were friends, I thought of it in too serious a manner not to speak about it. I did not know where to apply first, but after mature consideration sent for the chaplain, and he coming to me, I desired he would give me the best intelligence he could about it. "My lady," said he, "you cannot be so unacquainted with the duty of my function, and the trust my lord has reposed in me, but you must know I shall go beyond my trust in relating anything of that nature to you; all that I can say on that head is, that I would have you make friends with my lord as soon as you possibly can, and get him to make another will, or else take the best care of yourself as lies in your power; for, I assure you, if his lordship dies, you are but poorly provided for."

These last words of the chaplain's most terribly alarmed me. I knew not what to do; and, at last, as if I was to be guided by nothing but the furies, I went to his chamber, and after inquiring how he did, and hearing that he was far from well, I told him I had heard he had made his will. "Yes," said he, "I have; and what then?" "Why, my lord," replied I, "I thought it would not have been derogatory to both our honours for you to have mentioned it to me before you did it, and have let me known in what manner you intended to settle your estate. This would have been but acting like a man to his wife, even if you had married me without a fortune; but as you received so handsomely with me, you ought to have considered it as my substance, as well as your own, that you were going to dispose of."

My lord looked somewhat staggered at what I had said, and pausing a little while, answered, that he thought, and also looked upon it as a granted opinion, that after a man married a woman, all that she was in possession of was his, excepting he had made a prior writing or settlement to her of any part or all she was then possessed of. "Besides, my lady," added he, "I have married both your children, and given them very noble fortunes, especially your son. I have also had great losses in trade, both by sea and land, since you delivered your fortune to me, and even at this time, notwithstanding the appearance we make in the world,

I am not worth a third of what I was when we came to settle in Holland; and then, here is our own son shall be provided for in a handsome manner by me; for I am thoroughly convinced there will be but little care taken of him if I leave anything in your power for that purpose: witness Thomas and Susanna."

"My lord," said I, "I am not come into your chamber to know what care you have taken of our child. I do not doubt but you have acted like a father by it. What I would be informed in is, what I am to depend upon in case of your decease; which I, however, hope may be a great many years off yet." "You need not concern yourself about that," said he; "your son will take care that you shall not want; but yet, I will tell you, too," said he, "that it may prevent your wishing for my death. I have, in my will, left all I am possessed of in the world to my son, excepting £1500; out of that there is £500 for you, £500 among my executors, and the other £500 is to bury me, pay my funeral expenses, and what is overplus I have ordered to be equally divided among my servants."

When I had heard him pronounce these words, I stared like one that was frightened out of his senses. "Five hundred pounds for me!" says I; "pray, what do you mean? What! am I, that brought you so handsome a fortune, to be under the curb of my son, and ask him for every penny I want? No, sir," said I, "I will not accept it. I expect to be left in full possession of one—half of your fortune, that I may live the remainder of my life like your wife." "Madam," replied my lord, "you may expect what you please. If you can make it appear since I found you out to be a jilt that I have looked upon you as my wife, everything shall be altered and settled just as you desire, which might then be called your will; but as the case now stands, the will is mine, and so it shall remain."

I thought I should have sunk when I had heard him make this solemn and premeditated declaration. I raved like a mad woman, and, at the end of my discourse, told him that I did not value what could happen to me, even if I was forced to beg my bread, for I would stand the test of my own character; and as I could get nothing by being an honest woman, so I should not scruple to declare that "the son you have left what you have to is a bastard you had by me several years before we were married."

"Oh," says he, "madam, do you think you can frighten me? no, not in the least; for if you ever mention anything of it, the title, as well as all the estate, will go to another branch of my family, and you will then be left to starve in good earnest, without having the least glimpse of hope to better your fortune; for," added he, "it is not very probable that you will be courted for a wife by any man of substance at these years; so if you have a mind to make yourself easy in your present circumstances, you must rest contented with what I have left you, and not prove yourself a whore to ruin your child, in whose power it will be to provide for you in a handsome manner, provided you behave yourself with that respect to him and me as you ought to do; for if any words arise about what I have done, I shall make a fresh will, and, as the laws of this nation will give me liberty, cut you off with a shilling."

My own unhappiness, and his strong and lasting resentment, had kept me at high words, and flowing in tears, for some time; and as I was unwilling anybody should see me in that unhappy condition, I stayed coolly talking to him, till our son, who had been to several gentlemen's houses about my lord's business, came home to tell his father the success he had met with abroad. He brought in with him bank-notes to the amount of £12,000, which he had received of some merchants he held a correspondence with; at which my lord was well pleased, for he was pretty near out of money at this juncture. After our son had delivered the accounts and bills, and had withdrawn, I asked my lord, in a calm tone, to give me the satisfaction of knowing in what manner the losses he had complained to have suffered consisted. "You must consider, my lord," said I, "that according to what you have been pleased to inform me of, we are upwards of £2000 per annum, besides about £17,000 ready money, poorer than we were when we first came to settle in Holland."

"You talk," replied my lord, "in a very odd manner. Do not you know that I had children of my own by a former wife? and of these I have taken so much care as to provide with very handsome fortunes, which are settled irrevocably upon them. I have, Providence be thanked, given each of them £5000, and that is laid in East India stock, sufficient to keep them genteelly, above the frowns of fortune, and free from the fear of want. This, joined to the money I mentioned to you before, as losses at sea, deaths, and bankruptcies, your children's fortunes, which are larger than my own children's, the buying the estate we live on, and several other things, which my receipts and notes will account for, as you may see after my decease. I have, to oblige you on this head, almost descended to particulars, which I never thought to have done; but as I have, rest yourself contented, and be well assured that I have not wilfully thrown any of your substance away."

I could not tell what he meant by saying he had not wilfully thrown any of my substance away. These words puzzled me, for I found by his discourse I was to have but £500 of all I had brought him, at his decease, which I looked upon to be near at hand. I had but one thing that was any satisfaction to me, which was this: I was assured by him that he had not bestowed above the £15,000 he mentioned to me, on his children by his former wife; and, on an exact calculation, he made it appear that he had bestowed on my son Thomas alone near £13,000 in buying the plantation, shares in vessels, and merchandise, besides several valuable presents sent to his wife, both by him and me; and as for my daughter Susanna, she was very well married to a factor, with a fortune of £2000 (which was a great sum of money for a woman to have who was immediately to go to the East Indies), besides some handsome presents given to her both by him and me. In fact, her fortune was, in proportion, as large as her brother's, for there is but very few women in England or Holland with £2000 fortune that would venture to the coast of Malabar, even to have married an Indian king, much more to have gone over with a person that no one could tell what reception he might meet with, or might be recalled at the pleasure of the Company upon the least distaste taken by the merchants against him. Neither would I, though her own mother, hinder her voyage, for she had been the author of all the misfortunes that happened to me; and if my speaking a word would have saved her from the greatest torment, I believe I should have been quite silent. And I had but one reason to allege for the girl's going so hazardous a voyage, which is, she knew that the match was proposed by my lord, and if he had not thought it would have been advantageous for her, he would never have given £2000 to her husband as a fortune; and again, as my lord was the only friend she had in our family, she was cunning enough to know that the bare disobliging of him would have been her ruin for ever after; to which I may add, that it is possible, as she had made so much mischief about me, she was glad to get what she could and go out of the way, for fear my lord and I should be friends; which, if that had happened, she would have been told never to come to our house any more.

As my lord's death began to be daily the discourse of the family, I thought that he might be more reconciled if I entered into the arguments again, pro and con, which we had together before. I did so, but all I could say was no satisfaction, till I importuned him on my knees, with a flood of tears. "Madam," said he, "what would you have me do?" "Do, my lord," said I, "only be so tender to my years and circumstances as to alter your will, or, at least, add a codicil to it; I desire nothing more, for I declare I had rather be a beggar, than live under my child's jurisdiction." To this he agreed with some reluctance, and he added a codicil to his will.

This pleased me greatly, and gave me comfort, for I dreaded nothing so much, after all my high living, as being under any person, relation or stranger, and whether they exercised any power over me or not.

I saw the lawyer come out of the chamber first, but was above asking him any questions; the next were the executors and chaplain. I asked the last how they came to have words. He did not answer me directly, but begged to know whose pleasure it was to have the codicil annexed. "It was mine, sir," replied I; "and it made me very uneasy before I could have the favour granted." He only replied by saying, "Ah! poor lady, the favour, as you are pleased to term it, is not calculated for any benefit to you; think the worst you can of it."

I was terribly uneasy at what the chaplain had said, but I imagined to myself that I could not be worse off than I thought I should be before the codicil was annexed; and as he withdrew without saying any more, I was fain to rest satisfied with what I had heard, and that amounted to nothing.

The next day after this the physicians that attended my lord told him it was time for him to settle his worldly affairs, and prepare himself for a hereafter. I now found all was over, and I had no other hopes of his life than the physicians' declaration of his being near his death. For it often happens that the gentlemen of the faculty give out that a man is near his death, to make the cure appear to be the effect of their great skill in distempers and medicine; as others, when they cannot find out the real disease, give out that a man's end is near, rather than discover their want of judgment; and this I thought might be the case with our doctors of physic.

Our son was still kept from the university, and lodged at the house of one of his future guardians; but when he heard that his father was so near his end, he was very little out of his presence, for he dearly loved him. My lord sent the day before his death to lock and seal up all the doors in his dwelling house at The Hague; and the steward had orders, in case of my lord's decease, not to let anybody come in, not even his lady (who had for some time lodged in the same house with her lord), without an order from the executors.

The keys of the doors were carried to him, and as he saw his death approach, he prepared for it, and, in fact, resigned up the keys of everything to the executors, and having bid them all a farewell, they were dismissed. The physicians waited; but as the verge of life approached, and it was out of their power to do him any service, he gave them a bill of £100 for the care they had taken of him, and dismissed them.

I now went into the chamber, and kneeling by his bedside, kissed him with great earnestness, and begged of him, if ever I had disobliged him in any respect, to forgive me. He sighed, and said he most freely forgave me everything that I had reason to think I had offended him in; but he added, "If you had been so open in your conversation to me before our marriage as to discover your family and way of life, I know not but that I should have married you as I did. I might now have been in a good state of health, and you many years have lived with all the honours due to the Countess de Wintselsheim." These words drew tears from my eyes, and they being the last of any consequence he said, they had the greater impression upon me. He faintly bid me a long farewell, and said, as he had but a few moments to live, he hoped I would retire, and leave him with our son and chaplain. I withdrew into my own chamber, almost drowned in tears, and my son soon followed me out, leaving the chaplain with his father, offering up his prayers to Heaven for the receiving of his soul into the blessed mansions of eternal bliss.

A few minutes after our son went into the chamber with me again, and received his father's last blessing. The chaplain now saw him departing, and was reading the prayer ordered by the Church for that occasion; and while he was doing it, my lord laid his head gently on the pillow, and turning on his left side, departed this life with all the calmness of a composed mind, without so much as a groan, in the fifty-seventh year of his age.

As soon as he was dead an undertaker was sent for, by order of the executors, who met together immediately to open his will, and take care of all my son's effects. I was present when it was opened and read; but how terribly I was frightened at hearing the codicil repeated any person may imagine by the substance of it, which was to this effect; that if I had given me any more after his decease than the £500 he had left me, the £500 left to his executors, and the £1000 of my son's estate (which was now a year's interest), was to be given to such poor families at The Hague as were judged to be in the greatest want of it; not to be divided into equal sums, but every family to have according to their merit and necessity. But this was not all. My son was tied down much harder; for if it was known that he gave me any relief, let my condition be ever so bad, either by himself, by his order, or in any manner of way, device, or contrivance that he could think of, one-half of his estate, which was particularly mentioned, was to devolve to the executors for ever; and if they granted me ever so small a favour, that sum was to be equally divided among the several parishes where they lived, for the benefit of the poor.

Any person would have been surprised to have seen how we all sat staring at each other; for though it was signed by all the executors, yet they did not know the substance of it till it was publicly read, excepting the chaplain; and he, as I mentioned before, had told me the codicil had better never have been added.

I was now in a fine dilemma; had the title of a countess, with £500, and nothing else to subsist on but a very good wardrobe of clothes, which were not looked upon by my son and the executors to be my late lord's property, and which were worth, indeed, more than treble the sum I had left me.

I immediately removed from the lodgings, and left them to bury the body when they thought proper, and retired to a lodging at a private gentleman's house, about a mile from The Hague. I was now resolved to find out Amy, being, as it were, at liberty; and accordingly went to the house where she had lived, and finding that empty, inquired for her among the neighbours, who gave various accounts of what had become of her; but one of them had a direction left at his house where she might be found. I went to the place and found the house shut up, and all the windows broken, the sign taken down, and the rails and benches pulled from before the door. I was quite ashamed to ask for her there, for it was a very scandalous neighbourhood, and I concluded that Amy had been brought to low circumstances, and had kept a house of ill-fame, and was either run away herself, or was forced to it by the officers of justice. However, as nobody knew me here, I went into a shop to buy some trifles, and asked who had lived in the opposite house (meaning Amy's). "Really, madam," says the woman, "I do not well know; but it was a woman who kept girls for gentlemen; she went on in that wickedness for some time, till a gentleman was robbed there of his watch and a diamond ring, on which the women were all taken up, and committed to the house of correction; but the young ones are now at liberty, and keep about the town." "Pray," said I, "what may have become of the old beast that could be the ruin of those young creatures?" "Why, I do not well know," says she; "but I have heard that, as all her goods were seized upon, she was sent to the poorhouse; but it soon after appearing that she had the French disease to a violent degree, was removed to a hospital to be taken care of, but I believe she will never live to come out; and if she should be so fortunate, the gentleman that was robbed, finding that she was the guilty person, intends to prosecute her to the utmost rigour of the law."

I was sadly surprised to hear this character of Amy; for I thought whatever house she might keep, that the heyday of her blood had been over. But I found that she had not been willing to be taken for an old woman, though near sixty years of age; and my not seeing or hearing from her for some time past was a confirmation of what had been told me.

I went home sadly dejected, considering how I might hear of her. I had known her for a faithful servant to me, in all my bad and good fortune, and was sorry that at the last such a miserable end should overtake her, though she, as well as I, deserved it several years before.

A few days after I went pretty near the place I had heard she was, and hired a poor woman to go and inquire how Amy —— did, and whether she was likely to do well. The woman returned, and told me that the matron, or mistress, said, the person I inquired after died in a salivation two days before, and was buried the last night in the cemetery belonging to the hospital.

I was very sorry to hear of Amy's unhappy and miserable death; for when she came first into my service she was really a sober girl, very witty and brisk, but never impudent, and her notions in general were good, till my forcing her, as it were, to have an intrigue with the jeweller. She had also lived with me between thirty and forty years, in the several stages of life as I had passed through; and as I had done nothing but what she was privy to, so she was the best person in the universal world to consult with and take advice from, as my circumstances now were.

I returned to my lodgings much chagrined, and very disconsolate; for as I had for several years lived at the pinnacle of splendour and satisfaction, it was a prodigious heart-break to me now to fall from upwards of £3000 per annum to a poor £500 principal.

A few days after this I went to see my son, the Earl of Wintselsheim. He received me in a very courteous (though far from a dutiful) manner. We talked together near an hour upon general things, but had no particular discourse about my late lord's effects, as I wanted to have. Among other things he told me that his guardians had advised him to go to the university for four years longer, when he would come of age, and his estate would be somewhat repaired; to which he said he had agreed; and for that purpose all the household goods and equipages were to be disposed of the next week, and the servants dismissed. I immediately asked if it would be looked upon as an encroachment upon his father's will if I took Isabel (who had been my waiting-maid ever since I came from England) to live with me. "No, my lady," very readily replied he; "as she will be dismissed from me, she is certainly at liberty and full freedom to do for herself as soon and in the best manner she possibly can." After this I stayed about a quarter of an hour with him, and then I sent for Isabel, to know if she would come and live with me on her dismission from her lord's. The girl readily consented, for I had always been a good mistress to her; and then I went to my own lodgings in my son's coach, which he had ordered to be got ready to carry me home.

Isabel came, according to appointment, about ten days after, and told me the house was quite cleared both of men and movables, but said her lord (meaning my son) was not gone to the university as yet, but was at one of his guardians' houses, where he would stay about a month, and that he intended to make a visit before his departure, which he did, attended by my late chaplain; and I, being in handsome lodgings, received them with all the complaisance and love as was possible, telling them that time and circumstances having greatly varied with me, whatever they saw amiss I hoped they would be so good as to look over it at that time, by considering the unhappy situation of my affairs.

After this visit was over, and I had myself and Isabel to provide for, handsome lodgings to keep (which were as expensive as they were fine), and nothing but my principal money to live on (I mean what I happened to have in my pocket at my lord's death, for I had not been paid my £500 as yet), I could not manage for a genteel maintenance as I had done some years before. I thought of divers things to lay my small sums out to advantage, but could fix on nothing; for it always happens that when people have but a trifle, they are very dubious in the disposal of it.

Having been long resolving in my mind, I at last fixed on merchandise as the most genteel and profitable of anything else. Accordingly I went to a merchant who was intimate with my late lord, and letting him know how my circumstances were, he heartily condoled with me, and told me he could help me to a share in two ships—one was going a trading voyage to the coast of Africa, and the other a-privateering. I was now in a dilemma, and was willing to have a share in the trader, but was dubious of being concerned in the privateer; for I had heard strange stories told of the gentlemen concerned in that way of business. Nay, I had been told, but with what certainty I cannot aver, that there was a set of men who took upon them to issue ships, and as they always knew to what port they are bound, notice was sent to their correspondent abroad to order out their privateers on the coast the other sailed, and they knowing the loading, and the numbers of hands and guns were on board, soon made prizes of the vessels, and the profits were equally divided, after paying what was paid for their insurance, among them all.

However, I at last resolved, by the merchant's advice, to have a share in the trader, and the next day he over-persuaded me to have a share in the privateer also. But that I may not lay out my money before I have it, it may not be amiss to observe that I went to the executors and received my £500 at an hour's notice, and then went to the merchant's to know what the shares would come to, and being told £1500, I was resolved to raise the money; so I went home, and, with my maid Isabel, in two days' time disposed of as many of my clothes as fetched me near £1100, which, joined to the above sum, I carried to the merchant's, where the writings were drawn, signed, sealed, and delivered to me in the presence of two witnesses, who went with me for that purpose. The ships were near ready for sailing; the trader was so well manned and armed, as well as the privateer, that the partners would not consent to insure them, and out they both sailed, though from different ports, and I depended on getting a good estate between them.

When I was about this last ship a letter came from the count, my son, full of tender expressions of his duty to me, in which I was informed that he was going again to the university at Paris, where he should remain four years; after that he intended to make the tour of Europe, and then come and settle at The Hague. I returned him thanks in a letter for his compliment, wished him all happiness, and a safe return to Holland, and desired that he would write to me from time to time that I might hear of his welfare, which was all I could now expect of him. But this was the last time I heard from him, or he from me.

In about a month's time the news came that the privateer (which sailed under British colours, and was divided into eight shares) had taken a ship, and was bringing it into the Texel, but that it accidentally foundered, and being chained to the privateer, had, in sinking, like to have lost that too. Two or three of the hands got on shore, and came to The Hague; but how terribly I was alarmed any one may judge, when I heard the ship the privateer had was the Newfoundland merchantman, as I had bought two shares in out of four. About two months after news was current about The Hague of a privateer or merchantman, one of them of the town, though not known which, having an engagement in the Mediterranean, in which action both the privateer and trader was lost. Soon after their names were publicly known, and, in the end, my partners heard that they were our ships, and unhappily sailing under false colours (a thing often practised in the time of war), and never having seen each other, had, at meeting, a very smart engagement, each fighting for life and honour, till two unfortunate shots; one of them, viz., the privateer, was sunk by a shot between wind and water, and the trader unhappily blown up by a ball falling in the powder-room. There were only two hands of the trader, and three of the privateer, that escaped, and they all fortunately met at one of the partners' houses, where they confirmed the truth of this melancholy story, and to me a fatal loss.

What was to be done now? I had no money, and but few clothes left; there, was no hope of subsistence from my son or his guardians; they were tied down to be spectators of my misfortunes, without affording me any redress, even if they would.

Isabel, though I was now reduced to the last penny, would live with me still, and, as I observed before and may now repeat, I was in a pretty situation to begin the world—upwards of sixty years of age, friendless, scanty of clothes, and but very little money.

I proposed to Isabel to remove from lodgings and retire to Amsterdam, where I was not known, and might turn myself into some little way of business, and work for that bread now which had been too often squandered away upon very trifles. And upon consideration I found myself in a worse condition than I thought, for I had nothing to recommend me to Heaven, either in works or thoughts; had even banished from my mind all the cardinal and moral virtues, and had much more reason to hide myself from the sight of God, if possible, than I had to leave The Hague, that I might not be known of my fellow-creatures. And farther to hasten our removing to Amsterdam, I recollected I was involved in debt for money to purchase a share in the Newfoundland trader, which was lost, and my creditors daily threatened me with an arrest to make me pay them.

I soon discharged my lodgings and went with Isabel to Amsterdam, where I thought, as I was advanced in years, to give up all I could raise in the world, and on the sale of everything I had to go into one of the Proveniers' houses, where I should be settled for life. But as I could not produce enough money for it, I turned it into a coffee-house near the Stadt-house, where I might have done well; but as soon as I was settled one of my Hague creditors arrested me for a debt of £75, and I not having a friend in the world of whom to raise the money, was, in a shameful condition, carried to the common jail, where poor Isabel followed me with showers of tears, and left me inconsolable for my great misfortunes. Here, without some very unforeseen accident, I shall never go out of it until I am carried to my grave, for which my much-offended God prepare me as soon as possible.

The continuation of the Life of Roxana, by Isabel Johnson, who had been her waiting-maid, from the time she was thrown into jail to the time of her death.

After my lady, as it was my duty to call her, was thrown into jail for a debt she was unable to pay, she gave her mind wholly up to devotion. Whether it was from a thorough sense of her wretched state, or any other reason, I could never learn; but this I may say, that she was a sincere penitent, and in every action had all the behaviour of a Christian. By degrees all the things she had in the world were sold, and she began to find an inward decay upon her spirits. In this interval she repeated all the passages of her ill-spent life to me, and thoroughly repented of every bad action, especially the little value she had for her children, which were honestly born and bred. And having, as she believed, made her peace with God, she died with mere grief on the 2nd of July 1742, in the sixty-fifth year of her age, and was decently buried by me in the churchyard belonging to the Lutherans, in the city of Amsterdam.

THE END.

ACCLAIM FOR *SOUL'S GATE*

"Truly a story about freedom from things that we hold onto, this tale will captivate readers and encourage a more active, dynamic spiritual life."

—*RT Book Reviews*, TOP PICK

"[A] spiritual-warfare thriller that brilliantly takes four perfectly normal people . . . on a journey that begins with skepticism and ends up in places they could never have imagined or predicted."

—*CBA Retailers + Resources*

"Readers with high blood pressure or heart conditions be warned: this is a seriously heart-thumping and satisfying read that goes to the edge, jumps off, and 'builds wings on the way down.'"

—*Publishers Weekly*

"Powerful storytelling. Rubart writes with a depth of understanding about a realm most of us never investigate, let alone delve into. A deep and mystical journey that will leave you thinking long after you finish the book."

—Ted Dekker, *New York Times* best-selling author of *The Circle Series* and *Forbidden* (with Tosca Lee)

"Tight, boiled-down writing and an intriguing premise that will make you reconsider what you think you know about the spiritual realm."

—Steven James, national best-selling author of *Placebo* and *Opening Moves*

"*Soul's Gate* takes readers on a wild flight of fantasy into the spiritual realm, where we find the battle for our souls is even wilder than we imagined—and very, very real. With vividly drawn characters, startling imagery, and the power of a spiritual air-raid siren, the story is at once entertaining and breathtakingly enlightening. James L. Rubart has crafted a stunning piece of work, a call to arms for everyone who yearns for the freedom of the abundant life Christ promises us—and is willing to fight for it. Rubart knocks it out of the park with this one."

—ROBERT LIPARULO, AUTHOR OF *THE 13TH TRIBE* AND *COMES A HORSEMAN*

"Don't read this unless you're ready to see with new eyes. Through evocative prose and masterful storytelling, Rubart transports you to the spiritual realm—a realm of vision, mystery, healing and power. A deep and thoughtful—and jet-propelled—spiritual journey of a book."

—TOSCA LEE, *NEW YORK TIMES* BEST-SELLING AUTHOR OF THE BOOKS OF MORTALS SERIES WITH TED DEKKER AND *DEMON: A MEMOIR*

"This book is provocative . . . It forces the reader to consider components of God's nature not normally focused on."

—CHURCH LIBRARIES

MEMORY'S DOOR

ALSO BY JAMES L. RUBART

Soul's Gate
(A Well Spring Novel, Book 1)

Rooms
Book of Days
The Chair

MEMORY'S DOOR

A WELL SPRING NOVEL, BOOK 2

JAMES L. RUBART

THOMAS NELSON
Since 1798

NASHVILLE   DALLAS   MEXICO CITY   RIO DE JANEIRO

Published in Nashville, Tennessee, by Thomas Nelson. Thomas Nelson is a registered trademark of Thomas Nelson, Inc.

The author is represented by the literary agency of Alive Communications, Inc., 7680 Goddard Street, Suite 200, Colorado Springs, CO 80920. www.alivecommunications.com.

Thomas Nelson, Inc., titles may be purchased in bulk for educational, business, fund-raising, or sales promotional use. For information, please e-mail SpecialMarkets@ThomasNelson.com.

Publisher's Note: This novel is a work of fiction. Names, characters, places, and incidents are either products of the author's imagination or used fictitiously. All characters are fictional, and any similarity to people living or dead is purely coincidental.

Scripture quotations are taken from the HOLY BIBLE: NEW INTERNATIONAL VERSION®. © 1973, 1978, 1984 by Biblica, Inc.™ Used by permission. All rights reserved worldwide. www. zondervan.com NEW AMERICAN STANDARD BIBLE®, © The Lockman Foundation 1960, 1962, 1963, 1968, 1971, 1972, 1973, 1975, 1977, 1995. Used by permission. THE ENGLISH STANDARD VERSION. © 2001 by Crossway Bibles, a division of Good News Publishers. HOLMAN CHRISTIAN STANDARD BIBLE. © 1999, 2000, 2002, 2003 by Broadman and Holman Publishers. All rights reserved. *The Message* by Eugene H. Peterson. © 1993, 1994, 1995, 1996, 2000. Used by permission of NavPress Publishing Group. All rights reserved.

Library of Congress Cataloging-in-Publication Data

Rubart, James L.
Memory's door / James L. Rubart.
      pages cm -- (A Well Spring Novel ; book 2)
   ISBN 978-1-4016-8607-9 (trade paper : alk. paper)
   I. Title.
   PS3618.U2326M46 2013
   813'.6--dc23

                              2013006908

Printed in the United States of America

13 14 15 16 17 RRD 6 5 4 3

FOR WILMA,
BECAUSE I KNOW YOU SEE IT;
SOMETHING NEW HAS HAPPENED

"We cannot live our lives constantly looking back, listening back, lest we be turned to pillars of longing and regret."

FREDERICK BUECHNER, *THE SACRED JOURNEY*

⊙NE

THE MOMENT HAD COME TO ACT. THERE WAS LITTLE doubt and the target was clear. They had to expose the lies being fostered on the world of believers and shout the truth till it reverberated off the highest mountains. He felt it. The others had to sense it as well. The resistance would be significant, but they were ready. All four of them. They fought well together; each complemented the gifting of the others. Three men. One woman. Each fulfilling their roles with precision and strength. And God was on their side. Who could stand against them?

"It is time." He raised his head and drew in the spring air, tinged with smoke from the fire the four of them encircled.

"Have you prayed about this?" The woman turned to her left as she raised her hands to let the flames warm them.

"I've prayed extensively, as I hope all of you have done." The man gazed at each of the others. "The growth can't be ignored any longer. The influence, the appeal . . . it spreads like a virus far beyond themselves, and the time has come to crush it. With God's help we will."

The man to his left adjusted his glasses, bent forward, and stirred the fire with a long piece of kindling. "How long do you anticipate this operation will take?"

"This is the first Sunday of May. I believe before we reach the first Sunday of July we will have won a great campaign."

"Rock and roll." The third man grinned and rubbed his knees. "I think we'll take 'em down even faster than that."

"Let's pray you're right," the woman said, then stood and brushed off her light blue jeans. "I have to go. Traffic gets worse by the day. But before we break, what's the first step? Tell the millions all about their little band and what they're up to?"

"No, we're going to do something even better." The man rose to join the others and gave a grim smile as he stared into the blood-red coals, then turned to the woman. "I believe in you. That you can make the impossible happen. I believe somehow, some way, you're going to figure out how to get the world-famous Brandon Scott to come on my program and talk about his music and singing career.

"I'll talk to him about those things for a few minutes—get him feeling comfortable—then I'll shift the subject to him and his new friends. I'll hit Brandon with a few questions that will slice and dice him so severely he'll feel like he fell into a shredder. And 14.8 million of my most favorite listeners will hear every word. The truth will come out and the stream of people going through their training will turn into a desert. By the time the show is over, God will have dealt the so-called Warriors Riding a blow they'll never recover from."

TWO ⊙

WARM SUNLIGHT ON HIS FOREHEAD WOKE REECE ON FRIDAY morning and he involuntarily tried to open his eyes. Impossible. They were gone, destroyed during the battle inside his soul ten months ago. The despair once again hit him like a wave but he pushed it aside and sat up, dropped his legs over the side of his bed, and rested his feet on the cool hardwood floor he could now only see in his mind.

God was in this. He had to be. Right? Reece's mind tried to sling the thought into his heart but it ricocheted off. He reached for the watch Doug had bought him, flipped open the hinged covering, and touched the face. Six . . . fifteen. Too early—it was always too early these days—but he wouldn't be able to get back to sleep.

Reece dressed, then shuffled into his hallway past the room his silver-haired mentor had moved into. Part of him longed for Doug to stay forever and another part wished he would leave this morning. Reece had lived alone ever since Olivia and Willow had died—murdered twenty-five years ago by the demon they knew as Zennon. To have someone, even Doug, take care of him was a bit nauseating.

Reece leaned his ear against his friend's door. A faint clicking sound interspersed with a long, low snore told him Doug was still sleeping. Reece shuffled down the stairs, his hand gripped hard on the railing, his foot reaching out into the emptiness in front of him,

3

not completely sure whether his foot would contact the stair below or never touch anything. An illogical thought. He could picture the stairs in his mind—exactly what his sight counselor had told him to do. But it didn't quench the tingling fear that one day he'd step down and find only empty air.

The thought was ludicrous. A man who had traveled deep into others' souls, as well as into spiritual realms only he and Doug knew about, scared of falling down the stairs? But Reece was. Life was not without irony.

And now the Spirit was telling him to take the other Warriors into those deeper spiritual realms in preparation to soon lead them against the Wolf. How could he do that without his eyesight? Yes, he'd jumped off cliffs and built wings on the way down all his life. But never without the ability to see. Lack of sight changed the game. He needed his part of the prophecy to be fulfilled now and have his eyes restored.

Reece breathed deep, finished his descent, and made his way into the kitchen. When he reached the coffeemaker, he fumbled for the button, flicked it on, and sat at his kitchen table waiting for it to brew. After pouring a cup, he lifted his camera off the kitchen counter and slung it around his neck. Crazy to bring it with him. But it was habit to take it with him during mornings at the fire pit. Even after these many months. Because this might be the morning healing would come and he would once again see the leaves on his towering maple trees lit up with morning sun. This might be the day he watched the fire spit out red sparks and grow dark red embers in its heart. And in that instant he would capture the memory of his vision returning and have it forever.

Reece crept over the grass in his backyard out to the fire pit a hundred yards away. When he reached it, he set his camera on the bench surrounding the fire pit and knelt on the stones in front of it. He fumbled for the kindling Doug had cut and laid in the pine box that now sat next to one of the benches. If Doug ever did leave, how would Reece make the kindling without cutting off a finger or

two? But the question was irrelevant. It wouldn't be much longer. He could feel it.

He crumpled up three sheets of old newspaper, put the kindling on top, then laid logs on top of the kindling. Reece lit the paper and sat back, waiting for the kindling to catch, folded his arms, and prayed for his eyes. Five minutes, ten, half an hour, but he sensed nothing, felt nothing from the Spirit.

His counselor said he'd start to feel the size of a room even without his sight. That his hearing and sense of touch would heighten when he stood close to a wall or when people were near. It wasn't happening. Reece had fumbled and cracked his head on his doorway just last night. Not hard enough to truly hurt, but enough to refuel his desire for the healing to come now.

He raised his sightless eyes to the sky. "How long will you tarry, Lord?"

The sound of the wind rustling the trees surrounded him, taunted him, and seemed to whisper, *It's over, Reece. What good are you to the Warriors now? What good are you to anyone?*

"No! I make no agreement with that." He lowered his head, stooped, fumbled for one of the kindling pieces at his feet, and put a stranglehold on the ax till his fingers ached. But didn't loosen his grip. "Heal me!"

Reece imagined a flicker of light and let the stick of wood tumble to the ground. Could the moment be now? He reached for his eyes even though it was foolishness. He laid the tips of his fingers on the scar tissue, then let his hands fall like stones. The voice in the wind was right. He was finished and his belief was burning up and turning into ashes like the wood in front of him.

He groped for his camera next to him on the bench, snatched it up, and flung it out over the yard. It landed with a dull thud mixed with the sound of metal and plastic crunching. He didn't care. Seconds later the silence was filled with the sound of footsteps padding up to him on the grass. Doug.

"Good morning, Reece." The sound of a chair creaking across

the pit told him Doug had sat. "This is a May morning with grand finery surrounding it, wouldn't you agree?"

Reece didn't answer.

"Perhaps you're not in the mood to chat, but regardless it seems there is a grave need for conversation."

THREE

"YOU NEED TO BE FULLY ENGAGED IN THE GAME, FRIEND." Doug's voice had an edge to it.

"I am in the game."

"Really? Is that why you 'dropped' your camera? Was that a result of being in the game?"

They sat without speaking and Reece took a sip of his now-cold coffee.

"You can go back to Colorado anytime you like, Doug. I only asked you to be here long enough to get me back on my feet again."

"I'll go when the Spirit says to. One of the advantages of being retired and a widower is the ability to stay in one place as long as necessary."

"I can take care of myself now. The calendar might say I've had sixty-two birthdays, but this body isn't any older than thirty-three. And I've figured out how to navigate without sight."

The silence returned.

"Is the Spirit in this quest we're both a part of or not, Reece?"

A clichéd question that didn't deserve an answer. If what he believed was true, then of course God was in it. If he wasn't, then his entire life had been a lie. His emotions raged against the small voice of truth buried in the center of his heart.

The sound of paper being unfolded filled Reece's ears. "What's that?"

"I believe if I offered you one guess, your speculation would prove correct."

"The prophecy."

"Of course."

"And you've brought it out for what purpose?"

"Let me read it to you."

Reece fell back and blew out a quick breath. "I know what it says."

"In your head, yes. But you need to hear it again with your heart." Doug's voice started as a whisper but grew as he voiced the words Reece first heard his friend prophesy over him on the shores of Lake Chelan over three decades back.

There will come a day when you will train them—they will be four. The Song, the Teacher, the Leader, the Temple. Keep your eyes open to see, your ears open to listen, your heart open to feel, and your mind open to discern.

When the time comes, the Spirit will reveal each of them to you. You will teach them the wonders of my power they can't yet imagine. And instruct these warriors how to go far inside the soul and marrow.

They will rise up and fight for the hearts of others. They will demolish strongholds in the heavens and grind their enemies to dust. Their victories will spread across the nations. You will pour out your life for them and lead them to freedom, and they will turn and bring healing to the broken and set the hearts of others free.

And when the Wolf rises, the four must war against him and bring about his destruction.

Only they have hope of victory.

And for one, their vision will grow clear,

And for one, the darkness of choice will rain on them,

And for one, the other world will become more real than this one,

And for one, death will come before the appointed time.

Doug didn't get his wish because the words seemed hollow and fluttered to the damp grass before getting anywhere near Reece's heart. He sat in silence, the darkness seeming to draw out the time longer than it probably was.

"Is Brandon still the Song, Reece?"

"Yes."

"And Dana remains the Leader, Marcus the Teacher?"

"Yes." Reece spoke the words to the ground.

"And are you still the Temple?"

Reece rubbed his eye sockets till the stars came. But it wasn't seeing. Only chemical reactions from his fingers stimulating neurons that fired a message to his brain that there were lights in front of him. "What do you want me to say?"

"Whatever you want to."

What could Reece tell his friend that he hadn't already said fifty times? That he wouldn't feel like the Temple again without his sight and waiting for the prophecy to come true was wearing him thin as tissue paper? That at night he dreamed of being on the Skykomish River at dawn, or in the mountains, or at the ocean taking shots no one else would capture in quite the same way?

It wasn't only the death of being able to take photos. An image of his walls of books slipped across his mind. No more grabbing his worn copy of *Pensées* or his heavily highlighted hardback first edition of *Mere Christianity*. No more sitting in the light of his reading lamp studying philosophy or theology till the grandfather clock in his hallway struck one in the morning. And no more leafing through the worn-out Bible he'd lived with for more than forty years.

The healing had to come quickly.

"And for one, their vision will grow clear . . ."

Reece had said it with such confidence the day he came home from the hospital and Dana, Marcus, Brandon, and Doug had stood against Zennon and defeated the demon. But that confidence had been shrinking every day and the fire was close to going out.

"No, I don't want to talk about it. We've talked about it enough. There's nothing more to say."

Doug didn't respond and Reece pictured his friend with a sympathetic smile. But it would soon be followed up with a penetrating question.

Doug's chair creaked as if announcing his inquiry. "When?"

"When what?" Reece grabbed a piece of wood, pictured the fire pit in his mind, and tossed it where the pit should be.

"Nice toss. Right in the center."

"I can't lead them like this."

"Which is the same thing you said to me nearly a year ago. So I'll repeat what I said then. You must. There is no other choice. It is time to tell the four about the Wolf, determine exactly what humans the Wolf will use against us, and strategize our plans of engagement."

Reece shoved his sunglasses higher on his nose. "Not like this. Not until the healing comes. The classes and training we've been doing at Well Spring over the past ten months have been potent. The number of our allies has grown, and those allies are taking the message back to their communities all over the country. There have been significant breakthroughs. Think of the letters and e-mails we get, Doug. It's happening. We'll keep doing that until—"

"You've pushed it off as long as possible. The Wolf grows more powerful daily."

"The Wolf has been growing more powerful daily for ages. We can wait. Give it a little more time, six weeks, a month at least. The Spirit will come through for me and I'll be healed."

"That may be, but we cannot wait. The time to act is now. What has the Spirit told you? I believe Jesus is on his white horse with fire in his eyes, a sword in his hand, his cloak dipped in blood, and he is telling us to ride."

Reece shifted in his chair. "How does the fire look?"

"The fire is fine." Doug sighed. "Reece, we need to—"

"Are we still planning on putting them through the test? To prepare them for the Wolf?"

"Yes."

"Without warning them about what they'll face."

"Yes."

"I don't know if they're ready for that."

"I don't know either. That's the point of them going through it." Doug rested his hand on Reece's arm. "Fret not for the other Warriors. Before the test I believe we should take them into the Wall of Colors. That will give them strength. And I want you to come with me."

"I won't go there without being able to see. It would be worse than not going at all."

"All right, friend. The choice is yours." Doug's chair squeaked and his voice came from above Reece. "Your time is coming. I don't know how it will play out, but have faith, Reece. He will never forsake you."

Reece waited till the sound of Doug's footsteps had long faded before rising from the bench and making his way back to his home. *Come on.* His friend was right. He needed to snap out of it—*had* to snap out of it. Marcus, Brandon, Dana, Doug, and he would gather two days from now, and Reece needed to be strong for them and for himself. This was exactly the web the enemy would want him to become ensnared in. Pity. Self-focus. Only worried about when his sight would be restored. His mind knew the truth of it, but his feelings didn't agree.

Reece breathed deep and sank inside himself. "Lord, speak. Please."

You must ride. This is not about you.

The Spirit's voice was as clear as he'd ever heard it.

"When will I be healed, Lord?"

This journey is not about you, and yours is not to know the future. Yours is to trust.

He took in another deep breath and held it as the truth reached his heart. *I surrender, Lord.*

Peace washed over him and he let the breath whoosh into the cool morning air. Doug was right. They needed to move forward and as impossible as it seemed, Reece would lead the charge.

As he stepped onto his back deck, his cell phone just inside his house spit out "Break On Through (To the Other Side)" by the Doors. He flicked open his watch and rubbed the face. Seven thirty-nine. Who was calling him this early? The song stopped as he opened the screen door. Doug must have picked up his cell.

"Hello?" The sound of Doug's footsteps came toward him. "No, this is his friend Doug. Who is calling please?" The footsteps stopped a few feet in front of Reece.

"Please wait and I'll see if he's available." Reece pictured Doug covering up the mouthpiece of his cell phone. "It's Tamera. Do you want to take it?"

Reece held out his hand and a moment later felt his cell phone settle into his palm. "Hello, Tamera."

"I need to come see you." Her voice was clipped and too loud.

"What would we talk about?"

"What happened to me at Well Spring during my training with the other new students."

"And what was that?" Reece eased through the back door and sat at his kitchen table. He didn't need this. She'd been pinging him every few weeks since she ran into Marcus last summer at the Space Needle about getting deeper in with the ministry.

The first time they'd talked, Reece suggested the best way to go deeper was to attend one of their training sessions in Colorado at Well Spring Ranch. She'd refused. He said the same thing the second time she called. The third time she said she'd go and she had. He hadn't been there, but Brandon, Marcus, and Dana said things went well.

"I'll explain when we meet. I just want to ask you a few questions."

Reece rubbed his forehead. "Can you ask them now?"

"In person would be better."

"This is a busy time for me, Tamera."

"It's been a busy time for you for the past six months. I went through the training as you suggested. You implied we could get together after I did."

"I did not."

"I think you did."

Reece sighed. "All right, how does Sunday at three o'clock sound?"

"Fine, where would you like to meet?"

"Can you come to my home?"

"Of course."

Reece hung up and squeezed his cell phone.

"What did she want?" Doug's voice came from his left.

"To make life more difficult."

"The enemy is not going to rest just because you are."

"I'm not resting."

"You're waiting. Holding back. You can't—we can't—afford for you to do so." Doug squeezed Reece's shoulder. "When the Warriors gather here on Sunday night, you need to be ready."

"I came to that same conclusion at the fire pit." Reece raised his face in the direction of Doug's voice. "I'll be ready for Sunday night."

"Really?"

"I'm done with the self-pity."

"Excellent."

Reece heard the smile in Doug's voice, but his tone grew somber a moment later.

"There is little doubt in my spirit that the enemy is going to step up his attack. If he knows we're soon to go after the Wolf and his associates, he'll be coming for all of us in greater measure."

"I agree. I've felt it. With more subtlety this time." The demon Zennon they'd faced ten months back wasn't overt, but he wasn't subtle either. He wouldn't make the same mistake again. And neither would the Wolf.

Reece pulled his beat-up Stetson down on his forehead. "Have you sensed the attack will be focused on any of us in particular?"

"The one who comes to mind with the greatest frequency is the professor."

FOUR

"DO OTHER REALITIES OR UNIVERSES TRULY EXIST?"

A roar of delight broke out on Friday mid-morning in Professor Marcus Amber's class in the physics and astronomy building on the University of Washington campus. He grinned as he stood at the podium in front of forty or so students who whooped and applauded at the question like they were rabid Brandon Scott fans.

That was the question Marcus's class had been waiting to hear. It was the main reason his Physics 401 class was always full, with at least another twenty-three students on the waiting list. It surprised him every quarter that there were people as drawn to the idea of alternate realities as he was. And this quarter it wasn't theory. Not that he truly believed alternate realities existed. Yes, he'd written a book on it—quantum mechanics supported the idea—but he didn't believe there were other universes where you could meet altered versions of yourself or your friends and family.

But he certainly now believed there were spiritual dimensions beyond what most Christians dreamed of, and that at least some of the most seemingly outlandish, mind-bending stories in the Bible were true. He was living them. And in a certain sense, they qualified as alternate realities.

Marcus held up his hand to quiet his students. "I'm going to ask you to boldly go where many classes have gone before. It's your turn to follow in the footsteps of twenty-one classes before you. It has

now fallen among you to prove or disprove the existence of other realities and universes."

A shout came from a student in the back of the room. "Do you believe in them, Professor?"

Marcus chuckled. "I take it you haven't read my book."

The young man stood. "No, I have read your book and you don't ever give a definitive answer."

Marcus jabbed his pen in the direction of the student. "I see we have a sharp one among us this quarter. 'Tis true. I do not divulge my personal position on the subject within the covers of my book."

"So are you going to tell us?"

"I understand a number of you already know where I stand with regard to my beliefs in the alternate realities, even though I have sworn all my previous students to secrecy. But even if you do know and they have explained to you why I believe what I believe, I will presume they didn't explain to you the same way I would and with the complete explanation I can. So hopefully you will be enlightened even if you do already know."

"In other words, you're not going to tell us now."

"Yes." Marcus slipped off his glasses and set them on the podium. "I believe in dimensions other than the one in which we typically reside."

The majority of the class cheered, but the student at the back wasn't finished. "And that we can get to them."

"Other dimensions, yes. Alternate realities, no."

"What do you mean by that?"

"There is a high probability that by the end of the quarter you'll find out."

Marcus slid his glasses back on, pulled up a slide on his computer, and pointed to the white screen on the back wall of the classroom. "In case you haven't already heard, here's how the class will work. Half of you will argue for the existence of alternate realities, the other half against. It doesn't matter to me if you believe what you're arguing or not. In fact, I suggest you choose to play for

the side whose argument to which you don't subscribe. To convince others of your way of thinking, you must understand completely what they believe, why they believe what they do, and be able to state it with clarity."

Marcus shut his laptop and put it in his satchel. "The rest of the class today will be spent dividing into teams. My capable TA will handle the details. I'll see you on Monday."

✠ ✠ ✠

As Marcus stood on a street corner just west of campus waiting for the light to change, a man a foot to his right shuffled closer. He didn't stop till his left shoulder was within two inches of Marcus's. A space invader. Great. Marcus wished he could zap the guy into oblivion just like he used to do with that ancient video game he played when he was a kid.

On an airplane? Yes, being jammed within centimeters of strangers was unavoidable due to the airline's penchant for making a profit. But on the corner of the Ave and 45th, it wasn't necessary for this man to snuggle up to him like Marcus and Kat did in front of their big screen on cold January nights.

Marcus grimaced and took a step to the left. So did the man. Marcus glanced to his left. The woman next to him stared at the proximity of his shoulder, then scowled at him. He sighed and willed the light to change.

The man to his right scooted another quarter inch closer, then crept forward till the middle of his shoes were on the edge of the curb. He balanced there, his feet rocking back and forth as if to keep his balance, the edge of his dark red shirt brushing Marcus's as he swayed.

Marcus studied the man's face. A thick black goatee splattered with gray took some of the attention away from his slightly oversized ears. His full head of hair was the same color as his goatee. His eyes were slate gray and the kind that always seemed to be laughing at some inside joke. Fifty? Fifty-five? Somewhere in that age range.

Marcus was about to step backward to get some breathing room when the man cocked his head, looked up, and spoke.

"Finally." He winked.

His gaze roamed Marcus's face as if he knew something secret and was proud of the fact.

Marcus frowned. "Excuse me?"

"We finally get to meet. You and me." He laced and unlaced his fingers three times and stared at them like they might fly away. "I've been waiting, and I'm not always the most patient person in this reality or any other. Especially this one. Because this is the real one. I think. Almost positively sure."

This reality? Oh boy. Either an ex-student or someone who had read his book and had come to believe crossing over into other realities was more than theory.

"I see."

"No, you don't, oh no, you don't. But you will." He smacked his lips and tapped his nose four times. "You will, Professor. I can spot 'em. People like you and me, you know? You've got it on you. He's coming after you. Because you're the key, you see."

"How do you know I'm a professor?"

The man poked his head with his thumb. "Lots of brain cells working overtime."

"And your name?" Marcus didn't offer his hand.

"That will be revealed in due time, *mon frère*."

"I wouldn't say we're friends."

"We will be." The man rubbed his hands together. "I'm almost positive of that. We could call it a fact. Upon which we should act."

A second later the light changed and Marcus pushed off into the street. Dr. Strange remained on the corner, still rocking on the edge of the curb.

"I'll see you again soon," he murmured as Marcus strode away.

"Is that so?" Marcus called over his shoulder.

"Yes. Absolutely. You need me, you do, you do. I promise it's true."

"Wonderful." Marcus marched forward and waved his hand but didn't turn. "I'm not sure I'll survive the anticipation of seeing you again."

"Nor I," the man called, "so I must be spry, because your choice could pass by in the blink of an eye."

Wow. The man had good hearing. When Marcus reached the other side of the street, he turned to see if the man still stood on the corner but he was gone. A moment later light flashed against the window of the Gingko Tea store and into Marcus's eyes. He squeezed them shut, all sound vanished, and his legs went to jelly. He expected to faint but his strength returned a second later and he opened his eyes.

He almost wished he hadn't. The street, the buildings, the cars, and everyone around him had all vanished.

FIVE

MARCUS FOUND HIMSELF STANDING ON THE EDGE OF A
soccer field full of young girls, the air filled with shouts from the
sparse crowd on either side. What was this? Where was this? He
spun in a slow circle. He was in a park surrounded by northwest
trees, and the place felt vaguely familiar but he didn't recognize it.
Was this a vision from the Spirit? Maybe. If so, it felt so much more
real than last time. Could he be in someone's soul? No, he knew that
feeling well and this didn't feel anything like that. Plus he'd never
gone in involuntarily. And never alone. *Where am I?*

He turned back and studied the girls on the field. Should he
know one of them? None of them looked . . . Wait! At the far end of
the field it was Abbie, wasn't it? If this was real maybe he'd been tele-
ported here. But why? As he stared at Abbie his stomach churned.
Something was off. She looked younger than she should. At least
two years. Maybe more.

One of her teammates passed Abbie the soccer ball. She moved
to her left, faked to her right, and skittered around a defender. A
second later she launched the ball toward the other team's goal. The
ball glanced off the goalie's outstretched fingertips and ricocheted
into the net.

The crowd cheered and Abbie's teammates hugged her as they
bounced up and down on their toes. She turned and scanned the
sidelines until she spotted Marcus. Abbie sprinted to him and when

she got there threw her arms around his stomach. "My first goal! And you were here!" She gave him another squeeze. "I love you, Dad!" She turned and loped back onto the field.

Marcus stared at her as he staggered toward the middle of the sideline, his mind trying to grasp the scenario. He glanced at the coach's clipboard and the sun flashed off of it, and he shut his eyes. When he opened them he stood staring across the street he'd just crossed.

His new friend was still there, in the center of Marcus's vision just over the top of the cars passing back and forth in front of him. The man leaned against the Compton Building, his arms folded, a big all-knowing grin laminated on his face. Something in his eyes said he knew exactly what had just happened.

As soon as his gaze met Marcus's, the man pushed himself off the wall and strode in the direction of the campus.

"Hey!" Marcus shouted at the man as he popped the crossing button like he was playing a video game, but to no avail. If the light took as long as last time, the guy would be to University Village before Marcus could cross. "Wait!"

The man waved over his shoulder and kept going. Marcus rubbed his thinning brown hair. Over the past year he'd gotten almost used to strange things happening, but this one was new. It didn't feel evil, it didn't feel good, but it certainly didn't feel normal.

A flashback? Doubtful. Even if it was, a flashback to what? He hadn't gone to any games when Abbie was that young. Was it the enemy trying to stir up the old regrets? About what a lousy father he'd— No. Take the thought captive. He'd put up a Dead End sign on the road of regrets and he wasn't going down that street ever again.

Marcus pushed the lingering emotions aside and glanced at his watch. He'd have to hurry if he wanted to drop in on Kat at the bakery and still make it to lunch with Tim Schwarzburg on time. He glanced at the street once more but the light still hadn't changed. The glint off an old steel car bumper flashed into his eyes and Marcus half expected to be back at the soccer field but nothing

changed this time. He wiped the perspiration from his forehead and marched north up the street.

✛ ✛ ✛

The bells on the bakery shop where Kat worked jangled as Marcus pushed the door open and the smell of recently baked scones filled his nose. How she stayed so trim was a certifiable mystery of the universe. If Marcus worked in her shop he'd look like the Michelin Man, but the rubber around his middle undoubtedly wouldn't be quite so firm.

"Hey, you made it." Kat appeared through the door leading from the kitchen to the display cases and clipped around a case filled with chocolate éclairs, apple strudels, and oversized maple bars. Her auburn hair was down, which meant she'd finished baking and decorating for the day.

"Did you have any doubts pertaining to my arrival?"

"Not at all." Her brown eyes flashed at him. "I just know how the first day of a new quarter usually goes, so I didn't know if you'd be able to stop by."

"I was, as you have now most assuredly witnessed." Marcus glanced around the shop. "I wouldn't miss your anniversary."

She frowned.

He opened his arms. "This is your six-month anniversary of joining the work force again."

"Nice of you to remember the date since I didn't." She smiled.

"Still pleased you made the choice to work here?"

"I love it. Lets me indulge my love of baking and get paid for it at the same time." Kat gave a mock curtsy. "And your visit today, oh spouse of mine, is well chosen, for I, your wife of many years, have created a new pastry sensation I'd like you to try."

"Is that so?" Marcus smiled. "By all means, make me the tasting subject of yonder new concoction, fair lady."

She scuttled up to him and poked a round, donut hole-like

something into his mouth. "You'll love this." She licked her fingers and stepped back and watched Marcus chew.

It tasted like a glazed donut but had a tinge of orange to it. Not too much, not too little. He swallowed the last of it and stood on his toes to look over the counter.

Kat smiled. "Ah, the gaze that says you'd like another."

"What do you call those?"

"OBs." She traipsed back around the counter.

"Out of Bounds? For the golfing crowd?"

"Orange Balls."

Marcus laughed. "I'd stick with OBs."

"You don't like Orange Balls?"

"Some people might . . . I'm simply suggesting . . . Actually I don't want to suggest anything. I'll simply say in certain circles it would be a conversation starter."

"And in others it'd be an ender." She laughed.

"Precisely."

"Then I shall stick with calling them OBs."

Kat picked up another OB and tossed it in the air toward him. Marcus threw back his head, stutter-stepped to the left, and the Orange Ball plopped into his mouth. "Nuffin' bud ned!"

"Nothing but net?"

Marcus nodded as he chewed on the little puff of paradise. "Remember when we used to do that with olives at your sister's Thanksgiving dinners?"

"It was always the highlight of the day for me."

"Not for her."

"Remember how she scolded us every single time?" Marcus laughed and pretended he held a sign. "And the signs! Do you remember them?"

"The 'Are You My Mother' signs? The ones we brought out when my sister started in on us the next year for the entire gathering to see? The signs that made her barely speak to me for a year?" Kat glared at him. "Those I will never forget."

"Hey, you made them."

"Who gave me the suggestion?"

"I can't remember."

Kat held up an OB and studied it as if it were a diamond and she was looking for flaws. "You really like them?"

To prove his palate had been conquered, he reached over the counter, held his palm up, and wiggled his fingers. Kat placed the OB in his hand and folded her arms, and for an instant the look he'd come to dread appeared on her face. It was only there for a nanosecond, but it was there. The look that said another kind of anniversary was approaching that would rip her heart out once again. And his more than she knew. More than she would ever know because he could never tell her the truth.

Marcus spoke in a whisper. "Do you want to talk about it?"

"About what?"

"You know." Marcus swallowed. "Layne."

She shook her head. "I just want to get through this week."

Relief and disgust flooded Marcus. Relief that he had asked the question like a dutiful husband should and disgust that he lacked the strength to tell her all the details of what had happened that day.

Every year on the anniversary of their son's death he asked Kat if she wanted to talk about it, and every year she said no. In the first months after the accident they talked about it incessantly. Late into every night. Began again early every morning. But as the serrated sting of losing their son turned into numbness and Kat's and his tears came less often, Kat's need or desire to talk about it faded as well. So often the death of a child ripped the parents apart. It hadn't happened to them. But it would if she knew what he'd done.

He buried the thought as he'd become so skilled at doing over the years. The regret so deep that no matter how far down the other Warriors or anyone else went into his soul, it would never be uncovered.

"Do you?" Kat sighed. "Want to talk about it?"

Marcus shook his head and stood in the sweltering silence not knowing what to say, not trusting himself to speak even if he did know what words to offer.

"I'll be okay." She brushed her hands on her tan slacks as if to flick the raw emotions they both carried onto the hard floor. "So will you. We'll get through it like we do every year."

Marcus stared at her slacks.

"Why are you staring at my pants?"

"Are you behind on the laundry? Or did you run out of clothes?"

"Why do you say that?"

"You're wearing the same shirt and pants as yesterday. In all our years together, I've never known you to wear the same outfit two days in a row."

She cocked her head and gave him a quizzical look. "I didn't wear this yesterday. I stepped out of my norm and wore a dress." Kat stepped closer to Marcus and tapped him on the head. "All the neurons firing in order today? You even predicted my tips would be bigger, which turned out to be true."

"That was two days ago." He popped the last piece of the OB into his mouth and savored its sugary coating.

"No, it was yesterday."

"Two days ago."

Kat narrowed her eyes. "Marcus, we had a long talk about choice, that our ability to choose was what separates us from the animals and how we alter our reality in every moment with every choice we make. Remember? You turned choosing a dress over pants into a quantum mechanics lesson."

"No, I didn't."

"Yes. You did." Kat gave him her dead-serious look.

His body felt like it went from 98.6 degrees to 104 instantly. She wasn't kidding. And he had no recollection of the conversation.

"No I didn't." His conviction crumbled and he didn't know what else to say.

"I'm not making this up, Marcus."

"I don't think you are, but we didn't talk about it."

"We did."

He glanced at his watch. "I have to go. I have a lunch with Tim Schwarzburg." Marcus turned to the door.

"Stop." Kat spun him around, her hands on his arms. "Look at me. Are you okay?"

"I'm fine."

"What's going on?"

"Nothing. I honestly don't remember the conversation. I'm probably processing an abundance of stress due to the start of the new quarter." He kissed her on her forehead and then on her lips. "Or possibly I fell asleep while we were conversing. Or maybe you dreamed of the conversation."

"No, I didn't—"

"Then maybe I did. I have to go." He pulled open the door and pretended the jangle of the bells kept him from hearing Kat call his name.

The heat that had started while in the shop grew into an all-out blaze inside Marcus's body. Even though he knew he wouldn't see the man, he still strode back to the corner of the Ave and 45th and stared at the spot where the man had stood. Whatever was going on had something to do with the flashes of light that had come off the window and the car bumper. So what? He couldn't make another flash of light happen because he wanted it to. As he stared across the street, a man to his right jostled him.

"Sorry, man. My fault." An Asian man raised his hands in apology and light flashed off his watch. There was no feeling of vertigo, no feeling anything had changed. But what if it had?

On impulse he pulled out his cell phone and called Tim. "I'm going to be late for lunch. Sorry."

Marcus slid his cell phone back into the front pocket of his jeans and half walked, half jogged back to Kat's shop. He didn't know how he'd react if he saw what he expected. But he had to check.

The bell jingled just as before when he pushed the door open, but that didn't stop his body from going numb because nothing else was the same.

"Hey, I didn't think you were going to stop by. I thought you had a lunch."

"I do. I ..."

Marcus wiped the sweat from his forehead. Kat wore a pair of black jeans and a white blouse. No tan slacks, no red shirt, and her hair was pulled back.

"What's going on with you?"

"I'm fine."

"And I'm Tinker Bell. What's wrong, Professor?"

"I don't know. My stomach seized up just now." He bent over. He didn't think she'd buy it, but if she didn't, she kept it to herself.

"Are you going to be okay?"

"Yeah, it's feeling better already. It's likely nothing more than my breakfast having a spirited debate within my intestines."

"Sorry."

"And it's certainly not enough to keep me from missing out on your new creation, so I'm hoping you're willing to give me a sample."

"What new creation?"

"The one you wanted to try on me today."

"Nice mind reading, bucko. How did you know I've been trying to find something new to make?"

"You haven't made it yet?" The heat returned.

"No. Why, you have an idea?"

Where had he been ten minutes ago? Not here, based on Kat's words and dress. But he *had* been here, there was no doubt in his mind. He needed time to analyze this. Ask the Spirit. Figure out what was going on.

"I said, you have an idea?"

Marcus blinked and frowned at her. "Yes. A glazed donut hole with a splash of orange mixed in. Call them OBs. They'll taste sensational. Trust me." Marcus turned and staggered out of the bakery.

For the second time that day Kat called after him and for the second time he ignored her.

He pulled his cell phone out of his pocket and texted Tim, canceling lunch, then dialed Brandon.

"Hey, brain boy, what's up?" Brandon almost shouted over the sound of music in the background. "Sorry about the noise, we're right in the middle of a sound check for tonight's concert."

"No problem."

"You all right?"

"Something . . . two incidents . . . just occurred that I can't even start to explain." Marcus trudged down the sidewalk, weaving in between other pedestrians, trying to breathe steady.

"You? Not able to explain something? It's a miracle. Did you call to celebrate?"

"This is serious."

"Talk to me."

Marcus explained about the strange man on the corner and what had happened with the soccer game and being in two different versions of the bakery where Kat worked.

"Were they visions?"

"I don't know. It didn't feel like that." He stood staring at the same corner where it had all started half an hour ago. Nothing looked unusual, but now everything seemed odd. The smells, the sounds of the street, the breeze in the air.

"Maybe it was teleportation. The Spirit took you there."

"That might explain my visit to the soccer game, but it doesn't elucidate why I was in two different editions of the bakery."

"Elucidate?"

"Clarify, expound, explicate . . ."

"You should have stopped at *expound*."

"Brandon! I need assistance here."

"Sorry." The music grew softer. The musician must be finding a place of solitude. "I have to go back to it being a vision then."

"As I said, it didn't feel at all like it did during my vision at Well

Spring. This was concrete. I know I was there physically both times." The light changed and Marcus crossed the street and strode back toward campus.

"Doesn't mean it wasn't one just because you felt it wasn't. Remember Paul going into the third heaven? He didn't know if it was in his body or in his spirit."

"I know this was in my body, but still you raise a valid point."

"Not a vision, not teleportation, how 'bout a demonic implant was shot into your brain and altered your reality?"

"I'm not exactly in the joking mood. This was strange."

"But we've been in the business of strange for the past year. Think of some of the things that have happened at Well Spring over the past six or seven months. This kind of stuff shouldn't surprise us. We should be more surprised when it isn't happening. I'd shake it off. Let it go."

"Good, good. That's why I needed to chat. To gain a modicum of perspective." The red hickory trees on the edge of campus loomed in front of him. Somehow it seemed getting underneath them would provide a sense of protection and comfort.

"Glad to assist."

Marcus slowed his pace as he stepped into the intermittent shadows of the trees. "And you? Anything unusual?"

The music grew louder again. "I need to get back to the sound check."

"I have a feeling there are abnormalities you've experienced lately as well."

Brandon paused. "It's true. I've got my own version of *Strange Tales* going on these days."

"Would you care to enlighten me?"

"Yeah, soon, but I think I'm going to wait till we all get to hang on Sunday night. I have a feeling by that time I'll be able to tell not only the beginning and middle of this story but the end as well."

SIX

CARSON TANNER SAT IN HIS BROADCAST STUDIO EARLY ON Friday afternoon cradling a scalding cup of black coffee and pulled up the web page for Warriors Riding training at Well Spring Ranch. There was nothing to it. Just a splash page with a picture of a large cabin and white-chalk mountains behind it that shot into a deep blue sky. The only other thing on the page was a contact e-mail.

If Reece and his pals were trying to grow their ministry, this site couldn't be very inspiring to potential trainees to think about signing up. But that was the problem. From what Carson had been able to research after hearing about the ministry from one of his watchdogs, even with almost nonexistent promotion the ministry was growing exponentially. The only time the general public could catch wind of it was at Brandon Scott's concerts. The musician asked people if they wanted to go deeper—told the audience a little about the training— and invited anyone interested to go to the site and e-mail for more information.

That was it and yet little Warriors Riding weekends had popped up all over the country like dandelions gone viral. Men and women who had gone through the training were doing their own retreats from San Diego to New York to Chicago to right here in his hometown of LA—spreading the heresy like rabbits in heat. In *ten* months!

He'd learned about what the Warriors Riding taught from tracking down a few of their more enthusiastic trainees, and it scared

Carson. Made him angry. Reece and his pals were a serious threat to Christianity that had to be stopped. And now, they had a target on their backs. He would find a way to get it lined up in his sights.

Carson grimaced and checked Internet stats for himself and his show. Another 2,300 Facebook likes since yesterday. Excellent. Next he checked his blog subscribers, then the number of new fans who had signed up to receive his e-mail newsletter. Just over five hundred during the past three days. Outstanding. The Warriors Riding might be racing to the forefront of Christian culture like an Olympic sprinter going for gold, but the influence of what Carson and his team were doing to bring truth to God's people continued to grow faster than bamboo. The Lord was moving and he would keep following as hard and fast as he could.

He sipped his coffee, letting the blistering liquid burn his lips. Just like God was using Carson's ministry to burn away the heretical elements of Christendom. A rap on the door frame of the studio startled him.

"Hey, a minute and a half till you go on." Sooz Latora, his executive producer, stood in the doorway, her brown hair pulled back hard from her sharp-angled face.

"This show would crash without you."

Sooz smiled.

"What about me?" Carson's IT guy poked his head through the door and pushed up his glasses.

"Absolutely." Carson pointed at the two of them. "Have either of you or Grey found anything yet on these so-called Warriors we can use? Or found any of their trainees who didn't have a fun camping experience at the retreat?"

"Not yet, but it's only been four days. Why don't you just go on air and talk about it? Tell people what they're doing. Or try to get this Reece Roth on the show."

"I don't think we're being led to just talk about it. I want to expose it. And having Reece on the show wouldn't do us much good. No one knows him. There wouldn't be any ripple effect. But if we

can take Brandon Scott down, word of mouth about the Warriors Riding will spread like wildfire. Any update on reaching him?"

"I've tried his manager, Kevin Kaison, multiple times already. E-mail and voice mail but no response yet."

"Keep trying. And go after Brandon directly. E-mail him. Call him. And dig harder for people who have gone through this warriors training. Find them. Interview them. Draw them out. There have to be some who didn't get sucked into their lies. It can't be that hard. Find ones who are ticked off, ones we can—"

"I know how to do my job, Carson." She frowned playfully at him.

"You're right." He held his hands up. "My apologies. There is no one better at this. You're phenomenal. But I know God is saying move fast on this one." He slid his headphones over his thick blond hair and scooted over to the microphone. "Forgive?"

She smiled, winked, and pointed at the on-air sign above his head. "You're on in thirty seconds."

Carson winked back, then turned to his mic. Sooz was an exceptional producer and exceptional woman. Kind. Smart. Spiritually attuned. A blessing to have her.

A few seconds later his show's pulsing musical intro blasted through his headphones, followed by the recorded voice-over that always pumped him full of adrenaline.

"You want the truth? Can you handle the truth? You can? Then you're in the right spot and you won't want to move a millimeter for the next three hours. Welcome to *The Carson Tanner Show*, where we expose the lies trying to seep into your brain from every direction. We'll inspire, educate, and make sure the truth will propagate! We might even make you mad. But we promise we'll never bore you, 'cause the excitement meter is always pegging on eleven. Now here's your host, best-selling author, internationally known speaker, and voice to almost fifteen million daily listeners—Carson Tanner!"

He waited for the music to fade, then clicked on his mic.

"Without you, my dear listeners, I'd be nothing. Without God I'd be nothing. Without his grace and mercy I'd be tossed in oil and boiled up like a French fry. But with his power we're moving mountains. We're demolishing lies like they're sand castles on the beach. And we are the tide. Relentless and strong. Because of him. Only because of him."

Carson glanced through the glass in front of him and winked again at Sooz. She smiled back and flashed a thumbs-up. It would be a good show. Just like every day.

"Today we're talking United States insanity, folks. Yep, the states are falling like dominoes, my beloved ladies and gentlemen. And that's not a good thing. I'm talking about reefer, Mary Jane, pot, weed, the Jolly Green . . . and the dominoes are the states that are legalizing this drug. Are you kidding me? Will we soon be able to walk into the grocery store and grab a little ganja along with our milk and eggs? What is this country coming to?

"Am I wrong? Talk to me. The lines are open. I don't want to hear from people who agree. I want to talk to those who think I need to open my brain wider. C'mon, tell me where I'm all soaking wet. We're going to a quick commercial break that gives you time to be quick with your fingers. Back in sixty."

By the time the break was over the phone lines were lit up like the running lights on an airstrip.

Carson glanced at his computer screen, then flipped his finger toward Sooz. "We're talking with Kelsey in Virginia. Kelsey, you're on."

"I think every state should legalize it. Why not? It's not even as bad as alcohol and some studies show it's better. Plus, where does it say in the Bible it's wrong? I understand where it's wrong if the government we're under says it's wrong, but now that it's legal, at least in some states, is it still wrong?"

"So you're thinking in the states where it's now legal we ought to do a little prayer, a little study of the Word, and a little lighting up together?"

The caller laughed. "No, I'm not saying I think Christians should necessarily be smoking dope—"

"Hang on, Kelsey. 'Necessarily'? So you think it's okay?"

"If it becomes legal, isn't it their choice?"

"Have you ever tried dope, Kelsey?"

"Personally, no. But I don't see what the big deal is if other people want to—even other Christians. How is it any worse than having a glass or two of wine? I'm simply saying people are going to do it regardless, so why not get some tax money that can offset some of our country's massive debt?"

Carson tapped his fingers on the arms of his chair. "Here's the problem: When you're drinking alcohol, it's not breaking federal law. Right now, if you smoke pot you're breaking federal law. I don't care what the states say. And there's a difference between someone hooked on alcohol and someone hooked on pot or cocaine or meth. The latter group is breaking the law, the former is not." Carson leaned in closer to his mic. "In other words, the fact it's lawbreaking to do drugs prevents some people from taking that step. We make smoking pot legal, it gives an excuse for a certain segment of our population to step over the line who never would have done so before. And like you just said, Kelsey, that includes Christians.

"There are some Christians who drink. They have a glass of wine and feel a little warm and a little buzzed. Today isn't a day to debate whether that's right or wrong. But I think we can all agree that sometimes, some Christians who drink, drink too much. Right?" Carson adjusted his headphones. "And if pot is legal, then you're going to have Christians taking a little hit of pot to feel a little buzz and get a little relaxed. And then they do a little too much weed. And then they get addicted. And that's a major problem. I'd tell you where that path could lead, but you already know, don't you? Hell. Thanks for the call, Kelsey."

Carson scrolled down his computer screen and looked at the names of the callers on hold. Sooz always typed in quick notes next

to their names. Where they were from, age range, and what they wanted to talk about. There. This guy would lob him a serve he could return to all his listeners at a hundred miles per hour.

"Allen, you're on *The Carson Tanner Show*."

"I don't think it's the pot smoking or drinking you're really worried about."

"Really. Why do you say that? Talk to me, Allen."

"I think you're worried about Christians always pushing the edge of what's permissible rather than pushing the edge of what's holy. They're getting as close as possible to the edge of the cliff rather than sticking to the middle of the road."

"Bingo." Carson raised his hand and snapped his fingers. "Sooz, do you mind getting Allen's address and sending him a free copy of my latest book?"

Carson jabbed his fingers toward the ceiling like they were guns. "You've nailed it, Allen. He's right, folks. He's sooooo right." Carson closed his eyes, took in a sharp breath, and let it out slowly. "We're to be lights, people! Different. We're to stand apart. Stand out based on the way we behave. Not push the boundaries of sin. The choices we make to stay unstained from the world will infect the world for righteousness! If, if, *if* we choose right. We need to live redemptive lives."

Carson picked up a laminated sheet of paper and wiggled it. "If you don't have our Redemptive Reminders list, what are you waiting for? It'll set you free. You don't know about the list? My bad if you don't. I'll tell you how to get it in a minute.

"It's real simple, folks. You want to be holy? You want to shine? Then think of the movies you're going to. Really? You'd be proud to take Jesus to those movies? Some of the books you're reading? Really? You'd read those out loud with Jesus sitting next to you?"

Carson's head bobbed back and forth as a surge of adrenaline kicked in. This was truth. This was what they needed to hear. "These so-called Christian men who get out on the golf course and stick a big skunk-smelling cigar in their mouths? Hello? That's Jesus? Show me the scripture to back that one up. Ya see, following

Jesus isn't just about the warm and fuzzies. It's about taking a stand on behaviors and attitudes. My actions. Your actions. My choices. Your choices.

"You're not in church every Sunday, and I mean *every* Sunday? Why not? They don't have churches where you went on vacation? You need to have your backside inside those four walls every week. When the Word says don't forsake the assembly of the brothers, it means don't forsake it. Not some of the time. All of the time. Don't sit on the beach on Sunday. Get to church. It's the thing you should be looking forward to most on vacation. A chance to fellowship with new brothers and sisters. The chance to hear a different pastor. Hot or cold, not lukewarm. It's time to get serious, folks.

"You're cussin' from time to time—I know some of you are—and you're calling yourself a Christian? Explain that one to me. How can scum-infested water and clear water flow from the same fountain? It can't."

Carson raised his fists toward the ceiling and pumped his arms. "I'm not trying to make you feel guilty. I'm trying to get you to repent. I want to get you through the narrow gate without scraping the skin off your shoulders as you go through.

"Jesus is coming back for what? A blemished bride? No, my faithful, he's returning for an *un*blemished bride. Unblemished!" Carson slumped back in his chair and went silent for ten seconds. Dead air. Radio 101 said never let there be dead air. But it was right. Let the message sink in. Let God's truth seep deep into their minds.

"Do you smoke an occasional cigarette? Some of you are shocked I'd even pose the question. Good for you. But I'm telling you, there are folks listening right now who just felt the conviction of the Holy Spirit because they're in the habit of lighting up, and I'm talking on a regular basis. Do you really want to be tarnishing the temple like that? Really? You don't, I know you don't. But you need help. You need a little motivation. That's where we come in.

"You don't drive a car without guidelines. There are rules of the road to follow. And the spiritual road we're driving down has more enticing-looking off-ramps than you can count. Off-ramps with lights that look like they're from heaven. But they're not. Get it together, folks. Get on the straight and narrow. Be worthy of your calling. Starting when?" Carson lifted his arms wide. "There is no tomorrow. There is only this moment. So start now. Are you with me? Are you?

"Maybe this is the first time you've listened to my show. Maybe you haven't heard of the Redemptive Reminders. It's nothing fancy. No bells and whistles, just seven simple reminders of what a child of God looks like. But I promise you, they'll change your life. Let me read 'em to you now. Open your mind and hear what the Holy Ghost is saying.

"No cursing. Ever. Let no unwholesome word proceed out of your mouth. Ephesians 4:29.

"No crude jokes. Ever. Same verse.

"No smoking. Ever, in any form. Cigars, pipes, cigarettes. Nothing. The body is the temple of the Holy Spirit. 1 Corinthians 6:19.

"Sin will grow at R-rated shows. Keep yourself unstained by the world. James 1:27.

"A sip at most *might* be fine, but any more is too much wine. Proverbs 20:1.

"No slander, no gossip about anyone. Ever. Proverbs 16:28.

"And the final Redemptive Reminder, no missing church. Ever. Be there every week or you'll grow weak. Hebrews 10:25.

"You can download this list from our website. It will cost you nothing but a click of your mouse. More than five million of you have downloaded it. But that means ten million of you haven't. Print out multiple copies. Put it on your refrigerator. Stick it to your bathroom mirror. Put it on your kids' mirrors. Put a copy in your car, at work. Rise up, friends, and have done with lesser things!

"Time for a break, folks, but one more thought. I'm not saying

these things to make you feel bad. It's because I care for you. God has put his love for you in me, and so with his love I love you. But sometimes love is tough. Sometimes love calls you to repentance. Stay strong, folks. And stay there. We're coming right back with more talk, more callers, more truth. This! is *The Carson Tanner Show!*"

SEVEN

BRANDON FINISHED THE SECOND-TO-LAST SONG OF HIS first set on Friday evening and scanned the back of the arena looking for the stalker. If the man had come again and kept his pattern the same, he'd stand and walk out within a few seconds. He'd done it every time for the past five concerts when the band finished "Running Free."

No one but Kevin and Brandon's bass player, Anthony, knew about the guy—Brandon hadn't even hinted about it to any of the Warriors except to Marcus earlier in the day. For one thing, he'd been on the road for three weeks and wanted to talk to all of them about it at the same time, and in person. For another, he wanted to figure out if it was just your friendly neighborhood wacko or something darker, like Zennon.

They'd seen little of the demon during the past ten months. Yes, there had been minor skirmishes, but most of their days had been filled with going deeper into the Spirit and helping set others free. But now? Maybe this was part of Zennon's resurgence. Maybe the stalker was Zennon. Brandon had asked the Spirit repeatedly about the tall, well-built man who stuck to the shadows of the halls they'd played in over the past two weeks, but he'd gotten no answer, not even a deeper insight into what action to take.

Brandon pushed back his longish, dirty-blond hair and squinted against the glare of the spotlights bathing his band and him in dark

reds and blues. Where was the guy? Was it over? Maybe he'd stopped coming. Brandon scoffed. Yeah, right.

"Wake up, Song Boy. One more tune." His bass player bumped his shoulder into Brandon's. "You with us?"

"In a second." Brandon scanned back over the crowd. Each time the guy sat on the left side of whatever hall Brandon was playing, two-thirds of the way back.

"Are you looking for the guy again?"

"Lucky guess."

Anthony thumped out a bass line, probably to keep the crowd from wondering why the concert had screeched to a halt. "If he was stalking you, he'd have approached you by now, sent a note, sent flowers, done something. Let it go. Maybe he's just a megafan."

"Yeah, a megafan who just happens to have an ax in the trunk of his car."

"Men don't stalk men."

"They don't?"

"Well." His bass player grinned. "Not typically."

"I'll be sure to mention that to the guy when he shows up knocking on my bedroom door at two in the morning with an Uzi in his pocket. I'll call you, hand the guy my cell, and you can tell him he shouldn't be there."

Brandon made another scan of the room. Nothing. Wait. There. Sitting five or six rows back from the spot he usually sat in. Was the guy blond? Wearing a T-shirt? Hard to tell with the lights in Brandon's eyes and the audience buried in shadows. Two concerts back Brandon asked security to talk to the guy, find out who he was, but they hadn't been able to corner the man. Which didn't make sense. He would be hard to miss. The guy had to be almost as tall as Reece.

If he was a stalker, why didn't he ever try to get to Brandon? And why spend the money to see the same concert over and over again? Tickets to his shows these days weren't cheap. Between plane fare

and buying a ticket for each show and food while traveling, the guy had to be dropping upward of five hundred dollars per city.

He'd had strange fans before. Those wanting him to sign non-PG areas of their bodies, those whom God supposedly told they were to become a member of his band; there were even a few who thought they were told to come to his house, set up tents, and pray for him every morning at five thirty because "Jesus rose early to pray, so we're following the path he has showed us." But something about this guy was different. He wasn't your ordinary whack job. Which meant the enemy was most likely involved.

Anthony bumped his shoulder again. "Did you see him?"

"Yeah."

"That's cool. Can we start playing again?"

"Sure." Brandon blew out a quick breath and called out the next song to the beat of his foot thumping on the stage. "One, two, three, go!"

An hour later the concert was over and Brandon stood in front of the stage praying with people, hearing their stories, signing autographs, and scanning the back of the room. There was no use—the stalker had never shown up after a show—but he couldn't help himself.

As the last concertgoer turned and waved one more time at Brandon, Kevin clicked up to him on his right. "Done?"

Brandon glanced at the crew milling around the stage, breaking down their gear. "The stalker was here again."

"Yeah, Anthony told me." Kevin nodded. "And we were ready. The guys watched hard."

"And?"

Kevin stepped closer and lowered his voice. "They saw him tonight."

"What?"

"Apparently he left from a door fifty feet from where two of them stood. They went after the guy."

"Talk to me." His heart pounding, Brandon stared at Kevin. "Who is he? What does he want? What'd the guy have to say?"

"They didn't get to talk to him."

"Hold it. They see the guy leave the concert, they're only fifty feet away, and they couldn't find him?"

Kevin shook his head. "I don't know what happened. They say they ran after him. Turned the same corner the guy did three seconds earlier, but when they got there the hall was empty. There were only two doors and both were locked."

Heat washed over Brandon. Zennon. Had to be. Or someone who had learned Reece's teleportation trick. The former was more likely. Fine. Zennon wanted to stalk him? Brandon would hunt the demon in return.

"Next concert I want security racked and stacked every ten yards. We're going to corner this guy and find out who he is. And if he's not human, I know who and what he is, so we'll get ready for that possibility as well."

"Something right here"—Kevin pointed to his stomach—"tells me there won't need to be a next time."

EIGHT

Brandon stared at Kevin and gave a slow nod. As he'd told Marcus that afternoon, his gut was saying the same thing.

Twenty minutes later Brandon hefted his Nike bag onto his shoulder and strode for the back door of the arena. Just before he got there, two of his bodyguards fell into step with him, their black steel-toed boots clicking on the concrete floor of the hallway.

"Thanks, guys."

"No problem, Mr. Scott."

"You keep calling me Mr. Scott, either of you, and I'm going to lay you both out with one punch."

The second bodyguard cleared his throat. "I have grave doubts you'd be able to accomplish that, Mr. Scott. I don't believe you could do it with ten punches."

The first bodyguard gave a mock cough. "Maybe twenty."

Brandon put his hand against the back door and grinned. "That's why I love being around you two. Let's go."

Brandon saw the man's moving silhouette the instant he stepped through the backstage door leading to the roped-off parking lot. The streetlight above and behind the man cast a long shadow of him that ended at the bottom of the steps in front of Brandon and his bodyguards. If the man saw them, he didn't acknowledge it and continued to saunter across the huge parking lot with his head down.

"Hey!" Brandon called.

The man stopped but didn't turn to face them until five seconds had passed. When he did, he lifted his head and gave a single nod.

Brandon glanced at his bodyguards. "That the guy from earlier tonight?"

"Without a doubt," the one on his right said.

"Ready to find out who he is?"

Brandon didn't wait for an answer and marched down the steps, guards at his sides, toward the man who stood staring at him, legs shoulder-length apart, hands behind his back, blond hair thick and cut short.

From the stage the man had looked close to Reece's height. Up close it was obvious the man was at least a few inches taller. At least six six.

Brandon stopped ten yards from the man. "Can I help you?"

"You're the one who called to me. So perhaps I'm the one who can assist you." The man folded his hands in front of him.

"You've been showing up at my concerts."

"Really?" The man tilted his head and gave an astonished smile. "I'm surprised you've spotted me. I tried to be more discreet than that."

"Is there something you want from me?"

The tall man studied each of them for at least ten seconds before responding. "No. Not yet." He turned to go.

"Who are you?"

"Someone who would rather talk to you another time."

"You've been coming to every one of my shows for two weeks now."

The man turned back around. "As I said before, I didn't realize you saw me. I've always left before your concert was over. I wouldn't want you to think you had a stalker, nothing as unsettling as that."

A hint of laughter in the man's eyes seemed to say this statement wasn't quite true.

"I think you did want me to spot you." Brandon glanced at his bodyguards who both looked ready to jump the guy. Good.

"This is true." The man clapped his hands together three times, softly enough that there was no sound. "Well done, Brandon Scott."

"Well done that I've seen you?"

"Yes. But to repeat myself, this is not the time to talk. But when it is time I wanted us to have met so you'd be more open to further conversation. I mean you no harm."

"If we had a conversation, what would it be about?"

The man stared at the sky as if waiting for instructions. "That would take more than a few moments to explain, and I'm sure you are exhausted."

"The only thing on my schedule tonight is going back to the hotel, and my energy level is peaking at the moment." He motioned to the bodyguards on his right and left. "My friends and I have plenty of time to hear why you've been tracking me. So start talking."

The man took a stride forward and glanced at Brandon's bodyguards. "Can we do so alone?"

"Not thinking that's going to happen."

The man pursed his lips. "It would be better if we spoke alone."

"Do you want me to repeat what I just said, or would you like to play it over in your head by yourself?"

"I understand." The man looked up to his left as if studying the bright quarter moon that cast a dim light on the parking lot. He glanced at Brandon's bodyguards, frowned, then turned back to Brandon but remained silent.

Brandon pulled his bag from his shoulder and reached into it. "Listen, how 'bout I give you a few signed CDs and a couple of signed photos and you stop following me around on tour."

"If that were possible, I would do it."

"Who are you?"

"One who would help you."

"Sure. Got it. You're going to help me."

"Yes. I would like to."

"Great. Then it's settled. Stop coming to my concerts. Thanks. That will help a lot." Brandon glanced at his guards. "Time to go."

"As you wish." The blond man put his hands behind his back again and stared at Brandon with eyes that seemed to cut holes in his head.

"Wait."

"Yes?"

"Are you Zennon?"

The man frowned and his eyes grew dark. "My name is Tristan, and I look forward to meeting with you again soon, as well as with the rest of your band."

"My band?"

"The Warriors Riding."

"How do you know about them?"

"In time I'll explain that to you."

Brandon slung his bag back on his shoulder and glared at the man. "Just Tristan? No last name?"

"Barrow. Tristan Barrow."

"And if I don't want to see you again?"

Tristan pointed to the sky. "That's not my choice, and not yours." He smiled. "Don't worry, I'm on your side."

Doug's e-mail yesterday with Sunday night's agenda had hinted that an increased attack from the enemy was coming. Maybe Reece's mentor was right: Brandon had Tristan the stalker, Marcus was seeing visions that seemed to be more than visions, and Reece was struggling with the loss of his eyes.

Dana flashed into his mind but that didn't mean the Spirit was giving Brandon a specific warning about her. She filled his thoughts unbidden on a daily basis. An hourly basis. And he didn't want her to leave his brain but he should. She'd made that abundantly clear after the fourth time he'd asked her to have coffee—just the two of them—and she'd made him promise to stop asking. There was no hope for them. Why couldn't he get that through his head?

Regardless, whatever kind of assault was coming against Reece, Marcus, and him would include her as well.

NINE

THE SAIL SNAPPED INTO PLACE SATURDAY AFTERNOON as the wind took hold and the boat surged forward, the San Juan Islands in the foreground, sun drenching the scene enough that Dana and Perry both wore sunglasses.

They sailed for a time in silence, the briny smell of the sea and the slap of the water against the hull of Perry's boat enough to fill Dana's mind and imagination. She'd been working too many hours at the radio station, battling to keep her job, battling the pressures of sales goals that never grew easier to meet. And anytime she wasn't there she spent working on the classes she taught at Well Spring to the ever-growing number of trainees. She needed this break.

When she and Perry had gotten together at the end of summer last year to talk things out it had been healing, better than expected, and their getting together every three or four weeks had been unexpected as well. He hadn't pushed her to go deeper during the past eight months, which of course made her go deeper with him at times than she'd intended. She liked him. Enough for a serious relationship? No. She didn't think about a future together. Today and maybe tomorrow was plenty.

They anchored off Friday Harbor and Perry motioned toward the front of the boat. "If you want to get comfortable up there, I'll go down here"—he pointed below deck—"and bring up some food and some adult refreshments."

Dana eased toward the bow as the wind whipped through her light brown hair and lifted it off her shoulders. She knew what she wanted. But what did Perry want? Did he think they were dating again? He hadn't tried to kiss her which was a bit shocking and a relief. She didn't want to be forced onto the path a kiss would certainly lead them down.

Stop it. Hadn't she just told herself to think about today only? She was having another relaxing afternoon with a friend. Nothing more. What was wrong with that? Even if she and Perry grew back into something more, what fault could that contain?

She reached the bow and stretched out, one leg over the other, leaned back on her elbows, and watched the green waves and the seagulls cantering on the wind, the sun lighting up their wings like snow. If heaven was better than this, she didn't think she'd be able to stand it.

Perry emerged from below a few minutes later with a plate of strawberries surrounding a small glass bowl of melted chocolate and a bottle of champagne, his dark curly hair begging for a trim. "Voilà!" He grinned and climbed out to the bow to join her. "This should keep us occupied for a few minutes at least."

As she stared at him and the strawberries and champagne, Dana didn't know whether to laugh or grab a life jacket and jump overboard. Strawberries and champagne? It was all too clichéd and over the top for just friends. Did she want more? Yes. No. The fickle nature of the undecided human heart, like a garden of flitting butterflies that can't decide where to touch down.

"You're not getting all romantic on me, are you?"

Perry reared back his head. "I'm shocked you would think that."

She laughed. "What am I doing here with you?"

"Soaking in the sun, the wind, the waves . . . soaking in each other. Same thing we've been doing for the past ten months."

"Nine months."

"Nine and a half."

"Fine." She took a sip of the champagne. "Soaking in the first three on your list can work, but the last one isn't on the menu. Sorry."

Perry grew silent and took off his sunglasses.

"What?"

"Can you take off your sunglasses?"

She did.

"I want to soak in each other."

"Don't go there, Per—"

"Don't blame it on me. You've changed. You're more open—way more open about what's going on inside you. You've cut up the sixty-foot pole that kept people away. There's a . . . peace around you that was never there before. It's like you flipped a switch. It's hard not to think of the future."

"Try harder and don't think about it. It's been nice the way it is. Let's keep it that way." She grabbed a strawberry and tossed it overboard.

"Hey!"

"It's symbolic of what I'm going to do if we don't take our relationship one day at a time."

Perry scratched his cheek and fiddled with the sunglasses he held. "I suppose if you jumped in, I could rescue you from drowning."

"Stop it."

They said nothing for five minutes or so, taking the time to dip the strawberries in the chocolate and savor their taste. When Perry spoke he thankfully changed the subject.

"Tell me more about this group of yours. The one you went to Colorado with and seem to meet with on a regular basis. Do they know we're seeing each other?"

So much for changing the subject. Dana sat up and dipped another strawberry in the chocolate. "We're not seeing each other."

"We're not?" Perry frowned.

"Do you want to hear about the Warriors Riding?"

He nodded.

"You haven't shown much interest all this time, and now you want to know about them?"

"I figure the question is long overdue."

"We're doing amazing things together. Things I never would have believed. My eyes have opened to the spiritual realm in ways I never even imagined could be true."

"This I need to hear about."

How much should she tell him? Probably more than a little, but much less than all. She didn't want to overload him, but without some concrete examples of what the Spirit had done her statements would be vague platitudes. So she told him about how God had spoken new names to each of them, talked about deep intercessory prayer and how each of their little band had been healed of some of their deepest wounds. But she didn't go so far as to tell him they'd sent their spirits inside each other's souls.

She told him about teleporting their bodies to various places around the country by the power of God's Spirit. About their experience fighting the vine that tried to burrow its way into Brandon's chest at his concert, and how they'd been running frequent four-day training sessions at Well Spring in Colorado for hundreds of those who wanted to go deeper into the things of the Spirit.

When she finished she took a long sip of her champagne and gazed at Perry. "Do you think I'm nuts?"

"Wow." Perry blinked and rapidly shook his head. "No, I don't think you're nuts, but wow. I'll have to take a little time to get my head around this."

"You think we're crazy."

"Maybe a little." Perry dipped a strawberry in the chocolate and bit off half of it and looked in her eyes. "One more question."

"Sure."

"You said one of the four of you is named Brandon Scott."

She nodded.

"But this isn't your ex-fiancé, Brandon Scott, is it? The names are just a coincidence, right?"

Dana shook her head and put her sunglasses back on.

"Are you kidding? You spent four days in Colorado with him?

And now you do training with him? And get together as a group on a frequent basis?"

She nodded again.

"Wow." Perry popped his strawberry into his mouth and took a long time to chew and swallow. "Isn't it kind of weird being around him?"

"It was at first." She folded her arms. "It still is a tiny bit, but not much. We worked it out."

"Worked it out? Really? How do you work out something like that?"

The memory of Brandon being in her soul and the war that they waged flooded her mind. The closeness she'd experienced. The fractions of seconds where it felt like it did when they were engaged. "It's part of the healing Jesus did. I'll tell you about it sometime."

"You're okay being around him a lot?"

"It's okay. It's even good." She hesitated. It was good at times. But then there were those moments when she didn't know what to feel. When she wished for . . . no. She wouldn't entertain insane thoughts about Brandon. "Most of the time it's good."

Perry folded his arms and stepped back. "Do you still have feelings for him?"

"They're gone." She turned and focused on a seagull flying low over the water to her right.

"You're sure?"

A tinge of warmth spread across her face and she hoped Perry couldn't see her blush. "Why is that so important?"

"Because if we're . . ." Perry took a sip of his champagne.

"If we're what? We're friends, right? Taking it one day at a time? I thought we just had this conversation."

Perry squinted out over the sound toward Lopez Island. "True. My apologies. Your feelings or lack thereof toward Brandon should be none of my business. For now." He glanced at her, then back to the island. "But if certain scenarios play out, it might become my business."

Once again her emotions whipped back and forth like a loose sail in a prevailing wind. She should feel good about Perry's thinly veiled insinuations about their future. For the first time in . . . forever, she didn't want a guy in her life. More important, she didn't *need* a guy in her life. Which made her want to have someone in her life. It made no sense and all the sense in the world.

"When's the next time you're going to see him?"

"Tomorrow night at our Warriors Riding meeting."

"I see." Perry sucked in a deep breath and let it out slowly.

What do you want? The Spirit spoke to her so softly she almost missed it.

I want to love again. She turned and gazed over the water.

Yes. I want that for you too. Is Perry the one?

It was a question she should be asking the Spirit, not the other way around. Right? No, she knew the truth. Knew the answer because it was as clear as the cobalt sky above her.

She turned and looked at Perry. "There's nothing going on between us." Nothing between her and anyone. Except for the gnawing feeling deep down inside that she wouldn't even tell herself about. She took off her sunglasses once more. "And there never will be. I don't think we should see each other again."

☩ ☩ ☩

They didn't speak on the way back to shore and their good-bye was short and tense. Where did she go from here? Not Perry. Certainly not Brandon. No way, never. If God truly wanted her to find love again he would have to create the painting of romance. Because as far as she could see, the canvas was utterly blank.

Dana shifted her mind to the meeting tomorrow night and the strange line Doug's cryptic e-mail portended for their meeting. "*. . . when we meet you will go deeper than you've ever gone before.*"

It sounded like the gathering would be one to remember.

TEN

REECE FELT THE HANDS OF HIS WATCH ON SUNDAY, WISHING his meeting with Tamera was already over. Twenty minutes till she arrived. He had a feel for what she wanted to talk about, and the answer he would give her certainly wouldn't be the one she wanted.

He sat on his back deck, the late afternoon sun on his face, the image of what the maple trees looked like at this time of year filling his mind, leaves full of light from the sky turning them a more brilliant green, tiny veins weaving through their form. How he missed seeing them.

Nineteen minutes later a knock came from the front of the cabin. Reece heard Doug invite Tamera in. A creaking came from the living room floor and Reece imagined the woman bouncing across the floor as if trying to burn off some of the perpetual energy she stored inside. Then closer, into the kitchen and out through the screen door that led onto the back deck. The shuffle of two pairs of shoes went silent.

"Tamera is here to see you."

Reece turned to the sound of his voice. "Thanks, Doug."

"My pleasure."

Reece imagined his friend giving a slight bow, a smile, and a flick of his upturned hand toward Tamera that would have fit into eighteenth-century England like an ivory-colored glove. Tamera

and everyone else who saw it wouldn't understand it was Doug's dry sense of humor on display for anyone who had eyes to see.

The sound of Tamera sitting in the chair across from him pushed the image of Doug from his mind. "Hey, stranger."

"Good afternoon, Tamera." He pictured her as he'd last seen her. Short blond hair, fair skin, in excellent shape of course.

"Thanks for taking time for me."

"Not a problem."

Her chair creaked. "But it has been a problem, hasn't it?"

"Excuse me?"

"It's been a workout trying to get a one-on-one audience with you. This is our first just-the-two-of-us meeting since . . . I don't remember when."

"Life has been busy. You know that. The training school at Well Spring. The mundane things of living taking longer due to this." He pointed to where his eyes used to be.

"I understand that, but the last time we really talked and I asked to be part of Warriors Riding, you said you'd most likely invite me into the inner circle once I went through the training at Well Spring."

"No, I did not say I'd 'most likely invite you in.' I said I'd consider it, pray about it. See where the Spirit led."

"So now I've been through the training at Well Spring. Well over three months ago."

"Yes?"

"Marcus, Brandon, and Dana said I had a number of substantial breakthroughs."

"They conveyed that to me."

"And since then I've been growing in the Spirit and seeing him do amazing things through me."

"I agree."

"I'm learning to love like I've never done before."

"Again, from what I've been told, I would agree."

"I'd like to join you."

"I don't understand. You have joined us. You're one of a select group of warriors Jesus is raising up."

"No, I want to join the inner circle. The one that was formed at Well Spring when you and the others went there a year ago. I blew it. I've told you that many times. I should have been there. It's something I regret every day. But stop making me pay for my mistake. Let me into the inner circle and be one of you like I was meant to be."

"That choice isn't up to me. It's up to the Spirit."

What sounded like Tamera slapping the side of her chair filled the air. "Cut it, Reece! That's such an easy cop-out. You don't want something to happen so you blame it on God and it's his fault."

"The truth is never a cop-out."

"You invited me to Well Spring. You chose me." Tamera's voice rose in volume and pitch. "I was one of the four and now I'm just another grunt in the tribe following the great man."

Reece let the silence grow till Tamera spoke again.

"You have no answer for me? Figures."

"You know about the prophecy, yes? During your training at Well Spring it was shared with you. And you heard of the truth that surprised all of us, most of all me. Do you remember what was told?"

"That you're supposedly the Temple and not me."

Reece uncrossed his legs. "You can still be an integral part of this mission but there are four to the prophecy, not five."

"If it had played out as you intended and I'd gone to Well Spring with you last year, it would right now be Dana, Marcus, Brandon, you, and myself. That's five. So why can't it be five now?"

"You chose not to come. I'm sorry for your regret and the weight of that, but the tapestry is what it is at this point. Neither you nor I can go back and unravel what has been done."

"That's not fair, Reece. Where is the grace you supposedly speak of so frequently when you train people at Well Spring?"

"This isn't about grace or absence of grace. It isn't about what the Spirit did back then, but what the Spirit is doing now. And in

this now, there are four Warriors Riding. Not five." Reece tapped his armrest in a slow cadence. "Is there anything else?"

"You're making a mistake, Reece."

"Oh?"

"I could do such powerful things for this ministry. I have my own exercise TV show. I have the ear of producers who would be able to put you in front of millions. I have a newsletter of more than seventy-five thousand people. I have a Facebook page with over thirty thousand likes. I have a book contract."

"I don't want to be in front of millions. I don't want be in front of thousands. I want to be in front of the remnant of warriors who want to go deeper and are willing to pay the price that will entail. There will never be many."

"I get that. But to get to the few, you need to get to the many. You need me, Reece. Think about it. If you're trying to find a needle in a haystack you have to figure out a way to spin through a lot of hay."

"Tamera, you've learned much and grown in love as we both said a moment ago but you've failed to realize your place in the tapestry."

"What's my place? I've found my place. I'm making huge changes in people's lives."

"Yes, I believe you are."

"And you need me to do the same for you."

"No, I don't need you, Tamera. You're not needed at all."

"What?" The scrape of Tamera's chair filled Reece's ears and her voice came from above him. "You're wrong. I have so much to offer you. I'm worth something."

"Sit down."

"How do you know I'm standing?"

"Sit down, friend, and listen. I don't need you just as he doesn't need me. His purposes will be accomplished with or without me. All God's offering is an invitation into his story, the greater story, the things he's doing on a grand and microscopic level."

"I want to be needed. I need to be needed. I want to feel like what I'm doing matters. That God is using me to make a difference, to create some kind of legacy. I want to know I'm worth something. Is that so wrong?"

"And what if the legacy you create is simply one of loving the Father, Son, and Holy Spirit with all your heart, mind, soul, and strength?"

"I couldn't live with that. I need to be able to point to something."

"Open your heart to my words, Tamera. Don't you understand what that means? It means he values you for who you are, not for what you've done or what you might do for him or others. There is no earning his favor, his grace, or his mercy. There is no action you can take to make him love you. He already does. More than you will ever imagine. But you're not wrong to want to know if you're worth something. You are worth something. More than something. You are worth his being crushed and broken, torn and scourged. Executed against a scorching sun and the utter scorn of those around him. You are worth so much."

The air went still and all Reece heard was a gentle wind in the trees. A few seconds later the cry of children playing floated over the air from far away. "Do you hear that? It's what we must become. No pride, no self-focused ambition, no—"

"I get the message." The volume of Tamera's voice dropped—Reece couldn't tell if it was from sadness or anger seething just below the surface. He wished he could see her eyes, to know if she was about to explode or let the truth in.

"Why is this so important to you? It sounds like you have a tremendous career in fitness going."

"Because I want the power you four have. I want to be around it. Learn more. Do the things you talked about that are on the fringe. I want to experience it all."

"I don't know which way the wind will blow tomorrow, Tamera, but the answer in this moment is to wait."

"I'm done waiting."

"I'm sorry. This is not about you or your worth before God. It's about what he is doing. It's possible I'm not hearing correctly from the Spirit, but I believe I am, and this is not the time and I don't know when it will be."

"You'll regret this, Reece. So will the others."

ELEVEN

MARCUS ARRIVED AT REECE'S HOUSE ON SUNDAY EVENING at 7:05 and scanned the driveway. Brandon's and Dana's cars were already here. He didn't get out. Should he tell them about the bizarre incidents that happened on Friday? Or just let it go like Brandon suggested?

Nothing similar had happened for the past two days. Perchance it was a result of stress or a dream that seemed so genuine he hadn't been able to distinguish it from the real world. A somewhat common occurrence in human dream states.

Marcus stepped out of his car, shut the door, and rubbed his hands as if ridding himself of his visions of Abbie and Kat from Friday afternoon. If Doug and Reece were finally going to tell them about the Wolf and they were about to set their strategy, the focus shouldn't be on his hallucinations. It should be on the coming melee.

✠ ✠ ✠

A firm rap on the front door of Reece's home startled Dana. She'd been wrapped up in studying a site map she'd developed for the Well Spring website. At some point they'd need to expand it beyond the splash page and she was hoping the Warriors would use some of the photos she took at the ranch.

She stood as Brandon opened the front door and ushered

Marcus inside. A few minutes after she greeted him, Doug descended Reece's lightly stained wooden stairs and settled onto the couch in the living room. He rubbed his hands together as if getting ready to sculpt an object out of the air in front of him.

"Remember me saying last spring after the victory you had in Reece's soul that you've just begun your journey into the vastness of God? That you've only started down the path of joy and freedom?"

Dana nodded along with Marcus and Brandon and she studied Doug's eyes. They were bright and playful like a little boy's, as if he were about to show them one of his favorite toys. She hadn't ever seen him this animated.

"Today I'm going to show you more of the path. You have seen marvelous things so far but going into souls is only part of what God has made available to us if we only believe and are willing to let the Spirit take us deeper. There are far more tantalizing wonders to be explored for those who want to fly on wings like eagles."

"Here we go again." Brandon smiled.

"Oh yes." Doug returned the Song's smile and laid his hands on his knees. "Most assuredly, yes."

"Are you telling us we're going flying?" Dana flapped her hands like a bird.

"Something far better, yet at the same time I think there might be a bit of flying involved. We will have to see where the Spirit takes us." He winked, opened his Bible, and for a few moments the only sound was the rustle of pages as he searched.

He stopped toward the front of the book and then glanced at each of them, his eyes even brighter. "Are you ready to hear this?" Doug started reading without waiting for a response. He read in a soft voice that built to a crescendo by the end of the passage.

"'How awesome is this place! This is none other than the house of God; this is the gate of heaven.' Genesis 28:17."

"Are you saying—?" Brandon pointed the forefingers of both hands at Doug and then at the sky.

Doug held up his hand and patted the air as if to silence Brandon

and used his other to paw toward the back of his Bible. "'I know a man in Christ who fourteen years ago was caught up to the third heaven. Whether it was in the body or out of the body, I do not know . . . I know that this man . . . was caught up to paradise.'"

Marcus looked up from his ever-present notepad and tapped the air in front of him with his pen. "In an effort to accurately summarize your insinuation, you're articulating the view that we can voyage into supplementary spiritual and heavenly realms with as little exertion as we've expended to journey into the souls of others."

Doug stared at him with a bemused look on his face.

Brandon laughed. "Come on, Professor, give it more effort next time. I'm sure you could have stuck five or six more words in there to make that sentence one only your fellow geek-brains could understand. As it was, I understood over a quarter of it."

"Sorry." Marcus shrugged. "You're saying we can send our spirits into spiritual dimensions other than souls?"

"Yes." Doug winked at Brandon. "I am, and we can."

Brandon stood and pretended to hand something to Doug. "I have to take the gold medal from the current record holder and hand it to you, Doug. I've always thought Reece was the outright winner of the On-the-Fringe Olympics, but you're clearly sprinting past him with this one."

Doug smiled. "This is probably true. But I accept the medal with a humble heart and assure you I was taught by another just as I'm about to teach you." He spread his arms wide. "This evening, my friends, we shall go through the gate and see wonders beyond wonders. Are you ready?"

Dana glanced at the others, then settled her gaze on Doug. "Where is Reece?"

"He's upstairs and he'll be praying for us during the time we leave our bodies and then join us toward the end of the evening when we talk about where we need to go from here."

"He's not coming with us." Dana said it more as a statement than a question.

"No."

"Why not?" Brandon said. "We've sent our spirits into seventy-four souls over the past ten months and he hasn't been along for the ride even once."

Doug hesitated before answering. "He says he feels for the moment he's to stay out of souls and the heavens. That the time hasn't come for him yet to reengage in that way. He feels the three of you are doing powerful work—setting others free, bringing them healing—but it's not for him to join in on that front yet."

Dana folded her arms. "In other words, he's letting the enemy convince him he'd be of no use inside a soul or anywhere else in the heavenly realms without his sight."

"Reece is strong and will join you again when he is ready. In the meantime, we shall extend our friend grace." Doug set down his Bible and held out his hands. "Now, let us have an adventure together that will be most enjoyable."

Dana reached for Marcus's hand on her right, then extended her other hand to Brandon on her left. The moment her fingers touched his, her body went weightless and Reece's living room vanished.

She blinked twice, then opened her eyes fully to find herself floating on a current of air. The sensation was like river rafting down a surging rapid, only faster, but there was no undulation in the atmosphere beneath her. A few feet ahead was Doug. Brandon and Marcus were on either side of her.

She looked down and saw they floated miles above an ocean smooth as glass that extended as far as her eyes could see in every direction. Lush green islands dotted the sea, some massive, some not more than an acre across. Far below, birds, seagulls maybe, rode the same currents that must be gliding them toward the horizon and a massive descending sun.

At first she didn't move, concerned the wind wouldn't hold her up if she did. But after a few minutes she twisted and realized no matter how she turned, it wouldn't affect the river of air around her. She turned to her side, then her back, then onto her stomach, and as

she did, laughter pushed out of her in waves. Dana spun and twisted and was a little girl again, rolling down the tiny green hill in the park near her school and then sailing to the heavens on her old, rusty, light blue swing set in her childhood backyard.

Dana looked for Brandon and spied him to her left and slightly behind doing somersaults through the air. "Whooo-hooooooooo! Try this, Dana!"

She did and her body raced with adrenaline. After seven rotations she stopped. Laughter burst out of her and she grinned at him. His eyes lit up like they did back in the days when they were engaged. Whoops. She needed to dial it back. Be careful. No mixed signals, even in here.

To her right, Marcus flew spread-eagled, the wind whipping around his clothes and through his thinning brown hair like a hurricane, his face a cascade of joy, laughter pouring out of his mouth in a torrent. Even Doug had joined the celebration, doing cartwheels through the air and yelling like a crazed U-Dub football fan.

The whole thing was so natural and so absurd, both at the same time. All fear of the future, all worry about what would happen with Perry and where Brandon fit in her life, the always-present strain of her job slipped away. And whatever scenario the Warriors would face with the Wolf melted away and joy unspeakable buried her.

As they cavorted through the sky, the river of air grew stronger and they picked up speed. After what seemed like hours, Dana squinted toward the horizon again. The sun had sunk lower in the sky and now she saw a thin smear of colors. As they streaked toward it the smear turned into a wall and grew larger till it towered above them, a mile at least, probably more.

The four of them were traveling so fast she doubted they would survive the same velocity on earth. The greens and blues below her blurred. She should be frightened but she couldn't touch even a hint of that emotion. Only an overwhelming sense of love and joy she was sure would explode out of her in seconds. And still they moved faster.

Then the wall of colors was before them, looming too far above to see the top and too far to the sides to take in its vastness. Only seconds now and they would slam into the crimson, emerald, turquoise, gold, and aqua wall and certainly be destroyed, but Dana didn't care. She stretched forward with her fingers and pulled at the air as if swimming, as if she could draw herself into the wall with more speed. And she was laughing and crying and shouting and coming closer to exploding every second.

Then in a flash she reached the wall and smashed into it and she slammed her eyes shut and waited for death to come but it didn't. As she burst through the wall, the sense of love she'd felt earlier was a drop in the Pacific Ocean compared to what she felt now. The colors wrapped themselves around her and pushed into her and through her and each color was a hand of God that held her in infinite tenderness and strength.

Their speed slowed and they flew lower and soon a landscape took form in front of them. She glanced at the others, their faces basking in the splendor of the moment, then back to the world appearing in front of her. Mountains and valleys and deserts and forests and seas grew and vanished as they flew over the splendor.

None of them tried to make conversation. What would they say? Words would crash to the ground in epic failure trying to describe what they'd experienced, what they were feeling, what they'd seen, what they were still seeing.

Finally the birthing of worlds around them slowed, and they stood on a plain that reminded Dana of the Australian outback but this one was more vibrant and the air tingled with . . . she didn't know how to describe it. Life was the only word that made sense.

"Where are we?" Marcus's voice sounded strange.

Doug opened his arms and turned 360 degrees before answering. "'The creation waits in eager expectation for the sons of God to be revealed. For the creation was subjected to frustration, not by its own choice, but by the will of the one who subjected it, in hope that the creation itself will be liberated from its bondage

to decay and brought into the glorious freedom of the children of God.' 'Then I saw a new heaven and a new earth, for the first heaven and the first earth had passed away . . .'"

"What?" Dana made her own turn. "Are you saying this is the new heaven and the new earth?"

Doug laughed. "No, no. That is yet to come. Our eyes will not see that till the age we live in ends and all the sons and daughters become the audience as the Great Artist once again creates what was to have been in the beginning and what will be again for ages to come." He made a sweeping gesture. "This is only a foretaste of what that world will be, and not nearly as glorious as what we will see then."

"This is a foretaste?" Brandon widened his eyes. "It'll be better than this?"

"Oh yes." Doug's eyes were white fire. "My educated guess and hope is what you just experienced is the smallest appetizer of what we shall experience at the wedding feast between Christ and his bride.

"C. S. Lewis had it right when he said, 'If we consider the unblushing promises of reward and the staggering nature of the rewards promised in the Gospels, it would seem that Our Lord finds our desire not too strong, but too weak. We are half-hearted creatures, fooling about with drink and sex and ambition when infinite joy is offered us, we are like ignorant children who want to continue making mud pies in a slum because we cannot imagine what is meant by the offer of a vacation at the sea. We are far too easily pleased.'"

The four of them went silent again, soaking in the world Doug had led them to. Then one by one they stood and walked in four opposite directions.

Dana didn't see the colors around her, she tasted them, didn't look on the water of the streams she passed, she was part of it. The air and light were like food and made the most succulent chocolate torte she'd ever tasted seem like dust by comparison.

Too soon Doug's voice called out from behind her. "It is with great regret I must tell you our time here is finished."

She turned and strolled back toward Doug, wanting each step to last forever, watching Marcus's and Brandon's same slow gait and realizing they felt the same.

When she reached him she stopped and frowned. "Why did you bring us here? I'm not sure the ache of going from this place will ever leave me."

"This is true, but knowing this ahead of time, would you have chosen not to come?"

Doug reached for their hands. "After we've returned we will chat about why I brought you here and the lessons to be learned from voyaging through this realm. Let us go."

The moment her fingers touched Doug's hands her surroundings vanished and her spirit slid back into her body in Reece's cabin. She slipped her hands to her sides and rested them on Reece's couch as she stared at the others' faces. They seemed to reflect light and were so alluring she almost gasped.

Doug chuckled. "You see it in the others, don't you, Dana?"

She shook her head and smiled. "'But we all, with unveiled faces, beholding as in a mirror the glory of the Lord, are being transformed into the same image from glory to glory, just as from the Lord, the Spirit.' From Paul's second letter to the Corinthians, chapter 18."

"Yes, Dana. Yes." Doug patted her hand. "That is right."

Marcus tilted his flushed and bright face toward Doug. "You indicated there was a greater intent behind taking us there than simply to experience utter joy."

"Yes." Doug paused and a cloud came over his eyes. "I wish the only reason was for you to taste that freedom, that joy to come. But it isn't. You needed to see that, to experience the heavenly realms so you know what you are fighting for. Because I fear you'll soon be traveling into other dimensions not so pleasant as the one we just came from. Realms as dark as the one you just experienced are light. Realms where you must take the battle, and where your experience there can inspire and give you strength."

"The Wolf. Doing battle with him," Dana said.

Doug nodded.

Brandon leaned forward in his chair. "Do you know when we'll have to start doing that?"

Doug stood. "Sooner than you or Reece and I would like, I'm afraid."

"Define sooner."

A voice came from the top of the stairs. "We think the attack on each of us will increase in intensity if it hasn't already." Reece clumped down the staircase and eased over to his leather chair. "That's not a surprise, at least it shouldn't be. I will admit I've been on the ropes for the past two or three weeks. And this afternoon I had a conversation indicative of what kinds of things we can expect from the people around us. Do you remember Tamera?" Reece paused. "She's not happy with us."

"Good to see you, Reece." Dana immediately regretted her phrasing but if Reece took offense it didn't show in his face or gestures.

"Why's she putting on the frowny face?" Brandon puckered his lips.

"She wants to be a deeper part of our fellowship than the Spirit wants her to be. I'm not worried about it, but it is an indication of the enemy trying to whack the hornet's nest. Which means we need to be on alert more than ever." He clapped his hands on the armrests of his chair. "Enough of that. It's good for all of us to be together again. I trust you enjoyed what Doug had to show you?"

Dana laughed and the others joined her. "You could say that."

"I'm glad." Reece smiled. "Next time I intend to go with you."

Doug meandered over to where Reece sat and laid a hand on his shoulder. "We welcome that with open hearts and great anticipation." He released Reece's shoulder and sat in the chair next to the big man. "Now, let's talk about next steps."

Marcus opened his notebook and clicked his mechanical pencil twice. "You're finally going to tell us about the Wolf?"

Reece turned his head toward Doug as if he could see him,

then turned back to the others. "We are very close to that day, yes. Very close. But first we have to take your training up a notch."

"Do you care to give a clarifying descriptor of 'up a notch'?" Marcus said.

"We'll meet again on Friday night, and during that time the three of you will face a rather arduous test. I don't think it prudent to share anything more than that, but I will encourage you to be in prayer and stay in close communion with the Spirit."

"Anything else?" Dana asked.

"Only this: if the test goes well, Doug and I will tell you what we know about the Wolf, and we will all begin to form our strategy for engaging him in battle."

As Dana drove home, Reece's words filled her thoughts. *Lord, how will the enemy come after me?* Just before she turned into her driveway, a picture of her radio station flashed into her mind and she had the distinct feeling she would soon have a great deal of free time on her hands.

TWELVE

"ROBERT IS WAITING FOR YOU."

Dana's executive assistant spoke the words softly on Monday afternoon but Rebecca might as well have shouted them. Dana had found out first thing that morning that her general manager wanted to meet with her and even though she'd had a premonition of this the night before, it still surprised her.

"Deep breath, face the music," Dana said under her breath as she walked toward Robert's office. "God is in this." The hallway smelled like carpet cleaners had been there the night before. A fitting symbol for the cleaning her GM was about to do. She reached his door and came to a halt. Another deep breath and a quick prayer for composure. She would find another job. Or Reece could subsidize her to become the official Well Spring photographer. She closed her eyes and imagined the scene about to unfold.

She would step inside, sit on her GM's plush leather couch, and after polite greetings he would say something like, "Although you've done a wonderful job for this company over the years, we think it's time for us to mutually agree it's best for all concerned parties if we go our separate ways."

Then they would negotiate a severance package both Corporate and she could live with, she would pack her things, head home, turn off her alarm, and sleep till noon.

The meeting shouldn't have shocked her. Dana couldn't blame them. All the time she'd been spending on Warriors Riding, all the trips she'd taken to Well Spring to take part in the training sessions had cut into her focus at the station. Her heart was torn between the Warriors and the station and her intensity at the station had waned as her heart and strength went more and more to the mission Reece and Doug were taking them on.

Sure, all the days she'd taken off were from accrued vacation time she'd earned but it didn't mean it was okay. And while her budgets had only been off 3 percent over the past three quarters, she was still 3 percent off. And when her goals were for 7 percent growth, it meant she and her team were consistently underperforming by 10 percent. Not acceptable. Stockholders didn't care if she had the time off coming. And neither did her GM.

She glanced at Robert's executive assistant and he nodded at the door. Dana knocked once and walked in. Oh boy. This wasn't a one-on-one meeting. Next to Robert stood the head of the Seattle division—Spencer Benning—the suit from Corporate who visited a few times a year at most. Great. Two against one.

Spencer smiled, strode over to her, and offered his hand. "Great to see you, Dana. It's been at least a year."

"I think you're right." She shook his hand and offered a thin smile. "It's good to see you as well."

Robert and Spencer sat and he motioned to the couch across from them. She sat in the middle, her hands clasped on her lap. "I'd like to make a request in regard to this meeting."

"All right." Spencer glanced at Robert, then back to her.

"Can we forgo the pleasantries and the details of why you're letting me go and get right to work on a severance package we both agree is fair?"

Spencer glanced at Robert again, then leaned forward, picked up two white folders, and handed one to Dana and one to her GM. "Before we do, I'd like to go over a few figures."

Dana bit her lower lip and stayed silent. This was exactly what

she had hoped to avoid but it was obvious her final wish would not be granted. *Go with it. Play the stupid game. It won't kill you.*

"Let's start by taking a look at your team's sales performance over the past four quarters—2 percent down, 3 percent down, 2 1/2 percent down, 1 percent down, and based on current budgets for this quarter you'll finish at 1 1/2 percent down over the previous year."

This was a complete waste of time. She didn't need to look at these figures. They'd been a splinter in her brain every day for the past year. It had irritated her and made her come up with sales and promotional packages that brought in more revenue than if she hadn't. But it wasn't as important as what was going on with the Warriors Riding and at Well Spring. A year ago she would have found a way to meet her sales goal. Whatever it took, it didn't matter. Now it mattered.

Dana nodded. "Yes, down a little less than 3 percent on average."

"That's correct." Spencer turned a page. "Look at the next page."

Dana turned the page and looked at a chart tracking her station's rating performance.

"You're probably intimately aware that we've had some programming challenges on your station. Changing program directors twice in one year has not helped. Regardless, budgets still need to be set and met. Not reaching them isn't an option."

Another recap of the obvious. Why were they putting her through this?

"This next page is the Miller Kaplan report for the past year— again a report you've probably glanced at more than once."

This time they were wrong. She hadn't looked at the Miller Kaplan for at least eighteen months. She wasn't sure why. Probably because Robert never paid it much attention and never used it to evaluate her performance. Did it matter what other stations were doing compared to hers? The goal was the goal was the goal as had just been stated.

"As you can see, you've outperformed every station with similar

ratings to yours and your revenue is even ahead of five stations who have up to 15 percent higher ratings."

He tossed the packet on the coffee table in front of him, sat back, and crossed his legs. "That includes three stations here in our own group."

"You're not going to fire me?" Dana blurted out the thought without giving consideration to how stupid it would sound. She glanced at her GM who offered an affirming smile.

"This is true. We had hoped to go in a bit different direction."

Robert slid a sheet of paper across the glass coffee table and tapped it twice. "Before you look at that sheet let me apologize. Based on your request at the start of this meeting we obviously have done a poor job of conveying our view of your performance and what we think of you. With that in mind, take a moment to peruse this sheet that will give you a better feel of what our thoughts are with regard to your future with this company."

Dana picked up the paper. It took only ten seconds to read but she stared at the words and figures for over a minute.

- Dana Raine new position: station general manager
- Salary: $285,000
- Vacation days: six weeks paid
- Bonus structure: Immediate $15,000, and $15,000 per percentage point over goal each quarter from the previous year
- Start date: May 20

Was this real? She looked up. "You're promoting me." Another obvious comment, but they didn't seem to take offense.

"Yes." Spencer smiled. "You've done an excellent job. And not only with the numbers. As surprising as this might seem we do care about more than the bottom line. We care how our leaders treat the people they lead. Why? Because people do better in an atmosphere where they feel encouraged, believed in, and fought for. We know

you've stood in the gap for your salespeople. We know you fight for them in promotion meetings. We know you've gone far above and way beyond to make sure they're appreciated. When people have a leader like that, most of them will overachieve. Which you can see from the Miller Kaplan, they have done and continue to do.

"I guess in that sense that brings us back to the numbers so maybe that is all we care about." He laughed. "We talked to your salespeople and eight of the nine said your leadership over the past ten months has been stellar. Better than it's ever been."

"I . . . I thought . . . I don't know what to say."

"Say yes to a significant advance in your career."

"I didn't apply for this. I didn't even know you were looking for a new GM."

Robert leaned forward, elbows on his knees. "They tell me I've had a good run here, Dana. Good enough that I'm being bumped up." He smiled and waved his thumb at Spencer. "I'm taking his role, so someone needs to fill mine. They're going to let me work out of Seattle, so we'll still get to work together." He pointed to the sheet in her hands. "So what do you say? Would you do me the honor of succeeding me?"

She glanced at the paper in her hands, then up to her GM. "Yes."

The rest of the meeting was a blur. She thanked both of them, shook their hands, and stood, her body numb. They told her to be expecting a contract on her desk in the morning and to take her time looking it over and have her attorney look it over as well.

Dana was still in a daze as she pushed open her office door and slumped against her desk. Really? Had she really just been offered the chance to run the station? She'd been noticed. She'd been seen.

And suddenly life was good.

Sure, it was balanced out on the negative side with wanting a special person in her life and having no prospects on the horizon, not to mention her weird quasi relationship with Brandon. But still, on the whole her life felt solid and the future was full of

hope. Warriors Riding continued to propel her deeper with Jesus than she'd ever imagined was possible and they were doing amazing things for the kingdom. The school at Well Spring was going extremely well and now this promotion? If this was the enemy's attack she wanted more.

THIRTEEN

MARCUS PUSHED THROUGH HIS FRONT DOOR AT SIX THIRTY on Monday evening, the smell of spaghetti filling the small entryway of his home. His gaze fell on the picture of an eight-year-old Layne sitting on the credenza next to the coat closet, reminding Marcus for the millionth time of what he'd done.

No, take every thought captive. It was over and he couldn't go back.

You've been forgiven.

The words of the Spirit were hollow in his mind, the pain in his soul like thunder. But he'd gut through it just like he always did this time of year.

Kat peered around the corner of the kitchen as he took off his shoes and pushed them toward the basket next to the front door. "Hey." She winked at him and disappeared back inside the kitchen.

He walked up to the kitchen door and stood in the entry. "I thought I was supposed to cook tonight."

"You were, but I got home early and figured I'd get things started."

"Sorry I'm late."

"You're not that late." Kat glanced at the clock on the wall above the breakfast nook. "How was your day stimulating young minds?"

"Not as strange as Friday." He set his satchel down on the kitchen counter and gave Kat a quick kiss. "I swear I stepped into

two different versions of your shop. It wasn't a dream. It wasn't a vision."

"But you decided to let it go. So do it."

"You're right, you're right, I know you're right."

"Then truly release it and enjoy the evening, okay? You haven't been sleeping. You've been stressed over this possible book deal with Tim, and you're always a little out of sorts on the first day of a new quarter. Isn't it possible your mind was playing tricks on you?"

"Yes."

"Could you say that with a little less enthusiasm?"

Marcus laughed and lifted his hands in surrender. "Let me change and I'll set the table."

"No need. We're eating in the dining room tonight."

"What?"

"We're having a dinner guest tonight and you're going to be nice." Kat glared at him, a paring knife in her right hand pointed directly at him.

A dinner guest? This couldn't be good. If he hadn't been consulted on the occasion it meant the guest was one of Abbie's or Jayla's friends. And it wouldn't be Jayla's. Her friends didn't come for dinner. Neither did Abbie's unless they happened to be over and Kat extended an impromptu invitation. Which gave high credence to the hypothesis that this guest was not female.

"There's a boy coming to dinner tonight? Here?"

"Come on." Kat put her hands on her hips. "How did you know that?"

"It didn't take a great deal of analytical prowess to reach that conclusion."

"Yes, it's a boy." Kat turned and stirred the spaghetti sauce.

"From where? How old is he?"

"A friend of Abbie's from high school. He's seventeen."

"I seem to have acquired a considerable amount of wax in my ears in the past two seconds. I thought you just said he was seventeen."

Kat spun and glared at Marcus again. "Your ears are fine."

"This *boy* is three years older than Abbie?"

"Yes, he's a senior this year."

"She's not going to date anyone, let alone a young *man* who is three years older than she is."

"She's not dating. This isn't a date. They're just getting to know each other. As friends."

"Coming to the parents' house is more than just getting to know each other. And no seventeen-year-old is simply a friend of a fourteen-year-old girl."

"Would you rather she hid it from us?"

"How long have you known about this?"

Kat set down the knife, sashayed over to Marcus, and slid her fingers under the collar of his shirt. "How old were you when you went on your first date?"

"If memory serves me accurately, twenty-three."

"We were married at twenty-three."

"Then my first date must have been at twenty-two."

"Do I need to remind you of what your father used to say about your dating habits during your teen years? That you had more girl-friends than fleas on a dirty dog's back?"

"That wasn't until I was at least . . . seventeen."

"Try fourteen. The same age as your daughter. I remember stuff like that, remember?"

"The dating equations that pertain to boys are severely different when applied to girls."

"Care to explain that?"

"I was that age once. I understand fully what is going through a teenage boy's mind."

"And what is that?"

"Have you met this kid who has hormones racing all through his body like a particle accelerator?"

Kat nodded.

"And?"

She took a loaf of sourdough bread off the counter and put it in the oven. "You'll like him the second you meet him, I promise."

"I'm sure I will." Marcus gritted his teeth. "And when will said senior in high school be arriving?"

"He's in the family room with Abbie. Dinner will be ready in ten minutes. Remember, be nice, if not for his sake, for the sake of your relationship with Abbie."

Marcus frowned. "It's not right."

"What's not right? Calen is charming, handsome, an athlete, gets decent grades from what Abbie says . . . goes to youth group—he's the total package."

"That's the kind of description that worries me."

"Why?"

"I don't like perfect people. They're usually not."

"Don't be worried. I'm sure he has flaws like the rest of us. And maybe this is God's way of bringing a little light into what has been an unusual past year, to say the least."

Marcus headed upstairs and tried to wrap his mind around the idea of Abbie dating a seventeen-year-old. It wouldn't be easy.

☩ ☩ ☩

"Good to meet you, Mr. Amber." The kid shook his hand with a firm grip and looked right in Marcus's eyes when he spoke. His smile was relaxed and he didn't hang back but wasn't overly eager.

"You too, Calen. Welcome to our home."

"Thanks." Calen hooked his thumbs on the front of his belt, then immediately released one of his hands and pointed at the bookshelves to his left. "I'm trying to read your book."

"Trying?"

Calen's face flushed a pinch. "I'm dyslexic and reading has always been a challenge. So it takes longer for me to read books than most people."

"Calen has a 3.75 GPA," Abbie said and smiled at Marcus.

Dyslexic? And still got good grades? Great. Could this situation get any more clichéd? Sir Calen was not only a star but circumvented his weaknesses to light the way for others with learning disabilities. When dinner was over, Marcus would be shocked if the kid didn't propose to clear the table and do all the dishes.

He needed to relax. Why couldn't he accept Kat's idea that God was bringing something good into Abbie's life? Because he wasn't ready for another male to waltz into Abbie's world and become her main influence at the same time he was starting to find his way back into her heart.

True, he'd alienated her by spending far too much time on his career at the university when she was younger, but he'd been more than on board for the past two years. And lately their relationship had grown significantly better.

After they were seated, Marcus said a quick prayer and watched Kat gracefully steer the conversation. "Abbie tells me you're new in town."

"Yeah, we've been here for only a month but it's been great so far." Calen glanced at Abbie. "But like it says in John's gospel, the wind blows where it will, and I have to think the Spirit brought us to Seattle for a reason." He glanced at Abbie again and she flushed and gave him a shy smile.

⊹ ⊹ ⊹

That night as they lay in bed Marcus tried to accept the fact Abbie wasn't ten anymore. Or even twelve.

"Don't blow it." Kat patted his leg.

"Something is off about this kid."

"No, for you there is. No one else. Something is going to be off for you with every guy Abbie brings home. It's okay to feel that way but your feelings don't make it true."

"A large part of me cannot comprehend that we're having this discussion."

"Be wise." Kat poked him in the shoulder. "I mean it. This is a good kid. Yes, he's a senior but he's good for her. Haven't you seen it? She's lighter than she's been in a year and it's good for your relationship with her. Tell me you saw that tonight. And that you're not going to crush her."

"What are you insinuating?"

"That he asked her to the prom tonight, and when she tells you, you're going to smile and congratulate her."

"What? Wait a minute. When did this turn from 'a friend' to going to the prom? Let me guess, you wanted to ease me into it? Meet the kid, agree he's great, then roll over and say yes?"

"You and Abbie have done pretty well over the past several months. If you're going to tell her she can't go with Calen I suggest you do it with a great deal of tenderness and tact."

"She's just a little girl."

"I wish that were true."

"It is true."

"It's not."

"I don't care if she's twenty."

Kat didn't answer and turned over. Within minutes she was asleep. Slumber didn't come for Marcus till nearly an hour later. And fifty minutes of prayer didn't get him any closer to knowing what he was going to do.

✠ ✠ ✠

The next evening at nine thirty Abbie slumped onto the couch in their family room next to Kat and skewered him with her eyes. "This is where you tell me I can't go to the prom with Calen, right?"

"I'm only saying I want to discuss it."

"Let's cut to the final scene, Dad. Do you approve or not approve? Can I go or not?"

"He seems like a nice kid but—"

"He's not a *kid*! He's a senior and he's almost eighteen years old. He's nearly an adult."

Marcus took a deep breath. "Exactly."

"What does that mean?"

"He seems like a nice *adult* but—"

"But I'm too young to date, he's too much older than me, blah, blah, blah, and I can't go to the prom with him."

"I'm just trying to—"

Abbie grabbed the back of her long red hair and pulled down, her eyes closed. "To what, Dad? Protect me? Keep me from getting my heart broken? I just want to go to a dance together and if that goes well maybe a movie. Take a hike in the mountains. Go to a Sounders game together. Hang out with him at youth group. I'm not going to bed the guy."

"Abbie!"

"What?" She kicked the coffee table and yanked her arms across her chest.

"Statistically young girls . . . women . . . who start dating early have a much greater chance of winding up in relationships that will hurt them and taint their marriages for years to come. I know emotionally this doesn't register with you, but please consider the logic of this." He glanced at Kat for support but she shook her head. "You're only fourteen years old and you'll have years of time to date when you're older."

"Technically I've lived on earth for fourteen years so I'm really in my fifteenth year of living."

"Abbie."

She scowled. "Marcus."

"Don't call me that."

"Then be my dad, not a professor lecturing me on the ills of holding hands with a boy at my age. Can't you trust me just a little bit? I've prayed about this by myself and with Mom and I'm not blind."

He stared at her pleading eyes and an image of the dinner

they'd had almost a year ago at the Space Needle flashed into his mind. And the times since then where they'd watched TV together, went for mountain bike rides, and how her face lit up for a few seconds when he framed a picture he'd taken of her playing soccer and gave it to her for no reason at all. He didn't want to lose the ground they'd gained.

And logic? Yes, it was logical to let her go. It was one date. She wasn't getting engaged. And he could keep a very close eye on where things went from here with Calen.

"Okay, you can go." The words sputtered out of his mouth, and the moment they did he wished he could take them back.

Abbie leaped from the couch and threw her arms around his shoulders. "Thanks, Dad. I'm so glad I don't have to cut you out of my will now."

Marcus tried to smile. "Me too." He stood and glanced at Kat who mouthed, *Well done*. Then he walked out of the room and upstairs, trying to ignore the sensation in his stomach telling him he'd made an extremely poor decision.

✠ ✠ ✠

Marcus sat at his desk in his den. *You made the appropriate choice.* But had he? Where was the line between being a strong father and protecting his daughter and letting her go? How much of their strained relationship played into it—should play into it? Had he let her go just to keep their relationship going in the right direction? Did it mean he'd always be a slave to Abbie's desires? The desires of a fourteen-year-old?

A shuffle of feet in his doorway made him look up. Kat, with a smile on her face.

"Thoughts?" he said.

"You hit a few bumps, swerved a few times, but got the car back on the road by the end of the conversation." Kat eased over to his walnut desk and leaned against it.

"I hope we're even supposed to be on this stretch of the highway."

"I'm thinking what's left of today still has enough to worry about, so why don't we put tomorrow's worries off till tomorrow?"

"Well said."

"Are you coming to bed?" She turned to go.

"In a few minutes. I need some time to wind down."

"Don't think too hard. It's all going to work out." As Kat left, his den light flashed off her wedding ring and Marcus glanced around his den. Everything looked exactly the same.

He leaned back in his chair, closed his eyes, and stayed that way for a long time. He needed to relax. Trust that God had Abbie in his hands. He repeated the idea to himself along with verses that seemed like clichés. Finally he opened his eyes and came forward. Time for bed. Kat was probably already asleep.

He pulled a couple of pens out of his pocket and tossed them onto his desk. They came to rest against a small stack of photos tucked underneath a book he'd been studying. He reached for them and slowly drew them closer. He didn't remember the photos being there the day before yesterday. Were they? Marcus lifted the stack and his pulse spiked. Whether the photos had been there or not was irrelevant because the one on the top of the stack shouldn't exist.

FOURTEEN

MARCUS SLUMPED BACK IN THE LEATHER CHAIR IN HIS den and stared at the photo clutched in his hand as if it were proof UFOs were real. Where had the shot been taken? He racked his brain for the answer but his mind offered no solutions.

The picture was of Dave Damrell and him standing on the top of a rocky, nondescript cliff, their arms wrapped around each other's shoulders, wide grins under their mirrored sunglasses. A sweeping view of snowcapped peaks forty or fifty miles behind them appeared to be an ideal backdrop to capture a memory of male bonding.

The only problem was, Marcus had no recollection of the picture being taken or where he and Dave were standing. He turned the photo over. Eight words on the back, scrawled in his handwriting, made his body go numb: *On top of Little Annapurna—Enchantments trip '93.*

Was this some kind of joke? The first four photos were of jade-green alpine lakes and sweeping mountain views and goats with molting fur. But the last one was of Dave and him on a trip in the summer of '93 he didn't go on.

The trip he'd regretted missing ever since. Dave, Ricky Totten, and Mark Effinger had all gone and raved about it for years afterward—needled him was a more accurate description—and he'd

never forgiven himself for canceling at the last minute so he could . . . Marcus couldn't even remember why he'd thrown the trip away. Probably studying for a test for his PhD.

He turned the other photos over. There was a lack of notation on them. He set the photo of Dave and him in the center of his desk and shoved the other pictures to his right. A thick sensation of dread grew in the center of his stomach. There was no logical explanation for how this photo could exist. But it did.

"Would you like to explain to me what has just occurred, Lord? Along with the scenes in the bakery? Are they tied together?"

He clutched the photos in his hands and tiptoed out of the den toward his bedroom. The door creaked as he opened it—he had to WD-40 those hinges. The lights were off and Kat's rhythmic breathing told him she was asleep. He turned and eased back to the den. He needed to talk to someone now. Reece? No. That would be a ghastly choice. Their leader didn't need anything reminding him that taking or looking at photos would likely not be in his immediate—let alone long-term—future.

Brandon. He was most likely still up and Marcus didn't have to explain what had happened on the Ave last Friday. He pulled out his phone and dialed the Song.

"Professor. You have a physics question for me?"

"Sorry to call late."

"I'll be up for another hour at least. Talk to me."

"I found a photo of myself standing on a mountain I couldn't have been standing on."

"Cool."

"No, not cool." Marcus explained what happened. "I need to know where that photo came from."

"Do you feel like something weird spiritually is going on?"

Nothing in his spirit felt off in the slightest. Once again the situation felt neutral. "It feels the same."

"What's he do for a living?"

"What does who do for a living?"

"Your pal Dave. How does he produce cash-o-la? Put bread on the table, you know?"

"He teaches computers and video production at a junior high school." Marcus leaned back, his leather chair bumping up against his bookshelves.

"Ah yes, that makes perfect sense. Which I believe gives us the answer to your one-question quiz."

"I'm not following you."

"Hello?" Brandon laughed. "I thought you were supposed to have the exceptional mind, Prof."

"Apparently stumbling upon photos I know weren't part of my life has stunted the flow of blood to my prefrontal cortex." Marcus bit his lower lip and continued to stare at the picture.

"Would it be in the nature of this buddy of yours to do some Photoshopping as a practical joke?"

"You're brilliant." Marcus smiled as relief flooded his body.

"Thank you very much . . ." Brandon did a bad Elvis impersonation. "Ol' Dave is a practical joker, huh?"

"He rightfully holds the title of emperor. The twentieth anniversary of the hike is coming up later this summer and this is precisely the kind of thing Dave would do to remind me of my . . ." Marcus trailed off.

"Regret?"

"Yeah."

"And even though Dave snuck the photos into your house and stuck them on your desk in fun, it's the perfect circumstance for the enemy to use to make you wallow in what didn't happen, right?"

"Well said." Marcus spun his chair back around and gazed out the window at the dark night.

"Take it captive. No regrets. Fight back. Speak truth and all that."

"Thank you, Brandon. I will." Marcus hung up and set his phone down. Finally, a mystery solved. As he hunched farther over his desk to examine the job Dave had done, the light from his emerald-green

banker's lamp flashed off his sliver letter opener. Marcus blinked against the glare, pulled his glasses off, and rubbed his eyes. When he opened them again perspiration broke out on the back of his neck and forehead. The photos were gone.

✠ ✠ ✠

Marcus grabbed his phone and redialed Brandon. "They vanished."

"Professor?"

"Yes, of course, who else?"

"What vanished?"

"The photos. They're gone. I closed my eyes, opened them, and they disappeared."

"Okay . . . I'm sure at some point you're going to tell me what you're talking about, but how 'bout you do it now?"

"I just talked to you!" Marcus wiped the sweat from his forehead. "The photos of the backpacking trip I didn't go on. Determining where they might have come from."

"You all right, Prof?"

The pounding of Marcus's heart filled his ears. "No."

"I'm guessing you had another one of whatever happened to you on the Ave the other day."

"Yes."

"Was it a vision this time? Maybe?" Brandon said. "Something the Spirit was taking you through to have you face a regret and work through it?"

"Not possible."

Brandon gave a fake cough. "So your vast experience of having one vision makes you an expert?"

"No, but this wasn't a vision. It happened. It was real."

"Just because you know it makes it true?"

"I had a conversation with you."

"That makes it not a vision? Why couldn't you have a conversation with someone in your vision? John talked to Jesus quite

extensively during the vision that became the book of Revelation." Brandon paused. "So in your wildest imagination, what do you think is going on?"

"A possibility I haven't wanted to admit to myself or anyone else since it happened the first time." Marcus sighed.

"That your book is more than theory? That you've been taking little jaunts into alternate realities?"

"Exactly."

"Anything else?"

"Yes. That this is only the beginning."

FIFTEEN

BRANDON GLANCED AT THE PARKING LOT ON WEDNESDAY evening, hoping Dana would show up first. He sat on the grass in the middle of Houghton Beach Park in Kirkland on the shores of Lake Washington, wanting to talk to her but not having a clue what he would say. He glanced at his watch. Six thirty-five. Dana and Marcus were both twenty minutes late.

Except for two couples and a family with a toddler, the vast green lawn in front of the water was empty. He stared at a boat making its way across the lake in front of the park and pictured Dana and him on it together with a couple of kids. Ridiculous. Would never happen.

"Hey."

Brandon turned at the sound. Dana. "Nice of you to show up."

"Thank you."

"You could have told me you'd be late."

Dana scowled, sat beside him, and pointed at his cell phone sitting between them. "I did."

Brandon tapped the text icon on his cell phone. There were two messages, one from Dana, one from Marcus. "Oh. Sorry to accuse you falsely." He slipped his phone into his pocket. "Marcus says he'll be here in five."

Brandon shifted forward and tried to ignore the fact this was the first time he'd been with Dana alone since last year on the way

to the hospital to see Reece after he lost his eyes. Sitting here alone with her felt right and awkward at the same time. Did she feel it? He certainly wasn't going to ask her.

"Did you get held up at the station again?"

"No, early dinner with a friend. I lost track of time."

"Anyone I know?"

Dana flushed and gazed at Lake Washington. Interesting. A tinge of jealousy flared inside Brandon. Stupid. There was no reason to be feeling anything. Why couldn't he get it through his thick head there would never be anything between them ever again? He pushed the emotion down, but it was like rubber and bounced right back to the surface.

"What's his name?"

"Why do you think it was a guy?"

"Because I know you."

"You don't. Not anymore."

Brandon grinned and wrapped his arms around his legs. "Yeah I do."

"I thought we were here to talk about Reece, Doug, and pray for strength for them as we get ready to go after the Wolf."

"I'm sure we will once Marcus gets here. Does your friend have a name?"

"Perry, but I'm not sure why that should concern you."

"No concern, just curious."

She was right. It was none of his business and there was no reason to press her about it. He should stop and change subjects, let it go. He pulled off his sunglasses. "Do you like him?"

She sighed and turned the back of her head to him. "At one point, yes. But now we're just friends and I needed to make sure he's going to keep it that way."

He stared at her till she turned her head back around, then raised one ear like he always used to do when he didn't believe her. It irked her in the old days and he could tell it irked her now.

"Can we please drop this?"

"Have you ever been more than friends with this guy? Have his lips been on yours in the past six months?"

Dana spun cross-legged on the grass till she faced him and pointed her forefinger at his chest. "If we weren't in the Warriors together I wouldn't even bother to answer you. But since we are, listen very closely. If I had put my lips on another man's during the time we were dating or the time we were engaged, it would have been your business. I would have asked Jesus for forgiveness and then asked for yours. But that's not the situation." She plucked a finger full of grass and tossed it into the breeze coming off the lake.

"So if you can explain to me why you should concern yourself with my social life, I'll give you all the details. But if you can't, please leave me alone on the subject of my love life."

Brandon widened his eyes and fell backward. "Okay!"

"Don't mock me."

"Sorry, I just thought we were doing better than this. That it might be okay if I asked what was going on with you outside of the Warriors. You know, the healing may be changing the way you relate to people and everything."

Dana scooted around so she faced the lake again. "That healing was one of the greatest moments of my life, and yes, we've worked well together but that doesn't mean you can try to peel back my dating life and probe me for answers like I'm on a witness stand."

"You're part of me because you're part of the team, one-fourth of the prophecy. I need to know how to pray for you and—"

"That's why you are asking? So you can pray for me better?"

"I'm only thinking about—"

"Yourself. You're wondering if our relationship could leap back onto the highway it used to be on because we've found some healing from the past. Right?"

Heat rose to Brandon's face and he didn't answer.

"You know me? Well I know you too, so let me help you out. Yes, we will be friends. Yes, we'll probably be connected for a long

time because of the prophecy and what God is doing with Warriors Riding. But you and I more than what we are now? No chance. Let it go. That time is irrevocably gone. I thought you would have figured that out over the past ten months."

"Dana, I—"

"Put it out of your mind. Whatever was wrong with me when you broke our engagement is probably still there."

"Come on. You know I didn't break up because of you, but because I was scared you'd leave after I gave you all of my heart." Brandon tugged his fingers through the turf. "Like my mom did."

"Give up the idea of us. Forever." Dana stared at the lake. "For both of our sakes."

Brandon blinked and didn't try to hide his pain. She would take one look at him and know it anyway. She'd always been able to read his eyes. She'd told him his eyes turned a shade darker when his sorrow ran deep, so they were probably two shades darker now. He thought he was over her, over them. Wrong. He turned to her, not sure what he would say, but as he started to speak he spied Marcus over her shoulder ambling toward them.

"There's the professor."

"Thank goodness," Dana muttered.

Marcus settled down next to them. "Everything okay?"

"Great," Brandon said.

"Fine." Dana gave the professor a thin smile.

"Liars."

Both Dana and Brandon laughed and it broke the tension.

"I apologize for being detained, and not to hurry things but can we get right to the subject at hand?"

"Yes." Dana placed her palms on the grass and stared at the ground. She opened her mouth to speak but stopped as she glanced over Brandon's shoulder.

Brandon turned. Two men strolled their direction. One had brown hair and was probably in his late twenties or early thirties. He was a little shorter than average with a lean build and a baseball

hat turned backward on his head. The man next to him looked like he'd probably enjoyed deluxe double-bacon cheeseburgers a few times too many and was trying to cover it up with a Hawaiian shirt straight out of the sixties. Reece would love it.

They stopped three yards away. "Are you Brandon Scott, the fiction writer?"

"The what?" Brandon laughed. "The writer?" He'd heard "the musician" thousands of times, but "the writer"? Never. Where in the world would they get that idea? He'd started a blog three weeks ago but his name wasn't on it and he hadn't told anyone about it. Not Kevin, not Doug. Not even Marcus, Dana, or Reece.

"Yeah, the writer or blogger or whatever it is. The one who writes at www.godeeper.me. Isn't that you?"

"Why do you think it's me?" Brandon frowned and apprehension shot through him.

The guy with the baseball hat flipped his thumb back and forth between himself and Hawaiian Shirt Man. "We're techies. And big fans of your music. So when we were doing a little searching online we found traces you left that identify you as the owner of the site."

"I didn't think I left a trail."

"Yeah, most non-techies think that."

"Right." Brandon grimmaced and glanced at Marcus and Dana, then back to the man.

"Are you kidding me?" Dana tapped him on the elbow. "You have a blog?"

The guy with the baseball cap continued, "You're prolific. Three posts a week with almost six hundred words each time—that's a lot of verbiage. And the story you're writing is certainly intriguing. The ideas in it are, uh, not commonplace within Christendom."

Dana leaned in. "What kind of story are you writing?"

"I'm a little in shock anyone is reading it."

Hawaiian Shirt Man smiled and motioned to his friend. "Both of us are reading it."

Brandon turned to Dana and Marcus. "I started writing a story on a blog."

"We deduced that rather easily," Marcus said. "But not as private as you intended. Why didn't you simply write it on your computer?"

"What inspired the name of the story?" Cap Man sat and the other man did as well. "Do you mind if we sit down?"

"Uh . . ." Brandon glanced at Dana and Marcus who stayed silent. "No, fine."

Dana poked Brandon's shoulder. "Let me guess. You're basically making a story out of everything that's happened to us over the past year in a thinly veiled exposé for the world to read and see?"

"No one is supposed to see it." Brandon shrugged. "At least not yet."

"Wonderful." Dana slumped back on her arms. "What's the tagline?"

Hawaiian Shirt Man grinned. "'Skating on the edge of the universe.'" He motioned to Cap Man. "We like it. It sounds like us." The man rubbed his hands together. "How close to the edge do you get?"

"Who are you guys?"

The man with the baseball cap said, "I'm Jotham, and this is Orson. We're both 'Softies' and we love the Mariners. Now you know our entire lives."

"Orson?" Brandon said.

"It's a nickname."

"Okay." Brandon pointed at Orson. "And you're 'Softies'?"

"Microsoft," Dana said. "They both work for Microsoft."

"Got it."

Jotham leaned forward. "So, how close to the edge?"

Something about these guys seemed . . . different. Not evil, just different.

"Close."

Jotham turned and grinned at Orson, then shifted his gaze back to Brandon. "Do you really believe all that stuff you're writing in the

story? I mean, have you really truly been going into other people's souls, or are you simply having fun?"

"It's a story, not nonfiction."

"Really? That surprises me. The way you're writing it gave me the impression it's more than a story to you."

"Why do you say that?"

"Let's just say I'm reading between the lines."

These guys were playing a game and were a lot smarter than they were letting on. "Let's just say you're going to tell me how you acquired your between-the-lines reading skills."

"It's pretty obvious for anyone with eyes to see."

Brandon glanced at Marcus and Dana, then back to Jotham and Orson. He still didn't get the sense these two were evil, but there was more to them under the surface and Brandon had a feeling the lake was deep. They liked the Mariners? Good. He decided to throw them a fastball.

"You're right, it's not fiction." He motioned toward Dana and Marcus. "My friends and I send our spirits inside other people's souls to help set them free."

Jotham nodded and the expression on his face didn't change. Either he didn't understand what Brandon had said or he was trying to play it cool. "Ah yes. That makes sense now given the story you've been telling."

"You're not surprised?"

"No."

"This is something you're familiar with?"

"I am." Jotham motioned again to his companion. "We are."

"Who are you guys again?" Dana said.

Before they could answer, the attention of all of them was stolen by a tall man who strode toward them over the grass, a big smile on his face. Brandon smirked. Why didn't it surprise him? Tristan Barrow, his own personal blond-haired stalker, had appeared once again.

He pulled up between all of them and glanced back and forth. "I see you've met my friends, Brandon." He sat and smiled at Marcus and Dana. "Can I meet yours?"

The guy was too comfortable, too confident, too assuming.

"Make yourself at home." Brandon glared at him.

"Thanks, I appreciate that." Tristan ignored Brandon's look and addressed Dana and Marcus. "Did Brandon tell you he and I met a few nights back after one of his concerts?"

Dana and the professor shook their heads and eyed Tristan with wariness, and Dana scooted a few inches backward. "And now you've bumped into him again. Something tells me this isn't a chance encounter."

"That's true, Dana. It's not."

Tristan didn't continue so Brandon asked the obvious follow-up question. "Then at what point are you going to explain why you're stalking me?"

"Not just you, Brandon, all three of you. And Reece as well. And to a lesser extent, Doug." Tristan smiled as he said it but no one else joined him.

Marcus pressed his glasses closer to his face and frowned. "Since you've been forthcoming with your behavior perhaps you would be so kind as to describe your intent."

"Simple." Tristan glanced at his friends. "To help you."

"And if we don't want your help?" Dana said.

Tristan winked, the look in his eyes playful, as if he were answering a child. "We've taken enough of your time. It's good to meet all of you." Tristan and the other two men stood in unison. "Maybe we'll run into you again someday."

"Yeah, maybe. Maybe not," Brandon said.

The three strolled out of the park as if they were on a tour of the Seattle Art Museum. As soon as they were out of earshot Dana said, "Demons? Angels? Christians? Overeager fans? New Agers? Something else?"

Brandon scoffed. "Not thinking those three are angels, and I

didn't get anything remotely demonic. Maybe they're just spiritu-ally attuned wackos."

"I didn't get anything either." Dana continued to watch the three walk away. "But they were pretty obvious even if they didn't feel demonic."

"Meaning?" Marcus asked.

"These guys should have *Monkey Wrench* stamped on their foreheads because that's what I'm thinking they're going to throw at us."

"Agreed," Marcus said.

Brandon got to his feet and took a step toward the parking lot. "Then are you two thinking what I'm thinking?"

Dana stood and brushed off her shorts. "Follow them."

"Exactly. I want to know what we're dealing with." He glanced at the professor. "Well?"

The three of them jogged to the sidewalk just beyond the parking lot and glanced left and right. "There!" Marcus pointed north. Tristan's head bobbed along the sidewalk seventy yards in front of them, Jotham and Orson on either side.

Marcus lunged forward and picked up speed with each stride, but Dana caught up to him and shoved an arm across his chest. "Let's not be spotted, okay? A discreet distance, don't you think?"

As they slowed down and followed the three, Dana asked the exact question spinning in Brandon's mind. "So if they're human, then what are they all about?"

Marcus pulled out his cell phone and stabbed his thumbs at the screen like a miniature jackhammer. "There's three possibilities. First, they are evil and our discernment of this is being hindered somehow. Second, we're out of touch with the Spirit and the sig-nals are there, but our reading ability has waned. Third, the Spirit is blocking us."

"What about what I just said? Just ordinary wackos who we will need to avoid?" Brandon said.

"That certainly seems incongruous with their behavior and

even a cursory examination of the evidence. First, there is no neutral zone for us these days. I doubt you would postulate this being a chance encounter. I believe it is either for evil or for good. Second, do you really think people asking those kinds of questions are ordinary people? And third—"

"Do you always have to lay out our options like a professor?" Brandon snapped his fingers.

Marcus's face turned red. "But I am a—"

"It's a joke, Prof. Relax."

"I am relaxed." Marcus slid his phone back into his pocket and pushed his glasses back up on his nose.

"Uh-huh. You're melted white chocolate, you're so silky smooth."

Up ahead, the man who called himself Orson crossed the street, leaving Jotham and Tristan on the other side. Another block up, Jotham crossed the street as well.

"Do we want to split up?" Dana asked.

"No, let's stay on Tristan."

Thirty seconds later Tristan stopped next to a gold Pontiac Grand Am and reached into his pocket.

"You think he can see us?" Brandon said.

"Unlikely at this distance and angle," Marcus replied.

Tristan opened the door of his car, then turned and waved at them before getting in.

"I think he spotted us," Dana said.

"How'd he know we were following?"

"First, we are not as skilled in subterfuge as we would like to believe we are. Second, we were—" Marcus stopped, pointed at Brandon, and laughed. "I'm going to stop doing that sometime in the next ten years, I assure you."

"I hope not." Brandon grinned and watched Tristan pull away.

"Of course." Marcus smiled, then looked skyward, a puzzled expression on his face.

"Why the strange look, Marcus?"

"Two items for contemplation."

"Spill it."

"First, the three of us didn't talk about Reece." The professor rubbed his temple. "But it appears the Spirit had another agenda in mind."

"True, and the second?"

"Your stalker reminds me of someone who might be stalking me. And I have the sensation he's getting ready for a second visit very soon."

SIXTEEN

MARCUS WRAPPED THINGS UP IN HIS OFFICE AT FOUR fifteen on Thursday afternoon, which meant the chance to get in a workout at his gym before heading home but he never got there.

He decided to walk through Red Square to break up his normal routine when heading for his car. It would take a few more minutes but that was fine. It would give him a little more thinking time—to continue to wrestle with the idea that he truly had switched into another reality on the Ave, at Kat's bakery, and in his den two nights ago.

It couldn't have truly transpired. But that's what he would have said about all the things Doug and Reece had shown them over the past year.

The campus smelled of summer trying to make itself known in the midst of the perpetual dampness of a Seattle spring. A few students wore shorts as if they could hasten its arrival. Others wore jackets, unconvinced of the power of the descending sun poking through thick white clouds.

Marcus strolled by a man he'd long ago dubbed Jeremiah and watched him speak to ten or eleven students in his soft, husky voice about how to experience heaven on earth. As he passed by, Marcus winked at him and Jeremiah returned the gesture. They'd chatted once or twice a month about life and even about a few of his experiences with the Warriors. Jeremiah always ended their

conversations by saying, "Go with it, I'll pray for you," and Marcus believed the man did.

In the far corner some spray-paint artists created images for the freshmen who stared at their works in fascination. The painters would be kicked off campus soon enough, but not before three or ten students "donated" thirty bucks to their art fund in exchange for a custom painting.

Directly in his path, in the far left corner of the square, a crowd of thirty, maybe thirty-five people stood in a semicircle around a man dressed in black. Marcus took three more strides toward him, then stopped as if he'd slammed into an iron door.

It was him. The man on the street corner who had tried to get cozy six days back. His prediction had come true. They were seeing each other again. At least Marcus was seeing him. He eased up to the back of the crowd and avoided the man's line of sight.

He was dressed the same as the other day: black jeans and a dark red shirt. The man darted back and forth from one side of the crowd to the other, shoulders slightly stooped, not from old age but because they followed his head and neck that were thrust forward as if he were a large bird looking for seeds among his audience.

Finally he stopped on the side of the group opposite Marcus and swept his gaze over the crowd. "Students of this university and students of life, you are about to see a miracle."

He made a quarter bow as if the miracle had already taken place, then stood straight with a broad grin washing across his face. The man turned to a short brunette and offered his empty right hand as if it held something. "You, take it, please." He turned over his hand in the air above hers. "Don't drop it, thank you. Now, take the deck and lift it up for everyone to see."

"I'm not holding—"

"It's invisible." He said it in a mock whisper, then leaned forward and winked at her. "You must believe."

She offered a droopy grin, raised her hand palm up, and the magician pointed at the invisible deck on top of it.

"If you would do me the favor of choosing a color: red or black."

"Red."

"Splendid. Please give the deck to the person to your right."

She pretended to hand the deck to a student who looked like Alfred Hitchcock must have looked like when he was young. "The color red offers us two choices: diamonds or hearts." The man glanced in Marcus's direction, then back to the student. "Please choose either, my young director."

Marcus squinted at the magician and took a few steps closer to the front. How did the man know Marcus was thinking the student looked like Hitchcock? It was either a disconcerting coincidence or an impressive bit of mind reading—and he didn't believe in the latter.

"Do you have it? You've chosen a suit, yes?" He rubbed his teeth across his lower lip.

"Diamonds," the student answered.

"Do you want to change your mind?" The magician shuffled one step to his left.

"No."

He shuffled back. "So you're saying you're happy with the mind you have?"

Mild laughter fluttered through the crowd.

"Yes. I'm quite satisfied with the mind I have." Young Hitchcock smiled.

"I'm sure you are. Now hand the deck to the person next to you."

After the student mimed the transfer, the magician spoke to the young bohemian-looking woman who now held the deck. "Please choose lower cards, middle cards, or upper cards."

"Upper."

"Wonderful. Splendid. Superb."

To the next holder of the invisible pack of cards he asked, "Will you give us the name of a card in the upper diamonds?"

"Jack."

"The jack of diamonds?"

"Yes."

He spun in a 360, arms out to the crowd. "Amazing. Truly astounding." The magician closed his eyes and gave little shakes of his head—a thin smile on his face. He took a deep breath, opened his eyes, and beamed at the crowd.

"The card we arrived at was completely random. It was completely unknown to any of us until this moment. The choice of card was utterly and undeniably free. Yes?"

He glanced at the crowd who murmured their agreement.

"And yet last night I had a dream of strange portents." He closed his eyes and bowed his head. When he looked up and opened them, he looked ready to explode. "I dreamt of a card, in a dream so vivid that when I woke I immediately grabbed a deck of cards, found that card I'd dreamed of, and reversed it in the pack. I didn't know what it meant. I didn't know why I was compelled to reverse the card. I simply knew it had to be done."

The magician reached into his back pocket and pulled out a red deck of cards by the tips of his thumb and forefinger. He set it on the palm of his hand and stared at it.

"Unbelievable," he muttered.

He pulled the deck from the case and spread it between his hands. "Look. All these cards are faceup. Aces and eights and kings and fours and every other card." He spread them farther. "All of them."

Marcus squinted to see and pushed to the front of the crowd.

"All except one." Toward the end of the spread a reversed card slid into view, its red back in stark contrast to the other cards. "Fifty-one faceup cards. One card facedown."

The magician grinned, slid it out of the pack, and held it up for the crowd to gawk at. Marcus knew what had to be coming next but it still surprised him. The magician turned the card around and held the jack of diamonds high in the air as he slowly waved it back and forth.

"You were amazing." He pointed at each of the people who had helped choose the card. "Well done. If you'd chosen any other color, any other suit, the lower or middle cards or any other high card, well"—he motioned toward a brown leather bag with green bills

overflowing from it—"I fear the others among you wouldn't be as kind with their donations as I'm hoping they will now be." He picked up the bag—the money still sticking over the edges—and passed it through the crowd.

As the bag circulated, the magician squatted and stared at the ground as if trying to figure out what to do next. When he sprang back to his feet, he grinned at the sky, then turned to Marcus. His slate-gray eyes seemed to bore into Marcus's brain and shout, "I told you we'd meet again today, of course I couldn't have it any other way." He spun in a slow circle on his heel, eyes closed, thumbs hooked over the front of his jeans.

When he opened them, he addressed the crowd but his gaze locked onto Marcus. "We're about to do an experiment. Not a magic trick, not some manipulation of your senses to force you to choose in the way I want you to, but a true experiment that might or might not work. Simply put, I'm going to read your mind." He nodded at the crowd as if he'd just offered all of them a winning lottery ticket they couldn't refuse.

"But before we begin I should warn you this experiment will change at least one of your lives in a significant way." He bowed his head and opened his palms. "So if you suspect it might be you and are wondering what to do . . . if you'd like to remain in the cocoon you call your life, I suggest you leave now and give no chance to stir up strife."

The sensation the magician was talking specifically about him surged through Marcus's brain like a rogue ocean wave, but he shrugged it off. Apparently not everyone could do so as about a quarter of the crowd shuffled away.

After the sound of their echoing steps off the red bricks of the square faded, the man lifted his head and sighed with seeming contentment. "Ah yes. The faithful remain." He rubbed his hands together. "Good, I think we're ready."

The street magician glanced at each of the remaining people as if evaluating pieces of machinery. When he'd finished he looked

up and to his left, then blinked three times at half speed. Then he turned and smiled at Marcus. "Would you like to help?"

"With what?"

"The experiment of course." He sauntered toward Marcus and stopped with three feet between them. "Are you ready to get on this pony and take a little jaunt together?"

"You're going to read my mind?"

"Yes. But without anything being written down as so many of my brethren must do and without asking you a single question. As I already said, this experiment is real. No smoke, no mirrors, no cheap trick thrill."

He glanced at the rest of the crowd, an expectant look on their faces.

"No thanks."

"No worries." He turned to Marcus's left. "Then let's do something else. Would anyone like to help me prove the existence of alternate realities and explain why a woman would wear the same outfit to her job at a bakery two days in a row?"

Marcus blinked. "What did you say?"

The magician spun back to him. "I don't believe your hearing failed you." He beckoned with his fingers. "Now, can I try to read your mind? I promise to be ever so kind."

"How do you know about that?"

"Do you want to help?"

"How did you know?"

He leaned toward Marcus and spoke in a stage whisper. "Are you sure we should have that conversation right now in front of students who will likely report on the details of what we talk about to others at this university, or should we arrange for a more appropriate time to chat?"

Marcus didn't answer. He wanted to grab the magician around the neck and shove him up against a wall until he told Marcus what he knew about Kat. All this guy needed was a gold coin to flip to convince him it was Zennon.

After a few minutes of pretending he was finding something in the battered leather briefcase at his feet, the magician asked once more, "Will you help?" His eyes said the only acceptable answer was yes. Marcus nodded.

"Splendid." He turned to the crowd and opened his arms wide. "Let us begin." He paced three steps to the right and then three back to the left, stroking his chin as if he were playing a vaudeville stage back in the 1920s.

"Please think of a photograph you own. Any will do. Concentrate on it. Form a picture of it in your head. Now attach an emotion to the picture. Anger, fear, happiness, regret—anything you like." He stopped pacing and stared at Marcus. "Ready?"

"Sure."

"You're thinking of a photograph of the Enchantments. Your arm is around a good friend and the emotion you're feeling is . . . regret."

Marcus stepped out from the crowd and turned to face them. "Show's over. My new friend and I are going to have a chat. Right now."

"Was he right?" a young man asked.

"Yes, he was right." Marcus stared at the magician and motioned him toward Drumheller Fountain at the south end of campus.

✛ ✛ ✛

Marcus stood next to the fountain, arms crossed, his gaze drilling the magician. "What's your name?"

"Simon."

"Last name?"

Simon waved his hand. "Simon is enough."

"Fine. I suppose I don't have to tell you mine then."

"No, you don't. I picked that up while reading your mind." The man grinned.

"I don't believe that."

"You're right, it was much easier to find it online in the U-Dub faculty directory."

Marcus glanced to his left and right. No one near. Good. "Are you Zennon? Or some other demon?"

"No. Who is Zennon?"

"I think you know full well who Zennon is."

"Maybe, maybe not, but I swear on the stars beyond the stars beyond the many layered realms of alternate realities that I am not him." Simon took a coin out of his pocket and rolled it over his fingers. "He uses a gold coin. As you can plainly see, mine is silver."

"Are you an angel?"

"No." Simon sat on the edge of the fountain and patted the beveled concrete. Marcus stayed standing.

"Then what are you?"

Simon leaned back and laughed. "Are you always this direct?" He didn't wait for an answer. "I meant it when I said we would become friends. Or I should say, I hope we become friends. So let's ease into things before we talk about diamond rings. Get to know each other a bit first. Chat about the mundane things of the world, then let the deeper things naturally unfurl." He leaned forward and looked at Marcus from under his eyebrows. "For example, wouldn't you like to ask me about the invisible deck trick?"

"I'd prefer to be enlightened on how you knew about the Enchantments photo."

Simon wiggled his fingers. "The deck first."

"Fine." If he had to play Simon's game for a spell, he would. "Were the people in the crowd plants? Did you tell them what card to finish with?"

"In other words, did I cheat in order to accomplish my stunning feat?"

"Yes."

"I did not."

"Then how could you anticipate they would pick the jack of diamonds?"

"I didn't."

"I don't understand."

"It doesn't matter what card they choose. It will always be the one reversed in the deck."

"So how did you accomplish the trick?"

"As my son said when he was young, 'maaa-gitch.'" Simon frowned and spoke more to himself than Marcus. "I think I had a son. I did, didn't I? I mean a real one."

"Simon, are you quite well?"

The magician whipped his head up and scratched his salt-and-pepper goatee. "Sorry, can't keep it all straight most of the time. I definitely had a real son." He smiled as if he'd figured out the meaning of quantum mechanics but then his face turned dark. "But he died when he was very young. Years later my wife died too and that's when—" Simon stopped and waved his hand as if to bat the thought away. "No, no, I won't be able to explain the trick." He looked apologetic and bowed his head. "I'm unable to break the magician's code. But it's only a trick—not real magic."

"It's one of the best I've seen." Granted, Marcus hadn't seen a lot of street magic, but if it was true, that the crowd could have picked any card, the trick seemed impossible.

Simon shook his head and chuckled.

"Is there something intrinsically humorous about my comment?"

"Many versed magicians look down on that trick because it's so common and so simple to do." He smiled and rubbed his thumbs together. "Overused they'd call it. Beneath them. It relies on a gimmick—trick cards. Not pure sleight of hand, they say."

"Regardless, the crowd was enamored. If they hadn't observed the trick previously—"

"Exactly." Simon snapped his fingers. "What is common for some is a miracle for others. It's all a matter of perspective."

"As was my perspective with the bakery incident or the photo of the Enchantments."

"Precisely. You're as bright as advertised." Simon rolled his

silver coin around his fingers again and it vanished on the second pass. "This switching. Common for you, common for me."

"Not so common for me."

"Or for most of mankind. But it should be for you. You wrote the book. And trust me, they will become more common for you. Of that I'm sure." He frowned. "Almost sure. Close to sure, you know? Can't ever tell for certain. When you've lived in over four hundred different realities, you can't be certain about anything."

"Four hundred realities?"

Simon gave a quick nod. "Maybe a few more than that. Lost count."

Marcus stared at Simon and asked the Spirit what he was. Human didn't come into his mind. But nothing else did either. A few seconds later the magician clapped his hands and handed Marcus a business card. All it contained was *Simon* and a cell phone number.

"Well now, that was an excellent first session together, don't you think? In our second session let's be sure to talk about the Wolf, okay?"

Heat rose to Marcus's face. "How do you know about the Wolf?"

"In time, Mr. Amber, in time." Simon picked up his leather bag and strolled off.

Whoever Simon was, he would obviously have a role in this play. Marcus glanced at his watch. In a little over twenty-four hours he'd be with the other Warriors. The time couldn't come soon enough.

As he walked toward the garage that held his car, he pulled up his calendar. Tomorrow night: Warriors. Saturday night: Calen over for dinner. What would that be like? Marcus let out a soft moan. He felt like Jesus was telling him it would be far from an ordinary family gathering.

SEVENTEEN

Reece sat at his fire pit on Friday evening at seven waiting for the others to arrive, knowing he would need to be exactly what Doug said he would need to be in the coming days: stronger than he imagined, able to hear the Spirit with ears that listened well, and fully engaged in their coming battle with the Wolf. He couldn't see. So what.

The Spirit had told him the confrontation with the Wolf would be far from what he expected. And that he needed to be ready for that. Wonderful. He had no idea what the battle would be like but he was supposed to anticipate what it would be like?

The sound of footsteps broke Reece out of his mulling. Had to be Doug. Amazing how he'd learned to identify people by the way their feet fell on grass or floors or ground.

"How is my fire, Doug? Did I build a good one?"

"Yes, can't you feel the heat?"

"Just checking." Reece held out his hands and let the flames warm them. "If we send them in tonight, it will be brutal."

"It will be brutal any night. They need to go through this," Doug said, his voice soft.

"I don't want to do it."

"Neither do I."

✛ ✛ ✛

When Dana arrived the others were already seated around the fire pit in Reece's backyard. She hated being late, but for some reason the emergencies at the station didn't care that she had other commitments on her calendar.

As soon as she sat next to the professor, Reece invited them all to describe what had been happening during the past week. First Marcus told what had happened at the bakery where Kat worked, about the Enchantments photo, and about the strange magician, Simon, he'd met in Red Square at the U-Dub.

Brandon was next, telling them about his first encounter with Tristan Barrow and then the second one in the park with Dana and Marcus. When he'd finished, Reece turned to Dana.

It felt odd for her not to have something to describe other than give her impression of the meeting in Kirkland with Tristan and his two companions. She felt as if she'd done something wrong since there was no specific weirdness she could point to. She told them about her promotion simply to have something to say and received congratulations from Brandon and Marcus, but Reece stayed silent. Doug didn't.

He cleared his throat. "Just because it isn't obvious, it doesn't mean you're not on the enemy's radar, Dana. And please consider the truth that a subtle attack can often be far more effective than a direct assault since an attack of subterfuge and nuance is often not noticed till the victim has crawled into the middle of the spider's web."

"Are you talking about my promotion?"

"Just be aware."

"Thanks. I think."

Reece slid forward on the bench and turned his head in a slow semicircle as if he could see each of them. "My own story is mundane. The enemy has tried to discourage me and belittle me due to my sight being gone. He's tried to tell me I'm no longer fit to be your guide. Not subtle. Not unexpected. But nonetheless effective at times. Whether the attack is more overt as in the case with Brandon and the professor or more subdued as with Dana and me,

the solution is the same. Stay close to Jesus. Listen to the truth of the Spirit and make no agreement with the lies of the enemy." Reece sat back. "Doug?"

"Well said." He sighed. "My own battle has been with dreams that bring terror to my heart and a lack of sleep that results. However, he is with me, you are with me, and I am with all of you. We must stay strong, dear friends."

Reece rubbed his knees. "As you know, if the attacks are intensifying, then we are making the enemy nervous. We need to take heart from that thought. And now let's get to the next phase of your training. Any additional thoughts, Doug, before the three go in?"

"We're going 'in' tonight? In where?" Brandon said.

Doug clasped his hands together. "Yes, you are. More on that in a moment." He turned and looked at Reece. "To answer your question, Reece, I do have a few thoughts. While we must be aware of the enemy's schemes, do not let your full concentration be on him. He is not the goal. He is not our focus. Do not give him more power than he has. Jesus is setting captives free, and those captives are stepping out of their chains. That is what we will celebrate and keep at the forefront of our minds. We will press deeper into the Lord daily. That is what will give us the strength and ability to advance with power as we step further into this war."

"So be it," Dana said.

Brandon pulled a bag of sunflower seeds out of his pocket. "Now about this exercise. This is part of us getting in shape to face the Wolf-man?"

"Yes." Reece sighed.

"I don't like the sigh, big guy." Brandon popped a handful of seeds into his mouth. "Are you coming with us? Is this the 'next time' you talked about?"

Reece shook his head and stayed silent.

Doug gazed for a few seconds at each of them. "This will be far from easy. But it won't last long. Seven minutes perhaps. Ten at the most."

"Any advance intel?" Brandon said.

"No." Doug shook his head. "I'm sorry."

"When will this excursion take place?"

Doug took a deep breath and looked at Reece. "Right now."

Instantly Reece's backyard vanished and the only thought in Dana's mind was it was the first time they'd gone into any spiritual realm without holding hands. Apparently it wasn't necessary. Might have been nice to know.

A moment later Brandon, Marcus, and she stood in a small meadow bordered on one side by cliffs of granite. The ground was charred as if a fire had recently swept over the ground and burned the grasses.

"I can see why Reece didn't want to come," Dana said.

Brandon poked at the burned ground with the toe of his shoe. "No kidding."

A cry pierced the air behind her. Dana spun and gasped. It wouldn't be fun dealing with what rushed toward them.

EIGHTEEN

THREE HAWKS OR FALCONS, DANA COULDN'T TELL, streaked down from the sky at them, screams pouring from their beaks. They were a hundred yards away, talons out. Even from this distance they looked razor sharp.

"Move!" Brandon grabbed her arm and dragged her toward a thick row of alder trees fifteen yards to their right. Marcus followed and they reached the trees, turned sideways, and pushed through the narrow opening between the trunks. The falcons would get through easily. Dana spun to face them with . . . what? They had no weapons.

But the birds raced by and banked hard to avoid the cliffs and flew off.

Dana stared at Brandon. "What, that was just to scare us?"

Brandon didn't answer. She turned to see what he was focused on. The air shimmered in front of them as if heat were moving toward them in waves. Then came wind. Hot. Searing.

The heat slammed into Dana and sent her to her knees. "Unhh!" She shut her eyes against the scorching current of air and tried to breathe steady. It was cooler near the ground, but the swirling air pushed particles of loose dirt into her mouth and nose. What kind of soul had Reece sent them into? And why?

Dana coughed and opened her eyes. Brandon and Marcus

knelt in front of her, both pulling in choking gasps of air as she was doing. "Are you all—?"

"Look out!" Brandon leaped toward her, grabbed her, and rolled over three times with her in his arms. The ground shuddered and Dana turned her head. A massive slab of granite sat two inches from her nose.

"Professor!" Brandon pushed off Dana and glanced behind him.

"I'm good." Marcus's head swiveled back and forth as he studied the cliff above them. "And I'd like to stay that way. Any theories on how that state of being can be assured are heartily welcomed."

Brandon stood and lifted Dana to her feet. "We have to get out of here now!"

Dana's throat tightened as she drew in the burning air. "Agreed, but it's going to be hard to stand and hold hands and get in a state of mind to get out of here when it's raining bus-sized rocks and breathing is like being on Venus."

"Reece's estimate was we'd be here seven minutes." Marcus shouted to be heard over the increasing intensity of the wind. "We've only been in here two."

"And if we stay for three we're going to die."

The sound of boulders cracking high above them split the air. She glanced up. The top of the granite wall shook. Dana clutched Brandon's shoulder and jabbed her finger at a clump of trees at the base of the cliff. "We have to go there. Now!"

As she staggered toward the rock wall, Marcus shouted, "It's inadvisable to head toward the source of the stone that seconds ago nearly—"

Dana kept running and shouted over her shoulder, "I don't have time to debate this right now, Professor. Come on!"

A dull splintering sound came from above, and two seconds later the ground trembled like a giant had jumped from the sky. She turned back to the spot they'd stood in five seconds earlier. A jagged boulder the size of a Volkswagen Beetle filled the space.

Wham! Another boulder slammed into the ground to their

right, then another landed and shook the ground to their left. They pushed through the trees to the base of the granite wall. Dana whipped her head back and forth, scanning the rock. "There!" She pointed to a thin, dark opening fifteen yards to their left. "Let's go."

"We're going in there?" Brandon said.

"No choice."

"You might get through that opening but what about Marcus and me?"

"You'll make it," Dana sputtered. "You have to."

The instant they sprinted for the opening, the ground shuddered with another rock that landed in the spot where they'd just been. Dana reached the dark slit in the rock first and flung herself to her belly.

"You first, Professor."

"No, you, Dana." He gave a weak smile. "No time to debate."

Brandon grabbed her shoulder. "Wait. How do we know this whole thing isn't going to come down on us if we crawl in here?"

"We don't." Dana turned her head sideways and put it flat on the ground. Maybe two inches to spare. She dragged herself forward with her elbows, inches at a time, the jagged rocks on the floor of the cave digging into her arms and torso and legs. Faster. She had to move faster, but it made her breathe deeper and breathing was almost impossible.

The air outside was a winter's day compared to the heat inside the cramped cave. Each breath felt like the air inside a sauna ten times hotter than she'd ever been in. But no boulders rained down inside the cave and a sense of peace told her what she'd felt the Spirit saying while they were outside: This cave was safe. That this was their eye of the tornado and their place to escape to. She needed it to be. They all needed it to be.

Dana reached for the ceiling. The height of the tiny cave was three feet at most. It didn't matter. She was alive. But where were Marcus and Brandon? She crouched and blinked against the light coming through the cave. *Keep them safe.*

She spun and laid her face at the entrance, but the wind and dust made her clamp her eyes closed. "Come on, guys. Get in here!"

No sound came back. No, this couldn't happen. *Your protection, Lord.*

"Brandon! Marcus!"

Again there was no response. *No, stay strong. He is our protector and shield.* Dana's chest tightened. Yes, she was safe. But it didn't matter if Brandon and the professor weren't. She couldn't stay if they were in trouble. Dana had just started to crawl back out when a head filled the light streaming into the shallow cave.

"You have to move aside, Dana!" Marcus moaned as he crawled in beside her.

"What took you so long!"

Marcus pulled himself farther in. "We had a slight disagreement as to who should enter the cave next."

"I would let out a disgusted, 'Men!' but it would be a waste of words and I don't have the energy."

Moments later Brandon crawled through, accompanied by assorted angry grunts. "Okay, we've all made it to the party room. What do we do now? There's obviously not enough room to dance."

It was an excellent question. There were no demons to overcome on this one. Their enemy inside this soul wasn't an entity they could focus on. It was nature attacking them and how could they fight that? But it was still the enemy causing the boulders to fall and the heat to assault them and they could fight against that, right? But how? Then again, maybe they didn't have to fight. Stay in here seven minutes? Forget it. It was time to go now.

"It's getting downright toasty in here," Brandon puffed out.

Dana sucked in a breath that felt like fire. "Which is making it harder to breathe in case you hadn't noticed."

"If these conditions accelerate"—Marcus coughed like he was dying—"we'll have no choice but to crawl back outside so we don't suffocate."

"We're not crawling anywhere. We're going back." Dana fumbled

to find Brandon's and Marcus's hands. "Grab hold, let's get literally the hell out of here." She clamped down on the others' palms and closed her eyes, then emptied her mind of everything around her and focused on the Spirit. "Take us." But nothing happened.

"This is not good," Brandon said.

"Why are we still here?" Dana ground her teeth. "We've been doing this without a hitch for ten months."

"This is not a soul," Marcus said.

In the next instant the ground right outside the cave shook like a bomb had been dropped, and the feeble amount of light that had come through the opening vanished. A moment later the sound of cracking started over their heads.

"I think there's a high probability this cave is about to collapse," Marcus said.

What was Reece thinking sending them in here? "We can get out of this. We have to," Dana puffed out. "Talk to me, Teacher. Now would be a good time for a quick lesson. Are you getting anything?"

Marcus started to mumble as if to himself, then paused and spoke clearly. "Going in and out of souls has been accomplished without incident—like strolling in a garden. We haven't had to think about it, concentrate on it, give it much thought or worry. It has ceased to require an element most would consider critical to a vibrant relationship with the Father, Son, and Holy Spirit. One Doug, Reece, and the three of us would acknowledge as—"

"Professor!" Dana grabbed Marcus's arm. "Can we get to the end of the lesson and get out of class? The bell is about to ring."

"Right, right, yes of course." Marcus coughed. "Faith is confidence in what we hope for and assurance about what we do not see. This is what the ancients were commended for. By faith we understand the universe was formed at God's command, so that what is seen was not made out of what was visible.

"'By faith Abel brought God a better offering than Cain did . . . By faith Enoch was taken from this life, so that he did not experience death . . . By faith Noah, when warned about things not yet seen, in

holy fear built an ark to save his family. By faith Abraham, when called to go to a place he would later receive as his inheritance, obeyed and went, even though he did not know where he was going.

"'By faith Abraham, when God tested him, offered Isaac as a sacrifice ... By faith Joseph, when his end was near, spoke about the exodus of the Israelites from Egypt ... By faith Moses' parents hid him for three months after he was born ... By faith the people passed through the Red Sea as on dry land. By faith the walls of Jericho fell, after the army had marched around them for seven days.

"'By faith the prostitute Rahab, because she welcomed the spies, was not killed with those who were disobedient ...' And without faith it is impossible to please God."

Marcus breathed deep. "A few verses from Hebrews chapter 11."

"Are you kidding me?" Brandon said. "How do you get all that Scripture to stick in your head? I've tried memorizing Romans 8 for years and haven't gotten more than ten verses in."

"I have most of the New Testament memorized. In multiple translations."

"Really?"

"The curse of a brain that retains almost everything I ever read."

"Guys! Talk more later." Dana grabbed their hands. "Let's. Get. Out. Of. Here. Now!" She ignored the stinging sweat trickling into her eyes and called out to the Spirit of God, "We acknowledge you are the one who takes us into and out of the spiritual realm. By faith in who you are. On our own we can do nothing, with you all things can be done. And nothing can be done if we don't believe." She paused and gripped Marcus's and Brandon's hands even tighter. "In faith, we ask, please take us home."

Instantly the familiar rush of going through a gate filled Dana's mind and heart and body. Her next breath was one of the cool air of Reece's Pacific Northwest backyard. Her breathing slowed and she glanced at Marcus and Brandon. The professor sat with wide eyes, but Brandon had already turned toward Reece, who now stood on the grass a few yards to the right of the fire pit. "What was that?"

Reece raised his eyebrows but didn't speak. Brandon glanced at Doug, then back to Reece. "What were you two thinking? Why did you send us in there? Do you know how close we came to being killed? There wasn't even time to figure out how we were supposed to fight. We're not even close to ready for something like that."

"Exactly," Reece said.

"You're insane, Reece." Brandon slumped back and folded his arms.

Marcus rocked back and forth on the bench. "My assessment is that's precisely why Reece sent us through that particular gate into that particular realm. I'm assuming he had no knowledge of the specific kind of attack that would come against us, but he knew it would be one we couldn't handle."

"Okay, Professor Genius, tell me why."

Dana leaned forward, elbows on her knees, and answered before Marcus could speak. "Exactly what we realized when we were inside. If we're going to take on the Wolf, we need our belief to grow. We need to rely on the Spirit more than ever before. We need to take to heart we can do nothing without Jesus."

"Yes, that's the most significant part of it, Dana." Reece eased back over and sat next to Brandon. "But there is another part as well."

"Which is?"

"As you know, I believe we're about to enter a phase of battle far more intense than we've experienced up till this point. You needed to see the severity of what the enemy can bring. You needed to see how the enemy can sometimes attack without a specific enemy to fight against. How do you fight against nature inside the spiritual realms? What are the weapons you can wield? If you think you can do it on your own, you will die.

"If you surrender to Jesus and put your faith in his providing what you need, those weapons and ideas will come precisely at the moment you have to have them. I could have told you these things, but would you have grasped the lesson and the need as thoroughly as you now have done? I think not. And you all need to grasp it firmly."

Reece stood. "I suggest we take a short break to allow the emotions of your journey to settle a bit more, get something to drink or eat from my kitchen, and then we'll gather here once again. Let's say in ten minutes."

"And the point of discussion?" Dana asked.

Reece cracked his knuckles. "It's time to tell you about the Wolf."

NINETEEN

Finally they'd get answers about the Wolf. Brandon snatched a grape Powerade out of the refrigerator and stepped onto Reece's back deck. Who it was or what it was. How they would go after it. What kind of attack plan they'd put together, and the steps on putting it in motion to destroy the beast. Brandon gazed toward the fire pit.

Part of him relished the idea of taking down the Wolf. And part—if he was brutally honest—was scared. He'd seen what the demons had done to Reece's eyes. What if the Wolf came after his voice? Or Marcus's brain? Could they be as strong as Reece seemed to be after losing one of his greatest pleasures—taking photos, seeing the beauty of the world all around him—if something happened to one of them?

A strange feeling swept through Brandon. That he would soon have to face that question. Was it a premonition? Or a thought from the enemy? Singing had been his life since he was fourteen. He was the Song. He had to sing, right?

The back door opened and Marcus shuffled up next to him. "Are you ready?"

"Yeah, let's go."

They made their way over the hundred yards to Reece's fire pit. The others were already there.

As he and Marcus settled into chairs, Doug rubbed his knees and glanced at all of them. "The past ten months have been stunning.

We've made significant progress and our numbers are growing. Of the ninety-six men and women who have gone through the training school at Well Spring, ninety-two say they want to go through the advanced training once we start those courses. And these men and women have taken the Warriors Riding message of freedom back to their friends, their families, their communities.

"They are leading their own retreats, in their churches, at retreat centers, in private homes, and in cabins across the nation. And over the past three weeks I've received e-mails from groups starting Warriors Riding retreats in Australia, South Africa, Wales, France, and Brazil. This message, dear friends, truly is starting to spread to the nations. The prophecy is coming true.

"But . . ." Doug clasped his hands. "The Wolf has risen and is growing stronger daily. The time has come for you to act on the reason you were brought together in the first place."

Doug glanced at Reece who somehow picked up that it was his turn to speak. The big man adjusted his sunglasses and pushed back his beat-up dark tan Stetson. "As you might have suspected, who and what the Wolf is isn't obvious. A direct assault, while often brutal, isn't the most efficient or most thorough way to destroy an enemy."

Marcus looked up from scribbling notes in his journal. "It's to accomplish it from the inside out. The most strategic course of action is to present seemingly important distractions or inconsequential battles to take the focus off the major assault."

"Exactly," Doug said. "While you're fighting the enemy attacking your home out front, there's another contingent setting charges in your crawl space and you don't realize it till it's too late."

Dana pulled her hair back. "In other words, you're saying the Wolf isn't something like the government trying to restrict religious freedoms, or Hollywood and some of the garbage they're putting out, or atheistic groups trying to shut down Christmas."

"Well said."

"I'm loving this intro and discussion, I really am, but can we get on with the show?" Brandon wheeled his forefingers around each

other in a circle. "You know? Go ahead and give us the name of the Wolf? Him, her, them, whatever?"

"The Wolf is not a human." Reece massaged his fist.

"I'm lost," Brandon said.

"But while we can't know with 100 percent certainty who the Wolf is, we believe the Spirit has shown us a specific person to go after."

"Now I'm not only lost, every map in the universe has vanished." Brandon ran his fingers through his hair. "The Wolf isn't a person, but he is a person. Do I have it straight?"

"Yes." Reece smiled.

"What? Am I the only one who feels like he's not making any sense?" Brandon glanced at the others, then broke into song. *"Just a sphere of perplexity, that's what the universe is these days . . ."*

"'Ball of Confusion,' the Temptations, 1970, Motown," Reece said.

"How do you do that? I didn't say the words even close to right, plus sang the wrong melody. I'm never going to stump you. You're a music encyclopedia."

"Only from 1962 through '78. After that all the good music died."

"Why '78?"

Doug cleared his throat. "Gentlemen."

Reece nodded and leaned forward, elbows on his knees. "Think back to last year when we went to church together and the professor's eyes were opened and he saw demons masquerading as mundane ushers. Remember how the pastor challenged his audience not to drink even a sip of alcohol or go to even one R-rated movie for a year? And how Marcus saw the demons putting stones inside the backpacks of the people in the congregation? There is nothing wrong with making a personal choice not to drink alcohol or go to R-rated movies. But for one Christian to weigh another down with rules and regulations that are not their own . . . that is the greatest enemy of Christianity. Religion. It's what Jesus hated the

most. What he fought against with the Pharisees. And his onslaught against religion is what got him killed.

"The spirit of religion is an enemy who is crushing churches, dividing fellowships and friends, turning God from a person into a manifesto of dos and don'ts that crush the spirit and turn Christianity into a program devoid of true godly power and devoid of love."

Brandon leaned back in his chair. "I like the speech, but I'm still tempted to sing another verse of the Temptations song."

Dana folded her arms. "I'm still confused as well. I get it about the spirit of religion, but there has to be a more clearly defined expression of the Wolf than that."

Reece turned to Marcus. "Professor?"

"I would surmise that in the spiritual realm the Wolf is the spirit of religion, but in the physical realm that spirit manifests itself in a variety of different ways, including that of human nature. So while the Wolf is a spirit we must be aware of, and probably at some point engage, it is highly likely the Wolf can also be manifested in human individuals who are being used by the Wolf to carry out its design." Marcus pushed his glasses up on his nose. "Is there any accuracy to my assessment of the situation?"

"Ever the teacher, eh, Professor?" Brandon grinned.

"And ever the student as well. It is difficult to teach if you are not open to learning those things you do not yet know."

"Yes, you are accurate, Professor," Reece said. "Completely."

"So even though there's no way the Wolf is using only one person, there is a person you've targeted. That we need to confront."

"Yes." Reece turned toward Doug and opened his palm.

Doug placed a piece of wood on the fire. "For over a year we've sensed the Spirit telling us the Wolf is using a man named Carson Tanner."

"The radio show host?" Dana sat up ramrod straight. "On the cover of *Christianity World*? Named one of the new century's most influential evangelicals? I met him at the National Association of

Broadcasters four years ago. He was just starting to get big, but now he's pulling in serious numbers. Plus he's got columns in two major magazines and is a frequent guest on TV shows and podcasts. People follow what he says. You're not serious when you say you think he's—"

"What about you, Brandon? Heard of him?"

"Yeah, don't know many people who haven't. The best-selling books, the filled arenas when he does his speaking tours . . . people love him. They call him hard-core. Radical. That he's getting people back to the Bible and to living a pure Christian life."

Dana laughed. "You're going to have to sell me hard on the idea of Carson being the Wolf, Doug. He's charming, smart, knows his Bible cold." Dana smiled. "He's handsome."

"What do his looks have to do with anything?" Brandon frowned. "I think we all know what he looks like. We don't need to dwell on—"

"I'm not dwelling on his thick blond hair, his tan skin, or his trim athletic build, Brandon. I'm thinking that Marcus might not know what he looks like, and I'm trying to give the professor a visual to work with."

"I'm aware of him," Marcus said.

Brandon snorted out a breath. "Yeah, Dana, I'm sure that's exactly what you were—"

"Enough." Reece raised his palm, the reflection of the flames of the fire pit turning it a dark red. "Have you ever listened to his program?"

"Yes," Dana said.

"How long ago?"

She shrugged. "I don't know, a year and a half ago. Maybe two and a half years."

"When he first started he did a lot of good for a lot of people. But as his audience grew, he changed. We don't think he's one of the most influential evangelicals today. He is *the* most influential. He is allowing the enemy—through his ministry—to put rocks in

his listeners' spiritual backpacks the size of Volkswagen Beetles. But let's be clear. Our enemy is Carson and it isn't Carson."

"Great. More confusion." Brandon rolled his eyes back in his head.

"Carson is only the Wolf because he's allowed the spirit of religion to embed its claws into his life and soul."

Dana pulled her sweatshirt tighter against the rapidly cooling evening. "All right, for argument's sake let's say Carson is the Wolf—what is our action plan?"

"We're going after him," Reece said. "The enemy has been hunting us, trying to take us out. Now the hunters will become the hunted."

Marcus twirled his pen. "Will we look for an opportunity to engage Carson directly, or try to gain permission to enter into his soul, or proceed into some other spiritual sphere to engage the spirit or spirits influencing Carson?"

"My suspicion is all three. But Doug and I haven't sought the Lord on the answer to that yet. Or our next steps."

"Why not?" Brandon said.

"Because we are the Warriors Riding plural, not the Warrior Riding singular. We will seek the answer together."

"Shouldn't we do something in the meantime?" Brandon stood and paced. "Like send out an e-mail blast to our trainees telling them to boycott the guy and tell their friends and family to do the same?"

"Crawl, walk, run," Reece said. "First we will pray about it. Together and individually. Then we'll gather to hear what the Spirit has said to each of us about what actions to take from here." Reece turned to Dana. "Are you with us here, Dana?"

"Yes, sorry." She slid her cell phone into her pocket and looked up. "Crazy days at the station."

Doug stared at her for a long moment. "Too much to handle?"

"No, it's going really well."

Reece stood. "My friends, as usual, it has been an intense

evening so let's bring it to a close. A reminder that we're headed to Well Spring next week for our next round of training. We'll see you all here at my house on Thursday at noon."

Brandon walked with Marcus to their cars. "You okay, Professor? Weirded out about the Wolf? Or still dealing with the whole thinking you might be switching back and forth between realities thing?"

"I've put that behind me. I don't have the bandwidth to analyze it at this point."

"Okay, way to go. So it's this going after the Wolf thing that's bugging you?"

"In a sense, yes, but I have another concern that is a more imminent threat that is occupying the vast majority of my prefrontal cortex."

"I'm guessing that's part of the brain."

"In rudimentary terms it's the area of the brain where we make decisions."

Brandon scrunched up his face and pressed his finger into his cheek. "What does *rudimentary* mean?"

"It means—"

"I'm kidding, Professor." Brandon laughed and punched Marcus playfully in the arm. "I did go to school for a few years, you know." As they walked on, Brandon said, "So what's the big decision?"

"Tomorrow night a young man who is dating Abbie is coming over for dinner for the second time."

"And you're trying to decide whether to be nice to him or not."

"Yes." Marcus stopped and turned toward Brandon. "How did you assess that?"

Brandon smiled. "Unlike you, I was a teenager once and had a lot of those dinners where the dad didn't like me. Or thought he didn't like me just because I was male."

"I assure you, I was a teenager once."

Brandon laughed again and shook his head. "No, I mean the meeting-a-girl's-dad thing. You told me you didn't have to face that gauntlet very often in high school."

"Then I misled you. I faced it far too frequently." Marcus turned and continued toward his car as he recalled a few times where he thought his date's father was going to take out a shotgun. "You're right. I should lighten up. He's a nice kid from what I've seen and Abbie seems quite enamored with him."

"Then be nice."

"Agreed." Marcus frowned. "But still, I would ask that you pray for the dinner and for my attitude toward Romeo once you wake up."

"Done. And don't worry, Prof. It'll be fine."

Brandon watched Marcus pull away as he sat in his car and pictured himself with a daughter Abbie's age. If he did have a girl he'd feel exactly like Marcus. Because if this kid coming over to the professor's house was anything like Brandon was in high school, Marcus should be worried.

TWENTY

Marcus stood at the window of his den on Saturday night looking down on the street, waiting for Calen to pull up in his beat-up Ford truck. Marcus glanced at his watch. Three minutes to six. Calen would be on time. He was a good kid. Which should make Marcus happy. But he wasn't. Fourteen was too young for Abbie to be dating.

At 5:59 Calen's truck chugged to a stop in front of the house and he stepped out, ran his hand over his hair, and stared at Marcus's house. The kid reached into his pocket, smiled, and pulled something out but kept his fist closed around the object.

Irritated. That was the emotion Marcus felt toward the kid. But he shouldn't. On the surface there was no good reason. Which irritated him more. Calen made Abbie happy and that made Abbie happier with Marcus.

Calen put his hand back in his pocket and released whatever object it was he'd held. For an unknown reason the movement reminded Marcus of someone, but he couldn't determine who.

Marcus went to his desk and prayed hard for five minutes, then strode out of his den to the top of the stairs and took two long breaths. He made a slow descent, the feeling of unease intensifying with each step. He felt like he'd slid into a gladiatorial arena where he had no sword and no shield.

Abbie stood in the entryway, her arms wrapped around Calen,

130

his wrapped around her. She turned and spotted Marcus. "Hey, Daddy, Calen is here."

"That I can see." Marcus reached the bottom of the stairs just as Kat stepped into the entryway.

Kat held out both hands and gripped Calen's. "Great to have you here again, Calen."

"Thanks, fun to be here." He smiled at all of them.

Marcus stepped forward. "Before dinner I want to have a brief chat with Calen."

Calen pointed at himself, eyes mock wide. "You want to chat with me?"

"Yes."

"Sure, sounds good." Calen grinned at Abbie and winked.

"Play fair, Dad." She poked him in the side and smiled.

Marcus stared at Abbie but didn't answer. "It didn't rain for once so why don't we go out back?"

He walked down the hall, through the kitchen, and through the back door onto the patio. Calen followed. Seconds after they settled into two of the patio chairs out back, Kat stepped outside with a glass of strawberry lemonade in each hand. "How can men talk without something to drink while they do so?"

Calen stood and gave a light bow as he accepted the drink from Kat.

"You don't have to stand—"

"My pleasure, Mrs. Amber. Thanks for the drink."

"You are entirely welcome." Kat turned and gave Marcus an isn't-he-a-catch smile.

Marcus whispered a prayer to himself as Calen sat back in his chair. *Show me what I cannot see and bring your truth.*

A flash of darkness shimmered across Calen and in the next instant Marcus knew what the object was that resided in the young man's back pocket. But was it him?

"So did you have something in particular you wanted to talk to me about, or is this just a chance to get to know each other a

little better since Abbie and I have been getting to know each other a lot better?"

"My hat is off to you." Marcus set his drink on the armrest of his chair and leaned forward, his gaze drilling Calen. "You're a master, Calen. I'm impressed. It took me a long time to figure you out. In fact the equation didn't fall into place till just now."

"And what is that?"

Marcus glanced at the kitchen windows. "I know what you are."

"A teenager in love?"

"No. You took an object out of your pocket as you approached my house. I know what it is."

Calen reached into the same pocket he had five minutes ago and pulled it out, but kept his fist closed. "You think you know, huh?"

"Show it to me."

"You're sure? You really think it will help the situation?"

"Show me."

Even though Marcus knew what was coming it still sent a chill down his back when Calen held out his fist and uncurled his fingers one at a time to reveal a gold coin. He flipped it in the air and caught it on the back of his hand and then spun it around his fingers just as he had done in Reece's backyard almost a year ago.

A sensation of ice spread down Marcus's arms, down his legs. Zennon. Sitting three feet from him. The demon who had tracked and assaulted each of the Warriors Riding a year ago. The one who had murdered Reece's wife and daughter. Who had appeared in Marcus's class at the U-Dub, showed up in Dana's office, and almost killed his daughter Jayla. Who had destroyed Reece's eyes ten months ago.

Calm. He had to stay focused. Act in the power of the Spirit. No fear. "Hello, Zennon. We knew you'd show up sooner or later."

"Congratulations." Calen set the coin on his armrest and slowly clapped three times like the gong of a grandfather clock striking three. "Now it's my turn to be impressed. You figured it out much quicker than I imagined you would. When did you first suspect?"

"In retrospect, the first night I met you. But as I said, I wasn't certain till a moment ago."

"I've been looking forward to the instant when you realized it was me."

"Sure you have."

Zennon didn't answer.

Marcus leaned forward and pressed into the fear trying to tear at his mind. "And it explains who Simon is as well."

"Does it?" Zennon rolled his finger around the edge of the gold coin but didn't take his gaze off Marcus. "He's not exactly like us."

"What is he then? Who is he? What part does he have in this?"

"Let him tell you."

"I'd like you to."

"Well, to paraphrase Mick Jagger from many years ago, we can't always get the things we desire, but if we try with diligence, we can often acquire what we need." Calen grinned and played an air guitar. "What, you're not a Rolling Stones fan? Reece is. You should borrow a few of his CDs sometime."

Adrenaline pumped through Marcus. "I need you to listen to me very closely."

"Hmm?" Calen picked up the coin and massaged it between his thumb and fingers.

"You're going to walk into my house and tell Abbie your relationship is over. You're not going to contact her from this point forward. You're going to leave this host body you're in and never bother Abbie or Kat or Jayla in any way, shape, or form ever again."

"That is certainly one option."

"That's the *only* option."

"Do you really think so?" Calen flipped the coin from one hand to the other. "I would respectfully disagree. I say there's another option, which is that I continue to worm my way into your daughter's and your wife's and your other daughter's lives till I have them precisely where I want them."

"You take option two, I'll tell her exactly what you are."

"That's your plan?" Calen leaned forward and downed half his lemonade. "I think that strategy is fraught with problems. Why? Because Abbie won't believe you, will she? Her first love, the boy who treats her like a princess, is a demon?

"The senior who treats her with more attention and tenderness than her father ever has just so happens to be a spiritual being out to destroy her and her family? She'll buy that trinket? Nay, I think not. She'd look at you like you're crazy and trying to steal from her the happiest season of her life."

A smoldering anger rose in Marcus. "She'll believe me."

"Really?" Calen pointed toward the house. "I think you're delusional. I think you'd have a hard time convincing Kat about what I am, let alone Abbie."

"You're going to leave and you're never going to see Abbie again if I have to be with her twenty-four hours a day."

"Okay, that's one option—and I won't even comment on how stupid that sounds since you have a job and your precious Warriors to attend to. Do it. Ban her from seeing me. Forbid her from texting me or talking on the phone. Make her swear to avoid me at school. Go to the principal and tell her you need a restraining order against me because I've . . . well, I've been . . . wow, nothing is coming to mind at the moment. Model student. Youth group leader . . . athlete, good grades, hmmm, any ideas?" Calen laughed.

"Sure, you can forbid her from seeing me, but I'm thinking that won't do wonders for your relationship." Calen shook his head. "So sad. Just when the ice was starting to crack between you two."

Marcus's mind raced with ways to respond. But each of them seemed preposterous. Zennon, or Calen, was right. Abbie wouldn't believe him. Neither would Kat.

"Just curious." Calen's eyes grew dark. "Does it bother you more to realize I've had my tongue down your daughter's throat, or that there's nothing you can do to stop me from doing it again?"

Marcus gripped the arms of his chair hard and came forward, his heart pounding.

"Would it bother you if I told you about the times I've touched her in areas I don't think would be pleasing for you to hear about?"

"You're lying."

"She's weakening. And she's going to give in very soon. I have extensive experience in these matters. I'm sure you can trust me on that."

Marcus flung his glass of lemonade to the patio and it shattered. A moment later the back door was flung open and Abbie lurched onto the deck. "Dad! What happened?" She glanced back and forth between him and Calen.

"Go back inside, Abbie. Now!"

"What is going on?"

"Nothing. We're fine. Calen and I have to conclude our conversation and then we'll be back inside."

Calen mouthed, *I love you*. Abbie smiled and returned the sentiment.

Calen glanced at the broken glass strewn across the patio. "In the second book of Timothy it says God gives Christians a spirit of self-control. Pity they skipped you on handout day."

He stood, sauntered over to one of the smaller pieces of glass, bent over, and picked it up. "This would hurt if someone swallowed it. I wouldn't want that to happen to Abbie." He tossed it in the air and watched it spin in the fading sunlight, sending off tiny reflections of light. "No, I've grown fond of Abbie." He glared at Marcus. "But Jayla? I barely know her. If she swallowed it, I don't think it would bother me at all."

"I'm going to kill you."

Calen's thin smile grew into a grin and he strolled back over to Marcus and patted his hand before he could yank it away. "No, you're not, because you know you can't kill me. You could wrap your hands around my neck right now or send a bullet through

my brain, but it wouldn't do a thing to me. No, what you're going to do is stand up, straighten your preppy little professor shirt, go back through those doors, and pretend everything is okay. And you're going to back off on the little spiritual adventures you and your pals have been having. You're going to tell Reece you're taking a little break from the group, but you'll probably be back in late fall. You're going to let the others go after the Wolf on their own. Because if you don't . . ." Calen pointed toward the house and circled his tongue over his lips. "Do we understand each other completely?"

Calen didn't wait for an answer. He tossed the glass into one of Kat's flowerpots on the edge of the patio and glided toward the back door. Abbie slid it open and smiled at him. "Good talk with my dad?"

"Yes. He's an amazing guy. We had a great chat." Calen turned and drilled Marcus with his gaze before spinning back to Abbie. "I think we're going to get along really, really well."

"Dad?" Abbie called to Marcus over Calen's shoulder. "Are you coming in? Dinner's just about ready."

Marcus nodded and stood. He'd never felt so alone and so inadequate. He had no idea what to do next. No clue how to fight Zennon in the form of Calen. But it didn't matter. He fought tonight for Abbie, so he would fight well. He would call on the Spirit and the Spirit would answer.

He strode for the back door with a confidence he didn't feel, because he chose to believe by the time he sat down at the table he would have a solution.

TWENTY·ONE

MARCUS SAT IN HIS DEN, CLENCHING HIS HANDS TOGETHER tighter and tighter till the strain on his fingers grew into a sharp pain. He released his fingers and leaned forward, arms on his desk, and tried to stop sucking in breaths like he'd just completed a four-minute mile.

He'd come in from outside with confidence the Spirit would give him an answer, but his mind was clouded as if the Spirit was speaking but his ears were too clogged to hear. All he could consider was how impossible it would be to sit through a meal with Calen three feet away, using his allure to draw Abbie, Kat, and even Jayla into his dark pit of hell. That was not going to happen.

But what could he do? Calen—no, not Calen—Zennon, was right. If he kicked the thing out of his house, then Zennon would use the scene to play Abbie against him. If Marcus tried to tell his family right there at the table what Calen was they would shoot him down like a clay pigeon.

But he had to show up. He had to get down there now. He couldn't stay up here and let his wife and daughters dine without him. He stood and walked toward the door of his den. He stopped and his gaze fell on two framed movie posters side by side.

One was of *The Matrix*, the other of *The Terminator*. What would it be like if Neo and the Terminator met in battle? If it was in the real world, Neo would be slaughtered just like Marcus had been

out on the back patio. But if it was inside the matrix, the outcome would be vastly different.

Of course. That was it. He'd been fighting in Zennon's arena. An intellectual one where he could never beat the demon. Arguing with him was like a billy club going up against a lightsaber. He needed a nuclear bomb. What was that verse Reece continually quoted? *"For the weapons of our warfare are not of the flesh but have divine power to destroy strongholds."*

Marcus almost laughed. Hadn't he learned anything over the past year? He clomped down the stairs knowing exactly what to do. As he stepped into the dining room, he recalled Isaiah 42:13, *"The LORD will go forth like a warrior, He will arouse His zeal like a man of war. He will utter a shout, yes, He will raise a war cry. He will prevail against His enemies." Be with me, Warrior God.*

Chicken Dijon was stacked on a plate in the middle of the table. Thin wisps of steam rose from a bowl of mashed potatoes sitting next to a Caesar salad and next to it a bowl of corn on the cob. Norman Rockwell would be proud. Such a picturesque meal. One he was about to destroy.

"Nice of you to join us, honey." Kat glared at him.

Marcus smiled as wide as he could, moved to the head of the table, and sat. Kat was to his left and Jayla was next to her. To his right sat Abbie and to her right was Calen.

Here we go.

"Forgive my slight delay. May it not hamper in any way the enjoyment of this fine dinner and the pleasure of having with us once again our stimulating guest, Calen." Marcus took a deep breath through his nose and spread his napkin on his lap. "Calen and I had an extremely illuminating chat out on the back deck, and I feel like we truly had the chance to get to know each other intimately." He stared at the demon and the irises of Calen's brown eyes grew till they filled his pupils and turned to the color of a moonless night at 3:00 a.m.

"Now, before we begin, we have a tradition around the dinner

table in our family that I'm starting tonight, and I know all of us would love to have you participate in it, Calen."

Abbie frowned at him. "What are you doing, Dad?"

Marcus held up his hand. "As you know, Calen, we are a family that follows Jesus and have surrendered our lives to him. Abbie told me that you have done the same, which is wonderful. And apparently you're an integral part of the youth group at your church, so what we're about to do will likely feel very comfortable to you.

"With that in mind, from this evening forward, we will go around the table and declare our commitment to the Father, Son, and Holy Spirit by saying the following: 'I confess now before you, Lord, as well as before the friends and family now near me, that Jesus Christ is God come in the flesh, the King of kings, and all authority, all rulers, all principalities are under his feet.'"

Marcus turned and drilled Calen with his gaze. "As our guest, I'd be honored if you would do us the favor of going first." The air seemed to freeze and no one spoke.

"Why are you doing this, Dad?"

Marcus looked at Abbie and narrowed his eyes. "I need you to be silent for a bit, Abbs. And I need you to trust me."

"Marcus?" Kat laid her hand on his arm and squeezed hard. "Do you really want to create a scene at this moment?"

"It's a good question, Mr. Amber," Calen said. "Why are you doing this? I think your saying a short word of grace should suffice for the meal, but anything more will likely make your entire family as well as me quite uncomfortable."

"I appreciate your opinion, Calen. But tonight that will not suffice." Marcus turned to Kat. "Trust me that this is true." He turned back to Calen. "We need to hear our guest tell us Jesus Christ has come in the flesh and that he is God. It's not a difficult request for one who has surrendered to the Nazarene."

Calen's eyes went dark and his breathing grew shallow. He gripped the table and his fingers turned white. "I choose to respectfully decline."

Marcus raised himself up to his full height, sitting in the chair ramrod straight. "I insist."

He glanced at Abbie, whose eyes pleaded for him to stop, and then at Kat, who looked like she'd just swallowed a mouthful of gravel. He gave a slight nod to each of them, and the look in his eyes must have been like steel because they both dropped their gazes to the table and stayed silent.

Calen pulled his hands off the table and laughed. "I'm so sorry, Mr. Amber. I realize it's not my place to say this, but I think you're embarrassing your family and you're making me feel a little awkward as well." He motioned toward Kat. "Your beautiful wife has cooked a wonderful meal and it's getting cold. And if I'm being totally candid, I've never been good at saying grace, and on top of that, I've forgotten the words you wanted me to say. Can you just say a word of thanks so we all can eat?"

"Please, Dad? Please?"

"Calen, humor me and take part in our new tradition. I'm not asking you to say grace. And there are no words for you to memorize. Simply in your own words tell us Jesus is the Son of God, and that he is God come in the flesh."

Marcus waited a moment, then leaped to his feet, and as his chair smashed into the china hutch behind him, he shouted, "I command you by the blood of Jesus Christ to confess that Jesus is Lord."

A shudder went across Calen's shoulders and saliva bubbled onto his lips. His eyes narrowed and he leaned toward Marcus. "You don't want to do this."

Marcus stepped around the corner of the table. "By the blood of Jesus Christ, the power of his resurrection, and the power of his ascension, I command you to tell us who you are and what your true name is. I bind you with the blood of the Lamb. I command you to do this by the authority of Jesus Christ our Lord."

Calen snarled and grabbed the table with both hands. "You have no idea what you're dealing with. You're in so far over your head, you're looking up from the bottom of the seabed."

"Tell us, Calen. I command you by the blood of the Lamb. Tell us who you are."

The demon's face distorted into that of an elderly woman, then to a middle-aged man, then back to the face of Calen. "You have no power over me." His breathing came in gasps now and his hands slid across the table into the mashed potatoes, which slid between Kat and Jayla over the edge and smashed onto the floor.

"Tell us!" Marcus thundered.

"I am . . . I am . . . Zennon." Calen stood, stumbled back, knocked over his chair, and pointed at Marcus. "You cannot stop us. I'm one of millions and we are not going to destroy you at some point in the future—we already have. And you don't even know it."

"Get out! In the name of Jesus! Go!"

The demon spun and flung his hands at the mirror on the wall. The glass shattered and rained down on them like hail.

"Daddy!"

Calen staggered out of the dining room and came to a halt at the front door. He turned and stared at Marcus. "You're going to lose this battle, Professor. You've already lost it. Just wait till you see what we've cooked up just for you. I worked on it personally. It'll have you wishing you'd never gotten near the hornet's nest. We're coming for you. And for the others. And it won't end till you're dead." He waved his finger at Abbie and Jayla. "And then they will join you."

"One more thing." Zennon opened the door and pointed at Kat. "If you don't tell her soon, we will. And she'll know what you did to him. She'll know the catastrophic secret you've kept hidden from her forever."

Marcus screamed and sprinted toward the front door, but before he could reach Zennon, the door slammed shut and Marcus thumped against it hard. Adrenaline pumped through him and the back of his shirt was damp with perspiration.

After three deep breaths with his eyes closed he opened them and turned to his family. Abbie sat on the floor curled up in a ball in a corner of the dining room, her body shaking. Jayla was still at the

table, eyes wide, face the color of copy paper. Kat's arms were spread wide, one in the direction of each girl, and her head darted back and forth as if she couldn't decide which of their daughters to go to first.

Marcus strode back into the dining room, slid down beside Abbie, and motioned Kat and Jayla to join them.

"It's okay. We won. He's gone. He's gone." Marcus prayed, stopped after a few minutes, then prayed again. Three or four minutes went by and he prayed a third time.

"I think I'm going to be sick." Abbie squeezed Marcus's hand. "I . . . I kissed him, Daddy."

"I'm so sorry, Abbs." He pulled her tighter into his chest. "I should have seen it. I should have warned you."

"You did. And I wouldn't listen."

"It's okay."

The four of them sat in silence for what seemed like a half hour. He finally looked at Kat, who stroked Jayla's hair in between kissing the top of her head. She looked up at him, tears in her eyes but also peace.

"You're right, Marcus. It's not going to be easy. But it's going to be okay."

✠ ✠ ✠

Marcus lay in bed that night pretending he didn't know the secret Zennon had spoken of. Of Layne's death. Of how Marcus could have prevented their son from dying.

Marcus turned over, his back to Kat, and tried to push the memory from his mind. If she knew the truth it could destroy everything. It was a door he thought he'd successfully locked and bolted shut. But if Zennon had his way it would be flung wide open and Kat would be standing there when it was.

TWENTY-TWO

As Brandon clipped toward the stage in Oregon on Sunday evening he popped three cherry-flavored throat lozenges into his mouth and prayed they would get him through the concert. In the back of his mind he knew he had more than a sore throat going on.

His voice strength had been waning for the past three weeks and he'd never had a sore throat hang on this long. But with everything going on at Well Spring and with Warriors Riding, plus a concert schedule that never seemed to slow down, there was little time to think about it, let alone get to a doctor. And if he told anyone about it they'd force him to go see someone, which would be a waste of time.

His voice was just tired. It needed a little rest. So did he. Another month and he'd get some. His last concert before a two-week break would be in his backyard, at Marymoor Park in Redmond, Washington. It was a prime spot to end the tour, in front of friends and family.

Brandon stepped onto the stage and the lights fired up and bathed the band and him in their brilliant yellows, reds, and blues. "Hello, Portland! Do you want to live with freedom?"

The crowd roared their answer and Brandon grinned, then turned to the band. "Slight change in the song order. I want to kick things off with 'Final Race,' okay?"

The band ran through their first set as tight as they'd ever been. God was there and the Spirit moved through the music to bring people into deep worship.

As Brandon started into their second set and reached to hit his falsetto on the chorus, a sliver of pain shot down his throat. Then another and his voice faded. He glanced at Anthony, his bass player, who gave a questioning look. Brandon tapped his throat and shook his head, then mouthed the words, *Voice is gone*. He pointed at Anthony, then his microphone. Anthony picked up the hint and finished the song.

"Sorry, folks," Brandon rasped out. "I've been fighting a sore throat lately and it looks like it just won. My voice is shot as you can hear, so Anthony is going to carry this concert the rest of the way home."

Anthony's solid voice boomed through the speakers out over the crowd and the concert ended strong. Afterward Brandon went out into the crowd and tried to greet the people, but he couldn't speak in more than a whisper.

When he reached his dressing room, his manager, Kevin Kaison, was standing outside of it, arms pulled tight across his lean frame. "You've been keeping this from me, haven't you?"

Brandon shrugged and sighed.

"How long?"

"Three weeks," Brandon rasped out.

"Not good, pal."

"I know."

He did know. Depending on what he'd done, he could be out anywhere from a few days to forever. He didn't mean to get dramatic, but if it was nodules on his throat and he'd pushed it too far, he might never sing again like he once did.

First Reece with his eyes and now Brandon's voice. It seemed his premonition might be right. What was next? The professor would sprain his mind? Dana would lose her ability to lead? He

needed to talk to Reece about it. Get the Warriors to pray for him. Get healed fast.

Brandon scowled at the floor, then glanced at Kevin. "It's no surprise. The enemy is trying to take me out. Reece said this would happen."

"Uh, maybe it's not the enemy." Kevin cocked his head. "Maybe it's just you being stupid."

"Wow, thanks for the sympathy."

Kevin tapped his foot in double time as he rubbed his brown hair. "Sorry to be harsh, but it's easy to blame the enemy on something you should have taken care of. You had to know it was more than a sore throat, but you kept it to yourself and kept pushing your voice till it snapped. Couldn't it be as simple as that?"

Brandon shrugged.

"I'd find out quick. I'm getting an appointment for you in the next day or two."

Brandon nodded.

He sat in his hotel room that night trying not to swallow and trying to figure out if Kevin was right. He hadn't taken care of his throat. So was it the enemy who did this to him, or just Brandon's neglect? Regardless of the cause, he had a feeling there was a deeper plan in the works that would make the sore throat a blip on the screen in comparison.

✠ ✠ ✠

On Tuesday afternoon, the doctor slid the images of Brandon's throat onto his table and grimaced.

"I don't like the look in your eyes, Doc."

"Yeah, I wouldn't either." He poked at the shots with a mechanical pencil. "But it's really not that bad."

"Define 'not that bad.'" Brandon rubbed the edge of his chair and braced himself. To him, not that bad would mean go home,

drink some tea with honey, and not sing for a few days. Anything else would be a disaster.

"The good news is, I think you'll be fine. This happens to singers more often than people hear about." The doctor nodded at the statement. "The bad is, you won't be belting out the hits for at least five weeks. And that's after the surgery."

"Surgery?" Brandon shook his head. "Not an option."

"You've been mightily unkind to your vocal cords. You could take care of this with six months of no singing—that's what Celine Dion did, but it sounds like you don't want to take that long. Plus, in your case I'd recommend the surgery anyway."

"I need to be singing faster than that."

"Nope. Sorry." The doctor leaned back and put his hands behind his head.

"I have a concert out in Redmond at Marymoor Park in three weeks."

"You'll be recovering from surgery three weeks from now, so unless you want to lip-synch—"

"Can I put off the surgery till the first part of September?"

"Sure." The doctor leaned forward and gathered the photos into a stack. "You can put off the surgery forever. But if you want to sing again, I'd recommend having the procedure done sooner than later."

"How soon is sooner?"

"Since I like your music, you could persuade me to do the surgery tomorrow."

"Tomorrow?"

"Yes."

"Don't you have to get prepped for something like this?"

"When Kevin called and set up the appointment, he persuaded me to act fast. I did. Plus I'd like to see you up and singing, maybe not as fast as you do, but pretty close. So are you in?"

TWENTY-THREE

"Outstanding work your first ten days in the new role, Dana." Robert popped his head into Dana's office on Wednesday mid-morning and grinned. "You made me look like a hero when you were a general sales manager and you're already making me look that way as GM."

"Already?"

"Yes. I've noticed the restructuring you've been doing."

"Thanks for pushing for my promotion."

He waved his hands. "Nope, I won't take any credit. The only thing I did was say yes when they asked if I thought you'd do a good job as general manager of the station."

"I appreciate it anyway."

"Listen, are you and Perry still on for joining my wife and me a week from tomorrow for dinner?"

"I'm not really seeing him anymore."

"Oh, is that right?"

She nodded, then waited for the invitation to be withdrawn. As a couple she was desirable. Single? Not so much. Dana knew how the game was played.

"So you're coming solo? That will still work if you're okay with it. We'll have a great time."

"I thought—" She stopped, not knowing how to put her thoughts into words.

"You thought we were just doing the polite couples thing?" Robert spread his arms wide, placed his palms on Dana's desk, and leaned forward. "We like you for you, Dana. Period. You don't have to have a date to be around us." He straightened up. "But if you want me to try to fix you up with someone . . ."

"No. I'm okay."

"Great."

Dana smiled as Robert whapped the door frame of her office and strode away. She'd always liked him, but before the promotion she wouldn't have described their relationship as a friendship. A good working acquaintance? Yes. But hanging out together and possibly becoming friends with Robert's wife? She hadn't ever considered it.

But even though it had only been ten days since her promotion, she already felt as if she'd been given membership in an exclusive club where there was no official card to get in, but there was a card nonetheless.

Her cell phone chimed and she glanced at the reminder. Oops. Ten minutes before the staff meeting and half an hour of work to do before she got there. She'd never worked harder than during the past week and never loved it more. Everyone in the station had responded positively to her promotion and a significant amount of revenue had been booked in the past week. Huge blessing.

A knock came on her door frame. Rebecca. "Your buddy Reece on line one."

"Thanks." She picked up the phone while reading an e-mail regarding a TV spot they were developing to promote their summer jam concert.

"Reece, hi."

"How are you?"

"Good, but busy. No time to talk."

"I'll be brief. Just confirming you're still coming to Well Spring next week to help train our next batch of recruits. We leave next Thursday at noon, back Sunday night late as usual."

Dana rubbed her eyes and moaned inside. "Didn't you get my e-mail?"

The line went silent for a few seconds. "E-mail isn't the most effective way to communicate with me these days."

"I thought you were going to set up computer reading software for your e-mails."

"I don't see much need when I'm sensing the Spirit is going to heal me soon. What did your e-mail say?"

"I can't go, Reece. I'm sorry."

"What?"

"I have another commitment." Dinner with her boss and his wife was a commitment? Yes, it was. She'd earned it. She needed it. She wanted it.

"The mission of training these people is critical, Dana."

"I'd love to hear of one mission over the past year that hasn't been critical."

"None, but that doesn't change the importance of the time and the fact the entire team needs to be there."

"Point taken, but that doesn't change the fact that I can't make it."

"Why can't you?"

Heat rose to her face. "I don't have time to get into it right now."

"I think you should make the time."

She glanced at her watch. Eight minutes till the meeting. "I'd love to be able to make time, create it out of nothing, and add it to the twenty-four hours I get every day, but I can't. Twenty-four is all there is and all there ever will be."

After she hung up, Dana glared at her phone and shoved it across her desk where it teetered on the edge, then dropped off and thumped onto the carpet. She was mad at Reece, mad at herself, mad at the emotional energy the Warriors and always fighting the enemy took, and mad that her excuse for not going to Well Spring would melt under any kind of honest scrutiny.

Was it so wrong that she finally felt like she belonged at the station and wasn't alone in her job? That a group of people she liked

didn't center around activities that exhausted every fiber of her? That she might get a social life going where she could enjoy simple pleasures like going to dinner or a play and maybe even at some point going on a blind date with one of Robert's friends?

She glanced at her watch. Six minutes till the meeting. She'd have to fake it. And try to ignore the tiny neon beacon in her heart telling her she was going the wrong way down a one-way street.

TWENTY-FOUR

KEVIN SAUNTERED INTO BRANDON'S HOSPITAL ROOM ON Wednesday evening, leaned against the wall, and pointed back into the hallway with his thumb. "They told me the surgery went well this morning. That it couldn't have gone better."

Brandon flashed a thumbs-up.

"That's the good news. The bad is, it sounds like we have to scrap the Marymoor concert."

Brandon shook his head as he motioned his manager-agent to come farther into the room. No, they wouldn't have to cancel. The solution was simple. As long as Kevin would go along with it, and Brandon didn't think it would take that much persuading to get his manager behind the idea.

"No?"

Brandon shook his head and beckoned Kevin closer. When he reached the hospital bed, Brandon rapped out a message on his laptop.

The show must go on.

"There's no way the doctor I just talked to will let you sing at Marymoor. It's too soon. I suppose you could stand up there and talk for two and a half hours, but I'm not thinking that's what the audience will be coming to hear."

We can still do the show.

"Let's get serious. You want to explain how that's going to happen without your being able to sing? The concert is in just under three weeks and the doc just told me he won't even let you speak till next Thursday, and singing again won't come for another four weeks at the earliest."

Brandon smiled and typed out another message.

I have an idea.

"Let me guess. You want me to play videos of you in concert on a big screen? Or are you going to lip-synch?"

Brandon shook his head, moved his mouth as if singing, played an air guitar, and then pointed at Kevin.

"Me?" Kevin shook his head.

Brandon nodded.

"Nah, nah, nah, no way."

Brandon grinned and typed out another line.

This could be a big step, a nice break for you.

"Yeah, right. Nice break like break my career into a million pieces before it starts? I'm not ready to headline an entire concert. Plus I'm not going to make my debut trying to step into the monstrous shoes of Brandon Scott. I'm telling you, they'd figure out really quickly I wasn't you."

Brandon whipped his fingers over the keyboard.

You have a hit song, bro. Big hit. They're singing it in churches. A lot of people are starting to know your name. You're working on an album so you have those songs as well. You'll sing yours and some of mine. You know all of them by heart. It'll be a combo pack. They'll love it. I've already worked out all the details with the band. They're ready

to rehearse. I've talked to the promoter, and she's good with it. And every ticket holder has been sent an e-mail explaining the situation, and they've been offered a full refund if they want.

Plus Spirit 105.3 is promoting it on air and on their website. And I convinced them to say, "Come hear Kevin Kaison, the inspiration behind Brandon Scott, the one who believed in him and cared for him and supported him and made him into the man he is today."

"What? That makes it sound like I'm your wife. They aren't really saying that."

The hospital bed shook and creaked from Brandon's silent laughter. He bent over his notebook computer again.

No. Not the last part, but they are pushing the concert.

"I don't know, man. That would be too weird to have me up there."

Pray about it. Think about it. I believe it's the right moment for a live crowd to discover Kevin Kaison and his stunning songwriting and singing ability. And "I'm scared" is not a valid excuse. Not after all the speeches you've given me over the years about pushing through fear.

Kevin's eyes grew brighter and Brandon knew his friend would accept.

"I need a day to mull this over."

Really?

"No, not really." Kevin stuck out his fist and bumped Brandon's. "I'm in."

You're going to kill. I guarantee it.

✚ ✚ ✚

"Tell me you got Brandon Scott to come on the show."

Sooz slouched against Carson Tanner's door frame, a few strands of her hair hanging in her face. She flashed a thumbs-up and smiled. "I got Brandon to come on the show."

"Are you serious?" Carson lurched forward in his chair, his knees bumping his thick glass desk.

"No. Of course I'm not serious. You know this is mission extremely improbable. You made multiple attempts yourself. Remember when you liked Brandon and his music and tried for months and months to get him to come on? He doesn't do interviews. He hasn't for a long, long time. No exceptions."

"I never stopped liking him, which is why I want him on the show. I'm trying to bring him back to the truth. Keep him from getting too wrapped up with this modern mystic Reece Roth wacko." Carson rocked back in his chair, cradled the back of his head with his hands, and stared at the ceiling. "I don't get Brandon. In this day and age where you're supposed to connect with your fans—have give-and-take—interact with them, and the guy won't—"

"He does connect with his fans. You should hear what he does after every concert. Apparently he stays for hours talking to people, praying with them. He just doesn't connect with interviewers. Like you."

"Any other discouraging news?"

"Yes. He just went in for some kind of vocal-cord surgery so he'll be out for who knows how long recovering from that. Probably step out of the public light for at least a couple of months."

"Those kinds of surgeries don't take that long to recover from." Carson tossed his pen across the room and it smacked into the wall.

"I'm just saying."

"I'm not giving up on this, Sooz. I'm going to keep believing God is in this because I know he is. And that he will make it happen."

"I still say you could get some of these people who are doing mini Warriors Riding retreats on the show—"

"There's no point in cutting off the heads of dandelions. We could do that all day and they'd just grow back. We have to take off the head of the snake. Dam up the river at the source."

"That's three metaphors. I think one will do."

"Just get him. Soon. Okay?"

"I'm not giving up either. And like you, I believe. This battle is God's and he will not fail us."

TWENTY-FIVE

AS REECE CLOMPED DOWN HIS STAIRS AT NOON EIGHT days later, he heard his front door open and a voice he didn't expect.

"Good morning, Reece."

He smiled at the sound of Dana's voice as she said hello to Brandon. A pleasant surprise. He'd put the odds of her showing up today to head for Well Spring with them at a hundred to one.

"You're going?" Reece asked.

"I am indeed going. Don't sound so shocked."

"You were able to get out of your seemingly unbreakable commitment?"

She hesitated. "Yes, I was."

The sound of the door opening again and footsteps on the wood floor of his entryway and a bag being set down filled his ears. It had to be the professor. "Looks like all members of the entourage are present."

"Where's Doug?" Dana asked.

"He's meeting us at the ranch."

"Hey, Marcus," Brandon said.

"Your voice is quiet, but overall sounds quite adequate," Marcus said. "All is well?"

"Yeah, the doc says I'm going to be fine. Won't be singing for a bit, but things look good and it shouldn't be long before I'm back onstage."

Reece took a step in the direction Dana's voice had come from. "Do you care to expand on how you escaped your obligation?"

"Not at all. Doug's words the other night were simple but profound when he said, 'A subtle attack can often be far more effective than a direct assault since an attack of subterfuge and nuance is often not noticed till the victim has crawled into the middle of the spider's web.'

"You all probably saw it the whole time. I don't know why I didn't. My promotion—obvious to everyone but me that the enemy was using it to distract me, distance me from the game."

"True." Relief fell on Reece. He'd expected a much longer struggle to get Dana back firing on all cylinders.

"Why didn't you try to tell me?"

"I did."

"I mean, tell me specifically that it was the enemy."

"Would you have listened?"

Reece heard Dana shift in her chair. "No."

"So what does this mean for your job?"

"I'm not sure, but I am sure I'm all in with the Warriors."

He took another step toward her and reached out for her shoulders. He wrapped an arm around them tight. "You're a treasure, Dana. Never forget that." He released her and motioned with his hands. "Gather 'round, let's get ourselves to Well Spring."

"I don't care how many times we've done this teleportation thing. It still feels very, very strange," Dana said to Brandon.

"I know." Reece heard the smile in Brandon's voice. "That's why it's such a cool rush. I'm ready. Beam me up, Reecy."

✠ ✠ ✠

After they settled in at Well Spring, they all gathered in the main cabin. Over lunch Marcus told of his encounter with Zennon. Dana tried to imagine what it would be like to have a daughter go through what Abbie had just endured. Sometimes not having children was a very good thing.

"Excellent," Reece said when the professor finished.

"Excellent?" Brandon said. "Are you kidding? I wouldn't describe what the prof and his family went through as excellent."

Doug set down his fork and patted Brandon's arm. "What Reece means is—"

"I know, I know . . . things are on the right track, we've got the enemy upset, my throat, Dana's promotion, Reece's eyes not being healed yet, Zennon's attack on the professor—how that's all a good thing because he's trying to take us out before we confront the Wolf, blah, blah, blah." Brandon glanced around the table. "But don't you ever get tired of the battle? Wouldn't you like some peace and quiet sometimes?"

"Yes." Reece smiled. "Absolutely. We all need a break. That's why we're going in this afternoon before the new recruits get here. To a place of peace. Refreshment." He laughed. "I wish I could see the stunned looks on your faces, which I'm positive are there. Yes, I'm finally going to go back in. Scout's honor." He held up his fingers in the traditional Boy Scout's salute.

"You feel prepared?" Brandon said.

"Funny," Reece said as his countenance grew serious. "Yes, I am prepared, for whatever the Spirit has for me."

Dana looked at her watch. One thirty. The new trainees wouldn't be here till six, so they had plenty of time to go into wherever Reece wanted to go, get back out, and make any necessary last-minute prep to the ranch. The guys of course thought the place looked great. Reece had an excuse now, but the others should be able to see a bit of touch-up was sorely needed. These were the moments she wished another woman was part of the Warriors.

"Are we ready?" Doug glanced around the room, a look of glee on his face.

Dana opened her Bible. "Can I read something first?"

"Please." Doug nodded.

She glanced at the others before focusing her gaze on Reece. "I don't want to create any false expectations or stir hope without

reason, Reece, but as I was unpacking before lunch I think I heard the Spirit saying when you went in again, you'd like what you found there." She flipped her Bible to Isaiah. "And then I saw this verse: 'I will lead the blind by a way they do not know, in paths they do not know I will guide them. I will make darkness into light before them and rugged places into plains. These are the things I will do, and I will not leave them undone.'"

Reece didn't comment but he nodded and put his hand on hers.

"Amen and so be it," Doug said. "Anyone else?" No one spoke. "Then let's do a quick cleanup and be off."

Ten minutes later they took hold of each other's hands. Dana closed her eyes and waited. Less than a moment later she opened her eyes and found herself standing on a beach that reminded her of Costa Rica, no, maybe it was more like Jamaica or Fiji. Tiny waves lapped at a white sand beach, the breeze off the crystal-blue water was perfect, and the warm sand felt like cotton against her bare feet.

As it had been in the realm of the Wall of Colors, the hues were far more brilliant here than on earth and they filled her soul with wonder. She turned to look at the tropical foliage behind her but was interrupted by the screams and roars of delight that poured out of Reece.

"I can see!" Reece bounded down the beach and sprinted through the water, his arms waving like he was trying to fly. He probably was flying, in his mind and heart and spirit at least.

Dana laughed and shouted, "Yes!" in chorus with the whoops and cheers of Doug, Brandon, and Marcus. She hadn't known this would happen, but she had known.

After a few minutes he splashed back toward them through the water and stopped five feet away. He grinned, reached for his glasses, and pulled them off like he was unveiling his greatest photograph. For the first time in almost a year she looked into his brilliant blue eyes. Amazing. Full of love, and joy, and freedom. And even more penetrating than when she'd last seen them, if that was possible.

Dana continued to grin as Reece danced in an awkward circle, kicking up sand and letting out another whoop. She turned to Doug and frowned. He was smiling, but there was a deep sadness in his eyes she didn't understand.

For the next ten minutes she and Marcus wandered up and down the beach. Brandon stepped into the sea and swam out to a tiny island of rocks sixty yards off the shore, and Doug pushed into the thick jungle behind them. It was exactly what Reece had said it would be. Refreshing, restorative, invigorating. Too soon Doug's voice rang out over the beach. "It's time to go back."

They gathered at the spot they'd started from, all of their faces radiant and full of life.

"Do you know what this means?" Reece pointed to his eyes and grinned.

Brandon pointed at the big man. "What happens in here—"

"Becomes reality in the physical world." Reece held his arms wide. "I'm healed. The prophecy has been fulfilled."

Doug didn't comment and motioned them together with his hands, his eyes down. "Are you ready?"

"You're kidding, right?" Reece grinned. "Not even close. Five more minutes, friend. This is a moment to celebrate. It's been a long time coming. I need to soak in a little more of this beauty."

"I wish it could be longer." The same look Dana had seen a few minutes ago passed over Doug's face. "A few more at most."

Reece walked to the water's edge and turned his head slowly from one side to the other. Three or four minutes later he turned and trudged back up the beach. "Okay, Doug, I know we need to go. Seeing here is nothing like seeing back on earth. But trust me, I'm not complaining. I have a lot of photography to make up for. So yes, let's go."

Doug didn't respond as he clasped Dana's hand on one side and Marcus's on the other. Reece grabbed the hands of Marcus and Brandon and an instant later they were back in the living room at Well Spring.

Dana whirled to find Reece. He was on his knees in the center of the room, his head resting on the area rug. "Are you okay, Reece?"

He didn't answer and she looked at Doug. His face was ashen, and as he returned her gaze she realized why. He'd known this was going to happen, but there was nothing he could have done. Nothing any of them could have done to prepare Reece for the emotions of the moment.

The big man lifted his head and turned to them. He whipped off his sunglasses and stared at her and the others with the black, seared tissue that a moment ago had been his brilliant blue eyes. Reece opened his mouth. No noise came from his lips, but Dana could imagine what it would sound like if it did. Utter anguish.

She looked at Brandon and Marcus. At first their faces registered shock, then understanding, then horror. Doug glanced at her, then waited till Brandon and Marcus looked at him as well. Then he stood and motioned her and the others outside. No one spoke as they shuffled through the front door. None of them spoke as they stepped away from each other, all in different directions. There was no need. All of them would ask the Spirit why Reece wasn't healed, and all of them would ask him to fall on Reece with a peace their guide couldn't ignore.

✛ ✛ ✛

That night after their first session—without Reece—and after the new students had settled into their cabins, Dana sat at the fire pit and stared at the coals as the last of them winked out. She lifted her gaze at the sound of shoes on the stone path to her right. Doug.

"May I join you?"

"Of course."

He sat next to Dana, hands clasped, concern etched on his face.

"You knew this would happen to Reece, didn't you?"

"I didn't know." He sighed. "But yes, I suspected."

"Why weren't his eyes healed here if they were healed there?"

"I don't know, Dana. But I do know this is not the final chapter of any of our stories."

✛ ✛ ✛

The Friday, Saturday, and Sunday sessions went well. There were breakthroughs for almost all of the students and Reece took part in every class. If he had been taken down by what happened—what didn't happen to him—nothing in what he said or did showed it. But still, he didn't seem himself.

Ninety percent of the trainees committed to being prayer allies and starting their own groups when they got home. On Saturday night Reece spoke powerfully about going deeper in the Spirit and where the students needed to go from here. But while his words resonated, the fire behind them had gone dim.

As the last of the cars with the trainees in them pulled out of the ranch on Sunday late morning, Dana turned and walked north along the river. She needed to get away. Find a slice of silence to sit in and let the intensity of the past three days slide off of her, along with the fear Reece's eyes would never be restored.

By the time she'd gone one hundred yards she felt better. By the time she'd gone two hundred a sense of hope welled up inside. It wasn't over yet, and until it was, she would keep praying for the healing of Reece's eyes and believing it would happen. She took five steps off the path toward the river to watch the currents as she prayed.

"Hey!"

Dana spun at the sound of the voice. Brandon sat twenty yards to her left behind three pine trees, smiling at her—the same smile that melted her heart when they'd first met. Ugh. She was not going to go there even for a second. She'd been down that path so often in the past year her footprints were stamped on the trail like concrete.

She was done with Brandon forever. She'd told him that. She meant it.

"Want to talk for bit?"

No, she didn't. Yes, she did. Why did she have to be so schizophrenic when it came to him? Probably the curse of once being in love with the idiot.

"Sure, why not."

TWENTY-SIX

"Do you think we'll survive when we go after the Wolf?" Brandon said as Dana shuffled toward him.

"Survive the Wolf?" Dana sat next to him and let out a puff of laughter. "I'm focused on recovering from the past four days."

He knew how she felt. The last of the new trainees had left the ranch an hour ago. It had gone extremely well. Each of the four retreats they'd done over the past year had brought great freedom and healing to the men and women who had come, and this one was no different. But the training left him feeling like an air mattress after all the air had been expelled.

He turned from his view of the river below and lifted his hand to block the late afternoon sun flowing around Dana and into his eyes. She sat with her arms wrapped around her knees, light brown hair pulled back and tied up with a red scrunchie. No makeup. No need for it. She was beautiful.

"I agree." Brandon stared at her eyes, hoping she would turn and look into his. "It's exhilarating and exhausting at the same time."

The sound of the river soothed him as if God were washing away the dirt that seemed to cling to his soul after every training session was over and the new recruits had gone home. Reece said the enemy tried to spread fear and sin to them like a virus from the people they were training and setting free, so there needed to be a time of restoration and refreshment. Brandon didn't understand

the theology behind the statement, but he did know he felt like he needed time to detox every time after they were done and it seemed Dana felt the same.

He turned and looked at Dana again till she returned his gaze. "Do you ever wish you could go back to the way your life was before Well Spring?"

She shifted and drew her finger along the pine needles they sat on. "Yes and no. Do I wish we weren't the ones leading the charge into a battle that probably won't end till we die? Yes. Do I wish I could slip back into the chains I wore before coming here a year ago? Not a chance. What about you?"

"Same. But there are some things I'd like to go back and do differently."

"Such as?"

Maybe someday he'd tell her. Not now. It would still be a long time before he stepped into that rowboat. But it didn't mean he couldn't explore the condition of the oars.

"How's Perry?"

Dana picked at a spot of pitch on her hand. "Are we going to get into this again?"

"Not at all." Brandon raised his palms in surrender. "I'm genuinely asking."

She frowned. "Why don't I believe you?"

"Hey, don't believe me. It's fine." Brandon watched a leaf move from as far up the river as he could see till it disappeared downstream before he spoke again. "Are you worried about Reece? Do you think he'll be okay, that he'll make it through this?"

"He's probably good."

"You think so? It helps to hear you say that, because to get his sight back, then come out and discover he didn't get healed. Wow."

"Perry is probably good. Once I told him there was no chance of anything more between us than friends, he stopped calling."

"What?" Brandon turned and grinned. "Sorry, I thought you were answering my question about—"

"I know." She offered him a rare smile and her green eyes danced like they used to in the age when they'd been together. "I figured that out."

"Sorry, I just—"

"I'm teasing." She nudged him with her elbow. "Yes, I'm worried about him."

"Why are you worried about Perry?"

"No, I'm not, I'm worried about—"

Brandon grinned. "Now I get to say I knew that."

They both laughed and leaned into each other, and as they did a shot of adrenaline surged through Brandon. Instantly it felt like it was four years earlier and his engagement ring was still on Dana's finger, and his resolve not to ask the question till ages had passed melted away. He stared at her till Dana met his gaze.

"I know I'm asking again. The question I'm not supposed to, but do you ever think about us? What might have been if I hadn't . . . ?"

She dropped her gaze to the ground, then raised it to once again look at the river. "Let's walk, okay?"

"Where?" They stood and dusted off their jeans.

Dana pointed west and they started out on the trail that led toward the cabins.

"That's what you'd do differently, isn't it?" She kicked at sticks and pinecones as they shuffled along the trail leading past the cabins toward the zip lines and ropes course. A team of workers had installed it last fall so students could learn to conquer physical fears in order to face spiritual fears. Reece hadn't talked about putting in a strip of burning coals. Yet.

The silence between them stretched and Brandon let the subject drop. "Tell me what you're thinking about Reece."

Dana stopped, put her hands on her hips, and laughed. "I'm impressed. We're having a fairly digressive conversation and yet you never lost any of the threads."

"As you might suspect, I've bumped into a few women over the course of my life, so I've had practice."

She frowned at him playfully. "You're saying women often can't talk in a straight line?"

"That's exactly what I'm saying."

Dana laughed and walked on. "Yes, of course I'm worried. As mature as Reece is in the faith, you can't lose your sight and your greatest passion, think you've been healed and find out you haven't, and not have it tear at your mind and push you into decisions you wouldn't have made before."

"Have you talked to Doug?"

"A little bit the other night."

"Did he have any insight?" Brandon blinked. "Sorry, wrong word."

"Not really, just to pray."

"You know, we could go crazy and pray for him right now."

She smiled. "Let's go crazy."

They settled down in a small grove of alder trees just past the ropes course and slipped into silence. They'd prayed so often together over the past eleven months neither needed either to start or even pray out loud. After five or so minutes, Brandon opened his eyes and gazed at Dana till she opened hers.

"What did you get? Anything?"

Dana nodded, her eyes wider than normal.

"I'm not liking the look on your face."

"I kept getting this feeling of imminent danger and a picture of a hockey team."

"A what?"

"I know, I've never even been to a hockey game and couldn't tell you one team name, but I had a clear picture of one, their uniforms, the colors. I could almost hear the scrape of their blades on the ice, their streaking toward the other team's goal. It was vivid."

"The hockey team was in danger?"

"No, not them, but they had something to do with the danger or were the cause of the danger."

"Wow. Left of left field."

"Yeah, I know. What about you? Anything?"

"Nothing." Brandon shrugged. "Except an image of something white."

"What was the something?"

"I don't know. It was white. That was it."

"Like ice? Were you seeing the hockey rink?"

"Sure. Maybe. I have no clue." Brandon glanced at his watch. "We should go. We're supposed to be meeting with Reece and Marcus and Doug in a few minutes. Final debrief before we get ready to head home."

They both rose and ambled back toward the main cabin, listening to a lark bunting warble out an afternoon song. Dana glanced at him, then turned her gaze to a blue sky speckled with wispy clouds.

"I'm not trying to avoid the question. I just don't know how to answer it."

"You mean the 'do you think about us' question?"

"Once again, I'm impressed."

"You don't have an answer, or you don't want to give it to me?"

"I have an answer, but not one I'm ready to speak out loud."

"How often?"

"What?"

"How often do you think about us?"

"That's a different question, Brandon."

"Yes."

"With work and Warriors Riding and the healing still going on inside me . . . I try not to think about how often I think about us, or what we used to be."

They walked the rest of the way back to the main cabin in silence. She hadn't given him an answer, yet at the same time she had. She did think about the two of them. How often? It

didn't matter. The two of them came into her mind—and for the moment it was enough to say.

When Dana reached for the doorknob, Brandon put his hand on top of hers and stopped her from opening it. "Dana, I—"

"Don't ask me about it anymore, okay?" She smiled but her eyes were full of sorrow. "I think about us, yes, but that life is over and I don't see it ever returning. That part of my heart is gone. I'm sorry if that's hard to hear, but you and I happened in another age." Dana sighed and lifted his hand off of hers. "We should get inside. Reece and Marcus are probably wondering where we are."

She turned the knob and stepped into the cabin. He waited for her to look back, to give him another sad smile or a glance that said she didn't truly mean what she'd said, but all he saw was the back of her head as she strolled into the cabin and turned the corner into the living room.

⊕ ⊕ ⊕

"Hey."

The sound of Dana's voice filled the main room of the cabin along with the clop of her shoes on the heated hardwood floor. Then Reece heard another pair of shoes. Had to be Brandon since the professor and Doug already sat around the fireplace.

"Glad you two are back. I want to talk about our plan for going after the Wolf. Find out what we've all heard from the Spirit. See how and where Jesus wants to take us next."

Reece heard Brandon and Dana take seats across from each other and a slow sigh from Brandon.

"How is the Song today?"

"He's doing awesome."

But Brandon wasn't good. His voice betrayed him. Interesting that although Reece could no longer see body language, his sense of hearing had been so heightened he could gauge people's emotional state by the slightest nuance in their tone of voice.

"You're sure?"

"Yup. I'm sure."

It had to be something going on with Dana. Or the lack of something going on. Even though Brandon rarely discussed Dana with him, it was clear to anyone with a modicum of perception that the musician still loved her. It was also clear she either didn't feel the same or was refusing to let her feelings surface.

Reece shook his head. No time to think about that now. They needed to move on to the Wolf. "Who wants to start?"

The tap of a pen on a notebook came from Reece's left. Marcus getting ready to speak.

"The impression I received was we were to take our first step by going right to the source."

Reece smiled. He'd gotten the same feeling. "You mean engage Carson directly?"

"Precisely." Marcus's tapping increased. "But I don't mean confront him. I mean watch him in action, get a sense for what surrounds him spiritually. Do a reconnaissance mission."

"I agree, but how do you suggest we do that? I doubt Carson has any idea who we are, and he's not going to invite someone he doesn't know to drop by for coffee and donuts."

Reece heard someone shift position on the couch. "Easy," Dana said.

"How so?" Reece cocked his head in her direction.

"Have Brandon go on his show."

Reece laughed. "Of course." Given Brandon's level of fame, Carson had to know who the musician was. "Does he interview musicians?"

"Often," Dana said.

"I don't do interviews." From the sound of Brandon's voice and the scrape of his clothes against his chair, it was apparent the Song had stood and turned his back to the group.

"Why is that?" Reece said.

"I haven't done one in over four years."

Dana scoffed, "Is that part of your branding? You want to stay mysterious to your fans?"

Reece heard Brandon's feet shuffling back and forth over the cabin floor. Finally his feet stopped and it sounded like he turned. "But if the rest of you think this is what the Spirit is saying, I'm in."

TWENTY-SEVEN

Sooz stood in Carson Tanner's doorway late Monday afternoon, grinning like the Cheshire cat and bouncing on her toes double time.

"That's a good news smile." He rose and sauntered over to her. "No, that's a great news smile."

"You're not going to believe this." She pointed toward the heavens.

"I believe, help my unbelief."

"Guess who just called me?"

"The only person I can't believe would ever call you is Brandon Scott."

"He asked if he could come on your show."

"Unreal. God comes through."

"I've booked him for June fourteenth. And get this. We're not talking a phone interview. We're talking he's going to be in town to see his label so he wants to come to the studio."

Carson shook his head and sniffed out a laugh. "Just making sure I heard you correctly here. He called you. Not his manager. Him. Asking to be on my show. Plus he wants to come into the studio? Here? In person?" He bent down and pounded the floor with his fist.

"Yes."

"Why?" Carson rose up. "Please tell me what changed."

"No idea."

"I have an idea." He grinned at Sooz. "God is most definitely on the move."

She nodded and laughed.

Carson lurched back around his desk and sat, his hands moving like a windmill. "We're going to promote the garbanzo beans out of this. I want a new audio stinger, thirty-second promos running four times an hour every day till the interview, notices on all our social media sites, the blog, and at least three e-mail blasts to our subscribers. We're going to have the biggest audience we've had in eons. And Brandon and what the enemy is doing through him and his buddies will be hit like a fleet of Mack trucks."

TWENTY-EIGHT

LATE AFTERNOON ON SATURDAY KEVIN KAISON STOOD
backstage at Marymoor Park, trying to keep his legs from bouncing.
Why did he tell Brandon yes? This was too much. Sure, he wanted
to do the concert. But unless his nerves quieted, he'd be so amped
up and nervous his voice would make a soprano sound like a bass.

He rubbed his hands together. Both were damp with perspiration. His hands would slide all over his guitar—and he didn't play
slide guitar. His mouth ached. He didn't realize he was clenching
his teeth till the pain worked its way up into his jaw. He was a basket
case.

Kevin slumped onto a stool, closed his eyes, and laid two fingers across his wrist. Wow. Relax. How could his heart race with
Indianapolis 500 speed when all he was doing was sitting?

✛ ✛ ✛

By seven the crowd started ambling in over the expansive grass of
the venue and picked spots to lay their blankets or set up their red
and blue and green folding chairs. And it was a crowd. He'd hoped
for three hundred people to show up; he'd expected a hundred. He
glanced at his watch. Still an hour till showtime and there had to be
at least seven hundred people already through the gates.

They knew Brandon wasn't playing, right? Then again, reducing

the ticket price by half might have something to do with people still turning out. But still, who would want to see Brandon Scott's manager? Yeah, Kevin had a hit song, but that was hit song, singular. Did they really want to plunk down hard cash to see some guy they'd barely heard of?

Anthony, who wasn't much thicker than a javelin, sauntered up to him as he sucked on a milk shake Kevin surmised was his usual concoction of ice cream, butterscotch, and a healthy dose of wheat germ.

"Looks like you've got a decent crowd shuffling in."

"Yeah, a few anyway."

"Nice guerilla marketing move, K2." Anthony took a big gulp of his shake.

"What move?"

"Sending everyone who bought a ticket an MP3 of your soon-to-be-released next song." He wiggled his forefinger at the crowd. "Looks like a few of them liked it."

"I didn't . . ."

Brandon. He must have sent the song out to the list. "They heard my next song."

"Uh, yeah."

Kevin grabbed his phone and called Brandon. He picked up on the second ring. "You sent out my second song?"

"Did it work?" A light chuckle floated through the phone.

"Yeah, I think it worked." Kevin snaked through the stack of amps at the back of the stage and settled into a chair next to his guitar.

"How many people in seats so far?"

"Getting close to a thousand."

"One thousand? Sweet. See you at the top, bro."

"I don't know what to say."

"Say thanks."

Kevin got up and went back to the front of the stage. He peered around the curtain hiding him from view of the crowd laying

blankets on the thick June grass and lying back and letting the late afternoon sun soak into them. "Why are you doing all this for me?"

"You're kidding, right? After all the years you believed in what we were trying to do—even when it was lean? Talking me off the ledge millions of times? Telling me I had it when no one believed it but you? This is a very small payback for all those years."

"Thanks."

"Now go out there and go crazy. Sing like there's no tomorrow because there isn't. There is only this moment. Take it. It's yours."

"I needed those words and to say I appreciate it sounds so . . . stupid."

"Rock it, bro."

Kevin let the growing rumble of the crowd's conversation seep into his heart. They weren't here for Brandon Scott. They were here for him. Kevin Kaison. Not the manager. Not the agent. The musician. "I should go."

"Something else," Brandon said. "This is important. Ready? You might want to make a note of this. I'm serious."

"I'm ready."

"Try your best when the moment comes, and you walk onto that stage . . . not to puke."

Kevin laughed. "I'll try."

"K2? One more thing. Serious this time."

"Yeah?"

"God is in this and since he is, nothing about tonight is about you. It's about him. And if it's about him and he is in it, whatever happens is gold."

"Love ya, bro."

"Same. Kick it hard. I'll be praying."

✝ ✝ ✝

As Kevin started the fifth song, something flickered in his peripheral vision. A thin line of something translucent with a light green

tinge to it slithered through the grass to his right and left and up toward the stage, but when he stared at the matted grass he saw nothing. A memory flashed through his mind. Of Brandon's concert last year where Reece's and Dana's and Marcus's spirits had shown up onstage to fight . . . he couldn't remember. A vine? Some kind of evil but what? Brandon had never really talked about it, and Kevin shook his head. He couldn't let himself get distracted. This was his shot.

The crowd had been appreciative up till now, but he felt a shift, saw it on their faces. They loved him. And he loved them. And if he could admit it, he loved that they loved him. For once in his life the praise wasn't all about the god of Christian music: Brandon Scott. The roars of the crowd were for Kevin Kaison, stepping into his glory. No. Leaping into his glory—with arms stretched to their limit.

For the rest of the concert he did exactly what Brandon had told him to. He went crazy, forgot about playing every chord right and hitting every note perfect and just played with abandon.

By the time the last chord on the last song filled the dusky night air, he knew he'd hit a grand-slam home run. He raised his guitar to the audience and loped offstage, adrenaline and sweat and exhilaration all pouring over him.

The roar of the crowd ended in shouts of "Encore!" and Kevin strutted back onto the stage and again raised his guitar high in the air. The crowd erupted and his grin felt like it wrapped around his head. He was home for the first time in his life and if he had anything to say about it, would never leave.

✠ ✠ ✠

An hour later Kevin sat alone in the center of the empty stage. The shouts of a late-evening soccer game under the Marymoor Park lights floated toward him from a half mile away. And the shouts of the crowd at the concert still echoed through his head. Cheering for him. Loving his music. His dream had come alive.

Holding the case his bass rested in with both hands, Anthony bounced over to Kevin. "Congratulations, K2. I knew you could do it. The band knew you could do it. Most of all Brandon knew you could. Well done."

"Thanks." Kevin gazed over the matted grass again, and an image of the crowd again filled his mind.

"How are you going to juggle being a rising star and being Brandon's manager slash agent at the same time?"

A surge of adrenaline filled him, but he shoved the emotion down. "Easy. This was a one-time thing—my hobby getting a few moments in the sun. Managing Brandon is my true calling."

"Do you practice that insipid line every day?"

Kevin turned to Anthony and stared at the bass player's grin. As he did, an impression formed in Kevin's mind. Anthony was right. He wouldn't be going back. His days were on the verge of change. He'd just hopped on a sixty-foot wave and his surfboard was pointed straight down—he was about to go on the ride of his life.

Kevin turned to look out over the venue as if in slow motion. "I'll do it for you, Anthony. Because I think you're right."

"Don't do it for me, or anyone else, do it for you. You deserve it. You've earned it." Anthony frowned. "What? You're worried about what Brandon will think?"

Yes, he was. Brandon had given him incredible support, so why was Kevin worried? Because he knew Brandon better than almost anyone. And while Brandon wanted him to succeed, he didn't want it to come at the expense of losing Kevin as his manager.

As he drove home that night, two questions wrestled for his attention. How soon should he tell Brandon, and how would Brandon react?

TWENTY-NINE

MARCUS FINISHED UP HIS LAST CLASS ON MONDAY afternoon and called Simon's cell phone again. This would be the third message without a callback, but Marcus didn't care. He wanted to talk to the magician again. Simon hadn't been on campus for the past three weeks, or if he had, Marcus hadn't seen him. The magician had implied they'd talk again but it hadn't happened.

He wanted to ask Simon why the switching had stopped and why it had happened in the first place. And he wanted to talk about the Wolf. How did Simon know about that? What part was God going to have the magician play in this game?

Marcus didn't trust him, but the conjurer had at least some kind of answers, of that Marcus had no doubt. And more than anyone else could offer. As Marcus walked toward Red Square, the call went to voice mail. *"Simon here. Do you believe in magic? The Lovin' Spoonful did. I do too. Leave a message."*

Marcus smiled. Reece would love that message.

"Simon, it's Marcus. I'd like to talk again. Call me. You have the number from my previous calls. I apologize for the persistence, but I want to continue our discussion from before."

Marcus trudged across the bricks that made up Red Square toward the parking garage but on a whim turned left and headed toward Drumheller Fountain. It's where he'd last seen Simon. Why not?

When he was still one hundred yards from the fountain, Marcus spotted what looked like Simon. It had to be the magician. Who else would be balancing on one leg, the other in the air along with his arms, reaching for the sky? And doing it up on the concrete ring of the fountain dressed in all black. When Marcus was still twenty-five yards away, Simon turned and hopped onto the ground like a cat.

"Professor of time and all it contains, what do you do when realities rain down all around you like lightning and snow, and when the bough breaks, where do you go?"

Simon hadn't mentioned his ability to look more than a little crazy while spouting his somehow-ingratiating rhymes. The magician's gaze darted from the fountain to Marcus to the sky to the ground back to the fountain.

"It's good to see you, Simon."

"Is it?" Simon blinked and rubbed his eyes. "Good to be seen in this reality. It is real, isn't it? I'm choosing to believe so."

"Did you receive my cell phone messages?"

Simon rubbed his head as if he were scrubbing a one-hundred-year-old grease spot off a silver chalice. "I've been having a tough few days. Not sure if I have a cell phone here. Can't remember."

"Here? As opposed to where?"

"Other places, the other places, the other places. Stop asking about it. I don't want to go there. Got free of that finally. Never going back."

Simon bent over and squeezed and unsqueezed his fists like pistons working overtime. "What do you want to say today, and hear with ears that might not listen, to flashes and glistens, that take your mind, to many lives of another kind?"

If this was the result of Simon's tough days, the days must have been difficult indeed.

"Are you with me here, Simon?"

"Most assuredly, yes. Ask me, ask me anything."

"I want to discuss my supposed forays into other realities. And the Wolf."

"The Wolf, the Wolf, the Wolf of confusion, he always spins a compelling illusion."

"Are you all right, Simon?"

"I'm good. I'm fine, really. It's just that it's a contusion, this ball of confusion." Simon straightened and fixed his gaze on the fountain. "Talk? You would, you would, and I think you should. We should, we could, and we should."

"Simon. Slow down."

The magician's head swiveled like his neck was made of rubber, his eyes moving everywhere except to look at Marcus.

"Tell me about the Wolf."

"Wolf bad. God good. Wolf bad, God is good. The Wolf is very, very bad. God is very, very good."

"What do you know about the Wolf—the spirit of religion?"

"I used to have cream with my coffee all the time." Simon paused and blinked again like he was sending a Morse code message with his eyes. "Or did I?" He stared hard at Marcus. "Do you know?" He dropped his gaze and seemed to study his palm. "Hard to keep track of what is real and what isn't. Too many layers. Hard to keep track. Very difficult to keep track."

Marcus leaned in. "Simon, are you sure you're all—?"

"Did you know in some realities they don't have crème brûlée creamer? How crazy is that? Very challenging to deal with." He bit his lower lip like a chipmunk trying to crack a nut. "Yes, I'm fine. I know what you're thinking. But I'm not. I'm not insane. Not. Not. Not. Just having a bad day today. Too many memories to keep track of. Makes me jumpy and talk gibberish. I know that. Don't you think I don't know that?" His eyes flashed anger.

"What happened, Simon?"

"Chose the wrong door, you see. No, that's not right. That's wrong. Reverse that. Strike that. Didn't choose the door. Should have gone through it but didn't. Didn't, didn't, didn't. Want to go back and walk through it, because I think it would be good, but I can't now. What's done is done. Over. Finished. I went the other way.

Didn't even put my hand on the knob." Simon looked up, his gaze darting back and forth between Marcus and the fountain and his shoes. "Had my chance."

With a mixture of fascination and horror pinging through his mind, Marcus stared at Simon. This wasn't the same man he'd watched perform in Red Square the other day.

"You'll have to make the choice someday, Marcus Amber, professor of physics. The Teacher will need to learn how important choices are. And the most difficult ones will, of course, without doubt, without question, teach him the most important lessons." Simon stopped fidgeting and his body went stiff. "Don't you agree?"

"The switching has stopped."

Simon laughed and clapped Marcus on the shoulder. "Sure. Sure it has. I believe you. It has, certainly. But of course it hasn't stopped and you know that down there." The magician jabbed his finger at Marcus's stomach. "And it won't stop till you choose."

"Choose what?"

"Can't tell you that. No sir, no can do. Not yet."

Simon rose and pulled a silver coin from his pocket and tossed it in the air. Marcus tried to follow the flight but it had vanished. A second later Simon reached behind Marcus's head and pulled the coin into view for a quarter second, then slapped it on the back of his wrist.

"Heads or tails?"

"Tails."

Simon grinned and slowly lifted his hand. The coin was gone, replaced by a small golden ticket. "You're just like Charlie. Willy Wonka is going to hand you a ticket, but you'll have to choose to go through the factory door."

THIRTY

"You were supposed to get me out of that, bro. Now I'm looking stupid."

Brandon tapped his sandal against his deck at his home near Snoqualmie Ridge on Thursday afternoon. Sandals in mid-June. Nice. The month was typically full of rainy days. But today was sun and low seventies. Perfect.

Brandon stared at the Douglas fir trees in his backyard and gripped his phone tighter. Ever since Brandon gave him the show at Marymoor Park, Kevin had dropped the proverbial ball multiple times. There'd been complaints from the road crew as well. Nothing big in and of itself, but added all together it bothered Brandon. His manager was slipping and the cause was pretty obvious.

"Get you out of what?"

"I get a phone call this morning from a producer down in LA wanting to know what time I want to meet on Friday to go over what my cameo is going to look like on their TV series. I told you I wasn't going to do it."

"But you're going to be in LA anyway to meet with your label."

"That's not the point. I asked you to cancel it. I'm not going on the show."

"Yeah," Kevin muttered.

"Yeah what?"

"I spaced."

"You never space." Brandon strolled onto his lawn. "And you haven't exactly been Speed Racer lately with e-mails or phone calls."

"You mean it takes me more than an hour to respond to an e-mail or voice mail?"

This conversation wasn't going to end well if Brandon didn't get off the track, but the road seemed to have rails on it with no place to exit. "Try seven or eight hours."

"I'm allowed to have a life, right?"

"One hit song and one successful concert and you're suddenly a superstar copping an attitude."

"Knock it off, Brandon. I'm trying to keep a million plates spinning."

"Too many are falling off the poles. I think your brain is in the wrong spot and you need to figure out where you want to be."

Kevin didn't respond and Brandon's gut agreed with what his mind had been telling him for the past five days. "When do you want to leave?"

"What?"

"Become my ex-manager."

Brandon heard Kevin's quick breath through the phone. "You're not ticked—"

"I knew we'd get here someday, didn't you?"

"No . . . I mean I hoped . . . but I didn't know how to tell you."

Brandon wandered back inside and stared at a photo of Kevin and him skiing up at Whistler. "But you have to find me someone as good as or better than you before you ditch me entirely. Which is, of course, an impossible task."

"I don't know what to say."

"Say you're looking forward to us going on tour together."

Kevin laughed. "All the way. That will be the top."

Brandon switched gears. "Reminder. I'm headed out to see the label tomorrow. Anything going on there you want to help me with? Anything you've said to them about me I should be aware of?"

"No, it's all good on all fronts. Just trying to get my album finished."

"Sweet."

Brandon hung up and walked toward his home studio. Yeah, Kevin was dropping a few plates only because his dreams were coming true. Brandon needed to relax. But he couldn't get the feeling out of his mind that one of the larger plates was about to drop on his head.

THIRTY-ONE

REECE'S CELL PHONE RANG ON TUESDAY EVENING WITH a generic ring, which meant he didn't know the caller. He'd assigned all his inner circle specific ring tones since he lost his sight, which meant he probably should let the call go to voice mail. But something told him to pick up.

"It's Reece."

"Hello, Reece Roth. This is Tristan Barrow."

Interesting. Brandon's stalker. The one who had found the Song, the Leader, and the Teacher down at Houghton Beach Park.

"Good morning, Tristan. I understand you're getting to know some of my friends."

"Trying, yes." The tone of Tristan's voice made it sound like he was smiling. Who was this guy?

"And what is your interest in them?"

"The same as my interest in you."

"Which is?"

"From what you've heard about me from the others, do you believe I'm here to help or here to hinder you in your quest?"

"Why don't you end the suspense and tell me."

"If I said I was here to help, would you believe me?"

"I'd like to look into your eyes as you said it."

"I'm sorry for your loss, Roy, but there is purpose in it."

Reece's pulse spiked. Roy? How did Tristan know the name

Jesus had given him a year and a half ago? Roy Hobbs from *The Natural*—Roy Hobbs who was washed out but stepped back into the game to fulfill his destiny. Just like Reece. Had one of the other Warriors told Tristan that name? Highly unlikely.

"How do you know about that?"

"Why don't we meet, Reece Roth, and we can talk about that and other things as well. Always better in person than over the phone."

The man's voice was powerful, his tone one of confidence but not cockiness.

Jesus?

The answer from the Spirit was immediate. *Go.*

"Will your two friends Jotham and Orson be joining us?"

"No, they have other duties they must attend to."

"Fine. Maltby Café on Friday morning at eleven o'clock."

"Excellent."

"And, Reece?"

"Yes."

Tristan went silent.

"Do you have something else to say?"

For a few more seconds the only sound was the hum of the phone. "You will see again."

"Enough. How do you know about the name? What do you know of the proph—?"

"I'll meet you at the café on Friday. I'd like to ask you a favor when we do." The line went dead.

THIRTY-TWO

WHEN BRANDON STEPPED THROUGH THE DOORS OF Windfire Records Friday morning at nine o'clock his stomach said something was wrong. A moment later the receptionist in the lobby confirmed the feeling.

"Take a seat. Audrey is wrapping up a meeting but should be done shortly. As soon as she is, someone will be right down to get you."

Take a seat? In the fifteen-plus times he'd been in this building over the past six years he'd never had to "take a seat." Sure, in the early days he'd waited, but that was ages ago. There had always been someone waiting for him and he was escorted immediately to whichever office he was visiting.

Fifteen minutes later Logan Hall stepped out of the elevator and clipped over to him. "Sorry, Brandon. I hate to keep people waiting—especially you." Logan patted Brandon's shoulder. "You look good, really good. You've been well?"

"Sure, and you?"

"Fine, yes, and tell me, how was your flight? And is your hotel okay? I tried to get you first class but it wasn't available, and they were booked at the Hilton. Next time it'll be back to normal, okay?"

They headed to the elevators and Brandon relaxed. Maybe nothing was wrong. Logan seemed normal, without any hint of

188

unease in his eyes. As they rode up the elevator, Logan kept up a monologue about the label, other labels, who would have the biggest release in the fall—the normal Logan commentary about everything and nothing.

It didn't hit Brandon till they passed the sixth floor that this was the first time in years there wasn't a sign at the front desk with his name on it welcoming him. He pushed the thought away. Big deal, so they forgot to put it up one time. Still . . . he tried to shake off the feeling something was off balance, but it didn't work. He needed to get his mind off himself and onto someone else.

"How is Kevin's single doing?"

"Record breaking." Logan smiled. "Big records."

"Really?"

"It's already gone gold. Platinum looks very attainable."

"Serious? That is so cool. Kevin didn't tell me."

"We've never had a single sell this big this fast. Everyone around here is so grateful to you for discovering Kevin."

"My pleasure."

The elevator doors opened and they strolled down the open, cubicle-filled ninth floor. Half the desks were filled; a few people were on the phone. Windfire's lead cover designer glanced up, gave Brandon a quick wave, and then picked up her cell phone and dialed. On his right, Katie Bostic, Windfire's publicist extraordinaire, met Brandon's gaze and instantly looked away and became fixed on a file on her desk. Was the staff avoiding him, or had his imagination shifted into overdrive?

A few seconds later they reached the office of Audrey Decket, head of Windfire Records. Logan did a 180-degree spin before giving a slight bow and motioning his hand toward her door. "Here you are, Brandon."

"Thanks, Logan. Always good to see you."

"Likewise."

Brandon turned, peered into Audrey's office, and grinned.

She looked up from her desk. "Long time, stranger."

"True." Brandon strolled inside and gave Audrey a quick hug. A framed, blown-up cover of his latest CD hung along the wall over her mini conference table along with seven or eight other artists. Same ones as last time, and the time before that. Wait. There was a new one on the end. Kevin Kaison's.

"You've already finished the cover art for K2's album."

"He's on the fast track. As well as his single has done, we need to get the CD out last week."

"Congrats."

Audrey smiled and nodded. "How are you, Brandon?" She settled back into her chair and steepled her fingers. "You look good."

"Is that the line today?"

"Hmmm?"

"Same thing Logan said to me."

"There was a memo from the parent company this morning telling us to greet everyone that way." Audrey got up and closed her door. "Ready to get to business?"

"Sure. Is there anything on the agenda other than starting talks on a new contract?" Brandon crossed his legs.

"Yes."

Brandon bit his lip. He didn't like the way Audrey said yes. "And that is?"

"The music industry is changing. Has changed. Is changing more."

"Yeah." The office seemed to grow warmer.

"Brandon, you've had a tremendous run. Phenomenal. But the past three albums have sold fewer units. Yes, I realize people aren't buying albums as much anymore, but you haven't had a breakout hit in almost two years, and no one is downloading your backlist. They used to. But the river of sales has become a trickle."

"Hold on. My concerts have been packed for the past eight months, and six out of my next eight shows are already sold out."

"Yes, that's true." Audrey walked to the window overlooking LA. "Congratulations." She turned back to Brandon. "But we don't

make a lot of money on the concerts, you know? You do. We need to make some cuts."

Brandon's gut went tight. "Define cuts."

"Budgets have to be overhauled from time to time, to get them in line. As you know, we lost money last year. And the year before that. And the year before that."

"You're cutting me."

Audrey ran her fingers over the surface of her desk. "Not really."

"What does 'not really' mean? That my latest album is the last one with Windfire?"

Audrey waved her hands. "No, this is coming out sounding far worse than it is. It's not like we're dropping you. We're even willing to look at a new contract. We definitely want to keep making records together, but the terms might be a little different."

"How different? And what about support for my upcoming album?"

"Only a slight change there. We're going to reduce the amount of marketing behind it."

"How much?"

"A portion."

"We've been together too long for games, Audrey." Brandon stood and folded his arms. "What percentage?"

She narrowed her eyes and her tone was flat. "Eighty percent."

"Eighty? You're cutting my marketing budget by eighty percent?" Brandon pointed at the album covers on Audrey's wall. "I've sold over eighteen million albums for this label."

"Sold. Past tense. If this next album does better than your last one, we can look at bringing your marketing funds back up to where they were."

"Unbelievable." Brandon stared out the window at the Los Angeles smog. "I need to talk to K2. He's going to take you to the mat on this one. We have a contract that clearly spells out what kind of marketing support you'll give me."

"No, that's not in the contract. It's in a memo."

"Same thing."

"You know it's not and besides, it's already done. We've funneled the money into a newer artist. I'm sorry. It wasn't my decision."

"What a crock! Maybe it wasn't your decision, but you approved it. You could have stopped it, blocked it, you're the head of the label." Brandon jabbed his finger onto her desk, his voice rising with each sentence. "At least talked to me before you lit the fuse!"

"It's been decided. As far as everyone around here is concerned, the question of whether we make the move or not is dead."

"When Kevin gets on the phone, it will be resurrected, trust me. There's no way he'll let this happen." Kevin was a superb manager and even better when he played the role of an agent. Kind? One of the kindest men he'd ever known when people were fair with him. But when they weren't, K2 was the Tasmanian Devil. Brandon was looking forward to setting the devil loose.

"I don't think bringing Kevin into this is a good idea."

"Yeah, I wouldn't either if I were you." He paced between the windows and the door.

"Would you like to sit down?"

"No." Brandon stopped and stared at Audrey's phone. "Let's get Kevin on the phone right now and get this thing worked out."

"Brandon?" Audrey leaned forward and lowered her voice. "Let's not."

"Let's do." Brandon pulled out his cell phone, set it on her desk, and put his face inches from hers. "Now."

"We're giving the money to another artist. End of story. Listen, Brandon, we've been friends a long time. I think we should end this meeting before one of us says something that will damage that relationship."

"Who is the other artist?" Brandon pulled back.

"That's not the point."

"Who is it?"

Audrey sighed and closed her eyes.

"What? Is it some big secret?"

She sat in her chair and pressed her lips together for a long time before opening her eyes. "It's Kevin. And he's okay with it."

The words felt like he'd been hit with a medicine ball in the gut. "Wha . . . what?"

"I'm sorry." Audrey tapped the tips of her fingers together. "After Kevin's concert at Marymoor Park, iTunes went nuts with downloads. We have to ride this horse hard. We're a for-profit business."

Brandon sat stunned. It felt like every ounce of his energy had spilled onto the carpet and melted through it to the floor below. "You're sorry? I don't believe this."

He left Audrey's office in a daze. All he needed was Reece or Marcus or Doug to stab him in the back and life would be complete. By the time he reached his car and slid behind the wheel, Brandon's numbness had morphed into a smoldering rage. As he turned out of the parking garage onto the street he pulled his cell phone out and dialed Kevin.

THIRTY-THREE

"KEVIN KAISON."

"Why do you answer like that? You know it's me." Brandon spit out the words.

"You all right?"

"Yeah, I'm great. Life is excellent. Couldn't be better. How 'bout you?"

"I'm picking up the slightest tinge of sarcasm. Want to tell me why?"

"I just called to offer my congratulations."

"For what?"

Brandon gunned the engine of his rental car and passed two cars in front of him. One of them laid on the horn and the other screamed words that would probably scorch his paint if he got too close.

"Getting my marketing funds. Nicely done."

"What?"

"I just finished with an interesting meeting with Audrey and she tells me you're getting my marketing funds for your debut album. When were you going to let me in on this?"

"What? Look—"

"Playing stupid doesn't look good on you, pal. I stood up and boldly told her, 'Kevin won't stand for this. He'll fight it.' And you've known about it all along. Just before leaving town I asked you if there was anything going on at the label concerning me, and you said no. Unbelievable."

"Slow down, Brandon. Yes, I knew they were taking funds from somewhere else, but I had no clue where it was from and no clue whatsoever it was coming from another artist and no idea it was coming from your budgets. All they said was they found some additional marketing funds to promote my first album. Why would I ask where the money came from?"

"They said you were okay with it. With getting the money, which meant you knew it was coming from me."

"Of course I told them I was okay with it. That doesn't mean I knew it came from you!"

"You're my manager and my agent. Don't add traitor to your job description. You're going to talk to Audrey and get it fixed."

"What does that mean?"

"You're going to get my money back. You're going to tell them you can't take it."

"Hang on, Brandon. We need to talk about this."

"You want a career in this industry? You need me, so you're going to stop talking and start acting."

"Really? You still think I need you? Are you blind? I'm in the middle of negotiating a multi-album deal that will make me very comfortable, and I'm getting invitations from venues and promoters all over the country. Need you? You want to know the truth? It's the fall of your career and winter is coming on fast."

"A year ago you were scared to play one song for me. We would not be having this conversation if not for me."

"Wow, praise Brandon. All glory to Brandon. God had nothing to do with it, huh?"

"Shut up, Kaison."

"I appreciate what you did, I really do, but don't make me the arsonist for a fire I didn't set."

Brandon pulled onto the freeway and revved his car up to seventy-five. "Get this thing fixed, Kevin, or you're gone."

Kevin's voice slowed and seemed to drop an octave. "Gone? What do you mean, 'gone'? I was leaving anyway."

Brandon wiped the perspiration from his forehead. "I just moved up the timetable. You're done as of now. You're finished, Kaison. So is our friendship."

He ended the call and tossed his cell phone to the floor of the passenger seat. After a few minutes he cooled and glanced at the phone. He'd call Kevin back right now. He'd lost it. Did he think Kevin was lying? No. Which meant he didn't know about the marketing funds.

Brandon glanced at his phone again. Now? No. Wait a few days. Give them both time to cool down. Weird. One of his best friends and he'd shredded the guy without hesitation. He gripped his steering wheel harder. But Kevin had shredded right back and his words seeped into the gash Windfire had made in his soul. Maybe a few days would turn into never.

What did Reece always say? "They drop the bombs where the enemy is the strongest." But Brandon didn't feel strong. It felt like his career was coming apart. And that a nuclear warhead had just detonated inside his soul.

THIRTY-FOUR

Tristan Barrow was charming when Reece joined him for their late breakfast on Friday. It didn't surprise Reece. His demeanor on the phone had been strangely engaging and Reece didn't expect his in-person persona to be any different.

The smell of one of the Maltby Café's giant cinnamon rolls filled Reece's nostrils as a waitress carried it by their table. Even someone without an acute sense of smell would know that aroma.

They'd talked for half an hour but Reece felt only inches closer to knowing the identity and nature of the man and what he was after. The words from Tristan about the work of the kingdom were right, his insights into what Reece and the Warriors were doing were penetrating and even challenging, but something didn't ring true about the man.

"Might I ask about the favor I spoke of on the phone?" Tristan said.

"Sure," Reece answered as he continued to work on his California eggs Benedict.

"Jotham, Orson, and I want to come to one of your training sessions at Well Spring."

Not the favor Reece had expected Tristan to ask for. Of course this didn't seem the type of man who was easily figured out. "And why is it that you'd like to come to Well Spring?"

"God told us to go." He said it as if it were the most obvious thing in the universe.

"I see." The scrape of forks and knives on plates and conversations from all over the restaurant filled Reece's ears. Not knowing who was listening made it more difficult to speak freely, but he hadn't wanted to meet Barrow without others around. "We would want to know more about you before accepting any of you as students."

"My fault." Tristan's fork clanked against his plate, and from the pronunciation of his words, Reece could tell the man was chewing. "I didn't communicate well our desire. We don't want to come as students. We want to come as support. To pray for protection for you. To counsel the trainees if needed. To fight for the success of the week in prayer as you do it through your teaching."

"I just met you and you think I would let you three come and be part of my team?"

"Yes."

"Your thinking was incorrect."

A chill seemed to sweep across Reece's hands as if a miniature air conditioner had been set on the table and turned on high. "Even if I did agree, why would you offer your services?"

"As I already said, God told us to."

"You did mention that."

"You're skeptical."

Was the man serious? Of course he was skeptical. The word Dana, Brandon, and Marcus had agreed on when describing Tristan, Jotham, and Orson was *enigmatic*. And so far, Reece agreed. Based on their conversation so far it was clear Tristan was well versed in all things spiritual. And something about the man was magnetic. But that didn't mean he was safe and it didn't mean he was of God.

"God has told many people many things throughout the ages and much of the fruit that came out of those ventures proved conclusively God wasn't the one who had spoken."

Tristan laughed. "I understand and most assuredly agree with you. I pledge to you, that is not the case this time. The Spirit is behind this request."

"How do I know you're not the Wolf?"

Reece heard Tristan take another bite, then a long drink before his glass or cup thunked to the table.

"You don't. That is a question you must take to the Spirit, because no matter what I answer, you will likely doubt my words."

The confidence in Tristan's voice made Reece want to invite him to Well Spring right then. But that's what worried him. The enemy was coming at them in all forms, and as an angel of light was always high on his tactical-maneuvers list. Everything the man had said about faith and freedom and warring for the souls of others was perfect, but that was far from enough. If only he could see the man's face, study his countenance, see what light or darkness danced behind his eyes.

They ended their breakfast and agreed to speak again, but Reece wasn't convinced he hadn't just told Tristan a lie. If they spoke again it would be Tristan initiating the conversation and even then Reece wasn't sure he would agree to be on the other end of the line.

As they parted, Tristan's voice rang out with a clarity Reece hadn't heard before. "I know you're going after the Wolf, which is a good thing. But remember, it's highly likely the Wolf is coming after you in return."

THIRTY-FIVE

ON FRIDAY AFTERNOON AT TWELVE FORTY-FIVE, BRANDON walked into the den of the Wolf. He pushed open the doors of Carson Tanner's offices and studio hoping his spiritual eyes and ears were wide open. His row with Kevin certainly wasn't the best warm-up, but he wasn't going to let that distract him. He'd worked through the emotions of his meeting with Windfire and his talk with Kevin. At least he told himself he had. He needed to be ready for this interview.

Could he live without doing albums anymore and huge concerts? Yes. He didn't need the money. And he could go back to indie recording and still do concerts. Not being able to sing would end him, but all he needed was his voice and his guitar. And those things would always be there.

"Excuse me." A woman who looked to be in her mid- to late thirties walked toward him. "I believe you're Brandon Scott." She extended her hand. "I'm Sooz Latora, the executive producer of Carson's show. Great to meet you. Thanks so much for coming."

"Good to meet you, and it's my pleasure."

"Right this way."

Sooz motioned him to follow her and they walked down a long hallway. Reece and Doug had said to play it cool, and that's exactly what Brandon planned on doing. No controversy, no uncomfortable conversations. Just the chance to get a feel for the spirit of the

place, get to know Carson Tanner, start getting an idea of the kind of game he played, and see if Brandon could find out who the players behind the players were. See where the spirit of religion lurked.

A door at the end of the hallway flew open and Carson popped out of it. He smiled and half walked, half jogged down the hallway till he reached Brandon.

"Sorry to keep you waiting." The host's booming voice filled the hallway and made Brandon think of a movie trailer he'd seen last week. Dana was right. The guy was fit and good looking.

"You didn't keep me waiting at all." Brandon offered his hand.

"Shoot, it would have made me look important." Carson shook his head, then Brandon's hand and laughed at his own joke. "Stupid, sorry. I'm just a little nervous. Big fan of yours and all that. I know I have almost fifteen million listeners these days and the books and the speaking tours, and I'm supposed to be some sort of big deal, but it doesn't feel like that. It still feels like I'm in my basement trying to create a radio show a few people might listen to someday."

"Congratulations on all the success you've had. I wish I could say I've listened to your show but—"

"No worries, there's only so much time, right?"

Carson led him to the studio where another of the host's producers set him up with headphones and positioned him to the left of one of two microphones directly across from Carson's board. The host settled into his chair and bounced up and down a few times before grinning at Brandon. "We're on the air in about forty-five seconds, so since we have all this time on our hands, do you mind signing this?"

Carson handed Brandon a black Sharpie and his latest CD. Brandon scrawled his signature across the case and handed it back. This guy was a fan. Which meant the interview should be cake, leaving him enough bandwidth to focus on the spiritual atmosphere of the place. Maybe the guy was the Wolf but so far he had poodle written all over him. If the wrong kind of spirits were camping out in the place, they were lying so low they were asleep.

After the show's prerecorded intro, Carson pointed at him and grinned. "Very special show today, folks! You've been waiting for it, so have we. He's here, five feet from me ready to talk about the truth—it's the man, the legend, the machine—multiplatinum recording artist Brandon Scott." Carson leaned back and clapped. "We're going to be talking about his music, his ministry, and of course anything you want to talk about.

"No question is off limits, so get on the phone and we'll get to you soon. But first I get to toss out some of my own questions to this ultrapopular, ultratalented musician. Great to have you here, Brandon." Carson winked and pointed at Brandon's mic.

"Great to be here."

"All right, we never waste time on my show so let's dive in. Talk to us about your most recent CD. The one that came out, what, six months back?"

"That's right."

"My friends say it's your strongest album to date. That the songs are fresh again, full of life. It feels like the Brandon Scott from the old days. I agree. Do you? And if your answer is yes, what's changed?"

"Yeah, I agree. I never thought I'd like an album more than my first one, but this has become my favorite."

"What happened with this one?"

"I've been singing about freedom for years, but for a while there that idea was more in my head than in my heart. Now it's more in my heart than my head. I've been changed. I feel like I've had a rebirth and I want others to have happen to them what's happened to me."

Carson adjusted his headphones and narrowed his eyes. "And this change came from . . . ?"

Brandon hesitated. How much should he say? How little? What Reece, Dana, Marcus, and he were doing wasn't a hard-and-fast secret, but it wasn't something to shout from the rooftops either. And if this guy was the Wolf . . .

The Spirit had told them to stay under the radar as much as

possible. And talking about going into other people's souls was completely off limits. Trying to explain that part of Warriors Riding would be like playing Russian roulette with a chamber full of bullets.

"I've been getting together with a group of friends for the past year. Deep healing has come out of it, and that's spilled over into my music."

"What about hearing from God?" Carson's eyes narrowed further.

"What do you mean?"

"Hearing his voice. Him telling you what to do, where to go, who to talk to, whether there are demons here or there or everywhere?" Carson's gaze had turned cold.

"Yes, I believe the Spirit speaks to us. That talking to God should be like any other conversation. A back-and-forth dialogue. In the gospel of John, Jesus says his sheep will hear—"

"That's a controversial idea among some Christians."

"Among some, sure."

"Have you had any kind of backlash?"

"Backlash? About trying to listen to God?" Brandon frowned. Where was Carson going with this?

"No, over the extrabiblical ideas you've gotten into lately. Your going way beyond the idea that God speaks."

"What are you talking about?" Brandon's body chilled.

"Ah, folks, this is going to be fun. Here's the scoop with a bright red cherry on top: Brandon Scott has been getting into some pretty wild and wacky ideas lately, but I didn't want to get into it without Brandon here to defend himself." Carson laughed as the sound effect of a drumroll blasted through Brandon's headphones. "Okay, heeeerrre we go."

Carson leaned in close to the mic and lowered his voice. "What I've heard, from reliable sources, is you and these new pals you mentioned a minute or two ago have immersed yourselves deeply in occult practices such as astral projection, soul travel, turning

invisible, hearing from the dead, and . . . wow!" Carson threw his hands up. "God knows what else."

Brandon's body went from ice to volcano. He stabbed a finger at Carson and spoke into his microphone to protest, but nothing came through his headphones. Carson had muted his mic. Brandon yanked the headphones off his head, tossed them onto the counter in front of him, and stepped toward Carson.

"Folks, I think we've hit a maaaaajor nerve here. You can't see this, but it looks like Brandon Scott is getting ready to rumm-mmble." The radio host grinned and raised both his fists in a mock boxing posture. "It's true! Brandon Scott is out of his chair and looks like he's ready to plant his fist into my jaw. Or are you just joshing around, Brandon?"

Brandon sat down hard in his chair and glared at Carson. He had to stay calm. Play the game. Get a chance to speak the truth. "Nah, just stretching my back." He squeezed out a laugh.

"That's what I thought." Carson stared at him with a look that was the exact opposite of his words. "Now, I gotta ask, haven't you been at all worried your fans will get wind of you wrapping yourself up in a bunch of New Age garbage?

"Aren't you worried people will discover you now believe you can turn invisible with some sort of real-life Harry Potter invisibility cloak? That you can instantly beam yourself across vast distances in some kind of spiritual *Star Trek* machine?"

Brandon's body went numb and he pulled shallow breaths in through his mouth. *Stay calm. Ride it out.*

"Have you given any thought to the fact that if it gets out that you're not just dabbling, but embracing the occult head-on that you'll lose some fans? Or even worse, shatter the faith of those who have looked up to you for so long?" Carson paused and raised his eyebrows. "And worst of all, you're teaching other believers this is truth, aren't you? You and your buddies have been doing training seminars out in Colorado for hundreds of people, and those people

have been doing retreats with your material all over the United States and even other parts of the world. The heresy is spreading like a rampant virus."

"Are you going to let me speak this time, Carson, or are you going to hit the mute button again?"

Carson waved his hand. "Oh, by all means, speak on, dear friend."

"I'd be curious who you've been talking to. Because what you're describing is not what my friends and I are exploring or what we are teaching others."

"So you are exploring something, hmm?"

Brandon gripped the sides of his chair. "Everything we do is based on Scripture—"

"Based on?" Carson leaned in. "Did you say 'based on'? Kinda like some movies are 'based on' a true story when only 10 percent of the story is true?"

"No." Brandon glared at Carson. "What we are doing is setting people free, healing them of wounds, helping them—"

"From the research I've done, I think you're full-out immersed in the kind of things people in the Old Testament were stoned for." Carson widened his eyes and cocked his head. "Right? C'mon now, Brandon. You're exploring dark parts of the forest that should be left for the animals and the Wiccans, not for Bible-believing Christians. What has happened to you?"

"You're badly mistaken." Sweat seeped down Brandon's back and his heart rate had to be over one hundred. From adrenaline. Anger. The poodle had indeed turned into the Wolf.

"Whatever you've heard has been distorted by someone with a vendetta against us. It's pure slander from those on the outside looking in who don't know what they're talking about."

"I don't think so. This ain't hearsay. We've talked to a friend of yours who told us not only are you delving into areas of darkness yourselves, but you're brainwashing others to think the same way.

Would you like to hear what they have to say?" Carson didn't wait for a response and pushed a button on his computer screen. A familiar voice Brandon couldn't quite place filled his headphones.

"I really truly think they're trying to do good things with their training out at Well Spring, but they've become a little misguided. Okay, they're a lot misguided. They've pulled a seriously large muscle in their spiritual physique. I mean, wow, they're telling people they can do stuff so far out there it makes the Wiccans and the New Agers look like they're Quakers."

"Like?" Carson's voice asked.

"Astral projection. Teleporting around the world like Star Trek gone mad. Going inside other people's minds and doing psychotherapy on them while they're inside, turning invisible in a crowd. Going inside other people's souls. This is where Reece Roth, Brandon Scott, and the others are telling people they need to take their walk with God. They're telling people this is real and right and true. And that scares me because their influence is growing like mad."

Carson tapped his computer again and stared at Brandon. "As you might have figured out, that was Tamera Miller who most of you out there probably know has a nationally known show on fitness. She's all about keeping the spirit healthy and keeping the body healthy. She has a book coming out this fall. She's well respected.

"In other words, this isn't some derelict off the street with a skewed view of Christianity. And you know her, don't you, Brandon? Of course you do. She went through your training. So how do you explain her comments? Did you teach her and other people the things she's talking about or didn't you?"

Brandon clenched his teeth and ignored the voice inside telling him to stay silent. "Yes, we have gathered select groups of people over the past eleven months and have taught them how to go deeper with God. And yes, Tamera went through our training. But she isn't happy with us because—" Brandon stopped. What could he say that would have any relevance to Carson's audience? That wouldn't come out sounding divisive? Plus it wasn't anyone's business why

Tamera wasn't part of their inner circle, and it would be pure gossip to talk about her this way.

"Wooo, love it! So you're saying this is a revenge move on Tamera's part? Wow, the soup gets thicker fast!" Carson grinned. "Doesn't sound like Tamera got set free."

Brandon's body felt like Jell-O. His phone vibrated with a text message and he struggled to lift his phone. It was from Dana. GET OFF THE AIR. THERE'S NO SALVAGING THIS. CARSON HOLDS ALL THE CARDS AND HE'S NOT PLAYING FAIR AND WON'T START ANYTIME SOON. AND SOMETHING DEMONIC IS FEEDING HIM HIS LINES.

Dana was probably right. It was unlikely Brandon could say anything to stop the tsunami that had just crashed on him. But he would try.

"We'll get to more of your thoughts in a few minutes, Brandon, but first let's take a few calls."

Carson snapped a finger toward the window in front of him behind which sat Sooz. He glanced at his computer and winked at Brandon. "Welcome to the show, Lisa. You have a question for Brandon Scott?"

"More of a statement than a question but—"

"Fire hard."

"Brandon, I've listened to your music since the beginning and have all of your albums, and I don't understand how you could have slipped away from Jesus into the occult. What happened to you? What went wrong? Do you realize how many people you might take to hell with you?"

The woman's voice echoed in Brandon's head as he grasped for words that would stop this nightmare.

"What we're doing at Well Spring isn't occult. It's being led by the Spirit of—"

"Wait, wait, wait, Brandon." Carson waved his hands. "I'm sorry, you know I love you, but I can't let that statement slide by.

You're talking about sending your spirit into other people's souls? You're talking about walking through walls? You're talking about beaming around the universe like Scotty? Are you trying to tell me that's from the Spirit of God?"

"I get it. I understand why you're skeptical. I was too until—"

"Until your brain got washed on the full load cycle?"

"If you look in your Bible, you'll find verses that support what we're—"

"Sure. Of course. Just like I can show you verses that teach you to kill babies, but I'm not thinking that's going to be happenin' in the church anytime soon. Or hey! Wait! Do you guys teach that too?"

"I know why you're coming after us, Carson, and you won't win."

"Just looking for the truth, baby, and keeping the sheep from being devoured by men like you."

Brandon started to respond but Carson had cut off his mic again. Brandon's phone vibrated for a second time and he glanced down. Another text message from Dana. DO YOU BELIEVE ME NOW? GET OUT!

He read the message a second time, then blinked as if coming out of a trance. As he pulled his headphones off his head a second time, he stared at Carson and again struggled not to leap across the five feet between them and strangle the man. Brandon stood and turned toward the studio door as Carson's deep bass voice seemed to vibrate through the room.

"Sorry, folks. Brandon Scott has tucked his tail firmly between his legs and appears to be heading for the hills. I'll be back after our sponsors talk about a few offers you'll probably like, and then I'll take a few calls on why you think Brandon and his band of merry men have strayed so far from the truth. And whether this is the beginning of the end of Brandon Scott's singing career. And finally, we'll talk about what you can do to shut down these Warriors Riding retreats that are popping up all over the country. It's about the truth, baby!"

Carson turned off his mic and slid off his headphones. "Thanks for coming on the show. That was a rough one, I know."

"The enemy has his claws deeply embedded in your life."

"Nah, just love a good show."

"You set me up. You have to know Tamera is a loose cannon. Why?"

"I'm only trying to get to the truth."

"What we're doing at Well Spring is the truth."

"The place you spread your lies. But not anymore. We just took a major step toward shutting off the lights."

"You don't know what you're talking about. You don't know the situation."

"I know a topic that needs to be discussed when I see it. You're one of the most famous musicians singing Christian music in the world today. You could lead a lot of people astray."

Brandon thought of five different responses and rejected them all. His wrestle was not against flesh and blood. He pulled open the door of Carson's studio and strode for the station lobby, his head down, muttering ideas of what to do next, his mind still swimming in an ocean of disbelief at what had just happened.

The sound of voices brought him out of his daze. A crowd of at least ten men and women milled about the lobby chatting with subdued voices as if they worried a stray microphone might pick up their scattered conversations.

"There he is!" A lady in a dark blue blouse and black slacks jabbed her finger in his direction. Great. Apparently the interview wasn't over. Brandon spun back the way he'd come and looked for an exit sign, but all he found was Carson standing in the middle of the hallway with a hand placed on the walls to his right and left, a wry grin on his face.

Brandon turned and strode toward the lobby. He had to be careful. If he pushed through the crowd, they'd say he fled the scene. But if he made any comments, they could easily be twisted into a negative and stories would pop up online and in magazines shredding the ministry. And shredding him. Carson was right. What would this do to his career? Audrey wasn't going to be giving him *any* marketing

funds after this. And another contract? Uh, no. He had to turn this thing around now.

He stopped and put his hands up to quiet the crowd, but as he did the Spirit spoke.

Let it go.

Did he hear that right?

Let it go, Brandon.

"I'm sorry. I don't have time to stop and chat at the moment, but let me assure you we are not what Carson implied we are. All I can say is seek the truth. Seek Jesus."

"Nice cop-out, Brandon," said a journalist with a smirk on his face. "If you think you can defend Carson's accusations, then tell us here and now."

Let it go.

Brandon gritted his teeth to keep from responding. There was no question the Spirit had spoken. The tough part was obeying. He blinked twice and turned to the journalist.

"Sorry, guys, not this time." He pushed through the throng and stepped through the lobby doors. A few reporters followed, but he took the stairs and quickly distanced himself from the questions they shouted as he descended.

The Wolf, one. Warriors, zero. And Brandon knew this was only a skirmish compared to what was coming.

THIRTY-SIX

THE NEXT NIGHT REECE GATHERED THE OTHER WARRIORS at his home and spent the first half hour debriefing on Brandon's encounter with Carson. The Song had not only taken that shot, but the one with his record label as well. But if it gnawed at him, it didn't show in his voice or the things he said.

"No, I don't need to talk about my pal Carson anymore." Brandon's footsteps echoed back and forth over Reece's hardwood floors. "We've been over it. I had a lot of time to think about it on the plane ride home. I was hammered, yes. But is that a shock? This Tristan character said . . . what'd he say at your breakfast, Reece? That we were going after the Wolf, but the Wolf was also coming after us?" The pacing stopped. "I certainly discovered that to be true. Which makes me more than ever want to know more about this Mr. Barrow, stalker, prophet . . . friend, enemy, whatever he is. I think it's about time we find out."

"I agree," Reece said. "Let's review each of your impressions about Tristan and his friends."

Brandon paced again. "I've never gotten anything. Good or evil. They're spiritual Switzerland."

"Marcus, isn't that what you felt with Zennon when he was trying to infiltrate your home using Abbie? That your spiritual eyes were dulled somewhat?"

"Yes and no. Even though my certainty wasn't complete till

the end, something about Calen, or Zennon, felt incongruent from the moment I met him. However, I attributed it to not wanting my daughter to date till she's older. With Tristan, Jotham, and Orson, I'm like Brandon. I've felt nothing."

"I agree," Dana said.

"So Tristan and his friends could be more powerful demons, who have a greater ability to shroud our spiritual eyes and ears," Brandon said.

"Yes."

"Just a thought," Dana said. "It seems unlikely Tristan and his friends would be blocking us if they're good, so can we assume they're not our pals the way they claim to be?"

"It's dangerous to assume." Reece opened the face of his watch and felt the hands. It had become a habit and he did it even when he didn't care what time it was. Maybe symbolic of time growing short and their need to act.

"There is one way to find out where they stand that will give us an undisputable answer," Dana said.

Marcus coughed. "And what would that plan entail?"

"We go in."

"Go through the gate and enter their souls?" Marcus asked.

"Yes."

Brandon laughed. "Whoa, Supergirl, I think you've been sucking on a kryptonite milk shake. It's weakened your brain. Aren't you always the one making sure we don't tear the envelope on the rules of engagement?"

Dana's voice rose. "Am I crazy, Reece?"

Reece didn't answer for a few seconds. "No, you're not. I've been mulling over the same question."

"You're thinking about doing it too?" Brandon sighed. "Are you nuts? What about rule number two? Never go into a soul without explicit permission. That's what got you into—tell me you're not serious."

"Yes, I am. But before we make a decision on that I propose we ask them for their permission to go in. It's a way to call their bluff."

"And if they say yes?" Brandon said.

"Then we will have received their permission and we ask the Spirit if we should go in."

"And if they say no?" Dana said.

"Then we'll have learned something and we'll ask Jesus what the next move is."

"When will you ask the question?" Marcus said.

Reece picked up his cell phone. "Right now." He set his phone on speaker and dialed the number.

Tristan answered on the second ring. "Hello, Reece. Are we coming to Well Spring with you?"

"Before we discuss that, want to talk about something else. You've offered to help us. I'd like to offer something to you in return."

"What is that?"

"We'd like to war for you. Help set you free in the deepest way possible."

"What exactly does that look like?" Tristan said.

"I think you already know what that looks like."

"I believe you're right, but for the sake of clarity can you state it for me now?" Tristan's voice was light, but somehow serious at the same time.

"We want to send our spirits into your soul."

The phone went quiet and all Reece heard was the ticking of his grandfather clock and Tristan's breathing. "And what would you do while you're inside?"

"See if there are any chains to be broken, any wounds to be healed, any freedom to be fought for."

"When done with the Spirit, that can be powerful."

"Indeed. So? May we?"

"Regretfully that cannot happen. While I appreciate the boldness of the request, that is a boundary I'm unable to let you cross."

"Unable or unwilling?" Brandon said.

"I'd like you to trust me."

"You didn't increase the likelihood of that with the choice you just made."

"Our choices are often not our own. Can you think of another way for us to earn your trust?"

"Not at the moment."

"I understand." Tristan cleared his throat. "Then I believe there's nothing further we can accomplish at the moment."

"Are you for us or against us? What do you want from the Warriors?"

"We are for you. And what do we want other than your trust? Nothing."

"Who are you?"

"As I've said to all of you, ones who would help."

Reece hung up and turned to the group. "Thoughts? Any impressions as I talked to him? Who do you think he is?"

Dana sighed. "Someone trying to distract us. I say we stay away till we're done with the Wolf, then we can worry about who Tristan is."

Reece turned toward Marcus. "Professor? Do you agree?"

"My conclusion is the same as Dana's. We put Tristan on hold for the time being."

"What about you, Song?" Reece asked.

Reece listened to the sound of Brandon shifting in the brown leather chair to the right. "This guy knows way too much to ignore him. I say we have to find out who he and Jotham and Orson are, now. The big war is coming and I want to know if there's someone who might be outflanking us or might be joining their forces with ours. But going into his soul without permission isn't the way to find out."

Reece didn't respond. He'd asked the Spirit who Tristan was three times and all he'd gotten was silence. But it wouldn't hurt to ask again. An answer came seconds later with stark clarity.

Go in and find out.

His soul, Lord? Without permission?

This time it is permitted. You will understand why.

If Reece could see his own face, he would guess it was pale.

"I believe the Spirit is telling us to go in."

"What?" The sound of Brandon smacking the sides of the chair he sat in echoed in the room. "Maybe you are. Not me."

"I will enter with you." The professor's voice sounded scared.

"As will I." Dana's voice was stronger. "I'm sensing we are to go in as well."

"Did I miss something?" Brandon said.

"Apparently so." Reece heard laughter in Dana's voice.

"Fine," Brandon said. "Let's go on this crazy plane ride once again. It's the only way to die."

THIRTY-SEVEN

REECE SPUN HIS WALKING STICK AROUND HIS HAND LIKE it was a sword as the four of them walked to the fire pit in his backyard. Dana caught the hint of a smile on his face. Of course there would be. She watched him as the others built a fire. Inside spiritual realms, Reece felt alive. Valuable. It was a place where he could see in all applications of the word.

After flames blazed from the pit, Reece pointed his stick at the fire. "Are you all ready to find out who we're dealing with? Find out what side of the battle their loyalties lie on?"

"I'm in," Brandon answered.

After Marcus and she said the same, Reece extended his arms. "Grab hands."

Dana slipped her damp hand into Reece's on her right and Brandon's on her left. She didn't exactly feel nervous—they'd done enough soul travel over the past year to make her almost comfortable with it—but still, this felt different. All the souls they'd gone into were known entities—good or evil. Tristan and his friends? They didn't know. And the fact the Spirit had stayed silent on which camp the strangers fell into made this excursion full of apprehension.

"You all right, Dana?" Brandon squeezed her hand.

"Fine."

"Then why is your hand sweating?"

"Because we have no idea what we're getting into."

"Do we ever?"

"We usually know what kind of a soul we're going into."

"But not always."

She dropped the conversation and tried to relax.

"You don't have to go, Dana," Reece said.

"I'm ready."

"You're sure?"

"Yes."

Reece bowed his head. "Get a picture of Tristan in your mind. Let your spirit fly, let the Spirit take you. Here we go."

Dana closed her eyes and let the sensation of falling in upon herself sweep through her. Her mind grew smaller and her spirit welled up from inside and filled her consciousness. The touch of Brandon's and Reece's hands grew lighter and stronger at the same time and the physical world faded and they were soaring. They would land any moment.

But the landing didn't come.

Going through any soul gate had never taken this long. Seconds turned into minutes and then Dana did something she'd never done when going through a gate, maybe because there had never been the time. Maybe because she'd never thought of it before. She opened her eyes.

Where were they? Stars rushed by her as they streaked through the heavens. Planets appeared, then vanished behind them. Galaxies rushed by her. It seemed they traveled far faster than the speed of light.

She squeezed Brandon's hand, then turned to look at him. No one was beside her. Dana spun to locate Reece, but although she still felt his hand, she saw nothing but the stars rushing by her. She looked down expecting to see her body, but nothing was there either. A particle of thought said this should bother her, but it didn't. She blinked again but didn't know if she'd done so in her mind or in reality. She laughed. How could she blink when she had no eyes to blink with?

They slowed and she found herself looking back on a massive collection of brilliant star clusters. Impossible. But she knew what it was. She'd seen something just like it in eastern Washington last summer on a moonless night. The cluster was made up of hundreds of galaxies, all of which contained billions of stars.

"Do you see this?" In her mind she pointed to the vast collection of light in front of them.

Both Brandon and Reece squeezed her hands. Had they heard her? She laughed. Of course they had—Marcus too. She stared at the galaxies, beyond awe, knowing God held the star systems in the palm of his hand. A moment later the stars vanished and solid ground formed under her feet.

"Wow, what a rush!" Brandon laughed and patted his body. "Nice to be back in my body."

Marcus shook his head. "You aren't in your body. You think you are, but you are not, as it is not possible. You're projecting a mental impression that your spirit has graciously translated into a physical image. Quite effectively if you've forgotten the accuracy of my statement."

"I know, I'm just saying it was weird coming through whatever kind of gate that was and not having any sense of form while we did it."

Dana looked into Reece's blue eyes. "Have you—?"

"No, I've never experienced anything even close to that."

"What was it?"

"A gift." Reece looked at each of them. "I believe we've just seen a glimpse of the heavens, and in our glorified bodies we'll take journeys like that with high frequency."

They stood on top of a tall hill covered by a thick blanket of heather. A soft wind brought a hint of lilacs and there was a touch of moisture in the wind that soothed her face. In the distance to their right were green cliffs thousands of feet high, reminiscent of Hawaii, with waterfalls dividing the mountains in sporadic sections. To their left was an arid plain spotted with massive red-rock

bridges and formations that made Sedona look like a one-sixteenth scale model by comparison.

And in front of them, stretched out across a green field dotted with small patches of the most exquisite trees Dana had ever seen, were rows of doors, thousands of rows, millions maybe. Door frames of gold and silver, ones that looked like they were carved from marble, others carved from concrete, others from stone. Thick wood frames and frames made of thin branches no thicker than a cattail. All different. All captivating in their beauty.

As she stared at them, Dana realized they were more than door frames and doors. They were gates. Could these be . . . ? Some gates appeared to be made of glass and some of ice and even some of swirling clouds.

Directly in front of them, a long, winding set of stairs led to a flat area about halfway down the hill that supported a wide platform made of dark wood. A group of figures—too far away to make out if they were men or women—moved across the large dais, stopping in front of each other for a few seconds, then moving on to descend the stairs on either side of the platform to the field of gates below.

The sensation of peace that surrounded them was so strong, Dana felt like she could taste it. A tang of honey and raspberry and smoky cheddar cheese all blended together.

She caught Brandon licking his lips. "You taste it too?"

"It's unreal." He grinned at her, then turned to Reece. "Quite a soul this Tristan Barrow has."

Dana sniffed out a laugh. "I'm thinking we made a wrong turn and probably didn't end up in Tristan's soul."

"Lucky guess," Brandon said.

"I think we need little confirmation we are not in Tristan's soul," Marcus said. "But that does solicit the question of where we have ended our journey."

"I have a very good idea." Reece smiled.

"So do I," Dana said.

"Come then, let's find out if we're right."

THIRTY-EIGHT

DANA WATCHED REECE STRIDE DOWN THE SMOOTH STEPS of the stairway, his shoulders back, a song on his lips. As they grew closer to the platform of people, a few of them raised their heads and smiled. When they reached it, a man who looked to be in his seventies strolled over to them. His hair was thin and almost silver, but his eyes were young. "Enter in, with freedom, with joy."

Reece bowed his head. "It is our honor to be here."

"No, the honor is mine." He motioned toward the other men and women passing them on the dais. "The honor is ours."

"Can you tell us where we are?"

The man's eyes sparkled. "You've always gone right through the gates, haven't you? Never stopped to examine what it was you were passing through."

"I didn't know it was possible," Reece said.

"Now you do." The man smiled and turned to Dana. "You see what they are, yes? That they are not simply door frames and doors?"

"They're the gates into people's souls."

"Yes."

She gazed over the field. "And do you know who all of the gates belong to?"

"Yes, every one. All six billion of them."

"What?" Brandon stepped closer to the man. "Six billion?"

"How can the number be any other than the one just stated?" Marcus pushed up his glasses. "A gate for every soul on earth."

Reece put his hands on his hips and stared at the field. "Can you show us a specific gate? Take us to it?"

"Of course. You are welcome here and anywhere within the fields. And while you are here, you will have safe passage. I can take you to any gate you like."

Brandon tapped the tips of his fingers together. "Not to be skeptical, but with the spacing you have with the gates we can see, means with six billion gates this field has to be—help me, Prof, with a rough guess—five thousand square miles?"

Marcus blinked and looked up and to his right. "My estimation would be closer to eight thousand one hundred and thirty-five square miles."

The man smiled at Marcus, then turned toward Reece, a questioning look in his eyes.

"We were attempting to enter the soul of a man named Tristan Barrow."

"Ah yes, Tristan." The man nodded. "I see."

"You know of him?"

"Of course. And I'm guessing if you met him, you've met his friends Jotham and Orson as well."

"Some of us have, yes." Reece shifted his weight. "Can you take us to Tristan's gate?"

"No, I cannot. There is none here for him. Nor for Jotham nor Orson in case you care to know."

Brandon jammed his finger into his ear and wiggled it. "Uh, the hearing must be going. Thought you said you'd take us to anyone's gate we wanted to get to."

"Tristan and his friends have no gate here in the field."

"They don't have a soul?"

A thin smile formed on the man's face as he glanced at Reece, then back to Brandon. "Not in the same sense you do."

Brandon spun to Reece. "Do you know what he's succeeding at not explaining very well?"

"Yes." Reece smiled. "I think it's obvious and the answer I've expected for a while now."

"Are you going to share the secret with the rest of us?" Brandon said.

"Why didn't we see it?" Marcus laughed. "The dilemma has been solved."

"I was hoping for an answer that was a bit more expansive," Brandon said. "Come on, Prof, want to enlighten your fellow Warrior?"

Marcus stepped up next to Brandon and rested his hands on the wooden railing of the platform overlooking the field. "Tristan is an angel, as are Jotham and Orson. The Spirit has sent them to fight for us and with us, which I suspect they've already been doing for a lengthy amount of time."

"Oh, wow." Brandon twisted to face Dana. "Did you know this?"

"I figured it out, yes. But not until we reached the platform."

Brandon spun on his heel and nodded with his arms raised to shoulder height. "So I'm the only stupid one here?"

Laughter broke out and even their host joined them.

"Marcus Amber is right. Tristan, Jotham, and Orson have been warring for you and will continue to do so."

For the next few minutes the men discussed the implications of that, but the conversation faded from Dana as she stared at the field. If she kept her eyes fixed on a certain area, her eyes acted like a telescope and gates that at first were far too distant to see grew close as if she stood right in front of them.

"Will you tell me what has captured your attention so completely?" The elderly man stepped next to her.

"I see a gate of magnificent splendor." She pointed.

"The one on the bank of a small stream next to the poppies. Right where the brook curves to the north."

"Yes, how did you know?" Dana smiled.

"This is a different realm than the one you live in."

Of course. Maybe here there were no secrets. Nothing hidden that wouldn't be known.

"Do you like that gate?"

"It's captivating." What looked like diamonds formed a border just inside the frame of the door, and inside that was another border made of rubies and sapphires. As she focused she could see the frame itself was made of a dark wood with splashes of lighter wood that spoke of strength and power.

"Yes, it is."

Its exquisiteness filled Dana, but along with the splendor came pain. A sense of loss rose up in her and soon overwhelmed the beauty.

"I don't understand." She looked into the man's eyes for the answer.

They were full of sorrow and a heaviness so great she was tempted to turn and run away. The sadness seemed to seep into her spirit and the weight of it threatened to crush her.

"Watch the gate, daughter." The man's tone grew somber. He braced himself on the railing as tears fell from his eyes and dropped onto his hands. "Watch the gate, Dana."

She turned and stared at the gate. It seemed to grow in stature— the jewels reflecting the sun like a kaleidoscope of light—but then shrank a moment later to half its former size. At the base of the gate a thick purple vine grew and entwined the gate as it snaked up the sides and over the top. The creeper's thorns grew deep into the wood and in seconds the gate vanished beneath the thickening vine.

Then the vine and gate exploded together and turned the jewels into a million shards of light that fell onto the grass like November rain. The remains of the jewels along with the twisting vines and what remained of the wood grew darker, then black, then seeped into the soil and vanished, leaving a charred gouge of soil where the gate had stood.

The grass grew over the scar in the ground and filled it with its

emerald carpet, and if Dana hadn't seen it, she could not have been convinced a gate had ever stood there.

"What happened to the gate? Why did it happen?"

"Every soul that is born must die. We cannot thrust immortality on them and force them to live forever. It is their choice alone."

Reece's voice sounded behind her. "Is this the only reason you brought us here?"

"No." The man pointed at the field. "Look to the very edge. Tell me what you see."

As before, as Dana stared over the field, the distance seemed to shrink, and her eyes could see far beyond what her normal vision could show her. Slowly a low ring of smoke or a cloud came into focus. It was twenty or thirty feet high and pulsed as if pushing to get to the gates. As she watched, a razor-thin column of the smoke shot out from the ring and circled one of the gates for a moment, then retreated. All along the ring, millions of tendrils shot out, crossing thousands of miles across the field in an instant, then merged back into the dark cloud.

"Do you know what that is, Reece Roth?"

The answer struck Dana just before Reece spoke it.

His voice was deep and sounded marinated in anger. "The spiritual manifestation of the Wolf. The spirit of religion."

"Yes." The man turned from the field and waited till all their eyes were on him. "I am praying for the time when you must confront it."

THIRTY-NINE

MARCUS ARRIVED HOME FROM THE UNIVERSITY AT SIX on Monday evening and reached for the doorknob as a ray from the sun flashed off of it. He stopped with his hand inches from the door. Had he just switched again? He couldn't tell. Nothing felt different. But it hadn't the other times either, so why would it now?

He grabbed the knob, opened the door, and stepped inside. Marcus knew immediately he'd switched. "Where's Layne's picture?" It popped out of his mouth before he could stop it. Marcus stared at the antique credenza in the entryway.

"Is anyone home?"

"Upstairs!" Kat's voice called out and then another higher voice spoke from the top of the stairs. "Hi, Daddy!"

Impossible. Marcus shuddered as the boy whipped down the stairs—a blur of green shorts and a white top.

He braced himself against the railing and croaked out, "Layne!"

The blur on the stairs slowed and came to a stop halfway down and pointed at his chest. "That's me!"

Words tried to bubble out of Marcus's mouth, but nothing came. His son. Too full of life, too vibrant to deny he wasn't real. His green eyes smiled at Marcus as if Layne hadn't seen him in forever. How true that was. His brown hair fell forward as he peered up at Marcus.

"Your face looks funny, Daddy."

"I imagine it does," Marcus sputtered out.

His knees weakened but he refused to go down. He'd clearly slipped into the alternate reality again. Layne held out his arms and Marcus didn't hesitate. He scooped up the young child and held him tight, his head buried in Marcus's chest, his lips raining kisses on his son's head.

He squirmed. "You're going to make my stuffing come out, Daddy."

He loosened his grip, tears pouring down his cheeks. "Sorry, I just haven't seen you in so long."

"I know. Between morning and now is a long time." Layne gave a goofy smile with his head tilted to the side.

Alive. The word kept ricocheting through his brain. Layne was alive. Marcus didn't care if this was an alternate reality. Here his son was breathing, laughing, living, and Marcus wanted to stay forever. How old was his son here? Four? Five? Would he die in this reality three years from now as he had in the real world?

He tried to swallow his emotions. "Today made it seem like a long time since I've seen you."

"Your eyes are leaking."

Marcus laughed through his tears. How could he have forgotten? In preschool a boy had made fun of Layne when he cried, so he and Marcus had come up with this terminology to describe it.

"Yes, they are." He squeezed Layne again. "And you're the one causing the leaks."

✢ ✢ ✢

Marcus sat in his den at eleven o'clock that night trying to figure out what to do. The previous switches hadn't lasted anywhere near this long. This one was going on five hours. He leafed through a stack of books on quantum mechanics trying to find a reason why these switches were happening, but he knew he wouldn't find an answer. He'd written a book giving those answers and they were all wrong.

The only light came from the lamp on his desk. Its forty-watt

bulb cast a warm gold glow on his scrambled mass of notes and on a glass of Coke the melted ice had diluted into thin, brown sugar water. But it wasn't his desk, wasn't his Coke. Marcus rubbed his hair and closed his eyes.

A rap on the door frame startled him, and he knocked a stack of books to the floor as he sat up straight. They sounded like thunder as they smacked into the hardwood floor of the den. Hardwood? The floor in his den was carpeted. Just another reminder he wasn't in Kansas at the moment.

He looked up to find Kat standing in the doorway.

"Are you okay?"

"Yes."

She eased into the room, her arms folded and her eyes narrowed. "Really?"

"I'm fine."

She strolled by his desk and slid onto the couch under the windows. "What happened today when you came home? Layne told me you acted funny. And then you almost wouldn't let me put him to bed tonight. And squeezed him like it was the last time you would ever see him."

"Nothing happened."

She glanced at her watch. "It's late and I don't want to drag the truth out of you. So if you'd just like me to leave, I can do that. But if you want to talk, I'm here, okay?" She scooted forward on the couch as if to stand.

"If I described what I'm thinking about, you'd call the gentlemen with the white coats." Marcus clasped his hands behind his head and stared at the notes on his desk.

"Try me."

"Right now I'm enamored to a much greater degree with this reality than the true one."

"This reality?" She looked around the room and laughed, the laugh that captured him decades ago. "It's the only one I know of. Do you know of others?"

"Yes."

"Is this something you're delving into in class, or is it an extra-curricular activity?"

"A smattering of both."

"How long are you planning to continue this somewhat boring line of conversation?"

"In other words, why don't I just come right out and tell you what is going on."

Kat nodded.

"You aren't real."

"I'm not?"

"No."

Kat squeezed her upper arm, her tan fingers a stark contrast to her white blouse. "It feels so lifelike."

"You're part of an alternate reality."

"What, like that movie *Family Man*, something like that?" She leaned back and put her arm along the top of the couch. "How wonderful."

"I'm dead serious."

"I see. Do we live in the same house in the other reality? Do I work at a bakery? Are you a physics professor?"

"Yes to all of the above."

"And how long have I been a projection of your imagination?"

"Not my imagination. To me it's as real as the other side."

"So Layne is a figment of your imagination as well?"

"It's why I reacted the way I did this afternoon." He gazed into her eyes. "In my true reality, Layne isn't alive."

For the first time since she'd come in, Kat grew serious. "That's not funny."

"I'm not laughing."

"What do you mean he isn't alive? That would devastate you."

"Yes." He turned and slumped back in his chair.

"I don't know why you're talking like this."

"You're right. I apologize." Marcus lurched forward. "Let's drop it."

"You've gone this far."

He swallowed and closed his eyes. "Could you forgive me?"

"For what?"

"If I was the cause of Layne's death. Could you stay with me if I'd done that?"

"But you didn't do that. Layne is alive, sleeping in his bed right now."

"But if I had."

"But you didn't—"

"Please, Kat. How would you respond?"

"Tell me what you think you did in this dream world of yours."

"It isn't a—"

"What happened?"

The memory rushed in on Marcus like a flash flood.

"Dad, look at this!"

Layne pumped his pedals and his bike shot toward a jump in a field at Matthews Beach Park. He and three older boys had set up a ramp and had been jumping off it for an hour. Layne's bike smacked into the ramp and launched his son three feet into the air. At eight years old it must have seemed like thirty feet. Marcus glanced down at the paper he was presenting at the university that coming week, then back at Layne as joy broke out on his face. He circled around and sped back toward Marcus.

"Did you see that? Did you see it!" Layne slammed on his pedals and his bike skidded to a stop right in front of Marcus. "I was sooooo high!"

"It was excellent. I'm flummoxed that you didn't scrape your head on the clouds." Marcus grinned and turned back to his paper. "Nicely done."

"Do you want to watch me do it again?"

"I would love to, Layne, but I'm right in the middle of finishing up a project here, okay?"

Layne's gaze fell to the ground. "Sure, I guess."

"But next weekend we can come back, and then I'll even bring

my camera and get some photos of you flying through the air. I promise. No, wait. I pinkie promise. How does that sound?"

"It sounds good." Layne looked up, a grin on his face. "But do you have your camera now? Could you take just one shot?"

"Layne." Marcus tapped his papers with his mechanical pencil. "I wish I could. I do. Unfortunately I have to concentrate right now, but next weekend I'll get a bazillion pictures and we'll make one of them into a poster and put it on your bedroom wall, okay?"

"Yeah, okay."

Layne pedaled off but was back two minutes later. Marcus set his pencil down, rubbed his eyes, and sighed.

"Dad?"

"Yes?"

Layne pointed to the three other boys he was jumping with. "Is it okay if I go with them to the store?"

"What store? Where is it?"

"Just up the road . . . it's not very far."

"That would be great."

"Really?"

"Yes. Just promise me you'll be careful."

"Of course I will be! Really, very extra careful."

"All right." Marcus glanced at his watch. "It's 2:33 now. I want you back here by three at the latest. Okay, buddy?"

Layne jumped off his bike and grabbed Marcus around the waist. "I love you, Daddy. You're the bestest in the westest."

Marcus smiled. Layne hadn't said *Daddy* for over a year. That wasn't a bad thing. It was good, an indication his son was growing up. But hearing Layne say *Daddy* reminded him there was a little boy still inside who would be a little boy for many years to come.

Three o'clock came and went without a whisper. At three fifteen, Marcus couldn't wait any longer. He pulled his keys from his pocket and strode for his car, trying to ignore the sick feeling growing like thistles in his stomach. As he inserted his key into his car

door, sirens sliced through the air of the summer day and the temperature seemed to drop thirty degrees.

Marcus looked up at Kat through eyes blurred with tears. "I never got a photo of him doing the jump."

"I don't understand what you think you did, Marcus." Kat took his hands in hers. "What could you have done? You let him ride his bike with his friends. How could you have known what would happen?"

"I did know. I did." Marcus wiped his eyes. "Something inside me said, 'Don't let him go.' It was as clear as anything I've ever heard. But I let him go anyway." Marcus rubbed the corners of his eyes with his thumb and forefinger for a long time. "I was so wrapped up in that idiotic paper, I paid no attention to the voice inside."

The pace of Marcus's breathing increased and he repeated the last words Layne ever said to him. "'You're the bestest in the westest.'" Their secret saying for each other.

Marcus went silent, and after a few minutes Kat slid closer and put her arms around his shoulders. "He got hit by a car."

Marcus nodded, his vision blurred by tears. Long minutes later he asked Kat again, "So could you? Forgive me?"

"I don't know." She turned and picked at her fingernails. "When a child is lost, marriages have a hard time surviving it. If I knew you could have prevented it . . . I would try, but I don't think—" Kat sat up straight and stared at him, fire in her eyes. "But it doesn't matter. You didn't do it, Marcus!

"If Layne was on a bike or a boat or a swing or a ski slope or . . . or anything, if you heard that voice inside, you wouldn't let him go. Neither of us would. You'd keep him from going and I'd never ever have to face what you say happened and you wouldn't either."

With that Kat pushed herself off the sofa and shuffled out of his den. In this Kat's world, he would never do what he'd done to Layne. It's the only perspective she could see—the only possible outcome. But in his true reality the angle of vision was much different.

Marcus sat in the silence for ten minutes, maybe fifteen, before slowly rising and easing into Layne's room. He lay next to his sleeping son, kissed his head, and pulled Layne to his chest. The last thought before sleep took Marcus was how his boy's hair smelled exactly how a five-year-old's should and that he would do almost anything not to lose it.

FORTY

"I NEED ANSWERS." MARCUS PACED IN FRONT OF SIMON AT Magnuson Park, his untucked shirt ruffled by the breeze coming off Lake Washington. "Why is this happening to me?"

"In case I haven't been clear enough, let me do so now." The magician's gray-streaked hair was pulled back in a ponytail and his usual black coat was replaced by a gray sweatshirt. "There are alternate realities within alternate realities. Layers upon layers upon layers. The deeper you go, the less you know."

"Know what?"

"What is real."

"But where I've been can't be real."

"They can't?" Simon reached in his pocket and brought out his silver coin. He twirled it around his fingers as he stared at Marcus. "Not true. Those alternate realities cause chemical reactions in the brain where we store memories. And once that memory is planted, how can we know if it's real or not? Too many memories of too many realities means sifting through too many scenarios, and it's almost impossible to keep them all straight."

"They're dreams, visions."

"You know they aren't."

Simon was right. Marcus did know. Holding Layne the other day wasn't a dream or his imagination. And it had stirred up a pain so deep it would bury him if he couldn't contain it again. "It's a malevolent act to shove me into other worlds without my permission."

Simon lurched backward as if he'd been struck. "Faugh! I'm not the one doing the shoving."

"Who is?"

"You'll figure that out. You need to."

"Is it God or Satan or something else? And what is your role in it? Are you my enemy?"

Simon spread his arms to his sides and smiled. "I am your friend."

"As if I can trust your answer to be the truth."

"I told you the switching would continue till you made the choice."

"What choice?"

"I bet he's going to give you lots of options to choose from." Simon pulled a deck of cards out of his pocket. "He did me. And I chose them all. I answered the call, of the siren's song that drew me along, into years of living, devoid of giving, my heart to the One who shines like the sun."

"Who?"

"Who what?" Simon blinked like he'd just woken.

"Who is going to give me myriad options from which to choose?"

Simon squinted and tilted his head back and to the side as if he were a gunman in the Old West about to suggest a duel at fifty paces. "Do you like card tricks?" Simon whipped his hand up. "Wait! Stop! Don't answer that. I'm going to show you a trick whether you like 'em or not, so your answer doesn't matter."

He slid eight or nine cards out of the deck case and spread them out for Marcus on the picnic table Simon sat at. Marcus stopped pacing and stepped up to the table. All of the cards were different.

"Here's what we're going to do, Professor. I want you to pick a card." He brought the pack together and one at a time pulled a card from the top and put it on the bottom. "Not with your hand, just tell me when the card you want comes to the top of the stack." Simon tapped his head. "But before you choose, let me warn you: I'm going to try to influence your choice. Yes, ladies and professors, there is

one card in particular I want you to choose and I'm going to use everything in my power to make you choose that card. Ready?"

Marcus nodded. What exactly were Simon's powers? He still didn't know if the magician was human or demonic or angelic. He was fairly confident he could strike the latter categorization from his list, but the other two were fifty-fifty in his mind.

Simon slowly took each card from the top and placed it on the bottom. When the three of clubs came to the top the second time, Marcus said, "Stop."

"This one? The three?" Simon flicked the edge of the card with his thumb twice, then pulled out the card that had appeared just before the three: the eight of diamonds. "You're sure you don't want the eight? The eight is a wonderful card."

"Yes."

"Positive? Not a doubt in your mind?"

It was just a magic trick. So why was there a part of him that wanted to choose the eight? Was Simon pushing him to choose the eight because he wanted him to or because he'd wanted him to choose the three and by pressing the eight it would cause him to stick with the three? Was it that simple for Simon to manipulate his thinking?

"Sure, you're right. The eight is a great card. Let's go with that one."

Simon brought the eight from the bottom of the stack and placed it on top of the three, then brought out the new bottom card—the ace of hearts—and put it on top of the pack. "Are you positive you don't want the ace?"

"Yes."

"The eight, not the ace?"

"The eight."

"At the risk of insult, I'll ask once more. You want the eight, not the ace."

Marcus frowned and nodded.

Simon placed the eight faceup on the table, then showed him

the backs of all the remaining cards in his hands. Each of them was red.

"It's fascinating to me that you chose the eight. But then again, it happens every time." Simon reached for the card and flipped it over. It had a blue back. "The only card among all of these with a blue back. Exactly the card I wanted you to choose."

Marcus had felt nothing in his mind. No manipulation from Simon. The choice was free. Yet there, staring him in the face, was the only card among the stack that didn't have a red back. His face grew hot.

Simon leaned in and whispered, "You play his game, the only choices are his. No choice is free. No choice with him comes without a significant price tag. I know. I paid. I'm still paying."

"What if I'd chosen the ace?"

"I'm glad you asked, Marcus, because I really do like you and I really am trying to help."

Simon placed the ace faceup on the table, then showed the backs of the other cards. All of them were now blue.

"How did you accomplish that?" Marcus stared at the cards. "That's impossible."

"It's a card trick, Marcus. A simple one. One you can find in twenty magic books in hundreds of libraries across America. What's important is the lesson it teaches: He doesn't play fair and every choice is his choice no matter how much it seems like it's yours. Every choice leads to death, okay?" He clapped his hands. "Can I see your phone for a moment?"

Marcus handed his cell phone to Simon who opened a calendar.

"Really! It's already Tuesday. Time certainly dies, doesn't it? I have to go."

"You mean time flies."

"No, it dies. And the chance for choice in that moment dies right along with the passing of the seconds. As I've said before, Marcus, your time for choice is coming. I pray you choose well and you do not allow the moment to die."

FORTY-ONE

Reece's watch beeped, telling him he'd been on the climbing machine for an hour. One more to go. He shifted the day pack full of weights and fumbled for the keypad that would increase the speed of the stairs under his feet. *More intensity. Make the lungs burn.* As if taxing his body to its maximum could distract him from the fact that this coming summer—for the first time in twenty-seven years—he wouldn't be climbing one of the Rockies' fifty-two tallest peaks. He'd tried hiking with a seeing partner, but within twenty minutes he knew it wouldn't work. The man had tried.

"Sorry, Reece! I didn't see that branch."

"You've done this before, right?"

"Not for this kind of hike."

Reece rose from the ground and rubbed his right knee where he'd taken the brunt of his fall and his fingers came away wet. Blood. "How bad is the cut?"

"Oh, wow, that doesn't look good. Let me see."

For the next five minutes the man had cleaned and bandaged the cut on Reece's knee. Then for the next half hour the man called out obstacles as they trudged along.

"Large rock middle of the path, three feet ahead."

"Tree branch at six feet high about four yards in front of you."

It would likely take years of bloody knees and hands to understand what "four yards ahead" really meant. And when they reached

237

a level, smooth part of the climb, Reece felt like a Ferrari following a Yugo. This guy was supposed to be in great shape? That wasn't fair. Reece didn't know many who could keep up with him—which made the dream of finding someone to hike with even more impossible.

Reece turned up the volume on his cell phone and tried to lose himself in the classic rock pulsing through his earbuds, but it was useless. He'd never listened to music in the mountains, why do it here? Because here there was nothing to see and too much to think about. It should be the perfect time to seek the Spirit and hear his counsel.

But it didn't work that way. Other people said exercise was their thinking time, being with and hearing from God time, the time answers to life's conundrums would show up in their minds and hearts. It had never been that way for Reece.

Part of the joy of hiking was pushing his body further than it thought it could go. But a tremendous amount of scaling mountain peaks was what he saw. That should have been obvious. Taking thousands of photos every minute with his eyes and reveling in the artistry of the Spirit. But Reece didn't realize the extent of that part till the enemy had destroyed his eyes and shredded the ability to immerse himself in his greatest passion.

It didn't matter. This wasn't about him. Wasn't about him. Wasn't about *him*.

A rap on the door of his recently constructed workout room spiked Reece's pulse and his Polar heart monitor beeped. Over the top range of where his heart rate should be. No matter how many times Doug or anyone else knocked on a door, Reece didn't think he'd get used to it.

"Come in." Reece pulled his earbuds out.

The door gave a slight creak as it opened and a moment later the sound of Doug's shoes padded across the workout room and stopped three feet to his right.

"How are your workouts progressing?"

"Progressing?"

"Yes." Doug sighed. "I've never known you to exercise without a goal in mind—most often which mountain you were going to climb next. I'm curious what object of motivation you have in mind currently."

Reece continued to pump away, his legs like pistons. The climber was now on the maximum resistance and still his breathing and heart rate weren't as high as he'd like them to be.

"My workouts are fine."

"That's not what I asked."

Reece's watch went off a second time. Good. He was done.

"I know." He stepped off, fumbled for the towel hung on the back of the machine, and turned toward the sound of Doug's voice. "My goal is for God to give me my eyes back. Being able to see inside the spiritual realm was a start. The first part. I expected too much, that the second part of the healing would come at the same time. The second part will be in this world. It's coming."

"And what if he doesn't heal you?"

"He will. I believe the prophecy. Don't you?"

Doug didn't answer.

"Fine, next subject. Have you been reading any of the e-mails that have been coming in from the website?"

"You mean the ones where people are threatening to find Well Spring and burn down the ranch if we don't stop the training sessions? Yes. A pristine example of the religious spirit at work. Carson is doing his job."

"He's replayed the interview with Brandon at least twelve times." Reece rubbed the sweat off his forehead.

"I think it will be played many more times before this is over."

"So do we shut him down?"

"How would you propose doing that?"

"I have no idea."

"Nor do I, but I have a sense Jesus is saying a way is coming that will surprise even you."

"I can't wait." Reece threw his towel over his shoulder and felt his way to the door. "I gotta take a shower."

"Did you say you were going to a place tomorrow night where you can see?"

"Yes. It'll be good for them. And good for me."

"Be careful, Reece."

"I'm always careful."

He climbed the stairs and latched onto the belief he would be healed. It would happen. He would see again. And in the meantime he would go to where his eyes still worked. The Warriors could use another jolt of refreshment before they went after the Wolf, and Reece sensed the time was approaching quickly when Jesus would tell them to go in and do battle. So tomorrow night he would take the Warriors into one of his favorite realms.

FORTY-TWO

"TELL ME THIS ISN'T ONE OF THE MOST SPECTACULAR views you've ever beheld?"

Dana smiled as she looked from Reece to the mountain ranges buried in snow for as far as she could see. If she was guessing she'd say every one of the peaks would dwarf Everest by miles. And breathing up here was like drinking water. Every breath filled her with life and peace. She studied Marcus off to her left and Brandon to her right. From their posture it was apparent the air was doing the same for them.

After what felt like another ten minutes, she turned to Reece. "How long have we been inside this realm?"

"Not nearly long enough," Reece said, a grin on his face.

"I'm serious. Aren't we getting close to the edge of needing to get back out?" Dana jammed her hands into the pockets of her coat. "You know it's time, Reece."

He gazed down on the vast ranges below them, then slowly turned his head ninety degrees, the blue light in his eyes blazing. "You're right. Absolutely right." But Reece didn't move except for his head, which continued to turn back and forth, a brilliant sunset lighting up his face like gold.

"Just a few more minutes. Take this in, Dana. It is a feast for the eyes from the true Artist. You and I can't take a photo of this, but

we can remain long enough to burn the image into our memories. I need this. We all do."

Reece motioned toward Marcus who stood forty yards to their left staring at the deepening red and orange clouds. "Look at the professor. I imagine he's doing the same as we are. Whatever is going on with him and these alternate realities, it's drained him. Let's not deprive him of rejuvenation and of obtaining a memory he'll hold forever, much as we are doing. A few more minutes is all I'm asking."

It wasn't right. It seemed right, it should be right, but staying here even a second longer was wrong. The strong, calm voice of the Spirit was shouting at her to leave. And for some reason she couldn't get the image of the hockey team she'd seen while at Well Spring out of her mind.

"No. Not a few more minutes. We have to get out now." She turned to her right. "Brandon! Let's go."

The Song turned and trudged through the pure snow toward her. When he reached them he said, "Yeah, I'm thinking and feeling you're right."

"Professor!" she called out over the snow. "We have to go now."

Marcus nodded and twisted toward them. He broke into a slow jog, but before he'd gone seven paces, a small crack appeared in the snow halfway between them and the snow under her feet shuddered.

"Hurry!"

"I see it." The professor broke into a run, but before he'd taken three more strides it was already too late. The crack grew as wide as a footpath, then to half the size of a country road. Within ten seconds it was the size of a four-lane freeway.

Dana stuttered up as close to the edge as she dared and peered down. The crevasse was too deep to see the bottom. She whipped her head up and stared at Marcus's horrified expression.

"It isn't possible for me to leap across an expanse that wide."

Reece shuffled up next to her on the right, Brandon did the same on her left.

"It's okay," Reece said. "We'll find a bridge or a way over it where the crevasse isn't as wide or where it ends."

Even as Reece spoke the words, Dana knew the attempt would be futile. She glanced at the massive gash in the snow as far as she could see in both directions. The crevasse didn't narrow, and she knew they would walk for miles and never find a way across.

"Ropes." Reece clenched his fists together as if he held a rope in both hands. "We have to create ropes or a bridge to lie across the gap. Or heal the rift and bring the edges back together. This will be a good exercise for us."

"Dana?" Brandon's face had gone almost as white as the snow they stood on, and he looked ill. "I think we might have a bigger problem than the crevasse."

"What's wrong?"

"Think back to Well Spring. When we prayed together in the grove of aspen trees for Reece. That's pinging so hot and heavy in my brain I can't picture anything else."

"Yes, I got it, get to the point."

"You saw a hockey team, right? And had an overwhelming feeling of danger. And I saw white."

"What does that have to do—?"

"What were the colors? What did the uniforms look like? Can you remember any symbols or markings on the jerseys?"

"Sure." She frowned. "They were red with blue sleeves and they had the initial A on the front."

"Oh boy." The remaining color drained from Brandon's face. "We should have figured it out. We should have stuck with it right then, pressed into it till we got the answer."

"Figured what out?"

"The hockey team you saw was the Colorado Avalanche."

"So?"

Brandon didn't answer except to turn and look up the slope to her left.

"No," Dana whispered. "You don't really think—"

"Yeah, I do."

She turned to Reece. "We need to get that bridge now and get Marcus over here so we can leave!"

Marcus stepped to the edge of the crevasse, his toes sticking over the edge. "Forget the bridge. Let's just go. Try to get out."

"Impossible," Dana said. "You know the answer, Professor. We must go together. All four of us have to be physically connected."

"But that one time . . ."

"Are you willing to take that chance this time? I'm not."

Reece cupped his hands over his mouth. "There would be no way for you to control where you end up when you go back through the gate. And no way for us to know where you've gone."

"Haven't you ever run into this type of situation before?" Marcus said. "Where someone is separated from the group but you have to get out?" The crevasse rumbled and widened by another two feet. "You have to have encountered this scenario previously."

"Yes. I have."

"And what happened?"

Reece pressed his lips together till they turned white, started to answer, then stopped. "We have to get you across to us or us across to you. And you and Dana are right, we need that bridge now."

As Reece finished speaking, a dull roar at the top of the mountain filled Dana's ears. She slowly turned her head toward the sound knowing exactly what she would see and wanting to pretend it wasn't happening.

Avalanche. A half mile above them. At least three hundred yards wide and picking up speed. A churning giant wall of snow and ice and granite shot out tendrils of smaller chunks that it consumed seconds later as it fed upon itself and grew larger. How long did they have? Forty-five seconds? A minute at most? Maybe. Maybe less. Unless they could build an instant way across, they would either die together or be separated and Marcus would end up in a place probably not even Reece could predict. What had they been thinking?

Stick together. Pretend you're a scuba diver. Make sure you're within one breath of your partner at all times. Reece had taught them that as rule number three or four—it didn't matter because they'd broken whichever rule it was and right now, unless the miraculous leaped up in front of them, they were going to lose the professor.

Reece had his head down, hands clenched in front of him. A moment later he threw his arms wide and a bundle of wood and rope appeared in his arms. "Yes!" he shouted and stepped up to the edge of the crevasse, half his boot over the side, teetering over the expanse.

"Here!" Reece called to Marcus across the chasm as he shook the rope and wood slats in his hands. The big man somehow had conjured a rope bridge, and he spun twice like a discus thrower, then flung it toward the professor. It streaked out from Reece's hands like a rifle shot and lay against the bright blue sky. It seemed to float in slow motion toward the professor while the river of snow thundering down on them to their left moved faster.

"Come on!" Brandon shouted.

But the bridge wasn't enough. Not even close to close. The edge of the ropes only reached halfway across the chasm where they fluttered down and bounced against the side of the crevasse they stood on.

"Longer, we have to make it longer." Reece staggered up to the edge of the crevasse, his boots sending tiny bunches of snow over the edge, and dragged the bridge up from the depths. "Concentrate with me. Believe! We have to believe."

What was Reece thinking? Even if a bridge appeared long enough to reach the other side it would take anyone but a world-class tightrope walker at least thirty seconds to cross a chasm that wide.

"If *any* of us are going to survive, we have to go now, Reece!" She grabbed Brandon's hand and stretched out her other for Reece. "Now!"

Reece's head heaved up and down like a buoy in an ocean storm

and his breaths came in gasps. "We can't leave him! If we go, he goes too, but we'll have no way of knowing where."

"We have no choice!" She grabbed Brandon's hand and reached out for Reece's. "Grab my hand, Reece!"

"What about Marcus?"

The pain in Reece's eyes said he didn't know and never would. He turned to Marcus and shouted, but how could the professor hear over the thunder of the avalanche from that far away? "Stay in prayer, trust no one, we will find you!"

The professor shouted a response that sounded like a question, but Dana couldn't make it out. Reece whipped his head toward her with a questioning look in his eyes. He hadn't heard it either. She shook her head violently and pointed at the wall of snow and ice and granite pounding toward them like a giant white wave. They had seconds.

"Marcus will go at the same time we do?"

"I don't know."

"What! I thought—"

An instant before the moving wall of jagged snow slammed into them, the rush of soul travel buried Dana, and the avalanche and the roar in her ears vanished. Brilliant light and myriad colors and the rush of warm wind and a sensation of spinning filled her senses. They'd made it out. In seconds they'd be back at the fire pit in Reece's backyard.

But the seconds stretched out like a blade and Dana felt a tearing in her soul and in her spirit. Why was it taking longer to get out? Because Marcus wasn't with them? Because the Spirit was joining the professor to them even though he hadn't been physically connected when they left? *Please, Lord, let it be so.*

Her spirit slid back into her body with a jerk, as if all of her bones had been given a sharp yank in opposite directions. "Ow!" Her eyes fluttered open and she glanced at Reece and Brandon. "Where'd that electric jolt come from?"

Reece sighed but didn't answer. Brandon pointed at Marcus's

prone body lying on the couch. "I'm guessing since one of us didn't get out, it made our reentry a little bumpier than normal. Reece?"

Again the big man didn't answer but gave a slight nod of his head.

Dana gave a tiny shake of hers. "So Marcus's body is here, but his spirit is somewhere else? And we don't know where that somewhere else is?"

"That's right." Another deep breath from the Temple and again, silence.

Brandon stood and paced, his gaze flitting back and forth between her and Reece. He shrugged and his eyes opened wider as if asking why Reece had gone comatose and what they should do about it.

"Are you sure he didn't get out?" She turned to Marcus, rubbed his shoulder, and bent down to his ear. "Professor, we're back." She turned to Reece. "Is there a chance he's here?"

Reece shook his head and his voice was soft. "Only his body."

"How can you be so calm? I told you we needed to get out. Why didn't you listen to me!"

Reece stared at her with his dark, unmoving scarred eyes.

"Didn't you learn anything twenty-five years ago?" The moment the words escaped she regretted them. His delay wasn't about arrogance. It was about being able to see again. Being able to soak in the desire that had been the driving passion for most of his life. The desire that had been ripped from him by the demons and the gift God had not stopped from being stolen. And she had not walked in those shoes.

"I'm so wrong for saying that, Reece. I'm so sorry."

"We'll find Marcus. I promise you we will."

Brandon folded his arms. "You said this happened before. And the outcome wasn't good. I could see it in your eyes when we were inside just now. Tell us."

"A long time ago I went into a soul with a number of others. We were separated and we didn't know about staying physically

connected. We came out, but two of our party did not. We weren't able to find their spirits and bring them back out."

Reece slipped his fingers around the sunglasses hanging around his neck and slid them over his eyes. "But this time we won't fail. I promise, we will find the professor. We have to."

"More than just because he's one of the Warriors?"

"Yes." Reece took a long breath. "The Spirit told me Marcus is critical to our success in the coming battle with the Wolf. Without him, we are lost."

FORTY-THREE

JUST BEFORE THE AVALANCHE SLAMMED INTO THE others, they vanished, or had Marcus vanished from them? The air swirled and the sound of crashing waves surrounded him as often transpired when they went in or out of spiritual worlds. For a moment he thought the similarity meant he would return to his body with the others. But when silence came and his eyes fluttered open, he wasn't back at Reece's home.

He stood on the ledge of a cliff, maybe twenty-five feet long and five feet wide. A breeze pushed through his hair and brought the smell of giant sequoia trees. The screech of a red-tailed hawk ripped through the air to his right.

Far below him—a rough estimate said five hundred feet down—three tree-soaked valleys wound away from him for miles till they ended at the base of a mountain range at least five thousand feet high. Strange. Not a hint of snow covered their tops. The feeling of an early fall afternoon was on the wind.

He should be at least apprehensive, but with each breath he seemed to be inhaling peace. He studied the cliff wall above him, then turned and stared over the edge. Getting off would be a challenge. Marcus looked at the sun. He had two, maybe three hours before the sun disappeared behind the peaks to the west and then? It could get cold. A night up on this ledge would not be pleasant.

A voice from above floated down on him. "Ho there!"

Marcus whipped his head up to find a man dressed in red-and-black climbing gear hanging from a rope at least two hundred feet above him. The man waved and smiled. For the next few minutes Marcus watched the man rappel down the mountain till he stood on the ledge and stepped out of his climbing gear.

"I hope I didn't startle you from above."

The man was short, not much over five four, and his brown eyes were intense but kind. Brown hair was parted on the side and a three-day-old beard was thick on his face. Not handsome, but not unattractive either.

"Not at all." Marcus glanced around the ledge. "Although I can't say I was expecting you."

"You probably had no idea what to expect." The man stepped to the edge of the cliff, sat, and took long, slow breaths.

"True." Marcus joined him.

"And"—he smiled at Marcus—"I imagine you're wondering where you are."

"I would say earth, based on the geology and plant life, but there's too much peace here."

"Aye, rightly you've called that one." The man grinned and wrapped his arms around his legs and gazed out over the valleys. "There's few places I'd rather be than right here."

"Am I inside someone's soul?"

"No, you know that feeling by now, and I think you realize you're in a place entirely different. Where were you before you came here?"

"I was inside a spiritual realm with three friends of mine. We were on the slope of a mountain together, but a crevasse opened up between us and prevented me from leaving with them."

"Why didn't you find a way across?"

"An avalanche was bearing down on all of us. We couldn't wait any longer."

"I see."

Marcus studied the man's face. He'd been answering every

question without hesitation and with complete openness. It's not that he trusted the man—he didn't know him—but something about his eyes drew answers out of Marcus like water.

"You must not worry, Professor. I am well versed in soul travel as well as the journeys to other parts of the spiritual realm. And I'm here to help you. Whether you accept that help or not is, of course, up to you."

Marcus nodded but didn't speak. It might be wise to talk less and listen more.

"What are your friends' names?" The man drew the name Marcus in the dirt between them.

"Reece, Dana, and Brandon."

He added the names underneath Marcus's.

"And what were you doing together on the side of the mountain?"

"We were finding refreshment from the battle we've been in for a long time now. We've all grown weary, and the enemy has been relentless lately with his attacks as we try to figure out what the Wolf is and how to destroy it."

So much for his resolve to say less. Maybe he was free with his answers because the man seemed so familiar. "Do we know each other?"

"Yes, of course we do." The man's smile went wide. "We just met."

"No, I mean before now, did we know each other?"

"I don't think so, unless you've been here before or to one of the other realms I frequently travel in. But I would have remembered you if you had, I'm sure of that. And I think you would have remembered me."

"It's just that—" Marcus stopped. Just that what? That part of him wanted to tell this man every secret? That whatever this being was, Marcus was ready to open his soul to the man and take whatever help he could offer without reservation?

"Just what?"

"Even though I just met you, I feel you're one I can trust."

"Ah, thank you, Marcus. I hope so. I would indeed like to help you."

Marcus leaned back on his hands and surveyed the valleys below. A low ridge separated each one. The middle was the widest; the other two were the same width. A town sat in the middle of each valley and the layout looked identical. Something about each of them drew Marcus as if he were destined to visit each of them and had no way to prevent that from happening.

"If this isn't earth and we're not inside someone's soul, we must be in one of the other spiritual realms you spoke of. So where are we?"

The man stood, closed his eyes, and drew in a breath as if he were drinking the air. "This is the place where dreams are seen—all dreams, the good and the bad—and where dreams can come true." He turned to Marcus and his smile seemed to make his face glow. "And where some things best forgotten can be. Forever."

"Are you a man?"

"No, but you already suspected that, didn't you?"

"What are you?"

"One who can help you shed your darkest regrets and restore your greatest dreams."

"And you know what those are?"

"Most certainly. I've watched you for a long time, Marcus."

"I thought you said we'd never met."

"Yes, I did, and we haven't. But that doesn't mean I haven't been your friend for ages."

"Then you know about my son?"

"Yes, of course." His eyes grew somber. "That's what I meant when I said, 'Some things best forgotten can be.' The thing buried so deep and so far the others saw no hint of it when they went inside your soul. The one you'd almost convinced yourself didn't happen. The one God has brought to the surface so it can be dealt with once and for all."

The full memory of that day snaked out of the depths, and this time Marcus couldn't stop it.

Marcus slumped forward and dug his fingers into his forehead, his eyes, his cheeks. "You brought that up out of me just now. Made me face it. So I can get rid of the guilt, the remorse, the condemnation, the regret."

"I assisted, yes. But you wanted to face it. So give yourself a bit of credit."

Marcus spotted three hikers climbing a steep trail half a mile below them, one with an oversized backpack that seemed to slow his progress to a crawl. Just like what he'd seen in that church a year ago. Just like he had in his own backpack: a stone he'd placed there that day long ago. And now it was time to get rid of it.

He stared at the man. "I have to tell Kat, don't I? It's time to come clean and beg for forgiveness."

The man smiled and spoke in a voice so soft, Marcus strained to hear it. "No, that's what I was trying to tell you. You don't. That's the beauty of this place." The man gazed at the sky and the valleys below them.

"But even so, I must warn you, it won't be easy. After we talk and your eyes are opened, you'll have to make a choice of great difficulty. I will help you with the choice and freely give you all the wisdom I have, but I cannot make the choice for you."

"When do we start?"

"We can start now if you like."

"Then let's go."

FORTY-FOUR

THE VALLEY IN THE MIDDLE SEEMED TO GROW IN SIZE, OR Marcus's eyes changed so he saw and heard things moving in it. As his focus zeroed in, Kat and he came into view. It was the early days of their marriage when they lived in a one-bedroom apartment with an ugly, swirling, pea green and dark green carpet, and a man downstairs who loved to play Frank Sinatra records at three in the morning with all the strength his speakers could provide.

Kat had no lines in her face and no sadness in her eyes. It was the time before Abbie and Jayla—days when even Layne was only a someday dream and the horror of losing him hadn't woven its fibers into every place in their hearts.

Marcus lounged on their ugly tan couch and tossed a pillow at Kat. "Have you considered the various options for us this weekend?"

"What are you talking about? The weekend is already fully booked. We're going to a movie tonight with Marty and Cindy, Sunday we're going over to my parents, and tomorrow we're watching Kelly and Cecil get engaged at the top of Mount Si."

Marcus leaned his head back and moaned. "I wish we were just watching. Carrying a table and chairs and champagne to the top of Mount Si and then hiding a ring under a rock so Cecil can 'discover' it and ask Kelly to marry him is not watching. It's working. Hard."

"My heart is breaking for you."

The look he'd seen in the mirror for so many years now was

gone, replaced by a lightness on his face that brought back the days before he'd made the mistake that had killed Layne. Those innocent, beautiful, ignorant days when life's biggest struggle was deciding what trail to mountain bike down or what new cheap restaurant they should try in the coming week.

Marcus leaned forward on the cliff toward the valley as if he could step into that world and take into his arms the Kat he saw below and start over again from those days. Replay all the years of regret and this time live them right.

"You can, you know."

"Can what?" Marcus glanced at the man, then back to the valley, but the vision of Kat and him was gone.

The man pointed to the valley. "I can offer you that life, Marcus. You can step into it and live it and I promise you will never remember what you did to Layne. It will disappear as if it never happened because in that life down there, it won't happen.

"It's a world where you went on the Enchantments hike with Dave and the others, where you're close to Abbie, and it's a world, Marcus . . . where you didn't lose Layne."

At the last words Marcus's heart tightened. "That's not true."

The man nodded. "Yes, you can have him back. Your son. Returned to you along with all your memories of his childhood. Just give me the word and it will happen immediately."

Marcus spun and stared at the man. "What's the catch? You said the choice would be made with great difficulty."

The man sighed. "Yes, I did. I also said your eyes need to be opened. So before I tell you about the price you would have to pay to live in this world, you must see what will happen if you don't choose the valley you've just witnessed." The man scooted closer to the edge and pointed to the valley on the left. "This valley is what will happen if you tell Kat about your role in Layne's death. Are you ready?"

Marcus nodded and again either they moved toward the valley or the valley moved toward them, and within seconds he watched

Kat as she stood in their kitchen, her back to him, her hand clutching the counter as if she'd fall over if she let go.

"Kat?"

She turned. "I want to get it done quick for the sake of the girls." She slid a manila envelope onto the kitchen table.

"Get what done?"

"I'm so sorry, Marcus. I just can't do it anymore. I can't get past it. I've tried for so many years." Tears formed in her eyes. "I've filed."

"You've what? Divorce? I can't believe you filed. I didn't think—"

"But you did think. You heard God tell you not to let him go and you thought about it and let him go anyway."

"Please, I don't want to lose us. I don't believe you want to—"

"I know, and you're right. You are." Kat wiped her tears. "There's part of me that wants to make it work, but I just can't. You allowed my son to die, Marcus, and I so wish I could let that go. But I've tried and tried and tried and it's never going to happen."

A moment later the valley morphed into a courtroom, the air stuffy, the smell of old papers swirling around the space as if pushed by an invisible fan. A judge sat hunched over her bench as if she'd just finished speaking.

"I'm sorry, Marcus." A woman placed her hand on his shoulder. "It's final."

"You're my attorney?"

The woman smiled sadly. "Not anymore, unless you plan on getting divorced again someday."

Marcus turned, his sweat-soaked dress shirt plastered to his back, and stared at Kat who stood and shuffled out of the courtroom.

The scene stopped and grew smaller. In seconds he was back on the ledge.

"And the third valley?" Marcus asked the man.

"Are you sure you want to see it?"

"No."

"You're sure?"

"Yes. I mean no, I want to see it."

"This might be the most painful of the three."

"Can you give me a warning, a precursor of what will be shown?"

"Yes, it is the valley if you choose to do nothing. What will happen if you stay in your current world, keep your silence, and Kat doesn't find out about what you did to your son."

Marcus nodded and sighed. "Show me."

He stood in the middle of their bedroom, Kat stood at their closet. She pulled down sweaters and jeans and shoes as if they each weighed sixty pounds.

"Are you going on a trip?"

"No."

"Then what are you doing?"

"I'm leaving. Going to my mom and dad's for a while. Sort some things out. Figure out what I'm going to do." She dropped a pair of shoes and they seemed to land on the carpet like bowling balls.

"Do about what?"

"Us."

"What do you mean, 'us'? What's wrong with us?"

Kat turned and dropped the clothes in her hands to the floor. "I'm not sure. But I know when it started. It was the night you discovered Calen was Zennon and fought him right there in our dining room." She paused and looked down and her voice dropped to a whisper. "He talked about a secret, about 'what you did to him.'" Kat looked up. "I can't get it out of my mind that he was talking about Layne."

Heat torched Marcus's face. She knew. At the least she suspected what he'd done.

She picked up the clothes. "Is there anything you want to tell me?"

Marcus tried to imagine saying the words. Confessing what he'd done. But there was no point. He'd already seen what would happen if he did. He stared at her but dropped his gaze as her sad, questioning eyes looked into his and then filled again with tears.

"Don't say it, Marcus. Don't tell me. I don't want to know." A

sorrow-tinged smile creased her face. "Just give me this time and who knows, maybe it will be okay."

The scene grew smaller and the sensation of moving backward came over Marcus again till the ground grew hard and he was back on the cliff staring at the three valleys below.

"I'm sorry you had to see that, Marcus." The man's eyes were moist. "So much pain."

Marcus swallowed and tried to swallow again without success, his throat raw and dry. "Why would you, why would God give me the gift of the middle valley? I don't deserve it. What I've done has earned me the valley on the right or the left instead."

"That is true." The man drew three lines in the thin dirt next to them.

"Then why?"

"Because he is good. In James it says every perfect gift comes from the Father . . ." The man hesitated. "And he longs to give good gifts to his children."

"But what will it cost me? You said when I'd seen all three valleys, you would tell me the price. And I believe the price will be high."

The man raised his head and stared at Marcus for over ten seconds before speaking. "Why do you think the price will be high?"

"Because I see it in your eyes."

"It is true." The man turned away and gazed at each of the three valleys. "Your perception serves you well, Professor. And the cost might be too great for you to bear."

"Tell me."

The man stood and walked to the edge of the cliff. "In the middle valley you will retain all of your healing and all of your memories except for the memory of that afternoon with Layne.

"Your life with Kat and the girls will be the one you've longed for since before they were born. Your career, everything will be all you've ever imagined it could be. And Layne will be alive and well and enjoying the full life of a sixteen-year-old."

The man paused and locked his gaze on Marcus. "But one significant element of your life will be missing." The man paused again. "Warriors Riding."

A chill washed through Marcus. "What about them? What do you mean, 'missing'?"

"Although all your memories of Reece and Dana and Brandon will be fully intact, their memories of you will not be. They will not know who you are and will have no recollection of what you've built and experienced together."

"How could they not remember?"

"It's the way it has to be."

"Can I make them remember?"

"No." The man shook his head. "I know it is hard to think of what that would be like. I'm sorry."

"Can I tell them things about themselves no one else would know? Can I convince them those things happened?"

"I don't know." The man's gaze swept across the valleys as if he were searching for the answer. "Over time you might convince them something happened in another reality, but you can never bring back their memories and emotions and convictions about what went on at the ranch or your lives together."

"What about the healings inside Dana and Reece? What about Brandon getting his name and stepping back into the freedom he once sang with?"

"They will not have happened."

"Does that mean they could still happen?"

The man shrugged. "It is possible."

"Where would I start with them?"

"You would have to start over from the very beginning. It would be as if the past year had never happened. Reece would come to you as he did the first time with an invitation."

"So we would all go to Well Spring again?"

"Yes."

"I'd have to relive all of it?"

"Are you up for the challenge of that? Can you live through those weeks again, knowing what is going to happen and not saying anything about it? Can you live with knowing Reece will lose his eyes and knowing you are not allowed to do anything to stop it?"

"I don't know."

"A fair answer."

"Will everything turn out the same?"

"That cannot be known. Man has free choice. The decisions you make and Reece and Brandon and Dana make might be different next time. As you know, theoretically, the movement of a butterfly's wing in the Amazon can cause a hurricane in Texas." The man hesitated. "But to answer your next question before you ask it, yes, it is highly likely things would turn out very similar to what they are now. Highly likely, but not guaranteed."

The man lapsed into silence and Marcus did the same. There should be more questions to ask—at least he felt there should be. But there weren't. He wanted a fourth option. How could he give up what the Spirit had led the Warriors into? If he went back to Well Spring, how could he fake it and not tell them what he knew? What if things turned out differently, turned into disaster, how could he live with that? Yet the other two valleys were certain death—one fast and one slow. And he couldn't live with either.

"Do I have to choose in this moment?"

The man laughed. "No, it's not like some late-night infomercial where you have to call now, or some business deal where you're offered the world and if you don't grab it, it instantly vanishes forever. This"—the man gestured with both hands toward the valleys—"is the place where the offer always stands, and you can choose it now, or choose it a millennium from now." He paused and stared at Marcus with eyes that made him want to climb the mountain behind him or leap off the cliff knowing he could fly. "But why would anyone want to put off living the life they've always wanted for even one more moment?"

"I need a few minutes to think and to pray."

"Take all the time necessary." The man stood and walked to the far right side of the ledge. "I'll be here interceding for you, that you will choose well."

FORTY-FIVE

TEN MINUTES LATER MARCUS SHUFFLED OVER TO
the man.

"Have you made your choice?" he asked.

"I want to see more of the valley to the right."

"The one where Kat is about to leave."

"Yes."

"Why is that, Marcus?" The man seemed to stare through
him—eyes full of kindness that seemed on the brink of tearing up.

"Because she said she needed time. She didn't say it was over.
That means if I stay in the reality I live in, there is hope for things to
work themselves out, if I stay silent and accept that God has forgiven
me and ignore the voice of the enemy screaming at me to tell her."

"Yes, you can see. But only a glimpse. Ten years from now." The
man tapped both feet on the ledge in a fast rhythm and stared at the
valleys. "I should warn you, it won't be easy. Are you sure you want
to go?"

His answer came out in a whisper. "Yes."

There was no movement this time. Marcus instantly stood in
front of a tunnel at the base of a smooth stone wall. And this time
the man was with him. "In there."

"After you?" Marcus said.

"No. You first." The man smiled and patted Marcus on the
shoulder. "But don't worry, I'll be right behind you."

Marcus shuffled down the tunnel, the click of his shoes echo-ing off the walls. It smelled like antiseptic gone bad. It seemed like there should be stagnant water on the floor of the tunnel but it was dry. Ahead of them, framed in the curve of the opening, sat a man at what looked like an old kitchen table, no tablecloth, the only chair the one he sat in.

Marcus gazed at the man as they moved slowly through the tunnel. "Is that me?"

"You know it is."

Marcus stared at the figure who was him but wasn't him, and a moment later he sat at the small table hunched over a baked potato smothered in sour cream and bacon bits. A glass of vodka sat next to a bottle of Stoli.

Under his left hand was a photo of a young woman who looked to be in her midtwenties with sad eyes holding a blond baby boy as they both sat on a park bench, the trees in the background bare of leaves. Something about her was familiar.

A ring of a cell phone shattered the silence and he jerked his head to the right and left searching for it. There! On the small microwave on the counter. He lurched out of the chair and picked up the phone. The face of the woman in the photo filled the screen. There was no button to push to answer. "Hello? Hello?"

"Dad, thank God I got you."

"Jayla?"

"Yeah . . ."

"My daughter Jayla?"

"No, Jayla your son. Who do you think it is?"

"I'm sorry, I just . . . it's just that—"

"You're not drunk again, are you? You just got out of rehab three months ago. At least make it last a little longer this time. The U-Dub has been pretty nice to you, but my guess is their patience is getting tissue-paper thin."

Marcus glanced at the bottle of Stoli again. "No. I'm clean."

"Glad to hear it. Okay, now I know I just asked, so no lectures,

okay? I need a little bit of cash. Just a little to get me through to next month. He says he'll get me two months' worth really soon."

"Who is he? And what do you need the cash for? I—"

"I told you not to start, Dad. Please. Kids cost money."

"Yes, I apologize. I mean if you need it, but . . . let me talk to Kat about this. She'll—"

"You're going to talk to Mom? Yeah, sure. And my ex is going to morph into Prince Charming and waltz through my front door this afternoon."

Perspiration broke out on Marcus's forehead. "I talk to her every day."

"Oh, I'm sure you do. I'm sure you and Mom and her new husband sit down over a nightly cup of Earl Grey tea and talk about how she's making millions in the pastry business and you're staggering through your classroom lectures." A sigh came through the phone. "Wow, Dad, I really thought you'd stay sober this time."

Marcus's back grew damp and his hands shook. "Kat is not married to someone—"

Jayla's voice went up three notches. "Listen to me. I know you probably won't remember this once the booze wears off, but once the truth came out about your choice causing Layne to die, she left you. For good. And she's never, ever coming back. Okay? But I'll tell her you said hello if that makes you feel any better."

Marcus's mind reeled. It wasn't true. He wasn't really here. It was the future. But it felt so real. "Your mom is married to me!"

"You are so living in fantasy land."

"No, I'm not. I'm—"

"Make it a good one this time, Dad. You just woke up, or you were immersed in a novel or a sci-fi film, or you are just about to prove Einstein wrong on his theory of relativity. Any of those will work as to why your brain took a vaction, or do you want to try another?"

"Where's Abbie?"

"Are you on crack? What is wrong with you? Just trying to drop another Stonehenge-size rock of pain into your mind? Dwelling on the might-have-beens?"

A sick feeling swept through Marcus and somehow he knew in whatever reality he was currently in, he'd never speak to his older daughter again. "Tell me where she is, Jayla."

"How should I know? Tibet or Bali or wherever she went when she cut us off entirely, forever and ever amen. If you think you'll ever find her, you're delusional. I mean, it's been eight years for you and three years for Mom and me without a peep from her. Now I don't mean to be rude, but can I have the money or not?"

Marcus spun to find the man who had brought him here, but no one was in the kitchen. His gaze scraped across the worn cabinets and the counter stacked with books and a collection of battered coffee cups. In the middle of the refrigerator a photo riveted his gaze. Kat, the girls, and he stood in front of the Disneyland castle, broad smiles on their faces, bright sun lighting up their Tigger, Winnie the Pooh, Peter Pan, and Snow White T-shirts. Marcus closed his eyes and let out a soft moan. Why would he put up that shot? To torture himself every time he wanted something to eat?

He opened his eyes and called out to the ceiling, then out the small window over the sink that framed a setting sun. "Get me out of here. I've seen enough. I've seen too much."

There was no answer and Marcus slumped back in his chair and over the next hour watched the sky turn to the color of ash, then to black. He stood, walked to the sink, and stared at his reflection in the window. His hair was thinner and streaked with gray, his face gaunt, lines etched into it. And his eyes. Hollow and dead as if their hue had been changed to black and white.

"Are you ready to go?"

Marcus jerked around. The man from the cliff stood in the kitchen doorway, a compassionate smile on his face.

"Where have you been?"

The man took a step into the kitchen and held out his hands.

"I'm sorry. In order to fully grasp what is to come, you needed to be alone in the emotion for a good amount of time. If I could have stayed I would have, but I needed to take care of a few other things while the scene played out for you."

"We can go now?"

"Yes, of course."

The man waved his hand and, as if in sped-up reverse motion, Marcus was whisked backward through the tunnel and in seconds sat again on the cliff with the man. Marcus tried to shake the scene from his mind. It wasn't real. But it was. He hadn't just seen it, he'd lived it, he'd been inside the body of the Marcus of the future with all the emotions and horror of that life.

Marcus stared into the valley they'd just come from, its green winding form and the silver snake of a river on its right-hand side belying the desolation that lay within it.

The man picked up a thin stick and broke it into three pieces, then laid them next to each other. One pointing to the left, one straight ahead, and one to the right. "Are you ready to make a choice, Marcus Amber?"

"Yes." Marcus's head slumped forward. "I have to be."

"And what will your choice be?"

The images of Reece, Dana, and Brandon swept across his mind's eye. Then images of all the people they'd set free and the students they'd trained. Then visions of what more they would achieve.

"The choice is difficult in the extreme."

"Yes. It is." The man slid the front of his foot over the edge of the cliff. "And this is the kind of choice where choosing not to choose isn't an option."

As the man's words faded, something inside Marcus snapped. The decision settled on him and lightness filled his mind. Why had it been so hard to choose? The choice was obvious. He turned to the man and began to speak.

FORTY-SIX

DANA REACHED OVER, GRABBED REECE'S KNEECAP, AND shook it. They'd been back from their razor-close call with the avalanche for ten minutes, and Reece had slipped into a prolonged silence. "Hey, we can't just sit here. We have to take action. Figure out a plan for finding Marcus and how to go after him."

Reece tilted his head toward her. "I am taking action. I'm asking the Spirit for forgiveness for my foolishness and asking for the location of the professor. I suggest you do the same."

She looked up at Brandon, then closed her eyes and prayed. Two words blazed into her mind like neon signs flashing on and off. *Mountain*. And *valley*. Then another word joined the first two: *abandoned*. Great. Her weak spot. Jesus had done such healing in her, but still, the scar was fresh and she knew there was more healing to be done in that part of her heart.

Dana opened her eyes. Brandon's head was bowed, but Reece's head was turned toward her. "Did you get anything?"

"Mountain. Valley. Abandoned."

"I saw the word *mountain* as well. I felt the Spirit saying he would take us to Marcus, and finally, that this won't be easy." Reece clasped his knees. "Brandon?"

The musician glanced at Marcus's body. "I saw a sprinter racing down a track, the field behind him crumbling into darkness inches

behind him. He strained to outrun the disintegrating track, but it was gaining on him."

"Interpretation?"

"Pretty straightforward I think." Brandon leaned toward Marcus's body. "If we want to save the professor, we have to hurry."

"I agree." Reece rubbed his forehead, pushing his hat back high on his head. "Our first step is to get through a kind of gate none of us has ever gone through. But the Spirit will take us through and get us to Marcus, although this journey will not be an easy one."

Brandon leaned back on the couch in Reece's home and grinned. "In other words there's a good chance of going down in spectacular flames, dying an excruciatingly painful death at the hands of the enemy, and winding up in heaven."

"Precisely."

"Or in other words, business as usual," Dana added.

Reece smiled and held out his hand to Dana. "Would you like to be my guide out to the fire pit? I think that's where we should go in from."

"An honor, yes."

She took his hand and the three stepped out through Reece's back door. As they walked the familiar path through Reece's backyard to the circle of stones surrounding the pit, Dana realized his request for her to lead him was more about her than him. Over the past eleven months, Reece had certainly taught himself the way to the fire pit without needing help. He didn't need her hand to guide him. But she needed the assurance of his touch. Strength seemed to flow through his giant hand into hers, and although imaginations of the battle they were about to enter into spilled across her mind, a peace settled there as well and it seemed to carry her without effort across the hundred yards to the spot from which they would try to rescue the professor.

After Brandon started a small fire, Reece sat forward and clasped his hands. "Another adventure together." He paused and his head turned down. "This is my doing, my fault, my selfishness, and

consequently my battle to wage. I've confessed this to Jesus; now I'm confessing it to you. And because of that, you two do not have to come."

Neither Brandon nor she spoke.

"I take it the answer you both would give if I demanded it from you is you want to come."

"Ahh, I'm not sure I would describe it as *want* to—" Brandon raised his eyebrows.

"I want to come," Dana said. "So does Brandon." She looked at him and winked.

"So be it." Reece lifted his head as he took her hand and Brandon's. "There's a Warrior from among us who is missing. It's time we go find him and bring him home. Strength, truth, hope, and love. Go before us, Lord, and take up guard behind us. Be below us and above. To our left and our right, fill us with life and wisdom and your vast, unending strength."

Reece gave her hand a light squeeze and then she was free-falling, her stomach seizing up as if she'd just leaped from a plane at twelve thousand feet, air rushing past her, the sound of a thousand waterfalls pressing in on her. Then a shaking in her body as if being pummeled by twenty-foot waves and being slammed into the sand only to be picked up by another swell and slammed back to the ground.

She had to hang on. It would be over in seconds. But it wasn't. The feeling intensified till her body felt like it couldn't last another five seconds without breaking apart. Where had Reece taken them? Maybe no one had ever gone through this gate because it was impossible to get through.

She tried to pull in a breath, but there was no air to breathe and she started to panic. But before the sensation could overwhelm her, the wind and the roar around her stopped and she stood on solid ground. Dana bent over, gasped for air, her legs numb and shaking. She let go of Brandon's and Reece's hands and tried to slow her breathing.

"I can't say I enjoyed that a whole lot," Brandon sputtered out.

"Are you all right, Dana?" Reece said.

"It felt like my body was about to explode, but yes, I'm okay. Why was, why did we . . . ?"

"There is little light in this realm. It is owned by the evil one and we are far from welcome here."

She stood up straight and blinked against a harsh sun low in a turquoise sky. Ten small thatched huts surrounded them. The ground at their feet was muddy and wet as if it had rained just before they arrived.

A thick smoke that smelled like burned fish seeped from crude chimneys on top of each hut but didn't rise. It slithered along the top, then fell slowly to the ground where it formed a circle around the outside of the huts and grew darker as more smoke spilled down the sides of the huts onto the ground.

Dana studied the opening of each hut. Most were four to five feet high, a few were taller, one was barely two feet tall. All were dark inside and the feeling she got from all of them made bile rise in her throat.

The sound of a small chime seemed to come from above them, and as the sound rang out, nine men came through the opening of each hut except for the one with the smallest passageway. Their faces were like gray stone, their eyes dark, hair dark or missing; gnarled hands and fingers stuck out of thin, dark brown tunics.

The garb of the men reminded her of the medieval renaissance fair she'd gone to out in Carnation a few summers back. But these people obviously weren't pretending.

Brandon looked behind him, then turned to Reece. "I'm guessing we go through one of those huts to get to Marcus."

Reece did a slow spin. "I'm thinking the same."

Dana glanced at the men's faces. "And I'm presuming our new friends won't be completely enthralled with that idea."

Reece did another slow spin, then addressed a stocky man with a shock of hair that looked like a bird's nest made of black roots and grasses. "We'd like your help."

The man stared at each of them for at least five seconds, his gaze finally settling on Reece. "Speak of this help."

"We have a friend we need to reach. I believe we need to go through one of your huts to get to him."

"You have spoken rightly." The man glanced at the others in front of each hut, then back to Reece. "That is the way for you to reach him."

"May we pass?"

"Yes."

Brandon turned to Dana and whispered, "It may have taken me a few times to get the lesson, but I think that sounds a little too easy."

Dana nodded but kept her eyes on the nine men.

Reece took a step toward the stocky man. "You won't offer resistance?"

"No, you are free to pass through whichever opening you choose." The hint of a smile appeared on the man's face and grew into a full-out grin. The men in front of the rest of the huts joined him, and then all of them burst into laughter. When their mirth finally subsided, the man who had spoken to them shuffled forward a few paces.

"Is there anything else we can assist you with?"

Dana looked at the smoke surrounding the outside of the huts, which had grown into an ink-black wall thirty feet high. Reece and Brandon were looking at it too, and she met both their gazes when they turned back. None of them needed to speak. Unless the Spirit decided to offer up a miracle, going outside the circle of huts wouldn't be their path to wherever Marcus was. Going into one of the huts was their only option.

"Which is the hut that will take us to our friend?"

"Have you not considered the possibility that the gates here are closed to travelers such as yourselves?"

"No, and there's no chance of us considering."

"I understand." The man motioned with his gnarled hand to each of the openings. "In that case please look on the ten passages

before you. One of them will take you to Marcus Amber. The others will take you to nothing. And if you pass through one of those gates, you will reside in that nothingness for eternity."

"Is there one you can recommend to us?"

"I am not afforded that honor." The man grinned for the second time and again his comrades joined in his laughter. "Only the one who made the huts has the right to show you which to choose."

Reece motioned Brandon and her toward him. He took their shoulders and drew them in close. "Which one—are either of you hearing anything?"

"Nothing," Brandon said.

"Dana?"

"Same." But a moment later she did and pointed to her right at a hut that sat back from the circle by only a foot, maybe less. "I have a sense that is our path."

"How sure are you?"

"It's only an impression."

Reece stood straight and stared at the opening, then leaned down again. "Since it's the only one any of us have received, we'll go with it."

"I'm thinking we might want to be a bit surer," Brandon said.

"That would certainly be nice." Reece strode toward the hut and stopped at the entrance, waiting for Brandon and her to join him.

The man they'd spoken to started to clap and one at a time the others joined him. Their rhythm was slow and the sound their hands produced was low as if each of their hands were made of tree trunks. Dana came to a halt five feet from the opening, squatted, and stared into the darkness. For an instant a thin ray of light inside the hut shot across her vision, then vanished.

A sign? Again she searched for confirmation from the Spirit and again there was no answer. She stood and walked up to the entrance. The smell of fish was stronger here and turned her stomach.

"Should we try another?" Dana peered at Reece. "It was only an impression and it's gone now."

"No, time is even less on our side here than in the other realms. We must act."

Dana nodded, ducked her head, and forced herself to step through the hut's opening. Again the shaft of light appeared, then vanished and hope stirred in her. But the instant Dana had cleared the opening, something from behind shoved her onto the dirt floor of the hut and she landed hard on her hands and knees. "Uhhhhh!" Then whatever had shoved her forward landed on her back and slammed her to the floor and knocked the wind out of her. She groped for air and struggled, face pushed into the putrid-smelling ground.

"Dana!" Brandon's muffled yell floated through the walls of the hut and she heard him push through the opening. She caught her breath and cried out, "No!" but too late. A second later Brandon lay sprawled out beside her.

"Reece, stay out!" But again she was too late and Reece lay quivering on his stomach next to them.

Desolation swept over her. The blackness inside the hut seemed to grow and her thoughts felt thick, as if the mud they'd stood in outside the huts had filled her mind. She tried to get to her knees, but whatever held her down was like iron. Sharp, tiny rocks sliced into her cheeks and tried to force their way into her eyes.

She reached up to block them, but her hands wouldn't move and the force behind her continued to shove her face harder into the ground. Her vision blurred and blackness started to seep into her mind. Then the ground gave way and she melted through the dirt floor and seemed to be floating down—for how long she didn't know. The darkness swallowed her and silence pressed in on her. She cried out but her voice made no sound. With each second the darkness seemed to grow thicker as if she were sinking into black glue.

Finally her feet came to rest on a damp, undulating surface as if she stood on an old waterbed leaking tar. Dana felt her face with two fingers. Wet. Blood she guessed, but the pain was minimal. The cuts couldn't be deep. Small consolation. A feeling of isolation rose up inside. She was alone in the nothingness. There was no doubt.

"Am I alone?" Brandon's voice, thin and hollow, flittered through the darkness and echoed in her head. Relief thundered through her. "No! I'm here. Reece? Are you there?"

A response came as if from miles away and it echoed. "Yes."

"Where are we?"

Neither Reece nor Brandon answered.

"I made the wrong choice."

"I don't think so," Reece said. "I'm not sure any of the huts would have led us to Marcus. In fact, I'm sure they wouldn't."

"Where are we?" she asked again.

"I don't know," Brandon said, his voice growing fainter.

"Don't leave me!" Dana strained to push through the darkness toward the sound of Brandon's voice.

"I won't."

But his voice came to her even softer than before.

"Spirit, come." She cradled her head in her hands.

"He's not here, Dana." Only a hint of Brandon's voice came to her now. "You want to know where we are? In nothing. Alone forever."

Her brain felt like it was stuffed with black cotton. "Reece, help me fight this!"

"Fight? Yes, we have to." His voice sounded thick and as if he spoke in slow motion.

"We have to get out of here. There has to be a way." The mud continued to fill her brain and tried to push out thoughts of escape. No, she wouldn't give in. *You say I can do all things with your strength, Lord? Now would be a good time to fill me up.*

"Stay with me, Reece. What would Marcus say if he were here? What would he teach us in this moment?"

"Marcus? The physics professor? He's the one we're trying to rescue, yes? Is that why we're here?"

"What would he say!" Dana screamed the words but the sound sounded like a whisper coming out of her mouth.

"That the observation of quantum events affects the outcome." Reece's words sounded like they came to her from oceans away.

"What else?"

"That in the same way, our faith affects the outcome of events."

"Like this one." The words crossed her lips and fell to the ground, but she had to get them out. And had to keep Reece talking. Speaking truth.

"Yes."

"So one of our greatest weapons is . . . ?"

"Faith," Reece said.

"Another?"

"Hope."

"And the greatest of these?"

Brandon's voice flittered through the darkness. "The greatest is love."

"Yes." It was the first word Dana had spoken since they reached the bottom of the pit that didn't feel like it had fifty-pound weights on it.

Brandon's voice grew fifty decibels in volume. "And the sword of the Spirit, which is the Word of God."

"And with it there has to be a way of escape." Reece sounded like he was right next to her.

A moment later it felt like ice had been shot into Dana's veins, and a voice that seemed to come from everywhere interrupted them. The tone was that of the stocky man they'd spoken to outside the huts.

"You are wrong. Here you will stay forever. You know this to be true. Separated from the people you love. Separated from your life on earth. And separated forever from the God you have so blindly and futilely served. You made the choice and now you will live with the decision in utter solitude. You know this to be true. After a month you will give up. In two you'll go mad. With thirst, with hunger, but you will not die. In three months you will tear each other apart. You know this to be true."

Dana's head snapped back. "It can't be. That can't be true. It's a lie."

"No, it is true," Brandon muttered.

"Do you think it's true, Reece? What do you believe, Temple?"

"No, I won't believe that . . ." The words sounded like Reece spoke underwater and he gasped for air as he pushed his thoughts out. "I believe this voice lies. I believe all that we see here is deception. I believe we have the power to take these thoughts of evil captive to the obedience of Christ."

The voice of the stocky man spoke again. "Pretending doesn't make things real. We told you before you went in that if you chose wrong, you would be separated from everything and everyone you've loved, forever. There was no deception on our part. You chose this destiny for yourselves. Now you must live with the consequences of your decision."

Dana sank to her knees. Her fault. They would stay here forever because of her. Despair buried her and tears came. She didn't know how long she stayed like that, but at some point Reece's voice reached her. "'And who shall separate us from the love of Christ?'"

She raised her head and opened her mouth, but the words wouldn't come. But Dana refused to surrender and she pushed the words out as if lifting a massive stone off her chest. "'Neither death nor life.'"

"'And who shall separate us from the love of Christ?'" Reece repeated slightly louder.

"'Neither angels nor demons,'" Dana said, the words more easily sliding off her tongue.

"'And who shall separate us from the love of Christ?'"

"'Neither the present nor the future.'"

"'And who shall separate us from the love of Christ?'" Reece's voice went up another notch.

This time Brandon answered. "'Nor any powers.'"

"'And who shall separate us from the love of Christ?'" The big man was almost shouting now.

"'Neither height nor depth, nor anything else in all creation,

will be able to separate us from the love of God that is in Christ Jesus our Lord.'"

"The voice lies." Reece's voice sounded out like a clock striking midnight, and the thick, constrictive air around Dana loosened. "Though we stay here forever, the unquenchable love of the Trinity will never leave us." Reece paused and she heard laughter in his voice. "'Though he slay me, yet will I hope in him.'"

Nothing changed in what Dana could see, and her feet were still mired in whatever she stood upon, but inside a peace grew till she knew if her face could be seen by the others it would be radiant.

She closed her eyes. "'Who shall separate us from the love of Christ? Shall trouble or hardship or persecution or famine or nakedness or danger or sword? . . . No, in all these things we are more than conquerors through him who loved us.'"

Dana repeated the verses and halfway through Reece joined in. The third time through, all three of them spoke the scriptures with power. As they began the verse for the sixth time, a light the size of a needle point appeared. So small yet so bright in the midst of the darkness it seemed like she stood right in front of a massive lighthouse, its mirrors throwing off a million beams of light. The pinprick of brightness grew to the size of a spotlight, then the light was a torrent, a giant vortex pulling them forward, drawing them into its tunnel.

The instant Dana passed the edge of the tunnel, a feeling of joy and power and love surged through her. Laughter broke from her mouth and she spun and raced through the light at a trillion miles an hour, and still she wanted to go faster.

Their speed slowed and the light parted in the middle of the tunnel, and they were now flying over a series of vast mountain ranges far taller than Mount Everest, then down into valleys that reminded Dana of Hawaii, but these valleys were far wilder, the greens deeper, the churning of the waterfalls much whiter, and the rivers running through them more powerful.

Their speed slowed more and she looked at a mountain maybe a

mile away, far below them. As they came closer, Dana spotted two dots on a ledge about halfway up the mountain that morphed into men, and then into Marcus and a man surrounded by a thin, swirling curtain of darkness.

She didn't need the Spirit to tell her they were about to go to war.

FORTY-SEVEN

"I'VE CHOSEN." AS MARCUS SPOKE, A THIN SMILE GREW ON the man's face. "I will release the Warriors, let them go. I can rebuild with them. I can't give up Kat or the girls . . . and to have Layne back . . ." The words tumbled out of Marcus's mouth as if they were tiny lead anchors, but even after he spoke them, his jaw still seemed to be weighed down.

"Excellent." The man clapped Marcus on the back and pointed behind him. "This is so good. I'm so happy for you. It will only be moments now till you're with them in that valley forever."

The man wrapped his fist in the palm of his other hand. "You've chosen the right pill this time."

"What?" Marcus frowned at the man. Was he quoting from—?

"Yes, Professor, I'm quoting from *The Matrix*. Some choose the blue pill, some choose the red. You know that scene by heart."

He did. It flashed into his mind fully formed and he saw Neo taking the red pill and turning his world into insanity and pain and great triumph and truth. Red pill. Blue pill. Red cards. Blue cards. Red backs, blue backs. Simon! The magician's words rushed into his mind. *"He doesn't play fair. Every choice is his. Every choice leads to death."*

Neo had chosen the truth. Marcus fell onto his knees, his hands and arms limp at his sides. And he, Marcus Amber, was about to choose a lie. He was about to insert himself into a world that would

lobotomize his memory and bury the lie so far down, it could never be dug up, but that was a lie too.

It didn't matter if Kat would never know. It didn't matter if even he himself couldn't remember it. It had happened. It was real. It was true. And nothing could wipe that out of existence. He stared at the man, his breaths came more rapidly, his hands formed into fists.

"Is there a problem?" The man eased toward Marcus.

"You can turn the backs of the cards whatever color you want to, can't you? It's your game and I can't win. The blue pill is the way of the lie."

"No, Marcus, it is the way of salvation for you, for your daughters, for your wife, and for Layne."

"Who are you?"

"I am your friend. And it's time for you to go." He glanced at something over Marcus's shoulder. "And if you don't go, I will help you for I am truly a man who desires the best for you." His eyes grew darker.

Marcus's heart pounded and perspiration seeped down his back. "I've allowed my eyes to be blinded." He stood and stepped back from the oncoming man.

"If you don't follow through on your decision, just like Reece, your eyes truly will be blinded." The man glanced over Marcus's head and reached out his hand as if he were about to grab Marcus around the neck. "Be it your choice or not, you will . . ."

The last of the man's words were drowned out as a flash of light and the sound of boulders smashing together filled the air. The concussion of sound thrust Marcus back and he slammed into the cliff wall. When he regained his balance, he looked up and found himself staring into the dirt- and blood-smeared faces of Reece, Dana, and Brandon.

Brandon strode forward and grabbed him in a firm hug. "It's good to see you, Professor. I hope you haven't been bored since we last saw you. We haven't been."

"I apologize for taking so long, Marcus." Reece riveted his gaze

on the man and spoke in a low voice. "Leave. Now, Zennon. In the name of the Christ."

"Hello, Reece, it's wonderful to see you. So sorry to disappoint, but I'm not going anywhere."

The demon stared at Reece, his eyes on fire, the veins in his head and arms pulsing. "You think you can control me? Tell me to leave with a simple sentence? No, Reece Roth. You have no power over me. Not here. Not in this place. Or have you forgotten what happened eleven months ago?" Zennon tapped his skin next to his right eye.

He grinned and stepped toward Reece and the others, his feet stopping with each step as if a great weight were wrapped around his ankles. "This is my domain, not yours. Your simple religious phrases are no help here."

"You have spoken truth. I have no power worth speaking of in this place or any place on heaven or earth or any other realm. But the authority I have in every place because of the Spirit that lives within me is far beyond your ability to fight. Go. By the blood of the Lamb, by the Son of the Creator of the heavens and the earth, and by the authority that rules the universe."

The demon kept coming but Reece didn't move.

"Really? You truly aspire to that belief? And when I reach out seconds from now and draw my finger across your heart and destroy more than your eyes this time, what will you believe?"

Another heavy step and the cliff seemed to tremble with the weight of the demon's foot. "I feel it." A guttural laugh sputtered out of Zennon's throat. "The fear racing up your legs into your torso and into your mind. Yes, embrace the fear, Reece, embrace the truth of my power over you."

Their leader shuddered and his brilliant blue eyes blinked again and again.

"I will have mercy on you and your friends. I will allow you and the others to live if you leave this place now, but I will not make this offer again." The air around them grew hot.

Reece staggered back two steps and glanced at Marcus, Brandon,

and Dana. Fear and strength were both reflected in Reece's eyes, but the strength seemed to flicker like a dying TV.

"The panic growing inside you is the truth." Zennon was now only five feet from Reece. "Make your choice. Leave or Die. I suggest you choose wisely." The demon turned and smiled at Marcus as the air around them grew hotter.

Marcus turned back to Reece. "He's right. Choose wisely. Choose truth."

Brandon stared at Marcus, the musician's face an odd mix of fear and confusion and wonder and risk as if something inside wanted to burst out, but Brandon wasn't sure if he wanted it to. Brandon's hands balled into fists—he closed his eyes and lifted his head to the heavens. He pulled in a long breath and held it.

A moment later Brandon opened his eyes and stared straight at the demon. He began to hum, a high lilting melody that couldn't have been more than four or five notes but somehow sounded like it was made up of thousands of crystals ringing out amid a soft wind.

The demon rose up, seeming to grow three inches taller, and growled. "Desist, Brandon Scott—before I rip your throat out."

Brandon sang it again, louder, and his voice didn't sound like the voice of a man but that of an instrument made of water and glass and air and forest. Reece grinned at Brandon. "Nice to have you back, Brandon." Then he stepped toward the demon, who stopped, labored breaths pouring out of his mouth. "More. You are the Song."

✠ ✠ ✠

Brandon grinned and joy spread across his face like a boy getting his first baseball glove. It was the first time he'd sung since his surgery, and the doubt Marcus saw moments earlier was gone.

Brandon glanced at each of them and his eyes shone with the knowledge his voice had been fully restored in the physical realm and that its power was even more potent here. He was the Song,

and the music poured out of him like it was the last time he would ever sing.

Brandon raised his hands high and the melody grew louder and more complex and somehow out of his mouth poured melody and harmonies that seemed to sweep around them in tighter and tighter circles. The demon's eyes grew darker—if that were possible—and he lifted a shuddering hand toward Brandon as if to crush his throat.

"No." Reece spoke the word in a whisper, then again louder. "No." The third time it was a shout that reverberated off the mountain like a cannon shot. "No!"

The big man stepped toward the demon, lightning in his eyes. "By the power of his resurrection and ascension, we come against you and your lies and the poison you've tried to spread. By the name of the King of all, Jesus Christ, I command you to leave!"

A low guttural scream came out of the demon. "This is not over. It will never be—!" Zennon vanished. There was no sound, no flash of light, and nothing left behind. A hawk cried far above them and the air cooled in seconds. Marcus slumped to the ground.

"I almost made a profoundly poor choice." A chill raced down Marcus's back as he stared at the valley he'd almost vanished into.

"As did I," Reece said. He stepped to the edge of the cliff and stared down at the valleys. "Forgive me, Marcus."

"For what?"

"For allowing this to happen. For letting my selfishness send you here."

Marcus clasped Reece's hands in both of his. "It's over. Forgiven. There was purpose in it."

"Let's get out of here," Dana said. Brandon, Reece, and she joined hands, but the professor held up a finger and walked to the edge of the cliff and stared down into the valleys below.

"Marcus?"

He turned, his heart heavy. "I have been rescued in this moment, but it doesn't change the future. I'm still faced with a choice I don't want to make. One I feel must be made soon."

"What is the choice?" Brandon asked.

"If I'm going to tell Kat."

"Tell her what?"

Marcus didn't answer, and he had no doubt his eyes were telling them not to ask again.

FORTY-EIGHT

"Whew. That was a ride on the far side of extreme." Brandon squeezed his legs as if he were feeling them for the first time. "Kinda, sorta, extremely glad that pup is over." His body felt like lead, and if he were home in his bed he had no doubt he could crash for twelve hours without moving. The workout they'd just completed in the spiritual realm had been fully absorbed into his physical body.

"It's not over." Reece lurched to his feet and strode away from the fire pit toward the back of his house as if the experience hadn't affected him at all.

Brandon slowly rose from the bench, Dana stood, and they followed. For a guy who couldn't see, Reece moved fast. Not over? Brandon felt like they'd just finished sudden-death overtime in the Super Bowl and they weren't done?

He broke into a sluggish jog till he caught up with Reece. "Care to expand on what 'not over' means?"

"Yes, as soon as the four of us are together. I want to make sure the professor is okay."

The three of them reached Reece's back door together and if Brandon didn't know better, he'd swear the big man was seeing again. He reached for the door handle without hesitation and pushed through.

"Marcus?" Reece called the professor's name twice before he got an answer.

"I'm here."

Brandon slogged into the living room and stared at Marcus. His complexion was paler than usual, but other than that the professor looked well. "You're all right, Prof?"

"I'm good."

He stood, then sat back down on the couch his body had been lying on for almost five hours. Marcus breathed like he'd just finished a marathon. Good, Brandon wasn't the only one ready for a break.

"It will take an abundance of time to process the complexity and spiritual implications of what I just experienced, but yes, I truly am well."

"Regretfully, for all of us, there isn't any time for processing." Reece stood like a statue, his long arms folded across his chest.

Marcus gazed up at him. "I don't understand."

"That's two of us, bro." Brandon eased over next to the professor.

A voice rang out from above them. "It's time to go after the Wolf in the heavens, Marcus."

Doug eased down the stairs and came to a stop next to Reece.

"Now?" Brandon said. He glanced at Dana. Her eyes told him she wondered the same thing.

The professor looked down, then raised his head slowly. "It's not."

"It is," Doug said. "I've never heard more clearly from the Spirit. The time is now. I believe Reece agrees."

Marcus shook his head. "Proceeding into that course of action is not a path I'm able to take."

"I realize you've been through a harrowing journey and need time to analyze what has happened." Reece lumbered toward Marcus. "I realize what we all just came out of has exhausted us physically and emotionally as well as spiritually. But there isn't time for recovery right now. You don't think you have it in you to enter

immediately into another battle, but you do. You have the strength, Professor, his strength."

Marcus shook his head. "That isn't what I meant to indicate." He rubbed his hair. "Confronting the Wolf is not my path."

"What?"

"I'm not to go in with you and the other Warriors."

"It's the path for all of those of the prophecy." Reece took a step forward, his arms still folded. "We cannot do this without you. The Spirit has told me more than once that you are the key to victory over the Wolf. That without you, we are lost."

"I'm sorry."

Reece turned. "Dana? Brandon? Am I missing something here?"

Brandon hesitated before answering. Missing something? Yeah. Any hint of sanity. Reece and Doug wanted them to go after the Wolf right now? After what each of them had been through? Brandon was at the point of collapse. Dana had to be as well. But it didn't seem that way when she spoke.

"I think Reece and Doug might be right. I feel like Jesus told me the same thing. The time to go after the Wolf is now. Believe me, I don't want to, but I have little doubt of what we are to do." She turned to Brandon and stared at him for several seconds before speaking again. "Brandon, have you asked the Spirit? If yes, what has he said?"

He hadn't even thought of asking the Spirit what their next move was. He was thinking of sleep. But in the next moment the answer came. *Now.* He turned to Marcus. "We gotta go in, bro."

"That might be the state of affairs for the three of you, but it isn't for me. I'm sorry."

Reece stood to his full six-foot-five height and raised his voice a notch above normal. "Marcus Amber, put down your own desires, your self, the thing you feel you should do, and take hold of the thing you know you must do!"

Marcus stared at Reece, his eyes more intense than Brandon had ever seen them, his countenance like granite. As he opened his mouth to speak, a thundering knock came from the front door.

"Well now, it looks like we have a party crasher who wants to join this friendly discussion." Brandon turned to Reece. "Were you expecting guests?"

He didn't wait for an answer and loped toward the front of the house. He glanced back at the others, then opened the door. Tristan Barrow stood on the wood porch, his arms folded and legs spread shoulder-width apart. Behind him and to either side stood Jotham and Orson.

"Hello, Song." Tristan grinned and gazed at the rest of the Warriors. "We're not interrupting anything, are we?"

Brandon stepped back and ushered them in. The three angels clomped down the two steps into Reece's sunken living room and stood in front of the fireplace, Tristan in the middle, Jotham and Orson to his sides.

"Welcome." Reece stood and gestured to the others. "No interruption at all. Your timing is impeccable. We're just about to go in to confront the Wolf."

"Yes, it is time for that." Tristan glanced around the room. "All of you are going in?"

"Yes."

"I see." Tristan looked at the floor for a moment, then raised his head and stared at Reece. "So you don't believe Marcus when he says he knows he's to take a different path?"

"I know what the prophecy says, that the four must face the Wolf."

"Let it go, Reece. Allow Marcus to hear from the Spirit as clearly as you do."

"He's not to go with us?"

✠ ✠ ✠

Marcus stared at Tristan. Even though he knew he wasn't to go with the other Warriors, he had little doubt no quarter of rest was being offered to him either.

Tristan turned to Marcus, arm outstretched, eyes full of joy. "Will you go with me?"

Marcus didn't respond. The laughter in Tristan's eyes drew him, but whatever journey the angel wanted to take him on would not be all joy. Far from it. Facing what he'd done to Layne and choosing to tell Kat about it were sure to be part of wherever Tristan wanted to take him, and Marcus wasn't ready. He was worn out, exhausted from his ordeal on the ledge with Zennon, and Marcus didn't know if he could face any more potential realities without his brain splitting open.

Because there was no answer this time, no solution he could analyze and formulate that would save him. No principle of quantum mechanics that could be applied to create a happily ever after. Each one of the paths ended in wrenching pain for him, for Kat . . . but where else could he go?

"Will you join me, Marcus Amber?"

He stared into Tristan's eyes, then into Brandon's and Dana's. He held her gaze. Strange. For just an instant it felt like he wasn't seeing Dana's eyes, but Kat's. And in that moment he saw the tiniest flicker of hope.

"Yes, I will join you."

Tristan grinned and his head tilted back as if he were about to laugh. "I am glad for you. This is the path of truth." He turned back to Reece. "Go. Battle the Wolf. Fulfill the prophecy. He is for you." Tristan reached his hand out. "Marcus?"

Marcus walked over and laid his palm in Tristan's. Tristan nodded at the remaining Warriors and an instant later Reece's living room vanished.

✢ ✢ ✢

No one spoke. What could any of them say? Dana considered the options. There was only one. Go in without Marcus, but she believed Reece was right. The four of them were to confront the

Wolf, not three. And if Reece was right about Marcus being the key to their overcoming the Wolf, should they wait to go in till the professor did whatever he had to do?

Brandon was the first to break the silence. "That kind of puts a kibosh on our plans."

Dana sighed. "Leave it to you to try to be funny at a time like this."

"It wasn't funny? I saw the distinct hint of a smile on Reece's face. Really. You didn't notice?"

"You heard what Tristan said." Reece reached out his hands. "We still go in."

"Are you sure?" Dana moved toward Reece, as did Brandon on his other side.

"Without question."

Brandon asked, "Are we going in from here?"

Reece shook his head. "But we need to get to where we're going in from." He smiled.

"Well Spring?" Dana said. "Really?"

"Yes. Where else?"

"Here we come, Scotty," Brandon said.

Dana moved her fingers toward Reece's hand like she was reaching out to touch a scared fawn. The instant their hands met, their surroundings vanished and the three of them stood on the white-stone porch down the path from the main cabin at Well Spring Ranch.

FORTY-NINE

MARCUS GASPED. THE RUSH THIS TIME WAS NOTHING LIKE traveling through a soul's gate. This was faster and more exhilarating than any other time he had voyaged into a spiritual realm. He wasn't in the eye of the hurricane. He was on the fringe, moving a million miles an hour, and he didn't want it to stop.

But within seconds, the earth—or something like the earth—grew solid under his feet and he spun to take in his surroundings. Laughter burst out of his mouth. "Elation beyond anything I've experienced."

"Yes," Tristan said. "Few taste this while still wrapped in the confines of their mortal coil."

To their right and below them a huge golden-hued meadow—of wheat? grass?—spread to a blue horizon. In front of them a massive waterfall thundered hundreds of feet into a pool so clear and so deep, it made Marcus blink to make sure it was real. To their left ran a forest, and in the middle of the fir trees lay a lake so still the water seemed not to be water but trees planted upside down.

"This place . . . the . . . everything . . . the colors are so . . . vivid."

Marcus laughed at himself. Describing the colors as vivid was as vast an understatement as he'd ever made. It was like saying the universe was somewhat large. The most brilliant blue on earth was dull compared to the azure and cobalt hues that were splashed across the sky and lake. The greens of the trees and gold in the meadow made

the richest emerald colors of the Pacific Ocean in midsummer and the deepest golden sun of Hawaii seem pale by comparison. And one breath of the air here rendered all the most-treasured fragrances of earth odorless.

Marcus did a slow spin. "Where are we?"

Tristan laughed. "A place every man and woman longs for even though it does not exist in their wildest imaginings."

"What place?"

"A land where lies cannot live even for a moment. It's a country where the truth is seen by all those who face it."

"Face it?" Marcus said.

Tristan's face grew sober. "Face what would have been if they had chosen differently."

Marcus closed his eyes and pressed hard on one side of his nose. Unbelievable. The answer shouldn't have surprised him—he knew this was coming—but still, the answer did.

"And if I choose to face this truth, what will be the outcome? Will the sorrow of what I would face be too much?"

"I cannot know what will happen to you if you choose to face the memories and then see what might have been. I've never had to face one of my regrets because I've not made a choice that would force that emotion upon me."

Marcus frowned. "How can you insinuate this is a place men and women long for when your description indicates the greatest pain I can imagine lies before me?"

"I invited you to come. It is your choice to face what might have been." Tristan grabbed Marcus's shoulders and peered into his eyes. "But though the truth may slay you, it will also set you free."

The truth would set him free. Did he believe that? Marcus stared at Tristan. "I will go with you."

The angel grinned at Marcus and his eyes seemed to throw off showers of light making the charge of anticipation and fear that pulsed through Marcus all the stronger.

Tristan held out his palm. "Grab my hand."

Marcus waited for another rush but this time it didn't come. There was no sensation of movement, no swirling around his mind and heart and body. The journey was instant. One moment he stood with the angel on the hill; the next he was in a grassland seemingly as vast as the one that held the field of doors—the souls of all people on earth.

Tristan pointed at a speck on the horizon. "Do you see the object rising out of the ground in the center of the field? Where the sky meets the grass?"

"Yes."

"That is our destination."

Tristan turned and strode off at a pace Marcus had to half walk, half jog to keep up with. After a few minutes a song rang out, and although it seemed to come from all directions at once, Marcus knew Tristan was the one singing. The words were in a language Marcus didn't know, but it didn't matter. His mind filled with images of warriors in great wars and vast fleets of ships battling through thirty-foot waves.

They covered ground quickly. Marcus still couldn't make out precisely what the object was, but it was rectangular in shape. A few minutes later he knew it was a door. When they were ten yards from it, Tristan stopped and folded his arms.

The door rested on a four-tiered concrete foundation. Each tier was smaller than the one underneath it—steps leading up to the door. The sides and frame of the door looked to be concrete as well, and the top was slightly wider than the frame on both sides. A smattering of daises grew out of the thick jade grass that surrounded the foundation.

Behind the door, ethereal trees moved in an unfelt breeze against a sea-green sky. An arched wooden lattice stood behind the door. The door itself opened in the middle and was made up of four-paneled wood. Enthralling. But what captured Marcus's imagination was the light that seemed to pour from the sides and back of the door in waves. Brilliant light he was sure would kill him if he touched it.

The air smelled of an early morning day in the beginning of summer, and he drank it in. The door seemed to beckon him, and yet he couldn't ignore the sense of dread that surrounded the structure.

"What door is this?"

"It's time to choose, Marcus."

"Choose what?" he said even though the answer was obvious.

"Whether you will go through the door . . ." Tristan stared at the structure. "Or turn and walk away. This time will be your only chance."

"What is inside?"

Tristan bent to one knee, his gaze fixed on the door. "You would like to know the answer before you step through?"

Did he want to know? Was it even permissible to ask? "I asked the question with little expectation of you giving me the answer."

"I will answer the question if you want me to."

"Tell me."

Tristan continued to stare at the door as he answered. "It is the door of your memories."

His memories? "I don't understand."

Tristan rose and turned to Marcus. "Inside you will find all of your memories. The ones of joy, the ones of devastation. Ones you have treasured and ones you have forgotten. Played out as real as when the moments happened."

Marcus staggered back a step.

"You will face the memories of what you have imagined the future to be, of what the past might have been, of what the future might have been had you chosen differently. All are contained within your door."

The memories of what Zennon showed him in the valleys flooded his mind—Kat trying to figure out if she could stay with him, and her divorcing him, and ten years from now with his life in shambles. He took another step backward on the thick grass.

"Will I see what my life and Kat's life truly would have been like

if I hadn't done what I did to Layne and he hadn't died? A memory still to come?"

"Yes." Tristan's face was like stone. "This you shall see."

Marcus's arms and legs grew cold. "I can't face that."

"I see." Tristan shifted his weight and went silent again, his thick arms still folded across his wide chest.

Marcus stepped toward the angel. "Guide me, lend me your counsel."

"The choice to step through the door is yours. None can make it for you, and none can give counsel for this decision but the One."

Marcus asked the Spirit but no answer came. *Jesus, please, tell me.* Again, nothing.

"Are you permitted to tell me what else lies beyond the door?"

"A choice."

"What choice?"

"Open the door and discover it for yourself."

Marcus walked to the door's foundation, closed his eyes, and prayed for strength. A strange mix of peace and dread settled on him. How could he be feeling both at the same time?

Must I, Lord?

This time the Spirit answered. *As my angel has said, it is your choice.*

Will I survive?

No answer.

What will happen to me if I don't go through?

I have already spoken of that to you.

Marcus shook his head. When? How could the Spirit have told him anything about the door, since until a few minutes ago Marcus didn't know it existed? The image of a coin flashed into Marcus's mind. Of course! How could he be so obtuse? He twisted to look at Tristan.

"Simon. That's the answer, isn't it?" Marcus turned back and stared at the door as the magician's words floated back to him once again.

"Chose the wrong door, you see. No, that's not right. That's wrong. Reverse that. Strike that. Didn't choose the door. Should have gone through it but didn't. Didn't, didn't, didn't. Want to go back and walk through it, because I think it would be good, but I can't now. What's done is done. Over. Finished. I went the other way. Had my chance.

"You're just like Charlie. Willy Wonka is going to hand you a ticket, but you'll have to choose to go through the factory door."

Marcus took a last look at Tristan and smiled. The angel didn't look a bit like Willy Wonka.

Marcus placed his foot on the first step and his legs shuddered. Or was it the concrete step he stood on that moved? A second step. A third, and then he eased his foot onto the last step. The light that emanated from the sides of the door swirled around him and seemed to pull him closer. He took a deep breath, held it, and pushed the door open. The pulsing light on the sides of the door burst out like a flood and immersed him. It felt like liquid, as if he could swim in its currents.

After a minute his eyes somehow adjusted to the brilliance of the light and he stepped forward. He was in a hallway made of stone walls and ceiling—it reminded him of the Alhambra in Granada, Spain. Arched windows were spaced every few feet and gave views of a green, rocky coastline on either side. The crash of waves and the briny smell of sea air filled his nostrils.

A seagull riding the currents to his left seemed to cry in rhythm with his footsteps on the dark stones at his feet as he eased forward. Ten yards ahead was another door. This one had a handle made of gold and it turned without a whisper. Marcus stepped through and stared at the splendor around him.

He was in a lush garden of flowering trees and tiny waterfalls. Was he still inside the structure he'd entered? Or outside? Marcus laughed at himself. Inside what structure? The door of his memories hadn't led to anywhere, but in another sense he knew it led to everywhere.

A path made of leaves wove through the center of the garden and he stepped onto it. The pad of his feet on the leaves was the only

sound. The path went on for fifteen yards before it turned hard to the right, then hard to the left for ten yards, then a gentle curve for forty paces before it turned straight.

A canopy of trees was now overhead. As he walked on, the canopy grew closer till he felt like he was walking down a hallway made for a Hobbit. After a few more steps, he had to stoop almost double to keep from brushing his head on the soft branches above him. He craned his neck and saw the end of the tunnel and through it a clearing.

Enter in.

He fell to his knees and crawled through. He was in the middle of a wide swath of Japanese maples. There was no underbrush here, just a carpet of emerald green moss that ran up to the base of the trees. In the center of the clearing, not more than twenty feet across, was a pool. A ring of thick jade grass surrounded it.

Look into the pool. You must see what it contains.

Marcus removed his socks and shoes, giving in to a sudden desire to feel the soft touch of the moss on his feet. There was no movement on the surface of the pool, no breeze in the air, no sound of his feet on the moss carpet.

When he reached the line where the moss and the grass met, he slid his toes onto the grass, the rest of his foot remaining on the moss. A tingling sensation seeped through his toes, into his feet, up his legs, slowly at first, then faster as it surged into his torso, his arms, and then his face and head. He wouldn't have been surprised if whatever it was had rocketed out of his fingertips, but it remained inside and filled him with thundering joy.

Marcus rocked back and forth from his toes to his heels as the feeling intensified as if ocean waves were crashing inside him— each wave made up of his wildest desires answered. The longer he stood soaking in the glory of the Spirit's presence, the more difficult it was to imagine having to gaze into the pool and see what his life could have been, would have been if he hadn't let Layne die. To see what his life with Kat would be in the coming days and years.

But he had to see. It was the only way to deal with the regret

once and for all, to slay the beast for all time. With the strength of the Spirit he could more than face it. He could destroy it just as so many of his regrets been vanquished last year when the three other Warriors had gone into some of the deepest parts of his soul and obliterated them.

But even with the truth of those thoughts ricocheting through his mind, Marcus couldn't make his lead-filled feet move toward the pool. The regret was so deep, so cutting. The consequences so severe. His son had died because of him, and no matter which path he chose, from this moment forward he would lose Kat as well. The memories of what he'd seen in the valleys buried him, and tears rose to the surface. He cried out to Jesus, but the voice that answered him was not the Spirit's, but Simon's once again.

"The Wolf, the Wolf, the Wolf of confusion, he always spins a compelling illusion."

For the second time the magician's words pulled the scales of deception from Marcus's eyes. Simon was right. Illusions. Alternate realities of the enemy's making. How could the enemy know his future? Or what would have happened if he hadn't let Layne go? Why would Zennon show him anything but lies laced with enough truth to draw him into darkness and assault his heart? Marcus closed his eyes and tried to receive the truth.

Are you ready to see?

The voice of the Spirit.

"To see what, Lord?"

You know.

"What my life would have truly been like if I'd kept Layne in the park that day?"

Yes.

No, he wasn't ready, but he never would be. "Though the truth slay me . . ."

Marcus breathed deep three times, once for each member of the Trinity, and lifted his foot, which now felt as light as a butterfly

rising off a daisy in the heart of summer. Then another step, then another, then one more, and he settled onto the grass at the edge of the pool and let his feet slip into the crystal waters.

Instantly the same sensation he'd felt when his toes first touched the grass rocketed through his body, this time with so much more intensity his body felt like it was on fire, burning him with a hint of pain that seemed to cleanse his body, mind, soul, and spirit. He must have shut his eyes again because he no longer saw the trees or the grass or the moss or the sun cascading into the glade like liquid, but instead he saw the universe and other worlds and beings of power and overwhelming light.

After moments or ages, the fire inside faded along with the visions and Marcus opened his eyes. The ripples on the surface of the pool were fading and seconds later it was glass again. He gazed at its surface without hesitation and without fear, the power of the Spirit surging through him, giving him the strength and faith to endure and press through whatever he was about to see.

Freedom comes.

Slowly a jumble of colors formed on the surface of the pool and began to form into thin shapes he could almost make out. They faded, replaced by other ethereal scenes of shapes flying and running that again vanished into the water without becoming clear. Over and over the hint of a face appeared, or a gathering of people, a woman, a man, a child, but none of them came into focus.

Each time it was as if a giant hand came and washed away the image before it could settle. And each time the colors and images were washed away, Marcus felt another wave of peace and another surge of freedom enter his heart till there was no fear, no regret, no worry about what was to come. The pool bubbled and churned and when it stopped, the sense of peace and contentment was overwhelming.

He was ready and he knew beyond a doubt that when the pool formed the next image, he would see what would have happened if he had chosen differently that day in the park with Layne.

Nothing came except a feeling of love that grew stronger. He waited, but the water only reflected his own image back to him. Marcus swished his foot through the water and watched the ripples build, then fade back into glass. It didn't make sense. Why wasn't Jesus showing him? There was nothing to see. Nothing to see. Nothing.

I have shown you, son of my heart.

Realization flooded over him as the implications of what he'd seen—or not seen—became clear. Was it possible? Was it true? His would-have-been life couldn't be shown because it didn't happen? The pain of what might have been had no hold over him unless he allowed it to. And the future was not set. Hope filled him as the truth washed over him again and again.

There is one more thing you must do.

"Yes, Lord?"

Offer forgiveness.

"To?" But Marcus didn't need to ask, and in an instant he forgave himself for the choice he'd made with Layne so many years before. Once again he was buried in tears, but this time they were ones of release and unrestrained freedom. Wave after wave of forgiveness engulfed him. After an age the Spirit spoke again.

It is time to go.

Marcus made his way back through the tunnel of trees, back through the garden, and up to the door of his memories that would lead him back to Tristan. As Marcus approached the door, his pace slowed. On the back of the door was carved a verse that shone like gold.

"Do not remember the past events, pay no attention to things of old. Look, I am about to do something new; even now it is coming. Do you not see it? Indeed, I will make a way in the wilderness, rivers in the desert." *Isaiah 43:18–19*

For a moment he was too stunned to move. Then Marcus ripped open the door and leaped from the top step to the grass,

then tumbled and rolled like he was four years old again. Finally he rose to his feet, rushed to Tristan, and grabbed the angel as laughter poured from his mouth. When he released Tristan, Marcus stepped back and his breaths came in gasps.

"Marcus Amber, son of the King, the goal of the enemy was to make you live in the might-have-beens, to dwell on them till they destroyed you and those closest to you. But now you have been set free and have been given a choice going forward. To believe the Word of God and live in that freedom, or take up the chains from the past and wrap them around your heart."

Tristan peered deep into Marcus's eyes. "My suggestion is you choose to believe what God has said."

"I choose to believe." Marcus adjusted his glasses and frowned at Tristan. "The alternate realities. Were they real? Was my physical body truly there?"

"Your body truly was there, yes. But were they real? No. As you now know, they were only a life of lies created by the enemy to destroy you." Tristan squeezed Marcus's shoulder. "It is time to go."

"A question before we do."

"Of course."

"Simon."

Tristan smiled. "Yes, a good man."

"He's human?"

"Yes. But years ago he did not make the same choice you made on the cliffs with Zennon, nor did he make the same choice you did at the door of your memories." Tristan squeezed Marcus's shoulder again. "But all is not lost and the day of restoration for Simon is coming. You have not seen the last of him. He has helped you, and I believe in the weeks and months to come you will have the chance to help him in return."

"So be it." Marcus nodded. "I'm ready to leave."

"You're not curious as to where I'm to guide you next?"

"No." He smiled. "I am not."

"Where then?"

"Home," Marcus said. "To Kat."

He took Tristan's hand and the field and the door of his memories vanished.

FIFTY

REECE MARCHED DOWN THE PATH TOWARD THE FIRE PIT at Well Spring as if his eyes had been restored and Dana and Brandon followed. The midday sun radiating off the stones was almost blinding. This was it. Excitement, fear, and resolve all competed for Brandon's emotional attention. As the others settled in around the pit, Brandon built a fire. Once it burned bright and hot, Reece cleared his throat.

"I believe this will be the defining moment of each of our lives. It will be the moment we step into a battle we've been destined for since before we were born. If we are successful, the strike against the enemy will be catastrophic for him."

"Do you still believe we can succeed? Without the four of us together?" Dana asked.

"If we obey the Spirit's call to go in and allow him to take us where he wants us to go, we will have succeeded. Anything after that is a bonus." Reece held a hand toward each of them as if to give a blessing. "This is our destiny. He is for us. We will ride together. We will ride with strength." He lowered his hands. "Any comments before we go in?"

"Yeah, if we die in there . . ." Brandon slapped his legs. "No, forget it. I'll tell you when we get out."

"Tell us now," Dana said.

"Okay." Brandon shrugged and smiled. "Warriors Riding is the

greatest thing that's ever happened to me." He looked at Dana and hoped his eyes conveyed a piece of what his heart felt and that his voice did the same for Reece.

"Me too," Dana said.

"I agree." Reece nodded. "Anything else?"

"I feel the Spirit saying time to go," Dana said.

"So be it." Reece extended his hands to Dana on one side, Brandon on the other. Brandon took his hand and extended his other to Dana. The instant his hand touched hers, Well Spring vanished and a moment later they stood on the edge of the field of doors where they'd first discovered Tristan's true identity. In front of them, not more than twenty yards away, lay the inky, pulsing ring of darkness that surrounded the entire field. The spirit of religion.

"What are you two getting?" Reece's penetrating blue eyes danced. It was clear the man was ready for battle.

Brandon rubbed his lower lip with his eyeteeth. "Strange as this might sound, I'm getting the impression we're supposed to go through the darkness and find out what's on the other side."

"Why strange?" Reece asked.

"Because if the black cloud is the spirit, wouldn't you think that's what we have to fight?"

"I'm not sure I know how to fight a cloud." Reece turned toward Dana. "Anything?"

"I think Brandon's right. We go through."

"So be it." Before the sound of Reece's words faded, a murky tunnel through the cloud opened up.

"This seems a little too easy," Brandon said.

Dana smiled at him. "It seems you've learned a lesson."

"Maybe."

Reece strode toward the tunnel. "Let's go." He walked toward the misty tunnel and reached it with three of his long strides. Two more and he vanished from sight. Dana went next, and then Brandon stepped into the swirling chaos.

The cloud grew thicker as he stepped farther in, and a sense of

evil radiated off of it like heat. Tendrils reached out as if to grab him and pull him into the cloud, but they only flickered near his arms and legs. They never took hold. Seven steps later Brandon was out the other side, breathing heavy, but fine other than that.

Too easy, Brandon thought again. It made no sense. Why would the spirit want them to get through if it's where they were supposed to go? He joined the others who were both staring at the cloud they'd just exited. The tunnel was closed.

"Why did it let us through?" Brandon said.

"I don't know." Reece stared at the cloud for a long time before turning and gazing at their surroundings.

They stood on a dry, hard-packed dirt road beneath a reddish-gray sky. Vast drifts of undulating red sand stretched out for miles on either side of the road. The land held no trees, no plants. No birds flew overhead. The air was still. The heat blistering. There was no sound but the shuffle of their boots and shoes on the dirt.

Wait. A faint buzzing in front of and above them. Brandon looked up. Streaking down on them was a shadowy cloud of . . . he couldn't tell. Birds? No, far too small. Then the sound of thousands of tiny wings reached his ears as the cloud came close enough for him to see what it was.

Wasps, moving faster than he'd ever seen in the physical world.

Dana staggered back. "I'm not a fan of wasps."

"Brandon?" Reece focused his gaze on him and shouted over the roar of the insects. "Do you remember the orbs of fire you conjured up when we were inside Marcus's soul a year ago?"

"Yeah."

"I think now would be a good time to bring them back. And Dana, if you remember how to do them as well, all the better. I'd appreciate it if you'd greet our new friends with a few of them."

Brandon and Dana stretched out their arms and an instant later two white-hot balls of fire rested in each of their hands. Brandon slung his fireballs at the swarm and Dana threw hers an instant later. They exploded as they hit the front of the attack.

They followed the first four with four more and seconds later all that was left of the wasps was a thin black column of smoke that cleared a few seconds later.

"Nicely done."

"I'm guessing there are more assaults where that one came from," Dana said.

"Maybe, maybe not. Expect the unexpected is a wise attitude to cultivate."

"Sometimes you talk almost as weird as the professor," Brandon said.

"Thanks, I've been working on it," Reece said.

Just ahead of them the road sloped downward and grew level in a small valley. Then it rose, with multiple switchbacks as it climbed to the base of a cliff that shot two or three hundred feet almost straight up. On top of a column of dark red rock was a fortress.

Reece turned. "Does this look familiar?"

Brandon stared at the red sand, then to the fortress, then at the road. "Very."

"Do you two realize where we are?" Reece turned to Brandon and Dana and winked.

"Unbelievable," Brandon said. "We're in the professor's vision, aren't we? The one he had a year ago when we first went to Well Spring. Where he saw the four of us riding through that demonic cloud on horses, with Jesus in front, and then the cloud lifted and he was freeing people alongside the road, and then we got to a fortress and Jesus took the enemy down, threw him into an ancient-looking box and then the whole land broke out into grass and trees."

"It appears so."

"So maybe we know how this thing is going to play out?" Dana put her hands on her hips.

"Maybe? I don't like 'maybe,'" Brandon said.

Reece turned and strode down the road. "I think it's going to be more involved this time."

For the next half hour they hiked toward the fortress in silence. Nothing more attacked them, but it gave Brandon no comfort. It only meant something else more ominous was coming their way.

Finally they crested the top of the last switchback and found themselves in a large courtyard of black stone. The air grew cooler as the sound of their shoes against the stones echoed off the castle walls. The pungent odor of rotting vegetation filled the air.

Brandon coughed out a laugh. "This is too cliché. Cue the creepy music and get a vampire to walk out the front door, or Dr. Frankenstein's monster, or a crew of one hundred zombies, or the Hunchback of—"

"We get it, Brandon," Dana said.

Reece looked behind them, then at the archway of the entrance to the fortress. "Are either of you getting anything from the Spirit?"

Dana and Brandon shook their heads. Reece stood and alternated between staring at them and the long corridor in front of them. "Neither am I. I have no direction on what we're to do."

Dana looked at Reece, then Brandon. "We go on." She walked through the archway and down the long corridor, Brandon and Reece on her heels.

The Leader leading once again. Brandon would probably follow her anywhere. The passageway led them to a door, a mass of dark planks bound together at the top and bottom to rough two-by-sixes, three spikes pounded through each piece of wood. Dana reached up, hands steady, placed her palms on the gnarled wood, then turned back to Reece.

"Barricaded?" Reece asked.

Dana shook her head. "I'm guessing the Wolf has been waiting for us to arrive and wouldn't feel the need to keep us from getting in even if they didn't know we were coming. We are the flies here, not the spider."

"No, Dana." Reece glanced at Brandon, then back to her. "That's exactly what they want us to think. But think back to what happened at the end of Marcus's vision. In the place we now stand,

307

Jesus defeated Satan with no more effort than flicking a crumb of bread off a table."

"But we're not Jesus."

"Yet he lives inside us and we sit with him at the right hand of the Father with all power and authority."

"Good," Brandon said. "'Cause I have a feeling we're gonna need it."

Dana pushed on the door and it swung open without a sound.

FIFTY-ONE

DID HE HAVE TO TELL HER? OF COURSE. BUT IT DIDN'T mean he had the desire to.

Marcus stood in his kitchen and stared through the window at Kat, who sat on their deck in the backyard, head back, eyes closed, listening to music, the late morning sun on her face. The weight of regret over what had happened to Layne had vanished, and forgiveness filled the place of pain, but there was no way to know how Kat would react when he told her what he'd done.

No, Zennon's illusions were not the truth, but that didn't mean the outcome would be positive.

He slid open the screen door in the kitchen, eased onto the deck, and sat in a chair across from her.

She opened her eyes, waved at him, then closed them again. "When Doug called and said you and the other Warriors were going to have a late night, I didn't think he meant this late. It's almost noon."

"He called you?"

"Last night and again this morning. He wanted me to know you were okay." Kat sat up and opened her eyes again. "Are you okay?"

"Fine." Marcus stared at the cherry tree to the right of the house as if it could give him an idea of how to start, what he would say in the middle, and what he would say at the end. Just like a good teacher should do. Work out the lecture in his mind first. Then

imagine giving it with confidence and clarity. Then deliver what he'd already practiced with perfection in his head.

But this wasn't class, Kat wasn't one of his students, and the only test was how she would react. "I thought you were working at the bakery today."

"I took the day off. I had a feeling I should. Was I right?"

"Yes, you were." It felt like he was sputtering out chunks of concrete. "I have to tell you something."

"What?" Kat pulled her earbuds out.

"I have to tell you some—"

"I heard you." She pulled her legs up so her feet rested on the edge of the chair and she wrapped her arms around them tight. "I meant what is it?"

"I don't know how to begin this. The words are having difficulty emerging from my mouth." His pulse felt like it was topping out at 180 beats per minute and cold sweat eked out along his forehead.

"Begin anywhere."

"I don't want to hurt us." Marcus sighed. "I don't want to lose everything we are."

Kat's face turned pale and then her eyes narrowed as if she suspected what he was about to say. But how could she know what he'd done?

"This is the secret the demon spoke of that night at dinner."

Marcus nodded and stared at the trees along the back edge of their property as they swayed in the breeze. He stopped and gripped his knees with the tips of his fingers. He was near the edge of the waterfall now. The air seemed too thin and Marcus had trouble breathing. He braced himself for what was about to be unleashed on her, then unleashed on him, then them. It didn't matter. It was the truth. *Jesus, let there be freedom in it.*

"I made a poor choice. The most devastating of my life. And I'm terrified to tell you because I know what will happen if I do. I've seen it—and I can't live with that—but I can't not tell you."

She slipped on her sunglasses even though it was growing dark

and pulled her legs in tighter. "If you tell me you had an affair, I won't believe you."

Marcus squeezed his eyes shut. "No, in some ways having an affair would be easier."

Kat went silent and when she spoke it was only two words. "Tell me."

Then he was over the edge of the waterfall hurtling down, the speed increasing as the words of what he'd done poured out of him. Kat's mouth didn't move, nor did her chin or her head or her hands or her body. When he finished, Marcus dragged his hands slowly over his head and slumped back in his chair.

A minute passed. Then another. Kat said nothing.

"Please forgive me. Can you? Is that desire of mine even remotely attainable?"

Still his wife didn't speak, the only sound her slow, steady breathing.

"Please . . ." The word was barely above a whisper. "Talk to me. Say something, anything."

She nodded but remained silent. Kat sighed, let go of her legs, and shifted so she sat crisscrossed. She gazed toward their home, then out over the lawn, then back to Marcus.

"It's stunning," Kat said, then lapsed back into silence.

"What is?"

"How long you've carried this and how effectively the enemy has used it to ravage your soul."

"I don't understand. What do you—?"

Kat held her finger up to her lips. "As brilliant as you are at most times, your mind and heart have been blinded."

"I don't—"

"Let me speak." Kat took his hands in hers. "Do you not have any understanding of the heart of a mother? I heard that voice in my mind from the moment Layne was born. I heard it when Abbie and Jayla were born, and it has never stopped whispering in my ear.

"I hear it now in almost every moment of every day. I second-guess myself. Don't let Abbie play soccer, she could be badly hurt. Don't let Jayla do gymnastics—she's too young. Don't let them ski or ice skate, or even go to a friend's house for an overnight stay."

Kat squeezed his hands tighter. "Do you remember what I went through the first time Abbie went to summer camp? I was certain a canoe would tip over and there wouldn't be a life guard there in time. Do you remember the first time each of the girls got on the school bus?"

Kat swung her legs down onto the patio and pulled Marcus closer. "Every time I say good-bye to the girls, I wonder if it's for the last time. You don't know, you don't know." She laughed. "If I'd listened to that voice every time it said to keep them from going somewhere or doing something with the slightest hint of danger, they'd have never left the house."

"But it doesn't change the fact I let him go for that ride. It doesn't change the fact I was so consumed with my presentation, I . . . wanted him to go." Fresh tears spilled onto Marcus's cheeks. "Do you understand what I'm saying? I wanted him to go."

"Yes, you did. But that doesn't change anything. The enemy has used that lie against you for the last time. Yes, maybe you wouldn't have let him go if you'd been more focused on the moment. Maybe. But would you have saved him that time and lost him the next? Our lives are in God's hands, our hours on this earth are his alone to hold. I'm not going to live my life with regrets because I said yes to my children living life."

"Still I . . ."

"Yes, you let him ride. Yes, I miss him horribly. It's rare for two days to go by without my crying about it during moments alone that you never see. And yes, this time of the year it grows far worse and I wonder how I'll get through the days before and after the anniversary. But that pain has nothing to do with the guilt the enemy has thrown on you.

"For you to have carried this burden all these years makes me

so sad. And angry. Such a lie from the pit of hell. Why didn't you talk to me about this years ago?"

Marcus rubbed his face. "It took so much out of you when it happened, and I was afraid if I ever told you, you would . . . leave."

Tears spilled onto Kat's cheeks. "Hear me when I say this, Marcus." She waited till he held her gaze and when she spoke the words came slowly. "I would have done the same thing. Hear me again. I would have let Layne go too."

Marcus sighed and pulled her into his chest and his tears mixed with hers. Neither spoke for a long time.

"You have to let it go." Kat leaned forward and planted her elbows on her knees. "Now listen to me. Hear my words and hear my heart. I mean every word: I forgive you, Marcus. I forgive you utterly and completely even though there is nothing and never has been anything to forgive. It's gone. Don't let it ever sink its claws into you again. Do you hear me?"

Marcus stared at her, tears again coming to his eyes. What was wrong with him? He'd cried more in the past eight hours than he'd cried in the past eight months. Finally he lifted her head and kissed her. "Freedom."

She smiled, the tears glistening on her cheeks making her more beautiful than ever. "Yes. It's what he does."

FIFTY-TWO⊙

Dana, Reece, and Brandon stepped through the curved doorway in the fortress and stopped just inside. Before them lay a long hallway with a low ceiling that ran for sixty yards before ending in front of a heavy blue curtain. They eased down the hallway and stopped in front of the curtain.

"Go on?" Brandon said.

Dana glanced at him. Of course they would go on. They didn't come this far to stop now. She pushed through the plush curtain and the others followed. Ten feet ahead was another curtain—wispy, that looked like it was made of a lace that had faded long ago. They stepped through it into a huge circular room twenty yards across. It towered above them so high, the ceiling faded into dimness. The floor of the room was made of green marble, the walls of a light wood, ash or maple.

In the exact center of the room sat a young-looking boy—nine, ten at the most—on an ivory chair. Thin blond hair framed a peaceful face. The boy wore dark jeans and a light blue T-shirt with a picture of an eagle on it. His feet were bare. He sat so still Dana couldn't tell if he was alive or a statue.

When they got to within ten feet of the boy, he turned. "Hello." His smile was innocent and full of wonder. "Finally you're here, but where is Marcus?"

Reece took a step in front of Dana and Brandon. "We know what you are."

"No, you don't, but that's okay. It really is. All will be made clear, all will be revealed very soon." He gazed at them with placid green eyes.

"You are the Wolf."

"No." The boy giggled. "It's so much better than you could have imagined. There will be a tiny bit of discomfort, but that is all. The rest will be so very, very good. Are you ready?"

Before the boy finished speaking, he and the stone walls around them faded. The floor under their feet turned from stone to soft grass. They stood on a wide hill that sloped down to a valley filled with cypress trees. Above them was an almost-cloudless blue sky and the air had a feeling of late spring and unbridled joy. Worry slipped off Dana like a lead coat falling to the ground.

"Wow." Brandon spun in a slow circle. "I'm having a hard time not liking it here. Are you guys feeling this?"

"Be careful. Stay alert," Reece said.

"Any idea what we do next?"

The big man answered by pointing to the end of the valley on their right. Dana squinted and saw a tiny cloud of dust rising and then the cause. A rider on a white horse streaked their way faster than would have been possible on earth.

"The Wolf cometh?" Brandon said.

"I'm not getting any sense of evil." Reece turned to Dana. "You?"

"*Triumph* is the word that comes to mind."

"Brandon?"

"Same."

They stood, each of them like stone, and watched the rider flash toward them. In seconds he reached the bottom of the hill. The garb of the man matched the color of his horse. His body was wrapped in a white cloak except for a dark crimson stain along the bottom. In one hand he held the reins of his horse. In the other he held a sword. A thin gold crown encircled his head.

It couldn't be. Brandon was the first one to say it, but Dana was thinking it. Reece had to be as well.

"Straight out of Rev," Brandon said. "'I looked, and there before me was a white horse! Its rider held a bow, and he was given a crown, and he rode out as a conqueror bent on conquest.'"

"Is it possible?" Dana stared in astonishment.

Reece voiced her next thought. "'I saw heaven standing open and there before me was a white horse, whose rider is called Faithful and True. With justice he judges and wages war. His eyes are like blazing fire . . . He is dressed in a robe dipped in blood, and his name is the Word of God.'"

An instant later the ground shook as the thundering hooves of the horse dug into the ground ten feet from them, and the rider pulled the stallion back onto two legs as a loud whinny erupted from its throat.

The rider brought his horse back to four hooves and trotted back and forth twice before coming to a stop. The apostle had it right with the blazing-eyes thing.

"Lord." Dana stared at the rider. The word came out as a statement, but in her mind it was a question. It made no sense. How could it be him? This was the lair of the Wolf. The arena in the heavens where they had been led to face him in battle.

The rider grinned as he glanced at all of them and opened his arms wide. "You have all fought so well and so long. Well done, my faithful servants."

"Who are you?" Reece's voice was tight. Controlled. No fear.

"Search your heart, Reece." The rider slid from his horse and stood next to it. "You know it is I."

"Prove it."

"You are right to be cautious, alert, testing the spirits, but the time for rest is upon you." The rider . . . the Lord? Was it truly him? "Come, let me show you something."

He walked to the opposite side of the hill and they followed him but kept a healthy distance between them. The rider pointed toward the horizon. A speck of darkness far away, almost too distant

to see, spread across the vast plain. Gold, red, and silver light flashed against the clouds like machine-gun fire.

"There the battle against the kingdom rages, a war with the spirit of religion and all the other members of the demonic host. Its fires will never go out till I come again to earth to bring my beloved bride home, but let us not speak of that for the moment. Yes, you have come to the lair of the Wolf, but it is out there." He pointed again toward the horizon. "Not here." He turned and smiled at them again. "It is so good to see you."

Reece glanced at Brandon and her. "No closer than ten yards till we know if it is really him."

The rider held out his nail-scarred hands. "'Come to Me, all who are weary and heavy-laden, and I will give you rest.'"

Reece's head moved side to side as if he were studying one of M. C. Escher's drawings and couldn't reconcile how a staircase could keep going up indefinitely. Confusion and joy wrestled on his face. "The Spirit brought us here to engage the Wolf, the spirit of religion."

"Are you sure of that, Reece?" The rider shook his head. "No, I brought you here to explain that you have already battled the Wolf—the spirit of religion—many times and you will continue to wage war against him for years to come."

"If that's true, then explain it."

"With great joy I will, for you all have done well." Laughter swept through Jesus' eyes. "Yes, the Wolf—the spirit of religion—has risen, but don't you see? For the past year you have advanced the kingdom in significant ways. With each soul you go into and set free, you have brought war against the Wolf and weakened his kingdom. With every four-day session of training you do at Well Spring, you damage the enemy more and advance the cause of freedom."

The rider stroked his horse with a strong hand. "The ones you've trained have taken the message of freedom back to their friends, their families, their churches. Think of the e-mails you receive! The phone calls. The cards. The stories of breakthrough and healing

and victory over religion and rote traditions. Think of the fruit that is being produced." Jesus raised his arms to his sides. "Don't you see it? What the Father is doing?"

Reece glanced at Brandon and her, but only for an instant, then turned his gaze back to Jesus. "Talk to me, Song. What are you sensing?"

"Relief. I was so geared up for this massive battle with this religious spirit—whatever that was." Brandon snorted out a laugh. "Actually I wasn't geared up. I was exhausted after rescuing Marcus. I have to say this is totally unexpected, but so glorious." He let his head fall backward and he closed his eyes. "Accept the gift of this moment."

Reece's body language softened. "I'm starting to agree. But we have to be sure." He turned to Dana. "Leader?"

What the rider said made sense. And how could she deny his words? She'd never heard Zennon talk like this. It would be so good to rest. To let go. But a small part of her wasn't convinced. "Why the big buildup? Why take us through the dark cloud? Why set us on the road that was in Marcus's vision and lead us to the fortress that he saw? Why not simply bring us here first?"

"Don't you understand, child? Don't you remember the end of Marcus's vision? In it, I defeated Satan. I locked him in the chest and tossed the chest into a crack in the ground so small human eyes would not be able to see it. But you only *heard* about Marcus's vision. And even he only went so far as to watch my victory from a great distance. I wanted you to experience the victory, step into it yourselves, and celebrate here with me rather than just being told about it. Think about what stirred inside you as I streaked toward you just now down in the valley below. Think of the joy and triumph you felt when you knew it was me! I wanted you to know that feeling because you have earned it."

Dana stared at Reece's face. It was full of peace and adoration. Brandon looked the same. So what was wrong with her? Why did doubts still swirl around her like a swarm of mosquitoes?

"Why haven't you restored Reece's eyesight?"

He smiled with compassion. "Oh, Dana, let your doubts slip away. Have you not understood yet what it says in Isaiah? How my ways are higher than yours and there is purpose in all of them?" He turned to Reece. "How often do I answer you in the way you do not expect?" He turned back to Dana. "Yes, the answer will come for Reece, and I will do what is to be done, but in my way, my timing, and in my wisdom."

"So that's the only reason you brought us here?" She narrowed her eyes. "So we could feel the victory?"

"Ah yes, now we come to it. Good for you, Dana. You've seen there is another reason we must speak of." The Lord's face turned somber. "A father disciplines and instructs every son and daughter he loves. And since you have done so much for the kingdom and sacrificed so much, I desired to bring you here to talk face-to-face about the areas in which you have grown weak."

"What areas?" Reece frowned, his face like a little boy who is told there are no presents for his birthday.

"You have opened the door of freedom to many, Reece. All of you have. But without care of the hinges, care of the foundation, care of the frame that holds the door, the door will tumble—and crush many with its fall."

"I don't understand."

"This might be hard to bear, but he who has ears, let him hear." Jesus glanced at Brandon and her, then back to Reece. "Carson Tanner is not your enemy."

What? Dana's mind felt thick. Slow. How could Carson not be their enemy? It was what the Spirit had shown them. His mission was to destroy the Warriors Riding. He'd shown that when Brandon was on air.

"He is not the Wolf, Dana." Jesus focused his gaze on her. "He is a good man, one of my beloved servants, trying to bring truth to the world. Is he mistaken in areas? Yes. Just as you are. Has he taken things too far? Yes. Did he take them too far with you, Brandon? You know that to be true. Does he have areas to grow in and areas where he needs to be reined in? Yes. But much of what he says is truth."

Reece blinked as if to throw off the bewilderment that must be in his mind as much or more than it was in hers.

"I understand your thoughts and your confusion. Why would Carson tear into the powerful work you've been doing at Well Spring? Exactly because it is so powerful. It is changing lives, Reece. But you've gone too far. Understand and accept that I used Carson to bring you to this place. I placed the idea in your mind that he was the Wolf so you would engage him and bring you here to this very moment so the wheat and the chaff of your lives could be separated. You would not have heard it otherwise. Although this might sound difficult, I want you to forgive what he has done to you and become his friend. Come alongside him and help him grow when he needs growth. And allow him to help you grow where you need growth. Together you can be a powerful force for the kingdom."

Jesus strolled back and forth in front of them. "You speak of freedom, my Warriors Riding, but where do you speak of the disciplines? Of fasting? Of solitude? Of regular gatherings of believers? Of memorizing Scripture? Of study?"

Reece shook his head. "We do speak of all those things. That's part of the training we take people through."

"Yes, but not enough. Your emphasis on freedom can lead people astray, and it has done so in some cases." Jesus opened his arms. "That is the reason I brought you here. To lend correction to your path, to strengthen you, to sharpen you, to make you more powerful for my kingdom than ever before. Will you come?"

Dana stared at the faces of the Temple and the Song. They each held a tinge of sorrow. As if Jesus' words had cut them because they knew the words were true. What was the expression on her own face? Undoubtedly confusion but she wasn't buying what this Jesus was selling. Something was off.

"Are you ready to be restored? Refreshed?" Reece and Brandon gave a slow nod. Jesus turned to her. "Are you ready to enter my rest, Dana?" He beckoned all of them. "Come, take my hands."

"Wait." Dana held her arms out as if to block Reece and Brandon from stepping forward.

"You have warred so hard, Dana. You have led so well. But it is time to rest. There is so much more to be done, and you shall do it, but for now it is time for reprieve and refreshment." Jesus reached out his arms. "Take hold, and I will take you to a place of respite. Come. Enter into my rest."

"No." Dana shook her head and drew her hands into fists. "I don't believe you are who you say you are."

"Why do you think this, Dana? What is your evidence? What can you point to that proves who I say I am is not true?"

There was nothing she could point to. Every fiber in her said this was Jesus. Every fiber but one. A fiber buried so deep in her spirit, she barely felt it. As if she were in darkness and it was the light of a candle a mile away. "I just know it. I feel it."

"Feelings are not truth, Dana. They are emotions only and emotions are not reality." The rider stepped toward her. "Do I speak in the style of our enemy? Do I look like him? Is there anything I've said that is not true? How would you have me prove myself to you?"

"I don't know."

"But I do. You can choose to doubt. It's all right." He smiled. "But come with me now and enter into the place I have created for the three of you, and then you will not be able to deny who I Am and your doubts will vanish in the warm breeze of that land." He reached out his hand. "Come."

"What if I refuse?"

Sadness spilled onto his face. "Then you will stay here and I will take the others, and when they return they will tell you of an ecstasy you will long for the rest of your days but will not experience till you join me for eternity in heaven." The rider had been talking softly, but now his voice grew loud. "Enough. We must go." He stared at her, his eyes kind but intense.

"Are you coming with the others, daughter?"

FIFTY-THREE

MARCUS HELD KAT FOR A FEW MORE SECONDS, THEN PULLED back to arm's length. "There's someone I'd like you to meet."

"What? Now?" Kat glanced around their backyard. "Someone is here?"

"Yes. They've been—"

"They've been here during our whole conversation? Where?"

"In the front yard but not listening. You'll understand when you meet him."

"I'd better." She cocked her head, a wry smile on her face.

Marcus turned and called out, "Tristan!"

The angel strode around the corner of the house a few seconds later, his grin as wide as Marcus had ever seen it.

"You?" Kat stared at him, mouth open.

Marcus glanced back and forth between Kat and Tristan. "You know him? How is that poss—?"

"Hello, Kat, it's good to see you."

"Hello, Tristan." She stared at him as her eyes twinkled. "Yes, I know him. We've met once before."

Tristan gave a nod of his head. "This is true."

"Care to enlighten me?" Marcus said.

"On the street, in Seattle's University District. You were the one who saved Jayla almost a year ago from being run over by the car."

"Unbelievable. Utterly unbelievable," Marcus muttered.

"Yes. I'm sorry we didn't have longer to talk that day. It wasn't time."

"I understand." She smiled. "I'm guessing you've taken my husband on some interesting adventures as of late."

"Indeed I have," Tristan said.

"Daddy?"

Marcus turned. Abbie stood in the doorway leading onto the deck. She hesitated, stepped forward, then ran toward him. She threw her arms around him and buried her head in his chest.

"Hi, Abbie girl."

"I'm glad you're okay."

"Why wouldn't I be?"

"I don't know." She lifted her head. "I prayed for you through the night last night."

"You did?"

"I don't know why. I couldn't sleep and I just felt like I was supposed to." She snuggled back into his chest. "Like you did for me with . . . the other day when . . . at dinner, you know? You fought for me. I felt like I needed to fight for you."

"You fought well, Abbs." Marcus blinked back tears as he squeezed Abbie tighter. "Really, really well."

"You all have." Tristan looked at Marcus, then Kat, and then Abbie. "But the fight is not over. I'm sorry to pull your husband from you and your father from you again so soon, but he is desperately needed a little longer." The angel held out his arm. "Take my hand, Professor. You're due on the radio in five minutes. I wouldn't want you to be late."

"What? I'm due where?"

"You're about to appear on *The Carson Tanner Show*. I believe you are more than ready."

✠ ✠ ✠

The air swirled and an instant later Marcus stood in a hallway that led to a thick gray door. Over the top of it was a red sign, lit up with the words *On the Air*.

Marcus stared at the door seven paces in front of them. "Carson's studio."

"Of course."

"He has no idea I'm here."

"No, that would ruin the surprise." Tristan smiled. "But have no doubt as soon as he sees you he'll be more than willing to scrap his intended show and welcome you on the air as his special guest."

They walked toward the door.

"Hey!" A voice rang out behind them. "You can't go in there."

Marcus turned to find a slender woman twenty paces back striding toward them.

"I'm guessing you're Sooz," Marcus said.

"Yeah, who are you?"

"Marcus Amber, one of the Warriors Riding."

Surprise splashed on Sooz's face, replaced quickly by a gleam in her eyes that shouted, *This is going to be very, very good.*

"A pleasure to meet you, Professor." She pointed over his shoulder toward the studio door. "I'm thinking you'd like to be a special surprise guest on Carson's show."

"If he can squeeze me in."

"I'm almost certain that can be arranged. Do you mind if I let Carson know you're here?" She slid by them on the right and stopped.

"Not at all."

Sooz fixed her gaze on the sign above the door, apparently waiting for it to go off. The three stood not moving, the silence growing awkward. Sooz glanced back at Tristan, then at Marcus. "Who is your friend here?"

"A friend."

"I see."

Sooz opened her mouth, probably to press for a more complete answer, but before she could, the red light above the door went off. "Stay here." She opened the studio door and stepped through.

Tristan put his hand on Marcus's shoulder. "You're about to walk through another door, Marcus Amber. A different kind, but still one

that will change you as your door of memories did. Are you ready?" Tristan smiled at him and it filled Marcus with hope and power.

A moment later Carson Tanner strode through his studio door, light laughter filling the hallway. "Wow! Talk about slapping a surprise on my forehead like a God Bless You tattoo. It's good to meet you, Professor, and I hope"—he motioned behind him—"to have you on my show. What do you say?"

"I gratefully accept your invitation."

"No, no, no." Carson waved his hands. "The gratitude is mine. Shall we?"

Forty-five seconds later Marcus sat across from Carson, a pair of headphones on his head, his mind racing, his heart pumping. To his right and behind him, leaning against the wall, stood Tristan. "Are you sure you want to be here, Professor Amber? We're on the air in thirty seconds."

"Why do you ask?"

"Love the sinner, hate the sin. Or put another way, I'm guessing you heard my interview with your buddy Brandon."

"I did."

"In an attitude of truth, since that's what we're all about here, I need to tell you this won't go well for you." Carson grinned. "You still want to go on?"

Marcus didn't answer and adjusted his headphones.

"I'll take that as a yes." Carson kept grinning as he pushed his mic button. "Shake it, bake it, but there's no way we'll take it." Carson shifted his weight back and forth on his chair like he was trying to dance sitting down and the microphone was his partner. "Take what? Lies. No thank you, we don't want 'em! On *The Carson Tanner Show* we're all about truth, and right now I have a very special guest in the studio who might be tempted to tell you mixed truth that isn't truth at all. Just warning you. Keep your minds sharp 'cause we've got with us right now in the studio one of the brightest minds in the country—professor of physics at the University of Washington, Marcus Amber! Welcome, Professor."

"Thank you."

"Folks, just to remind you, we've been talking about this cult-like group called Warriors Riding that Brandon Scott got himself caught up in. That they're spreading their heresy all over the country with their training, and the Lord has told us to do our part in stopping it. Did you catch my interview with Brandon where we exposed the lies? Worth listening to."

Carson grinned and pointed at Marcus. "The professor here is part of the leadership of this group, and I had no idea till three—yeah, three minutes ago we were going to get the chance to talk to him. So let's get to it, Professor. What are you doing here?"

Marcus stared at Carson. It was an excellent question. Why was he here? Tristan obviously knew, but there hadn't been time to ask the angel what the purpose was in bringing him onto the show. He opened his mouth to confess to Carson he didn't know, but the words that spilled out were not an admittance of ignorance.

"I'm here to speak to you about truth and confront the lies of the spirit that have been controlling you. I'm here to talk about true freedom."

"Controlling me? Yeah, baby! That's what I'm talking about." Carson slapped his chair. "See why this stuff these Warriors are spouting about is so deceptive? Didn't the professor sound sincere?" He pointed at Marcus. "Okay, Professor, let's get right to it. What's the truth you think I'm missing?"

Again Marcus didn't have the words, and again he opened his mouth and spoke, his gaze fixed on Carson's eyes. "'You foolish Galatians! Who has bewitched you? Before your very eyes Jesus Christ was clearly portrayed as crucified. I would like to learn just one thing from you: Did you receive the Spirit by the works of the law, or by believing what you heard?'"

"Professor? You okay?" Carson whipped his head back and forth. "No Galatians in the studio here, and not thinking we have too many, if any among our fifteen million listeners. Want to try again?"

Marcus leaned forward. "Carson, 'Are you so foolish? After

beginning with the Spirit, are you now trying to attain your goal by human effort? Have you suffered so much for nothing—if it really was for nothing? Does God give you his Spirit and work miracles among you because you observe the law, or because you believe what you heard?'"

Carson blinked and a look of confusion flitted across his face. "We're not trying to attain anything by our own effort, Prof. We're simply trying to show people what a righteous lifestyle looks like. We're giving Christians a set of standards they can aspire to live up to every day."

"'Christ has set us free to live a free life. So take your stand! Never again let anyone put a harness of slavery on you. I am emphatic about this. The moment any one of you submits to circumcision or any other rule-keeping system, at that same moment Christ's hard-won gift of freedom is squandered.'"

Again a look of puzzlement appeared on Carson's face and it stayed longer this time. "We're not promoting a rule-keeping system. And we're not talking about whether Christians should have their baby boys circumcised or not. What does circumcision have to do with—?"

"'I repeat my warning: The person who accepts the ways of circumcision trades all the advantages of the free life in Christ for the obligations of the slave life of the law.'"

A thick sheen of sweat appeared on Carson's forehead and he struggled to speak. "Professor, I don't know where you're going with this circumcision thing, but my ministry was founded on the idea of drawing people deeper into Christ. Showing them how to walk the path."

Carson gripped the armrests of his chair. "My Redemptive Reminders are in churches and homes all across America. People memorize them and use them to lead their families and congregations."

"'Why don't you choose to be led by the Spirit and so escape the erratic compulsions of a law-dominated existence?'"

Marcus stood and took a step toward Carson. "'I suspect you would never intend this, but this is what happens. When you attempt to live by your own religious plans and projects, you are cut off from Christ, you fall out of grace.'"

"I'm in his grace, don't try to tell me I'm not." Carson wiped the perspiration off his forehead. "Without religion, Christianity gets out of control. Read Corinthians. They went nuts. Religion is to be regarded, respected, and revered."

Marcus took another step toward the radio show host, the cord of his headphones stretching to its full length. "'In Christ, neither our most conscientious religion nor disregard of religion amounts to anything. What matters is something far more interior: faith expressed in love.'"

Marcus blinked. A translucent curtain of darkness appeared and seemed to surround Carson as if he were inside a cocoon. It shuddered every few seconds as if being struck by a hammer.

"I have faith. I have love. I started this show with nothing, no one believed it would happen. No one. I've brought people stability. Guidelines. Principles. Challenges. They need it! They want it. Maybe some people don't like it, but it's the truth! And it will make people more moral, more righteous; it will purify their hearts. It will make them holy."

Marcus spoke in a whisper. "'Legalism is helpless in bringing this about; it only gets in the way.'"

The look now etched into Carson's face said he no longer believed what he just said was the truth, but he was holding on to it like a man drowning. "They need an ideology they can apply to their lives and their kids' lives. Rules are not a bad thing!"

The words poured from Marcus's mouth with power. "'For everything we know about God's Word is summed up in a single sentence: Love others as you love yourself. That's an act of true freedom. If you bite and ravage each other, watch out—in no time at all you will be annihilating each other, and where will your precious freedom be then?'"

The curtain around Carson shattered as if made of glass and the shards floated to the floor. Carson's eyes went wide and his breaths came quicker. "I'm doing a good work here, Professor. I'm not trying to divide people. We're changing lives. How do I know? Nearly fifteen million listeners tell me I am."

"I believe you, Carson. From what I've heard, 'you were running superbly. Who cut in on you, deflecting you from the true course of obedience? This detour doesn't come from the One who called you into the race in the first place. And please don't toss this off as insignificant. It only takes a minute amount of yeast, you know, to permeate an entire loaf of bread. Deep down, the Master has given me confidence that you will not defect. But the one who is upsetting you, whoever he is, will bear the divine judgment.'"

Carson's face went blank. He opened his mouth to speak three times, and three times he stopped. Five seconds passed. Ten. Twenty. Marcus prayed the power of the Spirit down on the room, but he didn't need to. The hold of the enemy had been shattered.

The dull sound of a fist pounding on glass floated toward them. Marcus turned. Sooz jabbed her finger at Carson's microphone and mouthed the words, *Get him back on the air!*

Marcus turned back toward Carson, the host's eyes desperate, pleading.

"I want to be free."

Marcus grinned and finished the passage from Galatians. "'It is absolutely clear that God has called you to a free life.'"

He turned and looked at Tristan. "I feel what the Spirit just accomplished has ramifications far beyond this studio."

"You have no idea how accurate you are, Professor." Tristan gripped Marcus's arm. "I have to go, but I'll be back soon. Wait here, yes?" The angel inclined his head toward Carson and smiled. "I think you'll find a friend to occupy your time till I return."

FIFTY-FOUR

THE RIDER SMILED, TOOK ANOTHER STEP TOWARD DANA, and repeated his question. "Are you coming with the other Warriors, daughter? Or will you stay here while they enter my rest?"

In the next moment three things happened in Dana's brain simultaneously. First, an image of the professor flashed into her mind. *Marcus, where are you?* He was talking into a microphone in some kind of studio with a man sitting near him. Carson Tanner? But somehow she knew the professor wasn't having a conversation. He was quoting Scripture. As the image intensified, a dark curtain surrounding him shattered into a million pieces, and the room the professor sat in filled with light.

Second, the words *confusion* and *deception* were plastered in brilliant white letters against a cloud of darkness. Third, she saw a picture of Jesus standing on a hill just like the one the three of them stood on now. More real, with more glory and power than the false Jesus in front of them could ever display. His words came in a whisper but also as loud as thunder. *Stay strong, Dana. For all of you.*

Peace and power flooded her. Whatever war the professor was waging in the physical realm had just saved them here.

"No!" She pointed her finger at the rider and took a step toward him.

"What is wrong with you?" Brandon grabbed her shoulders. "This is more than we could ever have hoped for."

"No." She bent over and pressed her temples as if to stop the migraine that had flared up seconds earlier. "He's not who he preten—"

"Be quiet, Dana!" She yanked her head up as the rider drilled her with his gaze. His eyes flashed dark for a nanosecond, then returned to light brown, full of life and joy. "Do not quench the Holy Spirit. I am giving you a gift. Do not neglect it. Do not refuse what you desperately need.

"The pain in your head is from the enemy, trying to distract and deceive you." The pretender motioned toward her head and the migraine vanished. "I long to bring you rest and healing, yet I will always give you a choice, even in this. You can turn from this now if you want and I will take Reece and Brandon without you. But I pray you do not. The Spirit desires to do a great work in all of you."

"Let's go, Dana." Brandon took her hand. "It's okay. Didn't he just heal you?"

"Yes." She rubbed her temple again. "But it's not him—"

"What more do you need to see? Let your doubt go. We need this. You need this."

She stepped back and pulled her hand from Brandon's. "I want you to do something for me."

"Sure." He gazed into her eyes and she looked back through the twin windows into his soul. His heart for her had never been this deep. "Anything."

"Be the Song."

"I am the—"

"Sing like you've never sung before. To Jesus. Not to this . . . this . . ." She pointed to the rider. "Close your eyes and sing to the Alpha and Omega with everything you are."

"Now? Right now? Even though my vocal cords aren't all the way back?" He grinned.

"Since we're in the spirit here, not in body, I think you'll sound wonderful." She returned his smile. "And even if you don't, I think it's about the heart behind the song, not how it sounds."

"I'm sorry." The rider shook his head. "There isn't time for Brandon to sing, Dana. Later, yes, we'll let the song of the Song echo through the heavens. But not now. If you want this gift, we must go."

"There is always time to bring adoration to the King. Always time to praise the one who holds eternity in the palm of his hand."

"So true, my friend." The rider opened his arms and smiled. "I welcome your song, Brandon. Then we will go."

"Sing, Brandon." Dana fixed her gaze on the rider. Maybe Reece and Brandon and this Jesus were right and the enemy was trying to pull her away. But more of her knew it was a lie.

Stay strong, Dana. For all of you. The words echoed in her mind again.

Brandon's song started soft and built, the melody strong and haunting.

Look.

The voice of the Spirit filled her heart and mind, and she intensified her focus on the rider. His arms were raised to the heavens and tears ran down his cheeks. His mouth moved silently along with Brandon's words. Despair flooded her. Was the vision she'd just seen of Marcus a lie? Was the rider who he claimed to be? Wait. Darkness shimmered across his chest so fast, she couldn't be sure if she'd seen it or imagined it.

The song ended and she grabbed Brandon by the collar. "Tell me you saw that!"

"Saw what? I was sing—"

"Reece?" She whirled toward the big man and clenched her fists. "Did you?"

"No." Reece shook his head and looked at Dana. "Brandon is right. Let go of your doubts and fears. It is time to go with him."

"Are you satisfied, Dana?" The rider smiled at her as his eyes danced like joy-filled lightning. There is so much I want to show you! Why did you doubt?"

Dana's legs shook. From fear? From adrenaline? She couldn't tell and didn't care. She knew what she'd seen, and yes, she doubted

it. But if she cried out and was wrong, there would be forgiveness from the Lord. If she was right . . . *Jesus, if this isn't you . . .*

Speak truth, dear one. I am with you.

She strode forward two paces—now only five feet from him—and pointed at the heart of the Jesus in front of them. "In the name of the true Christ, King of all realms in heaven and on earth, the crucified, ascended, and glorified Jesus Messiah, I command you to reveal yourself."

For a moment nothing happened. But an instant later the sky darkened and fat rain fell from the heavens and pelted them like liquid BBs. The drops fell on her arms and hands and face and head, but the sensation wasn't like liquid, it was like drops of fire that seared her skin.

"Arrrgh!" Brandon tried to shield his head from the rain, but it only exposed more of his bare arms. Tiny red welts appeared on his skin and on hers as well. But the drops didn't seem to be affecting Reece.

"Reece!"

The big man drew close to Brandon and her and covered them with his arms and body. "You have to fight this just like the three of you did during the testing Doug and I sent you on."

"No caves around here to escape into this time." Dana ground her teeth. "You couldn't just tell us how to fight this, could you?"

"What did you use then?"

"The sword of the Spirit." She closed her eyes against the pain and her body tightened.

"Yes."

Dana's brain spun as the rain fell harder. It pounded into the ground and splashed up onto her ankles and through her pants. The drops seemed to seep like acid through her skin into her bones. It was like white-hot needles were being stuck into her body in a thousand places.

"Reece!"

"Put on the armor."

A moment later she had it. "Ephesians. Faith . . . 'Take up the shield of faith, with which you can extinguish all the flaming arrows of the evil one.'" Her words rang out and seemed to surround them. She stared at Brandon and shouted through the pain, "Faith. We must believe he is with us. 'The LORD is a warrior, the LORD is his name!'"

His eyes widened and he nodded. She held his gaze and watched determination and belief grow inside and his pain grow into anger. He glanced at Reece, then stepped out from under the big man's covering. The drops of rain pounding down on them didn't lessen, but now they seemed to have no effect on Brandon.

She turned to her own arms in surprise. She'd been so focused on Brandon, Dana hadn't noticed the rain was bouncing off her arms as if a thin invisible force field surrounded her body. She looked up at Reece.

"Well done, both of you."

"Yes, well done."

Dana spun at the sound of the dark voice. Where the rider had stood was a man with thick dark hair and a gruesome smile on his face. "Your precious faith might have protected your skin, but it won't save you from what is about to be unleashed." He was taller, broader in his shoulders, his eyes somehow darker than the tar black they'd always been, but there was no doubt it was Zennon.

"I'm going to take my time killing you for revealing who I am, Dana."

"Zennon." Reece shook the rain from his face, his countenance one of granite.

"I really thought all of you had fallen for it." The demon cocked his head and pulled his gold coin out of his pocket and flipped it in the air. The raindrops bounced off it like miniature pinballs. "I really did. Why? Because you're stupid. Easily deceived." He slapped the coin onto the back of his hand. "Wow, heads. You all die." He looked up and zeroed his gaze in on Dana. "I'm curious, though. What tipped you off, dear?"

"I'm sorry, Dana." Brandon's words were full of shock.

"The Leader." Reece shifted in the mud at their feet and leveled his gaze on Zennon. "How many times do we have to vanquish you before you will leave us alone forever?"

Zennon scratched at a small scab on his left wrist. He pulled it off and fresh blood formed on his skin. The demon touched his finger to the blood, then brought it to his mouth and licked it off. "I'm guessing yours will taste better, Dana."

She shuddered. "Your strength, Jesus."

As she spoke Jesus' name, Zennon took a step back and pain streaked across his face for an instant. The demon turned to Reece. "What is it like to see again, blind man, knowing you can't see any place but the spiritual realms? What is it like to realize the answer to the prophecy isn't what you thought it would be? Does it claw at your mind in the still night hours? Does it make you wonder what else you're wrong about?" The demon held a finger over the spot where he'd ripped the scab off and pressed down. "Do you miss taking your precious photographs, Reece? I took your eyes last time, but of course I wanted to take much more. Now I will."

"Is there anything else you want to say before we destroy you?" Reece thundered one step forward.

"You and your petty desires. You believe yourself to be this mighty warrior, yet you're consumed with the idea of getting your eyes back. You let it blind you. Your choice to marinate in your selfishness on that mountain almost cost Marcus his sanity, and yet you still pretend you are worthy of being at the head of this band of pretenders."

Zennon turned his gaze on Brandon. "And you, Song. You think yourself worthy of that name? Hardly. Are you proud of your reaction at your record label? Toward Kevin? How would you like me to play a tape of that for all your adoring fans? And what about those fans? So you go out and shake a few hands after your concerts. Say a few insipid prayers. Do you really think that makes a difference in their lives? Come now. The prayers you offer all sound the

same. Why not make a recording and have someone else play it over and over again? Face the truth. Your singing career has been about you. Always about you trying to fill the hole left vacant from your childhood."

He turned to her. "My dear Dana. Filling your empty heart with the attention of your boss. Wondering what would happen if his wife were to leave him. I know you've had those thoughts. They've come and you've allowed them to linger in your mind. And you are alone, so alone in this life, and it will always be so."

"Enough!" The cry roared out of Reece's mouth with power. "Accuser of the brethren, you will stop. Be silent, in the name of Jesus."

Again pain flitted across Zennon's face.

"Jesus!"

Reece spoke the name again, and again Zennon stepped back, anger flashing. The demon breathed as if fire would erupt from his lungs but calmed a few moments later. "You have no idea what you're dealing with, Reece. But I think it's time you found out."

Zennon's face quivered. "I might be wrong about this, but I don't think so. I get the feeling you think I'm the spirit of religion." He paused and looked at each of them. "Ah yes, I see I am right." Zennon laughed and clapped his hands softly. "Wrong. I am not the spirit of religion. But since he is the one you came to see, let us delay no further and commence with the introductions, shall we?"

Zennon motioned to his right and left as if he were conducting an orchestra. "Warriors, I'd like you to meet a friend of mine. And I predict he'll want you to meet his army."

An icy gust of wind tore into Dana's clothes and as a second blast slammed into her back, a figure appeared next to Zennon. His height was eight feet plus. Black leather pants covered his legs, and his chest was bare and gleaming with dark sweat. Black hair was matted to his forehead and he held a curved white sword in his hand.

When he spoke, the sound rumbled out of his mouth like two trains smashing into each other head-on. "You will die."

"Nice voice, don't you think? I love it. Scares even people like you three." Zennon laughed. "Now it's time to pick the order. Hmm, let's see." He pointed at her. "Because of the stunt you pulled, Dana—making me show my true nature—you receive the honor of dying first."

Dana sucked air into her lungs in huge gulps and stumbled backward in step with the others. "Jesus!"

Zennon shuddered and his body grew thinner, his skin turned pale, and he grabbed the arm of the demon next to him. But the massive demon at his side only laughed and pointed to something over their heads. She spun. Advancing toward them from the back of the hill were hundreds of demons.

She glanced down the sides of the hill to the valleys on the left and right. Hundreds more climbed toward them with methodical steps. In unison the horde of demons marched up the sides of the hill, their white, dead eyes fixed on the three of them. A low screech filled the air and grew louder every second.

"We underestimated you last time, Reece," Zennon said, his voice laced with rage. "I hope it's obvious that isn't a mistake we've made a second time."

"Believe!" Reece shouted and instantly swords appeared in their hands.

Dana turned back to Zennon and the huge demon next to him who snarled out, "No escape."

The words ripped into her heart and a cloud of overwhelming fear filled her mind. The demon advanced on her, sword raised as iron hands gripped her arms from behind and knocked the sword from her hand. Dana yanked her head to the right. Reece shouted the name of Jesus over and over as he spun and ducked and slashed at the demons attacking him, his boots flinging mud and water into the air. The demons fell before Reece's blade like the rain pounding down on them from the sky, but an instant later more took the place of those who had fallen.

To her right came Brandon's voice, singing like lightning, and

the sound of his sword was like a hammer ringing against an anvil, but there were too many of the demons. They came like thundering waves.

She turned to look at Brandon, but one of the demons behind her jerked her head back by her hair before she could spot him—her throat now exposed. The white blade of the demon flashed above her. It was over. She closed her eyes. *I come, Lord Jesus, I come.*

The crash of metal on metal ripped into the air followed by a ragged scream. Her eyes flew open. Brandon stood between her and the demon for a moment before he slumped to his knees. His body shuddered. He dropped his sword and clutched for his throat. The demon stood over Brandon grinning.

"Such a touching sacrifice, boy." The demon's eyes shifted to Dana. "But it won't save her."

Brandon made a half turn and fixed his gaze on her. Blood oozed from a deep gash across his throat. The light in his eyes was fading and he gasped for air.

"No!" She reached for him but was wrenched back and held again by the demons. She looked up and stared at Zennon and the other massive demon. "I bind all of you by the blood and power of Jesus Christ, Son of the most high God. He is our shield and I claim it now against you!"

The demons behind her let go and Zennon staggered backward a step, a guttural snarl coming from his throat. An instant later Reece leaped between her and Zennon, his sword flashing at them, then in back of her at the horde coming from behind. They too had been buffeted back by her words, but how long would that last before they regrouped and attacked again? Any hope of victory seeped out of her and she shivered as fear coursed through her body.

But an instant later the sky flashed with a brilliance that would have blinded her on earth and all the demons surrounding them were flung to the ground. Then a voice rang out, crisp and clear as the dawn, "'The LORD is a warrior; the LORD is his name.'"

Tristan, Jotham, and Orson stood before them, eyes on fire, blazing swords in their hands.

Tristan glanced at her. "Trust in him, Dana."

"Will Brandon die?"

"Our lives are in God's hands."

Laughter from the massive demon echoed over the hill. "And your life is in my hand, Tristan Barrow. How long has it been? A millennium? Two? It is good to see you. It is a good day for you to die."

"I think not."

The giant demon laughed again. "You think the three of you can defeat my army?" He paced two steps to the right, then back to the left. "The three of you couldn't defeat me alone. You know this to be true. Give up the humans and we will let you remain."

Tristan, Jotham, and Orson together slowly raised their swords and stood back to back, Jotham facing to the right, Orson to the left, and Tristan straight ahead. Tristan's face turned to granite. "'I saw Satan fall like lightning from heaven.'"

He stepped toward the massive demon—at least a foot and a half taller—and its face contorted, but Dana couldn't tell if it was from fear or rage. Jotham and Orson stayed anchored to the ground, their swords ready. The demons in front of each of them stared at Tristan and their leader.

"Leave!" Tristan thundered.

"I've waited long to destroy you." The demon raised his sword, the end of its blade now only two feet from Tristan's. "But I offer one more chance, for old times, when the ages were different and there was no animosity between you and me. Go from us now."

"So you can destroy my friends?" Tristan grew more like stone if that were possible. "Leave."

The demon answered by swinging his blade toward Tristan so fast it blurred. The angel's body didn't move—just his hands and arms. He easily parried the demon's blow, then stepped to the right. The demon's face registered surprise but only for an instant. The two warriors circled each other, the demon feinting as if to

strike. Tristan did not respond and gave no false movement of his own.

Once, twice, then three times the two engaged, their swords exploding against each other, the impact reverberating over the hillside. The two fell back, Tristan's face expressionless but his breaths more rapid. They circled again, both faces like steel. The only sound was their boots sloshing through the mud.

Then so fast Dana almost couldn't follow the movement, the demon flung his sword like a spear toward Tristan's chest. The angel yanked his body to the side but not in time. The demon's sword pierced the angel's side and blood spilled out. Tristan stumbled to his knees, head down.

The demon leaped toward Tristan, yanked his sword out of Tristan's side, and raised it high above his head. The demon's bare torso gleamed with sweat and rain, his face full of triumph. "It is finished."

Dana tried to crawl to the angel but her arms and hands somehow wouldn't move. Time seemed to slow as the demon's blade swung in a wide arc toward Tristan's head. The cold blue steel of the sword threw off a darkness that reached Tristan's neck before the blade. Was what the demon said true? Could Tristan Barrow die? She stared in morbid fascination as the blade streaked toward Tristan's neck. It would be over in an instant. How could this happen?

But just before the blade reached Tristan, the angel moved faster than Dana thought possible, ducked underneath it, spun onto his back, and sliced his sword like lightning through the demon's legs.

The demon screamed—a mixture of pain and rage that reverberated across the sky. The demon crashed to the ground and blood gushed from what was left of his legs. He glanced up at Tristan and raised his sword to strike, but the angel was again too fast.

Tristan leaped forward and plunged his sword into the demon's

heart with a scream of his own. Seconds later the giant demon lay facedown in the mud, his lifeless body between them and Zennon.

Tristan fixed his gaze on Zennon. "You will not escape."

"Don't try to steal my line." Zennon motioned to his right and left and instantly the demon horde began to circle them and close in.

"Now! Open the eyes of all remaining on the field of battle, Lord of the heavens," Tristan shouted and the land shuddered.

Dana glanced around the field of battle. A vast ring of angels sat on horses encircling the demon army. All had swords drawn. Their horses pawed the ground and strained against their reins. The radiance coming off the horses and riders was like a thousand suns and many of the demons shielded their eyes against the light.

Tristan lifted his sword high and his shout rang over the hillside. "Engage!"

The next three minutes seemed to move in slow motion as Tristan, Jotham, Orson, and the angel army descended on the demons. Their swords flashed and rang out and the demons fell like water. Dana stood over Brandon as she watched Reece join the angels, his sword decimating as many of the demons as any of the angels'.

Then it was over, and as Tristan, Jotham, Orson, and Reece joined her on top of the hill, the skies cleared and the sun shone down on them.

Dana stared at Tristan. "Second Kings 6:5–17."

"Yes, the army has been here, waiting to be summoned." He shook his head. "Getting here was far more difficult than I anticipated." He glanced at Dana. "I am sorry we did not arrive sooner. We were detained."

She dropped to her knees and took Brandon's arms. "Talk to me."

A voice she didn't recognize rasped out of his mouth. "It probably looks worse than it is."

"Brandon, no."

He gave her a weak smile and closed his eyes. "I'll live."

Maybe he would. But this was about more than his life. Was his throat not as damaged as it looked? And while Brandon might sing again, she somehow knew his voice would never be the same. She glanced up at Tristan and the angel's eyes confirmed it. Tears spilled onto her cheeks and she held Brandon's hand tight.

"We need to get you out of here."

FIFTY-FIVE

MARCUS SAT WITH CARSON IN HIS OFFICE, NEITHER OF them speaking. Tristan had left after instructing Marcus to call on the Spirit to be taken to Well Spring when he was done talking to the radio host but told him there was no hurry. That he should take as much time as was needed with the host.

Carson stared out the window at the LA skyline, his face still wet from the tears that had streamed down his cheeks a few minutes earlier. Marcus held his tongue. He expected a man with Carson's ability to speak would speak when ready, but not before.

"That wasn't the show I was expecting." Carson massaged his knuckles. His voice grew soft. "I've been a fool. I allowed myself to be made into a god. Set up to lead people on the crooked and wide path."

He sniffed out a disgusted laugh. "I started the race well. Back then I talked a balanced mix of justice and grace." He dropped his face to his hands and rubbed his eyes. "I can't point to the moment we started sliding down the icy slope. If I could, I might have stopped it. Where do I go from here?"

"Jesus longs to restore you."

"And how do I forgive myself? Let the past go?"

"That is a choice only you can make." An image of his door of memories flashed into Marcus's mind. "And the choice is this: Will you believe that God wants you not to remember the past events

and pay no attention to things of old? Will you choose to believe it when he says, 'Look, I am about to do something new; even now it is coming. Do you not see it?' Will you hold on to his statement that he will make a way in the wilderness, rivers in the desert?"

Carson sighed. "Isaiah 43:18–19. I've quoted those verses many times."

"My assessment of your situation is the moment has come to embrace the verse with a liberal dose of belief. Not here." Marcus pointed to Carson's head, then his heart. "But here."

Carson laughed, tears forming again in the corners of his eyes. "Do you talk to everyone like that, or just people you're barely beginning to like?"

"Only those I'm giving strong consideration to liking."

Carson laughed again. "I know you need to go. Any final thoughts?"

"Might I suggest you give serious deliberation to at some point during the next few months coming to join the Warriors Riding at a small ranch in Colorado called Well Spring."

"After what I tried to do to you?" Carson shook his head. "You can't be serious."

Marcus slipped his card onto the conference room table and pushed it toward Carson. "We would be honored if you choose to come someday."

✠ ✠ ✠

Late that night Reece, Dana, Brandon, Doug, and Marcus sat in the family room at Well Spring and celebrated their victories. They talked about Marcus's conversation with Kat and how it freed him, about his experience with Carson in the studio and how what he had broken there had broken Zennon's hold on Reece, Brandon, and her in the spiritual realm. They heard what happened when Marcus went through the door of his memories. And talked about Reece's,

Brandon's, and her battle with Zennon and the other demons and how Tristan, Jotham, and Orson had warred for them.

But while part of her reveled in what they'd done and the triumph Jesus had brought them, another part couldn't get Brandon out of her mind. Would he make it without being able to sing? Once again, the enemy had dealt a devastating blow to one of the Warriors. Brandon was the Song. How could he be anything else? How would he live without his music?

He didn't say much as they talked. How could he? The gash across his throat would take time to heal, if it healed at all. The doctor who had worked on him in the emergency room at St. Vincent Hospital in Buena Vista earlier in the day said he would keep his voice but gave little hope Brandon would ever sing again like he once did. Ever sing at all. His voice at this point was only a whisper, and it was probably painful to talk.

Dana went to sleep that night trying to accept what he had done for her. In the morning she would talk to him. And say the things that needed to be said.

FIFTY-SIX

THE NEXT MORNING AFTER TAKING A HOT SHOWER AND spending a half hour alone down by the river, Dana strolled up to Piñon Bothy—the cabin Brandon stayed in last night—and knocked on the door. He opened the door a few seconds later and stood in the door frame, a look of surprise on his face.

"How is your throat?"

"I'll be okay." His whisper was a bit louder than the night before, and it gave her hope.

"Will you join me down at the listening post?"

He smiled, nodded, grabbed a coat off his bed, then stepped outside. They didn't speak till they'd reached the listening post and settled into chairs on the edge of the patio overlooking the river.

"I suppose you know what I want to talk about."

"Maybe." Brandon smiled.

"I think you know. Because you know me. Better than anyone." She immediately regretted the admission and then a moment later didn't. It was true. He did know her better than anyone else and it was nice to be known.

"You want to talk about what happened during the battle?"

"Sure."

Would she get used to Brandon's new voice? Before, so smooth, now little more than a rasp, like he'd eaten sandpaper for breakfast,

lunch, dinner, and midnight snacks. Yes, she would get used to it because with every syllable it would remind her of what he'd done for her. And that made his voice more beautiful than ever.

"What you did . . ." She couldn't say the words.

"You would have done the same."

Would she have? Dana watched the leaves on the aspen trees starting to bud, their green shoots speaking of new life to come.

"Did you know what would happen to you?"

Brandon stared at her. "In that moment time slowed, and yes, somehow I knew what might happen."

"But you did it anyway."

He leaned forward, elbows on his knees, and nodded.

"Was it worth it? Saving me? Knowing what you know now about your voice?" What was she asking for? For him to tell her he loved her again? *Maybe.* She chided herself for allowing the flame deep inside to flicker to life. Of course she'd known it had never completely gone out.

Over the past year she'd figured out how to frequently douse it with water. But like those birthday candles that stayed lit no matter how hard you blew, whatever emotions she still carried for Brandon simply wouldn't die. Dana reached out, put her hand on top of his, and held it there too long before pulling it away. "I don't know how to thank you without it sounding lame."

"Yes, I would do it again. I knew in that moment that I had to choose. My life or yours."

"Why did you choose mine?"

"You know why."

She did. The only sound for the next five minutes was the rush of the river and the wind through the trees.

"Another part of the prophecy comes true," Brandon finally said.

"What do you mean?"

"'And for one, death will come before the appointed time.'"

"The death of your career?"

"It's better than the alternative." Brandon picked up a tiny

pebble and rolled it between his fingers. "I always thought the part of the prophecy about one of us dying was literal."

"In some ways this is worse." In that moment Dana admitted how much she loved Brandon's music—how much she had missed it after they ended their engagement. "It will be hard not hearing new songs from you."

He let out a scratchy laugh. "Like I just said, I'm not dying. I can still write songs—it's just not going to work to sing them like I used to."

"That's the best part—hearing your voice. No one sings . . ." She hesitated. Should she be that blunt? "No one sang like you."

He didn't respond but he didn't need to. She glanced at him and spoke the words she'd considered since they sat down. "You've asked me to have coffee with you six times over the past year."

He nodded.

She leaned closer to him. "I'm told seven is the perfect number."

"I've heard that too." He smiled at her, his eyes bright.

They lapsed back into silence, but now they shared it and it felt so right. She didn't worry about what would happen with the two of them in the future. There was only this moment and she would live in it fully and let the days come as they may.

Brandon stood and stepped to the edge of the patio, hands in his back pockets, the sun framing his body and hair. "Does it frighten you to realize how close you came to dying?"

"Not anymore. I've seen too much. Think of the field of doors. Our gates are gone in a breath. We are such glorious flowers that fade from this earth so quickly. Lush grass that withers with one pass of the sun.

"If my door crumbles early, it's nothing in the scope of eternity. And I choose to believe I'm indestructible till my time has come." She stood and stepped next to Brandon. "What about you?"

"We're dead already if we're in Christ. But there is a Life inside me, a new being that is immortal and can never be destroyed." He turned to her and laughed, a choking, raspy laugh, but one filled

with joy. "You know what was going through my mind after I dove in front of you and lay with my throat spilling blood into the mud? 'He is no fool who gives what he cannot keep to gain that which he cannot lose.'"

"Jim Elliot."

"You impress me yet again," Brandon said.

"No greater love than to lay your life down for a friend."

"We have seen the unspeakable, Dana. We're four ordinary people who have seen far beyond the extraordinary. And maybe this is what you're feeling too. That those glories of eternity draw me deeper into the here and now and at the same time deeper into the life to come. I'm looking forward to going home."

Brandon turned and pointed toward the main Well Spring cabin. "Ready?"

"Yes."

"Can I ask you something?" Brandon said as they ambled up the path of white stones.

Dana nodded.

"Was what Zennon said true? Have you ever had thoughts about your boss?"

Dana laughed. "Not for an instant. Zennon was grasping for anything. Trying to put thoughts in your head maybe. I don't know." She paused. Should she say it? "There's only one person I've thought of from time to time lately."

Thankfully he didn't ask who it was, but that was only because he didn't have to. She wouldn't have answered if he asked. She'd already said more than enough.

FIFTY-SEVEN

"WHERE DO WE GO FROM HERE?" DANA SAID.

"Home. Bed," Brandon rasped. "Sleep for nine days. Repeat."

Reece smiled as they all sat around the fire pit for a few more minutes before they headed back to Seattle. It wasn't a bad plan, and certainly one he could support. They'd all earned it. But first they needed to do a final debrief on their battle in the heavens.

"My friends, my fellow Warriors, the spirit of religion is still out there. Our victory over him was major, but it was one battle in a larger war."

"There is more than one spirit of religion?" Brandon said.

"Many."

"So what will be our strategy as we venture on?" Marcus asked.

"It might sound strange, but the answer came from both Zennon and Carson Tanner during the time Brandon was on his show."

"And that is?" Dana asked.

"We continue to train. We continue to raise up other warriors here at Well Spring. We equip others to take the message of freedom to those around them. Here in the US, and around the globe."

Marcus smiled. "I know of a new ally I believe can become a significant warrior on our behalf."

"Who is that, Professor?" Doug said.

"Might I read you something before I reveal who it is?"

"Of course."

"I received an e-mail while we were in Buena Vista at the hospital with Brandon. It is titled 'Reminders for True Life.'" Marcus pulled out his cell phone and began to read. "When you speak, speak words of truth and life and love. All around you are parched souls longing for the living water of the Holy Spirit, and your words can guide them to the place where the water flows.

"Your body is a temple. Worship him through the way you care for it. Offer it as a living sacrifice that you might use it to advance his kingdom in great measure.

"Grow in wholeness—let him into your deepest wounds and fully surrender to his lordship and you will find holiness and will throw off the chains the world and the enemy try to entangle you in.

"Seek the pleasures of this age as shadows, as a foretaste to set your mind on the age to come where we will delight in his gifts in full measure and reign with him in eternity.

"Seek him with all your heart, all your mind, all your soul, all your strength.

"And finally, love your brothers and sisters deep and well, because this is the greatest command and love covers a multitude of sins."

"So be it," Dana said. "Who wrote it?"

"Has to be Carson Tanner." Reece grinned. "I would say he has been set free from the spirit of religion."

"Most assuredly." Marcus smiled as well. "If he stays on the air, I have little doubt his show will take a radical turn from what he has been doing. And I believe in the not-too-distant future he'll sit with us around this very fire pit."

"What!" Brandon's raspy laugh sounded more like a cough.

"During our time in the studio, I invited him to come to one of our Well Spring trainings. I have little doubt he will accept."

"Any other revelations, Marcus?" Dana said.

"Yes, I believe so. During my journey with Tristan, I received the distinct impression we will be visiting the field of doors again soon."

The others asked for details with excited voices. Marcus talked

talked of how he felt the Spirit told him they would all return within the next year. Reece listened to the conversation with a deep sense of peace. The warriors had done well. And he knew all of them would be willing to step into any new quest the Spirit brought them.

He breathed deep, drawing in the smell of burning pinyon pine. The rush of the river was the rhythm guitar to this rock-and-roll symphony of smells and sounds, and a deep joy seeped into every fiber of his body. Brandon would be okay. He would learn to live without his voice being what it once was. He was still the Song and always would be.

"It's time." Reece stood. "Take a few more minutes here, please. Just the three of you. Then grab your things. We'll meet back here in fifteen minutes. Let's go home."

He strode up to the main cabin. When he reached the nine-foot sliding door, Doug's voice spoke out from behind.

"Is there anything you'd like to share with me?"

Reece turned. "What do you mean?"

"I mean, friend, either you've gotten extremely confident with the repetition of walking these grounds, or something rather miraculous is going on with your eyes."

"The latter description is the most accurate." Reece pulled off his sunglasses. "But you're wondering how that can be when all you can see is two scars where my eyes used to be."

"Yes."

Reece turned his head back toward where the others sat around the fire pit and talked with animated voices. "The prophecy has come true. I can see again, Doug." Reece cocked his head toward his friend. "Not in the same way I used to. Not in the way a normal person does. But I see shapes, outlines—of the mountains, the cabin, the river—in impressions of light and darkness. And not all the time—but often—I can see the angelic warriors and the demonic host all around us."

"How often?"

"In fits and starts. Most of the time it's muddled and fuzzy. But even then I can see enough to orient myself. Don't worry; I'm not going to be driving a car anytime soon."

"What do you see right now?"

Reece turned again toward the fire. Three angels surrounded the fire pit behind the Warriors. "Our new friends are here."

"Tristan, Jotham, and Orson?"

"Yes."

"Fascinating." Doug put his hand on Reece's arm. "Then it's probably time to give you something."

"What?"

"Your journal. I found it out at the fire pit back home behind one of the benches."

"But didn't give it to me because it would be too difficult for me not to be able to read it."

"Yes."

Doug handed him the journal and Reece caressed the leather cover. "I still can't read it."

"Maybe not at this moment, but with your new vision that might change."

"True. Thank you; this was the perfect moment to return it." Reece turned his head toward his old friend. A faint gold outline of light gave a distinct shape to his body. "This kind of sight could be extremely useful and extremely terrifying in the days to come."

Reece took Doug's forearm. "I thought this would be the Warriors' last battle together. I thought finding the Wolf and confronting him was the end. The prophecy fulfilled. But now I'm not so sure. I think more freedom is coming if we desire it. For us, and for others."

Reece focused on where Doug's face should be. "You're smiling. I can see it."

"Yes, friend, I am." Doug chuckled. "Because you're right. There is more coming. Much more. The paths of freedom are breaking out all around us, and he has called you and the Warriors to ride."

READING GROUP GUIDE

1. Which character could you relate to most in *Memory's Door*? Was it Reece, Brandon, Dana, Marcus, or maybe even Simon? Explain.

2. Tristan, Jotham, and Orson turn out to be angels. Do you think angels can be involved in the lives of Christians as they were with the main characters?

3. One of the major themes of *Memory's Door* is finding freedom from regret. Do you have regrets from your past? If so, have you allowed them to keep you from truly living in the present?

4. Why do you think it's so tempting for us to look back on our mistakes?

5. Does the verse from Isaiah 43:18–19—"Do not remember the past events, pay no attention to things of old. Look, I am about to do something new; even now it is coming. Do you not see it? Indeed, I will make a way in the wilderness, rivers in the desert"—seem too good to be true? Do you think we really can forget the former things and that God can do and is doing a new thing in our lives? Why or why not?

6. If God has "made a way in the wilderness" or "rivers in the desert" for you, can you describe them? Are there others you see coming?

7. At the end of *Memory's Door*, Reece gets his sight back, but not in the way he was expecting. Have you ever realized God has given you an answer, but it's far different from what you expected? Was it a good different or a hard different? Why?

8. Brandon lost his voice in the final battle against the Wolf. Have you ever lost something like he did and felt like your life was over?

9. Toward the book's end, a Jesus appears that turns out to be a counterfeit. How can we know if we are hearing the true voice of the Spirit and not a false one?

10. Carson Tanner had a list of "Redemptive Reminders" he promoted on his radio show. Do you know people who seem to carry a list like that even if it's only in their heads? Do they bring freedom to the people around them and themselves or bondage?

11. Have you ever "carried" a list of dos and don'ts in your mind? Has it kept you from freedom or brought you freedom?

12. What do you need to do in your life right now that will bring you more freedom?

ACKNOWLEDGMENTS

SIGNIFICANT THANKS GOES OUT TO MY AGENT, LEE HOUGH; my brainstorming friend Ruth Voetmann; my prayer team; all of my team at Thomas Nelson; my editors, Amanda Bostic and Julee Schwarzburg; collaborator Allen Arnold; my sons, Taylor and Micah; my wife, Darci; and last but most certainly far from least, the passionate readers of my novels.

AUTHOR'S NOTE

Dear friends,

The response to *Soul's Gate* has thrilled me. Authors are frequently too close to their novels to know if a story has worked or not, so it's been a rush to hear the book is making a serious impact on people's lives. Some authors write to entertain. I do too, but I also want people to come away from reading one of my books with more freedom than when they started as well as full of the hope that their life can be transformed in significant ways.

With *Memory's Door*, I had the tremendous privilege of continuing to be with characters who have become a large part of my life and I was eager to see where their story would go. I don't use an outline when I write. I just transcribe the movie playing in my head, which allows me to experience the story for the first time just as you do.

Yet at the same time, my stories are never a complete surprise because they spring from my subconscious. What I see on my mental movie screen is a part of me. I've been asked if there are elements of me in Reece, Dana, Brandon, and Marcus. Yes, without question.

Consequently their struggles are (in part) my struggles. As an author friend of mine says, "My novels are just my personal journals in published form. I'm working the things out in my own life that wind up in my books."

That statement resonated with me at the time he said it and

it resonates strongly within the framework of *Memory's Door*. I went through a significant personal and spiritual crisis—and then rebirth—during the time I wrote the novel. It forced me to ask the same question Marcus faces. Can I forget the past, the things of old? Will I open my eyes despite the pain of what has been, in order to see the new thing(s) God is doing and has already done? Can I believe he can and will create rivers in the desert? My answer is yes, I can, because I did believe. And God came through.

My hope for you is you can open your eyes as I did, to see the good he is doing in your life. I don't know where you are on your journey through this reality, but I do know we have a choice every day and in every moment to enter boldly into the unquenchable love, grace, and mercy the One offers to our hearts, our minds, and our souls.

To your joy and freedom,
James L. Rubart
2013

Don't miss the conclusion to the Well Spring series

The Spirit Bridge

ARRIVING IN STORES
MAY 2014

ABOUT THE AUTHOR

Photo by Christophoto, Bothell, WA

JAMES L. RUBART IS A PROFESSIONAL MARKETER
and speaker. He is the author of the best-selling novel *Rooms*
as well as *Book of Days*, *The Chair*, and *Soul's Gate*. He lives
with his wife and sons in the Pacific Northwest.